Sofala

R H O D E S I A

Zimbabwe (ruins) ∴

Limpopo River

M
O
Ç
A
M
B
I
Q
U
E

Phalaborwa •

T r a n s v a a l

osega

Pretoria •

Johannesburg •

Vrymeer • • Venloo

Chrissie Meer

Waterval-Boven •

SWAZI-
LAND

Lourenço Marques •

Vaal River

Veg Kop •

Blood River •

ange

S t a t e

Kerkenberg

Spion
× *Kop*

Tugela R.

*Umfolozi
R.*

Dingane's Kraal •

oemfontein •

Blaauwkrantz •

aba Nchu •

LESOTHO

A

Durban (Port Natal) •

D
R
A
K
E
N
S
B
E
R
G

N
a
t
a
l

I
N
D
I
A
N

O
C
E
A
N

n Fish R.

• Grahamstown

ay

The Nations of South Africa
and Surrounding Lands

Jean Paul Tremblay

THE COVENANT

Volume 2

THE COVENANT

Volume 2

James A. Michener

Random House New York

Chapter drawings in the style of
Bushmen art by Lois Lowenstein

Cartography by Jean Paul Tremblay

Drawing of baobab
by Carole Lowenstein

Manufactured in the United States of America

Contents

VIII.	The Voortrekkers	Sable Antelope	531
IX.	The Englishmen	Zebra	643
X.	The Venloo Commando	Basuto Pony	727
XI.	Education of a Puritan	Springbok	819
XII.	Achievement of a Puritan	Elephant	895
XIII.	Apartheid	Cape Buffalo	950
XIV.	Diamonds	Giraffe	1018
	Glossary		1127
	Genealogical Charts		1129

VIII. The Voortrekkers

IN 1828 Tjaart van Doorn was about as happy as a man could be. His farm at De Kraal was flourishing. His second wife, Jakoba, had begun to soften her harsh ways. And his daughter Minna was as pleasing a child as a father could have in his middle years. He was thirty-nine, stout, stocky, with a full black beard that started near his ears, covered his cheeks and chin, but left his upper lip clear. He wore heavy clothes: short jacket, calfskin vest, tieless shirt and stiff pants made of moleskin, with a huge flap that came across his middle and buttoned at his right hip. The pants were held up by a wide belt and stout suspenders, but the characteristic that identified him immediately, wherever he stood, was a low-crowned hat, with a very wide, sloping brim, whose underside was bright blue.

Since he was a man of few words most of the time, having been overawed by his volcanic father Lodevicus, he gave the impression of a gruff, grumpy man with a firm-set countenance. He did not, however, seem a large man; there were many in his district who were taller, but few were more sturdy.

He had a right to take pride in his farm; from the fine start his father had given, he had augmented De Kraal in all respects. The basic holding was still that splendid valley set within protecting hills, with the copious stream running from the southwest right through the middle of the land to an opening at the northeast, from which it wandered on to make junction with the Great Fish River some miles farther on.

What Tjaart had done was to acquire from the government the right to use pasturage beyond the hills, and with the proceeds from his large herds, add to the clay-and-stone buildings that formed the heart of the farm. The house now had a spacious kitchen in which Jakoba could supervise the cooking; the servants and slaves occupied a chain of eight small huts linked together; calves had kraals with stone walls; and hay was stored in a spacious barn. Smaller buildings had proliferated for the safe holding of farm tools, feed and chicken roosts.

The farm contained the original nine thousand acres within the hills, but it now controlled an additional sixteen thousand acres to which he did not have legal title, but which his Coloured stockmen could use in herding cattle and flocks of sheep. Although he rarely saw much formal money, he had made himself into a man of considerable wealth and could look forward to a prosperous and placid old age.

Of course, most Boers grumbled about the English administration, its creeping modifications of law and custom, but such complaints were offset by the fact that the stalwart English settlers were now sharing the dangers of frontier life. The struggle had been harsh, as one Englishman noted in his diary:

> My wheat, two months ago the most promising I ever saw, is now cut down and in heaps for burning. The rust has utterly destroyed it. My barley, because of a grub which attacks the blade and the drought, produced little more than I sowed. All my other crops have practically been destroyed by the caterpillar and lice. My cows are dry from want of grass. Twenty of my flock of twenty-seven sheep were killed in a single night by a pack of wild dogs. My little girl has been bitten by a snake. I stood for a moment thinking of my misery, of my dying child, of my blasted crops, of my ruined flocks. God's will be done! I have need of fortitude to bear up against such accumulated misery.

And always there were the blacks invading the lands of Boer and Englishman alike. Tjaart, veldkornet of his district, had frequently taken his men to Grahamstown to help those settlers repel cattle raiders, and in many actions, had fought beside Richard Saltwood, ivory merchant, and Thomas Carleton, master wagon builder. He had found them an honorable pair and had invited them to hunting parties at De Kraal. Saltwood had proved himself not only a fine shot but a congenial guest who lacked all the mannerisms that irritated the Boers. He had even told Tjaart on departing at the end of the last hunt, 'This must be the best farm I've ever seen,' and with that he handed Mevrouw Jakoba two bottles of Trianon wine he had been hoarding.

And then the camaraderie was endangered. Lukas de Groot, Tjaart's neighbor nineteen miles to the north, stopped by one day on his way home from the port on that wild stretch of coast at which the English settlers had come ashore, and shocked Tjaart by showing him a copy of the Grahamstown newspaper: Dr. Simon Keer, the philanthropic leader in London, had published his second book, called *The Infamy of the Dutch Slaveholder,* and its appearance was guaranteed to cause trouble, for it was a savage assault against South African life and a shameless emotional appeal to the English Parliament to pass laws which Keer had long been advocating.

Keer's pressure came at a time when agitation for abolishing slavery throughout the British Empire was gaining momentum; it signaled the beginning of the final battle to demolish what many Boers considered their God-granted right: that all men of color should labor for them six days a week and sometimes seven, whether slave or free.

Keer's grand strategy of waging this war with propaganda in England had thus triumphed over Hilary Saltwood's tactic of cherishing and saving souls on the spot. The inspired lecturer with his flaming oratory had vanquished the modest missionary who had actually married one of his charges to prove that he loved them all. What Keer said in his new book was this:

> The oppression of free persons of color under the yoke of their Boer masters makes the idea of English fairness and justice a mockery. From birth till death the suffering native is held in bondage through a system of apprenticeship of his children born on Boer farms and through a contract that binds him and his family to Boer servitude. He is unable to move freely about the land, he is unequal in the eyes of the law, he is without protection from the scourge of Boer tyranny.

Was there any truth in these charges? Some. Was there gross exaggeration? A great deal. But from the indictment came a law which radically altered life on the frontier. 'Look what Keer and his fellow saints have done to us!' De Groot raged as he showed Tjaart the new provisions. 'It makes the Coloureds, the Hottentots, the Bushmen the exact equal to us Boers. They have all the rights we have. No further apprenticeship of the young. No work contracts. They don't have to have fixed abodes. Magistrates can no longer whip them as won't-works. From now on, damnit, Van Doorn, a man of color has all the rights I have.'

'That's terribly wrong!' Jakoba interrupted as the men talked. 'That's not what God intended at all.'

What Reverend Keer intended was a softening of the harsh laws that restricted servants; what he got was a disastrous dislocation; and the immediate burden fell on Lukas and Rachel de Groot, for when their herders and farm hands got word of their new status, twenty of thirty-six laborers took off, and it was a group of these homeless, roaming vagrants who ravaged their daughter.

To the big Boer she was Blommetjie, 'Little Flower,' a fragile girl of fourteen who spent most of her time among the trees and blooms of the veld. The three men found her beside a small stream, humming softly. She did not get home for the midday meal, and when she still wasn't back by late afternoon, De Groot went looking for her—and found a wild, deranged creature dragging herself across a mealie field.

He left the child with Rachel, said not a word and asked no one to accompany him as he rode out at dusk. Two of the guilty men had fled and would never again be seen in that district, but the third lay drunk in one of the deserted huts on De Groot's farm—and when the Boer discovered him, he pulled the man into the open, and for a moment stood over him.

'Get up, you devil!' he said grimly, and the man stood, swaying unsteadily, looking dazedly at his baas. With a wild cry of anguish, De Groot brought his gun up, and then the man realized what was happening, but as he backed away, a bullet slammed into his chest. He fell to the ground, not quite dead, and as he lay there De Groot pumped bullets into him, again and again.

As veldkornet, it was Tjaart's duty to report on the incident, and he duly swore that the vagrant had been shot while attempting to flee after having stolen mealies. The case was closed, but the wound in De Groot's heart remained open.

The seasons passed and no one said much about Blommetjie; they trusted that one day soon she would be able to move about the veld again. There was no improvement, either, in the labor situation, and in-

creasingly Tjaart and his sons had to go out with the herds, much like
the Van Doorns of four generations ago. And then, on a certain day in
October when spring flowers made the veld a garden, Tjaart said at
table, 'We shall go to the next Nachtmaal.'

The news created wild happiness among the women: Jakoba would
be able to see friends she had not talked with for two long years; the
slave women who would go along to do the cooking would enjoy the
chance to meet with other slaves and to cook dishes they preferred; and
little Minna, now thirteen and already worrying about how she would
find a husband in this great emptiness, conjured up visions of a bright
lad named Ryk Naudé, whom she had last seen at the Nachtmaal: 'May
I have a new dress, Mama? I mustn't go in my old one.'

So the slave women, who cherished the girl, set about the pleasant
task of fitting her out for a dress which would compare favorably with
the fashions in Grahamstown: turned-down collar, wide sleeves fastened at the wrists, flounces around the lower part of the skirt, and a
general sauciness to catch the eyes of young men. As they worked,
Tjaart saw how much joy his daughter was deriving from the process.
She was not a beautiful child, no one had ever claimed that, but she
was a fine stout lass, strong in body and character. The fact that she
was illiterate did not mean that she was stupid, for she could recite long
passages from the Bible. There was little in the repertory of a good
Boer *vrouw* that she could not do, and whereas in the western part of
the colony girls her age often had two or three slaves of their own and
never raised a finger except in rebuke, Minna was an industrious young
woman, adept at anything from making soap and candles to spinning
her father's wool into strong thread.

By rumor she had learned that several of the girls she had met at
the last Nachtmaal were already married at ages fourteen and fifteen,
and two were mothers, so it was understandable that she should become
apprehensive about her prospects. She had only one, really, the Naudé
boy from a farm far to the northeast, and she began to worry each night
when the family went to bed that the Naudés might not be attending
this Nachtmaal, and one night when Tjaart could not sleep he heard her
whimpering and strode over to her room: 'What's the worry, Min-
natjie?'

'I dreamed it was already Nachtmaal and Ryk Naudé didn't come.'

'Don't you worry, little lady. Lukas de Groot assured me he'd tell
Ryk.'

'Oh, Father!' That her father had anticipated her concern without her voicing it was most unexpected and it pleased her greatly. Grasping his hand in the darkness, she brought it to her lips and kissed it. 'Such a Nachtmaal we'll have! And I with a new dress.'

Touched by her childish gratitude, he bent down and kissed her twice. 'Did you think Mama and I would forget the necessary things?'

The next days were marked with butchering and the first steps in making an abundance of biltong for the trip to Graaff-Reinet, ninety-two miles to the northwest. Tjaart owned three transport wagons, long flat-bedded affairs, and he kept them in fine condition for journeys to market, but the family wagon was a rickety bone-shaker. As it was being washed down and greased, Tjaart instructed the servants as to how they must mind the farm during his absence and care for his mother, Ouma Wilhelmina, who would remain behind.

When all was ready, an English settler came posting in with disturbing news: a band of Xhosa had broken across the Fish and were committing depredations. The messenger said that Lukas de Groot was collecting Boers to the north and would meet Tjaart halfway to form a substantial commando for assistance to Grahamstown.

Without hesitating, Tjaart saddled up, called for four of his Coloureds to join him, and galloped east. Counting the massive battle of 1819, when he had helped save Grahamstown, this was the sixth time he had joined with fellow Boers to quell a border disturbance.

There were two reasons for their being so willing to help defend the English. As sensible men, they knew that in protecting the forward English farms they were protecting their own. But also, there was the acknowledgment that deplorable English mistakes, such as Slagter's Nek and the recent turning of Coloured servants loose to become vagrants and banditti, were the acts of English officialdom and the philanthropicals and not those of Englishmen on the frontier. Indeed, the settlers in Grahamstown suffered as much from these laws as did the Boers, which is why they cheered whenever the Boer commandos reported. There was harmony of interests.

The Stevens Affair of 1832 was a brief, fierce clash, and as unfortunate an incident as could have been devised. On a small farm six miles west of the Great Fish, there was an outcropping of red-paint earth with such a powerful impregnation of pyritic elements that it glowed handsomely when dried on a black man's skin. For generations untold the Xhosa had come to this spot to collect the clay treasured by circumcision boys and warriors, and the fact that a family from rural England had crossed the ocean to establish Stevens Farm did not diminish their desire—one might say spiritual need—to scrape up the earth and carry it back across the Great Fish.

Usually the expeditions were silent affairs, a few warriors braving considerable dangers to penetrate what had become English property and sneaking away without having done the white men harm. But in the spring of 1832 careless Xhosa, some drunk on Kaffir beer, had gone to the Stevens farm to collect not only red earth but also quite a few white sheep. A scuffle had ensued, with dead bodies, and now the Xhosa must be punished.

'What we'll do,' Major Saltwood of the Grahamstown Irregulars proposed as the men assembled, 'is ride east, cross the river at Trompetter's Drift, and take them in the rear.'

But the local Xhosa who rallied to the defense of the raiders were a battle-hardened group, a hundred veterans of many skirmishes with the English and Boers, and were not likely to be surprised by any flanking action. So when Saltwood led the men forward at a gallop, Xhosa warriors in ambush peppered them with spears and bullets from the few guns they had been able to beg, trade or capture.

That was the first skirmish, with the white men losing. The second was inconclusive, but the third was quite a different affair. Major Saltwood, Tjaart van Doorn and Lukas de Groot concocted a plan that would smash the Xhosa from three sides, and everything worked to perfection except that a hiding spearman stabbed Thomas Carleton deeply in the left thigh, dragged him from his horse, and was about to kill him when Van Doorn saw the danger, wheeled in midflight and roared back to brain the black with his rifle butt. It was a near thing, and when Carleton realized that he was saved, and that the wound in his leg was much bigger than he could tend, he quietly fainted in Van Doorn's arms, and the two men stayed on the ground till Saltwood and some others doubled back to find them.

When they returned to Grahamstown—victors, but with serious losses—Carleton was so effusive in his praise of Van Doorn's heroism, and repeated it so often, that Richard Saltwood told his wife, Julie, with some asperity, 'You'd think he'd let it rest.' Then he added, with no malice, 'But of course, poor Carleton's not a gentleman. He hasn't had the training.'

'Nor am I a lady,' Julie snapped. 'So I can't be expected to know, either. And I think it's a thrilling story. So does poor Vera, because without it she'd be a widow.'

'But you must admit, he does overplay it, rather.'

'If I'm in trouble, first I'd want you to come riding up to rescue me. But next in line, Van Doorn.'

The victory celebrations were so congenial, with many of the English volunteers offering toasts in reasonably good Dutch, that Van Doorn and De Groot lingered, and this delayed their arrival at the Graaff-Reinet Nachtmaal.

When De Groot and Van Doorn, accompanied by their Coloureds, who had fought bravely, prepared for the ride home they were joined by a veldkornet who had conducted himself, as always, with notable dignity. It was Piet Retief, a farmer from the Winterberg far north; thin, tallish, with a small beard, he was a friendly, outspoken man in his fifties, but when Saltwood and Carleton came out to bid the Boers thanks and farewell, he stood apart.

Carleton hobbled over to Van Doorn's horse, grasped Tjaart fervently, and said, 'Old chap, you carry my life in your saddle. May God bless you for what you did.'

'I'd expect the same from you,' Tjaart said, and the Boers left town.

For a day and half they were accompanied by Retief, and came to understand the perplexities that gnawed at him. He was a strange mixture, an esteemed commando leader from a Huguenot family, but also a reckless business adventurer who seemed destined to overreach himself. 'The English sued me when the barracks collapsed,' he grumbled, referring to a disastrous construction venture in Grahamstown.

'But you had it complete,' Van Doorn said, 'I saw it, and you did a fine job on the magistrate's office.'

'I ran out of money. And do you know why I hadn't any? I was always absent fighting the Xhosa to protect the very people that sued me.'

'You lost everything?'

'Everything. It always seems to happen that way.'

Van Doorn thought it best not to ask about the other disasters; what he wanted to hear was Retief's attitude toward the English government, for he was a man whose voice was being heard more and more. He spoke often about what he considered 'the persecution of the Boers.'

'The English will never give up until farmers like the three of us are ruined. Finished.'

'Why would any government adopt such a policy?'

'Because Keer will make them. His pressure will never cease until the Kaffirs control all the land. Look at your servants running wild over the veld . . .' His voice tapered off at the sight of De Groot's expression. 'They're not satisfied with robbing us of belongings and blood.

They want to steal our good name, too. I see that as the English program.'

'Wait, wait!' Tjaart protested. 'You've seen that men like Saltwood and Carleton are decent.'

'They are good men, but they're here in Grahamstown. Keer is in London, and every law he proposes favors the Kaffirs at our expense. The philanthropist ladies in their London parlors will continue to bleat when they hear we Boers are trying to defend our wives and children against their Kaffir darlings.'

Van Doorn was unable to decide how much of Retief's grievance was justified, how much an understandable animosity springing from his ruined business contracts, but before they parted, Retief raised a new bold topic about which there could be no ambiguity: 'Tjaart, would you contribute rix-dollars to a project that Pieter Uys is contemplating? You know Uys, a very good man.'

Van Doorn did not know him, but De Groot did, and most favorably: 'Maybe the best Boer along the sea. What's his plan?'

'He thinks to go on an exploring trip. Up the coast into the fertile valleys along the Indian Ocean.'

'Why?'

'He thinks that one day the Boers might have to move there. I don't want to quit my farm. And I know you wouldn't want to, Tjaart. But it might be prudent if we looked.'

'To what purpose?' Van Doorn asked, and in years that were to come he would never forget Retief's reply. They had reached a landmark where Retief must turn north for his farm among the mountain ranges. Up there lay the kind of place no man would willingly leave, but Retief said, 'I fear the English are determined to drive us into the ground. Did you read Keer's reports?'

'You know I can't read English,' De Groot said.

'Well, I read them all,' Retief said with great force, 'and you know what I think? After next year there will be no more slavery. They'll take our Coloureds away from us, too, and then how will we farm?'

'What has Pieter Uys to do with this?' De Groot asked.

'A wise man considers many plans,' Retief replied. 'Not for me or you. We can manage. But for the poor Boers who are going to be pressed down by English laws. Uys will look at the lands in Natal and tell us if we can farm them.'

'Aren't the lands already taken?' De Groot asked.

'To the north, the Zulu. To the south, a few Englishmen. But in be-tween, magnificent valleys with ample water, trees, good land.'

He asked again for contributions to the Uys expedition, and Tjaart had to say, 'I have no money now. Advance it for me and I'll pay back.' The English had recently introduced their own monetary system, think-ing to replace the Dutch that everyone used, and De Groot did have some of the crisp notes. When he handed his offering to Retief the latter took it, held it in his two hands, and allowed the sun to play upon it.

'I do not like this money,' he said.

Nachtmaal (night meal) was Holy Communion. It was held four times each year, and those living near the church were expected to attend each one. But Boers in remote areas were forgiven if they missed en-tirely for three or four years, because at the first opportunity they would come swarming in on pilgrimages that might last a month. With them they brought children to be baptized, young lovers to be married, and elders who whispered, 'This might be my last Nachtmaal.'

For such travelers, there could be nothing more exciting and spiritu-ally satisfying than this joyous celebration of the Dutch Reformed Church, for in its companionship there was social renewal and in its religious services a deepened pledge to Calvinist doctrine. A week of Nachtmaal lent grace and harmony to the lives of the Boers and ex-plained why they formed such a cohesive group.

The rite was carefully structured: church service each day for four days, the one on Sunday lasting four hours; public weddings and bap-tisms; acceptance of new members into the fellowship; much time set aside for buying and selling of properties; and wonderful singing parties at which youths were almost challenged to fall in love.

But what everyone cherished about Nachtmaal was the strengthened friendship of families who had shared common struggles: almost every man had been on commando; almost every woman had lost a baby, or a husband; and all had pondered during the difficult years their rela-tionship to God. In the English community there was nothing similar to Nachtmaal, which was one reason why the English could never be mistaken for Dutchmen.

In 1833 the Van Doorn wagon was not of the best for this long journey: ninety-two miles over a demanding terrain, with the sixteen oxen able to do at best eight miles a day. The cart had worn wheels and such a tattered canvas that Tjaart had been saying for some years, 'We must find ourselves a new wagon.' Upon his arrival at Graaff-Reinet, capital of the northeast, he was determined to acquire the best wagon possible, even if he had to trade all the sheep he was driving to the town to get it.

But his excitement in heading north was nothing compared to his daughter's, for she had convinced herself that when the Van Doorn wagon overtook the De Groots' in the far middle of nothingness, they would form a kind of royal procession, and at the entrance to Graaff-Reinet, near the miraculous mountain, they would meet Ryk Naudé, who would be waiting for her like a young prince. She had practiced her speech of welcome: 'Good afternoon, Ryk. How pleasant it is to see you again.' She would speak to him as if their parting had been two days ago, not two years. She experimented with charcoal to make her eyebrows darker and red clay from the Stevens' farm to touch her cheeks. She pestered her mother and the slave women to convince herself that she would be acceptable in Ryk's eyes, and they assured her that she was a proper little lady whom any man would be pleased to have.

She was experiencing the wonderful days of awakening, and no one watched her with more approval than Tjaart. And he told his wife, 'Jakoba, when a girl is almost fourteen she better think about catching herself a husband. You almost waited too long.' She had been all of sixteen when the Widower van Doorn rode seventy miles to find her, and she could remember how worried she had been. 'Minna's just right for her age, Tjaart. She has a good head.'

The senior members of the family had also been attending to their appearance: Jakoba had made herself a new dress, a new bonnet, and had ordered new shoes for herself and Tjaart from Koos, an old cobbler who moved from farm to farm. Tjaart, in turn, had unpacked his one fine suit of dark clothes: coat, vest, trousers with a big front flap, felt hat with enormous brim. On the final evening, when all the attractive things were spread on the floor prior to being wrapped for the dusty journey, he took down the brassbound Bible and opened it to Isaiah, where he read: ' "Who is this that cometh from Edom, with dyed garments from Bozrah, this that is glorious in his apparel, traveling in the greatness of his strength?" ' And he answered the rhetorical question by saying in his own words, 'It is the family of Tjaart van Doorn. Traveling to Graaff-Reinet for Nachtmaal, to do You honor.'

In the morning they started—father, mother, two sons and their families, and the girl Minna—all in their oldest, roughest clothes, the three men in broad-brimmed hats, the women in sunbonnets to protect their complexions from the sun. Four Coloureds accompanied them to tend the sixteen oxen, pitch the tents at night, and guard the large flock of sheep Tjaart intended to trade for his new wagon, and three women slaves to do the cooking and watch after the needs of the travelers. They stopped by midafternoon, for the oxen had to be outspanned in daylight hours so they could forage on the rich but sparse grass.

They were traveling over a route with which the Van Doorn people had been acquainted for many years. Their course was a strict north-northwest, but it deviated sharply at times to allow the crossing of ravines or the circumvention of large hills; so at night, when the Southern Cross appeared, Tjaart had to correct his heading, which he did with confidence that on the morrow they would see familiar hills.

The slow movement of the oxen—each of which responded only to its individual name—the swaying of the wagon, the soft singing of the slaves and the rhythmic walk of the men produced a kind of timeless lethargy in which there was constant movement but little change, just the grand emptiness of the veld across which not even animals moved at this time of year.

But there was excitement! Minna, alert to the increasing nearness of Graaff-Reinet, began to display nervousness; for one thing, she kept strictly in the shade so that her complexion would be as light as possible, for she knew that Boer men treasured this in their women. When the afternoon sun threatened her face, she produced a light goatskin mask which she wore as a shield. At intervals she also smoothed her rough traveling dress as if she were already preparing to meet young Naudé. And often she joined the slave women in their singing, for her heart was fluttering and sought release. She might not be beautiful, but she was inspiring to see as she blossomed in the veld like a gray flower expanding after a long drought, and Tjaart reveled in her happiness.

Her nervousness was caused in part by the delayed departure for Nachtmaal, which meant that the Van Doorns and De Groots would arrive not on the Wednesday as planned, but only on Friday itself, when the ceremonies would be beginning; and it was in those preliminary days, before the preaching began, that the young people conducted much of their courting.

'Minna!' her father assured her. 'He'll appreciate you more when you do arrive. He'll be hungry to see you.'

And then came the small miracle which enlivened the prospect of Nachtmaal as nothing else could have done, for out of the east, at a far distance, rose a faint sign of dust: it must have been fifteen miles away, two days of travel, but there it was, a mark in the sky. And all that first day the Van Doorns watched the pillar of dust, and at night they strained their eyes for any indication of light—a campfire perhaps—but none showed, and on the second day they looked with joy as the pillar expanded and assumed the thickness that would be caused by a large team of oxen.

It was the De Groots, coming out of the northeast, leading a herd of cows to Nachtmaal, converging their course with that of the Van Doorns, and before evening the juncture had been made. There were kisses among the women, backslapping for the men, and the jollity of renewed friendships for the servants and slaves. The two wagons rode together for the next four days, at the end of which De Groot said with some confidence, 'Tomorrow we'll see Spandau Kop,' and Minna was walking at the head of the procession when she cried, 'There it is!'

Tjaart had first seen this incredibly beautiful hill as a child, traveling to Nachtmaal with Lodevicus the Hammer, and to him it signified the beacons which God had placed in all deserts of the world for the guidance of His people. Abraham, coming out of Babylonia, had seen such reassuring signals, and Joseph, traveling home from Egypt, had seen the same. But what Tjaart had not appreciated as a child was the many-turreted chain of taller mountains that rimmed Graaff-Reinet, forming a kind of amphitheater of protection. When one came in from the flat veld, the physical appearance of this little town was overwhelming, and Tjaart saw with pleasure that his daughter was relishing the sight as he had done at her age.

The entire town was given over to the canopied wagons of men and women who had traveled vast distances for this religious ceremony: sixty groups had already arrived, their canvas tents pitched beside their wagons, their oxen grazing in the nearby meadows, attended by the herdsmen, who were enjoying the noise and the beer as much as their white masters.

The large square in front of the church was crammed with wagons by the time the Van Doorns arrived, but there was a tree-lined street leading to the parsonage which in some ways was preferable, for one's wagon was not surrounded by neighbors, and here the Van Doorns and the De Groots settled down.

It was Friday morning, and before Minna had time to seek out young Ryk Naudé, everyone had to convene in the famous white-walled church. The Van Doorns arrived just as the first long service was to begin, and they met with two situations that shocked them. The resident dominee, a Scotsman who had married a Boer girl, spoke more Dutch than English, and would have six sons, five of whom would be ordained at Graaff-Reinet, and five daughters, four of whom would marry dominees—this beloved man, a better Boer than many Boers, was absent in Cape Town, and in his place served a large, red-faced preacher from Glasgow who could barely speak intelligible Dutch; it was something to hear the burgeoning local patois delivered in a heavy Scots accent.

And then Minna saw to her horror that Ryk was sitting with a family that had a girl fifteen or sixteen years old and of remarkable beauty.

'Oh!' she sighed, and when her father asked what was the matter, all she could do was point with trembling finger across the church. It was unfortunate that she did so, for now Tjaart saw the girl, and for the duration of the service he could not take his eyes away. She was a glorious child, and at the same time a woman; her skin was fair, but touched with red at the cheeks; her face was broad and perfectly proportioned; her neck and shoulders were frighteningly suggestive, and despite the fact that he knew he was committing sin, he began to undress her in his mind, and the fall of her clothes was more provocative than anything he had previously known.

'Look at her!' Minna whispered, and he blinked his eyes and began to look at her in a different way, and what he saw boded unhappiness for his daughter, for this girl, whoever she was, had obviously decided that she was destined to marry Ryk Naudé, and by every feminine device, was ingratiating herself to him. Tilt of head, movement of arm, deep convincing smile, flash of white teeth—she used them all until the young man seemed quite bewildered by what was happening. Tjaart, himself so profoundly affected by the girl, knew that Minna had lost her young man, and to quieten both himself and his daughter he took her hand, and felt its trembling.

None of the Van Doorns paid much attention to the Scots minister, who was delivering one of the dullest sermons they had ever heard; he lacked the fire of a true Calvinist predikant, keeping his voice to a monotone, with none of the tumultuous raging the Boers liked, and often his words could not be easily understood. The true fire that day rested on the benches occupied by Ryk Naudé and his new girl.

When the sermon ended and the Boers had come out into the square, Minna, without any sense of shame, moved swiftly toward Naudé, posted herself where he could not escape her, and said boldly, 'Hello, Ryk. I've been waiting to see you.'

He nodded bleakly, well aware that he had promised two years ago to attend Minna at the next Nachtmaal they shared, but also aware that any such promises had been obviated by the dramatic arrival in town of the girl he now presented: 'This is Aletta.' He did not give her last name, for he had already determined that before this Nachtmaal ended, she would take his.

Aletta was as charming to Minna as she had been to Ryk during the service, and when Minna's father lumbered up, she was equally gracious, extending her hand and greeting him with a ravishing smile: 'I'm Aletta Probenius. My father keeps a store.'

'He's the man I seek,' Tjaart said, pleased that his business would keep him in touch with this exciting girl. 'Is it true that he has a wagon for sale?'

'He has almost everything,' Aletta said with a fetching toss of her head, and in the various events that accompanied Nachtmaal she demonstrated that, like her father in his store, she, too, had almost everything: smiles, witticisms, grace, and enormous sexual magnetism.

For Minna that first Friday was agony. One close look at the radiant Aletta warned her that chances for catching Ryk Naudé had vanished, and this so confused her that she did a series of things that made her look quite foolish. First she sought Ryk at his wagon to remind him of what he had promised her two years ago . . . 'We were children then,' he said.

'But you told me.'

'Things have happened.'

'But you told me,' she repeated, clutching at his hand, and when he tried to pull away, she grabbed at him. She wanted him, desperately she wanted him, terrified by the prospect of returning to isolated De Kraal for another span of years, after which she might be too old to catch herself a husband.

Ryk, at eighteen, had never experienced anything like this, for Aletta had permitted him only to hold her hand; he became so confused he did not know what to do, but his mother came up, deduced what was happening, and said calmly, 'Hello, Minna. Hadn't you better be joining your parents?'

'Ryk said that he—'

'Minna,' Mevrouw Naudé said, 'you'd better go—now.'

'But he promised—'

'Minna! Go home!' And she thrust the bewildered child away.

The following days were torment. In church Minna, like her father, stared at Aletta, and one evening as service ended she followed the girl to her father's store and confronted her: 'Ryk Naudé is promised to me.'

'Minna, don't be foolish. Ryk and I are going to be married.'

'No! He told me . . .'

'Whatever he told you,' Aletta said with a sweetness that would have mollified anyone else, 'was two years ago. You were children, and now he's a man and he's going to marry me.'

'I won't let you!' Minna cried, her voice rising so sharply that Mijnheer Probenius came out from his shop to see his daughter being assaulted by a strange girl much her junior in years.

'What goes on here?' he cried, and when it became apparent that the girls were fighting over a man, he laughed heartily and said, 'You ask me, that Ryk's not worth the trouble. You'd both be better off without him.'

Placing his arms about the two girls, he sat with them, telling Minna, 'You can't be more than thirteen. In Holland, where I came from, girls don't marry till they're twenty. Minna, you have seven years.'

'Not in the wilderness. And Ryk promised me . . .'

'Men promise a lot of things,' Probenius said. 'In Holland right now are three girls I promised to marry when I returned home to Haarlem. And here I am in Graaff-Reinet with a daughter sixteen years old who's to be married on Tuesday.'

'Married!' Minna cried, and she dissolved into tears, the shattering, soul-wrenching tears of a little girl striving to act like a woman.

To her surprise, Probenius took her round, tear-spattered face in his two hands, brought it up, and kissed it. 'Minna, this world is full of young men who need a wife like you.'

'Not in the wilderness,' she repeated stubbornly as Probenius got her to her feet, saying, 'Let's no one speak of this.' And he gently moved her along toward her parents' wagon.

Of course, everyone spoke of it, and when Tjaart reported at the store to dicker about the exchange of his sheep for a new wagon, he found Probenius, a man somewhat older than himself, disturbed that gossip should have struck so hard at little Minna: 'She's a fine child, Van Doorn, and I'm sorry this has happened. But she'll find a host of young men.'

'Her heart was set on Ryk. What kind of fellow is he?'

'The usual. Talks big. Acts little.'

'Are you happy with him?'

'Are parents ever happy with anyone?'

'Aletta's an impressive girl.'

'I sometimes fear for her. Back in Haarlem she'd be all right. Many young men to court her, for she is pretty. But also many young women just as attractive to break her heart now and then.'

'How are things in Holland?'

'Like everywhere, confused.'

'Will you go back?'

'Me? Leave paradise for those cold winters?' He came from behind his counter and stood with Tjaart. 'They warned us that after Jan Compagnie gave your land to the English, no Dutchman from Holland would be welcomed here. We came anyway. You should give thanks every day that you live in this wonderland.'

In trading, Probenius was a hard man, which accounted for his conspicuous success, but Tjaart was equally difficult, which explained his successful farm. At the end of the Friday negotiation no agreement had ever been approached: Tjaart had some of the finest sheep Graaff-Reinet had seen, and Probenius had a new wagon superior in every way to what Van Doorn had been using.

'You don't build wagons,' Tjaart said. 'Where'd you get it?'

'From an Englishman in Grahamstown named Thomas Carleton.'

'I know Carleton. I could get it cheaper by going to Grahamstown.'

'True, but your sheep are here. So you must trade here. And the price is what I said.'

On Saturday, Tjaart brought his family to inspect the wagon, and they found it to be even better than Tjaart had reported. It was a handsome piece of workmanship, so constructed that it could be disassembled for transporting down ravines, and then reassembled easily. It was nicely balanced, too, and the disselboom was so attached to the front axle that the whole would respond quickly to any turning of the oxen. Even the curved hoops that covered the body and to which canvas would be applied were nicely sanded to remove rough edges. It was in every respect superior, and the Van Doorns needed it.

There could be no bargaining on Sunday, of course, nor would there have been much time for it, for in addition to the four-hour service and the acceptance of new members, the predikant offered to conduct a special service for the baptism of those babies who had missed the Saturday rite, and the entire Van Doorn family had to attend because the De

Groots were offering their new son for baptism. He was Paulus, a lusty, squared-off little boy with powerful lungs and a rowdy nature. The Scots minister was so taken with him that at the conclusion of the service he kissed the little fellow on the forehead, saying, 'This one will be a staunch fighter for the Lord.' The De Groots were not entirely happy that their son had been welcomed into the Boer church by this Scotsman, but nevertheless they gave the dominee two sheep in thanks for the special service.

On Monday, Tjaart returned to the store for some serious bargaining, and as it happened, Probenius himself was not there, but his daughter Aletta was, and for the better part of an hour Tjaart talked with this lively, attractive girl, noting every particular. She had a musical voice and laughed easily when assuring him that her father never reduced a price, once set: 'You'll face difficulties, Mijnheer, if you pursue that line.'

'I face difficulties in all I do,' he assured her, watching the enchanting way her gingham dress defined her figure when she reached for articles on the higher shelves. 'You people in Graaff-Reinet—you're getting to be a real town. Must be three, four hundred houses here.'

'But it's not like Cape Town, is it? That's where I'd like to go.'

'I wouldn't know. I've never been there.'

At the conclusion of their conversation Tjaart thought that he had never before met a girl so totally charming, and he was somewhat irritated when her father appeared to talk about the wagon: 'Let's get one thing straight, Van Doorn. Once I set a price, I never lower it.'

'Let's get a second thing straight,' Tjaart responded. 'I am perfectly prepared to herd my sheep right back home and go to Grahamstown myself. You may not know it, but last month I served on commando with young Carleton, and when I left, his wife said that I would always be welcomed back. Can you guess why she said that?'

There were in South African life two events that struck terror in the hearts of ordinary men: when two bull elephants raged in low scrub, knocking down trees in their feud; and when two Boers engaged in a business deal. Awed Englishmen, watching the trickery, the deceit, the conniving, the bluster and the outright falsification of evidence that occurred when one artful Boer was trying to outsmart another, sometimes wondered how the new nation survived the passions and near-strangulations. 'I do believe,' Richard Saltwood wrote home to his brother in Parliament, 'that they are the most contrary people I've met. Rather than yield the slightest advantage, they dig their heels in like a dozen stubborn mules and won't budge, neither back nor forward, not till kingdom come.'

'The reason why the Carletons would welcome me back,' Tjaart was saying offhandedly, 'and offer me their best wagon at a low price, is that during the commando I saved his life.'

'Then you should certainly drove your sheep back one hundred miles and drove them another fifty for the slight advantage you'd get.'

'I'm prepared to do just that,' Tjaart said, and at this point he should have left the store to allow Probenius time to consider his folly—for he knew that the storekeeper needed the sheep—but now Aletta returned, and she was so like a gazelle resting along a stream that he was imprisoned. He stayed, and her father quickly understood why, and while she was there he did not mention the wagon, but when she left he said, 'Now, when will you be delivering the sheep?' and Tjaart said, 'Never, at your prices.' And he stomped from the store, exactly as Boer custom required.

On Tuesday there was no negotiation, because that was the day of the marriages, when gaunt couples in from the distant hills stepped before the predikant with their three and four children to have their unions recognized of God and confirmed by the community. It was a solemn time; the frontier church was filled with witnesses who used this ceremony to renew their own vows, and girls nine and ten watched wide-eyed as the words were said and the marriages were blessed.

But the highlight of the day was more traditional, for at the conclusion of the marriages already in existence came the young couples, and on this Tuesday, Ryk Naudé, a handsome fellow, was taking as his bride the bewitching Aletta Probenius. They stood before the predikant like two golden creatures, blessed in all ways, and their youthful beauty lent grace to all the ceremonies that had gone before; they represented what marriage should be, and Minna van Doorn wept as they were wed.

On Wednesday, Probenius the storekeeper came to Tjaart's wagon, kicked at the wheels and said, 'Do you seriously think you could get this thing back to De Kraal?'

'Yes,' Tjaart said, 'because once you tell me our business is ended, I drive my wagon to Viljoen the blacksmith and have him tighten it up.'

'Did you see Viljoen at Nachtmaal? Didn't anyone tell you that he is carting ivory back to Cape Town?'

'Didn't anyone tell you that I knew this, and made arrangements for my boys to use Viljoen's forge to make the repairs?'

Who was lying? In a Boer negotiation that could never be deter-

mined, for truth was elastic, and what men hoped would happen became a prediction which had to be weighed in scales quite different
from those used by a jeweler in weighing gold. Boer commercial truth
was negotiable, and after judging the situation carefully, Probenius said
with a show of honest summation, 'Tjaart, you need my wagon.' Here
he kicked a wheel with such force that it nearly fell apart. 'And I could
use your sheep, scrawny though they may be. Let's talk seriously of a
proper price.'

'But we must not think only of Graaff-Reinet,' Tjaart countered
with the same display of absolute honesty, 'because I am not forced to
trade my fat, prime sheep. I can still take them back to Grahamstown
for a better bargain.'

'I don't want to see you waste your time,' Probenius said as if he
were engaged in a transaction with his own mother. And he offered a
new price.

Fortunately, at this moment an extraordinary man came along looking for Van Doorn, and this gave Tjaart an excuse to defer the negotiations: 'Think it over, Probenius.' And he threw out a price markedly
lower than the one the storekeeper had just proposed, but not enough to
be insulting. 'I promised to talk with this gentleman.'

It was a curious use of words, for if there was anyone at the Nachtmaal who was not a gentleman, it was this odd fellow Theunis Nel,
forty-eight years old, short, rumpled, unshaven, poorly dressed, and
with a pitiful little mustache that made his upper lip tremble when he
talked. Three times during Nachtmaal he had come seeking guidance
from Tjaart, and thrice he had been put off. Now he arrived at a time
when Tjaart found it convenient to interrupt his bargaining with Probenius, and to the little man's surprise, he was welcomed warmly.

'Theunis, my trusted friend, what can I do for you?'

In addition to his other infirmities, Nel had two which irritated
many persons: he lisped slightly, and his left eye was both cocked and
watery, so that anyone speaking with him had a confusing time looking
first at one eye and then the other without ever knowing which one was
functioning, and whenever a decision was reached, Theunis would interrupt the conversation by taking out a grubby handkerchief and wiping
his eye: 'I have a cold, you know.' Now he said in pleading voice,
'Tjaart, please speak one more time with the predikant.'

'It's quite useless, dear fellow.'

'Maybe things have changed. Maybe he'll be more compassionate.'

'Haven't you got a job? Aren't you eating?'

'Oh, yes! I'm teaching school . . . for several families . . . beyond the mountains.'

'I'm very happy that you have work, Theunis.'

And then the terrible fire that burned in the heart of this little man manifested itself. In words that tumbled upon each other, and with his lisp worse than usual, he said, 'Tjaart, I am indeed called of God. I have a mission. I feel driven to pass through this community, helping and praying. Tjaart, God has spoken to me. His voice echoes in my ears. For His sake if not for mine, beg the predikant to ordain me.'

He was a pitiful man; refused entrance to any real theological school back in Holland, he had been half trained at a kind of missionary school in Germany. He was certainly not a predikant, which was why he sought ordination so compulsively, but he was not a layman either, because he had been on his way to Java to work in a mission when the last Dutch governor at the Cape had plucked him off his ship to serve in that capacity in South Africa. Itinerant teacher, wandering scholar, frontier sick-comforter, busybody, aspirant, his only virtue was that of all the Dutch sick-comforters in Africa and Java, he was the one who truly brought comfort to the dying. Insignificant, without pomp or pretense, but convinced that he was touched directly by the finger of God, he came into the meanest frontier hut and said, 'Life runs its course, Stephanus, and now the commando saddles up for the last charge. I have watched you for a dozen years, down and up, and I am convinced that God has His eye upon you. Death has not yet come. You have days and days to reflect upon the providential life you've enjoyed. Those children. The fields. Stephanus, you are quitting one glory to enter another, and I wish I could go with you, hand in hand, to see what you're about to see. Spend these last days in reflection. Would you like me to read you a sermon preached in Amsterdam about the nature of heaven?'

And that was the constant anguish! As a sick-comforter, Theunis Nel could read the sermons of others but never preach one of his own; the church laws which governed his deportment were severe. If he had ever presumed to preach in those early days when Holland governed, he would have been thrown in jail; now, under English law, he would escape jail but not the ostracism of his own people. So he carried with him always a small book of sermons, which he had memorized but which prudently he continued to read, because only this was permitted.

'Please, Tjaart, the years slip by and I am not yet ordained. Will you speak with the predikant?'

'Have you a Bible?' Tjaart asked. Theunis nodded eagerly, so they went to his wagon, and there in Leviticus, Tjaart found the citation he needed; it was terrifyingly explicit:

> And the Lord spake unto Moses saying . . . Whosoever . . . that hath any blemish, let him not approach to offer the bread of his God . . . Or crookbackt, or a dwarf, or that hath a blemish in his eye, or hath his stones broken . . . he shall not come nigh unto the altar, because he hath a blemish; that he profane not my sanctuaries.

Leaving the book open so that Theunis could see for himself, if he so wished, Tjaart said, 'There it is. You have a blemished eye. You give the impression of being crookbackt. It's impossible for you to be a predikant.'

'It's just a cold,' the little man said, daubing at his offending eye. And then the pretense ended and he scratched at his eye, crying, 'I would to God I could pluck it out.'

'Then you'd be blind,' Tjaart said, 'and the blemish would be even greater.'

'What can I do?' Nel pleaded, and all Tjaart could say was 'You're a teacher. You are God's sick-comforter. That's the way you must serve.'

'But I could do so much more. Tjaart, did you hear those dreadful sermons the fat Scotsman gave? No fire. No touch of God. It's a disgrace.'

'For reasons of His own, God has forbidden you to preach. Be content.'

And he shoved the difficult little man away, watching him as he returned to the wagon that would carry him to the four farms where he conducted his school, and when those children were grown, to four other farms, and then four others, until some younger sick-comforter should in due course come to him to ease his dying. He was the man of God whom God rejected.

On the way back to De Kraal in the new wagon, Tjaart thought several times that he would burst into tears before his entire family, something he had never done. But his anguish over the despair of little Minna was almost more than he could bear, and even as he tried to console her he felt himself coming apart, and he would leave before he made a fool of himself. Walking beside the lead oxen, he would try not to think of her sorrow, and his mind would fix on Aletta as she worked in the store, stretching to find a box, or as she appeared on the day of her wedding like a spirit risen from the veld, all gold and smiles and enchantment. He was entertaining such visions one afternoon when he heard a sudden cry from the wagon, and when he rushed back he found that Minna had undone the cloth in which her new dress was being carried and was tearing the garment apart, throwing the bits upon the veld.

'Daughter!' he cried in rage. 'What are you doing?'

'It's no use! I am lost!'

Climbing into the wagon beside her, he took her in his arms and told the slave women to recover the bits of cloth and take the dress away; it could be mended. He was not so sure about his daughter's heart, for in the days that followed she fell into a fever and lay in the wagon shivering and not caring whether she lived or died. The women had several remedies for such afflictions, but none sufficed, and on the third night Tjaart crept into bed with her, and kept her warm and comforted her, and when the dawn broke he said a strange thing: 'We must both forget Nachtmaal.'

Ironically, it was Van Doorn's oldest slave who announced the long-awaited decision on slavery. 'Baas, Baas!' he cried. 'Die big baas Cuyler, he here.' And that remarkable man from Albany, New York, Colonel Jacob Glen Cuyler, strode heavily into the De Kraal farm-house. The two men with him did not presume to enter, but remained respectfully outside: Saul, the Xhosa deacon at Golan, and Pieter, son of Dikkop. The first was old and gray, the second hastening in that direction.

They were at the first stage of an incredible venture: Cuyler had fetched them from the mission village and was taking them to Port Elizabeth, whence they would go by ship to London as guests of Dr. Simon Keer, who wanted them to participate in one of his grand lecture tours. Hesitant about entering the home of a Boer, they would be entertained at Buckingham Palace.

Colonel Cuyler, now a respected magistrate and soon to be a lieutenant-general, had a message which was brief and shocking: 'Parliament have passed a law that says all slaves will be emancipated next

year. On December 31, 1834, every slave in the empire will be freed.'
'Good God!' Tjaart cried. 'That's revolution!'
'Oh, you'll be compensated, fully. Every penny you spent. And the slaves must work for you during the first four years, so they can move in an orderly way into their freedom.'

Cuyler saluted and departed. For three days the Van Doorns and their neighbors discussed the new laws, and at the end of that time they still could not grasp the full meaning of this radical change—that it defined a whole new way of life—and to their surprise it was not any of the men who saw clearly the new landscape, but Jakoba van Doorn, the quiet, unlettered woman who had been ignored both at Nachtmaal and in these discussions. Now she spoke with fierce determination: 'The Bible says that the sons of Ham shall work for us and be our slaves. The Bible says there shall be a proper difference between master and slave. The Bible says we shall keep apart, His people to themselves, the Canaanites to themselves. I have never struck a slave. I have always tended my slaves and my Coloureds when they were sick. And I think I have shown that I love them. But I do not want them at my table and I do not like the sight of them in my church. For God has ordered me to live otherwise.'

Driven by her forcefulness, the illiterate men urged Tjaart to consult the Bible, desiring to hear for themselves what the strictures of good Christian life ought to be, and he found and recited those satisfying passages upon which their social order was so securely founded:

'And he said, Cursed be Canaan; a servant of servants shall he be unto his brethren . . . Now therefore ye are cursed, and there shall none of you be freed from being bondmen, and hewers of wood and drawers of water for the house of my God . . .'

After he had read a dozen such passages, which proved conclusively that God had ordained and blessed the institution of slavery, Jakoba, a woman fierce in righteousness, demanded that he seek further for two verses which predikants had explained to her, for upon them she based her belief that the Boers were special people, set free by God to behave in their own special way. After some searching in Leviticus, a book whose laws governed Boer life, Tjaart uttered the statement:

'And ye shall be holy unto me: for I the Lord am holy, and have severed you from other people, that ye should be mine.'

'See,' Jakoba cried with grim satisfaction, 'God Himself wanted us to be apart. We have special obligations, special privileges.' And she urged her husband to uncover that particular verse on which she hung the main body of her belief. He could not find it, and with some impatience she riffled the large pages of the book she could not read, then pushed the Bible back to Tjaart, with the command: 'Find it. It deals with tribute.'

It was this word that reminded Tjaart of a passage in Judges dealing with the establishment of Israel in a new land—an exact parallel to the situation of the Boers—and with a good deal of useless help from the men, he finally located what Jakoba wanted to hear:

'And it came to pass, when Israel was strong, that they put the Canaanites to tribute, and did not utterly drive them out . . . but the Canaanites dwelt among them and became tributaries.'

'And that,' said Jakoba, 'is how it should be. We have conquered the land. We live here. We are to be just to the Kaffirs, but they are tribute to us.'

'The English say that's all done for.'

'The English know nothing about Kaffirs,' Jakoba said. She was a small woman, daughter of a trekboer who had defended his land eleven times against black marauders, and in the harshness of her family's hut she had learned the principles by which a Christian lives, and to such a life she was committed. She was honest, hard-working, a good mother both to her own daughter and to Tjaart's children by his first marriage, and although she could not attend church each Sunday, for the nearest was many miles away, she did hold personal services in which she thanked God for His merciful guidance. What He wanted in the matter of relationships between white masters and black slaves was so clear that an idiot could understand, and she proposed that she, her family and her nation obey those precepts.

'We will not abide by English laws,' she said as she left the men, 'if they run counter to the word of God,' and when she was gone, Tjaart called after her, 'What have you in mind?' and from the kitchen she replied, 'Leave here. Go over the mountains and form a nation of our own.'

*   *   *

Late one morning as Tjaart returned from inspecting his flocks he was alarmed to find five horses tethered at his house, and he assumed that new troubles had erupted on the frontier: 'Damn! Another commando!'

But when he entered the kitchen he found no sense of urgency. Five neighbors were drinking gin and joking with Jakoba and Minna as the two brought large platters of food. 'Veldkornet!' the men cried noisily as Tjaart entered, and there was ribald joking as to why he had been absent when they arrived.

Leader of the group was Balthazar Bronk, a man Tjaart instinctively distrusted. Bronk endeavored to be two quite different persons at the same time: with superiors he was obsequious; with others he tried to dominate in various pompous ways; and sometimes he was downright objectionable. He could never be simply Balthazar Bronk, farmer.

'Veldkornet,' he said humbly as Tjaart reached for a glass of gin. 'We've come to enlist your services.'

'No commando. I'm tired of fighting those damned Xhosa.'

The men laughed, for they knew that the first man to saddle up if trouble came would be Van Doorn, but Bronk continued: 'We're worried, Veldkornet. With English rule—'

'Stop right there!' Van Doorn snapped, slamming his two hands down on the table. 'The English are in command, and slowly they're learning to do things right. Accept them.'

'Exactly what I said,' Bronk cried eagerly, and when he looked to the others for confirmation, they nodded. Then he coughed, adjusted things on the table, and went on: 'Under English rule our children will have to know more—to compete, to make us proud.'

Tjaart could not guess what would come next, but a quiet member of the group said, 'You're the only one of us who can read. None of our children can read—'

'We need a teacher,' Bronk interrupted. 'Find us a teacher.'

'Who would pay him?' Tjaart asked cautiously.

'All of us. We have so many children.'

A census was taken, and when the numbers were announced they gave a good picture of Boer life: 'Eleven, nine, nine, seven.' And proudly Bronk declared: 'Seventeen.'

'You mean they all want to go to school?'

'Only the young ones,' Bronk said. 'Six of mine are married.' Then he smiled unctuously at Tjaart and said, 'You have how many?'

Tjaart swigged on his gin, then said, 'First wife, two boys. They're past schooling, but they have children. Jakoba, tell them how many you have.'

Wiping her hands on her apron, she said, 'Minna here.'

Five heads turned toward the girl, who blushed deeply, for she could see that they were thinking: Why isn't she married?

'Mejuffrouw Minna is not for school,' Bronk said with a wide smile, and the others returned to the task of finding a master, and as expected, Tjaart was of help: 'At Nachtmaal, I was speaking with Theunis Nel . . .'

Bronk groaned. 'We want a real teacher. Not a squint-eye.'

Another said, 'We must have a school. Go see him, Van Doorn.'

When Tjaart reined his horse at the northern farm of Gerrit Viljoen, he was astonished by what the owner said: 'Welcome! Have you come to talk with us about emigrating north?'

'Why do you ask that?'

'Six wagons passed here the other day. Men like you and me.'

'Why would you go north?'

'Freedom.'

'I'm staying where I am.'

'I'd expect you to. All those good stone buildings.'

'They are good,' Tjaart agreed, not catching the challenge to his worldliness.

'You might have to reach a decision sooner than you think, Tjaart.'

'Why?'

'Freedom. Boers love freedom. And ours is being stolen from us.'

'Gerrit,' Tjaart said abruptly. 'I came here to steal your school-master.'

'No complaint from me. He's about done his job at these farms.'

'Do you recommend him?'

'I do. I do. Knows his numbers. Knows his Bible.'

'Have I your permission to speak with him?'

'I'd be relieved if he found a good job.' He paused. 'A man so ill-favored needs help.'

Viljoen dispatched a slave to fetch the itinerant teacher, and when Tjaart saw the man again—crookbackt, and almost fifty years old—he shuddered: This man could never teach! But when he consulted the families, he found that all spoke of Nel with affection. One mother said, 'He's small and he has a high voice, but he's a man of God,' and the oldest Viljoen boy said, 'Any of us in class could have whipped him, but he kept order.'

'How?'

'He told us that Jesus was a teacher, too, and we listened.'

That night Tjaart offered Nel the job, and the little man wiped his watery eye and blessed him. 'But if I handle the children well, will you ask the predikant to ordain me?'

'Theunis,' Van Doorn said as if talking with a child, although the schoolmaster was older than he, 'you'll never be a dominee. I've told you that. We need you as a schoolmaster.'

'How many children?'

'Thirty, maybe.' Tjaart was afraid this might sound like too many, but Nel smiled broadly.

'It's better when there's lots. Then the school doesn't end too soon.'

'How many schools have you conducted?'

'Eleven.' Quickly he added, 'I was never discharged. The children grew up and I moved on.' He looked at the two farmers. 'I move on,' he said.

During Tjaart's absence it had been agreed that the new master, if found, would live with Balthazar Bronk and his many children, but when Jakoba heard of the arrangement she snorted: 'No charity there. Bronk wants him to help discipline the children. They're rhinoceroses.' And when Nel saw where he was to domicile, he, too, understood.

Bronk's farm lay nine miles east of De Kraal and proved quite suitable; it was central to the participating families, and had a small whitewashed storage shed that could be converted into a schoolroom. Here Theunis collected his thirty-three youngsters to teach the alphabet, the Bible and the counting tables. Nel had only the slightest knowledge of history, literature, geography and such related subjects, so he did not presume to teach them, but whatever he did attempt carried a heavy overlay of moral instruction.

'Bronk, Dieter. Stand and recite the First Psalm.' After the oafish lad had stumbled through, Nel would ask, 'Bronk, Dieter, suppose you walked in the counsel of the ungodly. What would you be doing?'

'I don't know, Master.'

'You would be breaking commandments.' And here Nel would launch into a small sermon about not lying, not stealing, not coveting another man's wife; though forbidden to deliver large sermons in church, he was free to deliver small ones in school.

All his pupils, age five to fourteen, met in one squarish room

furnished only with benches, and often the school seemed more riot
than rote, but patiently Nel established order, and with various groups
sequestered in odd corners, he taught first the five-to-seven, then the
eight-to-eleven, then the twelve-to-fourteen, but the best part came each
morning at eleven and each afternoon at three, for then he assembled
the students in one big group. In the morning he discussed the Bible, especially the Book of Joshua, which proved that God had chosen the
Boers for some special task; in the afternoon he taught Dutch, or
rather, the semi-Dutch of the frontier. He was a lively actor and would
tell his children, 'I can speak English as well as anyone at Graaff-
Reinet.' And here he would become a magistrate or a Scots minister,
offering a fairly garbled English. 'But when I am a true man, I speak
Dutch. Learn this manly language. Hold on to it.'

In a year of Nel's teaching a child might learn what he or she could
have mastered in two weeks at a real school, but would certainly learn a
wealth of moral instruction which children in better schools never acquired.

He had one weakness as a schoolmaster, and the farmers who employed him could not correct it. 'I am,' he told them, 'first and last a
sick-comforter,' and if anyone in the region fell ill or approached death,
he felt obligated to appear at the bedside. This meant that his school
went unattended, and for this he was rebuked, but he told Balthazar
Bronk, 'God has two concerns in the Graaff-Reinet district. That his
young people get started right on their journey through life. That his old
people get started right on their journey to heaven. In both instances I
am the teacher.'

He was indeed a sick-comforter. With dying men he recalled their
vigorous contributions to Boer society; with women he reminded them
of the essential role they played in producing and rearing good people.
He made the termination of life respectable, proper, inevitable, a thing
to be as much appreciated as a beginning: 'You have seen the meadows
fill with grain. You have seen six cattle multiply to sixty-six. These have
been the signs of a good life, and through them God has marked you for
salvation.'

In strict obedience to John Calvin's teaching, he was convinced that
every human being he met was destined either for heaven or for hell,
and he usually knew which; but this did not mean that he treated the
condemned with any less benevolence than he treated the saved, and in
the final moments whenever a dying person asked, 'Dominee, am I to be
saved?' he replied, 'I am not a dominee, and I often wonder whether I

am saved. This crooked back. This blemished eye. All I know about you is what I know about myself. In this life God has been just to me, and I'm sure He will be so in the next.'

The Van Doorns became personally affected by Nel's dual functions when the old grandmother fell ill. Wilhelmina was past sixty and her life was ending in a painful sickness. Nel, hearing of this, closed school and rode the horse his farmers had given him over to De Kraal, where he said simply, 'I am told Ouma is dying.'

'She is,' Tjaart said, tears marring his broad face and beard. 'She built this farm.' He led Nel to the dark room in which the old woman lay, and the first thing Theunis did was open the blinds and the windows. He then stepped to the bedside and spoke to Wilhelmina as if she were one of his scholars: 'Now tell me how you got this farm,' and when she had spoken only a few words, he interrupted, ran to the kitchen and told Tjaart, 'You must assemble all the children, immediately. Ouma wants to talk with them.'

She had in no way indicated that she wished to speak with her grandchildren, but Nel recognized that she possessed words of importance which ought to be passed from one generation to the next. So when they were all assembled, Nel arranged them in the sickroom and said, 'The generations of man are but as the winnowing of grain, and when the chaff is blown aside, the wheat must be treasured.'

'What in hell is he talking about?' Tjaart whispered.

'This Ouma who lies here with us has had a powerful life, and you must know about it, and tell it to your children's children.' And with this he started Wilhelmina on the story of how she had come to De Kraal.

In a wispy voice, sensing that she had only hours to live, she began: 'I lived by the sea in a family that knew not God, and a passing smous told me that up north a good man had lost his wife, so I got on my horse, and without saying goodbye to anyone I left that wrong house, rode north and told your father . . .' She was speaking to Tjaart, who listened dumfounded.

'They called your father the Hammer, which was an ugly name, really, and not at all the proud one he thought. But we needed a Hammer. Forty times or more he rode off, and always I prayed that I would see him come back.'

One thing worried her: 'Lodevicus died because he did a wrong thing. He offered to betray his government. I am ashamed . . .' Here she broke down momentarily, then said an unfortunate thing: 'I want to tell you about Nachtmaal at Graaff-Reinet. We went four times, I think, and the farmers . . .'

At the mention of Nachtmaal, Tjaart thought hungrily of that exquisite girl, but he stopped when he became aware that someone near him was sobbing. It was Minna. Death she could tolerate, but Nachtmaal carried memories too bitter to accept. Dashing from the death-room, she ran from the house and toward the hills that protected De Kraal.

'You must find her a husband,' the dying Ouma said. 'I rode alone more than a hundred miles to find your father, Tjaart.'

One of the children asked, 'Were there lions when you rode, Ouma?'

'There were lions,' she said.

When Theunis Nel began riding over to the Van Doorn farm after the death of Wilhelmina, it was ostensibly to report on the progress of the children, but after a third visit Jakoba took Tjaart aside: 'When he first came I thought it was to have a good meal. You know how the Bronks scrimp on food.'

'He eats practically nothing.'

'Do you know why? He's courting Minna. It's ridiculous. Tell him to stay away.'

'Minna!' Tjaart sat down heavily. 'Do you think . . .'

That afternoon he rode over to the school and invited Theunis Nel to dine, and the eagerness with which the little schoolmaster accepted convinced Tjaart that Jakoba had made a shrewd guess. That night both the Van Doorns scanned the teacher as he toyed with his food, and after he departed they whispered together.

'It's wrong, Tjaart. He's older than you.'

'I'm not so old.'

'But Minna's—'

'I know what Minna is. She's nearly sixteen, a woman without a man. And she's not so well-favored that she'll easily catch a good one now.'

These blunt truths brought tears, and Jakoba asked, 'What can we do?'

'We can encourage Theunis Nel.'

'You can't mean . . . to marry her?'

'That's exactly what I mean.'

'But she's a girl. He's an old man.'

'Any woman past fifteen is thirty years old, or forty, or fifty, or whatever is required. When Nel comes to sit with Minna, you make him welcome.'

But how to inform the schoolmaster that he was free to sit with Mejuffrouw van Doorn in the opening stages of a formal courtship? Tjaart solved the problem in what he deemed a subtle way: 'Theunis, I've ridden over here to tell you that you've done wonders with our grandchildren. I have a daughter, you may have met her, I think. She ought to learn her letters, too, and we will pay you extra . . .'

'I'm sure I could arrange some free time,' Nel said, and he entered upon the most hectic period of his life: school all day, sick-comforting many nights, nine miles to De Kraal; instructing Minna at night; and helping everywhere on unforeseen tasks.

Sometimes Tjaart and Jakoba would peer into the kitchen, and there would be the schoolmaster, gazing raptly at Minna as she laboriously copied her alphabet. 'I wonder if she knows?' Tjaart asked, and Jakoba said, 'Women always know.'

And one night after Nel had departed, so weary that he fell asleep on his horse and allowed the beast to take him back to the school, Minna told her parents, 'I think he wants to speak with you, Father.' But having reported this, as she had promised Theunis she would, she burst into tears. 'But I'm in love with Ryk Naudé. I always will be.'

'Minna,' her mother said sternly, 'he's gone.'

'But I can't marry that schoolmaster.'

Jakoba shook her and said, 'When a woman's past fifteen she must make the best bargain.'

'You want me to marry him?'

'You heard what Nel said. "The generations of man are but as the winnowing of wheat."'

'I still don't know what that means,' Tjaart protested.

'It means a woman must do what she has to,' Jakoba said.

Two nights later Theunis Nel, wearing the best clothes he could command, appeared in the kitchen, and when Minna spread her papers, he brushed them aside: 'Tonight I speak with you, Mijnheer van Doorn.'

'Yes?' Tjaart said.

'Mijnheer van Doorn'—the schoolmaster spoke as if he were sixteen and Tjaart seventy—'I have the great honor of asking whether I might have the hand of your daughter Minna . . .'

When Minna heard these fateful words and saw the pitiful man that

spoke them she might have broken into a sob had not her mother anticipated such a scene and grabbed her daughter's wrist furiously, as if to
say, You cannot.

'I am older,' Nel continued, 'and have no farm . . .'

'But you're a good man,' Jakoba said, and she pushed her daughter
forward.

'Theunis,' Tjaart said, 'we welcome you into our family.'

'Oh!' the schoolmaster gasped. Recovering his composure, he said,
'Can we all ride to Graaff-Reinet for the wedding?'

'Not in these troubled times,' Tjaart said, 'but you can start the
marriage, and whenever a dominee comes this way . . .'

'I could not,' the devout little man protested, unable to imagine living with a woman before vows had been solemnized. 'I must pray on
this.'

'Go ahead,' Tjaart said, eager to have his daughter married. 'But
I've noticed that whenever men pray on this subject, the answer's always yes. Do you want Minna to ride with you to Bronk's?'

'I must pray.'

It was Minna who answered that particular prayer. 'You heard what
Wilhelmina did when she married Lodevicus. She rode one hundred
miles. The school's nine miles. I'm riding with you.' Tjaart van Doorn
had found a son-in-law.

In December 1834 it seemed as if all of Tjaart's uncertainties were laid
to rest. Theunis and Minna returned to help run the farm, and the English government began to show common sense in running the country.
But almost immediately trouble resumed, for the Xhosa launched a
series of forays deep into Boer country, and all commandos were summoned to Grahamstown to strengthen the English regular troops and
their civilian helpers like Saltwood. 'We're dealing not with hundreds of
Xhosa warriors,' the commanding officer said, 'but thousands. An invasion of our colony is under way.'

After fourteen rugged days in the saddle, Tjaart's men were given a
week's furlough; they were farmers, not soldiers, and their first responsibility lay in ensuring the safety of their homestead and flocks. As the
tired men rode back to Grahamstown, a place Tjaart had grown to love
for its hospitality, Saltwood spoke seriously: 'Piet Retief is talking
about pulling out of here and emigrating north. If that good man leaves,

it's obvious to me you'll all go. I think that's a mistake. You and I have proved that Boers and Englishmen can live together.'

'Your laws go against the Bible.'

'Against the Old Bible, not the New.'

'It's the Old that counts.'

'Be that as it may, if you ever decide to go north, I'd be very interested in your farm. It's the best in this area.'

'I'd not care to sell.'

'Then why did you buy that new wagon?'

Tjaart reflected on this. He refused to concede that he had acquired the wagon in order to emigrate, even though his wife had been counseling this for some time. 'I bought it because a farmer needs good tools,' he had told his sons. But gradually he admitted that he might also have done so because there was in the air a desire for life unimpeded by English law and custom. Perhaps Jakoba had been right. Perhaps they should go north and form a new nation.

But such thoughts fled from him when he and De Groot came over the last hill to De Kraal, for from its summit they looked down on a scene of devastation: all parts of the barn that were not of stone were burned away; the wooden shed attached to the house was burned; and in the space between barn and house stood what had been the new wagon, all parts charred and shattered.

'Great God!' Tjaart shouted, spurring his horse to find what might have happened to his family. 'De Groot!' he cried from the ashes. 'They've all been killed.'

But a search of the ruins uncovered no bodies, and now Tjaart feared that his family had been taken captive. A wide-ranging search for spoor finally disclosed a trail leading to a faraway glen, and there they found Theunis Nel, the women, the children and the slaves—safe and hungry. His sons had been slain.

'Theunis saved us,' Jakoba said quietly when Tjaart embraced her.

'How?'

A Coloured servant, grateful that he was still alive, replied, 'Two guns. We fight one hour. We move back, step by step. We kill many. They go.'

Theunis had supervised the brilliant retreat which had saved the remnants of the Van Doorn family. Curiously, he had fired neither of the guns; Jakoba had used one, a Coloured shepherd the other. But it had been Theunis who had kept the group together and picked the route of their escape.

When Tjaart asked the would-be dominee, 'How did you find the courage, Theunis?' Nel replied, 'I had to. Minna's pregnant, you know.'

Six hundred miles away in Cape Town it was New Year's Eve, and guests at the Governor's Ball were saying it was the finest entertainment ever staged at the Cape. The ladies and gentlemen of the capital were resplendent in modish suits and gowns, but what really gave dazzling romance to the occasion were the immaculately uniformed English officers who moved through the festive crowd like valiant princes. The guests had come from every corner of the western Cape, and among them were the Trianon Van Doorns, one of the most prosperous of the older Cape Dutch families.

There were now more than twenty thousand people in the bustling town, a chaotic mix of wild irreverent seaport and nascent commercial center. Shops offering the fashions of Europe, fine blended teas and spices of Ceylon and Java, exquisite silks from China; little nooks where silversmiths crafted their precious wares; and a gentleman like Baron von Ludwig, who could advise on snuffs and tobaccos—all flourished. Comfortable hotels and clubs where the latest news from 'home' could be pondered at leisure stood alongside bawdy taverns with their Gentoo hostesses, stable yards, chandlers, the workshops of Malay carpenters, alleys jammed with the shacks of Coloureds and poor whites.

The gentry lived well in their fine town houses or in the gabled grandeur of their farms, devoting their energies to establishing the great Cape families of the future while debating such disparate subjects as the vexatious loss of their slaves and the newfangled bathing machine that would enable them to immerse their bodies in the Atlantic, 'a process which guarantees medicinal benefit.'

Much of the talk on this night at the ball centered upon the hunt, that New Year's Day event featuring scarlet-jacketed men led by the governor himself in thunderous pursuit of the fox of the veld, the jackal. 'Damn good job, too,' one crusty major cried. 'Gives one a touch of the old country, eh, what? Helps rid the farmer of his pests. Sporting show, what? Takes an English countryman to show these Boers how to make the best of this country.' He sealed his opinion with a mighty draught of port.

Outside the Castle, this New Year's was special too; the black and brown slaves were enjoying their first day of freedom. A huge crowd of these persons, with a horde of children, had gathered at the Lutheran church, their eye on the steeple clock that would announce the New Year. The children were whooping and yelling, impatient for the giant fireworks promised for midnight. At dawn next day they would receive their presents, as always.

At Government House the regimental band, augmented by the best town musicians, struck up another waltz, and there was an enthusiastic cheer as the garrison's lieutenant-colonel led his pretty wife onto the floor. Henry George Wakelyn Smith was a reedy, hawk-faced young officer whose reputation pleased both his soldiers and the Cape civilians. He had conducted himself with rare bravery while serving under the Duke of Wellington in the Spanish campaign against Napoleon, and had been honored, but he insisted upon being known as plain Harry Smith, one of fourteen children from an impoverished family. And he positively loved playing at war.

If the locals were proud of Harry, they adored his wife. Everyone knew of the gallant manner in which he had won her. At the siege of Badajoz, when he led his troops in their final assault on that city, two Spanish children, one a young girl, came running from the French-held lines in tears: 'Soldiers have killed our parents. And look! They've ripped the rings from our ears.'

Young Smith took one look at Juanita and declared to a friend, 'There has never been a lovelier lady.' And forthwith he married her, even though she was only fourteen and a Catholic. They formed one of the notable married couples in history, a marvelous, well-matched pair. He entertained the public with his bravery, she with her guitar. Years after this first sojourn at the Cape, Sir Harry would return as governor, and Juanita would be worshipped by everyone.

On this night, as he waltzed with her, Harry saw one of the governor's aides enter the hall and with grave gestures beckon him. Graciously he deposited his lady with friends, and without betraying any excitement, walked slowly to the governor's study.

'The Kaffirs have broken through all our frontier lines. Grahamstown and the Boer commandos can't hold them back. They're destroying everything in their path. Burning and pillaging.'

Without hesitation Harry said, 'I shall go.'

'It will be weeks before a warship can get you there.'

'Forget the damned navy. I'll ride.' Then he bowed slightly. 'Sir, midnight is almost here. Would it not be proper for us to rejoin the ladies?'

In the ballroom, as the eleventh hour ended, a great cheer went up and the band played that exquisite song of nostalgia 'Auld Lang Syne.' Harry Smith, aware that he must soon be off across the continent, clasped Juanita tightly as he voiced with her the words of Robert Burns:

> 'We twa hae run about the braes,
> And pu'd the gowans fine;
> But we've wandered mony a weary foot
> Sin' auld lang syne.
>
> We twa hae paidl'd in the burn,
> Frae morning sun till dine;
> But seas between us braid hae roar'd
> Sin' auld lang syne.'

From outside came the explosion of fireworks and cries of delight from those who welcomed 1835.

Harry and Juanita left the dance immediately. After a brief three hours' rest he kissed her farewell, buckled on his saber, picked up dispatches for the frontier, and rode out into the night as the citizens slept soundly in preparation for the next day's revelry.

At dawn Smith was well east of Cape Town, and in six days he covered the six hundred miles to Grahamstown, where, without resting, he took command.

The governor, Sir Benjamin D'Urban, sorely frightened by the Xhosa invasion, arrived himself on January 14, and soon Englishmen and Boers, two thousand strong, were ready, accompanied by their three hundred Coloured militiamen. 'We shall thrash the Kaffirs,' Smith said, but it took seven months to make good his threat. However, with men like Tjaart van Doorn and Richard Saltwood at his side he proved tireless . . . and merciless. After one three-week push, he announced with satisfaction, 'I have burned two thousand, seven hundred and sixteen huts. That'll teach 'em.' But in a more sober mood he estimated correctly: 'It would take me one hundred thousand of England's finest to crush these Xhosa.'

When finally he had forced them back to their own territory he returned to Grahamstown, where triumphal arches lauded him as the victor of the frontier, the subduer of the rebellion. 'We shall now have peace,' he declared.

But peace depended primarily upon the actions of Sir Benjamin, who had arrived at the Cape filled with the preachments of Dr. Simon Keer. However, service with a realist like Harry Smith, plus personal experience on the battlefront, had induced a radical change of mind. In his perceptive report on the Sixth Kaffir War he informed London that 'this fertile and beautiful province is almost a desert, and the murders which have gone hand in hand with this work of pillage and rapine have deeply aggravated its atrocity.' He added that in his opinion the Kaffirs were irreclaimable savages: 'Merciless barbarians who have driven our seven thousand farmers to utter destitution.'

Desirous of preventing a repetition, and eager, as an honest man, to formulate a just settlement, he annexed a vast territory, erected a chain of forts, and moved every man he could to garrison the land. Friendly blacks who had not participated in the war were invited to remain where they were, and new lands would be opened up for Boer and English settlers.

It was a sensible solution and went a long way toward compensating the farmers for their grievous losses, but when the costs of the war had been totted up, Sir Benjamin stuck assegais in a large map to indicate the extent of the huge losses suffered by the white men: 100 slain, 800 farms burned, 119,000 cattle stolen, 161,000 sheep missing. Coloured suffered comparably.

When news of this prudent settlement reached London, Dr. Keer stormed Parliament: 'The blacks were fully justified in their attempts to reclaim lands that were rightfully theirs. Three thousand of these gentle, helpless people are dead, martyrs in their struggle against the systematic injustice of the Boer and his new ally, the scum of England who live along the frontier.'

Keer won the propaganda war. The sensible peace arranged by D'Urban and Smith was annulled, with the annexed territory being returned to the blacks. D'Urban was recalled in semi-disgrace, and Harry Smith was left powerless: 'How am I to eat up Kaffirs with a lawbook?'

Keer and his philanthropicals had a simple answer: 'Send considerate English officials to live among our black friends and make good English citizens of them.' They also suggested the establishment of a dozen new Golans in which missionaries could offer refuge.

It didn't work. The frontier slipped back into tension and anxiety, and in region after region the Boers, now smitten by a vicious drought that withered their crops, met quietly, some amid the ruins of the farms, and said, 'To hell with these Englishmen!'

Tjaart's attention to these grievances was diverted when his daughter Minna, about to deliver her first child, became persuaded that because of her husband's imperfect appearance, her baby would be a misshapen monster: 'I can feel him in my belly. He's fighting to get out. Because he's grotesque and evil.'

She became so convinced that she was about to bear some hideous thing, and that the fault was her husband's, that she could not tolerate his presence. 'I look at him,' she whimpered, 'and all I see is that crook-backt. Then he stares at me like a wounded bird and I see that pitiful eye, always weeping. God cursed him, and now Theunis has passed the curse along to our son.'

She often became hysterical, and when Tjaart heard of her rantings he grew angry: 'Damnit, Minna, thousands of women have babies every year. Mevrouw Bronk has how many?'

'This wife has twelve'—Minna sniffed—'but her husband is a whole man.'

'So is your husband. He saved your life, didn't he?'

'He couldn't even fire a gun. Mama had to. I know my son is going to be all bent and twisted.'

Her obsession grew so strong that as time for delivery approached, Theunis had to leave the poor hut that served as their temporary home, taking residence with a Du Toit family that had three boys in school. These boys heard about their teacher's troubles at home, and even the cause, and rowdier lads began to torment Nel, but when Tjaart heard of this he stormed into the school, brusquely told Theunis to wait outside, and threatened to thrash the entire student body if there was any more of this nonsense.

'Your teacher is my friend,' he growled. 'A good, decent man, and as you've been whispering, he's going to be a father in a few days.'

'Du Toit says the thing's going to be a monster.'

'Who's Du Toit?' And when that boy stood, Tjaart rushed at him, stopping with his face close to the boy's: 'If I hit you, you'd bounce through that wall.'

No one laughed, for the menace was real. But immediately Tjaart relaxed and said quietly, 'Du Toit, go fetch the master.' And when the bewildered teacher returned, dabbing at his eye, Tjaart said, 'Boys, his son will be my grandson. And my father was Lodevicus the Hammer. We raise only the best.'

He quieted the schoolboys but not his daughter, and now her apprehensions contaminated him, so that when Minna was about to have her baby, and women filled the hut, he fell into a sweat greater than any he had known when his own children were being born. As he paced near the doorway during the agonizing wait, he could see ill-formed cripples drifting across his vision, and he prayed that this child would be whole: God, this is an empty land. We need all the young ones we can get, and we need them strong.

Cries came from inside, then women running out: 'A beautiful baby girl!'

Brushing people out of his way, he rushed into the hut, then slowly went to the cot and picked up the naked infant. Holding it aloft by its heels, he inspected it from all angles, satisfied himself that it was perfect, then returned it gently to Minna's arms: 'Thank you, daughter. Not a blemish. I must tell Theunis.'

He galloped the miles to the school, where he crashed into the room, shouting, 'Theunis! It's a girl. Perfect in every detail.' Then he pointed at the Du Toit boy who had led the disturbances: 'You, fetch some water.' For although Theunis was grinning happily, it was apparent that he might faint.

The Boer frontiersmen could have withstood the drought and resisted the renewed Xhosa incursions, but now the English government insulted them with the disgraceful business of the slave payments. The Van Doorns and their Boer neighbors had been long prepared for the ultimate freeing of their slaves, and they did not object in principle, but they did sometimes wonder why England was so insistent when countries equally moral—Holland, the United States, for example—were content to hold on to their slaves.

What happened was difficult to explain and impossible to justify. The English Parliament, even though Sir Peter Saltwood, M.P., as manager of the bill had promised otherwise, refused to provide the £3,000,000 which would have compensated the Cape slaveholders for their financial losses. Such a miserly amount was voted that Tjaart would receive for his six legally owned slaves not the £600 promised, but a grudging £180. And then, because the rules were mindful of London-based magnates with vast holdings in the West Indies, it was stipulated that no Cape farmer could receive even his diminished allowance unless he traveled personally to London to collect it.

'I don't understand,' Tjaart said, endeavoring to unravel these incredible instructions.

'It's simple,' Lukas de Groot said as he listened to the law with a group of Boers. 'Instead of six hundred pounds, you get one-third. And to get this, you have to trek to Cape Town, six weeks, then take a ship to London, four months, then back by ship, then trek back home. Better part of a year.' And the reader added, 'Look at this line at the bottom.' There it was: *Any claimant who comes to London must pay a filing fee of £1-10-6 per slave to cover the cost of drafting the papers.*

Tjaart was outraged. Under these insane regulations, there could not be in the entire region east of Stellenbosch one Boer slaveowner who could collect the compensation due him, and it became obvious that this had been London's intention. Who could absent himself from his farm for most of a year? And who, if he did get to London, could argue before the claims court in English, the required language?

It was such a gross injustice that it encouraged a brood of unsavory types to circulate through the hinterlands, offering to buy up the farmers' rights at nine shillings to the pound; some of these scavengers were Englishmen who had failed at proper work and who saw this as a device for paying their passage back to London. The chances that any Boer would receive his funds from this gang of thieves was remote. 'But look, Tjaart,' one of them weasled, 'I make the trek to Cape Town for you. I sail to London for you. I spend days in the claims courts and urge your case in English. I earn my fee.'

'But the government owes me the whole amount,' Tjaart argued in Dutch. 'Why should I have to pay you more than fifty per centum?'

'Because you will be here, on a farm, and I'll be in London, in court.'

'It's so unfair.'

'It's the law,' the would-be agent said with a bland smile, and Tjaart, realizing how impotent he was to press his legal rights, would probably have accepted the offer and received less than one-sixth of what he had originally been promised had not a deputation ridden in from Grahamstown to prevent this injustice.

It was composed of three Englishmen at whose side Tjaart had fought in the Xhosa war, and two of them were his special friends: Saltwood and Carleton. 'Have you signed any papers?' Saltwood cried as he rode in.

'No.'

'Thank God. Now you, sir, leave this district or be horsewhipped.'

'I have my rights,' the man whined.

With a snap of his short hippopotamus whip, Saltwood flicked the intruder's saddle and called to Carleton, 'Show him what you can do.' And with a somewhat longer whip the wagon builder also struck the saddle.

'You'd better ride on,' Saltwood said, and when the man started to protest that he had legal rights, Saltwood snapped his whip and caught him on the leg. 'Thief, ride out of here,' he said, and the man, now thoroughly frightened, hurried away. Throwing threats, but only after he was at a safe distance from the whips, he started across country to other farms whose rights he would try to buy at nine shillings to the pound.

'Disgraceful,' Saltwood said as he explained what he and Carleton were proposing to their Boer friends: 'You've been our good allies. Without you we'd have no town back there, and we can't stand by and see you robbed. So you give us your claims and I'll send them to my brother in Parliament. I promise you nothing, Tjaart, except an honest deal. We may win, we may not, but at least you have a chance.'

As they were discussing the matter, Carleton happened to see Van Doorn's scorched wagon and identified it as one of his: 'How did you get it?'

'Traded for it at Graaff-Reinet.'

'You should have come to me. I'd have given you a proper price.'

'My sheep were in Graaff-Reinet.'

Carleton picked up one of the charred timbers and pointed to a small rubric carved into the wood: TC–36 (Thomas Carleton–Wagon 36). Had he been satisfied to work rapidly and without careful attention, this wagon might have been numbered in the 80s.

'You'll need a new wagon,' he said. 'When you trek north.'

Tjaart looked at him strangely. First it had been Jakoba, years ago; then Saltwood, when they were returning from the Xhosa war; and now Carleton—all saying that the Van Doorns must emigrate north, as though there were no alternative.

'Who's trekking north?' he asked.

'Haven't you heard? Hendrick Potgieter departed last week.'

'For where?'

'The north. That's all he said.'

'Alone?'

'No, he had forty or fifty people with him. Sarel Cilliers left with him, you know. And Louis Trichardt left with Van Rensburg. Months ago. Maybe ninety people and seventy or eighty servants.'

Tjaart felt weak. Things were happening at a speed and magnitude he could not comprehend, and reluctantly he conceded that perhaps his neighbors were right.

Saltwood said, 'We thought that if men like you and Piet Retief do finally decide to leave us, you must not depart with ill feelings toward us. Hell, Tjaart, you fought with us—side by side.'

So an agreement was made, whereby Saltwood took the warrants of several Boers—among them, Van Doorn and De Groot—promising to send them to Sir Peter in London to collect whatever the government might allow, but in order for the transaction to be legal, it was necessary for the Boers to sign away their rights for one shilling each, relying upon the good faith of their English friends. This the men did with absolute assurance that an honest reporting would be made, for the participants in this arrangement had fought as brothers in defense of their homes. That the Boers were now thinking of quitting those homes was as distressing to the Englishmen as it was to the Boers themselves.

Tjaart was deeply moved by the sympathy shown by Saltwood and Carleton during their visit to his still-ruined farm. In the war he had volunteered to protect the English establishments, yet the government had shown itself powerless to save Boer farms; hundreds had been ravaged, and now the government sided with the Kaffirs. However, he was convinced that the Grahamstown fighters like Saltwood genuinely sought his friendship and deplored the losses they had suffered. As he moved among the charred timbers of his barn he pondered seriously what he should do. Seeking Jakoba's counsel, he asked, 'Shall we build a new house?'

'We must go north,' she said bluntly. 'To seek free land.'

When Lukas and Rachel de Groot came south to report on the sad condition of their farm they fortified Jakoba's advice: 'We haven't the heart to build again. We're leaving.'

'To where?'

'Cross the Orange River. Then down into Natal.'

'I think I shall stay here,' Tjaart said deliberately. 'This is a good farm in a good region. I think the English will govern it well, one day.'

When the De Groots volunteered to stay and help him rebuild, he had an opportunity to see what a fine lad their boy Paulus had become.

He was four, a stocky little man who wore heavy trousers like his father's. His copious blond hair was cut straight across his forehead, bobbing this way and that when he ran, and his sturdy limbs indicated the strength he already had.

In the repairs to the farm the boy took to himself many tasks that might have gone to men, such as struggling with broken timbers and keeping the cattle to their proper areas. Tjaart, looking at the lad, thought: How splendid it would be if that boy married Minna's daughter. But when his thoughts ran in this pattern they were sooner or later diverted to that dazzling girl up north, Aletta Naudé, and he wondered if he would ever see her again. He pictured the inadequacy of Ryk, and imagined various ways in which he might come to a bad end: he proved a coward and Xhosa slew him; he stole money and an English officer shot him; he led a hunting party and an elephant crushed him. Always he disappeared, leaving Aletta to be saved by Tjaart van Doorn. The years would pass, but she would never age; never do household tasks. She was forever the nubile girl he had seen in her father's shop at Graaff-Reinet.

That name came up in the conversation quite often these days. From the first Theunis Nel had felt uncomfortable about living with a girl to whom he was not married, and when she became pregnant he felt downright immoral. But now that he was the father of the beautiful girl Sybilla, he began to nag Tjaart about taking the family to Nachtmaal, 'so that we can become acceptable in the sight of the Lord.' But Tjaart had no wagon and he was loath to borrow a neighbor's; still, Theunis was so insistent in his desire to sanctify his marriage, that Tjaart had to respect him, for in his own marriages he had experienced the same emotion. He was not an overly religious man, and certainly his two wives were rugged, rough women accustomed to frontier exigencies, but they had felt vaguely uneasy until their marriages were solemnized; there was something about living with a person of the other sex which had mysterious overtones: the passing of the month, the spacing of fertility, the birth of a child, the establishment of a home, the blessing of a barn to prevent lightning. These mysteries deserved attention, and prudent men gauged their lives accordingly. If Theunis Nel, a man of God, found himself enmeshed in these human complications and sought verification, Tjaart van Doorn was not going to ridicule him, even though sanctification lay ninety-two miles away, with no wagon to cover the distance.

Slowly, slowly in the rugged mind of this stubborn Boer his enthusiasm for rebuilding De Kraal waned and another stratagem began to coalesce: If we did go to Nachtmaal, Theunis and Minna could be married and Sybilla baptized, and we'd already be well on our way to the north. Three days' turning to the east, we'd be on the track the others took. The De Groots could ride in their good wagon. And I'm sure he'd help me build something usable on the burned frame.

Once he came close to weeping when he thought of that fine wagon, charred to dust in the ruin of his farm. But something could be built. The rims of the wheels were there, some of the fittings.

Very cautiously he said to Theunis, 'You are right. We must have a marriage and a baptism. In Graaff-Reinet.' That's all that was said, but everyone within the enfolding hills at De Kraal understood that the Van Doorns were preparing to abandon the farm they had spent sixty years in perfecting. The women began to sort away things for which they would have no space. The men sold off the weaker cattle. And little Paulus, approaching five, carried a hammer and banged away at everything.

No one mentioned a date for their leaving, but someone said casually that Nachtmaal would start in seven weeks. No one picked up the comment, yet day by day departure became more inevitable, and one day when Tjaart came upon his wife gathering eggs he saw that she was close to weeping. 'What a woman! You shout at me, "Go north!" and when I start, you weep.' She denied this.

He had a bad moment himself one morning when two Coloured herdsmen shouted, 'Baas! Baas! Look what come!' There, entering the farmlands from the hills at the southwest, came seventeen sable antelope, the most beautiful creatures in Africa, stately dark animals with white blazes across their faces and incredible scimitar horns that curved backward from the head, reaching forty, fifty inches. No purpose for these horns had ever been demonstrated; they swung so far back that they could not possibly be used in fighting. Perhaps, just perhaps, they were intended merely to be beautiful.

All the Van Doorns came from the house to witness this elegant parade. 'They must be the last ones south of the Orange River,' Tjaart said. 'See how gently they lift their feet.' How beautiful they were, how stately, this remnant of a great herd now diminished. Never before had they been seen at De Kraal, and their quiet passage across the farm seemed to presage a similar movement of the Van Doorns.

That night, while the majesty of the sables lingered in the valley, Tjaart said simply, 'We'll be following them north. Our life, too, has been used up here,' and once these words were thrown into the air, Jakoba and Minna felt free to weep.

If ever a group of people entered their exile with heavy hearts and moral reluctance it was the Van Doorns, and they spent one night drafting a letter of justification to their English neighbors in Grahamstown and their Boer friends in Graaff-Reinet. Tjaart began by saying, 'I think we've all heard the statement the Americans made when they broke away from England. I'm sure we must do the same.' And with ample guidance from Theunis, plus an occasional strong remark from Lukas de Groot, he compiled these thoughts which appeared in the papers of each community:

> When in the course of human events a group of people decide to leave their homes, they must, out of decent respect for their neighbors, explain why they are doing so. We leave our farms with sadness, our neighbors with deep regret, but we can do no other. Our reasons for leaving will be adjudged by all good men to be just and reasonable.
>
> The ravages of the past war show to the world that this Government is incapable of protecting our farmers against invasions of the Kaffir, and it has removed the last hope for an effective barrier to keep these hordes out of the colony.
>
> Government has taken our slaves from us without compensating us adequately or honestly. It has ridiculed our traditional way of handling slaves and has listened only to contumelious adversaries who parade up and down England preaching lies and defamations. The honest citizens of this land, who live with the problem, have not been listened to.
>
> Government has placed in the pulpits of our church predikants unfamiliar with our language. It has sent us officials to try our law cases who cannot understand the words we speak in our defense. It fills our schools with teachers who erase our children's knowledge of their mother tongue.
>
> We leave soil claimed by the English Government without rancor, or threats, or ill will. We pay testimony to the good people of English heritage who have befriended us and we wish them

and their nation well. We are satisfied in our hearts that we owe England no further obligations, and we are sure that the Government will allow us to depart in peace, for all we seek is to establish in the north a nation more obedient to God's rule.

Well after midnight, when five of the six participants judged that they had made a complete and honest statement, Jakoba startled them by pointing out that they had omitted their most important grievance, and when Tjaart asked, 'What might that be?' she explained. And after prayerful discussion her husband obediently added this paragraph, which came closer to the truth than any of the others; for that reason it would be widely quoted throughout the world:

> Through a series of unfortunate laws Government has tried to alter the natural relationship between the races, exalting the savage and debasing the Christian. It has asked us to form a society in which the proper distance between master and servant is not respected. This is against the teaching of God Himself and we cannot surrender to it. God has said that there shall be master and servant, and that each shall keep his proper place, and we propose to form a new nation in obedience to that law, one in which people of all color shall have their proper place, under the guidance of those whom God has elected to lead them.

At four that morning the Van Doorns and De Groots, a trivial group in the large movements of mankind, confirmed with prayer the fact that they were heading not only to the Nachtmaal at Graaff-Reinet, but on to a world they could not even imagine. The Great Trek was under way. The Voortrekkers were in motion.

On the afternoon that Tjaart's letter appeared in the *Graham's Town Journal,* Major Richard Saltwood and Thomas Carleton saddled their horses, rasped out a series of orders to their servants, and galloped westward to intercept the Voortrekkers before they left De Kraal.

They arrived in time to see the wagons loaded, and they stood in shock to witness the pitiful thing in which Van Doorn proposed to carry his worldly goods into exile: 'Those wheels won't get them to Graaff-Reinet.' But of this they said nothing.

'We can't let you go away like this,' Saltwood said. 'You've been our brothers-in-arms.'

With a sweep of his hand Van Doorn indicated the ramshackle buildings: 'This is what is left of generations of Van Doorns.'

'I know,' Saltwood said.

'And the slave money. Will we ever get our share?'

'There's no word from London, Tjaart. These things take time.'

'We have no more time.'

'Tjaart, how old are you?'

'Forty-seven.'

'I thought so. You and I are twins. Same year. You are my brother, and I want to buy your farm, because I respect it.'

'This?' The two men looked about them.

'Yes. I can finish rebuilding it. I want my home here.'

'You would pay for this?'

'Yes. We made a kind of deal, last year. It wasn't your fault the facts changed.'

So they spent that day discussing what a fair price would be, and where the road north would take them, and whether they would ever return. Evening prayers were held, with Theunis Nel translating the Bible in his own inspired way, one-third Bible, two-thirds Theunis.

In the morning it became apparent that for some reason the Englishmen were reluctant to depart, and their stay was so protracted that finally Jakoba asked bluntly, 'When are you leaving?' and Carleton said, 'We have a present for you,' and after a painful hour, over the eastern rim of hills appeared twelve oxen dragging a new Carleton wagon with a tidy disselboom, a fine set of patented brakes, and a double canvas cover to keep out the rain and heat. On a board under the body was burned the rubric TC-43.

'I need my sheep for the journey north,' Tjaart said.

'You owe us no sheep,' Carleton replied. 'You helped us start our colony. We help you start yours.'

'I think we should have a prayer,' Theunis said, and from Exodus he wrenched four timely texts about Israelites moving across the Red Sea and toward their promised land. 'We are the new Israelites,' he said, whereupon the men who had fought together so many times started their farewells.

When the new wagon was packed and the five men were preparing to go their separate ways—two Englishmen back to Grahamstown, three Boer families north to lands unknown—an incident occurred which seemed at the time to be of no significance, whereas in fact it altered the history of South Africa.

A bold and cunning Xhosa prophet named Mhlakaza, with a ridged scar across his forehead, had taken advantage of the confusion following the war to slip into the area to spy out the amount of damage done in the recent raids. Not realizing that five armed men were ahorse, he suddenly appeared on the horizon in a silhouette so exposed that any one of the men could have shot and killed him.

Automatically Tjaart van Doorn raised his rifle to do so, but his son-in-law Theunis grabbed at his arm and cried, 'No! He's done nothing.' So Tjaart lowered his gun, and the Xhosa, laughing derisively, disappeared from view.

If Tjaart had killed him, and in the presence of two Englishmen, word would certainly have filtered back to London; Dr. Keer would have asked persistent questions; a scandal would have ensued, proving once more the heartlessness of the Boer; and quite possibly Tjaart would have been hanged. So it was fortunate that Theunis restrained him.

On the other hand, if Tjaart *had* killed this crafty man, the lives of many thousands of Xhosa would have been saved, a noble people would have been preserved at full strength, and the history of this area would have been dramatically modified.

On 15 March 1836 the Van Doorn party, as it came to be called, crossed the Orange River—that moody giant between banks of sand—leaving the jurisdiction of England and heading into those vast lands which Mal Adriaan had explored seventy years earlier.

Through gradual accretions the group now consisted of nineteen families with seventeen wagons. The latter number was most significant in that it was the smallest number that would allow the formation of a proper cordon, or laager, inside which women, children and cattle could be protected.

The emigrant party contained nineteen grown men, but this included Theunis Nel, deemed largely useless despite his heroic performance when the Xhosa overran De Kraal, and an equal number of mature women, making thirty-eight adults, all battle-tested. They had among them ninety-eight children: some, like the daughter of Theunis and Minna, mere infants; others, like the older sons of some of the families, almost men, well capable of handling a gun.

So there were a hundred and thirty-six white people, but they were attended by two hundred Coloureds and blacks. In most cases these servants had received reasonably good treatment on the farms and had come to accept that they belonged with the Boers, not in the way a slave belongs to an owner, but in a paternalistic pattern, as much a part of the white family as the children.

These servants had remained loyal when others had run off, and they saw no reason to leave the baas now. His life was theirs; they would find no other work they liked better; they were as excited as he by this adventure of heading into unexplored lands. They'd accept an old pair of shoes or a tattered jacket with a smiling 'Dankie, Baas,' a scolding with a great show of misery. And between the good and the bad, if they met with other Coloureds or blacks, they would argue that their baas was the best in the land. To show that they meant it, most were prepared to die for 'their' white people.

Each of the seventeen wagons had a span of from twelve to sixteen oxen, plus half a dozen spares; all men, most boys and many of the Coloureds had horses. And the party as a whole had two thousand cattle and eleven hundred sheep, which explained why the Voortrekkers were lucky if they covered six miles a day.

Of the hundred and thirty-six Boers, only two men could read, Tjaart van Doorn and Theunis Nel, but all could recite long passages from the Bible, and as they prepared to enter a new land, they compared themselves constantly with the ancient Hebrews who appeared in the Book of Joshua. Night after night, when the wagons were assembled, not in laager, for there was as yet no enemy, Theunis Nel, in the manner of a predikant, would read from that chapter and apply the lessons of that noble journey to conditions faced by the Voortrekkers. Inevitably the Boers came to believe that they were a reincarnation of Joshua's army and that God watched over them, too:

Now therefore arise, go over this Jordan, thou, and all this people, unto the land which I do give to them, even to the children of Israel. Every place that the sole of your foot shall tread upon, that I have given unto you . . . There shall not any man be able to stand before thee all the days of thy life . . . I will not fail thee, nor forsake thee . . . Only be thou strong and very courageous, that thou mayest observe to do according to all the law . . . turn not from it to the right hand or to the left, that thou mayest prosper withersoever thou goest.

One other characteristic of the Voortrekkers applied particularly to the Van Doorn party: all the adult men, except the unfortunate Theunis Nel, had had more than one wife, and he was lucky to have any. If one took seven leaders of seven representative groups, the number of their wives would be 2-2-3-3-3-4-5, and seven typical ages for the brides would be 13-13-14-15-29-31-34, the first series proving that men liked their wives young, the last indicating that no woman was allowed to remain a widow long. When men were Old Testament patriarchs, as these men were, they used up their women.

They were in general an intransigent, opinionated group of Dutchmen whose isolation had caused them to turn their backs on the liberalizing influences of the eighteenth century, except that Tjaart himself had quoted from the American Declaration of Independence in laying forth his reasons for emigrating. They felt no need for Rousseau, Locke, Kant or the German theologians who had begun to expose the mythological elements in the Old Testament. They were satisfied with the fundamentals their Dutch and Huguenot ancestors had brought with them in the middle 1600s and rejected any new ideas imported by the English. Above all, they were self-confident, so that when one Voortrekker came upon a little stream running due north, he had no hesitation in announcing, 'This is the beginning of the Nile River,' even though that body lay a good two thousand miles away—and forthwith he christened it Nylstroom (Nile Stream).

The wagons in which they would live for the next two or three years were special affairs, not at all like the great lumbering things that crossed the American prairies. They were small, only twelve to fifteen feet long, and rather low to the ground, except that when a canvas shelter was thrown over the top, they appeared higher. They were surprisingly narrow, and were so packed with family possessions that there was no room to sleep inside, except for the mother, who made a rough bed for herself atop the baggage. The iron-banded wheels were invariable: small front ones with ten spokes, larger back ones with fourteen.

A superior feature of the Voortrekker wagon was its disselboom, the pivoted main shaft that was so fixed to the front axle that it provided maximum flexibility in both guiding and in riding easily over the bumpy trail. But only the last pair of oxen were harnessed to the disselboom; all others pulled against chains and harness that were attached to the wagon in various ways.

Since nearly two thousand wagons would participate in the early move to the north, trails became marked across the veld, but many par-

ties like the Van Doorn struck off on their own, making their way over
the veld from one conspicuous flat-topped hill to the next.

It was a habit of the Voortrekkers to linger at any congenial spot,
sometimes for a week, at other times for a month. Then the wagons
would be brought into proximity, but not in laager, and the men would
ride far afield to hunt while the women tended to sewing, and the making of needed articles, and the baking of special dishes. Jakoba was particularly pleased when the wagons halted at some spot which contained
a good supply of ant hills, for as a girl she had learned how to utilize
these remarkable constructions that rose two and three feet above the
veld, shining like little red-sand mountains.

Selecting a sturdy one off by itself, she would take a heavy stick and
break open a small hole at the spot where the side of the dome touched
the earth; she was careful not to disturb the upper part of the ant hill,
for it was this dome which ensured fruitful use. When the hole was broken, a flood of small black ants scurried about the landscape and soon
disappeared. Then the opening was crammed with sticks, leaves and
other flammable debris and set afire; for an hour or so it blazed and
smoldered, becoming in due course an effective, excellent oven in which
all kinds of food could be prepared.

Jakoba liked to bake her bread in such ovens, but she also knew
how to prepare a delicious toasted curry dish made of antelope strips
bathed in a sauce flavored with dried onions. The men were so fond of
this that as they traveled they kept an eye alert for ant hills, and the
women learned that when such were plentiful, there would probably be
a restful halt. And if there were no hills, they prepared a bobotie.

The determined movement of these Voortrekkers must not be
thought of as a gallop across the landscape toward a known, specific
destination; it was more like the slow displacement of a small village—
with all the utensils, the babies' cribs, and the cattle moving patiently
along.

But in one startling aspect the trek did not resemble the slow displacement of a town: among the fourteen thousand Boers who would
ultimately travel north, there was not one clergyman. The Dutch Reformed Church, which had played, and would play, so significant a role
in the history of the Boers, refused to sanction the mass exodus, and for
substantial reasons: it suspected that the exiles represented a revolutionary spirit, and Calvinism could not tolerate that; it feared that the
farmers were moving away from church influence, and this had to be
opposed; and it felt uneasy about unauthorized movement into unex-

plored territory, since in such unfamiliar land the dominance of the church might be diminished. Resolutely the church turned its back on the emigrants, castigated them as revolutionaries and ignored their pleas for assistance.

More remarkable was the fact that in the most significant event in South African history, individual predikants also cut themselves off from the people, with many dominees flatly refusing to accompany the wanderers. The Voortrekkers, one of the most religious people on earth, with a profound reliance upon the Bible, were thus rejected by their own church. There could be no baptisms, marriages, solemnized burials, or even weekly services, yet at the end of the travail the Voortrekkers would be even more solidly supportive of their church than they had been at the beginning, and after having refused the travelers the services of religion, the Dutch Reformed Church would gather the emigrants back into its hands, converting the whole nation into a theocracy.

The man who suffered most in this strange development was Theunis Nel. Acutely aware of the Voortrekkers' spiritual needs, and grieved by the refusal of his church to help, he volunteered at various intervals to serve as substitute predikant, but invariably the majority rejected him on the grounds of his blemished eye and crookbackt.

He did not complain. Patiently he bore his wife's scorn, the ridicule of his fellow travelers, the lack of support from leaders like Van Doorn and De Groot. He tended the sick, tried to teach the children, and recited prayers at the graves of those who died. At one funeral, when an old man was being buried short of the new home he had hoped to reach, Theunis was overcome by emotion and launched into a graveside homily, a sort of informal sermon about the transitory nature of human life, and after the burial party had left the site, Balthazar Bronk, who took religion most seriously, asked Theunis and Tjaart to stand aside, and when the others had left, he berated the sick-comforter.

'You're not to preach. You're not a predikant.'

'We were burying a poor old man.'

'Bury him. And keep your mouth shut.'

'But, Mijnheer Bronk—'

'Tjaart, tell this simpleton to obey the rules.'

And when two young people from another party wanted to marry and came to Nel soliciting his assistance, he was willing to comply, but again Bronk intruded: 'Bedamned, I've warned you five times against posing as a predikant.'

'But these young people want to start their new life—'

'Let them wait till a real minister comes along.' And he was so adamant that the couple had to depart, their union unsanctified. But when
Bronk was not spying, Theunis rode after the pair and told them, 'God
wants his children to marry and multiply. I name you man and wife,
and when a true predikant does arrive, ask him to bless your marriage
properly.' When one did come after three years, he was able to baptize
two children also.

Where was this exodus heading? No one worried. The families were
more concerned with leaving English rule than with their destination:
some proposed to cut east across the Drakensberg Mountains, which
had hemmed Shaka's empire. Others, like Tjaart van Doorn, were determined to head north, cross the Vaal River and settle in remote
valleys.

But where in the north? One of Tjaart's earliest memories was of
the tales told about his grandfather Adriaan, who had gone into that
northland with a Hottentot named Dikkop and a tame hyena named
Swarts: 'He said he grew frightened at the Limpopo River and turned
back, and found a lake which he called Vrijmeer, and on its bank he
buried Dikkop.' Tjaart believed he was destined to reach that lake.

But regardless of whether a Voortrekker elected Natal as his destination or the unexplored north, all trails converged at the foot of a mountain with a fanciful name, Thaba Nchu. The Voortrekkers called it *Ta-
ban'-choo,* and so many wanderers found rest here that for some years
it formed a major settlement.

It was here that they met the first major black tribe north of the Orange River. In the first days of their trek they had encountered small
groups of blacks and a few Coloureds, but at Thaba Nchu, there was a
tribe of five thousand who welcomed them as allies against a mortal
enemy to the north: Mzilikazi, Great Bull Elephant of the Matabele,
one of the architects of Mfecane.

On 13 June 1836 wagons of the Van Doorn party rolled into Thaba
Nchu, where five or six hundred earlier arrivals were waiting for their
leaders to reach some decision, and they rested there, and there was
time for new friendships to develop. Especially active was young Paulus
de Groot, who ran with boys twice his age and wrestled with them, too.
He talked little, was savagely protective of his rights, and seemed to
prefer the companionship of Tjaart van Doorn above that of his own fa-

ther, and this was understandable, for the lad showed signs of growing into the kind of man Tjaart was: solid, cautious, devout. When young Paulus said his prayers his large squarish face glowed with religious fervor, for it seemed to him that God was listening.

Despite this natural inclination toward devotion, Paulus disliked Theunis Nel, the self-appointed representative of religion, for the boy sensed the ridicule in which the sick-comforter was held. One morning, when Tjaart suggested that Paulus start learning his letters from Theunis, the effect of Tjaart's sponsorship was destroyed when Minna came out of her tent screaming at her husband, calling him disrespectful names and conveying to the boy the community's reaction to the cock-eyed fellow. No man could discipline a strong-minded boy like Paulus de Groot if he could not first discipline his own wife.

Tjaart, hoping to see this promising lad grow into a leader of men, took it upon himself to teach the alphabet and instruct in numbers, and one morning he was seated on a log drilling the boy when Lukas de Groot came past, taking offense at the idea of another man instructing his son: 'He don't need to read. I don't read and I do all right.'

'All boys should learn to read.'

'Your boys didn't.'

'That's right. They were to live at De Kraal all their lives, and it didn't signify.'

'Why does it signify now?'

'Because we're moving into a new world. Your son may be needed as the leader of a great community. If he can't read, the leadership goes to someone else.'

The discussion might have become ardent had not Minna wandered by to inform her father that he must go out to shoot antelope, for the supply of biltong was depleted; and as she stood speaking to the two men, they saw that of a sudden her face changed from its normal sullen expression, and a frown gave way to a smile of broadening radiance. They turned to see what effected this change, and De Groot spoke for both men: 'Look who comes to join us!'

Among the newcomers to Thaba Nchu were sixteen families who had joined the main stream of Voortrekkers just south of the Orange River, and in the lead was Ryk Naudé, the handsome young farmer, and his pretty wife, Aletta. For Minna Nel, the return of the one man she could love was prophetic: God had used this exodus to bring them back together; for Tjaart, the arrival of Aletta meant that his tormented imaginings were given life. She was even more enticing than he had remembered, older now and more the woman, and his eyes would never leave her.

Wherever Aletta Naudé moved in these days when the leaders were trying to reach decisions, Tjaart endeavored to place himself so that she would have to see him, and after a while she became aware that he was doing this. It irritated her. She was nineteen years old and happily married, while he was forty-seven, with a second wife and a grandchild. He looked silly when he mooned at her, and one afternoon when he had succeeded in interposing himself between her and her tent, she said sharply, 'Mijnheer van Doorn, you're making yourself ridiculous,' and this so embarrassed him that he kept away from her for some days, but then the terrible fascination manifested itself again, and once more she had to avoid him.

The arrival at Thaba Nchu of so many new emigrants caused other troubles. Ryk Naudé and his wife announced that they had decided to cross the Drakensberg and go down to Natal, and this encouraged Lukas de Groot to choose the same option, which meant that Tjaart would be separated both from the girl he loved and from his long-time associate. With profound seriousness he contemplated relinquishing his idea of settlement in the north so as to remain with people he preferred, and he might have surrendered to this temptation had not the affair of the lion skin shown him what fearful temptations threatened his family.

Minna had been less discreet than her father. She was overjoyed to meet with Ryk again and was not ashamed to display her affection. She did everything but embrace him in public, and when he told the clustered emigrants that he and some friends were moving east to see if they could shoot some lions for their skins, she openly ran to him, imploring him to be careful, and when he was gone she moped. This so irritated Jakoba that she told Tjaart, 'You must speak with her. She's becoming a Jezebel.'

So Tjaart took his daughter aside and gave her blunt warning: 'You're married to a good man. He cherishes you and little Sybilla, and you owe him a decent respect. Minna, behave yourself.'

'But Ryk promised me. In the new land, somehow he will be set free.'

'You're married forever. In the eyes of God. Before the predikant at Graaff-Reinet. Obey your vows.'

Tearfully, but with stubborn determination, she said, 'Father, if Ryk and Aletta were separated. Somehow. In God's wisdom. How happy you and I would be.'

Tjaart was stung by her probing of his secret, by her shrewd connivance in bringing it out. What he replied was 'They're heading east over the mountain, we're going north over the Vaal—and we'll never meet again.'

But when Ryk came back to camp with four lion skins and gave Minna one of them, she was certain that this proved his devotion to her, and she convinced herself that he was as hungry for her as she was for him, and at night, when others were asleep, she crept to his tent and quietly, lest Aletta hear, called him out, and coaxed him beyond the wagons. There she poured out her love, and helped him to undress, and encouraged him to join with her three times. It was an explosion of love unlike any he had ever known with Aletta, beautiful as she was, and an invitation to endless future repetitions.

In the days that followed, even Tjaart, who was not quick to perceive nuances, became aware that something gravely wrong was occurring in his family, and one evening he followed Minna, and from a hiding spot, saw with astonishment his daughter's brazen conduct. Shame prevented him from breaking in upon the lovers, but next morning, after the cattle were tended, he went to his daughter's tent, told Theunis to go teach his class, and then confronted Minna.

'I know what you're doing. I saw you behind the wagons.'

'I can't live without him, Father. I'm going down into Natal.'

The possibility that a child of his should be guilty of disobedience was more than he could tolerate; a red haze flooded his eyes, and he recalled instructions from the Bible: 'If a child be disobedient, he shall be killed. If a woman commit adultery, she shall be stoned to death.' In his befuddlement he knew not what to say, so with a wild sweep of his arm he knocked her to the ground, then stormed at her, calling her names from the Old Testament, threatening to drag her before the public to be humiliated.

When his rage subsided, and some kind of sanity returned, he lifted her from the earth and held her as she trembled from the fury of his blow: 'Minna, God has tempted you and me. We have both been guilty of great sin. Tomorrow we go north to prevent the destruction of our souls. And tonight you sleep in my tent, because you are precious to me and I cannot bear to lose you.'

Next morning, 6 July 1836, Tjaart van Doorn, Theunis Nel, Balthazar Bronk and four other families not in the original group formed a new unit to cross the Vaal River and start a fresh community dedicated to the rule of God, the proper relationship between master and servant, and the strict separation of races. It took them eighteen days to reach the river, and with each tramp of the oxen's hooves, Minna Nel and her father felt more and more desolate, for they would never again see the persons they loved.

Only once did either of them mention the mournful separation; Minna said as she walked beside her father, 'My heart seems to break at every step. I realize now that he is gone. I heard a trekker describe the Drakensberg. Once a man crosses those mountains, he will not come back.'

Tjaart, desperately hungry for someone to talk with at this crisis in his life, confessed: 'Because of what you saw, you will find this hard to believe. But my heart yearns for three people. Most of all, little Paulus de Groot. I should love to watch him grow into a man. His possibilities are endless. And I will miss Lukas, too. And after them, Aletta, in a different way.'

'We'll never know.' And that was all she said, plodding her way toward the Vaal.

When they reached the river they found it swollen by an unexpected flood, and were forced to camp on the south bank, where they found several other parties also waiting for the water to subside. At first Tjaart was vexed by the forced delay, but one day the assembled Voortrekkers saw a heavy cloud of dust to the south, and as it approached they discerned four wagons accompanied by the complement of Coloureds, blacks and cattle.

It was Lukas de Groot, hurrying north to overtake his friend, and when the two men met, there was unspoken apology, silent acceptance. 'When I thought about it,' De Groot said, 'I knew my fate was to the north.' He did not add, 'With you,' but the joy his son Paulus displayed at being reunited with Tjaart spoke for the entire family. It was a happy, sensible reunion, and not even when De Groot spoke thoughtlessly of the Ryk Naudés—'They're heading into Natal, fine pair'—was there any recurrence of the earlier irritation.

Indeed, when the river lowered and the seventy-odd Voortrekkers completed the crossing, Lukas easily consented when little Paulus asked, 'Can I stay with Tjaart tonight?' The Van Doorns camped much farther to the west than the De Groots, so that late at night when frenzied messengers galloped in from the northeast, they reached the latter family first.

'Where'd you come from?' two dusty, tired men shouted, scarcely halting to rest their horses.

'Thaba Nchu,' De Groot replied.

'Go into laager immediately. Kaffirs on the rampage.'

Before Lukas could interrogate the men they disappeared, spurring
their horses westward and leaving the De Groot family with a difficult
decision. They had nine wagons, not enough for a proper laager, and
even these were well scattered. To assemble them would necessitate
much maneuvering, and there was no certainty that blacks would come
their way. Besides, the hurried trek up from Thaba Nchu had tired the
men, so it was decided to wait till morning.

When the messengers took a last look back and realized that the
Voortrekkers were not protecting themselves, they were appalled; rein-
ing in their horses, they returned to shout, 'Damnit, go into laager—
now!' But again the De Groots ignored the warning, for as Lukas
pointed out, 'Those men are not our friends. They're Englishmen, and
they're trying to scare us into turning back.'

In disgust the messengers galloped westward along the Vaal River
until they came to the Van Doorn encampment: 'Go into laager at
once. Kaffirs.'

'What Kaffirs?' Tjaart shouted back.

'Mzilikazi!'

It was a name to strike terror among those acquainted with the
north, and although the Van Doorns had known no one who had contact with the Bull Elephant, as he was now called, they had heard
around the campfires at Thaba Nchu reports of his annihilations. One
hunter who knew the area north of the Vaal had said, 'Mzilikazi was
the shrewdest of the Zulus. Three times they came after him and three
times he beat them off. To protect himself he has cleared an area,
maybe two thousand square miles. Killed everything. Men, women, cattle, wild animals. Only thing I saw in fourteen days' travel—hyenas,
jackals, a few small birds. I've spotted his scouts south of the Vaal, not
far from here. He's watching us every day, the Great Bull Elephant.'

'Is that the Mzilikazi we were warned against?' Tjaart asked.

'The same. He has twenty thousand warriors.'

'Good God! If they all come at us . . .'

'They're spread across the area. It will be only a small detachment.'
The two Englishmen, who had been hunting in the north, accepted a
drink of water, and asked, 'Any other companies of you Dutchmen?'

'Three others. Farther west.' So off the two messengers went, spurring their horses.

Even before they were gone, Tjaart had started bringing his eleven wagons into an abbreviated laager, and this consisted of jamming the front of one against the rear of the one ahead, guiding the disselboom almost completely under the front wagon and fastening it with the trek chains, then lashing the wheels together and sending children out to gather thorn bushes, which the boys cut and the girls carried back to their mothers, who wove the prickly wood into spokes and wheels and each crevice along the outside perimeter. When they were finished, no enemy could sneak up to the laager and force his way either through or between or under the wagons, for he would face a wall of wood and canvas and thorn. One small opening was provided, and for it a gate of thorn was hastily built. Nine of the sixteen Coloured servants were sent back toward the river with the cattle and sheep; the other seven would fight alongside their masters.

Two people watched the construction of the laager with keen interest: Tjaart van Doorn and little Paulus de Groot, too young to help cut the thorn branches, not old enough to herd the cattle. What he did was stay at Tjaart's heels, running errands for him. Later he would carry lead to the women so that they could swiftly reload the rifles. Each adult man needed three guns, because as soon as he fired one it was useless, and he would have to pass it with his left hand to his daughter, while reaching out with his empty right hand to his wife. 'Give!' was all he would say, and the loaded second rifle would be slapped into his hand for the next shot. Tjaart's two women could load the guns just fast enough to keep one of them ready, and little Paulus could run bags of powder to them.

Dawn came without any sign of Mzilikazi's men, but toward nine Tjaart heard a dreadful hissing sound to the east and then the ominous stamping of heavy feet on the earth, and a deafening cry of 'Mzilikazi!' followed by a titanic rush of near-naked soldiers and a flight of deadly spears.

'Do not fire!' he ordered the thirteen trekkers and the seven Coloureds. 'Let them come closer . . . closer.' And he heard the hissing sound again, the stomp of many feet and the same cry 'Mzilikazi!' Also, he heard one lonely voice inside the laager praying: 'Almighty God, we are few, but we wear Your armor. We are not afraid, for we have tried to be righteous men. Almighty God, they are many but You are with us. Guide us in this battle.' It was Theunis Nel, gun in hand, waiting for the charge.

'Mzilikazi!' shouted the warriors, rushing at the small concentration of wagons, expecting to overrun it.

'Fire!' Tjaart cried, and twenty guns blazed directly into the face of Mzilikazi's men.

The carnage was horrendous, but after the first ranks fell, wave after wave replaced them.

'Fire!' Tjaart cried again, and then the Voortrekker men passed along their empty guns, reaching back for the next loaded one.

'Fire!' Tjaart cried again and again, but still the intrepid enemy kept rushing at the laager.

'Tjaart!' a boyish voice called. 'Under the wagon!' But before Paulus could attract his captain's attention, Jakoba had chopped at the head of a black crawling into the laager, cleaving his skull.

For ninety terrible minutes the assault continued, with every man holding his position between the wheels of the wagons, continuing to fire while women loaded the rifles.

When the Matabele warriors slowly retreated, a few infuriated veterans of other battles refused to believe that this handful of trekkers had been able to stand them off. Enraged by their defeat, they reformed at a safe distance, shouted for the last time 'Mzilikazi!' and dashed right into the muzzles of the guns. They died with their hands touching the wagons, but none broke through.

At dusk Tjaart went out with little Paulus to find the dead and count them: 'One hundred and sixty-seven. On our side, none.'

Theunis Nel, hearing these figures, called upon the entire party to kneel, and as they did he intoned an impassioned prayer, rocking back and forth, daubing his left eye now and then with his fingers. He reviewed the godliness of the Voortrekkers, the loyal faith of their grandfathers, their heroism in entering a strange new land, and he concluded:

'Almighty God, when we looked across the veld and saw those dark and fearful forms, more than the mind could count, against thirteen of us, we knew that victory would be possible only if You were with us. The victory was not ours, but Yours.'

And every man and woman and child listening, even the seven servants not included in the prayer, knew that what Theunis was saying had to be true.

But when the final tally was taken, the Voortrekkers had gained no victory. Not at all. Of the two companies camping to the west, one had been overrun, the other had not been annihilated but had lost four men. And at the De Groot camp, which had refused to go into laager, all fifty-two people were slain—children, Coloureds, former slaves—and all were horribly mutilated.

'You mustn't go there, Paulus,' Tjaart said, tears in his eyes at the horror of the massacre. 'Your father and mother and sisters are dead.'

'I want to go,' the little survivor said, and he rode back with Tjaart and the gravediggers to see what was left of his family. He recognized them, and did not vomit at the sight the way some of the adults did. He walked solemnly along the line of their eight bare feet, for they were stripped naked, and saw the manner of their deaths. Not a tear came to his eyes, and as the shallow graves were dug—just enough to keep the hyenas away—he placed a stone upon the chest of each person he had loved.

The rampaging of Mzilikazi's regiments forced all Voortrekkers to change their plans. The few like Tjaart who had ventured north of the Vaal River had to retreat hastily well beyond the south bank, and all along the line of advance the emigrants took stock of their perilous state as they awaited the Great Bull Elephant's next move.

Two members of a black tribe suppressed by Mzilikazi crept down with reports that the Matabele were assembling a mighty army that would overwhelm the Boers, with a superiority of one hundred and fifty blacks to one Voortrekker.

The English government chose this moment of dread to deliver, by means of late arrivals at the camp, its latest proclamation against the Voortrekkers; it stated that even though the fugitives had fled English soil, they must not think that they had escaped English law, because any wrong-doing committed south of the twenty-fifth parallel would be construed as having taken place within English jurisdiction and would be punished accordingly. Since the Vaal River lay well south of that parallel, the battle in which the Van Doorns had defended themselves could be interpreted as an unwarranted aggression, and Tjaart could be hanged.

The document was of course printed in English, but after it had been translated to the astonished Voortrekkers, Tjaart asked to see it. Even though his English was sparse, he could pick out some of the insulting words, and as his lips framed them they created in him a violent bitterness, for he could still envision the mutilated bodies of Lukas de Groot and his people.

It was typical of Tjaart's slow, stubborn awakening to any problem that for two days he said nothing, just carried the proclamation with him, pausing occasionally to reread the offensive lines, but on the third day he assembled all members of his party, and such others as he could reach, to deliver his judgment:

'We know from the Book of Joshua that we are doing God's work, in obedience to His commands. But at every turn we are opposed by the English. My father, whom you knew, Lodevicus the Hammer, he was dragged before the Black Circuit and accused by English missionaries of murder. Bezuidenhout here, his people were hanged at Slagter's Nek after God Himself broke their ropes and granted them reprieve. The English have stolen our language, the pulpits in our churches, our slaves. And now they send these laws after us to warn us that we can never escape them.

'I say "To hell with all the English." I say to my son Paulus, "Remember this day when the Voortrekkers, facing death at the hands of Mzilikazi, swore an oath to be free men." '

Somberly the members of the party whispered, 'I swear!' And all knew that any further compromise with any Englishman had become impossible. From that day, the break must be total.

But on the very next day a smous arrived from Thaba Nchu, and Tjaart was thrown into sad confusion. The peddler brought not only supplies, but also small packets addressed to Tjaart van Doorn and Lukas de Groot.

'Major Saltwood in Grahamstown asked me to deliver these,' the nervous little trader said.

'De Groot's dead.'

'Oh, dear!' The smous was terrified. 'Mzilikazi?'

'Yes. What shall we do with this?'

'Did any of his family survive?'

'His boy, Paulus.'

'Then we'd better give it to him. Because I made a solemn promise to deliver . . .'

They called Paulus and handed him the last message ever sent to his father, and when the boy opened the wrapping, there lay a pile of crisp English pounds. Every penny owed for the De Groot slaves had been paid in full, with no commission subtracted.

When Tjaart opened his packet he found the same. He was perplexed. His English friends had proved their trustworthiness, yet he had
sworn open enmity toward them, and he did not know what to say, but
after he gave Jakoba the two bundles of money for safekeeping he
walked for long hours alone, then sought out the smous and asked, 'Did
Major Saltwood pay you for bringing me the money?' And the peddler
said, 'Yes, two pounds.' Awkwardly Tjaart translated this into rix-
dollars, and he was amazed that Saltwood had spent so much of his
own money to forward the funds.

He was confused on other matters, too, for in these days of anxiety
when no one knew how soon Mzilikazi would strike again, he learned to
his disgust that Ryk Naudé had not crossed the Drakensberg but had
encamped some miles away. On several nights Tjaart had ridden over to
seek Minna, and again spied on their love-making and he was bewildered: Why would a man with a wonderful wife like Aletta bother to
plow the furrow with someone like Minna? He loved his daughter and
had worked diligently to find her a husband, but he could never delude
himself into thinking that she was in any way the equal of Aletta. Yet
here was this young no-good imperiling his marriage by sneaking out at
night to make love to a plain and married woman.

Tjaart became so disturbed by his daughter's misbehavior, relating it
always to his own renewed infatuation for Aletta, that one day he
resolutely confronted Ryk to upbraid him for his adultery: 'Ryk, we're
about to engage Mzilikazi in a battle where we might all die. If God
turns against us for our sins, we might perish. Don't you feel any responsibility?'

'I feel love for your daughter.'

'Love?'

'Yes, I should have married her, as she said.'

'But you have a beautiful wife . . .'

'Old man, tend to your battle. Guns will win it, not commandments.'

This was so blasphemous that Tjaart could not decide how to respond, but Ryk saved him: 'In two days we march north—to face Mzilikazi. We may all be killed, but I'll be happy knowing that Minna . . .'
He did not finish this extraordinary statement, just walked off to prepare his horses.

Tjaart was angered by the young man's insolence, and surprised,
too, for he had not thought of Ryk as brave enough to oppose an elder.
More tantalizing were some of the deductions that could be made from
what the young husband had said: if Ryk did not think much of his

wife, if he did not want her, what wrong could there be if someone else approached her? None, he concluded, and as to the adultery he would be committing, he avoided any consideration of this by simply erasing Jakoba from his mind.

So he resumed his old habit of placing himself in Aletta's path, a foolish, dumpy man in belt and suspenders offering himself to the most beautiful young woman among the trekkers. He was ridiculous, and he knew it, but he was powerless to stop. One afternoon he waited till she was apart from the others, then grabbed her, pulled her behind some wagons, and started kissing her furiously.

To his surprise, she did not resist, nor did she participate. She simply leaned against him, even lovelier than in his dreams, smiling between the kisses and whispering at the end, 'You're not such a silly old man, after all.' And with that she walked slowly away, completely untouched by his embraces.

The encounter was an agony for Tjaart. During one spell he railed silently against his son-in-law: Why doesn't that damned fool Theunis manage his wife? Where in God's hell did I find such a man to bring into my family? And for more than an hour he mentally reviled the little sick-comforter as the cause of his own malaise.

Then he envisioned the forthcoming battle against Mzilikazi, and when he recalled the fearlessness with which those first Matabele had kept storming the laager, he grew frightened: If twice that many, three times that many, come at us, what shall we do? Then he recalled the mutilated bodies of De Groot's people, and a sickening rage overcame him: We must slay them, slay them! No Voortrekker ever raised a finger against Mzilikazi, and he did that to us. We must destroy him.

And then he paused, and like all Boers, reflected on the fact that even self-protection, let alone victory, would be impossible without God's help, and he became totally contrite, taking upon himself the burden of sin that he had tried to throw upon the adulterous Ryk Naudé. Lighting an oil lamp, he took down his Bible and looked through Proverbs till he came upon the passage which spoke definitively of his transgression:

> For the commandment is a lamp; and the law is light; and reproofs of instruction are the way of life: to keep thee from . . . the flattery of the tongue of a strange woman. Lust not after her beauty in thine heart; neither let her take thee with her eyelids . . . Can a man take fire in his bosom, and his clothes not be

burned? Can one go upon hot coals, and his feet not be burned? So he that goeth in to his neighbour's wife; whosoever toucheth her shall not be innocent.

He was about to close the book when he realized that he required much more help than he could find by himself, and he sought out Theunis Nel, sleeping alone, for his wife was away committing sin, and he said to the sick-comforter, 'Come read the Bible with me and instruct me.'

Always prepared for such calls, Theunis rose, wrapped himself in a blanket, and accompanied Tjaart to where the Bible stood open under the lamp, and he grasped at once the significance of Tjaart's having been reading Proverbs Six. But he said nothing of adultery or lusting in one's heart.

'Theunis, this time we face terrible odds.'

'We did last time.'

'But then we didn't know. Now, with the De Groots dead, we do.'

'God rides with us.'

'Are you sure?'

The little man quickly turned the pages from Proverbs and closed the book, then placed his hands upon it and said, 'I know that God intends our people to establish a new nation in His image. If He sends us on this mission, surely He will protect us.'

'Then why didn't he send his predikants to accompany us? To give us guidance in His word?'

'I've wondered about that, Tjaart. I think He sent common folk like you and me because He wanted His word to work up slowly from the ground. Not thundering down in sermons written by learned Scottish predikants.'

'Is that a possibility?'

In the flickering shadows the sick-comforter said, 'If we had with us a learned dominee, we'd put all the burdens on him, let him tell us what God intended. This way, it's simple people like you and me. And when we work out our solutions, they will come from the heart of the Voortrekker, not from outside.' Rising and striding about the tent, if a man so slight could be said to stride, he told Tjaart, 'You will gain victory. You will slay the Canaanites. You will lead us across Jordan into our inheritance.'

And these two unhappy men—the stronger torn apart by sin and confusion, the weaker desolated by the misconduct of his wife—knelt and prayed.

* * *

In these years Mzilikazi commanded fifty-six regiments of highly trained infantry, so that had he wished, he might have sent twenty thousand men against the Voortrekkers, but despite his losses at the Van Doorn laager, he still could not believe that white men with guns and horses and interlocked wagons could prevail against his power. So he sent south only some six thousand men, not all of whom would be in position to attack the main laager when the battle joined.

A resolute body of Voortrekkers, consisting of some forty men, an equal number of women, about sixty-five children and the normal proportion of Coloureds, had moved to institute a massive laager of fifty-one wagons securely tied together and protected by solid interweavings of heavy thorn. Peculiar to this laager, where all participants knew that they must triumph or they would perish in hideous mutilation, was a block of four wagons kept at the center and covered with boards and heavy canvas: in these the women and children would take refuge during the battle, but it was foreseen that steadfast women like Jakoba van Doorn and Minna Nel would stay outside to help in the fighting, while many boys like Paulus de Groot would be at the barricades, firing guns at times and running powder to their mothers.

The leaders had chosen a flattish area at the base of a small hill, which meant that Mzilikazi's regiments would have to attack up a slight slope or down a steep one; at either point they would be at a disadvantage. To the surprise of the Voortrekkers, the enemy chose the steep southwest slope, and there they established an enormous camp, preparing methodically for the assault that must destroy the laager and all within it.

For two days the regiments sharpened their assegais and perfected their signals for the big thrust. During this time the Voortrekkers could see the enemy and hear him attending his duties; at night the Matabele campfires flared, and men wondered: Will the attack come at dawn?

On 16 October 1836 the Matabele were ready, and started slowly toward a position opposite the laager, whereupon Tjaart asked Theunis to lead the defenders in prayer, but once again Balthazar Bronk objected on the grounds that the defense might be imperiled if an improper clergyman was allowed to utter his own prayers. To this Tjaart responded, 'The enemy is ten minutes from us and we need God's help,' but Bronk was insistent: 'God is perfect. His church is perfect. Neither can tolerate a blemished man.' So Theunis was silenced, but Tjaart himself was encouraged to lead a prayer, which was short, impassioned, and a mighty solace to those who kept one eye open to watch the remorseless approach of some six thousand battle-hardened Matabele.

The leaders resolved to approach the Matabele in a startling way. A fearless patriarch named Hendrik Potgieter, famed for having had five wives in rapid succession, proposed that a sortie of twenty to thirty men —more than half the entire force—ride out into the middle of the black commanders and try to reason with them. It was this kind of action only an idiot would devise, or a man who felt the touch of God upon his shoulder.

'I'll go!' Tjaart said.

'I'll go!' Theunis Nel echoed.

Soon Potgieter had twenty-four volunteers besides himself, and then a twenty-fifth. It was Balthazar Bronk, whom Jakoba had shamed into joining: 'Are you afraid to die?' Reluctantly accepting the gun she thrust at him, he joined the suicide patrol.

On signal from Potgieter, these daring men left the safety of their laager, spurred their horses, and rode at breakneck speed directly at the heart of the enemy. One of the Coloureds in the laager had served with a hunter in Matabele lands, and through him, Potgieter addressed the warriors: 'Why do you wish to attack us? We come in friendship.'

'You come to steal our lands,' a commander shouted.

'No! We come to live in peace.'

'Mzilikazi, the Great Bull Elephant, is angry. His word is that you must die.' One commander raised his assegai and shouted the war cry 'Mzilikazi!'

At this signal the regiments started running toward the Voortrekkers, who sped back to the safety of their laager. That they made it could only be attributed to God's providence, for the odds against them were crushing. But they succeeded, firing from the saddle at the advancing Matabele.

Not all entered the laager. Five men, totally demoralized by the hordes of black warriors and withered by fear as assegais flew about them, reached the entrance with the others, but then ahead of them they saw an escape route which would carry them all the way to Thaba Nchu and safety. Without consciously intending to be cowards, they accepted this invitation so enticingly put before them. They took flight.

Young Paulus de Groot, standing by the entrance to welcome the returning Voortrekkers, saw with amazement that they were quitting the fight, and cried, 'They're running away.' And these five became known in Voortrekker history as the Fear Commando. In their lead as they fled was Balthazar Bronk, his face ashen with awful dread.

'May God have mercy upon our children,' Jakoba muttered, and then no further prayers were said, for with a single, terrifying scream the black soldiers fell upon the laager.

At every moment for more than a hour it seemed that the chain of wagons must crumble, and so many assegais fell upon the four wagons in the middle that Paulus ran out and collected more than twenty. Selecting the one that seemed strongest, he took position at a point where the wagons seemed most likely to collapse and stabbed at any Matabele who tried to penetrate.

The laager held. The barrels of the guns were burning hot from overfiring, but those courageous women who were helping in the fight kept on—exhausted, sweating, fearful. And the wagons held. One group of six was pushed back two feet, so powerful were the attacking Matabele, but in the end even those wagons held, their disselbooms shattered, their sides peppered with assegais, their canvas torn.

Veg Kop, they called this fight, Battle Hill, where less than fifty determined Voortrekkers, aided by their remarkable women and their loyal Coloured servants, defeated more than six thousand attackers. When Tjaart rode over the battlefield he counted four hundred and thirty-one dead Matabele, and he knew that only two Voortrekkers had been killed. But he also knew that there was hardly a member of the laager that did not have some wound to show; Paulus de Groot had been cut twice by flashing assegais, and he was proud of this, but he had to agree when a girl pointed out that he had given himself one of the wounds by his awkward handling of an enemy spear which he was trying to wrench free from the wagon it had pierced.

Jakoba had a painful cut in the left hand, but this had not impeded her handling of ammunition, and Minna had a gash in her leg which required bandaging. Tjaart was untouched, but he found to his dismay that during the attack Theunis Nel had taken two serious stabs. The man who comforted the sick was himself put to bed, and during the waiting period, when the Matabele had quit the fight but not the battlefield, he was visited by many who told him that as a man of courage and devotion he ought to be proclaimed the Voortrekkers' dominee; but there were just as many, and more obstinate, who refused to countenance such a move, for as they repeated: 'God Himself forbade such an ordination.'

* * *

The Voortrekkers had won the Battle of Veg Kop, but when the cost was counted, they found that the Matabele had slain every Coloured herdsman and had driven off every animal they possessed. For eighteen hungry days they were unable to move from their laager, and their plight might have grown even more perilous had not help arrived from an unexpected quarter: the black chief at Thaba Nchu, hearing of their predicament, decided that he must help the brave people who had smitten his enemy. He sent trek oxen north with food for the Boers, oxen for their wagons, and an invitation to return to the safety of Thaba Nchu, which they accepted.

Despite the loss of their livestock, they felt such joyousness of spirit that there was celebration for many days, with the somberness that marked the aftermath of battle giving way to drinking and raucous singing. When Tjaart growled, 'What I want is to find Balthazar Bronk and those others who fled,' he was told to forget them: 'They galloped in here telling us what heroes they had been. Then scuttled across the mountains, where they can still be heroes.' The smous, relieved that he had escaped the Matabele, produced a French accordion, which he hoped to sell to some wandering family, and on it played a series of old Cape ballads, and while the others danced, Tjaart took from the peddler's wagon a random supply of sugar, raisins, dried fruits and spices, to which he added such odds and ends as Jakoba could supply. In his brown-gold pot he baked a bread pudding which, with some pride, he contributed to the festivities.

Among those who took a cupful was Aletta Naudé. Carefully adding a little milk, she dusted her portion with sugar, then, keeping the mug close to her lips but not eating, and with a spoon clutched in her right hand, she looked over the rim at Tjaart and smiled. Slowly, provocatively she lowered the mug, dug out a spoonful of the pudding and took it to her lips; she delicately tasted the stuff and smiled again.

Tjaart was so entranced by Aletta, so held by the spell of her smile, that when he finally reached for his share of the pudding, there was none, but he could taste it whenever Aletta took a spoonful, and as she neared the end of her portion he moved toward her, and without speaking, indicated that she must accompany him.

Once clear of the celebration, he guided her behind a set of wagons, and while the accordion filled the night with revelry, pulled her to the ground and hungrily tore aside her clothes. Never before had he known what an overwhelming thing sex could be, and he was so preoccupied with his own violent experience that he failed to notice that Aletta was merely smiling at his ridiculous performance.

When it ended, and he lay back watching her impassive dressing, he made no attempt to reconcile his adulterous action in taking another man's wife with his profound gratitude to God for having protected the Voortrekkers in their laager. These were two unrelated things, and he was not obligated to harmonize them, for as he said to himself: King David had the same problem.

In April 1837 Tjaart encountered once again the man who was to become the memorable figure of the trek, Piet Retief, the frontier farmer with whom he had ridden so often on commando, and they talked of those heroic days: 'Remember how we did it, Tjaart? Fifty of us, two hundred Xhosa, a skirmish, a retreat. I understand that with the Matabele, it was different.'

Tjaart shivered. 'Five thousand coming at once. Six thousand. And every man prepared to die. For hours we fired point-blank into their faces.'

'That's finished,' Retief said. 'You're to come down into Natal with me. The Zulu will leave us alone. They have a sensible king, Dingane by name. We can deal with him.'

'I would hate to leave the plateau. Mzilikazi remains a threat, but I still want to go north.'

'The ones who did, they didn't fare too well. I think they're all dead.'

Retief was right. The toll had been heavy, and he advanced so many other sound reasons in support of Natal that Tjaart wavered, but Jakoba stiffened his determination to cross the Vaal: 'You've always wanted to search out that lake your grandfather spoke of. Do it. Natal is for weaklings like Bronk and Naudé.' It was the first time she referred to the family with which her own was so sorely enmeshed, and she said no more.

He accepted her counsel and informed Retief that the Van Doorn party would not go down into Natal, but that evening as he was heading back to his own tent, Aletta Naudé appeared mysteriously from behind a row of transport wagons, and almost before he knew what was happening, he was clutching at her, rolling with her in the stubble. When he lay exhausted, she ran her fingers through his beard and whispered, 'We're crossing over the mountains. Come down into Natal with us.'

That night he informed Jakoba that Retief had convinced him; they were moving east. She said, 'It's a mistake,' and in the morning she learned that Ryk Naudé and his wife were going, too.

It was a journey into springtime and into some of the most difficult land the Van Doorns would traverse. In their slow migration from De Kraal they had climbed unnoticed from near sea level to well over five thousand feet, so that for some time now they had been operating on what the men called 'the plateau.' It was high land, dipping to lower levels where rivers passed through. But now they were required to climb toward eight thousand feet, then drop precipitously down to sea level. The upward climb would be easy, the downward plunge frightful.

Eleven wagons gathered to make the attempt, and as they climbed the gentle western face of the Drakensberg they could not foresee the problems that awaited them, because Ryk Naudé assured them: 'Retief has gone ahead to scout a safe pass down. It can be done.'

But when they reached the summit and saw for the first time what lay ahead, even Tjaart blanched. To take a Voortrekker wagon down those steep slopes would be impossible, regardless of how many oxen a man had to help hold the wagons back. And when the beasts saw the cliffs they refused to go down them even without the wagons. On this route, Tjaart had to agree, descent was hopeless.

So he and Theunis searched for other trails. They found them, plenty of them. They descended easily, ran along relatively flat ground, then *boom!* A sheer cliff two hundred feet high.

Try the next trail. Fine descent, a reassuring spread of land sloping easily down, then a fairly sharp but negotiable stretch ending in another cliff.

For three weeks, as spring continued to blossom—a wild assortment of mountain flowers and baby animals and birds all around them—the Voortrekkers tried fruitlessly to locate that one pass through the mountains that would allow them to reach the lush pastures they knew existed below. Always the enticing avenue, always the sheer cliff.

In the fourth week Tjaart saw a lesser trail leading well to the north, and its conspicuous difference reassured him, for at no point was it inviting or easy; it was cruelly difficult, but as he descended, scraping shins, he gave a shout of triumph when he saw that the pass continued right down to level land. But could wagons traverse it? He thought so.

Accordingly, he hurried back to his beleaguered group and told them, 'We can go much of the distance in our present condition. But for about two miles we'll have to take the wagons apart and carry them, piece by piece.' Ryk Naudé thought this impossible, whereupon, with disgust, Jakoba pointed back over the route they had come: 'Then go back.' After much hemming and hawing, he decided to trust his luck with the others.

For two difficult days eleven wagons slipped and slid down grassy inclines, then rattled over stony ones. Theunis Nel conceived the good idea of reversing wheels, so that the big ones were in front of the wagon, where they could be better controlled on the really steep slopes, and another man devised a trick for replacing the big aft wheels altogether, and substituting heavy timbers which would drag along the ground under the axletree, providing an effective brake: the oxen did not like this, and when they saw the heavy branches being moved into place, grew restless; the Coloureds talked to them by name, treating them as pampered individuals, each with its own catalogue of complaints. It was remarkable how a few soothing words gave the hardworked beasts the encouragement they needed.

But every yard that was successfully traversed brought the Voortrekkers closer to the low cliffs that could never be negotiated by any wagon. There the procession halted while Tjaart pointed out the grand and easy path that awaited them, once they cleared these cliffs, and when he had consoled them with his assurances, he led them off to the north to a prominence below which lay the rolling pasture lands that reached to the Indian Ocean. It was an introduction to a homeland that would never be excelled, a promise of grandeur and fruition: 'There lies Natal. There rests your home.' He did not, Jakoba noted, refer to it as their home, and for this she was grateful, for she remembered the cleaner, harder land of the Transvaal.

It was a hellish nineteen days. Theunis discovered a footpath by which he could lead the oxen down to the pastures, where they flourished. Every man, woman and child, Boer and servant alike, strained and sweated on the horrendous descent of the berg.

It was murderous work. Unpacking a heavy wagon and then disassembling it was difficult enough, but back-packing all items down the steep inclines where feet slipped on pebbles was exhausting, and reassembling the wagons and then repacking them was exhausting. The Voortrekkers accepted the challenge; even Paulus de Groot, hardly as tall as a wheel, sought responsibility for guiding one of Tjaart's wheels down the grade, but did not listen when Van Doorn warned him not to let it get going too fast. Before long Tjaart saw with dismay his precious wheel thundering down the grade and about to break to pieces. Fortunately, it stopped itself in bushes, and Tjaart had to laugh as he watched the lad wrestling with it to get it back on the path.

Ryk Naudé was less energetic. He complained of the route Tjaart had chosen, arguing that one farther south would have been better, and when he grudgingly carried an item down the cliff, he was most tardy in returning for another, and on one of his own trips Tjaart spotted Ryk and Minna kissing behind some rocks. He was turning out to be what Jakoba had predicted, a selfish, inconsiderate young man, and the older Voortrekkers were disgusted with him.

Jakoba was indefatigable, slipping and sliding as she descended with baskets, puffing with determination as she climbed back. For all those days she worked harder than any of the oxen, supervising the passage not only of her own wagon but also those of her neighbors. When she saw Aletta shirking, she spoke harshly: 'You needn't linger so long down there. Work's to be done.' But Aletta only smiled at her with the knowing grin of a younger woman who has captivated an older woman's man.

When this part of the descent was accomplished, the Voortrekkers were so exhausted they rested for five days, during which Tjaart made a fortunate discovery. While checking the last portion of the trail, to satisfy himself that it would be as easy as he had judged at first, he came upon a place so majestic that he had to conclude that God Himself had set this aside for his weary travelers. Because of its cathedral shape, he named it Kerkenberg (Church-in-the-Mountain), and to it he led his people.

It was a series of shallow caves and beautiful flat areas rimmed by towering granite boulders. From the outside it appeared to be a collection of mighty rocks assembled in accordance with some plan; from the inside it was a cathedral with the boulders inclining slightly toward the center and open to the sky; from every aperture the worshipper could look down to see the beautiful plains of Natal.

When the Voortrekkers entered this sanctified place, they were overawed by its rough majesty and almost simultaneously they knelt in prayer, thanking God for His many deliverances, and while they were on their knees, Tjaart summoned Theunis Nel and uttered the words the little man had waited so long to hear: 'Theunis, by your valor and devotion you have earned the title *predikant*. You are now our dominee, and you are to lead us in prayer.' And this time no one tried to deny him.

Nel, fifty-two years old, rose and stood with his blemished face looking upward; this was a church beyond his greatest hope, an ordination nobler than any he had dreamed of, for it came from the people in the heat of their travail. His prayer was short, an acknowledgment that these Boers could not have survived the regiments of Mzilikazi, the dangers of the veld, the descent of these hills without God's assistance. The joy they felt at their deliverance was attributable to Him, and they thanked Him in advance for leading them into this land of peace and prosperity.

'Amen!' Tjaart cried, and when the people rose, he said, 'We have missed many Sundays. Theunis, you shall preach to us.' The crookbackt man looked apprehensively at the congregation and became unnerved for a moment when two older men led their families from the church in the rocks, for it was against their belief that a man so marked should serve as dominee. But when the noise of their departure subsided, Tjaart nodded quietly toward his little friend, and Theunis, set free at last, entered upon a sermon of transcendent power, and when he finished he left the worshippers and walked to where the dissident families stood beside tall rocks.

'Please join us now,' he said. 'The preaching part has ended.'

In November, Van Doorn terminated theological discussion; he was required to leave Kerkenberg and go alone to the lower levels, where he hoped to find a permanent home for his people. He was not happy about leaving, for Balthazar Bronk, the craven hero of the Fear Commando, had returned, and in Tjaart's absence, would assume charge, and he was a man not to be trusted. But Tjaart had work to do, so he descended to the Tugela River, along whose banks Shaka had conducted so many of his battles, and there he met again with Piet Retief: 'What a fearful descent we made over the mountains.'

'Once down, never up,' Retief said.

'Has the king agreed to give us the land?'

'No. And that's why I am so pleased to see you here with me, because soon we shall go to see Dingane.'

Retief was now fifty-seven years old, whip-thin, bearded, and eager to put a capstone to his life's work: he would establish the Voortrekkers in a solid, fruitful home, then send to the Cape for predikants and watch the founding of a new nation obedient to God's instructions. To accomplish this, he needed only the final approval of the King of the Zulu, who had already agreed in principle to the proposal which Retief had offered.

The two men, accompanied by assistants, rode north from the Tugela River toward the Umfolozi, the historic river of the Zulu, and near its southern banks they came upon Dingane's Kraal, the established capital town of the Zulu.

Dingane was no black Napoleon like his half brother Shaka; he was a Nero, a tyrannical despot caring more for entertainment and intrigue than solid governance. His town was big, a dwelling place for forty thousand people. It contained row upon row of beehive huts, large parade grounds, a royal hut with ceilings twenty feet high and a reception hall with a vast dome roof supported by more than twenty pillars, each completely covered with intricate beadwork.

Retief and Van Doorn were led to the cattle kraal, the center of Zulu life, but before they could enter it and stand in the presence of the king, they had to divest themselves of all arms and come as humble supplicants. They were astounded by the extent of the place and the obvious desire of the king to impress any visitors. 'When the king appears, you must fall on your bellies and crawl like snakes to his feet,' an attendant explained in good English, acquired from a mission station.

'That we will not do,' Retief said.

'Then you will be killed.'

'No. Because you will explain to the king that Boers do not crawl.'

'But I could never address the king, unless he spoke first. He would kill me.'

'And if you don't, we will kill you.'

The man began to sweat so copiously that Tjaart realized he could never bring himself to tell the king anything, so he was dismissed, and the two Boers remained standing.

In a flurry of excitement, a score of lesser attendants rushed about the far end of the kraal, whereupon all the Zulu present fell to their knees while King Dingane entered, smiled at the Boers, whom he had expected to remain standing, and took his seat in a remarkable throne. It was an armchair ornately carved in Grahamstown and presented to the Zulu king by an English trader.

It was now nine years since Dingane had murdered his half brother Shaka, and then his fellow conspirator and full brother, Mhlangana, and then his uncle, and his other full brother Ngwadi, and nineteen other relatives and counselors. The years had been good to him; he weighed some two hundred and sixty pounds, had over three hundred wives, and an insight and a sense of what might happen next, which compensated somewhat for his treacherous ways, and it fell to him to confront the white men who kept coming over the Drakensberg.

He had already mastered the art of dealing with the Englishmen who clustered at the seaside; since they had ships which kept them in contact with London and Cape Town, they had to be treated with respect on the one hand and harsh indifference on the other. As he explained to one of the head councillors, Dambuza, with whom he often shared responsibilities: 'With the English it's all right to kick them, so long as you salute their flag and speak well of their new queen.'

The Boers were a much different problem. They owed no allegiance to any ruler in Europe, and apparently none to the government in Cape Town. They were self-ruled and obstinate. They did not wear badges like the English, and they did not summon ships from across the ocean to assist them in time of trouble. As he told Dambuza, 'They are like their oxen, patient and pressing. I can live with the English, for I know what they will do next. But I am afraid of these Boers, who come at me from across the mountains that you told me could not be passed.'

When Dingane was seated in his great chair he signaled, and sixteen of his brides were brought in to arrange themselves at his feet. A dozen of the women were beautiful, dressed in silky garments which the king had personally designed, but the other four were tremendous women, weighing almost as much as their king; on them the garments seemed ridiculous.

The king indicated that he was now ready to open his bargaining session, whereupon six older men were summoned to flank him, and while he smiled at the Voortrekkers these official flatterers, as they were called, poured forth their praises: 'Oh, Great and Mighty Slayer of the Matabele, Wise Master Elephant of the Deepest Jungles, He whose Footfall Causes the Earth to Tremble, Wisest of the Planners, He Who Orders the Wizards to be Impaled . . .' The interpreter, in bored monotone, rattled off an additional dozen descriptions, after which Dingane silenced the flatterers, who were prepared to go on all day if necessary; they knew how to keep a ruler happy.

When Dingane finally spoke, Retief learned with disappointment that no real negotiation would occur that day; what the king had in mind was a series of displays calculated to impress the visitors with his power and their own insignificance, and to launch this exhibition, he used a device that had awed earlier visitors. In a compelling voice he cried, 'Tell the warriors to appear.' And then he raised his left hand to his mouth and spit upon his wrist. 'And all is to be done before the spit dries on my wrist.'

'What happens if the spit dries?' Tjaart asked the interpreter.

'The messenger who received the order is strangled.'

The warriors were ready. From numerous openings more than two thousand Zulu fighting men rushed into the cattle kraal bearing tall white shields, which they flashed this way and that in a dazzling display. Then, with three mighty stompings of their right feet, they shouted 'Bayete!' and the earth reverberated. They then began a warriors' dance, swaying gently at times, leaping into the air at others; it was an awesome performance, kept in such perfect synchronization that Retief whispered, 'I doubt if any European army could do the same.'

The first day was spent in this manner, and when it ended Retief said, through the interpreter, 'Tomorrow we shall talk.'

That was not Dingane's plan, for on the morrow he sat with his guests in the royal cattle kraal, where, like an Oriental ruler showing his jewels to impress a visitor, or a European his collection of paintings, he prepared to display his conspicuous wealth. Again he spit on his wrist, whereupon servants led enormous herds of cattle past in silent defile. One herd of more than two thousand consisted of alternate rows of black and red; another of somewhat smaller size was all brown.

When the handsome beasts departed and a scurry of men cleaned up the droppings, Dingane signaled once more, and now came an incredible performance. Filing through the entrance to the kraal came two hundred snow-white oxen garbed majestically in garlands and caparisons and all without horns. Each was attended by an ebony warrior who stayed at the beast's head but never touched it.

Tjaart assumed that this was another march-past, and he was sufficiently impressed by the beauty of these matched animals to nod approvingly to the king, who held up one hand to indicate that the real performance would now begin.

Slowly, to the Boers' amazement, the two hundred oxen began to dance with the warriors, following a set of rather intricate steps, forming large patterns and then regrouping, without ever a command that Tjaart could hear. Gradually, as Dingane had intended, the effect became hypnotic and wonderfully African: these huge beasts delicately stepping off their patterns, turning majestically and coming back, hesitating, twisting, and then moving forward at their slow purposeful pace.

Each animal looked as if he alone were performing the dance, as if the eyes of all spectators were following him, and each displayed obvious satisfaction in dancing so well.

That night Retief told Tjaart, 'Tomorrow we talk.'

This time he was right. They talked, but not about the grant of land. Dingane, listening attentively to every word the interpreter said, asked, 'What happened when your people met with Mzilikazi?'

Delighted at this opportunity to instruct a pagan king, Retief expounded enthusiastically on the Boer triumphs: 'A handful of us . . . Van Doorn here was one of them. He'll tell you—'

'Tell me what?' the king interrupted.

Tjaart knew instinctively that he must not boast of his victories over the Great Bull Elephant, even though Mzilikazi was Dingane's enemy, for to do so would raise questions in the king's mind, so he replied modestly, 'We fought him twice, and he was powerful.'

'That's not the story!' Retief protested, and while Dingane kept his pudgy fingers pressed against his lips, the Boer leader cried, 'Forty of our men held off five thousand of his. Wave after wave of his soldiers came at our men, and we shot them down till they lay like ripe pumpkins in the veld.'

'So few of you, so many of them?'

'Yes, Mighty King, because when a ruler disobeys the commands of our God, he is struck down. Remember that.'

Dingane did not change his expression, but Tjaart noticed that he kept his fingertips pressed hard against his lips, as if he were controlling himself lest he say too much, and when the two Voortrekkers took their seats for this day's entertainment, Tjaart said, 'I wish you had not been so bold,' but Retief, in some exhilaration, replied, 'From time to time you must teach these pagan kings a lesson.' When Tjaart tried to remonstrate, Retief said, 'Look!'

More than two thousand Zulu warriors in full battle dress, with distinctive ox tails tied about their upper arms and knees, had run onto the parade ground, taken position and stamped their feet, shouting 'Bayete!' Then came a stylized battle show replete with cries, stabbing exercises and mock attacks. Tjaart, who had experienced the real thing, was repelled by the display, but Retief was riveted by the performance, and told the king, 'Your men are mighty warriors.' Dingane nodded, then replied, 'They live at my command. They kill at my command.'

On the fourth day the king finally consented to talk seriously with the Boers, and assured them that he was viewing favorably their application for a large grant of land south of his own domains. He asked Retief to prove his responsibility as a possible settler by recovering some cattle stolen from him by a distant chief, and more or less assured him that once this mission was accomplished, the land grant would be quickly arranged during Retief's next visit. After a long speech of farewell, with foot-stomping and a graceful exit of his sixteen favorite wives, the king nodded and departed, leaving Retief and Van Doorn free to return to their company of waiting Voortrekkers. But before the men left the area, an English missionary, who had been living near Dingane's kraal for some months, hurried up to them and said, 'Friends, your lives are my concern.'

'Ours too,' Retief said lightly, for he was pleased by the promising results of his first official visit with the king.

'Did he invite you back for another visit?'

'Yes, in January, if we could complete a small matter for him. If not, in February.'

'Friends, in the name of God, do not come back.'

'Foolishness. He's going to give us the grant we seek.'

'Friends, believe me. I live with these people. Every sign I saw proved to me that he intends killing you.'

'We Boers do not hold much with missionaries,' Retief said, and Tjaart nodded. Neither of the men could tolerate the philanthropists, and they saw in this meddling man one more troublemaker.

'Friends, regardless of what you think of me as a missionary, I warn you as a guide. Dingane means to kill you. If you return to his kraal, you will never leave.'

Retief had grown impatient with the intrusion. Brushing the missionary aside, he said as he strode past, 'Say no prayers on our account. We're not Englishmen. We're Dutchmen. We know how to deal with Kaffirs.'

When Tjaart returned to the Kerkenberg he found the place deserted except for one boy shepherding a flock left there for utilization by chance travelers. He said that Mijnheer Bronk had prevailed upon the group to complete the descent into the valley of the Blaauwkrantz River.

Tjaart was at first angry that Bronk should have made such a bold decision alone, but when he saw the new site he had to admit that it was an improvement on the aerie in the hills. Kerkenberg had been for resting; the Blaauwkrantz was for living. It had ample water, good drain-age, and a promise of the fine pastures which the Voortrekkers would occupy for the remainder of their lives. Tjaart went to Bronk and said, 'You have chosen well.'

In December 1837 new arrivals struggling down the Drakensberg brought the Voortrekkers an unexpected Christmas present: 'We have defeated Mzilikazi. He's fled north of the Limpopo, gone forever.' And three men who had participated in the final running battle elaborated: 'We caught him in retreat and kept at his heels. Overpowered him. Four thousand of his men dead. Two of ours.'

Brave beyond the demands of normal warfare, these black troops without guns or horses had tried to combat a white army that had both, and the day had come when the Great Bull Elephant had to face the fact that his regiments could no longer dominate the vast area they had delineated for themselves, and his kraals could not hold out against the Boer and Coloured horsemen who came thundering through the huts at dawn. As one of the arriving Boers said, 'Like an enraged elephant, he thrashed about the veld, then slowly withdrew.' He crossed the Lim-popo, passing that grand and gloomy collection of ruins at Zimbabwe and establishing his permanent kingdom of the Matabele in the western reaches of that olden empire. For Mzilikazi, the great odyssey of his people, which had left such a trail of blood, was ended.

But even as Jakoba heard of this victory, she shared with Tjaart her apprehensions over the way things had been going ever since Balthazar Bronk had led the Voortrekkers to lower ground: 'I don't feel safe here. We've worked so hard to come this far, and I think it's all wrong.'

'What do you propose?'

'We should go back to higher ground.'

'We can't move all these people back to the Kerkenberg.'

'I mean all the way back. To the plateau where we belong.'

Tjaart was astounded. 'You'd go back up that mountain?'

'I would. Right now.'

'We'd never get our wagon up.'

'Leave it. Let's go back to Thaba Nchu and join some other group moving north.'

The idea was appealing. Tjaart had not liked what he saw at Din-gane's Kraal, for if the Zulu king controlled that number of well-trained men, what would keep him from acting like Mzilikazi if he became angry? And why had he been so nervously concerned about the defeat of his arch-rival in the early skirmishes if he were not applying that experience to himself? Surely, if the Voortrekkers had heard of the Bull Elephant's final expulsion, Dingane must have heard too, and must be wondering whether a handful of Boers could do the same to him.

'I fear the English missionary may have been correct,' he confided to Jakoba. 'I think Retief might do well to avoid that kraal.'

'Warn him.'

'He listens to no man. Never has.'

'Tjaart, I think we should leave here. Let Bronk command. Did you know that during your absence he expelled Theunis from the Kerkenberg?'

'He what?' Such graceless behavior in the name of religion nauseated Tjaart, and he sought the sick-comforter to assure him that many of the men in the company, those who had faced death repeatedly and had not run away, appreciated his spiritual assistance: 'Theunis, when a man faces odds of a thousand to one, and when the cattle have been stolen and the horses stampeded, he needs God's assurance. On this trek you have been more important than four guns. Stay close to us, for I fear that harsh days lie ahead.'

'As bad as on the Vaal River?'

'Worse. Mzilikazi was wily and brilliant. Dingane is terrible and undisciplined. If I'm ever absent, keep the wagons in laager.'

'We haven't been in laager for months.'

'I've seen Dingane,' Tjaart said. 'I've seen his kraal. This man is a king, and kings invade.'

Three times in the next days he contemplated following his wife's advice and leaving this encampment, and he even went so far as to consult with his son-in-law: 'Theunis, how would you respond to Jakoba's belief that we should leave here, climb the mountain and go north, as we proposed?'

'I would go tomorrow.'

'Why?'

'Balthazar Bronk, he's a tyrant. He's not a man to lead other men.'

Tjaart laughed. 'You're angry with him for demoting you.'

'That's one reason,' Theunis confessed. 'But we're in a new land, new problems. Desperately this people needs a predikant. Our church has refused to countenance us, so we should establish our own rules.'

'I tried. You saw me try, and we were defeated.'

'I would like to go north with you, Tjaart, and find our own land. Believe me, this Natal is contaminated.'

It was contaminated in ways that the sick-comforter either did not

know or refused to recognize, for Minna, always fearful that the trek
might split and take Ryk Naudé from her permanently, was stealing out
to see him at every opportunity, and he seemed as eager as she for these
assignations. This left Aletta free, and for reasons that no one could
have explained, and certainly not the participants, she threw herself in
Tjaart's way, knowing that he was hungry for her. It was a strange and
ugly situation, the more so in that the aggrieved parties, Jakoba and
Theunis, were among the strongest of the Voortrekkers, and the best.
They never spoke to each other of their private griefs, but in their family prayers little Theunis, twisted to one side, sometimes became elo-
quent when he invoked God on behalf of the Voortrekkers, seeking for
them a strength unusual, a devotion unworldly. Often at the end of his
protracted prayers tears would spring from both his eyes, not only from
the blemished one.

The Van Doorns were not able to leave Blaauwkrantz, because Piet
Retief came riding into camp with an urgent request: 'I need a hundred
men to accompany me to Dingane's Kraal. And they must be good
horsemen.'

'Why?' a murmur of voices asked.

'Tjaart knows why,' and he asked Van Doorn to describe the exhibitions Dingane had provided for his visitors during the last meeting: the
military drills, the dancing of the oxen. 'I want our horsemen to show
that king something he's never even imagined. Boer strength. Our
horsemen in their speediest drill.'

He was not able to enlist the full hundred, but he did get seventy-
one skilled horsemen, including himself and his son. Of course, some
thirty-one Coloureds rode along, for the Voortrekkers engaged in not a
single operation, warlike or peaceful, without their usual complement of
assistants. Besides, some of the Coloured were exciting horsemen, and
Retief was counting on them to adorn the display he had in mind.

Added to the roster were Tjaart and Paulus de Groot, two weeks
short of six years old and already a practiced horseman; as Tjaart said
farewell to Jakoba and the Nels, he promised them that he would protect the boy and be home soon with an agreement giving the Voortrekkers rights in Natal. Plans for seeking a safer home in the north
were abandoned.

It was a beautiful summer's journey down to the Tugela and across
it into the heart of Zululand, but it was dangerously seductive, for the
Voortrekkers had convinced themselves that no harm could befall them.

Even Tjaart, who had been warned by the missionary and cautioned by his wife, forgot his apprehensions.

'What could happen to us?' he asked his friends. 'Dingane wanted us to recover his stolen cattle, and there they are, trailing along behind us. He'll welcome us and sign the papers we want.'

They arrived at the great kraal on Saturday morning, 3 February 1838, and the festivities began at once. Paulus encountered a pleasure of which no one had told him, for in the royal town there had been for some time an English lad named William Wood, twelve years old, whom King Dingane treated as a kind of pet, a precious curiosity who lived with the nearby missionaries but who had the run of the capital. This lad took Paulus under his protection, showing him the intricacies of the royal huts and even the forbidden quarters, vast in extent, in which the king's wives were sequestered.

At the end of the first day Paulus was exhausted but delighted: 'Father Tjaart, this is the best.' And memories of his parents' mutilation by the regiments of another king like Dingane were dulled.

On the second day Retief offered the king a surprise, calling upon his horsemen to go through their maneuvers. Into the vast arena, populated by at least four thousand Zulu warriors, came the Boer horsemen, two by two, rifles across their saddles, blank loadings in position. Slowly the horses circled the arena, came down the middle, performing convolutions and raising a stirring clatter. The warriors were entranced, for although they had danced with the oxen, their beautiful beasts had been slow and ponderous; these horses flowed with magic, leaping and twisting at command.

And then, again from a signal by Retief, which Dingane carefully noted, the horsemen broke into a gallop, formed one phalanx, dashed straight at the ebony armchair-throne and discharged their rifles. The effect was overwhelming, and so startled Dingane that he whispered to an attendant, 'These men are indeed wizards.'

William Wood overheard this remark, and as soon as the affair ended he sought out Tjaart and told him of the awful thing the king had said: 'He whispered that you were indeed wizards.'

'In a way we are,' Tjaart agreed.

'Ssssh! It means he's going to kill you.'

Tjaart frowned. 'What's your name again?'

'William Wood. I know Dingane. Mr. van Doorn, he's going to kill all of you.'

The boy's face was so woebegone that Tjaart felt he must inform

Retief of the incident, but the commander laughed it off: 'One of the English missionaries said the same thing. But you must remember they're English. They're afraid of Kaffirs.'

But Tjaart was so impressed by William's warning that he suggested leaving the area that night, and he argued so persuasively that Retief might have ordered his people home had not King Dingane himself suddenly appeared: 'I want to ask two questions. First, is it true that your people have finally defeated Mzilikazi?'

'Yes,' Retief replied expansively. 'We killed five thousand of his men. Drove him right across the Limpopo.' He looked threateningly at Dingane, and added, 'A similar defeat awaits any king who opposes the will of God.'

'Who decides that the will of your God has been opposed?' the interpreter asked.

'We will know,' Retief said.

'My second question. Is it true that your Coloured people can ride horses the way you do?' Retief answered, 'Tomorrow you'll see. And as you watch them, remember that you might be given horses, too, once we move into our land.' Dingane nodded.

On Monday, February 5, the show was held, and although the Coloured riders lacked the military precision of the Boers, they rode with such joyous abandon that they more than compensated for the deficiency. William Wood, sitting near the king, heard him grumble to his advisors, 'If the Coloured can ride horses, so can the Zulu. We must keep careful watch on these wizards.'

When the performance ended, William hurried to the Voortrekkers, warning them for the second time: 'Dingane means to kill you either tonight or tomorrow.' But again Retief refused to heed the caution, pointing out: 'A treaty is to be signed in the morning. We'll leave immediately thereafter.'

'Too late,' the boy said, but Retief dismissed him, turning to Tjaart: 'What we might do, Tjaart, is for you to speed back to the Blaauwkrantz. Tell our people that we've been granted the land. Get them packed and ready to take possession before Dingane changes his mind.'

From a small leather pouch he brought forth the precious paper, showing it to Tjaart in a kind of triumph. 'Tell them you saw this. Tell them the Kaffir will sign it tomorrow and then the land is peacefully ours.'

So Tjaart and Paulus saddled their horses, and prepared to serve as bearers of sweet tidings. At last the Voortrekkers would have a home of their own, but before Paulus mounted his horse, William Wood slipped up to him, grasped his hand and whispered, 'I'm glad you're going. Because tomorrow the others will all be dead.'

On Tuesday morning, 6 February 1838, Piet Retief, accompanied by seventy Boer horsemen, rode up to the gates of Dingane's Kraal, where Zulu commanders ordered them to dismount, tether their horses and deposit their weapons in a pile, which would be guarded by one of the regiments: 'Out of respect for the king. He was frightened by that sudden blast the other day.' To these arrangements Retief, as a gentleman, agreed.

The seventy-one white men, including Retief, entered the great arena, followed by their thirty-one Coloureds—one hundred and two in all. Since the day was extremely hot, the visitors were given those areas where the breeze was most likely to move the air, and they seated themselves and accepted the gourds of sorghum beer provided by Dambuza, the king's chief councillor. The land deed was presented to Dingane, who with a flourishing gesture put his mark on it and returned it to Retief. Then the dancing began, two regiments unarmed and wonderfully muscular performing intricate steps and maneuvers.

It was as peaceful a dance as the Zulu could have offered, and it pleased Retief and his men, but the boy William Wood, seeing that beyond the dancers three other regiments were silently moving into position, ran from the arena and told the people at the mission station, 'They are all going to be killed.'

'Hush,' a woman said. 'You've been reprimanded before for spreading rumors.'

The king, watching carefully the progress of the dance, decided that it had reached the designated moment, so while the steps continued he rose and proposed a toast, putting it into Zulu verse, which he composed on the spot:

> 'Let the white lips that thirst,
>   Thirst no more!
> Let the eyes that want everything,
>   See no more!
> Let the white hearts that beat . . .
>   Be still!'

Retief, understanding none of the words, nodded graciously to the king and raised his gourd. At that instant Dingane shouted, 'Seize them, my warriors! Slay the wizards!'

A thousand voices repeated the king's command, and the dancing regiments stepped aside, allowing the real soldiers to leap forward, assegais in hand. With these daggers pointing at their throats, the bewildered Boers stumbled to their feet, whipped out what knives they had, and tried to defend themselves. It was useless. Four, six, ten Zulu grabbed at each Boer, wrestled him to the floor, then, holding him by the legs, dragged him out of the kraal and along a climbing footpath to the place of execution. There on a hill, as William Wood and the missionary women watched from their homes, the Boers were clubbed to death, one by one, knobkerries rising and falling.

The Coloureds also were slain to a man. Piet Retief, pinioned, had to watch his own son being tortured to death before he, too, was clubbed mercilessly until his skull was shattered and he fell upon the heaped bodies of his comrades.

The Zulu commander who had supervised the killings cried, 'Cut out the liver and the heart of this man. Bury them in the middle of the road he traveled.'

So ended Piet Retief, a man who had led his people into the wilderness to build a country of their own, a man who trusted those he met and placed his faith in God. His laager was destroyed; his son was slain; his far designs left unattained. A failure in much that he attempted, he came to a terrible end, but it was also a noble beginning, for his legend would inspire a nation.

On the day ten months later when other Boers came upon his body, they would find in the leather pouch near his bones a document carefully marked by Dingane, King of the Zulu, granting him:

> the Place called Port Natal together with all the Land annexed, that is to say from Dogeela to the River westward and from the Sea to the North as far as the Land may be Useful and in my possession for their Everlasting property.
>
> De merk + + van de Koning Dingane

Tjaart and Paulus, riding quietly along the banks of the Tugela River, could not know that their fellow Voortrekkers were being massacred, but the boy suffered powerful premonitions and said, 'Father, I do think the king is going to kill all our men. Should we turn back to warn them?'

'No one would dare do a thing like that.'

'But William knows the king. Twice he heard him say that we were wizards.'

'He meant wise men. Because we defeated Mzilikazi.'

'But William has seen wizards put to death. Men hammer stakes into them.'

The boy was so insistent that Tjaart had to pay attention; he became more alert, and it was fortunate that he did, because toward noon he detected to the rear a rise of dust along the trail they had just traveled, and from a hiding place, saw with horror the better part of two regiments, assegais glistening, flash past, headed in the general direction of the Blaauwkrantz River.

Instantly Tjaart realized that they must somehow move ahead of the running column to alert the encampments and the hundreds of Voortrekkers who would not be in laager, but no matter how cleverly they tried to speed along unused trails, invariably they were forestalled by detachments of Zulu who were fanning out across the countryside, murdering any Boers they found.

At four different isolated camps, Tjaart and Paulus found only smoldering ruins and gutted Boers. In an agony of fear, they fought to circumvent the Zulu lines and sound an alarm, but always they failed; once when it seemed that they could slip down a canyon, they watched in dismay as a third regiment of Dingane's men crept in, attacking a lonely wagon and killing everyone.

Belatedly, Tjaart had to acknowledge aloud that Retief and all his men were probably dead. He looked blankly at Paulus, and the boy nodded. He had known all along how great would be the disaster, for William Wood had told him, and now, distraught, he said, 'And before we left, William told me that every Boer in Zululand would be killed. We must hurry to the river.'

'I've been trying!' Tjaart cried, and once again he sought to outflank the Zulu lines, and failed.

At sunset on Friday, 16 February 1838, they were still far short of the Blaauwkrantz, their warning signal undelivered. That night, along an unprotected stretch eleven miles in length, the scattered wagons of the Voortrekkers stood in formless array, and near them the women and children of the men already slaughtered went carelessly to sleep.

Additional families, only recently arrived from Thaba Nchu, were spending their first nights in their promised land and staring at the stars which had brought them safely home. It was a quiet night, with only a few dogs barking sporadically.

At one o'clock in the morning three full regiments of Zulu warriors stormed forth in a surprise attack and reached the sleeping wagons and tents before anyone could sound an alarm. In the first wave they slaughtered everyone at the eastern end of the line, except two members of the Bezuidenhout family. The younger Bezuidenhout, barely able to grasp the fact that all but one of his kin were slain, enabled others farther westward to survive the assault by heroically riding through the night, breaking miraculously through one concentration of Zulu warriors after another.

Among the groups he wakened was the Van Doorn encampment: Jakoba, Minna and Theunis, their three-year-old daughter Sybilla and their five servants. These nine had just enough time to take frenzied precautions before the screaming Zulu fell upon them, and in these moments of terror Theunis Nel did a remarkable thing: he took Sybilla and hid her behind a tree, well away from the wagons, and as he left her, trembling with a fear he could not control, he whispered, 'Sybilla, remember when we played the game? You must not make a sound.'

Running back to the wagons, he supervised the distribution of guns and knives and boards, and with these futile weapons and a heroism unmatched, his people defended themselves, the women firing their rifles until there was no more gunpowder, then standing side by side with their Coloureds, chopping at the deadly enemy. Minna went down first, cut to pieces. One by one the fearless, faithful Coloureds died. Then Jakoba and Theunis stood with their hands touching in love and farewell, fighting with whatever they could grab, and finally there was Theunis alone, a pathetic little man swinging a club.

When he saw fresh hordes descending upon him and realized that they might stumble upon his hidden daughter, he ran before them, leading away from her tree, and as the warriors overtook him, each stabbed at him with an assegai. But still he ran, to lead them as far away as possible, and shouting to warn the other wagons. When he felt his knees failing and blood choking his lungs, he turned to face his assailants, grabbed at their assegais, and died of many wounds.

Balthazar Bronk, who had so relentlessly denied him his ordination, had managed, as such men often do, to be at the far end of the encampment, where the Zulu did not reach.

* * *

Tjaart arrived at Blaauwkrantz before dawn, and searching in the ghostly light, he and Paulus saw the awful desolation: men hacked to pieces, women and children chopped down, brown and black servants who had surrendered their lives defending the people for whom they worked.

'Father!' Paulus cried. 'Our wagons!'

Recognizing the burned-out frames, Tjaart rushed over—and found his family massacred: Jakoba lay with six dead Zulu at her feet, Minna with three, all the servants, their bodies slashed by assegais. But no Sybilla. And no Theunis.

'Child!' Tjaart roared, hoping that she might somehow have escaped. There was no response, so he started shouting for Theunis, cursing him for having run away and deserted his women.

'Goddamn you, Nel!' he bellowed, and then suddenly he was surrounded by women, jabbering that Theunis had saved their lives: 'He was dying, but he ran nearly half a mile, shouting to us, warning us . . .' 'He was stabbed so many times . . .'

'Was Sybilla with him?'

'He was alone with the spears.' They led him to where the crookbackt sick-comforter lay, uncovered, and Tjaart fell beside him and cried, 'Theunis, where is your daughter?'

Paulus de Groot, now six, looked at the dead body of his second mother, then at Aunt Minna, and he was about to move on to see where Uncle Theunis lay when he sensed a movement among the trees, and although he was terrified by the dreadful things of this night, he walked toward the sound, and there beneath a tree sat Sybilla. She had witnessed everything that happened, but she knew from what her father had told her in those last moments that she must not make a sound.

She made none now, and even when Paulus reached down to take her hands, she followed him mutely, and with Paulus walking backward and guiding her, they left the tree and started to where Tjaart was grieving over the body of her father. But when Paulus had her well on the way, she suddenly halted, pulling her hands free, and when she was thus released she walked purposefully to where her mother and Ouma Jakoba lay. When she stood over them she did not weep, nor did she kneel to kiss them. She simply stood there, and after a while she turned to her friend Paulus and placed her hands again in his. Vaguely she had always known that his father and mother had been killed, and now she knew that hers had died, too. He was the person she could trust. He was the one who understood.

They were standing thus when someone informed Tjaart that his granddaughter was alive. 'Sybilla!' he shouted, but when he dashed back to lift her in his arms, crying, 'Thank God, thank God!' she merely looked at him. Her father had warned her not to speak, and it would be some days before she did.

As soon as Jakoba and the Nels were buried, Tjaart headed for the far end of the wagon line to ascertain what had happened to the Ryk Naudés, and as he walked, dozens of Voortrekkers halted him to ask, 'What news of Retief?' and he was afraid to tell them of Paulus' conviction that the entire party had been slain.

When he found the Naudé wagon, the people of that group were engaged in burying thirteen of their dead. Among them was Ryk; that feckless youth had refused to put his wagons into laager, had been out sporting with some new girl, and had rushed back in time to face a circle of Zulu, who hacked him to pieces.

At the end of the common grave Tjaart found Aletta, her arm in a sling, her face scarred by a long gash; as always, she stood there betraying no emotion, and even when Tjaart signaled to her across the fallen bodies, she merely nodded. Since the Voortrekkers were still without a clergyman, a layman was needed to read from the Bible, and Balthazar Bronk volunteered; he offered a fine prayer and the mass grave was closed.

Then, as if a mighty hand were pushing him from the back, Tjaart stepped around the grave, walked solemnly to where Aletta stood, and addressed her before some other womanless man might lay claim: 'You can't live alone, Aletta.'

'It would be impossible,' she said.

Her husband was dead. Her wagon was burned. She had no place to sleep, no clothes other than those she wore. She had no money, no food, no relatives. She was alone on unprotected land which the Zulu might overrun at any moment, so with a last tearless look at the grave, she held out her good hand, encouraging Tjaart to take it and guide her down the long line of wagons till they reached his.

With dismay she saw that he, too, had nothing: no bed, no box of Jakoba's clothes, no wagon ready for the road—nothing but a brown-gold pot and a Bible. There was no Dutch minister to marry them, but this widow and this widower were wed of their own determination; and as they started retrieving the possessions scattered about, messengers came crying: 'Retief and all his men are slain.'

It was obvious that God had struck His chosen people with a series of punishing blows. For their arrogance and their sins he had chastised them, and as they huddled in their depleted laagers, awaiting the next assault of the Zulu, they tried to unravel the mystery of their wrongdoing.

Every man who died at Dingane's Kraal had loved God and had endeavored to live according to His laws, yet all had perished. Every woman and child murdered at Blaauwkrantz had been faithful to the Bible, but they had been slaughtered. If ever an assembly of people had just cause to rebel against their deity, it was the Voortrekkers that summer of 1838, but they reacted quite differently.

Spiritually they sought within themselves the reasons for their reverses, and decided that they had been lax in their attention to worship and in the keeping of the commandments. For example, Tjaart van Doorn knew in his heart that the adulteries in his family had been the cause of the savage retribution he had suffered, and yet—why had he been saved and faultless Jakoba punished?

Aletta continued to perplex him. In the days following the massacre, her principal concern had been with the cut across her cheek: 'Will it leave a scar?' Wives showed her how to sterilize the wound with cow's urine and salve it with butter, and when she was assured that it would heal without a major blemish, she was satisfied. In her relations with Tjaart she continued as she had always been—completely passive, interested in nothing, absorbed only in herself. Once when he returned to their tent exhausted from digging trenches, he wanted to discuss the problem of finding someone who might lead them against the Zulu, but she had no opinions on any of the men. In some exasperation he asked, 'How about Balthazar Bronk?' and she put her hand to her chin, studied the matter, and said, 'He might be the one,' even though she knew he had run away at Veg Kop.

In the hard task of erecting some sort of defense he noticed this peculiarity: that the boy Paulus toiled like a man while the woman Aletta behaved like a child. He could not help comparing her with Jakoba, who would have been at his side as the new barricades were being built, and he began to understand why Ryk Naudé, married to this extremely beautiful girl, had nevertheless preferred Minna.

When, thanks to Tjaart's stubborn work, these Voortrekkers felt moderately safe from Zulu attack, they returned to the Book of Joshua to review the steps by which he had triumphed at Jericho over his Canaanite enemies, and now the loss of Theunis Nel was felt, for he would have been eager to explicate such matters. In his absence, Tjaart had to serve as principal guide, bending over the charred cover of his Bible to read the relevant verses:

> 'And it came to pass . . . that the people went up into the city, every man straight before him, and they took the city. And they utterly destroyed all that was in the city, both man and woman, young and old, and ox, and sheep, and ass, with the edge of the sword.'

Then he swore grimly: 'That's what we'll do to Dingane's Kraal. Total destruction.' By what specific steps this would be accomplished he did not know, for he considered himself inadequate to lead. What he could do was reflect the stubborn Boer determination to see this job finished, and if any man wavered, he laid forth the damning statistics: 'At the kraal, one hundred and two of our men killed. Here at Blaauwkrantz, two hundred and eighty-two. Out in the countryside, at least seventy more slain in their sleep. We demand retribution.'

'How can we attain it,' Balthazar Bronk asked, 'when we are so few and they so many?'

'I don't know,' Tjaart said, 'but I'm sure God will show us a way.'

And then into camp rode the man who would achieve miracles. He was Andries Pretorius, clean-shaven, younger than the other leaders, a person of substance in Graaff-Reinet. He was extremely tall and bulky, slow to reach decisions but resolute when he had done so. Like most of the leaders, he had been married more than once, with eight children by his first wife, three by his second. A grave, thoughtful man, he had hurried north in response to a summons from the beleaguered Voortrekkers. With his gun, his pistols and a thick-bladed cutlass, he strode into camp on 22 November 1838 and said simply, 'I have come to help you. Within the week we shall ride forth to destroy Dingane.'

The first thing he did was follow the cautious precept of Joshua: 'I want two men to spy out the enemy,' and he designated a curious pair— Tjaart van Doorn, whom he trusted because of his determined commandos against the Xhosa, and Balthazar Bronk, who had behaved so badly in previous battles. He wanted Tjaart because he knew how to fight, Bronk because he was a clever, wily man.

Together the two men left Blaauwkrantz, eased themselves cautiously northward, and returned to camp with the somber news that Dingane had begun to assemble his regiments for a massive strike: 'He will have twelve thousand men to throw against us. How many will we have?'

Pretorius, like Joshua, had gathered all available soldiers, and he told them, 'The odds against us will be thirty-to-one. But we will carry the fight to them. We will select the place of battle.'

Only five days after the arrival of this dynamic man, the commando was in motion. It consisted of four hundred and sixty-four men, with the ususal complement of Coloureds and blacks. About half had fought against the Zulu in one capacity or another; half had never opposed any black regiment. With them they had sixty-four wagons, absolutely essential in the plan Pretorius had devised. In the forefront was the rebuilt TC-43, now a sturdy, clean war vehicle with reinforced sides and fourteen highly trained oxen who seemed to take pride in setting the pace; if another wagon threatened to assume the lead, these oxen quickened their steps to stay in front.

By this swift movement General Pretorius appropriated tactical advantage; the battle would be fought where he decided, and on terrain favorable to his design. With brilliance he selected a steeply banked corner where a deep gully joined a small river; and in this fortunate area he placed his laager beside a deep pool which recently had been used by hippopotamuses for their bathing (Seekoei Gat, the Boers called it, Sea-cow Hole). He was thus protected on the south by the deep gully, on the east by the hippo pool, and to the north and west by the chain of sixty-four wagons, which he lashed together with enormous thongs, trek chains and great accumulations of thorn bush. At points along the perimeter, and positioned so they would face the maximum number of Zulu rushing to attack the laager, he placed four small cannon capable of firing an immense load of pellets, iron bits, chain links and rocks.

'We are ready,' he said at dusk on Saturday, 15 December 1838, and that night was the longest that these embattled Boers would ever know. They were few, and on the hills surrounding them on all sides gathered the Zulu regiments, men who had fought across the face of Africa, sweeping all before them. Inside the laager the nine hundred trek oxen lowed, hundreds of horses fretted, disturbed by the fires the

Zulu maintained, worried by the sounds that encroached on all sides. Pretorius, moving among his troops, told them, 'We must station our men along the entire perimeter, for if we fire only from one direction, the animals, especially our horses, will swarm away from the noise, and they might escape through upset wagons. Without horses, tomorrow we would be lost.'

When all the details were perfected, the time was ripe for the crucial moment in Boer history. With the death of Theunis Nel, the Voortrekkers had no one who even presumed to be a predikant, but they had numerous men who knew the Old Testament almost by heart, and one of these was Sarel Cilliers, an educated farmer of deep religious conviction, and upon him fell the responsibility of reminding his fellow Voortrekkers of the sacred mission upon which they were engaged, and he recited those passages from the thundering Book of Joshua which presaged the forthcoming battle:

> 'And the Lord said unto Joshua, Be not afraid because of them: for tomorrow about this time will I deliver them up all slain before Israel: thou shalt hough their horses and burn their chariots with fire . . . One man of you shall chase a thousand: for the Lord your God, he it is that fighteth for you, as he hath promised you.'

Then Cilliers climbed upon the carriage on which a beloved cannon named Ou Grietjie (Old Gertie) rested, and repeated for the last time the covenant upon which the Voortrekkers had agreed:

> 'Almighty God, at this dark moment we stand before You, promising that if You will protect us and deliver the enemy into our hands, we shall forever after live in obedience to Your divine law. If You enable us to triumph, we shall observe this day as an anniversary in each year, a day of thanksgiving and remembrance, even for all our posterity. And if anyone sees difficulty in this, let him retire from the battlefield.'

In the darkness the Voortrekkers whispered their Amens; they were now a nation established by God, in pursuit of His objectives, and those who were able to sleep the few hours before dawn did so with easy consciences, for they knew that God Himself had brought them to this river to face odds that would have terrified ordinary men.

* * *

The Battle of Blood River, as it came understandably to be called, had no parallel in recent world history. Twelve thousand, five hundred highly trained and capable Zulu threw themselves over a period of two hours at a cleverly entrenched foe, and without modern weapons of any kind, attempted to overwhelm a group of tough, resolute men armed with rifles, pistols and cannon. It was a hideous affair. The Zulu warriors stamped their feet, shouted their war cries, and drove straight at the laager. The men inside stood firm, waited for the enemy to come within six feet of the wagons, then fired into their chests. Those warriors fell, but others replaced them, expecting their cowhide shields to protect them, and they, too, marched right into the muzzles of the guns, and they, too, fell.

A thousand Zulu died in this way, then two thousand, but still they came on. Within the first hour the Zulu generals, supposing that the white men inside the laager must be depleted, decided to throw at them their two finest regiments, those entitled to wear all-white shields, white armlets and knee decorations, and it was awesome to see these excellent men, all of an age and a height, march unswervingly over the bodies of their fallen comrades, straight at the laager.

Inside, General Pretorius told his men, 'This may be the flood tide. Hold your fire.' So the riflemen waited while the gunners loaded Ou Grietjie with a murderous load of scrap and leaden slugs; and when these crack regiments had marched directly to the muzzles of these creaking guns, Pretorius gave the signal. Ou Grietjie and her three ugly sisters spewed out their lethal dose right into the faces of the Zulu, while riflemen from the flanks poured hot fire at them.

Not even the White Shields could absorb punishment like this, but they did not falter or run. They simply came on, and died.

Now Pretorius made an astounding decision: 'Mount your horses. We shall drive them from the field.' So about a hundred Voortrekkers leaped upon their steeds, waited till riflemen opened a gateway through the laager, and galloped out in a firing, slashing foray that startled the Zulu. Down one front the Voortrekkers rode, killing at a fantastic rate; then along another, cutting and firing; then deep into the heart of the enemy concentration, galloping like wild avengers; then back and forth three times, as if they were immortal.

After slaying hundreds of the enemy, they galloped back inside the laager; the only rider in this amazing sortie to suffer a wound was General Pretorius. He had his hand cut by an assegai.

Now Ou Grietjie was moved from her position along the wagon arc and dragged by hand to one of the corners, from which she could fire straight down the gully into which four hundred Zulu had crept, hoping in this way to cut in behind the wagons. Then the cannon was loaded with an assortment of nails and scrap, and pointed directly into the gully and discharged. It was loaded again, and fired. And before the hidden Zulu could clamber out, a third salvo hit, killing the remnants.

Still the amazing Zulu pressed on; the ground was littered with broken bodies, but on they marched, throwing themselves against the wagons, trying in vain to move close enough to use their stabbing assegais, and falling back only when they were dead.

At the end of two hours the black generals sought to rally their regiments by gathering in one spot all White Shield survivors and giving them the simple command: 'Break through and slay the wizards.' Without hesitation these splendid warriors adjusted the shields, borrowed extra assegais, and began a stately march right at the spot from which Ou Grietjie had been removed. They came in panoply, they fought in glory. Wave after wave marched almost to the wagons and fell to the blazing guns. Yet on they came, men trained all their lives to obey, but when the final ranks hit the wagons, they accomplished nothing. Silently the generals signaled retreat and the punished regiments withdrew, defeated but still obedient to command. A new power had replaced them in Zululand, and it had come to stay.

Before dusk the Voortrekkers came out of their laager to inspect the battlefield, on which they counted over three thousand dead. Another seven hundred died of wounds at a distance and could not be verified. Still others would die later.

What can be said of a battle in which the casualties were over four thousand dead on one side, a cut hand on the other? Not one man in the Voortrekker laager was killed; not one was seriously injured; counting even the scratches, only three were touched in this incredible battle. Four thousand-to-nothing, what kind of warfare is that? The answer would come years later from a troubled Dutch Reformed minister: 'It was not a battle. It was an execution.'

But Blood River, terrible though it was, must not be considered by itself; it was merely the culminating battle in the campaign that included the massacres at Dingane's Kraal and Blaauwkrantz. If those unwarranted deaths are counted, plus the many casualties at unprotected farms, the real nature of this continuing battle can be apprehended: at first, overwhelming Zulu victories; at the end, a Voortrekker triumph so one-sided as to be grotesque; but on balance, a ferocious battle with many casualties on each side.

The real victor at Blood River was not the Voortrekker commando, but the spirit of the covenant that assured their triumph. As Tjaart said when he led prayers after the battle: 'Almighty God, only You enabled us to win. We were faithful to You, and You fought at our side. In obedience to the covenant You offered us and which You honored, we shall henceforth abide as Your people in the land You have given us.'

What the Voortrekkers failed to realize in their moment of victory was that they had offered the covenant to God, not He to them. Any group of people anywhere in the world was free to propose a covenant on whatever terms they pleased, but this did not obligate God to accept that covenant, and especially not if their unilateral terms contravened His basic teachings to the detriment of another race whom He loved equally. Nevertheless, in obedience to the covenant as they understood it, they had won a signal victory, which confirmed their belief that He had accepted their offer and had personally intervened on their behalf. No matter what happened henceforth, men like Tjaart van Doorn were convinced that whatever they did was done in consonance with His wishes. The Boer nation had become a theocracy, and would so remain.

General Pretorius knew he must not allow King Dingane a chance to regroup his regiments; he realized that Zulu learned quickly and that in the next great battle they would present him with difficult tactics, so he scoured the landscape, seeking the devious ruler who had committed the murders. He did not catch him. Before fleeing, Dingane set fire to his famous kraal, destroying the treasures accumulated since the reign of Shaka. Among the items found by the Boers in the kraal were two cannon, a gift from a treaty-seeker. They had been allowed to rust, unused; had they been operating at Blood River, they might have offset Ou Grietjie and her three sisters.

Dingane fled far to the north, where he established a new kraal and waited in fright for the Boers to come seeking retribution. A younger brother, Mpande, seized the chance to ally himself with the Boers and suggested a joint expedition against his brother's battered regiments. But before this campaign could be launched, Dingane sent his chief councillor, Dambuza, and a subordinate to the Voortrekkers, offering them two hundred of his finest cattle.

'Dingane seeks peace,' Dambuza entreated. 'The lands Retief sought are yours.'

Mpande, who attended this meeting, always seeking an opportunity to increase his standing with the whites, screamed at Dambuza, 'You lie! There will be no peace if Dingane lives. Who are you to speak, Dambuza? Were you not at his side when he killed Retief and his men? Were you not shouting, "They are wizards"?'

So ferocious was Mpande's indictment that Pretorius ordered the envoys stripped naked and cast into chains. Shortly, both were on trial before a military court, where the chief witness was Mpande. On his testimony, both envoys were sentenced to death, even though they were diplomats visiting a host country, as it were.

Dambuza did not beg, but he did plead for his subordinate: 'Spare him. He's a young man with no guilt.'

There was no mercy. Tjaart van Doorn, present throughout the hearing, saw Balthazar Bronk, eager to serve on the firing squad, prepare his rifle. The two condemned blacks were dragged into the open, and Bronk's marksmen lined up.

'Wait!' Pretorius cried. Striding swiftly toward the envoys, he said, 'Dambuza, you must ask forgiveness from God. Tell Him you're sorry, and He'll listen.'

The tall, powerful black said slowly, 'I know not your God, Boer. King Dingane is my chief. I did what he ordered. But I do plead for my aide. Release him.'

'Shoot them,' Pretorius barked, turning away from the scene of execution.

Bronk and his men assumed position. Their gunfire splattered, and the two blacks fell. Then the miracle happened. Councillor Dambuza, only slightly wounded, rose to his feet.

'He is spared,' someone shouted. 'God has saved him for his courage.'

'Reload,' Bronk shouted.

Tjaart van Doorn said not a word as Dambuza faced the firing squad for a second time, but he did think of a grim day long ago at a place called Slagter's Nek, and in his mind he saw a scrawny English missionary, brother to his friend in Grahamstown, pleading for mercy for men whom God had reprieved when the ropes at their necks broke.

'Fire!' Bronk shouted, and this time the aim of the executioners was sure.

Within months Dingane himself was dead, assassinated perhaps at the instigation of his brother Mpande, who ascended the throne with the help of his Boer allies. It had been Dingane's fate to wrest the kingdom from his half brother Shaka at the time in history when confrontation with a new and powerful force was inescapable, and he had never had a glimmer as to how adjustments should be made. He was an evil, pitiful man; he was also a powerful, wise and cunning manipulator; and the best that can be said of him is that his errors did not destroy the Zulu people. On the ashes of Dingane's Kraal a mighty nation would arise, powerful enough within a few decades to challenge the British Empire, and within a century to contest with the Boer nation for the leadership of southern Africa.

When victory was complete, Tjaart studied the situation carefully; desperately he wished that Lukas de Groot were still alive so that he might compare assessments with that sage farmer, for he needed help. He also missed Jakoba, whose stubborn advice had always been so sensible; she would have been a good one to talk with, but her successor, Aletta, was quite hopeless. Whatever Tjaart elected to do suited her; her principal concern was finding enough cloth and stiffeners to make a sunbonnet large enough to keep the sun's rays from her face, which she hoped to keep as fair as possible.

Once, in dismay, Tjaart said, 'Aletta, I think we ought to go back over the mountains to land we know. I don't like it here. Sooner or later the English are going to come at us . . .'

'That's a good idea,' Aletta agreed, but when he took the first steps to effectuate the plan, she whimpered, 'I wouldn't want to carry our wagon back up those cliffs.' He did not remind her that she had carried precious little down, but he was confused by her vacillations, and one day he asked, 'Aletta, where would you like to spend the rest of your life?'

The bluntness of this question startled her, for she had not reached the age when the phrase 'the rest of your life' had any meaning; it was then that she awakened fully to the fact that she was married to a man over fifty years old and that he had only a limited number of years remaining. But where would she like to live? 'Cape Town,' she said honestly, whereupon he ended the discussion.

He had about decided to stay in Natal with General Pretorius, whom he admired immensely, when two trivial things intervened: an English merchant came up from Port Natal with news that an English force would soon be arriving to take the port under their command; and young Paulus, now a tall and vigorous lad, said casually, 'I would like to go hunting lions.' And the vision of an untrammeled veld came back to haunt Tjaart. He appreciated Natal, especially these good fields along the Tugela River, but like many Voortrekkers, once he had seen the vast open sweep of the Transvaal, all other land seemed puny. He, too, longed to see lions and rhinoceroses and perhaps the sable antelope. He was homesick for loneliness, and the presence of so many Boers erecting villages and towns oppressed him.

Even so, Aletta's obvious preference for the maturing life of Natal might have kept him there had not a ridiculous situation developed: one morning he was awakened by a clatter outside his tent, and there was Balthazar Bronk, a man he despised. 'Van Doorn,' he said as soon as Tjaart wiped the sleeping-sand out of his eyes, 'what they say is true. "Wherever a ship can sail, an Englishman will come." I think we ought to get out of here.'

'To where?'

'Back up on the plateau.' From the tent, young Paulus cried, 'Hooray! We'll go back and hunt lions.'

The more Balthazar talked, the more sense he made, and by the time Aletta got out of bed, the two men had convinced themselves that they must start quickly toward the mountains; Natal was not for them. But when Aletta heard the decision she began to pout and said that she did not intend to help carry this wagon back up those hills. 'No necessity,' Bronk assured her. 'There's a good trail now. General Pretorius crossed the peaks in three days.'

'Why didn't we use it?' she said.

'It wasn't known then.'

For a three-day period it looked as if Aletta might leave Tjaart; she was not legally married to him yet, and there were other men in the new settlements who needed wives. It was her strong desire to remain here with the other women and not climb back to the highveld where her life would be lonely and short. But then an American missionary—a gawky young Baptist from Indiana—wandered into the settlements, and the hunger of the Voortrekkers for a predikant manifested itself. Tjaart joined a committee of five which interrogated the young man to see if he might be willing to perfect his Dutch and transfer his allegiance to the Dutch Reformed Church.

'I am not too good at languages,' he said in English.

'Did you attend seminary?' Tjaart asked in Dutch.

'Yes.'

'And were you approved?'

'Yes.'

'Then you can learn.'

'But you ought to have a Dutch minister.'

'That's right,' Tjaart said, 'but the Dutch ministers have outlawed us,' and he showed the young man the latest copy of the Cape Town newspaper, *The South African Commercial Advertiser,* in which spokesmen for the church reiterated the charge that the Voortrekkers were fugitives acting in disobedience to organized society, that they were no doubt spiritual degenerates and should be shunned by all good people.

'Of course it would be better if we had Dutch predikants,' Tjaart summarized, 'but what we want to know is can you accept our doctrines?'

'Well,' the young fellow said brightly, 'seems to me that the Dutch Reformed Church is pretty much what we in America call Lutherans.'

'Nothing of the kind!' Tjaart roared. 'That's Martin Luther. We're John Calvin.'

'Aren't they the same?'

'Good God!' Tjaart grumbled, and he took no further part in the interrogation, but when the other four had completed their questioning, it became apparent that here was a true man of God, called to the frontier from a vast distance, one who would grace any community. Without consulting Tjaart, they made him a definite offer, and he finally accepted.

But it was Tjaart who gave him his first two commissions: 'Will you perform a marriage?'

'I would be proud to do so, Mr. van Doorn.'

'I'm never a mister,' Tjaart growled, whereupon the young minister said, 'But you are a man of strong calling, and that I like.'

The two men walked to Tjaart's wagon, where Aletta was summoned, and when she heard that this strange fellow was a minister she turned pale, for during the past several nights she had been secretly meeting a young man whose love-making she fancied, and she had been about to inform Tjaart of her new preference. He, seeing her paleness, surmised what the situation might be, for he had met with her when she was married to another and he knew her irresponsibility; but he also knew that moving to the north without a wife would be impossible, and he was still captivated by her beauty. So he reached out, grasped her harshly by the wrist, and pulled her before the new predikant.

'Marry us,' he said, and there in the Natal sunlight the new clergyman performed his first ritual, knowing well that it was somehow faulty and that this was not a good union.

His second rite was a strange one. Tjaart, with the approval of some of his neighbors, asked the missionary, 'Sir, can you honor us by ordaining a dead man?'

'Quite unheard of.' But when Van Doorn led the party to a narrow grave marked by a few stones and explained to the new predikant who Theunis Nel had been, and how he had died, and why he had always wanted to be an ordained clergyman, the young fellow said, 'He won his ordination of God. It would ill behoove me to deprive him of it.'

So at the graveside he prayed for the soul of . . . 'What's the name again?' 'Theunis Nel,' Tjaart whispered. '. . . The soul of Thy servant Theunis Nel. I became a minister by studying at seminary in Pennsylvania. Theunis became one by sacrificing his life for others.'

'Can you pray in Dutch?' Tjaart asked.

'I'm learning.'

'Well, say a few words. Theunis spoke Dutch.'

In halting phrases the young predikant asked for the blessing of all upon this man who had served so faithfully, the true minister of the faith, after which Tjaart said defiantly, 'Now he's a predikant,' but Balthazar Bronk, following this nonsense from a distance, whispered to his cronies, 'He was Tjaart's son-in-law. That explains it.'

Nevertheless, when Tjaart and his legal wife inspanned their oxen and set their rebuilt wagon on the journey west, Bronk was with them, and six other families. With the English once more breathing down their necks, this time in Natal, they knew they had yet to find the promised land they sought.

On 26 March 1841 they reached the foothills of the Drakensberg, where they rested for three weeks prior to the assault. Bronk had been correct in stating that a new pass had been found over the peaks, but even so, it required almost a month for the wagons slowly to retrace their way to Thaba Nchu, where hundreds of Voortrekkers had assembled. Here, too, they rested through the cold months of June and July, acquiring goods, listening to tales about the land across the Vaal River.

Two of their families defected, but four new ones joined, and it was in a party of ten wagons that they started their serious penetration of the veld. Vast areas depopulated by Mzilikazi's early depredations had slowly started their recovery, but the journey in late winter of that year was still appalling: they came upon the roots of villages which had been totally destroyed. Not a hut remained, not an animal, only bleached bones. Tjaart said, 'It's as if a Biblical plague had wasted the land and its people.'

One morning as the wagons moved across the empty veld with Tjaart and Paulus in the lead, Aletta broke into laughter, and when others asked the reason, she pointed at the two figures and said, 'They look like two flat-topped hills moving across the landscape,' and when the others studied them, they did indeed resemble walking mounds: heavy shoes, thick ragged trousers, bulking shoulders and flat hats with enormous brims—Tjaart ponderous and heavy, Paulus a true child of the veld. They were the walking mountains on whom a new society would be built.

In October they reached as far north as the Pienaars River, where Paulus shot a large hippopotamus, providing meat for two weeks of their stay in that congenial place. They had now been in uncharted territory for three months, with no idea at all of where they would settle, but no one complained. This was so much better than the early days of the Mzilikazi terror, or those later days in Natal when massacres were frequent; here there was only loneliness and swift death if illness attacked; there was also food, and safety at night, and the incredible beauty of the veld.

On 17 November 1841 Tjaart reached a major decision: 'We're going up to the Limpopo. I've always been told it's the best part of Africa.' Such a journey might require six months, eight months. But there was nothing else to do, so the ten wagons slowly pressed northward, into the land of the baobabs, the land of enormous antelope herds. On the southern shore of the river Paulus de Groot shot his lion. Of course, Tjaart and Balthazar stood behind him and shot at the same instant so as to avoid leaving a cripple to ravage the area, but they did not tell Paulus of this and all agreed that he had brought down the beast.

These Voortrekkers spent from January 1842 to September exploring north of the Limpopo, moving out cautiously to ascertain whether or not the land which looked so peaceful contained enemy tribes, and at the conclusion of the fourth such probe, Tjaart said, 'The Kaffirs we've met all speak of a great city to the north. Zimbabwe. I think we should go see.'

The other families, including Aletta, counseled against this, saying, 'Mzilikazi lies in wait up there.' But to Tjaart's surprise he was supported by Balthazar Bronk, who had heard rumors that Zimbabwe was paved with gold: 'I've asked the Kaffirs. They say Mzilikazi moved far west.' So Tjaart, Balthazar, Paulus and two blacks set forth with six horses to reach Zimbabwe, and as they traveled through low scrub, decorated with euphorbias that looked like Christmas trees with a thousand upright candles, they caught something of the grandeur of this region; it was quite unlike land to the south of the Limpopo, but they noticed also that their horses were weakening, as if some new disease were striking them, and they began to hurry, eager to see Zimbabwe with its golden streets.

At last they could view on the far horizon the vast hills of granite with their exfoliated layers of smooth stone, and they guessed that they were in the general region of the city, but when their horses faltered, they felt that they must turn back, and a serious conclave was held, with Balthazar wanting to return and Tjaart wishing to forge ahead just a little farther. Paulus, too, wanted to try, and his vote decided; Bronk would stay with the sick horses while the two others walked for three days: 'If you see nothing by then, you must come back.'

'Agreed.'

So Tjaart, Paulus and the two servants walked the last miles, and from a hill they saw Zimbabwe, not the flourishing city paved with gold, but the ruins of a notable site, overgrown with trees, captured by vines, and populated by a tribe that knew nothing of past glories. On the ruins where great kings had knelt and along the overgrown streets which Arab traders had trod with bags of gold, baboons played and warthogs shuffled along, grunting and rooting among the fallen stones.

It was a gloomy, sad place and Tjaart said, 'Poor Balthazar. No gold here.'

When they rejoined Bronk, he informed them that two of the horses had died: 'I think a fly is biting them.'

'It's not biting us,' Tjaart said.

'The trip's proved nothing,' Balthazar complained.

'It's proved we don't want to live up here. No gold for you, either.'

So they returned south, three Voortrekkers leading four sick horses, and by the time they reached the Limpopo, two more were dead. Something in the vicinity of this river was inimical to horses, and when they rejoined their families, they found that the oxen were wasting away, too.

'We must leave here,' Tjaart said, and on 20 September 1842 they started slowly south, oppressed by a sense of defeat, which was exacerbated for Tjaart when Aletta began to show a distinct dislike for her granddaughter Sybilla. Because the little girl, now seven years old, was so extraordinarily beautiful, so fragile and so enticing, Aletta saw her as a reminder of her own aging. She was twenty-five now and the hated life of the frontier had attacked both her beauty and her figure, so that she sometimes considered herself actually ugly. 'Won't we ever settle in some town, Tjaart? I want to live with other people.' When he rebuffed her, she took her discomfort out on little Sybilla, who proved a most infuriating child; for when Aletta berated her for some imagined fault, she merely looked at her grandmother, listened obediently, then walked away to find Paulus, who comforted her after such assaults.

It angered Aletta to see the two children together, for obviously they inhabited a private world from which she would always be excluded; Sybilla's habit of clinging to the boy's hand, as she had done that awful night, irritated her, and whenever she saw this she shouted, 'Sybilla, come in here. Girls don't play with boys that way.' And the little girl would just stare at her.

On the southward journey Tjaart kept his group well to the east, and by the middle of November 1842 they had reached a protected valley some hundred miles south of the Limpopo. Here they camped for three months, collecting ivory from the vast herds of elephants that roamed off to the east in the dense forests that presumably led down to the distant ocean. They were quite content to stay clear of those rich lands: 'We want no more lowlands. Boers are meant to live on the highveld with the gazelles.'

On 10 February 1843, in the middle of a promising summer, the ten wagons, loaded with ivory, resumed their drift south, and after four weeks of easy travel, Paulus shouted one dawn, 'Look at them come!'

Startled, still half-asleep, they did not know what to expect. They had been so long removed from enemy tribes that they were quite unprepared for laagers, and none were now necessary, for from the veld to the west came a line of the finest sable antelope any of these wanderers had ever seen. They were larger, sleeker than those that had crossed De Kraal before the trek, and their coats were of a warmer hue.

The white of their bellies shone in the morning sunlight, as did the distinctive blaze across their faces. But it was their horns which dominated —forty, fifty inches long, gracefully back-curved and awesome.

'Look at them!' Tjaart said, echoing the boy's delight. Even Aletta showed interest in the splendid beasts as they moved gracefully, unconcernedly away from the wagons.

'Where are they going?' Bronk asked, and Tjaart said, 'I think they're leading us home.' And he turned the wagons eastward, not trying to follow the sables, for they might gallop off at any moment. For some reason, the animals were not frightened by the wagons, so for part of that morning the two groups moved together, sables majestically in front, their horns shining in sunlight, the men and women behind, praying that they might soon reach the end of their wandering.

And then from the low and level fields that lay to the west of the lake, the Voortrekkers saw for the first time the quiet beauty of Vrij-meer, with its protecting mountains and the two signal hills. After seven full years of wandering, they had come home to what in the developing new language would henceforth be called Vrymeer.

They were not alone, for as they approached the lake they saw at the eastern end the collection of huts and lean-tos occupied by Nxumalo and his complicated family.

'Enemy!' Bronk cried, reaching for his gun.

'Wait!' Tjaart advised, after which he walked forward cautiously, gun at the ready, primed to defend himself if need be but also ready to accept friendship if that were proffered.

From his rondavel Nxumalo saw the white people approaching, and prudently he took down his stabbing assegai, and almost naked, strode forth to meet the newcomers.

Slowly, cautiously the two men approached each other, and in the heart of each there was a weariness with killing. Tjaart wanted no more rivers of blood and sorrow; Nxumalo had fled the excesses of King Shaka and the evil force of Mzilikazi. They were older men now, Tjaart fifty-four, Nxumalo one year more, and they sought repose beside some lake. Fate, at the end of wars and tribulations, had brought them to the same spot, and it would be madness for them to contest it.

Passing his gun back to Paulus, Tjaart extended his hands to show that he carried no weapons, and at this gesture of friendliness, Nxumalo, now white-haired, handed his assegai to his son. Paulus and the black boy waited as the two men moved cautiously forward, stopped an arm's length apart, and stared at each other. Finally, Nxumalo, on whose land this meeting was taking place, pointed to the lake and said that it was a safe, strong place. Tjaart, knowing little of the Zulu language, said haltingly that he had had this lake in his heart for all the years of his life, that his grandfather had discovered it and passed along remembrances of it. Pointing to the rondavels, he indicated that his people would build theirs at this spot, too, and this Nxumalo understood.

'There is room,' he said. In the days before King Shaka had run wild he had seen many tribes living side by side, and it could be done again.

But Tjaart, whose ten wagons represented just about the same population power as Nxumalo's accumulation, felt it necessary to demonstrate that the white men had certain advantages which the blacks would be wise to respect. Turning to Paulus, he told the boy, 'Shoot us a bird. Or an antelope.'

At that moment the sables elected to move on, and in doing so, came into range of the little fellow, who took careful aim, fired, and dropped the last in line. Nxumalo was dutifully impressed by two things: that the white man could kill at such a distance and that he would want to kill an animal as splendid as the sable antelope.

When the hartebeest huts were finished, identical with the rude sheds occupied by Hendrik van Doorn one hundred and forty-nine years earlier, a most fortunate thing occurred, one which Balthazar Bronk was able to utilize to the general advantage of the white community.

Relations with Nxumalo's tribe had prospered, and it was apparent that whites and blacks could share Vrymeer in harmony. There was no trouble about land, nor hunting rights, nor anything else; Nxumalo tried to make it clear, as he learned bits of Dutch, that his Zulu would in no way become vassals of the white men, nor would they work for them on any regular basis like their Coloured servants; they, too, were free and proud of that. But when during the building of the huts the blacks volunteered much labor and showed the newcomers how best to utilize the terrain for drainage, Tjaart said confidently, 'They'll soon be working for us.' It was a happy, prosperous relationship, with the Voortrekkers providing an occasional antelope for Nxumalo's pots and with certain women of the tribe volunteering to care for the white babies while their mothers worked at other tasks.

The situation did not exactly please Bronk and his group; they wanted the blacks to become slaves, as the Bible directed, and there was even some talk of eliminating Nxumalo's tribe altogether, in obedience to the precepts of Joshua, which Balthazar was skilled in quoting:

> 'And they smote all the souls that were therein with the edge of the sword, utterly destroying them: and there was not any left to breathe: and he burnt Hazor with fire . . . And all the spoil of these cities, and the cattle, the children of Israel took.'

To the surprise of all, Tjaart opposed this draconian solution, whereupon Bronk countered with the suggestion that the blacks be converted into servants, as the Bible ordered in so many places, but this, too, Tjaart rejected, saying, 'We have searched so long for a place in which we can live in peace, let us do so here.' And since he was the acknowledged leader of the group, this counsel was accepted.

But then the fortunate stroke came, and the whole problem was neatly settled. One night cattle thieves broke into the Van Doorn kraal and made away with some twenty oxen, half of them belonging to Balthazar, who threatened to annihilate the black settlement, but when Tjaart and Paulus went to investigate, they found that none of Nxumalo's people had touched the cattle: 'It's the village far over the hill. They steal our cattle, too.'

So a retaliatory commando was enlisted, and under the leadership of Balthazar Bronk it ranged far, following the spoor of the stolen cattle and coming at last upon a meager village of some forty people. There, in the kraals, stood the Van Doorn cattle, so with a mighty shout the horsemen burst into the heart of the village, massacring everyone.

'Not the children!' Bronk shouted. 'Save the children!'

In obedience to his command, eleven black children were saved, and these were driven back to the white camp, where they were distributed among the families to work for the rest of their lives. They were not slaves; the law forbade any further slavery and every Voortrekker constitution for a new republic outlawed it. But the Bible had expressly authorized Israelites to take children from the Canaanites and raise them as servants:

> Moreover of the children of the strangers that do sojourn among you, of them shall ye buy, and of their families that are with you, which they begat in your land: and they shall be your possession.

> And ye shall take them as an inheritance for your children after
> you, to inherit them for a possession; they shall be your bondmen
> for ever . . .

Cleverly the Voortrekkers reconciled this Biblical injunction with the
new English law: No slavery, but if a black child is left orphaned in
battle, it must as an act of charity be taken into a white home, where it
shall serve as helper till the age of twenty-one, without wages but with
Christian instruction and wholesome Kaffir food. After that, of course,
the black would have nowhere to go, really, so it would be logical for
him to stay on, at whatever compensation the master saw fit to offer.

So the sensible thing to do on commando was to see that there were
orphans, and Balthazar Bronk had done so. Tjaart argued mildly
against what seemed to him an evasion, but his wife was so pleased to
receive the two children assigned to her that he said nothing, for even
though he was disposed to ask Aletta not to keep them, there in his
Bible were the instructions commanding him to keep the children, and
to accept others when they came his way.

Now that the great fixed battles had ended, Tjaart could think of the
blacks against whom he had fought so incessantly—Xhosa, Matabele,
Zulu—as men of enviable courage. He had been awed by their willingness to keep coming forward into the face of certain death, and he
prayed that the time had come when blacks and Voortrekkers could
share peace. In both religion and tradition he had been taught that no
black could ever attain the cultural or moral level achieved by the most
ordinary white man, and he was now satisfied that they were intended to
be servants. The Boer leaders referred to them as 'the inferior race,' and
he saw no reason to alter that assessment, but he also knew they could
be wonderful friends and trusted associates. In his lifetime he had been
forced to kill well over one hundred and sixty individual blacks himself,
and he could think of not a single instance in which he had been in any
way at fault. It was strange that not once did he fire a gun at a black
without having at his elbow one of his Hottentot or Xhosa servants,
who had helped him track the enemy and prepare the guns. And no
matter where he traveled, in peace or war, he never went anywhere
without blacks who had elected of their own volition to stay with him.
On numerous occasions he risked his life to preserve his personal freedom, but if anyone had told him that blacks would do the same, he

would have been dumfounded, for he believed that they welcomed the
coming of the white man and preferred an orderly progress in servitude
and self-development, much as the oxen yoked to his wagon liked to be
told where to go.

Aletta was now completely disenchanted with Tjaart, finding him a mo-
notonous, single-minded man whose rigorous attitudes toward life grew
tedious. He had been exciting as an alternative to her pusillanimous
Ryk Naudé, but as a legal husband, he was tiresome. Much more to her
taste was a man like Balthazar Bronk, younger, livelier, more fun by the
lakeside, and before long she was seeing this flamboyant gentleman with
some regularity.

Paulus alerted his father as to what was happening: 'Aletta goes to
the fields.'

'Who with?'

'Balthazar.'

As always, Tjaart studied the matter cautiously, and when he
proved to his satisfaction that his wife had returned to her customary
deceptions, he went into seclusion for several days, during which he calculated the remaining probabilities of his life: I'm an old man now, and
all my children are dead. My two sons slain at De Kraal. Minna dead at
Blaauwkrantz. If I lose Aletta, I'll never leave any sons. This Paulus is
a man among boys, finest lad I've ever known. I'll care for him and get
him started, but damnit, he's not mine.

Here he paused, for from his window he could see Paulus and his
grandchild Sybilla, twelve and nine, walking beside the lake, and as always, she held on to his hand. Impulsively, Tjaart set aside his own
miseries and prayed: God, protect those two. They are the seed of our
nation.

Then he returned to himself: The years roll past so swiftly, and we
are so many miles from the families we knew at De Kraal and Graaff-
Reinet. I'm alone, and I need this woman, whatever her behavior, and I
shall keep her.

Strong in his resolve, he stormed back into community life with fire
and terror. Grabbing his gun and marching to the hut of Balthazar
Bronk, he called him out, aimed the rifle directly at his heart, and cried
in loud voice, 'Balthazar, pack your wagon and leave within the hour.
Elsewise, I shoot you dead.'

'But what . . .' It was Bronk's wife, peering out from the hut.

'He knows' was all Tjaart would say. And he stood there while the Bronk family packed and sorted out their cattle from the common herd.

'Where shall I go?' Bronk said in a whining voice.

'I care not,' Tjaart snapped, and he called for Paulus to fetch another gun and stand guard with him till the wagon was rolling.

'Give them our biltong,' Tjaart growled, and Paulus ran to fetch the Van Doorn supplies. When the wagon started to move, Tjaart waited till it was well under way, then fired shots over it to warn the Bronks that they must not turn back, but on the second volley Aletta appeared, crying that she must run to join them.

Once again Tjaart, who could manage men so ably, flew into a red fury when called upon to reason with a woman. Throwing his gun to Paulus, he grabbed his wife by the arm, swung her about, and used the only logic he knew: he struck her three times across the face, and when she fell into the dust, he reached down, pulled her back to her feet, and struck her again.

'Into the hut!' he commanded, and all that day the neighbors watched as he sat by the door, gun in hand, saying nothing.

At sunset he went inside, and when he undressed for bed and stood before his wife, she burst into uncontrollable tears: 'You're old and fat and you have a big belly. Ryk was so young and strong. I despise you.'

With a great swing of his arm he knocked her down once more, so that she ran screaming from the hut, with him chasing her in only his pantalets.

'I shall go after him,' she wailed.

'Do,' he shouted. 'Go into the darkness, with the lions waiting.'

And when she had taken only a few steps, she saw the eyes of those animals who came to the lake at night, and she heard strange sounds and the muffled roaring of a distant lion, so terrifying that she hurried back to the protection of the village, and after a while, into her own hut.

Tjaart was waiting. With compassion and a profound unexplainable love, he took her in his arms and said, 'Ryk was young and beautiful, but he's dead. I'm old and fat, but I'm alive. That's how it is.' And that night Aletta conceived the boy Jakob, named after Tjaart's revered second wife.

IX. The Englishmen

I

N the middle years of the nineteenth century a chain of unlikely
events inspired Queen Victoria to confer a knighthood on Major
Richard Saltwood, of De Kraal, Cape Colony, and when this occurred, cartoonists of South Africa and England lampooned him in a
congenial way as Sir Cupid. He was a hero, and his investiture became
an act of warm celebration, uniting the colony more firmly to the
mother country.

Saltwood's personal good luck began in 1856 when he was cata-
pulted into national prominence because of a disaster which riveted
the attention of the world. It began one autumn morning in May 1856
when a short, frail girl of fourteen went to a pool in a stream east of the
Great Fish River and saw therein a ghostly assembly of figures accompanied by swirling mists.

This might have had no aftermath had not the girl, Nongqause, happened to be the niece of that cunning seer Mhlakaza, whom Tjaart van
Doorn had come close to shooting back in 1836. Now, after twenty additional years of chicanery and nefarious behavior, this shifty man saw
in his niece an opportunity to set himself up as the great prophet of the
Xhosa people.

Mhlakaza interrogated the child at length, but found her answers
confused and vague. She recited a rambling account of her walk to the
pool and kept referring to a hornbill that had flown near her—'certain

omen of disaster, for it brings droughts'—but he did not interrupt her until she said something startling: 'They were strangers, my Uncle. Some with black skins like Xhosa. But others in the mists . . . I am frightened!'

'What others?' he asked reassuringly.

'White men rising from the mists, my Uncle.'

Mhlakaza did not press her. Placing his hand gently on her shoulder, he said, 'Go to your hut, Nongqause, and tell no one of this.' He watched until she disappeared through the low entrance of her parents' place; then he stole from the village to inspect this pool.

It was four hours before he returned, and his slightest movement was watched, especially by older men and women who concerned themselves in such matters. For months he had been promising that the Xhosa would hear words of importance from his lips, and now his secretive behavior indicated that the prophet was ready.

When he stalked silently to his hut, word spread that no one was to approach him for two days and nights: the spirits had ordered him to do certain things. No questions were to be asked of the diviners, and young people were not to speculate on what his forthcoming revelation might be. If they did, their chatter might interrupt his communication with those who dwelt in the sky.

Alone, within his hut, Mhlakaza burned herbs and medicines to thwart witchcraft, then sat naked as the acrid smoke fumed about his body, causing his eyes to stream. He swallowed powerful emetics to purge himself, daubed his skin with red ocher and white clay, and entered into long incantations, begging the spirits to unleash forces that would prepare him for the great role he was about to play.

On the third day he came out from his seclusion, and with the entire village at his heels, strode to the cattle kraal, where he chose the plumpest beast from his own herd. Prodding it with an assegai, he pierced the skin until the animal bellowed with rage. He loved that sound; it meant the spirits were speaking to him. Then, with a vicious thrust, he drove the iron tip deep into the neck of the ox. Next he cut out the stomach and bladder, anointing his body with their contents, and to the delight of the witnesses, ordered the ox to be roasted and eaten. He was purified.

On the fourth day Mhlakaza returned alone to the stream long before first light, and his vigil ended when he uttered a mighty cry, as if things deep within him were released. There in the gray dawn stood an older brother who had died in the 1835 war against the English. 'Draw near, Mhlakaza, my good brother who is chosen for great deeds' came the voice. 'Our child Nongqause is chosen with you to lead our people to victory. To you, members of my family, will be shown the Xhosa strength.'

And then, just as Nongqause had seen the strangers in the pool, so did he! Regiment upon regiment of Xhosa heroes, risen from the dead, marched triumphantly through a great valley where no English or Boer face was to be seen. But with the black legions rode the white strangers who had come from overseas to help the Xhosa.

A dazed, wild-eyed Mhlakaza staggered back to the village, where his followers were not disappointed, for he told them that he, too, had seen the strangers who had first shown themselves to Nongqause. They had, he said, ordered him to purify himself before talking with them, and had not everyone seen him do this?

'We saw! We saw! The nights of smoke. The days of prayer.'

'Those that wait by the pool say this: "There is a valley of desolation, with the bones of many animals, with baskets empty of grain."'

A frightful cry rose from the listeners, wails and groans at so grim a vision.

'But look further, my friends. Open your eyes. And this land of death begins to blossom like a paradise. The cattle rise and are fat. The fields burst with the finest corn.'

'Aieee, Mhlakaza! How wonderful!'

'Say the ones at the pool, "All this is yours if you obey us." I saw a million Xhosa ready for battle. And with them came a regiment of strangers who fight alongside us as brothers.' Flecks of spittle hung at the corners of his mouth as he revealed his startling visions: 'They will slay the English! They will trample the Boers!'

When the roar of approval died, he added, 'The Xhosa will inherit everything. All the farms in this land will be yours. You will never again know a cattle shortage. Your grain baskets will overflow forever.'

Now, it so happened that Mhlakaza had recently traveled through the frontier districts, moving along the fringe of settlement as on that morning at De Kraal when Van Doorn wanted to shoot him. And as he moved about he listened: 'In lands beyond the sea there is a body of warriors called Russians. They are like the Xhosa, except they have white skins, but like us, they fight the English.'

'They're afraid of these Russians,' a servant whispered. 'In one battle they struck down the best commando of the English. Killed six hundred when the English ran at them on horses, with stabbing sticks.'

He picked up what additional information he could about the disastrous charge of the English brigade at Balaklava, and one fact began to burn in his mind: his enemy England had another enemy, the Russians.

Mhlakaza took Nongqause aside and explained the mystery of her visions: 'The Xhosa will be reinforced by the white strangers you saw, the Russians. We must hurry to the pool to get further instructions.' And when these words were locked in her childish mind, he took her to the kraal of the great chief, Kreli, where she stood before the councillors of the area: 'To prove your faith in the ancestors who spoke with me, you must do two things. Kill all your cattle. Burn all your mealies. Only when you are purified in this way will the ghosts march to help us.'

Chief Kreli, bewildered by such instructions, said, 'Step forward, child, and let us see who it is our ancestors speak with.'

Nudged by her uncle, Nongqause moved timidly toward Kreli, her large hazel eyes meeting those of the great chief.

'Tell them the white soldiers are ready to march with us,' Mhlakaza said.

'It is so, my Chief.'

'They have come across the sea to fight for us?' Kreli asked.

'They have,' she said quietly, going on to describe in detail the heroics of the Russians in their battle against the English. As she spoke, a chatter ran through the crowd, for if Mhlakaza vouched for her as a true Mother of Greatness, she must be listened to.

'The cattle are to be killed,' she said again. 'The baskets empty. The land bare. When that is done, the Russians and the Xhosa will drive the English and the Boers into the sea.'

The idea of slaughtering all cattle was so infamous, threatening as it did the very existence of the Xhosa, that older councillors scorned both Nongqause and her prophecy. One white-haired advisor protested: 'Where was this nonsense seen?'

'At the pool,' Mhlakaza said. 'She saw it first. Then I did.'

'This talk of a day when all people, dead and alive, shall come together. Isn't that what they say at the Christian mission at Golan?' the old man asked. 'Isn't that where you heard it?'

'It is the word of our ancestors,' Mhlakaza insisted.

'You bring us missionary ideas,' the old councillor persisted. 'The tribes of the dead coming back to earth, bringing paradise with them.'

'Our ancestors told me. At the pool.'

Chief Kreli, an artful, determined leader, had long sought some tactic that would unite his Xhosa, and he surmised that this young girl's visions might be the answer. Organizing a pilgrimage to the pool, he allowed his councillors to see Nongqause talking with the departed leaders and hear her speaking with the waiting Russians. When she reiterated the ghostly commands, that all foodstuffs be destroyed, he began to believe that if this were done, the Russians would arrive by ship and unite with the long-dead chieftains to expel the white men from the land.

'We shall do it!' Kreli announced, and for nine months Nongqause and her uncle paraded west and east, to the Xhosa and all adjoining tribes, assuring everyone that the day of revelation was at hand and the miracle about to occur, if only they would slay their cattle and let their fields lie barren. 'The ghosts wait there behind the clouds, all the victorious warriors of the past, eager to help us regain our pastures. But you must do as they command.'

It was a powerful doctrine, made more compulsory when Mhlakaza boldly predicted the precise day on which the miracle would happen: 'On the eighteenth day of February 1857 the ghosts will return, driving millions of plump cattle before them and bringing us untold baskets filled with grain.'

When reports of the cattle killing reached government agencies at Grahamstown, there was initial disbelief that such hysteria could ensnare an entire people, especially on the word of a child who could not possibly know where Russia was or what the name represented, but a tremor did run through the colony, for twice before, fanatic prophets had incited the Xhosa masses, whipping the kraals into a frenzy and leading them to disaster. In the first attack on Grahamstown a prophet had assured his people of victory, and not long ago another prophet had convinced his warriors that white men's bullets would be no stronger than raindrops if only the Xhosa killed all cream-colored cattle.

Now the government received proof indisputable that entire villages were engaging in an orgy of cattle slaughter, and serious attention had to be paid, for the people in Grahamstown had now lived side-by-side with the Xhosa for two generations and knew how much they revered their cattle. 'If they're actually killing them, something desperate's afoot,' a new district officer said, and Major Saltwood of De Kraal was sent for.

'What's it all about?' he asked when he reported for consultations.

'A crazy prophet named Mhlakaza has been preaching that the Xhosa must slay their cattle.'

'Mhlakaza?' Saltwood asked. 'Isn't he that fellow who gave us so much trouble over access to one of the rivers? Ten, fifteen years ago?'

'The same. This time he claims his niece, a stupid little girl of fourteen or fifteen . . . I've seen her. Squinched-up face. Doesn't weigh ninety pounds. She claims she was visited by all the dead Xhosa chiefs—Hintsa, Ndlambe, the lot. She says they told her to slay all the cattle, burn all the crops, and they'd come storming back to throw us English into the sea.'

'What's this about the Russians?' Saltwood asked. He was sixty-eight years old, tall, lean, white-haired, very much an English military man in retirement, and because of his service on the Afghan frontier, perpetually interested in Russian trickery.

'Oh, Mhlakaza seems to have picked up some nonsense about the Crimean War. All he knows is that Russia fought against us. Because of our loss at Balaklava, he's convinced himself that Russia won and that she wants to invade Grahamstown to complete her victory. Frightful mess he peddles.'

'Don't underestimate their prophets,' Saltwood warned. 'They can whip a countryside into frenzy.'

'To what purpose?'

'They're in cahoots with the schemers and plotters in the nation. Men like Kreli. I've survived two wars launched by fanatics, and it's serious business. If they do kill all their cattle, they'll have to find others. I hardly need tell you where they'll start looking.'

'What about the little girl?'

'She's a mystic of some sort. Hears voices. He's using her.'

'As simple as that?'

'Carson's the only one who's actually seen her. What's your story?'

A young Oxford graduate, whose first job had been at Grahamstown, had made a minor name for himself by learning the Xhosa language and something of the tribe's internal politics. The Xhosa trusted him, and on one of his recent trips into the heartland of the region they had allowed him to talk with Nongqause. 'She's illiterate, has no idea of our government at Cape Town, and couldn't possibly have any concept of Russia. But she has been remarkably consistent in her visions and has told only one clear story: "Kill everything, burn everything, and the spirits will come to free us." '

'Does she speak specifically against us?' Saltwood asked.

'Never heard her say as much. She has only a generic enemy, but it's got to be us.'

'She's not preaching armed rebellion?'

'The spirits are going to handle that end of it. But of course, the living Xhosa must be prepared to follow them, so I suppose that in the end we must expect armed invasion.'

'Good God,' the new district officer said.

'Do you take it that seriously?' one of the officials asked Saltwood.

'I do. You must remember, gentlemen, that these men you're talking about have been fighting us for nearly half a century. They've learned all the tricks. They're brave, and when their prophets preach a holy war they can become quite fanatical. I think we're in for trouble.'

Saltwood's perceptive observation about blended heroism and fanaticism gained such wide circulation that the government asked him to see what he could do to minimize or even halt the cattle killing, and he left Grahamstown with two Xhosa men who worked for him at De Kraal to enter the regions where Nongqause's preachments were having their strongest effect.

He was not prepared for what he saw. Entire fields lay covered with dead animals, and anyone who knew the Xhosa had to be appalled at this wanton sacrifice. On two different occasions his Xhosa companions broke into tears at the sheer waste, but when Saltwood talked with the men who had done the killing, he found them in a state of euphoria—smiling, happy, marking time till the eighteenth of February when every dead animal would be returned a hundredfold.

'Tell them it cannot happen,' Saltwood urged his men, but when they endeavored to persuade the other Xhosa not to kill any more cattle, the tribesmen smiled benignly and said, 'You wouldn't understand,' and the slaughter continued.

At the end of five days Saltwood had seen more than twenty thousand dead animals, and he sent one of his companions running back to Grahamstown with this brief message: 'The rumors we heard were one-tenth of the story. I truly fear that all cattle may be slain and that thousands of people will face starvation. Begin to assemble foodstuffs immediately.'

Distraught, uncertain, he decided to seek out a village where one of his former workers lived, a man named Mpedi, fine and trustworthy, hoping to use him as a wedge into the heart of the problem. But when he reached Mpedi's hut he found the man, a sensible fellow in his sixties, mesmerized by the glorious thing that was about to happen: 'Baas, you cannot know what we shall be doing. All the great chiefs coming back to help us. A hundred . . . a thousand warriors waiting in the rivers to rise up and lead us into our inheritance.'

'Mpedi, wake up!' Saltwood begged. 'Do you think your dead cattle will be replaced? Do you think food will come from the sky?'

'It will come, Baas.'

'Can't you see that you're about to starve?'

'There will be food for all, Baas.'

'Goddamnit!' Saltwood raged. 'Open your eyes!'

'They are open, Baas. And on the eighteenth of February yours will be opened, too.'

Saltwood shook his old herdsman, a man who loved cattle. 'Mpedi, if you kill the rest of your cattle, you're going to starve.'

'Baas,' the herdsman said with deep affection, 'I want you to leave this village and go back across the Great Fish, where you belong. Go to De Kraal and get your family. Hurry to Port Elizabeth and get aboard a ship and go away. Because the risen chiefs are going to march right to headquarters and kill all the white people who have stolen our land from us. I don't want you to die, Baas, because you've been a good man to us.'

Saltwood was so shaken by his inability to bring sense into the discussion that he tried a new tack: 'Mpedi, I'm not here as your friend. Remember how many times I went out on commando against you men.'

'Ah!' the herdsman said with a broad smile. 'That was war, Baas. I shoot you. You shoot me. Who cares? It was in peace that you were so good to us. Now please leave.'

And while Saltwood stood there, this man whose life had centered upon the building up of a small herd of cattle went back into his fields and resumed slaying the docile creatures whose existence represented the only chance of keeping that village alive in the awful days that loomed.

During the first two weeks of February, Saltwood penetrated to most areas of the western Xhosa, and what he saw sickened him so that he returned to Mpedi's village, now stripped of all food except what was in the pots for the few days remaining till the miracle. 'Can you take me to Nongqause?' he asked his former workman.

'No good, Baas. She sits by the pool waiting for the generals to rise from the waters.'

'I must talk with her.'

'No good, Baas. She just sits there, waiting!'

'Damnit, Mpedi. I'm trying to save enough animals to keep you idiots alive.'

'No good, but if you want to hear from her own lips . . .'

He led Saltwood a day's journey eastward to the Gxara River, where a delirious crowd of Xhosa had gathered to be near the prophetess when the chiefs arose to greet her, and enough people knew Saltwood's good reputation to allow him to pass through the multitude to talk with the little girl. She had a pinched face, no beauty whatever, and large watery eyes. She was quite oblivious of the furor she was causing, and when Saltwood had been in her presence only a few minutes he was satisfied that she did indeed see visions. When he spoke to her, she did not respond coherently but rather with a dreamy indifference, for she knew that the day of revelation was at hand.

'Nongqause, there's still time to save enough cattle to feed the people during the coming winter. Stop the killing, I beg you.'

'When all are dead, then the new will arrive.'

'Can't you see that you're bringing desolation to the Xhosa?'

'When the grain is all burned, the new will arrive.'

'Nongqause! You're destroying your people.'

'When the chiefs arise, it is the enemy who will be destroyed.' She pointed to the calm, dark surface of the pool as if she expected Saltwood to see what she saw: the cattle waiting to fill the pastures, the boundless supplies of grain, the great chiefs dressed in battle array, with the Russians somehow behind them.

'Do you know where Russia is?' Saltwood asked.

As soon as he said this word, an older man moved in to insert himself between the little prophetess and this English intruder. It was Mhlakaza, but neither he nor Saltwood was aware that they had met one fateful morning back in 1836 on the hill at De Kraal when Tjaart van Doorn was prevented from shooting him.

'Why do you come here?' he asked in good English.

'I come to beg the little girl to stop the cattle killing.'

'The spirits demand it.'

'Who are you?' Saltwood asked.

'Mhlakaza, he who speaks for the spirits.'

'Don't you realize that you're all going to starve?'

'There will be two hundred cattle for every Xhosa.'

'Don't be a damned fool. Your meadows couldn't hold them.'

'There will be food for all.'

Saltwood was so disgusted with this crazy man that he tried to return to the little girl, but this Mhlakaza would not permit. Keeping himself face-to-face with the Englishman, he nudged him farther and farther away from the pool. In desperation Saltwood asked, 'Mhlakaza, do you know who I am?'

'Are you Saltwood of De Kraal?'

'Yes. And Mpedi here will assure you that I'm a friend of the Xhosa. I've fought against you in clean battle. I've worked with you. Tell him, Mpedi.'

Mpedi nodded, whereupon Saltwood asked, 'Mhlakaza, do you know where Russia is?'

'The ships are already on the sea, coming to join us.'

'But do you know what it is? A city? A town? A group of kraals?'

'It is Russia,' the prophet said. 'They will be here next week.'

'And what will you do?'

'Greet them at the shore. Then march to Grahamstown.'

Having said this, Mhlakaza spoke in Xhosa to Mpedi: 'Take this man away. See that he reaches home safely.' In English he said, 'Saltwood, hurry home and leave the country. We do not wish to kill you when the Russians come.'

In frustration and despair Saltwood left the Gxara River and its magical pool. Wherever he moved through Xhosa land he saw the slaughtered cattle, the burning piles of grain. He calculated that about twenty-five thousand blacks would starve in the months ahead, and that figure represented only the western lands which he had seen. In the eastern areas, where white men rarely penetrated, there would be, he supposed, perhaps another fifty thousand. Mpedi would surely die, and Nongqause the innocent cause, and Mhlakaza the effective cause. The Xhosa nation would be so prostrated that it could never recover, and this was happening in the year 1857 when sensible nations ought to be able to halt such insanity.

When he returned to Grahamstown he dispatched reports to Cape Town and London, warning the governments that by the first week in March starvation would be rampant and that at least fifty thousand deaths must be anticipated. He urged immediate shipment to Grahamstown of all surplus food supplies and suggested that they be doled out slowly, for the starving period was bound to last at least a year and a half.

Tired, weak from inadequate food and sleep, he felt both his advanced age and the dreadful tragedy about to descend upon this region. He wanted very much to hurry back to De Kraal and prepare his farm for the wandering skeletons who would soon be spreading over the countryside, but he felt obligated to go back among the Xhosa, and he was at Mpedi's desolated village on the evening of 17 February 1857. It was one of those calm, sweet summer nights when birds sang and the earth seemed impatient for the coming of dawn.

The eighteenth was a bright, clear day, with visibility so unsullied that every mountaintop stood clear. If ever there was a day for beneficent miracles, this was it. The sun rose without a cloud across its face; the air was quiet, with no hint of storm; and had any cattle been alive in the valleys, they would have been lowing.

Ten o'clock came, and the sun reached toward its apex, increasing in strength. Since it was generally believed that the dead would rise at high noon, crowds began to gather, looking in various directions to catch the first sight of marching armies and the arriving cattle.

Noon came, and silence. Slowly the sun passed its zenith and began its long descent to the horizon, and with every hour the suspicion grew that neither the chiefs nor the cattle were going to arrive. By five o'clock, when shadows were conspicuously lengthening, Mpedi came to Saltwood and asked, 'Will they come in darkness? They wouldn't do that, would they?'

'They are not coming,' Saltwood said, his eyes touched with tears.

'You mean . . .'

'I mean that when the hunger strikes, old friend, come back to De Kraal.'

At six, while there was still plenty of daylight if the chiefs and the Russians wanted to fulfill their pledges, everyone became anxious, and by seven there was panic. When the sun vanished and the fateful day was gone, many began to wail, and by midnight there was consternation throughout the little villages. All food was gone; the Russians had not come; and slowly the Xhosa realized that on the morning of the nineteenth they were going to face problems more terrible than any they had so far imagined.

The next two months were horror. To the headquarters in Grahamstown came reports that chilled even the most hardened veterans: 'I visited six villages and found only seven people alive.' Entire river systems, including even their tiny branches, had not a single person surviving along their banks. Corpses of people rotted in the veld beside the older corpses of their cattle. The land lay devastated, as if Plague had swept in with his Scythe.

Many who survived owed their existence to Richard Saltwood, who marshaled his inadequate food supplies with brilliance, squeezing the maximum good from the mealies allowed him. He organized relief teams, went himself into the bleakest areas, and prevailed upon his neighbors to accept on their farms as many wandering Xhosa as they could.

He became inured to death, and hardened himself to make decisions which meant that this village would survive and that perish. For vast numbers in the Xhosa heartland, there was simply nothing to be done; there death was universal.

When he surveyed the western areas in late April he found that his estimates of the tragedy had been accurate: at least twenty-five thousand corpses could be seen lying about unburied; and he had been correct in guessing that a greater number lay dead in the eastern areas to which he could not go. Seventy, eighty thousand of the finest blacks in Africa had probably died, some two hundred thousand cattle were slain, because a little girl had visions which her unscrupulous uncle had used to reach for goals not even he could fully understand.

In the midst of this desolation Saltwood kept thinking of his old friend Mpedi; the herdsman had not reported to De Kraal, where some fifty Xhosa were being sheltered at Saltwood's expense, so he set out to rescue Mpedi—if he still lived.

The journey to that village was one he would later try to strike from his mind: corpses scattered in the sun like dead autumn flowers; pastures forlorn and empty of cattle that should have been producing calves; stench and dust and loneliness. But at the village itself the ultimate horror, for there he found six adults who had survived, and Mpedi off in a hut by himself, trembling and near death from starvation.

'Old friend,' Saltwood cried, tears coming to his eyes despite the fact that he had seen thousands of others dying. Mpedi was an individual man, a good herdsman who had tended De Kraal cattle faithfully, and his death would be a personal grief.

'Old friend,' Saltwood repeated. 'Why are you not sharing the food with the others?'

Shivering in terror, the herdsman drew back. He could not trust even his old baas. He wanted only to die.

'Mpedi!' Saltwood said, somewhat irritated at this rebuff. 'Why do you lie here alone?'

'They are eating their children,' the old man said, and when Saltwood stormed from the hut and kicked the ashes under the pot and upset everything, he saw human bones.

Mpedi starved to death, as did the fool Mhlakaza, responsible for it all. Nongqause did not starve; as a frail child she required little food, and her admirers supplied that. She lived another forty-one years, a curiosity gossiped about but rarely seen, for the Xhosa eventually realized that she was the instrument of their disaster. In the midst of a later famine she fled for her life when her identity became known. Among her intimates, however, she was pleased to talk about the great days when all the world listened to her preachments, and she seemed to have no realization of what she had done. In later years she assumed a new name, which she felt was more appropriate to her position. She rechristened herself Victoria Regina.

The Crimean War had been in part responsible for agitating the mind of Mhlakaza and creating the fatuous idea that Russia would shortly invade the Cape Colony; one year later it was directly responsible for Richard Saltwood's new name, Cupid.

When the Russians in Sebastopol stubbornly held out against the British, causing thereby the infamous Charge of the Light Brigade at nearby Balaklava, a serious crisis developed in the British army. Enlistments at home failed to provide enough new troops to replace those dying from Russian bullets and English malfeasance. Various devices were suggested for replenishing the ranks, but in the end the only thing that made sense was a return to the system used so effectively in 1776 against American rebels and in 1809 against Napoleon: the English army sent recruiting agents to Germany, where for substantial bonuses a first-class mercenary legion was employed.

The Germans had to be under twenty-five years old, over sixty-two inches tall, and unmarried. They proved a superb lot, and would surely have conducted themselves bravely in the Crimea except that peace came before they could be shipped out of England. This created a serious problem; the English had an army, trained and paid for, with no war in which to engage it.

Queen Victoria, herself of German extraction, and her husband Prince Albert of Saxe-Coburg-Gotha were naturally concerned about what might happen to their young compatriots and were delighted when plans were announced whereby the entire contingent was offered passage to the Cape as military settlers, to establish homes and secure posts along the recently disrupted Xhosa frontier. A strategy somewhat like this had been advocated in 1820 with English colonists, and there was no reason why it could not be duplicated in 1857 with Germans.

A vast scheme was initiated whereby nine thousand of the mercenaries, plus such new wives as they could acquire, would be shipped to the same port used by the English when they landed. But now a snag developed. The Germans had such an excellent reputation for soldiering that numerous other nations were eager to employ them; they received offers from the King of Naples, the Dutch in Java, the Argentinian government and seven revolutionary juntas across Europe, who felt that if only they could enroll these crack troops, they could overthrow reactionary governments. About a quarter of the recruits, 2,350 officers and men, were left over to emigrate to the Cape.

Since Queen Victoria and her husband were most eager that this settlement prove successful, they wrote to South Africa, asking that Major Richard Saltwood, who had distinguished himself during the cattle killing, come to London to supervise the emigration. He was delighted with this opportunity to visit with his brother Sir Peter, and within two days of receiving the invitation, was on his way.

To his astonishment, when he disembarked at Tilbury, he was whisked immediately to Buckingham Palace, where the queen herself discussed the emigration. She was a shortish, round woman with no chin, and when meeting strangers, liked to defer to her husband's judgment; they both displayed a keen interest in her South African colonies —Cape and Natal—and were enchanted by the various stories told of Saltwood's life on the frontier. They said that he must hurry to Southampton to make certain that the German embarkation moved smoothly, and Victoria added that she would hold Richard personally responsible.

She was in the process of adding that she preferred only married emigrants, for this ensured family stability, when a charming boy of thirteen burst into the room, stopped in embarrassment, and started to withdraw. 'Alfred, come here,' the queen said, 'this gentleman is from the land of lions and elephants.' The lad stopped, turned, and bowed low like a Prussian officer.

'I am most pleased to meet you, sir,' he said, whereupon Major Saltwood extended his hand, took the boy's, and drew him back into the room.

'You must come to my farm one day, and see the animals.'

'That I should like to do,' Alfred said, and the brief meeting ended.

In Southampton the authorities were mustering the mercenaries for the voyage to the Cape, and they found themselves with a sterling group of husky young men, but they were not having much success with getting wives. This omission worried Saltwood, since the queen had specifically stated that she preferred complete families in her colonies, so he made a special effort to visit all the nearby towns, seeking women for the young Germans. He was not successful, and when the last of the ships was ready to sail, the rickety old *Alice Grace,* he informed the captain that it must not depart until a final effort had been made to find more brides.

'Who am I?' the captain demanded. 'Cupid?'

'No,' Saltwood replied evenly, 'but you do have a commission to perform.'

'My commission is sailing this ship,' the captain replied. 'Not finding wives,' and the adventure would have ended poorly had not Saltwood been a man of ingenuity and humanity.

'You have over two hundred fine young men aboard this ship,' he told the captain. 'I want them all on deck. Now!'

When they assembled on the afterdeck he told them bluntly, 'Men, it would be most improvident to travel to the Cape without women, so the captain has agreed to hold his ship here for two days. You must circulate through the town and find wives. You'll be married before we sail.'

Saltwood added his own imaginative touch to the quest. Finding himself only a short distance from Salisbury, he hurried there by train, burst into Sentinels and cried, 'I can use all the spare women in town.' His brother was absent, attending Parliament, but his wife was there, and she organized a hunt which produced five young women who had only bleak prospects at home. One ill-favored lass named Maggie began to whimper, 'I don't want no South Aferkee.'

'That's where you're going,' Saltwood said sternly, herding his charges onto the train, which frightened them just as much as the prospective sea voyage.

At the ship two chaotic days were spent in a grand sorting-out, but since many of the Germans and some of the women were drunk, when dawn came on the third day and the passengers awoke to see the horrible choices they had made in the dark, there was rebellion.

This man did not intend to spend his life with that woman, and this woman who could speak no German knew that a substitute husband had been fobbed off on her in the confusion. A wild scene ensued, which the two German ministers aboard could not resolve, and it seemed as if the whole plan might go smash when Saltwood grabbed a whistle, blew it shrilly, and ordered the men to line up on one side of the ship, the women on the other. Then he addressed them: 'Gentlemen, do you wish to spend your lives alone?' When the interpreter repeated this question, many men said 'No.' And Saltwood continued: 'Well, if you don't find your wives this day, you won't find any out there for three or four or a dozen years. Is that what you want?' The interpreter handled this message with brutal frankness, and the German men looked at the deck, saying nothing.

Saltwood then directed his words at the English women: 'You haven't had good lives here. I can see that. Now you have a chance to go to a bright new land, with hope and a good husband. Are you daft, that you would surrender this?'

Before his chastened listeners could dredge up excuses, he ordered the men and women to remain in lines, facing each other, upon which he blew his whistle three times, then said, his finger pointing, 'You, at the head of the line. This is your woman!' And that couple moved forward.

'You!' the interpreter repeated in German. 'This is your woman.'

He went down the entire roster, arbitrarily deciding who was to be married to whom, and at his signal, Reverend Johannes Oppermann stepped forward and in one grand ceremony married the lot. The two hundred and forty couples spent three months together aboard the old *Alice Grace,* and when they reached their destination they established some of the strongest families in South Africa.

The London press delighted in the spectacle of a brother to the sobersides member of Parliament, Sir Peter Saltwood, engaged in so amorous a royal commission, and a *Punch* caricaturist fleshed Richard considerably, plumped up his cheeks, stripped off his clothing but added a discreet diaper, gave him a little bow and arrow, and christened him Cupid.

*　*　*

When officials at Cape Town implored Queen Victoria to send some member of the royal family out to the colony to show the flag and instill patriotism in the hearts of the English segment of the population, she found herself in something of a quandary. She herself would not think of leaving England, and Prince Albert was in failing health. Five of their nine children were girls, and deemed unsuitable for foreign travel among lions and elephants. That left four sons, but the youngest two were ten and seven, hardly appropriate for diplomatic service, while the oldest boy, the Prince of Wales, was visiting the United States and Canada that year. That left only the second son, Alfred, but he was only sixteen. Still, South Africa was a country of farmers and shopkeepers, not a real country like Canada, so little Alfred might do.

He was a popular lad, and within the royal family it had been agreed that he would be the Sailor Prince, with newspapers making a great fuss over the fact that while serving as a midshipman he went barefoot on deck. He was not very bright, which was never a handicap in the English system, but he did love guns; all in all he seemed a sensible solution to the South African problem, and the queen wrote to her friend Major Richard Saltwood of De Kraal, asking him to look after her boy and to 'arrange for him a grand battue, if that be possible.'

It would indeed be possible. Richard knew an English farmer near Bloemfontein who could enlist enough blacks to put on a real battue for the young prince, and all was arranged. Saltwood was at the dock at the Cape when the young fellow landed, and after a round of receptions he sailed with him along the coast to Port Elizabeth, where the royal party disembarked and mounted horses for an adventure inland which would cover twelve hundred miles of saddle-riding over the roughest terrain.

When Saltwood first saw the entourage that proposed to make this journey, he was appalled by its magnitude: the prince, his toothy equerry Friddley, a company of fourteen from the ship, a company of twenty-six from the local government, several score of grooms to tend the spare horses, twenty-seven wagons with drivers to haul the gear, and a professional photographer, Mr. Yorke, to record events on a ponderous camera that required a wagon of its own. All this to enable a boy of sixteen to enjoy a battue.

But it was a no-nonsense expedition, as the riders learned that first day when they rode twenty-two miles without a major stop. The next day they covered forty-six and were dusty-tired when they pulled into De Kraal, where they would rest for two days with the Saltwoods.

It was a splendid respite, with the prince delighted by his first acquaintance with an African farm. De Kraal had been much improved in recent years when the Saltwood fortunes prospered. All the stone buildings dating back to the 1780s had been enlarged and beautified; the grounds had been spruced up with flower gardens; and the fences had been regularized; but the charm of the place, as young Alfred remarked, was still the handsome setting within the hills and the wandering stream that cut diagonally across the holding.

In acreage the farm was somewhat diminished since the days when Tjaart van Doorn operated it: still the nine thousand acres within the hills, but only four thousand outside. 'What I enjoy so much,' the boy prince told Saltwood, 'is the mix of closed-in and open.' He also enjoyed the hunting and proved his reputation by bringing down several smaller antelope.

At dinner on the first night the young man was embarrassed when one of the black maids brought in a bawling white infant to be presented to royalty. 'It's my grandson,' Saltwood explained. 'Seven months old and lord of the manor.'

'What's his name?' the prince asked, holding the baby awkwardly. 'Frank.'

'Frank, I christen thee Sir Bawler,' and that became the child's nickname.

From De Kraal the party headed east to Grahamstown, where Friddley cried, 'What a delightful place! So English. Even the Dutchmen who live here look like our Surrey squires!'

Friddley was a new experience for Saltwood; as the nephew of a duke, he felt entitled to say whatever came into his mind, and he did so in a flush of patriotic emotion which often raced ahead of his grammar. At the opening reception in Grahamstown he gave a far-ranging toast: 'To the loyal citizens of this brave frontier city whose English pluck and heroic perseverance, which shall ever animate our noble race, and who love the queen with a devotion unparalleled and thank her for sharing with you her son, the gallant Sailor Prince . . .' He dropped that sentence and launched fervently into another: 'I say, it was your loyalty to our beloved queen and her beloved consort, the father of our beloved Sailor Prince who does us such honor by this timely visit to the most loyal of his mother's colonies, and I have seen him barefooted on the deck of his ship, discharging his tasks like any other decent, red-blooded sailor on whom the safety of our nation depends . . .' He seemed to run out of breath, but then shouted, 'I drink to the brave English hearts that protected this town against fierce savages.'

'Hear, hear!' the audience cried, but Saltwood asked his neighbor, Carleton the wagon builder, who served as mayor of the little town, 'What about the Boers?' and Carleton whispered, 'Tonight Boers don't count,' and Saltwood chuckled. 'Without them, he wouldn't be standing here tonight.'

At each step Friddley was eager to orate, dwelling upon the nobility of the queen in allowing her young son to come so far to receive the plaudits of the colony; he served the same purpose as the official flatterers at the court of King Dingane and his words were equally empty. But the prince was not diverted by this constant aggrandizement. 'When do we get to the battue?' he asked repeatedly, and once Grahamstown was passed, he stayed in the saddle for fifty miles a day.

Behind him the entourage rode in clouds of dust; the wagons creaked; the grooms helped along the horses gone lame; and Mr. Yorke performed heroics in keeping his cumbersome photographic wagon within striking distance of the others. When they slept in cots in their tents, he lay curled up in his wagon.

After a final ride of fifty-six miles in one day, they came at last to a large farm east of Bloemfontein, where an enormous plain a hundred miles in circumference lay hemmed in by low hills. Days before, at every pass through which game might escape, blacks had been stationed, one thousand in all, and on the late afternoon of 23 August 1860 these beaters began slowly moving toward the central area which the prince would occupy next morning. As they moved, they drove ahead of them from all compass directions a monstrous herd of zebras, blesbok, eland, hartebeest, wildebeest, kudu, ostriches and the soon-to-be-extinct quagga. How many animals did the herd contain? Perhaps two hundred thousand, perhaps less, for no one could count the beasts as they moved in toward the center, then out to the perimeter. Some escaped through unguarded valleys; most were kept penned in by the multitude of beaters.

At dawn the prince, accompanied by twenty-four other guns, moved to the hunting ground, where Friddley laid down the rules: 'I shall ride at the prince's left, Major Saltwood to his right. We will not shoot. Our job will be to hand the prince freshly loaded guns as he fires at the beasts. Your Royal Highness, reach first to me on the left, then to Saltwood on the right. Now I want six good shots to ride behind us in a semicircle. You gentlemen may fire at the game occasionally, but your main task is to protect the prince, should any beast come at him. Is that understood?'

Just as the sun came up, the twenty-five guns took their positions, plus Friddley and Saltwood as handlers, plus ninety black servants, many with guns, plus eighteen white factotums, plus one thousand beaters out on the plains to get everything in readiness for 'the greatest hunt in history.' Only then did Friddley flash a signal, and the grand battue was under way.

The beaters close in raised a hullabaloo, whereupon the frightened animals in that quarter started to rush in the general direction of the waiting hunters. First a score of zebras rushed past, then a scattered flight of leaping springbok, then the main body of the herd. They came in turmoil, hundreds of them, thousands. At first they veered away from the hunters, and many escaped, but when the crush became sheer chaos, they galloped by within ten paces of the gunners, great concentrations of large animals running in terror.

The firing never ceased. 'Here, your Highness!' Friddley cried as he took the prince's empty gun, thrusting a freshly loaded one into his hands. After firing from ten feet into the side of a zebra, the prince would thrust his gun in Saltwood's general direction, and without even looking, reach for a fresh one, which he would again discharge at animals not ten paces away.

Meantime, the twenty-four other sportsmen were also surrounded by fleeing beasts, often throwing up dust in their faces, and they, too, were firing as rapidly as they could, right into the chests of the rushing animals.

After an hour of incessant slaughter the herd reeled in confusion, whereupon the factotums rode their horses out into various parts of the plain, encouraging the beaters to accelerate their movement, and this threw a really tremendous flight of animals right past the waiting prince. Indeed, the great beasts now came so close that firing guns at them was senseless, if not impossible, for the barrels could scarcely be raised against the pressure of the animals.

This delighted Friddley, who shouted, 'Your Highness, let's use the blades!' And he took away the prince's gun, thrusting into his hand a short-handled hog-hunting spear, so sharp that Friddley had named it 'the Paget blade,' after the surgeon who attended Queen Victoria and her family. The young prince used it with some skill; he and Friddley spurred their horses and charged the stampeding beasts, stabbing at them as they roared past. Within minutes both Friddley and the prince were splattered with blood from the frequent stabbings and the fall of the animals.

The two men used their lances for the better part of an hour, with the six precautionary gunmen ranged behind them to fire in the event that some confused beast turned to threaten the royal hunter. Saltwood, without either gun or hog-spear, watched with a kind of detached horror as one great animal after another stumbled to its knees, gushing blood; at numerous times he could hold out his hand and touch the stampeding antelope sweeping past. The only danger a child would have had in that mad affair would be if it stumbled beneath the flying hooves or got in the way of some sportsman's rifle.

'Enough!' someone finally shouted, and when Saltwood got to the prince to take away the bladed-spear, he saw that he was completely covered with blood, like some inept country butcher. In the celebration that followed, one local gentleman shot off his own arm while firing a salute in honor of the heroic young visitor, and Friddley gave a stirring address of thanks to the hundreds of Bloemfontein people who had arranged the shoot: 'On this day we have slain six hundred and forty animals, each larger than a horse, plus thousands of smaller beasts we will not bother to register. Our glorious Sailor Prince proved that he is as brave on land as he is at sea, and we can assure the queen that we watched with manly pride the extreme courage he displayed when faced by the thunder of those enraged beasts. We are sorry that His Royal Highness was deprived of his lion, which we have no doubt he will confront and shoot before he leaves these shores.'

As an afterthought he added, 'This great onslaught was no willful waste of God's creatures. Our faithful Kaffirs need not go hungry this night.'

And since there was no stopping Friddley once he got going, he went on to observe: 'It was a very exciting day, and were His Royal Highness to live for a hundred years, I do not believe he could ever see such a scene again, for the game in these parts is fast disappearing.'

Prince Alfred sent his mother such a glowing account of Richard Saltwood's hospitality that when her prime minister raised a matter of importance which concerned both India and Natal, she put forward the name of the master of De Kraal, pointing out: 'Saltwood's familiar with both places. Give him the job.' And thus she granted Cupid one more chance to launch his arrows.

At the age of seventy-one Richard was approached by the Natal government on a negotiation which would require some delicacy: 'Natal's a great land for sugar, but there's damned little we can accomplish unless we find labor.'

'You've got the Zulu,' Richard said. 'Put them to work.'

'Zulu don't tame easy, old chap. Not like your Xhosa after this cattle madness. No Zulu will work in the fields; won't use his hands. Says it's undignified. Women do such work. We've brought in a couple of Chinese, but the damned Chinamen won't work for the ten shillings a month we offer. They want to save money and buy their own shops.'

'So you're suggesting Indians?'

'Couple of thousand of them, ten shillings a head, we won't know what to do with all the sugar. They've been a success in Mauritius and the West Indies. Why not Natal?'

'What am I to do?'

'The necessary laws have been passed. Now we must go to India and collect them in an orderly way. You did a fine job with those German chappies, and we're sure you can do the same with Indians.'

At his age, Richard would have preferred keeping close to De Kraal with his young grandson, but he had the energy to accept this arduous task, and when he learned that the queen herself had recommended him, he had to accept.

More than forty years had passed since he fought in India, and when his ship reached Madras he was struck by the changes, for he entered that port barely eighteen months after the terrible Indian Mutiny. That bloody uprising had been suppressed after grievous loss on both sides, and it was a jittery peace that prevailed.

'Soldiers that we trained,' an officer at Government House recited, 'turned against us. Burning, looting, murdering. And do you know why? Because of those damned bullets at Dumdum.' Noticing Saltwood's quizzical look, he added, 'The new cartridges for the Enfields were greased at one end and had to be bitten—before use in muzzle loaders, that is. Rumor spread that the grease was pig fat, and the Muslims wouldn't touch it. Said we did it to humiliate their religion.'

'Our problem was red earth,' Saltwood muttered to himself.

'Whassat?'

'Our Kaffirs fought us because they needed red earth from one of our farms for their ceremonies. Hundreds died for red earth.'

More significant for Saltwood was the disappearance of John Company from the Indian scene. Even before the mutiny was quelled, Queen Victoria had signed the act which transferred the subcontinent to the crown, and after two centuries of deadly rivalry with the Dutch, the English company was dead.

'Maybe the businessmen should have retained power,' the officer said.

'Why?'

'They'd have dealt differently with the rebels.' The bitterness of the traditional colonial officer came through: 'A few of the leaders—the really bad ones who killed our people—they were hanged. But we have hundreds walking around with the blood of Englishmen on their hands. "Clemency Canning" they call our viceroy. By gad, his father, the real Canning, he'd have given them clemency at the end of a rope. Our Canning said it wouldn't do to make martyrs of them. More trouble than greased cartridges. Saltwood, I saw our women and children at Allahabad—hacked to death or tossed into a well still breathing. "Clemency Canning," damn him.' Saltwood was to hear endless repetition of these complaints.

He was furiously busy during his stay at Madras, ironing out the hitches in the labor contracts, consulting with recruiting agents; nevertheless, he was able to accomplish his commission, and one afternoon he stood in a large compound at the edge of town where nine hundred Indians squatted on the ground, each praying that he would be chosen to fill one of the two hundred vacancies that would enable him to escape the poverty of India. In less than two hours Saltwood had made his selection, but as he strode out of the compound, the three Desai brothers grabbed at him: 'Please, Sahib, Great Master, we go to your country, too.'

'All places taken. You'll have to wait for the next ship.'

'Please, Great Sahib!' And in the time remaining before his departure, these Desais dogged his steps, walking for miles behind his carriage, waiting at the gates to Government House, desperately striving to keep themselves before him. They would nod, break a pathway for him through crowds, repeat their names, tug at his arm: 'Please, Great Sahib, it is a matter of life and death.'

And always they grinned, showing very white teeth. Eventually they wore Saltwood down, so that he asked the captain of the *Limerick,* 'Got space for three more?'

'Well, my friend, that's a question,' the captain said. 'This is not a slave ship I run.'

'Captain, Captain!' the three Desais cried, bleating like injured sheep. 'You are a very great captain. Surely you can arrange . . .'

'Well, maybe I can fit them in.' The Desais kissed his hands, came weeping to do the same with Saltwood. 'You will never regret this,' they assured him.

So two hundred and three Indian men were certified for passage to Natal on ten-year contracts, after which they were to return home, but when Saltwood reported to the *Limerick* to see her off, he found some five or six hundred Indians ready to sail, many of them women. The three Desai brothers, grinning happily, had five extremely attractive women in tow.

'Our wives,' they explained.

'You're not Muslim,' Saltwood growled. 'You don't have more than one wife.'

'These two,' the Desais said. 'Our wives' sisters.'

'They can't sail with you. Men only. You work ten years, then come back to your wives.'

There was no great wailing. Life in India, especially after the mutiny, was difficult, and if this was the way these men were to earn their living, so be it. But that night at Government House, Saltwood raised the question with an official, who coughed and said, 'Well, there is some rubbish in the law about taking wives to Natal. But you certainly don't want that, do you? Take wives along, every man will have ten children in ten years.'

'Do you want them to live without women for ten years?'

'Do some of them good.'

'We have found in South Africa that it's inhuman to keep men separated from their women, and I'll have none of it.' His arguments prevailed; the government conceded that in future, women should accompany their men and work with them in the sugar fields, and it was then that some wag posted a letter to *Punch* detailing the further adventures of Cupid Saltwood, and soon the caricaturist had a new series showing the diapered Saltwood hovering with his bow and arrow over Indian couples working the sugar in the fields of Natal.

His successful mission to India, and the subsequent landing of young, healthy coolies with their wives, added the final complexity to the South African racial crucible: Bushman, Hottentot, Xhosa, Zulu, Afrikaner, Englishman, Coloured, and now the Indian.

When the cane workers, arriving under contract, were in place, 'passenger Indians' who paid their own way to Natal set themselves up as shopkeepers, and together, these initial groups grew to three-quarters of a million within the century. And though all were repeatedly offered free passage and bonus money if they would return to India, few were foolish enough to accept. They had found life so sweet in the land of Shaka that they intended staying.

Richard had succeeded beyond expectations. The Indians were happy to be in Natal and the white farmers were glad to have them. For his enterprise in handling this migration, and especially his foresight in also bringing wives, he received from the queen herself a letter which formed the capstone to his life: 'Because of your generous services to the Royal Family and the Throne, and in so many capacities, we wish you to come to London to receive a knighthood from our hands.'

When the ceremonies at court ended, Sir Richard Saltwood of De Kraal boarded his first train and rode down to Salisbury, where in the ancient hang-tile house beneath the sentinel oaks and chestnuts he sat with his older brother, Sir Peter, looking across the river at the still-glorious cathedral. They spoke of many things; Sir Peter was no longer in Parliament, having surrendered that seat to his son, but like all the Saltwoods, he was interested in everything.

'Tell me, Richard, what's to be done with the Dutchmen out there?'

'The Boers, or Afrikaners as some call them. They're a special breed. A real Dutchman came out not long ago, a clergyman from Amsterdam, intending to make his life there. I knew him well, and after six months he sat in my house and said, "I'm going back to civilization. These people don't even speak proper Dutch. They worship in a fashion we discarded two centuries ago. Few have read any book but the Bible, and even there, only the Old Testament." And he returned to Holland.'

'What did the locals say?'

'That's where it gets complicated. You've got to understand that the visiting Dutchman was talking about emigrant farmers who trekked—maybe fourteen thousand of them. But you must remember there were other thousands who did not trek. They still form the majority in the colony, and they don't know whether to love or hate their brothers up north. Our Amsterdam clergyman was trying to change the trekker Boers, but they are set in their ways. It'll take more than a Holland predikant to push that lot into the nineteenth century.'

'Are their ways so old?'

Sir Richard sat with his fingers propping his chin, and hesitated about answering, because what he said next would determine the nature of his reply to Sir Peter's major question about the probable future, and he knew that Peter still carried much weight in London. Very carefully he said, 'The ways of the Boer are very old indeed. And the ways of the Englishman are very modern. Sooner or later the two must come into real conflict.'

'War?'

'I don't know. If somehow we could maintain relations with them, the chasm could be bridged. But look at what happened to Tjaart van Doorn, the man who sold me his farm. Peter, you should come to South Africa and see it. No cathedrals visible from it, but a glorious place.'

'What about Van Doorn?'

'Same age as me. Same degree of energy. Splendid fellow—he stood at my side in forty skirmishes against the Kaffirs.'

'But what about him?'

'When he emigrated from our area . . . wrote a first-class letter giving his reasons. He battled Mzilikazi, then stormed down into Natal and helped destroy Dingane. Then fled to some valley far and gone. Lives there with Kaffirs, a few families like his own. No books, no newspapers, no ideas. None of the children can read. Lost. Lost.'

'But if he's fallen back into the bush, why fear him?'

'Because the Tjaart van Doorn I knew was a powerful man. You don't have men like that in England. Carved out of solid rock. Peter, if your government insults this man, or enrages him, there could be hell to pay.'

'What do you want us to do?'

'Conciliate.'

'Bosh.'

Without discussing the matter openly, the brothers agreed that since this would probably be the last time they would ever meet, they ought to take a traditional family excursion to Stonehenge and perhaps on to Oriel College in Oxford, where Sir Richard's grandson would one day be a student, like the three grandsons of Sir Peter. They arranged their schedules, told the grooms to prepare the horses, and one morning Peter said, 'Shall we saddle up and see the Stones?'

'Capital!' And within the hour they were on their way with a small retinue of servants.

They halted at Election Elm at Old Sarum, and under its branches Sir Peter said, 'I was the last member of Parliament to come from this wonderful borough. Back in 1832 I think it was. When Sir John Russell proposed his bill outlawing the rotten boroughs, I amazed everyone by supporting it. The day for that kind of privilege had passed.' He sighed.

'But this old tree sent some sterling men to Parliament, none better than Father.' He chuckled. 'Did you hear how I got the seat?' He told how the Proprietor had brought him here, grumbling all the while, then handed him the ballot with his name inscribed. 'He said he feared I was one of those young radicals. I must have been forty, but he liked members to be in their seventies. Said that by then they had some sense.'

By the time they reached Stonehenge the two old men were tired, and they decided not to try the longer ride to Oxford. 'It was a dear place,' Sir Peter said. 'I collected all my ideas at Oriel. They weren't very good, really, but they sufficed. My son feels the same way. And your grandson will, too. How old is the boy?'

'Two.'

'Is he bright?'

'Average, like all of us.'

After Richard said this the brothers fell silent, and finally Peter, with tears in his eyes, asked, 'Did you ever hear anything about David in America?'

'He disappeared somewhere in Indiana.'

There was prolonged silence as the brothers looked at the fallen stones on which their mother and their grandmother had sat during family picnics. Then Peter said, 'Tell me about Hilary,' but before Richard could speak, he added, 'You know, I suppose, that his visit home with that nigger wife was a disaster.'

'It was a disaster everywhere,' Richard said. 'Poor fellow, they both had their throats cut one night. No one ever knew who did it.'

'Those two dead. We two, knights of the realm. I think Mother would have been satisfied. She was dreadfully practical, you know.' He stared at the ancient stones so loved by his family and repeated what he had told Richard almost sixty years ago: 'This is always to be your home. I mean, here and Sentinels. Do come back.' But each brother knew there would be no revisiting, not for them. But for their children's children this would always be a lodestar.

When Frank Saltwood, grandson of Sir Richard, attended Oriel College during the years 1879–1881, he found it to be a luminous center for theological discussion, but like his forebears, he avoided any deep intellectual discussion. In the Michaelmas Term of his final year he began to take notice of a curious scholar who flitted in and out of Oxford, now attending lectures, now arguing in pubs, and then disappearing for months. Frank was not even certain what college this person belonged to, or whether he was a tutor or a fellow student.

Since he appeared so much older, Frank assumed he must be some itinerant lecturer attached temporarily to a prestigious college like Balliol or Christ Church, a retiring man of poor family whose clothes seemed out of place, whose coat was always buttoned to the chin, and whose trousers were invariably of an odd fabric. He had dark reddish hair, a heavyset body and watery blue eyes, which he shifted away from any direct stare.

As the time approached when he must take his final examinations and leave Oriel, Frank felt keenly the unique beauty of Oxford, and on days when he should have been studying he wandered along the Thames, listening to birds he had not known in South Africa, and wasted his time looking back at the profile of the city, with its domes and towers standing as proudly as they had four hundred years ago. He was oppressed by the ancient dignity of this place as compared to the raw youth of his homeland, and he began to generate that ambivalence which all South Africans experienced who came here for their studies.

In fact, he fell into quite a funk, the sharp direction which he had known up to now blunted by his oscillations between Oxford and De Kraal. For whole days he wandered the streets of Oxford, leaving his rooms at Oriel and aimlessly visiting the nearby colleges, not for intellectual enrichment in preparation for his exams, but rather to look at the great quadrangles as if he were leaving a place he cherished, never to see it again.

He would enter the gateway to some college in which he had never attended a lecture and stand there like a tripper down from London, staring at the beautiful façades of the buildings that outlined the square, imagining the great men who had lived in those rooms or studied in those halls. He was not good at political or literary history, and he certainly could not associate the notable graduates of Oxford with their colleges, but from the conversation of his father and from hints picked up during his residence at Oriel, he vaguely knew that great men of England had come to their studies in this city: Samuel Johnson, Cardinal Wolsey, Charles James Fox and the two Williams, Penn and Pitt, who had left Oxford to represent Old Sarum in Parliament.

When he returned to his own college and entered its gate and saw the low, squat outline of its rugged buildings, he could not believe that any famous men had come from its confines. Legend said that Sir

Walter Raleigh had studied here, but he doubted it. Some of the professors made a fuss over an Oriel man named Gilbert White, but Frank
had no idea who he was or what he had done. No, what came from this
college was an endless procession of Saltwoods, men of solid worth who
never stood at the head of any list but who had a penchant for doing
the right thing. They had managed their business in Salisbury, and extended it into various profitable fields; they had served in Parliament
when Old Sarum was a rotten borough and then stood for honest election when it was abolished; and like his grandfather's brother Hilary,
they had followed God into strange and tragic callings.

Three weeks before his examinations were to begin he fell into a
deep melancholy, obsessed by his thoughts of Hilary Saltwood, and he
wondered what had motivated him. He had died with his throat cut,
Frank knew, and images of the old man . . . He assumed that Hilary
had been old, for he had lived long ago, and the old man's ghost
haunted him so persistently that he began to wonder if this might not be
a call to holy orders. Was God speaking to him, soliciting his assistance
in some distant missionary field?

He might have gone quite sour and missed his examinations altogether had not the curious scholar come bursting back to Oriel, feverishly preparing for his own final examinations, as strange as ever,
those watery blue eyes still deceptive. They seemed somnolent, like a
snake's; actually, they burned with an incandescent fire on the few occasions when he looked directly at a newcomer.

This happened one afternoon at tea when a friend said in banter,
'Saltwood, you're beginning to look like a missionary.'

Frank blushed, but was spared the embarrassment of reply by the
peripatetic scholar, who hunched his shoulders forward, stared right at
him, and asked in a soft, high-pitched voice, 'Why would you elect to be
a missionary in strange quarters when there's so much real work to be
done in your homeland?'

'What do you mean?' Frank stammered.

'I mean South Africa. Don't you live there?'

'I . . . I do. But what's that got to do with it?'

Suddenly the stranger put down his cup, rose awkwardly and
stomped from the room, volunteering not another word.

'Who is that fellow?' one of the Oriel men asked.

'Odd duck. Been studying here for his degree since 1873.'

'Eight years to do three years' work. Is he stupid?'

'I don't know. Those are the first words I've ever heard him speak.'

A younger student interrupted: 'He's not stupid at all, although he sometimes seems so.'

Another disagreed: 'He tried to enter a real college, you know. Balliol, I think, but he couldn't pass the exams. So Balliol sent him over here, and our provost said, "It's always the same. All the colleges send me their failures." And Oriel accepted him.' The speaker laughed nervously. 'Same thing happened with me.'

The first young man continued: 'He lives in South Africa, I'm told, and that's why he's been able to attend only on a hit-or-miss basis.'

'I don't understand,' Frank said.

'His health fails. His lungs. Our Oxford climate threatens him and he must hurry home to recuperate. He's had a very broken career, you know.'

'I'd hardly call that a career,' one student said derisively. 'I say, Saltwood, you're from South Africa. You know the blighter?'

'First time he spoke to me,' Frank said.

'Well, he owns diamond mines in South Africa, and caring for them's the real reason he flits back and forth.'

Three days later Frank again met the stranger, and was impelled to speak with him: 'You said I should not become a missionary?'

'What I meant to say—why don't you knuckle down and quit this foolishness? Why don't you act like a man, pass your examinations?'

The stranger's tone of voice was so peremptory that it sounded like a father's, and Frank said rebelliously, 'They tell me it's taken you eight years to pass yours.'

The man showed no resentment. A bright smile animated his face and he grasped Frank by the arm. 'You spend three years and come away with a degree. I spend eight years and return home with an empire.'

'What kind?'

'Every kind you can imagine. Political, business, mining, but mostly power.' The man started to leave, then turned back, taking Frank's arm again and holding it firmly. 'For God's sake, man, buckle down, finish the job, pass your examinations. Then brood about what to do.'

He spoke with such force and moral imperative that Frank became curious and tried to find out by what strange route this man had come to his final week at Oriel, but none of Frank's friends knew, or even whether he was English-born or a native South African. Later, when everyone dressed in formal attire—black suit, bow tie, black shoes, cap and gown—and filed into the stately Examination Schools adjoining the

Bodleian Library, there was the stranger, older than any of the other examinees and older also than many of the proctors. For an entire week he scribbled furiously, never looking up, and when the ordeal ended he disappeared.

Because of this man's rude intervention, Frank had pulled himself together, accomplishing exactly what all his Saltwood predecessors had achieved at Oriel: a pass without distinction or honors of any kind. He had not been exactly educated at Oxford; he had been ordained into the fellowship of English country gentlemen, not bright enough to lead but steady enough to be good followers.

With his degree in hand, Frank hired a horse and wagon and started the long journey to Stonehenge, then south to Old Sarum, and finally into the stately cathedral town where his ancestral home stood quietly beside the river. For generations the South African Saltwoods would bring their diplomas home in this way, for until they were registered before admiring family at Sentinels, with John Constable's fine watercolor of the cathedral filling the hall with radiance, they were not truly graduated or ready to start their life's work in the colony.

Frank was so enchanted with the Saltwood home, and he enjoyed so much the civilized life of taking tea under the great oaks, that all thought of becoming a missionary vanished, but he did tell his cousin, Sir Victor Saltwood, M.P., of the curious experience he had had of going into a blue funk, from which he was rescued only by this forceful stranger. 'I'm indebted to him. He quite saved me, you know.'

He was therefore surprised and not a little pleased when he boarded his ship at Southampton to find that one of the first-class cabins was occupied by this belated graduate of Oxford, and with uncharacteristic boldness he presented himself before the man, saying, 'I must thank you for having saved my life.'

The stranger knew immediately who he was and remembered the brief conversation. 'I saw you buckling down to your examinations. I was pleased.'

'I say, if we're to travel so long together, shouldn't I know your name? Mine's Saltwood.'

'I know. De Kraal. Sir Richard, the old fool Hilary. I'm C. J. Rhodes.'

'Thank you for what you did, Mr. Rhodes.'

The brusque man extended no invitation either to call him by something other than Mr. Rhodes or to walk with him, and the conversation ended. Since Frank's quarters were at the farther end of the ship, during the first week he saw his fellow graduate no more, but during the second week some older men were gathered in a salon, engaged in heated conversation, and when they saw Frank passing, one of them called, 'I say, Saltwood. You live at De Kraal, don't you?'

'I do.'

'Stop with us a moment.' Place was made for him, and when he was seated, the man who had hailed him said, 'Do you think of South Africa as rich or poor?'

For several moments Frank compared images of rural England as he had come to know it with those of the veld, and he had to confess: 'I would say on the poor side.'

'He's right!' an excited, high-pitched voice cried. 'I tell you, South Africa's an impoverished land. Only hard work and imagination will save it.'

Mr. Rhodes spoke with a book of maps on his knees, and as the men listened he outlined his basic thesis, slapping at the maps with a stubby hand as he made his points. 'Look at the map, man. Look at what nature did.' And with a pudgy forefinger he showed how South Africa ended at a degree of latitude where the more fortunate continents were just beginning. 'Nature robbed us, savagely.' And he demonstrated how Africa was the continent that hugged closest to the equator, as if afraid to venture down into colder waters. 'We're the only continent that lacks a substantial percentage of its land in the temperate zone where farming can flourish and industry thrive. Look how we compare with South America, which shares the same oceans with us. It reaches south to the fifty-sixth parallel. We're cut short at the thirty-fifth. Measure it out on the scale. They extend fourteen hundred miles farther into the good climates than we do.'

As he became more excited, his voice rose until it was a complaining wail. Flicking the maps, he invited his companions to see for themselves how their continent had been defrauded. 'It's only when you compare us with Asia, Europe and North America that our impoverishment becomes clear. If those continents had been cut off the way we've been, look at the civilization they'd have lost!'

With the men following his finger closely, he demonstrated how Asia would have had to surrender Kyoto, Tokyo, Peking, Tehran and most of Turkey. 'Every good thing done in those civilizations lost forever. But look at Europe!' Here he showed how the entire continent would have been lost had it been as truncated as South Africa. 'And when we reach America, the same story.' Carefully he drew the line which would have run south of Chattanooga, Memphis, Oklahoma City, Amarillo and Albuquerque. 'Those cities and all the places to the north that you've heard of—St. Louis, Seattle, Detroit, New York, Boston. None of them would have existed.'

He passed his atlas to his listeners, and as they studied the facts he said solemnly, 'If the rest of the world were as deprived as we are, civilization would consist of Los Angeles, Mexico City, Jerusalem and Delhi. Our cathedrals would not have been built, our plays would not have been written, and neither Beethoven nor Shakespeare would have existed.'

He spoke with great passion, then recovered his atlas and opened it to South Africa itself to make his final points. 'We've been sorely cheated by nature . . .'

'Why are you afraid to say that it was God who cheated us?' a man asked.

'God?' Rhodes said, twisting the palm of his right hand up and down like a bargainer. 'I give Him fifty-fifty. He may exist. He may not. I never fight with Him, and if you want to say God where I say nature, so be it.' He returned to the map and said, 'We can't move northwest because the Kalahari Desert impedes us. And we can't move south because our land ends. What we can do, is make the most of what nature has given us.'

He became quite poetical as he outlined the South African promise: 'We have people with wonderful vitality. Forests with some of the most fertile lands on earth. Flowers that have no equal. And herds of great animals that are inexhaustible. In a week's journey you can see hippos and rhinos, lions and elephants. I've seen the land rolling with zebra and eland and gemsbok. It's a treasury with boundaries unlimited.'

Then he plumped his fingers upon the area about Kimberley, where his mining interests lay. 'Nature is rarely unfair. If she cheats us in extension, she compensates by allowing us to dig deep. She's given us the finest concentration of diamonds in the world. And they've already found gold, too. But the real gold lies up here.'

As he said this, he pointed to the empty lands north of the Limpopo; at least the map showed them as empty, a vague Matabeleland governed by a son of the famous Mzilikazi. 'And here, too,' he said gravely, indicating land north of the Zambezi. With a sudden movement of his right hand he covered the entire segment of Africa with his palm. 'This map should all be red.' He meant that it should become part of the British Empire.

'How could that happen?' one of the listeners asked.

'It's your job to make it happen,' he said.

The next weeks determined the pattern of Frank Saltwood's life. He had intended going to South Africa for only a brief visit with his parents, then returning to London for legal training, but as he moved about the ship he became aware that Mr. Rhodes was keeping an eye on him, and at various intervals they met in discussion, and once Rhodes asked bluntly, 'Why would you pursue the law when you could be exercising your power directly?'

'What do you mean?'

'When you were at Oxford, did you ever read John Ruskin's charge to the young men of the university? You didn't? You should have been required to memorize it. Wait here.' He ran to his cabin, a rather heavy man moving with agility, and within a few moments was back with a dog-eared pamphlet of Ruskin's famous Oxford address of 1870, a few years before Rhodes matriculated. 'Read this,' he said peremptorily, 'and we'll talk about it after dinner.' In Mr. Rhodes' chair on deck, Frank read the intoxicating challenge:

> Will you youths of England make your country again a royal throne of kings, a sceptered isle, for all the world a source of light, a center of Peace; a mistress of learning and of the Arts, faithful guardian of time-tried principles? This is what England must do or perish. She must found colonies as fast and as far as she is able, formed of her most energetic and worthiest men; seizing any piece of fruitful waste ground she can set her foot on, and there teaching these her colonists that their chief virtue is to be fidelity to their country, and their first aim is to advance the power of England by land and sea. All that I ask of you is to have a fixed purpose of some kind for your country and for yourselves, no matter how restricted, so that it be fixed and unselfish.

When Mr. Rhodes returned after dinner, the sun had set behind the western horizon, but its invisible disk still sent golden rays to illuminate the clouds that stood guard over Africa, making the eastern Atlantic a scene of glory. He asked only one question: 'Saltwood, have you discovered your fixed purpose?'

'Not really, sir.'

'Isn't it about time you did?'

'As you know, I've been thinking of law.'

'You've *been thinking of!*' He spat out the words with distaste. 'At Oriel you were thinking of missionary work. And next week you'll be thinking of something else. Why not come to solid grips with real problems?'

'What do you mean, sir?'

'Come to work for me. There's so much to be done, so little time to do it.'

Darkness fell upon the ship, and as it sailed southward to the realm of stars that Frank knew well, Rhodes talked insistently. 'I need help, Saltwood. I need the energy of young men.'

'How old are you, sir?'

'Twenty-nine. But I feel thirty-nine. Have you any idea, Saltwood, of the empire I control?'

'No, sir.'

'I told few at Oxford. I was embarrassed. But I mean to control all the diamonds in the world.'

'To what purpose?'

'The map, Saltwood. The map. I mean to turn it all red. To make places you and I have never seen part of the British Empire.'

'Can that be done?'

'Never ask such a question!' Rhodes exploded. 'Anything can be done if men of good principle determine that it shall be done. Have you the courage to strike for immortal goals?'

In the darkness of midnight Frank had no estimate whatever of his courage, and he said so. 'Then you must come to work for me,' Rhodes said, 'and I'll show you how much courage a young man can develop.'

Through the night they talked of the Limpopo and the Zambezi, of the Matabele, and when the moon hung low upon the waves Rhodes introduced a new word: 'Zimbabwe. Ever heard of it?'

'Yes.'

'A fabulous city. Some idiots are beginning to argue that it was built by blacks, but those who know are convinced it's Ophir of the Bible. The Queen of Sheba may have built it, or the Phoenicians. One day we must go to Zimbabwe to show the world that this is the Queen of Sheba's city.' Immediately he enlarged on the subject: 'Matabeleland, ancient cities, gold mines . . . They're nothing, Saltwood. The obligation of mankind is to improve society, and no people have stepped upon this earth more qualified to perform this task than well-bred Englishmen. Will you work with me?'

The night was gone, the sun was coming up over Africa—and young Saltwood was bewildered. 'I must discuss these matters with my parents.'

'Saltwood! A man forges his destiny of himself, not of his parents' wishes. If I'd listened to my father—' He stopped abruptly. 'Fine old man. Village preacher. Nine children. Much loved by his parishioners, and do you know why? No sermon he ever preached was more than ten minutes long.'

'You have eight brothers and sisters?'

'Yes, and a half sister.'

'All of them married?'

'One,' and he said this with such fierce finality, as if a sore point had been touched, that Frank was not surprised when he stalked off. Then he recollected that not once during the entire voyage had he seen Rhodes talking with any of the lady passengers or acknowledging in any way that they existed.

In the days that followed that conversation Rhodes spent his time with a group of male passengers, discussing only one topic: England and her glory. 'Join us,' he called one morning to Saltwood, and when Frank sat with the men he was peppered with questions about South Africa, the future of ranching at De Kraal, and the likelihood that Zulu warriors might once more challenge English armies.

Rhodes liked his answers, and when the others left he kept Saltwood beside him: 'You're the only one who made sense.' Then he became excited. He did not speak, he orated—in a high voice that grew higher as his enthusiasm flamed. He sat on his hands, rocking back and forth, and always he returned to the subject of Africa and the extension of empire: 'Germany is coming at us from the west, and Portugal's dug in on the east. It will be our responsibility to fend them both off. Push the channels north. Always north till we reach Cairo. The world can be saved only by Englishmen standing together. Saltwood, I need your help.'

'What about the Boers?' Frank evaded. 'Can they, too, be used?'

'The Boers are some of the finest people on earth. United with them, we could form a nation of unsurpassed strength.'

'Why don't we invite them to join us?'

Mr. Rhodes frowned and rubbed his chin. 'You know, I'm a member of Parliament. And what kind of district elected me, if you please? Heavily Boer. I work with them, I collect their votes—and damnit, I know them no better than when I started. And those who emigrated north I understand even less.'

'Is there a mystery?'

'Yes. They huddle in their little republics and refuse to join the mainstream of the human race. They keep away on their farms and leave the running of the world to us.'

'You speak as if you intend to rule the world.'

'Nothing less.' Quickly he added, 'If that sounds arrogant, I mean that the empire I shall put together for England must rule the world.' He dropped his voice: 'So your task will be to bring the Boers in with us.'

Then he became so impassioned on this point that he asked Saltwood to wait by the railing, and while other passengers were heading for the dining room, he ran to his cabin and returned with a rumpled piece of paper. It was a holograph of his will, and when Saltwood read it he was shocked: C. J. Rhodes was donating all his possessions to two minor officials of the English government, commissioning them to bring into the British Empire countries as diverse as the United States, the east coast of China and the whole continent of Africa, the Voortrekker republics not excluded.

'Can this really be done?' Frank asked.

'It must be,' Rhodes said, 'and you're to be part of it.'

When the volatile man disappeared into his cabin, Saltwood reflected on his curious behavior: he was offering a young Oriel graduate, whom he scarcely knew, a part in governing the world, but he never invited him to his cabin, or to his table, or to any other event of which he was a part. And one afternoon when he saw Frank talking with an attractive girl on her way home to Cape Town, he actually scowled and turned away in disgust. For some days thereafter he did not speak to Frank, and when he finally did he muttered, 'I hope you're not making silly promises to some silly girl,' and only when Saltwood replied, 'Hardly,' did he resume his friendship.

When the ship docked at Port Elizabeth, Frank headed immediately north for his family's farm, and he supposed that he would never again see C. J. Rhodes, but one afternoon as he and his parents sat at tea on a veranda overlooking the pastures and the stream, a dusty cart clattered up to the gate, and Mr. Rhodes strode up to the porch. After the most perfunctory acknowledgment of Frank's parents, he asked bluntly, 'Well, Saltwood, are you prepared to come with me?'

'I haven't really . . .'

'You're not mooning about the law, are you? With so much work to be done?'

Frank tried to avoid a harsh answer that would send Mr. Rhodes away permanently, and once he vacillated, Rhodes sprang at him like a tiger: 'Good! We're off to Kimberley in the morning.' Only then did he bother with the older Saltwoods: 'I'll watch over him. He'll be at the heart of things, and when you next see him he'll be a man.'

The next day they drove to Graaff-Reinet, where they caught the stagecoach to Kimberley, whose violent activity was bewildering. Frank would never forget his first sight of the diamond mines, for as he wrote to his mother, they were like nothing else on earth:

> Each prospector is entitled to a square of precious land, thirty-one feet to a side, but of this land he must leave a narrow path for others to use. Since Miner A had dug his plot forty feet down, and Miner B twenty feet, poor Miner C who has not dug at all finds himself atop a square with such precipitous sides that any fall is fatal. Also, at night irresponsible men cut underneath the footpaths, causing them to collapse. All is chaos.

> But what catches the eye is a massive nest of cobwebs which looks as if ten thousand Arachnes had been spinning. They are the wires and ropes leading from the edge of the mine down to each of the individual holdings. On them buckets are drawn up, bearing the diamantiferous soil, and this immense tangle of lines, the buckets rising and falling are the signs of a diamond mine at Kimberley.

> It is Mr. Rhodes' fervent hope that he can bring some order into this madness, and to this end he has quietly been buying up plots here and there, endeavoring to consolidate them into some kind of reasonable concentration. If he can do so, he will command the industry and will become even more rich and powerful than he now is. It is my job to cut down to the same level all the contiguous plots he acquires, and I am finding many diamonds in the soil left for the footpaths. But for the moment the chaos continues, with one block fifty feet up in the air, the one beside it fifty feet down, and no order anywhere except in those areas he con-

trols. It is a race between reason and anarchy, and he assures me that where men of good sense are concerned, reason always wins. He intends to.

Frank did not tell his mother what might have been the two most interesting bits of information. In the cottage occupied by Mr. Rhodes just as much chaos reigned as in the mines; a tin-roofed affair, it was Spartan-like, with not a single adornment to grace it, clothes pitched everywhere, dishes unwashed and furniture about to collapse. No woman was ever allowed in the house, which Rhodes shared with a gifted, sickly young man a few years younger than he. Frank found that he wasn't the only one in his early twenties selected to advance Mr. Rhodes' many interests; a squad of bright, eager recruits submerged their personal interests in those of this dreamer who visualized a Union Jack over every territory from the Cape to Cairo.

He invariably called his young men by their first names: Neville, Sandys, Percival, Bob, Johnny, and often he encouraged them to engage in hearty pranks, as if they were in grammar school. They were free to entertain such women as they could find in the diamond town, but there was an unwritten law that ladies were to be flirted with, and perhaps frolicked with, but quickly forgotten. Far greater things were in store for 'my young gentlemen,' as he referred to them, and like Shaka, he wanted his regiments to keep their hearts on the great tasks ahead and not on the bosoms of their wives.

Frank noticed that up to the time of his formal employment, Rhodes addressed him with a curt 'Saltwood,' but once he accepted his assignment he became 'Frank,' and so he would remain, perpetually young, perpetually smiling. Like all the young gentlemen, he was paid well.

The second interesting bit involved Mr. Rhodes' chief rival in diamonds, an extraordinary chap who never stopped amazing the young gentlemen and the public at large. He was as different from Mr. Rhodes as a man could be, but was equally ruthless in hounding a business opportunity, and he alone stood between Rhodes and true riches.

Barnett Isaacs was a year older than Rhodes, a Jew born in one of the worst slums of London; in the midst of an undistinguished career as a frowzy vaudeville comedian and tap-dancer, he decided in a stroke of pure genius to make his fortune in the mines of South Africa. With only his nerve and some boxes of cheap cigars purchased near the docks at Cape Town, he talked his way north to Kimberley, peddled his 'six-penny-satisfiers,' and earned a pitiful living entertaining the miners with deplorable jokes, ridiculous acrobatics, and whatever else came to his mind when he stood before them in one cheap hall or another.

But Barnett Isaacs was an inspired listener, and while he clowned he picked up choice bits of negotiable information: who was going broke, who wanted to return to London, who had stolen whose claim. And bit by bit he pulled this information together, acquiring a horse and cart and prowling the diggings as a kopje-walloper, a kind of money-minded vulture looking to snap up the discarded pickings off other men's sorting tables. He soon got his hands on valuable rights, and one day Kimberley woke to find that Isaacs was one of the richest men on the diamond fields.

He thereupon changed his name to Barney Barnato, bought himself several suits of slick clothes, and indulged in a fancy which had tantalized many an earlier vaudevillian.

At a considerable personal cost, he assembled a moderately good theatrical company, purchased himself a set of Shakespearean costumes, and offered South Africa its first performance of *Othello,* with himself in the title role. Frank arrived at the mines too late to see the opening performance, but when all the young gentlemen purchased tickets to a subsequent exhibition, he went along to a steaming tin-roofed shed crowded with a noisy audience that cheered madly when 'Our Barney' strode onstage. His Desdemona, unfortunately, was six inches taller than he and appeared to be wrestling with him whenever they embraced; also, his makeup was so black and so thick that when she touched him her skin came away smeared while his showed white empty spaces.

'But he's rather good!' Frank whispered to the men beside him.

'Wait till the afterpiece!'

'What happens?'

'You won't believe it.'

When the final curtain fell, with Desdemona dead and pretty well besmudged, the young actor who played Cassio came forward to announce that in response to unusual demand, Mr. Barnato, who had already excelled in *Othello,* would now give his classic rendition of Hamlet's soliloquy, at which the crowd began to roar and whistle. After a few minutes Mr. Barnato, his face wiped clean, appeared in a whole new costume. 'Watch this!' the young gentlemen whispered.

While Frank gaped, Mr. Barnato nimbly gave a flip-flop and ended standing on his head. Maintaining perfect balance for a surprisingly long time, he began to recite the soliloquy, but as he came to the better lines, he gave wild gestures with his hands, stabbing at 'bare bodkin' and waving madly at 'fly to others that we know not of.' At the concluding words 'and lose the name of action' he gave an amazing flip and landed back on his feet. The applause was shattering, for as Mr. Rhodes admitted acidly when his young men returned, 'The remarkable thing is not that he can do it, but that whilst on his head he can speak so powerfully and deliver such convincing gestures. I've never seen a better Hamlet.'

These two titans, Rhodes the taciturn plotter, Barnato the vaudevillian, fought each other for years, and then one night they stood face-to-face in the cottage of a man destined to be famous in South African history: Dr. Leander Starr Jameson. At four in the morning, after eighteen hours of tense bargaining, a deal was struck whereby Othello would eventually surrender all his control to Mars for a check whose photograph would be widely displayed throughout the world: £5,338,650. As Barnato capitulated, bleary-eyed and worn down, he said, 'Some people have a fancy for one thing, some for another. You, Rhodes, have a fancy for building an empire. Well, I suppose I must give in to you.' But he refrained from doing so until Rhodes promised that he would personally sponsor Barnato for membership in the ultra-exclusive Kimberley Club, where no Jewish Othello from Whitechapel would normally be welcomed.

If Barney's recitation of *Hamlet* had been surprising to Frank, his campaign for election to Parliament was stupefying: he purchased a whole new set of Paris suits, an imperial landau pulled by four dappled horses, European gilded uniforms for six footmen, a handsome costume for a postillion who rode ahead blowing a long trumpet, and a brass band of eighteen to follow behind. 'I voted for him,' Frank told the young gentlemen, and to his delight he found that they had, too. And he suspected that Mr. Rhodes had done the same, for as he once said, 'There are few men in this world who achieve everything they seek. Barney Barnato is one. He's played *Othello* to applause. He's recited *Hamlet* on his head. He's won the boxing championship of the diamond mines for his weight. He's had his own imperial guard. He's been elected to office. And he's the richest Jew in the country, with a full-fledged membership in the Kimberley Club. What more could he want?'

The young gentlemen were saddened when they heard that this man who had conquered the world by courage and sheer brazenness had committed suicide by throwing himself off the England-bound *Scot* in the middle of the Atlantic.

* * *

When Cecil Rhodes acquired control of the diamond fields, his attention was free to focus on the greater goals of his life; mere money, of which he now had prodigious supplies, interested him little except as a path to power. In the years when he was one of the richest men in the world, he continued to live with his young gentlemen in austere surroundings. 'Every man has his price,' he assured Saltwood, 'and often it's a hankering for luxury. With enough money you can buy any man. For example, the king up in Matabeleland wants guns. Above everything else, he wants guns. So let's see that he gets them.'

Selecting a team from among his Kimberley staff, he began to suborn the king, and this left him free to study the perpetual problem: 'Frank, we have at our end of the continent a priceless land governed by three races. English—who ought to rule. Boers—who don't know how to rule. And Kaffirs—who should never be allowed to rule. What's to be done?'

He allowed Frank to study this problem for some days, then gave his own answer: 'It's clear that England was intended to govern all of Africa. We're people of vision, decency, honor. We know how to govern, and to everyone we govern we bring added virtues. So we must gain control.

'The Boers? I love them. In some ways they're sturdier than the English. But they lack vision. They will never be able to provide good government. The republics they occupy must become part of our enterprise, and I think I see ways of accomplishing this. When they join us, they must be given every consideration, for we need them. But join they must.

'The Kaffirs? I stand ready to offer full citizenship to any man regardless of his color, so long as he is civilized. Would it be proper for them to have the vote while they remain in barbarism? I say they must be treated as children, and we must do something for the minds and brains the Almighty has given them.' He added, 'We must lord it over them until they gain civilization. Above all, Frank, never let them have alcohol.'

Upon analysis, Frank found that all of Mr. Rhodes' basic beliefs were debatable: at Majuba the Boer armies had knocked the devil out of regular British troops; Germany was moving defiantly into Africa and had already annexed the southwest lands along the Atlantic Ocean, her moves outsmarting the English; in the mines, Kaffir workmen were proving at least as capable as whites. But Mr. Rhodes had several million pounds to support his objectives, and Saltwood had none, so it was the former's views that prevailed.

To Rhodes, diamonds were the fire of his life, the glittering foundation of his fortune, so it was not surprising that he had been lukewarm to the discovery of gold two years earlier on the Witwatersrand (White Water Ridge), some five hundred miles to the north in the heart of the Boer republics. He did, however, stake his claim to a share of the golden fortunes, launching a great company that made him a Croesus, with unlimited power to undermine the Boers, keep the blacks obedient, and drive his highway of empire straight to the heart of Africa.

What happened next was inexplicable. In the Cape Parliament, Cecil Rhodes invariably sponsored full partnership for any Afrikaners who resided in the province, and they reciprocated by electing him to office, and would do so till he died. They liked his courage and admired his abilities. But now he decided to destroy the Boer republics in the north because, as he explained to Saltwood, 'They must come in with us.'

'But if they don't want to?'

'Then we shall force them.'

His reasoning was simple. The diamond mines at Kimberley were located on farmland which the English by infamous chicanery had forced to become part of their colony; English law governed the diamond fields. But the gold mines were located within the boundaries of one of the Boer republics; here Boer law prevailed, and this raised problems.

In the gold fields, which proliferated at a rate far greater than that seen in either Australia or California, there were Englishmen galore, and hundreds of Australians, and many Frenchmen, and Italians and Canadians and not a few American citizens who flocked in on ships from all the ports of the world. They were noisy, undisciplined, and a menace to the stolid Boers who wanted to be left alone on their farms; they swooped down on Witwatersrand like vultures finding a carcass on the highveld, and with them they brought contention, violence and every possible threat to the phlegmatic Boer way of life.

The self-governing Boers retaliated with the most imprudent laws: an Uitlander (Outlander) could vote for the Volksraad only after fourteen years' residence; before that apprenticeship he remained a second-class citizen, entitled to cast his ballot only for a separate assembly subject to Boer veto; dynamite required in mining was made by a Boer-favored monopoly, and prices for it became prohibitive; any infraction of a score of meticulous laws must be judged in a Dutch-speaking court according to laws not promulgated in English. Investment of money, movement of men and the mining of gold all fell under Boer law, and no concessions to reason were granted.

Rhodes, with his relentless determination to bring disparate elements in Africa under English rule, was convinced that the arrogant conduct of the Boers was ill-advised and must lead to rebellion unless modified. He decided to intervene personally with the forbidding Boer leader, Stephanus Johannes Paulus Kruger, that rumbling volcano of a man who ruled his little world from the stoep of his unpretentious dwelling on a tree-lined street in Pretoria.

'I will go to him privately this time,' he told his young men, 'and invite him like a gentleman to join with us.'

'What can you offer him in return?' someone asked.

'Membership in the British Empire,' Rhodes said without hesitating. 'What more could a ruler of a petty state want?'

Before any of the young men could point out that many nations about the world wanted a good deal more, Rhodes continued: 'I will see President Kruger next week, and we will talk like two grown-up men. Frank, you will come with me, so make sure you learn all there is to know about him.' During the next days Saltwood sought out anyone in Kimberley with knowledge of the titanic man with whom Cecil Rhodes was about to grapple. The diamond magnate had met the Boer leader before, in his capacity as a Cape politician; this time he would go unofficially as a private citizen, with his eye not on local affairs but on world empire.

'First of all,' one of the young gentlemen told Saltwood, 'he's known as Oom Paul, Uncle Paul. He's twenty-eight years older than Mr. Rhodes and will demand due respect. He's very vain, you know.'

'And ugly as sin,' another said. 'His face is all crags without the grandeur of mountains. His nose is marked with bumps, and his eyes are hooded. He stands leaning backward, with his great belly projecting forward. But because of his height . . . He's much taller than Mr. Rhodes and will treat him like a little boy.'

The first instructor resumed: 'He was in the Great Trek, you know. Killed some of Mzilikazi's warriors. Extraordinary strength. Extraordinary bravery. He's fought in all the wars.'

'But what you must remember, in all his life he's had only three months of schooling. He boasts, "Only book I ever read was the Bible, but since that contains all knowledge worth knowing, it's enough." '

'Do not,' the first man warned, 'react in any way if he mentions the earth.'

'I don't understand,' Frank said, seeking to build up his portrait of the Boer leader.

'Oom Paul believes the earth is flat. The Bible says so. And if he finds that either you or Mr. Rhodes holds it to be round, he'll stomp out of the room. He's also convinced that the Boers have been given their republics by God Himself, so Mr. Rhodes will be forced to prove that joining our empire is what God proposed, not Mr. Rhodes.'

'The one thing in your advantage, Frank, is that even though Kruger hates colonial Englishmen, he despises Uitlanders. Calls them the atheistic rabble stealing his land. He sees the English miners, Australians and Americans as impious and immoral, and he's not going to concede them anything. But if Mr. Rhodes can insinuate that he feels the same way about the Uitlanders . . .'

'It must be done with tact,' the oldest of the gentlemen warned. 'Oom Paul is beloved by his Boers. He's a dictator, because he knows he has total support, no matter what he does. He'll be imperious, objectionable, insulting and infuriating. But consistently he outsmarts the Uitlanders sent to deal with him. He's a brilliant manipulator. You are not meeting an ordinary man.'

One of the younger men added, 'And remember, the world is flat.'

Frank went to sleep that Thursday night with three adjectives reverberating: *'Stubborn, opinionated, God-driven,'* and he concluded that in contesting with Oom Paul, Mr. Rhodes might be in for a difficult tussle, but then the adjectives that depicted Mr. Rhodes began echoing: *'Relentless, self-assured, empire-driven,'* and he began to wonder if perhaps it might be President Kruger who would need help. Before he fell asleep he recalled the description of Kruger's appearance: 'Ugly as sin,' and he reflected that spiritually Mr. Rhodes might be described with those same words.

Late on a Friday afternoon they arrived in Pretoria in Mr. Rhodes' private coach, and they retired early so as to be up fresh and ready for their important meeting; Frank observed that Mr. Rhodes took special care with his shaving, as if he were seeing a princess, and adjusted his tie and high-collared coat so as to make the best appearance. In a carriage they rode through this extremely Boer town until, on a handsome street, they came upon an unpretentious cottage, somewhat Oriental in style, marked by a wide stoep on which stood a comfortable armchair. In it, so that all Pretoria could see him consulting with his people, sat Oom Paul himself, a hulking giant of a man, shoulders hunched forward, belly out, legs spread wide, his hooded eyes inscrutable, his beard framing his massive face. He was holding court for whoever chanced to pass by.

Rhodes stopped the carriage a respectful distance from the cottage. 'He's a difficult man, Frank. You go and prepare the way. Be courteous.'

When Frank approached the stoep he was astounded at how massive Kruger was and how ugly; he seemed a cartoonist's caricature of an illiterate Boer farmer, but when Frank fell in line and had a chance to witness how Kruger handled his complaining burghers, it was obvious that here was a man of tremendous animal magnetism and resolute force.

'What brings you?' the president asked abruptly.

'Mr. Cecil Rhodes is waiting in the carriage. He asks permission to have words with you, sir.'

Without even looking in the direction of the carriage, Kruger grumbled, 'This is Nachtmaal.'

'I was not aware of that, sir.'

'My burghers are. For years they've known they can talk with me at Nachtmaal. Schalk Wessels here has come a hundred and ten miles, haven't you, Schalk?'

When the man nodded, Kruger said, 'This day is sacred to the burghers. I might have a few free minutes on Monday.'

'On Monday, Mr. Rhodes has other appointments. Can't he possibly see you today? Or tomorrow, perhaps?'

President Kruger rose from his chair, demonstrating the great dignity he could command when necessary, and in a gracious voice explained: 'Today is Nachtmaal Saturday. It's reserved for the burghers. Tomorrow is Sabbath. It's reserved for the Lord. No matter how important Mr. Rhodes' problems, they can wait till Monday, and so can he.'

Without thinking, Frank replied in words which imitated Kruger's urbanity: 'Mr. Rhodes waits for no man.' Turning smartly on his heel, he left the stoep.

But by the time he reached the waiting carriage, he was alarmed by what he had done and asked Mr. Rhodes, 'Shall I return and apologize?'

'Never! You behaved with spirit. I meant to give that old devil a chance, but I refuse to crawl on my knees. We shall proceed without him.'

Back in his offices, Mr. Rhodes referred so frequently to 'that obstinate, Bible-quoting Boer' that Frank speculated on what his response to his humiliation might be. Then he discovered that Mr. Rhodes was making many cautious inquiries on various aspects of Boer strength, for as he told his young gentlemen, 'A man must never move until he can assess the full power of his opponent.'

'Are you spying out the enemy?' one of the young fellows asked.

'I have no enemies,' Rhodes snapped. 'Only opponents. The day after we settle our differences we become mutual friends.' And Frank recollected a dozen instances in which this rule had prevailed. For three years Rhodes had fought Barney Barnato, and when the fight was settled, had welcomed him to his board of directors. Now Rhodes promised: 'The morning after President Kruger agrees to our plans, I will offer myself as his assistant in governing our joint territories.'

Suddenly, one morning, he wheeled about and fixed Saltwood with his watery eyes, which could become so fiery when he wished. 'Zimbabwe! Frank, I've always wanted to know who built it. I'm convinced in my own mind it must have been the Queen of Sheba, as the Bible indicates. What I want you to do is organize an expedition to search out the place and report to me what you find. Because we must nail down the truth before some German adventurer proves that the stone castles were built by Kaffirs. Hideous thought.'

Since Frank could not decipher what Mr. Rhodes was up to, he asked, 'What has this to do with your plans?'

'There's a man living far east of here, next to the farm they call Vrymeer. They say he went to Zimbabwe as a boy. Saw the turrets close up. I want you to interrogate that man, check his truthfulness . . .' Rhodes hesitated, then added, 'Take a measure of him.'

'Who is he?'

'Paulus de Groot.'

Frank did not allow his countenance to change, but like a bomb lighting up the night, Mr. Rhodes' intentions became clear. 'I'll go see General de Groot. Sound him out.'

Paulus de Groot was that giant of a man, six feet five, with stooped shoulders and massive red head, who had led one of the charges at Majuba in 1881 when the Boers defeated the best troops in the British Empire. He was a man who could enlist the support of other men; he was also without vanity, for when the great battles ended he returned to his farm, where he was reported to be living in stark simplicity. The Boer rulers in Pretoria begged him to join the government, but he told them, 'Riding a horse up a hill doesn't make a man sagacious.' And he remained a farmer.

What Mr. Rhodes wanted to know was whether General de Groot had the capacity and the fire to resist an English attempt at taking over the Boer republics. 'He's said to be past sixty, much too old to be leading troops. But he's also said to be a very active man, good with horses and guns. Find out about him.'

'Then you're not interested in Zimbabwe? Not really?'

Mr. Rhodes changed his attitude completely. Grasping Saltwood by the shoulder, he said quietly, 'Frank, I'm interested in everything. I want to pursue everything. You're off to Zimbabwe in the morning. By way of Vrymeer.'

It was this variety of interests which almost destroyed the pleasant relationship between Mr. Rhodes and Frank, because that night a cable from London reached South Africa, informing Rhodes that a business friend of some importance was sending his niece on vacation to Cape Town and using her to deliver a packet of documents that he wanted Rhodes to study. Someone must meet the young woman, Maud Turner, not only to receive the documents, but also to see that she was properly ensconced.

No one knew anything about Miss Turner except that her uncle was powerful, but there was a strong suspicion that she must be rather unattractive, else why would her uncle be sending her to Cape Town? Through the years English families had developed the pleasant and prudent habit of managing by one device or another to ship their unmarriageable females either to India or to Australia, on the principle that 'if she can't get married out where the competition is so thin, she'll never make it.' This trickle of gaunt, unlovely creatures was regularly dispatched to the far colonies in hopes that most would never return, or at least, not till they had sons of a proper age for Eton or Harrow.

'You must attend her, Frank,' Rhodes said peremptorily.

'But I'm heading for Zimbabwe.'

'It can wait. It's been waiting three thousand years.'

So Frank Saltwood, now in his thirties, clean and trim, with the affectations of an Oxford education, boarded the smoky train at Kimberley and headed south over the empty spaces of the Great Karroo.

He realized from the start that this could be a much more dangerous mission than going north to Zimbabwe, because of the inviolate rule that governed Mr. Rhodes' young gentlemen: once a man displayed serious interest in a young woman, he was quarantined from decisions of importance, and if he actually married her, he could be fired that day. Indeed, Frank wondered if Mr. Rhodes' choice of him to attend Miss Turner had not been some kind of signal that his days in diamonds and gold were nearing an end. Because he enjoyed his work and wanted to continue it, he was determined to handle the young lady with aloofness, accept her documents, sign her into the Mount Nelson, and hurry back to Kimberley and his more important work. He certainly would not risk employment he'd liked for so many years by becoming entangled with a woman.

He had not counted on the duplicity of his Salisbury cousin, Sir Victor Saltwood, who had ascertained that young Frank was still without a wife or prospects of any. It was he who had gone to Maud Turner's uncle, proposing that his charming, gifted niece, twenty-three years old, be dispatched to Cape Town with papers for Cecil Rhodes, and it was he who drafted the cable which Rhodes received. Families of importance saw to it that their young men and women met marriageable people of their own kind, and if girls had to ship all the way to Australia or Cape Town, so be it. Sir Victor could not have devised that Frank himself should meet the ship, but he certainly expected him to meet Miss Turner sooner rather than later.

He had a right to expect favorable results, for he had sent one of the finest young women of the Salisbury district, member of a strong family, heiress to a modest fortune, and recipient of one of the most practical educations possible: she had been allowed to listen to the lively conversation of her elders, who were interested in politics, morals, business and empire. She was reasonably pretty, unreasonably clever with her tongue, and a person to whom an adventure like Cape Town was irresistibly attractive as something to do before settling down in Salisbury.

She half suspected that Sir Victor and her uncle were conspiring in some way to get her to meet this or that young man; they were always conspiring about bills in Parliament or reforms in the church, but this did not mean that she had to accede to their rough-and-ready stratagems. She would deliver the papers, go on an elephant hunt, and return to England to marry whom she pleased. In performing these duties she would see as much of South Africa as possible, and have a rattling good time doing so.

At the end of the voyage out she could have married any one of three quite ordinary men who had courted her, and she felt confident that on the voyage home she could do better, so she was in no hurry to accept whomever it was that her uncle had selected for her, but when she saw on the dock awaiting her a young man of obvious charm and vitality, she was interested.

'Halloo!' she cried in a very unladylike shout. 'Are you Mr. Rhodes' emissary?'

'I am. Saltwood's the name.'

'Meet me over there, Saltwood,' and without assistance from the pursers she found the gangway and was one of the first off the ship.

Frank, watching her come skipping down the sloping stairs, saw at once what a remarkable young woman she was. 'She seemed all of a piece,' he wrote to his mother. 'From her buttoned shoes to the sway of her skirt, from the broad cloth belt about her waist to the perfection of her blouse, she was a harmony, but what I liked most was the way she coiled her hair. No man could have deciphered just how she did it, all auburn and glowing in the sunlight.'

Still, he might have resisted her allure had it not been for the added seductiveness of the Mount Nelson Hotel. This fine edifice stood at the edge of the gardens laid out by Jan van Riebeeck two hundred and forty years before. It was the glory of Cape Town, a spacious inn with lovely grounds, ornate hallways, excellent kitchens and muted servants who seemed to be either Malay or Coloured. A chilled Trianon wine from the Van Doorn vineyards, a small helping of a spicy bobotie, followed by roast duiker and an orange soufflé at the Mount Nelson might addle any young man's good judgment, but when a lively young woman like Maud Turner sat sharing it and throwing her witty barbs, it became a Lucullan feast. He telegraphed Mr. Rhodes: BUSINESS COMPLICATIONS NECESSITATE THREE MORE DAYS.

During these three days he was captivated by the levels of interest and understanding she displayed, and he found that she was honestly 'all of a piece,' as he had written, a beautifully organized person whose individuality matched her intelligence. In curious ways she resembled Mr. Rhodes, for absolutely everything interested her: 'How will the blacks ever learn if there aren't enough schools for them?' She developed a special affinity for the Cape Afrikaners and sought them out. 'How could you, Frank, have lived here so long and known so few of them? They're far more interesting than your English friends . . . What, for heaven's sake, have you been doing all this time?'

'Working with Mr. Rhodes.'

'What I mean, Saltwood. The English in South Africa. Another decade, you'll have been here a century, and what have you achieved? You've driven the Boers to set up their own republics. And the ones left behind here in the Cape are talking about an Afrikaner Bond, or something. What have you English got to show?'

Frank laughed. 'My dear Maud, almost everything you've seen has been the result of English effort. The port you entered. The railroad you took to Stellenbosch. The passes over the mountains. The schools, the hospitals, the free press. All English-inspired.'

'It may be as you say,' she conceded, inwardly proud of the accomplishments he kept rattling off. 'But the Afrikaners I met at the coffee-house don't seem to recognize any of it.'

'Nor did they ever recognize what Hilary was trying to do.'

'Your granduncle, was it? The missionary with the . . .'

'Black woman?'

'I didn't mean to say it that way, Frank.'

'I understand. But don't be surprised if you live to believe that what Hilary tried to do was right. That he saw the salvation of this land.'

'Do you think of this as your land? The way the Boers say they do?'

'I was born here. I've made it my home, even if your Afrikaner friends won't acknowledge my joint ownership. Just because they were here first doesn't mean that God gave them the land in some kind of deal. That's what the Boers up north preach, but mark my words, the English progress they despise will catch up with them. Perhaps very soon.'

'You're getting too serious, Frank Saltwood. Tell me about elephant hunting. Is it dangerous?'

She really did want to go on an elephant hunt, and if that proved impractical, a lion would do. When he informed her that both animals had quit these parts generations ago, she said simply, 'Then let's go after them. I have a small allowance, but I think it might suffice.'

When he disappointed her by saying that he could not remove himself from Kimberley, she said, 'Good, I've always wanted to see how they dig for diamonds. Silly stones—wouldn't want one myself.'

He pointed out that it would be quite improper for her to journey to Kimberley either with him or by herself, but she snapped, 'Nonsense! I carry with me letters to the most respectable families on the diamond fields.' And she organized the delivery of her two trunks to the railway and the purchase of her sleeping compartment to Kimberley. Frank was free to tag along, if he so wished.

The journey north was as pleasing as any he would ever know, a revelation of what a young woman could be. She was neither flirtatious nor coy; whenever an interesting topic arose, her expressive face revealed pretty much what she was thinking; and she sought out people for animated discussion. In the dining car, on the first evening, she invited an older couple to join them. With charming frankness she explained that she was not married to Frank, then went on to say that he was an important part of the diamond industry. From them she elicited the fact that they had a nephew working the gold fields and that he believed there was need, in the new town of Johannesburg, for a tailor. Normally they could not have afforded first-class accommodations on the train, but he had sent so much money that they had decided to splurge.

'Are you Jewish?' Maud asked abruptly.

'Yes. From Germany, our fathers, years ago.'

'Would you ever consider returning to Germany?'

'No. That happens to other people, not us.'

'Do you think Germany will try to take South Africa from us?'

'Germany will try to take everything,' they said.

On the second day she invited an Australian couple to dine with them, and again she explained that she was not married to Frank, whereupon the wife asked, 'Isn't it a mite risky? I mean, traveling with a young man?'

'Not if he's a nice young man, like Frank.' But as she patted his hand she added, 'Of course, he's not so young, really. How old are you, Frank?'

'Past thirty,' he said.

'Time to be taking the plunge,' the man said, at which Frank blushed uncontrollably.

'He'll do the right thing at the right time,' Maud said.

'With you?' the Australian woman asked.

'Goodness, we hardly know each other.' And by the time the train reached Kimberley, all the passengers knew that this fine-looking young woman was traveling with a young man she scarcely knew.

Mr. Rhodes took one look at the couple and realized that young Saltwood had better be dispatched at once, or he was going to fall into irreversible error, so once the introductions were made, he said, 'Saltwood, your conveyances are waiting. You'd better be off . . . this afternoon.'

'I shall leave day after tomorrow,' Frank said with some force, and that was the beginning of the estrangement, for Mr. Rhodes realized with dismay that one of his young gentlemen had got himself seriously mixed up with a woman.

In the time he had stolen for himself, Frank demonstrated attractively his deep feelings for Miss Turner. He deposited her trunks at the local hotel, then escorted her about the town, showing her the mighty hole in the earth where he had worked, and the donkey engines which kept the water out. He took her into the countryside and to the local church, and as the second day ended he asked, 'Are you promised to anyone?' When she said, 'I am not,' he asked, 'Would you keep yourself free till I return from Zimbabwe?'

'And where's that?' she parried. When he told her, she wanted to accompany him on the safari, but this suggestion he rejected forcibly. 'I understand,' she teased. 'Mr. Rhodes wouldn't like it.'

'Conditions are far too rough, Maud.'

'I understand. Mr. Rhodes lays down very strict conditions for his employees. No women.' She expected him to say something, and when he didn't, she said boldly, 'But if I did wait, wouldn't Mr. Rhodes discharge you?'

'Yes. So when I married you, I'd have to find other employment.'

'Could you do so?'

'I'm a young man. I can work. I know diamonds and gold.'

Very quietly she said, 'I shall cancel my steamship.'

'What will you do?'

'I am going on an elephant shoot.'

'With whom?' he asked in amazement.

'With three gentlemen at the hotel.'

'My God, Maud!'

'I said I would wait, Frank. I didn't say I was going to sit on my hands.'

'But . . . but, three men from the hotel!'

'My uncle sent letters to two of them.' And then she kissed him, not a peck on the cheek, but the full passionate kiss of a liberated young woman who had found the kind of man she was willing to wait for.

From Pretoria, Frank took the new train leading down to Lourenço Marques on Delagoa Bay, but after a full day's journey he disembarked at the small station of Waterval-Boven, where a wagon awaited him. It was a fifteen-mile drive south, with a black man who gave his name as

Micah Nxumalo. The first part came from the Bible, he explained in broken English, the second part from his grandfather, who had come here from Zululand in the time of troubles.

'Did Mr. van Doorn own the land then?'

'No. It was our land.'

'But how did Mr. van Doorn acquire it?' The word was too big for Micah and he asked what it meant. 'Get. How did he get the land?'

A puzzled look came over the black man's face and he said, 'At first it was ours, then after a while it was his.'

When they reached the town of Venloo, Frank expected to be dropped at a lodging place before visiting Vrymeer, but Micah informed him that he was to room at the lake. 'With whom?' Saltwood asked. 'The De Groots or the Van Doorns?'

'Nobody stays with the De Groots,' Micah explained. 'They have only a very small place.' And when the horses climbed to the top of the rise that separated Venloo from the lake, Frank understood, for to the north stood a mean collection of wattle-and-daub structures in the center of unkempt fields, while to the east unfolded a substantial farm with an interesting mixture of barns for animals, kraals for holding areas, a rambling whitewashed farmhouse with a corrugated iron roof, and at some distance a handsome collection of rondavels for the Nxumalos and the other blacks who worked the land.

The farm was obviously prosperous and looked inviting, but what captured Saltwood's eye was the inconsequential little stream that debouched from the hills, ran among the farm buildings and broadened out to a beautiful lake on which ducks abounded and flamingos. What Saltwood could not see, approaching by this road, were the two rounded mountains that gave the site distinction; as they came slowly into view, Micah pointed them out and said, 'Sannie's Tits.'

'Who's Sannie?'

'Girl that used to live here. My father's time. She loved a young man. He died. She died.'

The little northern dwellings were occupied by General de Groot, the big farm by the Van Doorns, and it was to the latter that Micah led the horses. 'Hello, there!' a rough voice called from the barn. 'You that Mr. Rhodes' man?' The English words came uneasily and with heavy accent.

'Yes. Frank Saltwood.'

'We don't hold much with that Mr. Rhodes. He's a bad one. But you're welcome.'

The farmer held out a big hand and said, 'Jakob van Doorn. Mama!'

From the house emerged not an older woman but three of the prettiest little girls Frank had ever seen. With a bang they burst onto the edge of the stoep—and then behaved quite differently. The oldest girl, about fifteen, stopped shyly when she saw the strange man and stood by a pillar, her blond pigtails reflecting the light. The two younger ones, who seemed to be about the same age, seven or eight, were not abashed by the stranger; they came rushing right down into the yard to embrace him, their pigtails flying.

'The twins!' Jakob said proudly. 'Anna and Sannah, but which is which you'll never know.'

The girls did not try to be cute or tease about their names. They simply took Frank by the hand and led him toward the stoep, where through the front door appeared Mevrou van Doorn, in her late thirties, holding an infant on her hip. 'This is my wife, Sara, and the ruler of our roost, little Detlev.'

With delighted tugging, the twins carried their baby brother about the stoep. 'Come in,' Mevrou van Doorn said. 'We wondered about your telegram.'

'Yes, I came to see the general. I understand he went to Zimbabwe once.'

'He was there. But only as a little boy.'

'Will he remember?'

'The general remembers everything,' Mevrou van Doorn replied.

'My father was there, too,' Van Doorn said. 'He led a party north of the Limpopo. Tsetse fly drove them back.'

'Will I run into the tsetse up there?'

'You will.' The Van Doorns took him into their house and showed him where he would sleep. As the twins helped him unpack, their mother made coffee and rusks, and then Jakob opened a bottle of witblits (white lightning), a fiery homemade brandy. 'We drink to your coming. Do you speak Dutch?'

'Alas, not much. I was brought up in the Grahamstown area, you know, where there were few Boers.' And before they could respond, he added, 'Our family bought De Kraal, you know.'

'You did!' Mevrou van Doorn cried. Vaguely the family had known that trustworthy English settlers had purchased the farm, but their name had been lost.

'Are you the family that collected the money from London for my father's slaves?' Van Doorn asked.

'Yes. I've heard that story.' Frank shook his head in disgust. 'What a bad thing the London government did to you people on the slave deal.'

'What do you mean, *deal?*' Van Doorn asked.

'The cheap way the slaves were paid for. Or not paid for.'

'That was a bad time,' Van Doorn said, but then he added brightly, 'You'll want to see the general right away, I suppose?' When Frank nodded, he cried, 'Come along, children,' and led a procession around the end of the lake.

Saltwood was totally unprepared for the primitive conditions in which this great general, a hero of the Boer republics, lived. But when De Groot came forward to extend a rough welcome, any thought of meanness or privation vanished. The man was a giant, but hunched over like some mountain denizen in a German fairy story. When he gripped Saltwood by the shoulder, his fingers were like steel.

Then he laughed heartily and said, 'I want you to meet my wife,' and from the rude hut came a handsome woman in her sixties, erect, white-haired, blue-eyed. As a girl she must have been beautiful, and even now her dignity was striking. 'This is Mevrou de Groot,' the general said, and as he spoke he took her hand, and they stood facing their visitor.

But then they saw the three Van Doorn girls, and Sybilla de Groot bent down to embrace the twins while the general bowed gallantly to Johanna. At this point Jakob said, 'This is Frank Saltwood. It was his grandfather who got us the payment for our slaves. He took our warrants, sent them to London, and got us every penny to which we were entitled. Not all that we should have had, but all that was allowed us.'

With a great slap of his hand on Frank's leg, De Groot said, 'I remember the day at Thaba Nchu. A smous came up from Graaff-Reinet with two packets. One for Van Doorn, one for my father. But my father had been killed by Mzilikazi. So the packet was given to me, and I can remember tearing it open and seeing the new bills, English bills, and I didn't like them. And do you know what I did with that money, young man?'

Frank said, 'I can't guess,' and the old general said, 'I saved it. Year after year I saved it, and in 1881, when we fought the English at Majuba, I spent it all to outfit my own commando. English money fighting English soldiers. I liked that.'

'Was the fighting hard—at Majuba?'

'Fighting is always hard, especially against you English. Your officers are stupid but your men are heroic.'

'Were you in command of the Boer forces?' Before the old man could respond, Frank added, 'I mean, they speak of you as one of the heroes of Majuba.'

With a big forefinger De Groot poked at his guest. 'No one is ever in command of Boers. Each man is his own general.'

'But everyone speaks of you as the general.'

'Yes. I raised the commando. And at night I asked if this or that approach might not be best. But if I ever gave an order, someone would have asked, "And who in hell are you?" And that,' he said, punctuating his remarks with his finger, 'would be a very . . .' He fumbled for a word and asked Van Doorn for help, using Dutch.

'Relevant,' Van Doorn suggested.

'Yes, that would be a relevant question. "Who in hell are you to give orders?" '

'How did you fight the battle?'

'Our Bible tells us that one Boer can defeat one thousand Canaanites. So we did it, that's how.'

'I don't remember any mention of Boers in my Bible,' Frank said, to which De Groot replied, 'That's your Bible.'

For nine days Frank studied these two families, and as he watched them in action he concluded that people like these would never conform to Mr. Rhodes' plans for them. When his departure neared, the Van Doorns announced that the De Groots would come over for a farewell supper with a surprise at the end, and Frank was perched on the stoep, trying to guess which little girl was Anna and which Sannah, when they suddenly cried, 'Here comes Ouma!' and Frank looked across the lake to see the De Groots approaching.

They came in an old cart pulled by one tired horse. General Paulus sat in front, the great bearded patriarch usurping the entire seat, while Sybilla sat deferentially behind, a big woman crammed into a little space. She sat not on a seat, but in the well of the cart on a pile of animal skins, and Saltwood had to suppress a grin, for she resembled a Queen Victoria of the veld, regal and rugged and triumphant.

When he went to the cart, this impression was reinforced, for she said quietly, 'How pleased we are to be with you again,' and he would have helped her down except that General de Groot calmly intruded, extending his hands as if it was his privilege, and his alone, to help this woman.

It was a substantial supper, one of Mevrou van Doorn's massive offerings of lamb stew, and as it ended, each of the four children, and the old people, too, began to show excitement, which reached a peak when Jakob went into the kitchen, reappearing with a brown-gold pot over whose rim showed a crusty pudding marked with citron, cherries and raisins. 'Bread pudding, style of Van Doorn,' Johanna cried, and when Frank tasted it he complimented Mevrou van Doorn.

'Not me! My man!' And she nodded at her husband, reverently touching the old ceramic pot as she did.

'Yes, in our family the men make the pudding,' Jakob said. 'This pot, 1680 maybe. Made in China, no doubt. Came over the mountains. Two farms were burned with it on the shelf. You ever hear of Blaauwkrantz? Well, it went through fire there, too.'

'We're an old people,' General de Groot said. 'We've been here a long time.'

After the meal the family grew quiet, and Van Doorn produced a Bible even older than the crock. 'Amsterdam, I think. Maybe 1630. The first pages were burned away.' And he prayed with his hand on the book.

Frank, who was paying close attention, began to suspect that these two families were trying to warn him about something, and his feeling was confirmed when the old general spoke: 'We were here more than a hundred and fifty years before you came, Saltwood. More than two hundred before Rhodes. We would not like interruptions.' Combing his heavy beard with his fingers, he stared right at the young Englishman, never for a moment conceding that Frank might be just as much a part of Africa as he.

On the last day Frank asked Jakob for a free space at the table, and there, with the twins looking over his shoulder, he wrote a long report to his employer, the crucial paragraph being this:

> One cannot talk with these men without becoming convinced that they would again take up arms in a minute if they thought their freedom was endangered. Van Doorn is probably in his fifties, but he would ride forth tomorrow if called upon. The general is well into his sixties, and I suppose he would not actually go into battle, but I am sure he would lend every support. One night we rode into the little town of Venloo, where we met with another

forty Boers who said specifically they were at all times ready to mount a commando on one hour's notice. I must therefore caution you doubly and trebly not to allow any of your associates to launch unwarranted or headstrong adventures. I would hate to see the rabble of the gold reef go up against these rocklike men, who would be fighting for their independence. I can hear you telling the others: 'Young Frank is frightened.' That would not be correct, because I am terrified. I am terrified that an imprudent or hasty action might bring disaster upon us all. I assure you that Paulus de Groot alone could take on eleven Australian and American floaters who have no concern with the land except to bleed it, and I suspect he could handle five or six Englishmen, too.

I am off to Zimbabwe. General de Groot was there more than fifty years ago, but he says he can still see every wall, every edifice. I wish he were on our side.

By the accidents of history, Frank Saltwood was about to traverse in 1895 the route that young Nxumalo had taken in 1457. He left Vrymeer and headed for the Limpopo, near whose banks the copper mine still flourished. Once more high water impeded the crossing, and when the north bank was reached, the baobab trees exerted their magic. 'I was quite unprepared for them,' he wrote his mother. 'Trees which seemed to be planted upside down by some mysterious force, their uplifted roots filled with birds. On two occasions we have slept inside the trees.'

Like Nxumalo, he came upon the great slabs of granite, their layers exfoliated into perfect building blocks, but unlike him, he did not have to carry samples to the king. In proper time he reached the hills from which the ancient city became visible, and there he paused to see for himself, without distraction of any kind, physical or historical, just what it was this strange, lost city represented. Lacking all prejudice, he studied the ruins from afar and saw that they were long overgrown with trees and climbing vines, that they must once have been imposing but were now in poor condition, and that nothing in their sad, majestic profile betrayed their origin.

He descended into a valley leading to the ruins, and came after a while to an impoverished group of blacks led by a Chief Mugabe, who could speak neither the Zulu nor the Sotho language of the bearers, but after a while one was found who had once drifted down to the diamond mines, and he could speak a kind of lingua franca.

'Zimbabwe?' He knew nothing of it.

'Who rules now?' No one, but Chief Mugabe had his kraal on the side of the hill on which the citadel rested.

'Who built the towers?' That had often been discussed.

'Can we inspect it?' Why not?

For two weeks Frank climbed over the ruins, uncovering not a single clue which would indicate origins. The pictures in the Bible his parents had given him on his twenty-first birthday came to mind, but they looked nothing like this. However, suppose that all those pictures had been of Jewish structures? Could not these ruins have been those of the Queen of Sheba, who would have built in a different manner? Or of the Phoenicians, who would have had their own style? And what authority did the pictures in the Bible have? Were they not merely some artist's imagination?

Whenever he pursued such thoughts, he stopped before reaching a logical conclusion, because he had to keep in mind the fact that his employer, Mr. Rhodes, desperately wanted these buildings to be the ancient Ophir, not because that would prove the Bible to have been accurate, but for a much subtler reason: to justify his own wrongdoing.

When he got nowhere with President Kruger in his plan to have a joint English-Boer occupation of the lands north of the Limpopo, he had leap-frogged the Boer republics and thrown his own pioneer column deep into Matabeleland, where Mzilikazi's son was overrun. When resistance developed, he dispatched a private army to crush it, then annexed the entire area. Even at this moment, grateful imperialists in London were proposing that this new British colony be called Rhodesia.

So now, if Rhodes could prove that no black society had ever been advanced enough to have built Zimbabwe, his theft of Matabeleland would seem more palatable. It would, after all, be rather ugly to have stolen a kingdom in order to bring it civilization if that kingdom had once been civilized.

Frank Saltwood was thus obligated to prove that Zimbabwe had been built far back, in the time of the Old Testament, and during his last three days on the site he remained in his tent, drafting another report to Mr. Rhodes:

> Every indication at Zimbabwe proves that it was of Phoenician origin. The grand design, the shape of the tower, the construction

of the high citadel, the way the now-vanished huts of the city must have been arranged, and especially the work of the stone-masons, combine to demonstrate a Mediterranean provenance. I could not find a shred of evidence that would support the claims of some that these walls had been erected by primitive black men, and to so argue seems preposterous.

I put these structures at the late Phoenician period, which means that they could well have been erected by artisans of that nation imported here by the Queen of Sheba in the days when King Solomon ruled in Jerusalem. Since there is strong and viable rec-ord of much gold coming from Zimbabwe, I think we can state with certainty that this is Ophir of the Bible and that from it Sheba obtained the gold she took with her on her journey to meet Solomon. The matter is closed.

But when the wagons were packed, and the last photograph taken, and the antelope shot for the food supply, Frank returned to the ruins alone, sickened by the shameful thing he had done, this profanation of every-thing he had learned at Oriel: 'A man must be true to the facts, and if the facts disprove his preconceptions, he must change his preconcep-tions, not the facts.'

What have I done? he asked himself as he studied the silent stones whose messages were crying out to be understood. Have I debased my-self to curry favor with an irascible man who perverts everything to his own purpose?

Cautiously he climbed a platform next to the tower to inspect once more the stonework, which now seemed so primitive, so unlike anything the Phoenicians or the Jews of Solomon's time might have done. After all, the basic stonework of Rome was being laid down in that age, and Greek masons already knew the major principles. Men trained in those schools could never have built these edifices.

But he found no proof of anything until the final moments, when he had left the tower and was standing at a point where two walls abutted, and he saw with amazement that the stones were not interlocked, as they would have been in any Mediterranean building: that is, the stones of the wall running east and west did not bind themselves into the stones of the wall running north and south, making each wall stronger. In crude fashion, one wall merely leaned against the other, acquiring only such added strength as proximity provided, and it occurred to him that masons had not used that childish device in Rome or Greece or Phoenicia or the Holy Land or Persia or Arabia for the past four thousand years.

'My God!' he whispered. 'They're right. These buildings were erected by black men who never heard of Ophir or the Queen of Sheba,' and he ran to all the corners where walls abutted, and in every instance one wall merely leaned against the other. With this knowledge, he hastened to the foot of the steep hill on which the citadel rested, and, though exhausted, ran up, breathing furiously until he reached the lonely top where the goldsmiths had worked and the great Mhondoro conversed with spirits. And there, too, the walls leaned one upon the other, and the stonework was primitive, with no sign of Mediterranean sophistication. These buildings, too, had been built by the ancestors of the Xhosa and the Zulu. The nonsense about the Queen of Sheba was a fatuous dream generated by men who had never seen the stones, and kept alive by fancifiers who loved the idea of ancient royalty and despised the actuality of black builders.

As he was about to leave the citadel he saw, partly hidden by the rubble, something he had missed on his earlier explorations: a beautifully carved narrow stone about six feet high, its bottom squared off for fitting into a socket, its top an intriguing bird, something like a falcon, something like an eagle. In not a single line did it betray Mediterranean influence; this was an artwork of black men, and when he called for servants to carry it down the hill for delivery to Mr. Rhodes, he thought: I have been forced to write that Zimbabwe is Phoenician, but this bird will proclaim the truth.

Back in his tent as it was about to be folded, he looked at his report and was tempted to destroy it, but he was restrained by the fact that Mr. Rhodes would like it in its present form and would be most distressed if he, Frank, modified it in accordance with his final discovery: I know what the truth is. Does what Mr. Rhodes thinks do any harm? And he carefully filed the papers that would set the intellectual patterns for the next eighty years. Zimbabwe had been stolen from the blacks.

When he neared civilization he began to hear rumors of turmoil, but exactly what caused them he could not ascertain. Black members of his safari spoke of a battle, but the white members could make nothing of this until a terrified English miner, obviously running for his life, intercepted them with the shocking news that Mr. Rhodes had shortly before declared war on the Boer republics. His ragtag army, led by the mercurial Dr. Leander Starr Jameson, had tried to take over the government but had been roundly defeated.

Anxiously, Frank interrogated the fugitive, who gave confirming details: Mr. Rhodes had done all the things which Frank had warned him against, and the consequences had been the disaster he had predicted.

When the safari reached Pretoria it was approached by an armed Boer commando whose leader shouted in English, 'You have a man named Saltwood?' and when Frank stepped forward, three Boers pinioned him, took his papers, and carted him off to jail.

'What's the charge?' Frank protested.

'You'll hear. Just before they hang you.'

He was thrown into a cell that contained an Australian member of Mr. Rhodes' revolutionary force, two Englishmen and a breezy, even-tempered American mining engineer named John Hays Hammond, who had helped organize the ridiculous affair. 'What happened?' Frank asked.

'Very simple,' Hammond explained. 'We had five hundred hand-picked men under Dr. Jameson, many more waiting in Johannesburg, but with no communication between them. We marched forth to capture the country, but suddenly Boer horsemen appeared from everywhere, led by this great whiskered brute of a man, General de Groot, riding a little Basuto pony. He said, "All right, boys, put down your guns." So our men put them down, and here we are—in jail.'

'You mean De Groot defeated your whole army?'

'Have you ever seen De Groot?'

'I have. They call him the Hero of Majuba.'

'He's a formidable man,' Hammond said.

'But what am I doing here?' Frank asked. 'I was north of the Limpopo when this happened.'

None of the prisoners, cell after cell of Uitlanders, who had called themselves Reformers, could explain why Saltwood had been arrested, but after days in the crowded jail he heard enough from the conspirators to assure himself that they were indeed guilty of insurrection and that the venture had been sorely botched.

'How could Mr. Rhodes have stumbled into this?' he asked repeatedly, and finally the Australian said, 'Because he had contempt for the Boers, like all of us did.'

'After what I wrote him?' Frank blurted out, and when these words echoed in the cell, all the prisoners looked at him.

'Oh,' one of the Englishmen said, 'you're the spy they kept asking about.'

'Spy?' Frank repeated. He suddenly realized that his prying visit to General de Groot, his chain of persistent questions and his note-taking could be interpreted as spying.

And at the trial, General de Groot and Jakob van Doorn both testified, with regret, that he had come to them some months before the raid as a friend, asking a series of probing questions relating to the rebellion. Van Doorn in particular could verify that he had written a long report which he admitted he was sending to Cecil Rhodes, and from hints that Van Doorn picked up, it concerned the military capabilities of the Boers.

'Did Mr. Saltwood appear at your farm in military uniform?'

'No, sir, he came as a spy.'

'Did he inform you that he was serving as the agent of a rebellion?'

'No, sir, he functioned as a spy.'

When the trial ended, the grim-faced judge placed on his head a small black cloth. One by one the prisoners were brought before him: 'John Hays Hammond, the court finds you guilty, and for your treasons you will be taken from jail and hanged.'

Frank felt his knees buckling as an ashen-faced Hammond was returned to the jail, and if the Australian had not held him, he might have collapsed. The Australian was sentenced, then the two Englishmen, and now it was Saltwood's turn, but as he was led into the dock a rude commotion erupted at the rear of the courtroom. Two policemen were trying to restrain an elderly Boer who was struggling with some heavy object.

When they led him before the bench, the judge looked down severely: 'Lang-Piet Bezuidenhout, what is this nonsense?'

'Forgive me, your Honor. But I bring something that might help your Honor punish these men.'

'Lang-Piet, this is a court for justice, not a place for cheap revenge. Go before I get angry.'

'But, your Honor, the men of my commando have been in the saddle many days to bring you this thing.'

'What thing?'

'Die balk van Slagter's Nek, Oom Gideon.'

And that was precisely what had happened. Lang-Piet Bezuidenhout and his cronies had ridden down to Graaff-Reinet to buy the wooden beam of the Slagter's Nek gallows from a family who had preserved the grim relic for some eighty years.

'The rebels must hang from this very beam,' the old man shouted as his cronies cheered. 'We want justice.'

The judge, Oom Gideon de Beer, said quietly, 'Lang-Piet, in these days we dispense a fairer kind of justice. Sit down and be silent.' Then he turned his attention to the man waiting in the dock: 'For your crimes you will be taken from jail and hanged.'

In this extremity, Maud Turner came to Frank's rescue. With bars separating her from the man she considered her fiancé, she listened intently as he told her every detail of what he had done since she had said farewell to him at Kimberley. When he explained what he had written in his Vrymeer report to Rhodes, she cried, 'But that would exonerate you!' And when he told her of the Zimbabwe report, which the Boer commando had taken from him, she was exultant: 'It proves you honestly were doing scientific work. That makes your Vrymeer questionings legitimate.'

But how to get possession of the two documents? The first was held by Rhodes, who would be further incriminated if its contents were revealed. The second was held by the Boers, who would not likely deliver it. There seemed no way to obtain the papers.

With no other recourse, and with the death of her fiancé imminent, she took the bold step of going directly to the president of the Boers, and she found him sitting on his stoep, wearing a top hat and making himself available to any complaining citizen. At first he terrified her: that face of monumental ugliness, the deep voice that rumbled like a volcano, the flecked beard that rimmed his features, the tight-fitting black frock coat. But after he heard her out, he spoke to her, in English, with a warmth that surprised her.

'You want me to save the young man's life?'

'I do!' she cried.

'You sit down here. You say two documents are in existence?'

'They are! They are!'

'And if I could see them, they would exonerate him?'

'They would, sir.'

'Then why don't you produce them?'

She took a deep breath. 'Because Mr. Rhodes has one. And you have the other. And you are both very stubborn men.'

He halted his interrogation and called for his wife to fetch them coffee, and when Mevrou Kruger appeared on the stoep, a heavy, wheezing housewife, she seemed more like a kindly grandmother than the first lady of a republic. Her Coloured servant handed Maud a gaudy cup and saucer, with a second saucer to hold a helping of rusks. To her husband, Mevrou Kruger handed a double portion of rusks, then sat beside him with hands folded.

'You say you are Miss Maud Turner?' the president asked.

'Yes.'

'And you planned to marry this young man? Before he was caught as a spy?'

'He was never a spy, sir.'

'But you yourself told me that in his first report he informed Mr. Rhodes of our strength.'

'That he did, but if you remember, he also warned Mr. Rhodes against any military adventure.'

Mevrou Kruger broke in: 'Do you still want to marry him?'

Before Maud could respond, President Kruger astounded her by breaking into a hearty laugh. 'My dear young lady! Do you think we Boers want to give the English a motive for revenge, such as they gave us at Slagter's Nek?' He paused. 'Have you ever heard of Slagter's Nek?'

'I've been there, twice. Do you know the role played by Frank's ancestor? Reverend Saltwood the missionary? Who tried to halt the hangings?'

'We Boers do not cite missionaries as evidence,' Kruger said, and again he broke into laughter. 'Miss Turner, early this afternoon I commuted all the sentences.' He reached over and patted her knee as Mevrou Kruger offered fresh coffee to both her husband and his guest.

'Yes,' Kruger said as Maud daubed at her eyes. 'He's free, if he can pay his fine.'

'How much?'

'Twenty-five thousand pounds.'

She gasped. This was more money than she had ever visualized, a vast fortune really, but she firmed her chin and said, 'Somehow I'll get it.'

'No need. Mr. Rhodes has already informed us that he'll pay it.'

'Then Frank is free?'

'Yes.'

Her fortitude deserted her. With trembling hands she put the saucers aside and buried her face in her hands. After a few moments

Mevrou Kruger came to her side and helped her to her feet. 'He was free when you arrived,' she said. 'My husband likes to talk with pretty women.'

When Mr. Rhodes learned that Frank was determined to marry Miss Turner, he was deeply distressed. The loss of any of his young gentlemen to matrimony was a calamity, but to have Frank leave when he was going to be so sorely needed was intolerable. Summoning Miss Turner to his offices in Kimberley, he put it boldly to her that she was ruining the young fellow's life by insisting upon marriage.

'Seems to me,' she snapped, 'it's you who've done the ruining.'

'Don't be pert, young woman,' he replied.

'I didn't land him in jail,' she retorted, and the debate was on.

Rhodes pointed out that if Frank stayed with him he would always have a fine job, at the center of things, helping to decide affairs of great moment, to which she replied, 'He decided how to get himself hanged.'

'I saved him,' Rhodes said, and he proceeded to depict the bright future that awaited this brilliant chap—

'He's not brilliant,' she cut in. 'He's not even bright, if you ask me, getting involved in your daydreams.'

Ignoring the interruption, Rhodes explained the dismal prospect that would await Frank if he married and lost his job, to which Maud asked, 'Why must he lose his job? If he does a sensible thing like marrying the woman of his choice?'

'Because no man can work as my personal assistant, and share the dreams I have, and cater to a woman, too.'

'Your dreams, Mr. Rhodes, are addled, and I'm taking Frank away from you before you turn him crazy, too.'

The threat was easier made than discharged, for when Frank was brought into the discussion, Rhodes pleaded for the young man's continued help, especially at this time of crisis: 'You must come with me to London. To help me face down the inquisitors.' And he made such a plaintive appeal, explaining the morass of legal problems he faced as a consequence of the rebellion, that Saltwood once more allowed himself to be entrapped by this man.

'Maud, I'll be gone only a short time. He needs me.'

'I need you,' she replied. 'And if you go, don't count on my waiting for you forever.'

'Maud!' It was a cry she did not hear, for she had left the offices, and in her stead Frank had in his hands a sheaf of legal papers which he must study before sailing from Cape Town.

Maud's patience was to be severely tested, for not only did Rhodes keep his hold on Frank during this time, with its involved lawsuits and frenzied meetings, but he dragged him into another set of extensive negotiations in an attempt to strengthen his empire. He had exited from his troubles with more power and money than before; he had engaged in criminal acts against both the Boer republics and his own government, but had emerged almost unscathed. He did have to resign as prime minister of Cape Colony, but he retained his seat in Parliament permanently.

He turned once more to his grand design. The map of Africa must be painted red; Rhodesia must be extended in all directions. German infiltrations must be halted and Belgium watched. He had a thousand schemes, plus a special one which lay entwined with his heart: this he discussed with Saltwood, whom he considered, all things in balance, to have been the very finest of his eighteen or so young gentlemen.

'What do you think of it?' he asked one morning during their second trip to London as he shoved at Frank a rumpled paper covered with ink scratches. It was the rough outline of a new last will and testament—seventh in line—explaining his involved plan for a perpetual trust. It would receive millions of pounds, to be doled out to bright young men in the British colonies and America to enable them to attend Oxford and there imbibe the instruction which would encourage them to go forth and make the world British.

Mr. Rhodes proposed four large criteria for identifying the perfect man: scholastic achievement; success in manly sports; exhibition of moral force and leadership; and what he called 'qualities of manhood,' which included truth, courage, devotion to duty, sympathy for the weak, kindliness, unselfishness and fellowship. Young men who exhibited these qualities were to be handsomely endowed with scholarship funds and given every advantage in gaining a start in life.

'Well?' Rhodes asked impatiently.

'You establish very high standards, sir.'

'You met them. All my young gentlemen at Kimberley met them.'

When this reference was added, Frank understood what Mr. Rhodes hoped to accomplish with his largesse: he wanted an endless supply of the young men who had served him so well—Neville, Richard, Edgar, Elmhirst, Gordon, Mountjoy, Johnny, and so on, through eternity, men with first names only, who did not bother with girls but who stood tall and tended the duties of empire. The list of attributes Mr. Rhodes had drawn up were those best calculated to produce just such men, and there would always be both a need and a place for them.

But even as Frank studied this description of himself he had to be amused by one incongruous aspect. 'What's funny?' Rhodes asked testily.

'Your criteria,' Frank said with a chuckle he could not repress. Tapping the paper, he said, 'Mr. Rhodes, you wouldn't qualify on a single item. You hate sports and ridicule us when we engage in them. You took nearly a decade to win your degree. You had little sympathy for the Matabele, until they were thrashed. And as for truth, I've heard you give quite wrong explanations of your acts. Courage you may have, but you weren't in the front line when your revolution took place. And damnit all, you showed no kindliness to Maud. Not only would you fail to win one of your scholarships, you wouldn't even be considered.'

Laughing heartily, Rhodes reached for his will, waved it under Frank's nose and said, 'These criteria are not meant to identify men like me. We who move the world are not pleasant people, but we need pleasant, inoffensive people to help us. These scholarships will uncover such people.' When Frank started to speak, Rhodes interrupted: 'Stay with me, most precious of my young gentlemen, and we shall attain the dreams. You're to administer the scholarships, you know.' As he started to leave the room he turned back to say, 'You're to find me an endless supply of decent chaps just like yourself.' Handing the will back to Frank, he said, 'Think about it.'

For some time Frank sat staring at the floor, anticipating the great times he could have in Oxford, administering the scholarships, but this opportunity vanished when two visitors to his hotel room changed everything.

The first was his cousin, Sir Victor Saltwood, M.P. for Salisbury. He was brief and harsh: 'You've behaved like a damned fool, Frank. I sent you one of the finest young women this world could produce, and what in hell do you do but leave her and go off to some pile of rubble in what they call Rhodesia. And when you come back you get yourself nearly hanged. Your life was saved by that girl, and yet you abandoned her.'

'Mr. Rhodes needed me. You've seen what happened in London.'

'Needed you, yes, but dictate to you how your life should be lived? If you had any gumption, you'd tell him to go to hell, get aboard the next ship, and marry Maud Turner.'

'I'm afraid I've lost her, Victor. I've hardly seen her these past years.'

'You haven't at all. She understands the pressure you were under. After you left her the first time she got herself involved with schools in the farm districts. She's done a splendid job. Her father tells me she's visited your folks at De Kraal, loves them, and is prepared to wait till you come to your senses. But she's only human, Frank, and others want to marry her. She writes me that she's giving you two months.'

'She is!' The world seemed to spin back from the abyss of loneliness which Frank had envisioned for himself. He had supposed that Maud was lost and his life was to be an endless extension of the present, but now his cousin was saying that he had been in communication . . .

'I want to send a cable,' he cried impulsively, and on the back of Mr. Rhodes' proposed will he scribbled: *Maud. Sailing home immediately. Marry me the day I arrive, please, please, and save my life.*

He was signing it when Mr. Rhodes returned to the room to fetch his will, but before he could reach for it, Frank thrust it at him, his words face up, and said, 'Sir, I think you should be the first to know.'

Displaying no emotion, the great financier read the proposed cable, smiled, and said to Sir Victor, 'Stated in plain language.' He summoned a bellhop and asked him to bring the manager of the hotel. When that gentleman arrived, Rhodes said, 'See that this telegram is filed instanter. And book us two staterooms on the *Scot* sailing on Friday.'

'No, sir,' Frank said with a firmness that pleased his cousin. 'I don't want you arguing with me all the way to Cape Town. My mind's quite made up, you know.'

'Of course it is, and properly so. I wish to be present at the wedding.' Turning to Sir Victor, he said, 'The best, I think. This boy was the best of the lot.'

'Was?' Sir Victor repeated.

'Yes. He won't be working with me any more. I had plans for him, but times change, plans change.' And he accompanied Sir Victor from the room, a bulky, tired man, only forty-six years old, whose weakened heart could not keep pace with his dreams.

Frank's second visitor was the managing director of the Union Line, which operated the mail ships to South Africa. It seemed strange that a man of such high position would be delivering the tickets, even to such a frequent customer as Mr. Rhodes, and Frank said so: 'I know he travels back and forth at least once a year, but this is most considerate of you. I shall tell him.'

'No! No!' the director said in real panic. 'My meeting with you is highly confidential.'

'What is it?' Frank asked.

'The princess. The Polish princess.'

'Who?'

'A lady of high rank. Berlin, Warsaw, St. Petersburg.'

'What's she got to do with Mr. Rhodes?'

'Ah, that's what we don't know.' Nervously he began to unfold an incredible yarn: 'I don't know whether it's a hoax or what. I don't know whether Mr. Rhodes is in some kind of danger or not. In fact, I don't know what I know.'

'Why not tell me what you think you know.'

'The Princess Radziwill—a real princess bearing a distinguished Polish name—for some time she's been visiting us to talk about a shadowy trip to Cape Town. Says she has interests there. It develops that her interest is Mr. Rhodes. She never buys a ticket. She's interested only in when Mr. Rhodes is sailing.'

'That seems harmless.'

'Yes, but yesterday, within fifteen minutes of your ordering the two tickets to Cape Town . . .'

'He did the ordering. Did it himself.'

'Even more suspicious. Someone in this hotel, or someone in our offices—someone notified Princess Radziwill. And as I said, within fifteen minutes she was in my office, wanting to know which stateroom he had and demanding the one next to it.'

'Now, that does pose problems,' Frank conceded. 'Who is this woman? Young? Adventurous?'

'Not at all. She is the true Princess Radziwill. Well vetted in the Almanaca de Gotha. Not young at all. In her forties maybe, fifties, and looks it. May have been a great beauty once, but too much Polish and Russian cooking. Dark hair, no streaks of gray. Speaks acceptable English, but also French, German and, of course, Polish and Russian.'

'Has she any funds?'

'There's my problem, Mr. Saltwood. I have absolutely nothing to go on, but from years of selling tickets for boat passages, I'd say the Princess Radziwill conforms in every detail to the typical woman passenger who is going to give us trouble. Why do I say this? I don't really know. But that woman has financial problems.'

'Is there any chance that I might see her before we sail? Not talk to her, you understand. Just see her. Because we don't want a scandal, do we?'

The managing director thought that he might summon her to the office at three, to confirm her passage, or something like that, and if Frank happened to chance by to pick up *his* tickets . . . 'You wouldn't approach my door, you understand. Just the outer office, like any ordinary passenger. You could see her as she exits.'

It was arranged, and from a shop across the street from the Union Line offices Frank watched a shortish, attractive, dark-haired woman step out of a cab and walk in to confirm her stateroom. Casually he crossed the street, moved to a counter, and engaged the young male clerk in conversation about a possible passage to Australia. From where he stood, he commanded a fine view of the manager's office and had a good chance to study the Princess Radziwill of Poland.

She seemed gracious, well groomed, interested in the details of her forthcoming voyage. She talked with animation, and whenever he caught sight of her face, it seemed quite pleasant. If she was an agent in some conspiracy against his employer, she masked it well.

She rose rather sooner than he expected, walked briskly from the inner office, spotted Frank immediately, and walked straight up to him. 'Frank Saltwood,' she said without hesitation. 'I am Princess Radziwill. And you are the cousin of my good friend Sir Victor. Liberal party. Salisbury. I believe we're to share the *Scot* together, this Friday. How very congenial.' With a slight bow she passed on.

Both the steamship management and young Saltwood deemed it best to inform Mr. Rhodes of this strange development, and he guffawed at their apprehensions. 'I like *grandes dames* like that. I talk to them roughly, introducing more profanity with each turn of the conversation. After a while they leave me alone.'

Frank had a premonition that this cavalier treatment might not succeed with royalty as determined as the Princess Radziwill, and he boarded the Union Line ship with trepidation, which was justified a few hours later at the evening meal. He cautioned Mr. Rhodes: 'We'll go in late, after she's chosen her table,' and they did so, but as they entered the salon Frank caught a glimpse of a lady in black waiting in the shadows, and no sooner had Mr. Rhodes taken his table, one with spare chairs so that he might entertain business acquaintances during the long voyage, than Princess Radziwill swept into the room, crying in a soft, ladylike voice, 'Oh, dear! Where shall I sit?'

Ignoring the chief steward, who hurried up to assist her, she let her hand fall upon one of the chairs at Rhodes' table and asked gently, 'Does this happen to be vacant?'

Frank started to say brusquely, 'It's taken, ma'am,' but before he could complete the sentence Mr. Rhodes said gallantly, but with obvious reluctance, 'It seems to be free, madam,' at which she seated herself with great firmness, indicating that this would be her place for the duration of the voyage.

She was an enchanting woman, much younger in spirit than her years, informed on everything and willing to deliver final judgments on politicians, writers, musicians and the state of the world. When Mr. Rhodes attempted to stifle her with his routine profanity, she responded with animated discussions of her digestive system, her bowel movements and episodes in her sex life. Very quickly Mr. Rhodes retreated to more casual conversation.

From the first she demonstrated an intense dislike of Frank Saltwood, assessing him accurately as a bar to whatever designs she might have on Mr. Rhodes. She scorned any statement he made, ridiculed his Oxford insularity and lampooned his general deportment. Specifically she wanted to know why he wasn't married, and when he tried to counter with questions about her own status, she deflated him with a forthright statement: 'I am the daughter of a great Polish nobleman, but my father and I have always considered ourselves Russians first, Poles second. I am married to a Radziwill, one of the proudest Polish names, but he has treated me abominably, and I am soon to be divorced from him. I am forty-one years old.'

She intimated that she was also a famous authoress: 'Five wellregarded books.'

When he made inquiries among the other passengers, he found that she was indeed a distinguished writer on political subjects and that she knew everyone in European society. Sensing that he doubted her statement about her writing, she appeared one noontime in the promenade café with two of her books, solid affairs dealing with European court life and its political intrigues. When she saw that Frank and, indirectly, Mr. Rhodes were sufficiently impressed, she said casually, 'You know, of course, that my aunt, Evelina Rzewuska, was the wife and financial salvation of Honoré de Balzac.'

'Who was he?' asked a young man from Kimberley who had recently been invited to join the Rhodes circle.

'Oh, my God!' she screamed so loudly that people at other tables turned to look. This pleased her, and she appealed to them: 'This young fool asks me who Honoré de Balzac was. It's like asking an Englishman who William Shakespeare was.' And with this she launched upon a recitation, with wild gestures, of the entire sonnet:

> 'When to the sessions of sweet silent thought
> I summon up remembrance of things past . . .'

When she was halfway through, Frank thought: What can this creature be up to? At the closing couplet he found out, for with a sudden drop in her voice, she gazed longingly at Mr. Rhodes and whispered:

> 'But if the while I think on thee, dear friend,
> All losses are restored and sorrows end.'

After a few demonstrations like this, Frank was so deflated that she could speak right past him when she wished to address Mr. Rhodes. But if she humbled the younger man, she exalted the older, praising him extravagantly and placing herself in his way whenever she moved on deck. When he sat down on a deck chair, he found that she had acquired the one next to it, and if he sought to rest because of his increasing heart unease, there she was, prepared to argue politics with him.

'What does that woman want with me?' Rhodes asked Frank in some dismay at the end of the fifth day.

'I think she wants to marry you, sir.'

'She's already married. Said so herself.'

'But she's getting a divorce. Said so herself.' Rhodes caught the mockery in his young friend's voice and burst into laughter. 'You have only one commission, Frank. Protect me from that woman.'

Saltwood's first stratagem backfired: 'We'll take our meals in your cabin. Let her have the table.' But before the first meal ended, the princess burst into the cabin, eyes aflutter, to assure herself that 'dear Mr. Rhodes is not suffering.' Deftly she maneuvered Frank out of the stateroom, fluffed up the pillows, and sat close beside Mr. Rhodes to help him eat his meal.

'Frank!' came the anguished cry. 'You said you'd bring the papers.' Grabbing anything at hand, Saltwood hurried back into the room, where the beleaguered man said, 'Sit here beside me,' and the princess was edged away.

The next afternoon, in their deck chairs, she chided Mr. Rhodes for having been so ungallant, and as she rose to spread a blanket for him she was seized with a mild fainting spell, which threw her gently into his arms.

'Frank!' he bellowed, and when Saltwood hurried up, he found his master embracing the inert body of the Polish princess.

During the entire voyage this charade continued, for no matter what maneuver the two men devised, the princess knew how to outsmart them, and one evening when persons at the bar said in her hearing, 'I do believe Mr. Rhodes, the woman hater, is having an affair with the princess,' she smiled.

It was when the *Scot* was one day out of Cape Town that Cecil Rhodes made the second great mistake of his life. In the presence of Frank Saltwood and two guests at his table he said casually to these business friends, 'When we reach the Cape you must visit me at Groote Schuur.'

'I shall be delighted!' the princess said.

He had scarcely unpacked his bags when a telegram arrived from the Mount Nelson Hotel announcing that the princess would be coming to dinner that night. At the meal, a party for the colony's political leaders, she assigned herself the seat as mistress of the establishment, and before long, cryptic notices began appearing in the Cape Town newspapers, sent to them anonymously in a woman's handwriting:

> The mighty Colossus whose armor has blunted all the arrows of Cupid seems to have been wounded by that sly huntsman, and we understand that wedding bells may soon be sounding, but who the fair partner is to be we cannot at this time divulge except to say that she is a titled dignitary much accustomed to the royal circles of Berlin, Warsaw and St. Petersburg.

Who was this cyclonic woman who had risked everything on a boat trip to South Africa in pursuit of the world's richest bachelor? Princess Radziwill was everything she claimed to be, and one thing more. She was the daughter of one of Poland's noblest families; her aunt had indeed been the salvation of Honoré de Balzac; she had written widely popular books; and she was divorcing her husband, a process that would require many years. But the salient fact was that she was almost penniless.

At forty-one, her hectic behavior had caused her expulsion from the courts of Europe, and several nations had denied her reentry. A waspish gossip, she had frittered away a dazzling life until members of her two families, who did have great wealth, wished to see her no more. With her pen she might have made herself a good life with respectable income, but this talent, too, she abused, and her publishers were weary of her broken promises and unfulfilled contracts. Like her talents, her beauty had begun to fade, and she sensed that she had only a few more good years, which she must use to advantage.

It was remarkable that at the nadir of her career she should have devised a plan so bold, with risks so tremendous, but one day as she was sitting in her mean Paris lodgings this splendid thought had come to her: Why not marry Cecil Rhodes? Unfree to marry because of her dragging divorce, without funds, with fewer good dresses than ever before in her life, she had nevertheless launched her assault. Now, at Groote Schurr, Rhodes' fine Cape Dutch mansion that would become the equivalent of South Africa's White House, she behaved like a first lady and made it clear that she intended assisting Mr. Rhodes in governing the nation.

'I need help,' the great man moaned one afternoon. 'Beg Frank Saltwood to come back.'

In the hectic days when Princess Radziwill was intent on capturing Groote Schurr, Frank was having the tenderest experience of his life. Upon disembarking from *Scot* and bidding Cecil Rhodes farewell for what he assumed was the last time, since he had been dismissed, he caught a cab and hurried to the Mount Nelson Hotel, where Maud Turner had come to greet him. Ascertaining from the desk clerk where her room was located, he hurried through the stately lobby, bounded up a flight of oaken stairs, and thumped loudly at her door. Quickly it was opened and quickly he was down on his knees for anyone in the hallway to see: 'Maud, can you forgive me?'

'Get up, you stupid boy.'

'Then you'll have me?'

'Not if you act like this.' And with a swift reach of her hand she grabbed his wrist and pulled him into the room, then kicked the door shut with her heel. 'I am so glad we found each other again,' she said, and she maneuvered Frank to the bed, telling him, when the impassioned interlude was over, 'Now, damnit, you've got to marry me.'

They took the train up through the Karroo, then south to a small siding convenient to De Kraal. It consisted of an iron shed and stock ramp marked by a deeply carved sign erected by Frank's father: HILARY. On the long journey Maud had discussed seriously the manner in which they should lead their lives: 'Forget Mr. Rhodes completely. We'll have no more to do with him. What kind of work can you do, Frank?'

'I know the business world. Bankers, diamonds, Parliament.'

'Could you be a manager of sorts?'

'I think so. But where shall we establish our headquarters?'

She had been thinking about this for over two years, and every selfish desire urged her to say Cape Town, for she considered this the fairest city she had ever seen, a place incomparably lovely, with its ocean, its mountain, its deep indented bays, its gorgeous wealth of flowers. This was a city she could love, but her business sense warned her that South African industry was bound to center in the north, near the diamonds and the gold, and it was there that a young man could make his way: 'I think we should work in Johannesburg.'

'What a grubby place. Have you ever seen it?'

'Grubby now, but we must think of the future. It's got to be Johannesburg.'

'But couldn't we . . .' He hesitated, rubbed his nose, and asked tentatively, 'Couldn't we . . . maybe . . . maintain an office also in Cape Town?'

As if the idea had never occurred to her, she pondered it, tickled him under the chin with her fingernail, and said, 'Frank, I think that's a capital idea.'

In the Cape cart sent from De Kraal to meet them at the Hilary siding they devised a rough pattern for their future: a secure farm investment in the countryside; a business office in Johannesburg to watch over banking, insurance, trading and stocks, which Boers ignored because they had little interest in intricate financial matters; a political footing in Cape Town to protect one's holdings; and a permanent link with 'home,' a spot back in England crammed with memories.

'We must never forget our families in Salisbury,' Maud said.

'Naturally. What do you have in mind?'

'I'd like to slip back home as often as I can. I do cherish my English heritage.'

'Sounds reasonable.'

The decisions reached by Maud and Frank Saltwood represented those of many Englishmen in South Africa at that time. For them, some cathedral town like Salisbury was 'home,' Stonehenge their playground, Oxford or Cambridge their natural inheritance. No matter how diligently Frank handled his finances in Johannesburg or his political connivings at Cape Town, he and Maud would always be drawn back to Salisbury, spiritually if not physically; and whenever an opportunity for a trip to England arose, they would be eager to renew the umbilical tie.

The Van Doorns, on the other hand, never returned to Holland. Not one of them would have known his or her way around the canals of Amsterdam; they rarely knew who was governing the land or what political disposition it had. And if they had gone, they would not have understood either the religion or the language. Huguenot descendants were the same: none of the Du Preez family remembered the Oudezijdsvoorburgwal or its significance to their ancestors; and even less, the French village of Caix where their history began; nor could they speak French. Both the Dutch Van Doorns and the Huguenot Du Preez were now Afrikaners, and proud to be so.

The Saltwoods were Europeans; the Boers were people of Africa. The Saltwoods would always have a refuge to scurry back to if trouble erupted; the Boers would not. If a Saltwood behaved moderately well, the English queen might call him back to London for a knighthood, but if a De Groot performed heroically, no royalty in Amsterdam would know of it, much less seek to ennoble him. Prudently the Saltwoods kept one foot in Salisbury; the Van Doorns kept both feet in Africa and did not even know of any alternative home to escape to. They rose or fell, lived or died according to what happened in Africa, and between these two types of people, the Europeans and the Afrikaners, the gulf would grow wider and wider.

Maud paid close attention to the wild rumors coming out of Cape Town regarding Mr. Rhodes and the Polish princess, and found naughty delight in the great man's discomfiture: 'Gossip says he told her she was not welcome at Groote Schuur and warned her to return to Europe.'

As the scandal worsened, Frank was forced to take notice, and he was grieved when the papers reported that the princess had forged Rhodes' name to bank paper to the extent of £23,000. 'Listen to this, Maud. "She seems to have copied his signature from a printed postcard sold in stationery stores." How bloody preposterous!'

'Who is this woman?' Maud asked.

'The most extraordinary liar I've ever met, except that everything she ever told me was true.' He delighted her with a brief sketch of the affair, explaining how the princess had maneuvered herself onto the *Scot* and into Mr. Rhodes' astonished arms. Then he became serious: 'If she claims she has letters which incriminate him, I'd say she has them. If she claims the financial papers are not forgeries, but were given to her by Rhodes, I'd hesitate to call her a liar in court. This woman is . . .' He fumbled for words, then came up with 'Stupendous.' He added that if the charge of forgery had to be ventilated in court, the entire Cape had better prepare itself for a hurricane.

'Should you offer your assistance, Frank?'

'To whom?'

'To Mr. Rhodes, of course,' she snapped.

'But he fired me.' He broke into laughter and fell into a chair, dragging his wife along with him. As she perched on his lap he said, 'You know, of course, that he has never in his life allowed a married man to work as his private secretary. You got me discharged, and it was damned well worth it.'

'But if he needs you . . .'

Maud Turner was the first of the famous Saltwood women; they formed a long line of strong-willed girls who had left secure homes in rural England, bringing with them to South Africa learning, musical ability, skill in drawing and high moral conscience. They accounted for the charity wards, the little schools tucked away in valleys, the libraries, the inadequate colleges, the books of reminiscences which would mean so much to later generations. Even during her stay in Cape Town, Maud Turner had already launched the Lady Anne Barnard Bowls Club, and near De Kraal she was using her own money to restore the ruins of Golan Mission. Women like her looked at their world, rolled up their sleeves, and tried to make it better.

Now Maud behaved with characteristic charity. Not forgetting that Mr. Rhodes had denigrated her and delayed her marriage for several years, she nevertheless told Frank, 'If that sad, confused man needs your help, we must offer it,' and they had already reached Grahamstown on their way to the Cape when a telegram intercepted them: NEED YOUR HELP. RHODES.

When they entered Groote Schuur they found it occupied only by a cadre of male servants and assistants, one of whom said, 'That woman's chasing him all the time. He's run away to Muizenberg.' At that little seafront village, well to the south of Cape Town, the great man had sequestered himself in a small corrugated-roof cottage wedged against tall trees. Viewed from the outside, it seemed to contain a few meager rooms and no amenities; it was scarcely a proper setting for what was becoming a major tragedy.

Maud expected to work in the cottage, providing what comfort she could, but as she walked up the narrow footpath two young men appeared at the door of the cottage, obviously determined to prevent her entrance: 'No women allowed.'

'But he sent a telegram for us,' and she produced the paper.

'That meant Frank, not you. Mr. Rhodes would be most distraught if you were to force your way in.'

'I never force my way,' she said quietly, but the men were adamant: 'No women.' So she drove back to Cape Town and her husband moved inside.

He was shocked. Mr. Rhodes, not yet fifty, sagged in all directions. His jowls were heavy and unshaven; his mustache, never attractive, was less so when untrimmed; his reddish hair was uncombed and matted with sweat; his arms and legs lay inert; but it was his eyes that sent the most alarming signals, for they were sodden, lids drooping and pupils unfocused. He behaved like a man in his painful eighties, forlorn and distressed. The bright young men still surrounded him; they seemed to come in endless supply: 'Yes, Mr. Rhodes. Yes, Mr. Rhodes.' But they gave him little sustenance.

'Is that you, Frank?'

'It is, Mr. Rhodes. What can I do to help?'

'You've already helped a great deal. See the Phoenician bird in the corner? He watches over me.' It would be intolerable to tell him now that the stone masterpiece was not Phoenician.

Rasping sounds came from the bed. It was Rhodes trying to make an important statement: 'Frank, to protect my honor I've got to defend myself against that damned woman.'

There was now no time for courtesies or blandishments: 'Sir, I must advise you most firmly that in proper English society a gentleman never brings suit against a lady.'

'I've never given a damn about English society. I'm not a gentleman. And that princess is certainly no lady. See the attorney-general, Frank, and urge him to file charges.'

'Oh, my God!' cried one of the young gentlemen. 'There she is again.'

And everyone in the cottage looked down the path to the roadway, where a woman dressed in stylish black, under an umbrella, walked slowly back and forth, staring at the cottage where the man she had wanted to marry lay dying.

'Drive her away!' Rhodes cried, but the young man said that they had tried this and the police had warned them that she had a right to walk on a public thoroughfare.

'But not to stare at me!' Rhodes wailed.

'She can walk and she can walk and she can look,' one of the young fellows said. 'All we can do is pray for rain.'

For weeks this tragicomedy continued. Rhodes lay in the cottage planning, while his lawyer and Frank Saltwood helped the attorney-general's office with their case against this brazen embezzler; she issued threatening releases to the newspapers and at dusk came down from Cape Town to walk back and forth, menacingly, silently before the cottage.

One evening Maud rode out to talk with the princess as she patrolled the roadway. 'Why do you torment him?'

'Because he has tormented me. He wants to send me to jail.'

'Did you forge the seven papers?'

'I have been Mr. Rhodes' staunchest supporter. He owes me enormous sums.'

'Didn't he pay your hotel bill when the Mount Nelson threatened to evict you?' Before the princess could respond, she added, 'And when you accepted the money, didn't you promise that you'd leave South Africa?'

'I did leave,' she protested like an insulted innocent, 'but I came back.'

'Princess, what can you hope to achieve by this ridiculous behavior?'

'Prison, I suppose. But men who ignore women, or treat them badly—they must be taught a lesson. When I'm through with Cecil Rhodes the entire world will be laughing at him.'

'They're already laughing at you. Have you seen the cartoons?'

'Cartoons are for today,' she huffed. 'I am for history.'

Maud achieved nothing, and when she drove off, the princess was still stalking back and forth in the shadows, casting a witchlike spell on the cottage and its inhabitants.

Despite all that the two Saltwoods tried to do to bring sanity into this mad affair, the criminal trial moved forward, complicated by civil trials on lesser matters, and the day came when the two protagonists faced each other before a judge sitting with his clerks at Groote Schuur, since Rhodes was too ill to appear in a regular Cape Town court. They met in bitterness, they testified in bitterness, with Rhodes stating categorically that he had never signed any papers on behalf of the princess, and that if she had peddled such promissory notes to the bankers and money lenders of Cape Town, she had done so as a forger.

His testimony, ungracious and unforgiving, condemned the woman to imprisonment; her testimony, malicious and biting, condemned him as a fool. Worse, it condemned him to death.

After appearing before the judge, he retreated to the miserable cottage, where Frank ordered a hole knocked in the bedroom wall so that Rhodes could catch the air for which he gasped continuously. If he lay down, he could not breathe; if he sat up, he could not rest. Still the princess marched back and forth, keeping her death watch; knowing that she could not escape incarceration, she showed no mercy. She would haunt this ungracious, unforgiving man to his death.

'Please go away,' Frank pleaded with her one night.

'This is my only freedom.'

'Have you any money left? Any at all?'

'I'm a pauper. I haven't enough to eat. I shall welcome the security of prison, for all my friends have abandoned me, a princess of the Russian court.' She pronounced the word *Rrrosshian*.

He gave her two pounds and told her to go to the Muizenberg Pavilion and eat, but she continued her vigil.

The breath of air Rhodes sought in that dreadfully hot March never reached him, and when he felt that death would overtake him before the criminal trial reached a conclusion, he dismissed her from his mind completely. Asking for his beloved atlas, he talked with Frank about those portions of his plans still to be realized: 'You must make the map red. Look how much we've done so far.'

When his hand fell upon Rhodesia, he looked up almost pitifully and asked, 'They never change the name of a country, do they?'

'No,' Frank said. 'That will always be Rhodesia. Your monument.'

But then Rhodes' eyes could not avoid the areas which represented his gnawing defeats: South-West Africa had fallen to the Germans; Moçambique still rested in Portuguese hands; the damned Belgians had proved their hearts were made of concrete. But worst of all, while Rhodes was suffering torment from the princess, a far greater agony had raged around him, for Boer and Englishman had finally come to fratricidal blows on the South African veld. His unwavering goal, the union of those two groups, seemed more impossible than ever, but his final words to Frank addressed that problem: 'Dear boy, when this war is over, spend your life trying to unite Boer and Englishman.'

When Rhodes died, Frank was in Cape Town giving a deposition in the trial, and when he heard of the death he felt an overwhelming sense of failure: he had tried to protect this great man from his blunders and from this fiasco with the princess, but he had accomplished little. He was told that Rhodes had died just at sunset on 26 March 1902, forty-nine years old, consumed by the volcanic fires that had driven him. As he died he uttered his own sardonic epitaph: 'So little done, so much to do.'

When the Princess Catherine Rzewuska Radziwill heard of Rhodes' death she was only forty-four, disgraced, penniless, and facing a two-year sentence in one of Cape Town's worst prisons. She said of Rhodes: 'I wanted only to help this lonely, miserable man. Had he attended to me, he might have been saved.'

In prison, her first demand was for a book of rules, which she mastered with such diligence that she became a notorious 'jailhouse lawyer,' arguing for the rights of all prisoners. Long before her sentence was completed, the warden petitioned the court that she be set free: 'Whenever I see her coming at me with that book of rules, I am threatened with twitches.'

The conniving princess would not accept freedom unless the government provided her with first-class steamship passage to London, and enough cash to allow her to live in a respectable London hotel for half a year. Since the senior authorities were also developing twitches, they bowed to her demands, then requisitioned a tug to ensure that she got aboard. To the Afrikaner lawyer who had enthusiastically defended her against the Colossus, they said, 'Do not give her a penny of the money. Hand it in a sealed envelope to the captain of the ship, to be delivered only when the vessel is far out to sea.'

She wrote more books, thirty in all; she lectured; when Prince Radziwill, her husband, finally died, she quickly married a Swedish gentleman whom no one ever saw; she was condemned by Russia to perpetual exile; and by some bizarre set of accidents she landed in New York, which she loved. As Princess Radziwill, she became the darling of royalty-hungry Americans and lived off them in various ingenious ways.

Never once during her long stay in that country did anyone uncover the fact that she had spent nearly two years in a South African prison as an embezzler.

Finally she wrote her autobiography, not one chapter of which was true; she enchanted new generations of New York society; and in 1941, at the age of eighty-three, she sat propped up in bed writing long letters to the rulers of Europe advising them how best to prosecute World War II. She signed her pronouncements: Princess Catherine Radziwill—and when she died she was surrounded by three American ladies-in-waiting.

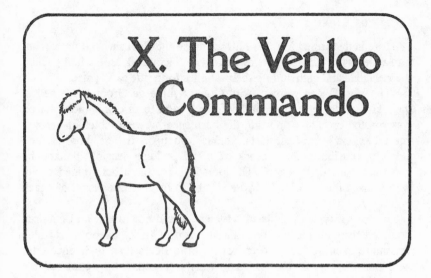

X. The Venloo Commando

FROM the throats of a hundred Boers, young and old, fair-faced and weather-beaten, came a merry song that carried far beyond the great barn at Vrymeer in which they were celebrating. The melody was that of an American Civil War song, 'Just Before the Battle, Mother,' but the Afrikaner version, popular in the eighties, had to do with love, not war:

> 'When will our marriage be, Gertjie?
> Why are you so very quiet?
> We've been betrothed so long, Gertjie!
> Now's the time for us to wed.
>
> Come then, Gertjie, for I shall not
> Be kept any longer on a string.
> Perhaps you think I cannot die,
> But my years are passing on!'

The grizzled warrior Paulus de Groot could not remember when last he had seen so many happy couples. 'Tonight, Jakob,' he shouted to the owner of the barn, 'there's many a heart will be lost under the stars of Vrymeer.' Van Doorn grinned back through a haze of smoke and dust.

General de Groot, as all thought of him, was guest of honor at the party, and with good reason, for in this very week back in February

1881 he had stormed Majuba Hill to thrash the English. And now, from fifty miles away and farther, as if it were Nachtmaal, Boers had packed their wagons and gathered up their families for a ride to Vrymeer.

The Van Doorn women, with Ouma Sybilla de Groot enthroned at their kitchen table, had prepared enough food for a commando. An ox was roasted on a spit opposite the barn; nearby were tables of bredies, vegetables, sweet dishes: tarts, koekies, pumpkin fritters, konfyts, and Jakob's contribution, the crock of bread pudding sensibly flanked by two bucketfuls of the same. Of course, there was a determined group who praised the pudding but passed it by in favor of the barrel of peach brandy.

It was a day the people of Vrymeer would not forget, and children bounded through the paradise like a troop of frisky baboons. Nothing was more exciting for a dozen robust little Boers than their encounter with the offspring of the Nxumalo family. Together they explored the secrets of Vrymeer, running screaming from the barn to the cave where the Bushmen's rhinoceros galloped. After a shouting circuit, they ran to the lake, tossed aside their clothes, and jumped in.

At nightfall the tallow candles along the walls of the barn were lit, the ant-hill floor gleamed, and a noisy trio of guitar, violin and concertina went to work. Even Ouma Sybilla managed, just once, to step out and do a few turns, not with her husband, who was tending the peach brandy, but with a young man who had his eye on Johanna van Doorn and thought courtesy to the old queen-buffalo would improve his chances.

The dancing was really for the young couples, and the floor was continuously crowded, for if the violin grew tired, the guitar and concertina kept going; and sometimes the squash-box performed alone. Johanna had agonized for some days over what to wear, and her efforts had proved most successful: she had donned a long skirt whose bottom hem was filled with kernels of corn to give it weight and make it flare out when she pirouetted.

'Watch your millstone, young fellow!' De Groot roared suddenly. 'You're grinding too rough.' He meant that the partner swinging Johanna had her dress so nearly parallel to the floor that bits of grain were flying loose.

It was past midnight and the concertina played a little more slowly as groups talked quietly or hummed old songs and Jakob mentioned the one sober question of this festive day: 'How long have our families lived here, Paulus?'

The general reflected: 'Fifty-eight years.'

'We should be grateful.'

'What for?' the old warrior asked.

'Many things, Paulus. Mostly we've been able to hold on to our ways . . . keep the Englishmen from changing us. But with so many Uitlanders moving in . . .'

'Oom Paul—it's his job to watch the English. If he wants to see you, like the telegram said, it must be important.'

'Ja, my Generaal!'

Earlier that week Jakob had been summoned to meet with President Kruger in Pretoria; he would take the train Monday morning, for he knew that something serious was brewing.

Jakob found the great man on the stoep, deep wrinkles in his face, a black top hat perched on his head and a tightly buttoned coat covering his enormous belly. He did not rise to greet one of his most trusted burghers but showed his pleasure at the visit.

'Jakob, there are troubles, there are dangers we must face,' he said, indicating a chair.

'The English, Oom Paul?'

'Always the English. They mean to steal our republics, them and the Uitlanders.'

'Not while this Van Doorn has a breath. We'll never allow that.'

'Nice words, Jakob. Nice words.' He spat over the edge of the stoep. 'I have a task for you, broeder. You have family at the Cape, not so? Van Doorns of Trianon. I want you to visit them. Hear what they have to say. What's on their minds if the English take up arms.'

'There's been talk of rebellion down there. Against the English government.'

'Ja, ja. But what do the people really think?' He rocked back and forth. 'Talk isn't enough. Where will the Van Doorns, the Du Preez, the Hofmeyrs stand the day we have to fight for our lives?'

'We'll need them all,' Jakob said.

'You are visiting family down there. Understand? You're not Oom Paul's official. Talk with anyone you like, but keep away from government people. We have enough troubles with them already.'

'I understand, Oom Paul.'

'Ja, now that's good, Jakob. Let's have some coffee while you tell me about Paulus de Groot. How's the old devil these days?'

Jakob was fifty-five years old that February, a man of medium height, heavy build and deliberate movement. He was delighted at the prospect of traveling to the Cape in a first-class carriage and at government expense, for he had never seen the Trianon of his ancestors and looked forward to meeting its occupants.

He conducted his interviews in Cape Town first, and was pleased to find that the wealthy Du Preez had not forgotten their links with his family. They were most congenial when recalling those days when the first De Prés shared the Trianon vineyards with the Van Doorns. 'We've both moved a long way.' But when he discovered their attitude toward participation in a possible war, he was unhappy to learn that they had no interest whatever in taking up arms to defend the Boers.

'Don't misunderstand us, Van Doorn. We have much sympathy for the republics, but not for war. Look at what we have here. It's all come since the English arrived. I realize you might not like the Uitlanders as neighbors, but damnit, man, you Boers wouldn't know how to handle gold. Not even with all the Hollanders and Germans you bring in to run your government.'

Jakob tried to argue that the freedom not only of the northern Boer but of the southern Afrikaner, too, would hang in the balance: 'That is, if war comes. You Cape Afrikaners would certainly—' They cut him off: 'We have all the freedom we need here in the Cape. More than you seem to have up north. You may not believe this, but we like it here. We won't march in your armies.'

A schoolteacher named Carolus Marais invited Jakob to walk with him to see various Afrikaner establishments in the area: schools, big churches, solid homes built on the slopes of Table Mountain. 'Our forefathers never did so well under Dutch rule. We elect our people to Parliament, protect ourselves from the Englishmen. We don't want war.'

'Neither do we!' Jakob exploded. 'But suppose the English force it on us. Surely, if you have any decency or courage, you'll support the republics.'

'Would you ride out in some silly war, at your age?'

'Of course. And the other burghers at Venloo, we'd ride with our commando if they call us. We'd lose everything if we didn't.'

'Then you'd be very foolish. You and I can gain everything we want from the English without firing a shot. They have laws, Van Doorn. They're a great people for putting everything down in laws. And when they do, they obey them.'

'But always on their own terms.'

'Jakob, be sensible! We Cape Afrikaners are fighting our own war, not with German guns and Boer commandos. With the laws the Englishmen give us. Go listen to our clever politicians in the House and you'll learn how to keep the English rulers on the run.'

After eight days of this, it dawned on Jakob that Pretoria's hopes of a Cape Afrikaner uprising were pointless. These sturdy people with their schools and coffeehouses and politics were not interested in supporting a rebellion.

'Wait a moment!' Du Preez protested when Jakob voiced his disappointment. 'At first you asked, "Will you support the republics?" Of course we'll support them. We'll argue your case in Parliament. We'll speak out for you in every meeting. We'll back you up with letters in our newspapers.'

'But will you support us with arms?'

'Good heavens, no!'

He did locate three young Afrikaners who offered to volunteer, but when he asked around about them he learned they were a bunch of ruffians unable to hold a job with any respectable English firm. The schoolteacher, Mr. Marais, said, 'I was unlucky enough to have two of them in my school. They're wild, like old Rooi van Valck.'

'Maybe that's what we need.'

'Good heavens, no! There are plenty of decent Afrikaners here who'd want to help you keep your independence. Some may even want to join your fight. Perhaps the Boers near your borders. But don't count on it. And the three rascals you have found won't help your army much.'

'We have no army. Only commandos.'

'Then you'll lose the war. Because the English surely will have an army, and that makes a difference.'

Jakob was glad to be rid of Cape Town. The Afrikaners there seemed more interested in playing political games than in fighting for their freedoms. Little things had irritated him, too, like Du Preez and Carolus Marais saying 'Good heavens!' as if they were proper Englishmen. He saw other manifestations of this pervasive English influence, all making him think that the local Afrikaners were corrupted by their long severance from the Boers of the north. It was impossible to imagine Paulus de Groot in the Cape setting, or his own vibrant father, Tjaart. There were apparently two groups of Afrikaners now, and the southern had fallen into the hands of the enemy.

The train puffed across the Cape flats to Stellenbosch, out beyond the broken hedge of bitter almond: it passed suburban backyards, small settlements and numerous farms. He had left Cape Town with no promises, but he felt confident that when he got among his own people at Trianon his reception would be different, for these Afrikaners lived outside the debilitating influences of the city, and he would be able to talk with them in specifics.

When he saw the lovely tree-lined streets of Stellenbosch and the low white buildings, he felt that he had come to a town that had always been his. He stopped at a small, very clean whitewashed inn, where he had a room overlooking the central square and better food than he had enjoyed in some time. Three other travelers shared his table, men in from farms near Swellendam, and they wanted to know his business. When he told them that he was a farmer, too, but from Venloo in the Zuid-Afrikaansche Republiek, they all leaned forward: 'What's Oom Paul doing up there?'

'He's facing down the English, and he better, or you'll all be losing your freedoms.'

'I wouldn't know what to do with more freedom if I had it,' one of the farmers said.

'I mean freedom to worship as you wish. Have Dutch taught to your children.'

'We have that now.'

Another broke in: 'You say your name's Van Doorn? One of our Van Doorns?'

'The same.'

'You're not going to talk to them about joining Kruger's ridiculous war?'

'It's the duty of every good Afrikaner to support Oom Paul.'

'Agreed,' the three men said at once. And one added, 'I liked it when he took the strap and belted those lords of Johannesburg and their cheeky Uitlanders. But war . . . against England . . . With her navy? And her empire? Your people can't be serious about that?'

'Aren't you?' Jakob asked.

'Good heavens, no.'

There was the phrase again, spoken in accented English, betraying the corruption that had overtaken these good people; they lived so far from the heartland of the Volk, where great decisions were being made, that they could not comprehend the problems facing them. He rose to leave this depressing assembly, but as he walked away one of the farmers warned him: 'Don't go talking rebellion to the ones at Trianon. They sell their wine to London.'

The warning was perceptive, for next morning when he hired a cart to carry him west to the winery, he could see that its vineyards were so substantial and so ancient that whoever owned them must perforce be a cautious man; but when the driver swung about in a large circle to approach the house from the west, and Jakob saw for the first time that magnificent entrance, with the white arms reaching out in welcome and the great house standing in pristine loveliness, he gasped.

'These are the Van Doorns of Trianon,' he whispered respectfully. The place was like some palace he might have seen in a children's book, all green grass and blue hills, white walls of an older society. When the cart approached the big house the driver blew a small whistle, which brought the occupants to the stoep.

'It's Jakob come from up north!' the master of the house shouted to his children, whereupon he leaped off the stoep, rushed to the cart, and embraced this almost-forgotten cousin.

'I am Coenraad van Doorn,' he said, pushing Jakob back so he could see him better. 'And this is my wife, Florrie. The two boys are Dirk and Gerrit and the baby is Clara. Now come in.'

With real enthusiasm the young master of the vineyards, only thirty years old, led Jakob through the front door and into the spacious line of rooms which comprised the forward leg of the H. In the center of this line stood the reception hall; to the left, a lofty-ceilinged room for meetings; to the right, the guest bedroom in which Jakob would stay. But once his bags were deposited, he was led back through the crossbar of the H and into the warm, lively room where meals were served, off which the family bedrooms ranged. What was so very pleasing about the arrangement of this house was that gardens proliferated in both squares, so that all rooms were surrounded by flowers. The place had an air of elegance that almost overwhelmed Jakob.

Young Coenraad showed himself to be an able fellow: 'My father died too soon, and someone had to take command. I feel quite submerged. I've never been to Europe, you know, and most of our accounts are there. I must trust the opinions of others.'

'Does the business prosper?'

'Famously. But I'm worried. If this war talk continues . . .'

'I don't think it will stop. Up north many people believe that war with England is inevitable.'

'Wrong decisions, Jakob, are never inevitable. A wise man can always turn back from a precipice.'

'Are you telling me—you, a Van Doorn—that we Boers must not fight when an enemy wants to steal our lands and oppress us?'

'What oppression?' He almost laughed as he spoke.

Jakob had no opportunity to pursue the matter, because young Coenraad saw his cousin's visit as an opportunity to unravel the mysteries of the Van Doorns in South Africa, and before Jakob knew what was happening, a large sheet of white paper was laid down before him, with names and lines indicating the various members of the family: 'Willem and Marthinus in the 1600s I have. It's the next generation that confuses us, isn't that right, Florrie?' His wife came to sit with the two men, explaining from the chart how the two sons of Marthinus had separated, one to father the Trianon wine-makers, the other to go out into the veld to form the Vrymeer line. 'But what was your ancestor's name?' Coenraad asked.

Without having the family Bible at hand, Jakob could not trace his line so far back: 'My great-grandfather was a trekboer called Mal Adriaan. There's something they say . . . he discovered Vrymeer. His father may have been the one who left Trianon, but I don't recall his name.'

'That must have been Hendrik. Who was your grandfather?'

'A famous fighter. They called him Lodevicus the Hammer. He had two or three wives. One was a Wilhelmina, I believe. My mother died only last year. Aletta, eighty-one years old; I think her maiden name was Probenius.'

Carefully Coenraad drew in the lines, making estimates to account for the lost generations. It was a spotty genealogy they constructed, detailed in the case of the Trianon Van Doorns, inaccurate regarding the trekkers.

'But we are cousins,' Coenraad said expansively. 'That much we know.' When Jakob tried again to bring up the question of volunteering during the forthcoming war, the wine-maker laughed easily and cut him off: 'No one at Trianon wants war. We have no quarrel with the English.' And when Jakob started to argue that no Afrikaner would ever be spiritually free till the English were subdued, Coenraad drew his children to his side of the table so that they could inspect the diagram of their family, and said firmly, 'That'll be your war, Jakob, not ours.' And he would permit no further discussion.

In September 1899 England began moving troops up to the Orange River and ordering home regiments and units from other colonies to reinforce the Cape and Natal garrisons. The two Boer republics loaded their arsenals also, importing Mausers from Krupp's and long-range guns for the State Artillery, their only regular military organization. Late in the month the word went out to the commandos: 'Opsaal, burghers!' And when the Boers were told to saddle up, they knew that danger was at hand.

One of the first to respond at Vrymeer was Micah Nxumalo: 'Baas, the Kaffirs at Groenkop, they got ponies. You want me to see if they're any good?'

Jakob nodded. 'What will those Kaffirs do in the war?'

'Nothing, Baas. Sit in their kraals and talk.'

The Groenkop blacks were a small group who occupied a valley far to the north; some of their people worked for Boers, but they had never entirely surrendered their tribal roots the way Nxumalo had done. They were, of course, part of the Boer republics, but no one took much notice of these pockets of blacks so long as they 'behaved' themselves. This would not be their war.

'Will your older boy be riding with us?' Van Doorn asked.

'No. He stay with his mother. I go with you, Baas.'

It never occurred to Micah that he had an option in this matter; if war came, he would naturally ride with the Venloo Commando. His affection for Van Doorn and his respect for the old general would dictate that.

Next morning Paulus de Groot came over to Vrymeer; he and Sybilla had left their miserable house and would stay with the Van Doorns until decisions were reached. His only concern was whether the Venloo men would keep him as leader of their commando, and when Jakob said, 'Of course they will. You were a general at Majuba,' he replied with some anxiety, 'With a commando, you never know. The burghers of Venloo will make up their own minds.'

In each district a new commandant was elected every five years, and because of his heroics at Majuba, De Groot had won the post every time, but save for a few Kaffir raids and the rout of Dr. Jameson's invaders, there had been eighteen years of peace, and there were a dozen young men claiming that they would be better at fighting the English.

De Groot and Van Doorn rode in to Venloo to meet with two hundred and sixty-seven other men who comprised the commando. They were a tough lot, burghers mostly in their thirties, but anywhere between sixteen and sixty, with De Groot the oldest, ignoring his seven years past normal retirement. They met at the church, but not in it, for they were many and each wanted his say. Under the big trees, in the shade, these men of the Boer nation discussed the looming war.

'We beat them at Majuba,' De Groot said, eager to establish his credentials early, 'and we'll donder them again. With these!' And he held up a Mauser. A wagonload of guns had arrived from Pretoria, and they were handed out.

The new weapons caused much excitement, and there was so much free firing that the war almost ended for three burghers who got in the way of the fusillades. But the problem of who would lead remained unsettled, and this was of grave importance for a commando. Tonight it had two hundred and sixty-nine members; tomorrow it might have four hundred or, if things went poorly, it could relapse into a veldkornetcy with less than a hundred fighters. It all depended upon how the war was progressing, conditions in Venloo, and what the burghers thought of their leader.

The law said that every male citizen had to serve when summoned, unless officially excused. The commandant-general, his assistant-generals and the combat commanders laid down the regulations, but the Boers had lost none of their independent Voortrekker spirit, nor their disregard for meddlesome authority. They might be ordered to serve in a commando, and Oom Paul might have a law which said they would be thrown in jail if they refused, but once they were in the saddle, they would recognize their leader only as chief among equals.

If he made one serious mistake, half his troops might ride off in disgust, and even if he were continuously brilliant, his burghers still might go home if they grew sick of the war or apprehensive about its outcome. Also, every fighting man considered himself free to quit the commando he was in and transfer to another, if he liked its fighting style better or considered its leader more apt to win his battles.

It was crucial, therefore, to select the right man at the beginning, and one burgher said, 'Naturally, we would want you to carry on as commandant, De Groot, a former general and all. But you're an old man now, and I doubt you could stand the chases.'

'He can ride better than me,' Jakob said.

'We need someone who can think quickly,' another said. 'You know, the English are going to throw their best generals into this fight.'

It was uncertain whether this speaker was for old Paulus or against him, but before he could clarify his statement, another said warmly, 'If De Groot did so well at Majuba, and when the Uitlander raiders came . . .'

'I think he's too old.'

Without a vote having been taken, it seemed that sentiment ran something like 180–89 in favor of the old man, but one of the complainants said with some force, 'This won't be Majuba or untrained Uitlanders. We need someone young, with strength in the saddle.'

The commando decided not to vote that night, but to think some more about the touchy problem; each burgher was convinced that war with England was only days away, that it would be demanding, and that they must have the best leader possible.

Some of the men wished to consult with Jakob, since he had been to both Cape Town and Pretoria: 'How does it look with the Boers at the Cape?'

'I found three boys who'll be cleaning their rifles tonight. But we can forget about real help from the south. They will not fight. Say they'll win their war on the floor of their Parliament, and that we're wasting our time with commandos.'

'Verdomp! We'll show them. God alone knows, we'll show the whole damn world, too.'

'Tell me, Van Doorn,' a thoughtful burgher asked. 'Who do you want as commandant?'

'We already have one—Paulus. He's a true leader.'

They left it at that, and De Groot slept that night at the Van Doorns'; before going to bed he said fervently, 'I would like to serve, Jakob. I have ideas about how to handle the English.'

'We'll have to wait and see. A lot of them think you're too old.'

'I am,' De Groot conceded quickly. 'But I'm the one with ideas.'

Next morning the burghers resumed discussion, and sentiment swung strongly to a vigorous young man who farmed east of Vrymeer, but someone pointed out that he was always talking about how clever the Hollanders in Pretoria were and how the Boers could learn some culture from them. That finished him, for while most Boers supported Oom Paul in anything he did, they distrusted the Amsterdam clique around him, the hundreds who had been imported to serve in the Boer government. Some Venloo men said, 'The damned Hollanders are almost as bad as the Uitlanders.'

The vote was taken that afternoon, and old Paulus de Groot was retained as commandant, 201–68, grudgingly by some, who mumbled,

'We wanted someone younger. But we'll give you a chance.' All he said
was 'Get your saddles ready.'

At Vrymeer the old man gathered everyone in the farmhouse
kitchen, and with his hands resting on the ancient Van Doorn Bible, he
said, 'When God chooses a people to do His work, He places on that
people many demands, but in our response He watches over us and always brings us victory. Sybilla, are you ready?' The old woman, her
hair drawn tight across her head, nodded. 'Sara, will you guard the farm
and the children?' The younger woman nodded, bringing her young son
closer to her side. 'Girls, will you defend this home against the Englishmen, if they come?'

'We will,' the twins said gravely, but Johanna, the older girl, merely
nodded.

'Then your father and I can go to war with easy hearts. Let us pray,'
and in the farmhouse, so far removed from conflict, the eight farm people bowed their heads and clasped their hands:

> 'Almighty God, we know that You have called us to this battle.
> We know that as Your chosen people we must obey the covenant
> You handed down to us. We are Your instrument in bringing
> Your kingdom into being on this earth, and we submit ourselves
> to Your care. Bring us the victory You gave us in the past.'

On the morning of October 7 word reached Venloo that their commando was to depart immediately for the Natal border, but not to cross
it until formal commencement of hostilities: 'You can stand with the
forefeet of your ponies touching enemy territory.' So the Venloo Commando formed up, and rode south.

This commando consisted of two hundred and sixty-nine Boers,
each mounted on a sturdy pony which he supplied. Since each man
dressed in whatever clothes he deemed appropriate for an extended stay
in the field, the file looked more like a rabble than an army company.
Some men wore heavy brown corduroys, some black, a few white. Most
wore vests, unbuttoned, and about half had heavy coats of a wild variety. They wore veldskoen, heavy homemade field shoes of softened
leather. The only item of clothing or equipment in which there was the
slightest standardization was the hat: most of the men preferred the
slouching Boer hat, which made them look like disgruntled sheepdogs.
But even hats weren't uniform, for some men chose bowlers, tweed caps

or almost any other available headgear. Behind them came some forty blacks, all mounted, leading twenty or thirty spare ponies.

What made the Venloo Commando unforgettable were the units front and rear. Ahead of his troops rode General Paulus de Groot, sixty-seven years old, big, hefty in chest and belly, bearded, wearing the uniform that had distinguished him at Majuba: a formal frock coat with silver buttons and a tall black top hat. The side of this hat was decorated with a small republican flag embroidered by Sybilla with the words: VIR GOD! VIR LAND! VIR JUSTISIE! His official rank was Commandant, but no one addressed him as anything but General.

At the rear, behind the blacks and the remounts, came the wagons containing the sixteen wives who would accompany their men to the front. Undisputed leader among them was Sybilla de Groot, sixty-four years old, who said, 'I must go with my man in his war against that woman across the sea.'

This was typical of the Boer army, little disciplined, less organized, paid not at all, but well able to live off the land it fought for, with a Mauser and six legs for each man, because everyone was mounted. Its task: to defeat the combined armies of the British Empire.

Ostensible blame for launching the Anglo-Boer War of 1899 was visible for all the world to see. At five o'clock on the afternoon of October 9 the Boer republics drafted an ultimatum which threw into the face of the British government demands of such an uncompromising nature that no self-respecting major power could possibly have accepted them.

Early in the morning of 10 October 1899 these demands were presented officially to the British cabinet, who reacted with surprise and delight: 'They've done it! They've given us a cast-iron case. They stand before the world as the aggressors.' That night the British government rejected the ultimatum, and when news of this reaction reached Pretoria on the afternoon of October 11, war officially began, and troops from both sides swung into action. A handful of rural Boers had brazenly challenged the might of an empire.

But the real cause of the war was much more complex than an exchange of cablegrams over demands for arbitration and troop withdrawals. It involved the same forces that had caused General de Groot's storming of Majuba in 1881, and those which had urged Cecil Rhodes to support the invasion of the Transvaal in 1895. The English wanted to control all of southern Africa in one grand union of states and peoples; the Boers wanted the freedom to conduct their own governments off to one side without interference from London. The English took up the case of the Uitlanders on the Golden Reef. The Boers saw these fortune-seekers as a threat to their way of life. These interests conflicted, aroused animosities, and inevitably goaded the two nations into combat.

If the Boers had not declared war on October 11, the English would probably have done so within a few days. The sanest judgment that can be passed on the genesis of this terrible war between two groups of friends is that it was the result of imperiousness on the English side and intransigence on the Boer.

Like rivulets wandering across a plain, coalescing at last to form a river, the various commandos heading toward Natal came together to create a Boer army. In time it contained some seventeen thousand men, and when they were assembled for the drive into English territory, old Commandant-General Joubert, in charge, decided to hold a review in honor of Oom Paul's birthday to inspirit the troops and put them in a military frame of mind, so while he sat astride his horse to take the salute, the commandos galloped past, each man executing what he called a salute in the distinctive style he favored. Some doffed their big hats; some merely touched the brim with a finger; some yelled Boer fighting words; some nodded; a few shook their own hands and grinned; and some made no other gesture than a wink. But each man signified that he was ready.

They galloped into Natal, prepared to sweep gloriously down to the Indian Ocean, capture Durban at the end of their ride, and deprive the English of a port through which to bring the reinforcements already on their way from London. General de Groot, with his Venloo Commando, tried to keep near the front of the advance, for he wished to lead the gallop down to the sea.

Two heavily garrisoned towns obstructed the path of the Boers as they entered Natal—Dundee and Ladysmith—and it was De Groot's urgent advice that they be by-passed: 'Give me a handful of commandos, we'll dash direct to Durban.' Had he been allowed to do this, he would have prevented English ships from landing reinforcements, and then, as he growled, 'Without supplies, the garrisons will wither up here and we can pluck them when we will.'

But the commandant-general felt that orderliness required that he capture these two strong points: 'We can't have thousands of English troops in our rear, can we?' De Groot insisted that his charging raid to the seaport might win the war, but he was silenced with a stern command: 'Take your burghers toward Ladysmith. You'll do your fighting there.'

So while thousands of Boers peeled off for the attack on Dundee, where the English commanding general was to be mortally wounded while his troops fled south, the Venloo Commando had to swing west, abandon the brilliant concept of a dash to the sea, and make for the hills overlooking Ladysmith.

The town acquired this remarkable name because of the exploits of a dashing young officer, Sir Harry Smith, who made his historic ride from Cape Town to the defense of Grahamstown back in 1835. He captivated the imagination of the local population. Later he returned to Cape Town as governor, and was enthusiastically welcomed by 'my children,' as he called the Boers and blacks. But just in case the Xhosa had any dream of re-creating the troubles they had caused him, he summoned two thousand to meet him, with their chiefs. Mounted on his horse Aliwal, he held in his right hand a brass-headed wand signifying peace, and in his left, a sergeant's stick representing war.

The chiefs were ordered to step forward and touch the wand or the stick, indicating the course they wished to follow. Peace was the victor, but at a price: 'Now, to show that you submit to me and my Great White Queen, you will kiss my foot.' They did, whereupon Sir Harry shook their hands and reported: 'We have secured permanent peace.' Alas, only three years later his Xhosa children invaded the frontier yet again, and once more he had to repulse them.

Sir Harry also had his troubles with the Voortrekkers who crossed the Orange River, but the dashing governor and his lovely Spanish wife continued to enjoy such adulation that the people named a series of towns after them: Harrismith; Aliwal, honoring his victory over the Sikhs at that place in India; and two different towns named Ladysmith, one of which Paulus de Groot and his Boers were about to invest.

Late on the second afternoon of the ride toward Ladysmith, a violent thunderstorm broke, making De Groot's drenched burghers curse as they pushed through the torrent. He rode up front with Van Doorn, head pulled in toward chest, a bitter anger darkening his face. 'Every step this horse takes,' he grumbled, 'we're farther away from the route to the sea. Damnit, Jakob! Even if we do reach Ladysmith in good order, we'll have to wait for the rest to catch up before we can attack.' Then he voiced his real complaint: 'We're missing the battles.'

He was mistaken. Two Boer scouts raced back and cried through the pelting rain, 'Die Engelese! They're fighting our men just beyond those gullies.'

'We join them!' De Groot shouted as he spurred his horse. The commando plunged into the eroded rift in the veld, ponies slipping and sliding in the quagmire, then struggling up the opposite side. They came out on the edge of a vast plain, but the rain cut visibility; through a small telescope De Groot could barely discern a company of Boers, far distant. To his dismay, they seemed to be retreating: 'Where in hell are they going? To the Transvaal?' Without waiting for an answer, he headed directly toward the fighting.

The Venloo burghers were thus projected into an experience which would go far in determining General de Groot's future actions. To begin with, their scouting had been inadequate: the two young fellows sent forward miscalculated the capacity of the enemy force, encouraging the Boer contingent to advance too rapidly, ill-prepared for the shock the English were about to deliver. Boer losses had already been heavy and the retreat was general.

De Groot judged that swift movement on his part might halt the rout, but as his men approached, the English commander unleashed a unit which up to now had been held in reserve: four hundred lancers roared onto the plain, sweeping toward the confused Boers. When they spotted the arrival of the Venloo Commando, half the force broke away and came directly at the new target.

The Boers rarely charged an enemy on horseback; they usually dismounted, tied their ponies, and fought on foot. Nor did they like the idea of one white man stabbing at another with bayonets and lances; to them, decent warfare permitted only bullets, with stabbing a savage tactic resorted to by Zulu and Xhosa. But now here came the English cavalry, galloping like fiends across the open space, their lances flashing in the sunlight that broke through the clouds.

It was a dreadful affray, those huge horses coming at the Boers, those long, sharp lances jabbing at the disorganized burghers caught unprepared in the open. Van Doorn narrowly escaped when a lance smacked into his saddle, jarring his pony to a deathly stop and tossing him to the ground. Luckily, he made it on foot to some rocks, but watched as a score of his fellow Boers were cut down. Because of the nature of a cavalry charge—fifteen, twenty, forty mounted men thundering one behind another along a single path—any Boer who was struck by one lance was apt to be hit by a dozen others, so that a dead body could be riddled.

The Venloo Commando was broken and scattered, which encouraged the Englishmen to launch a second and third charge. On and on they came, yelling and shouting and spewing obscenities; Van Doorn heard one young officer cry, 'What a glorious pig-sticking!' His khaki uniform was splattered with blood; this was a grand battue all over again, a wild and savage slaughter.

Aside from the group of rocks in which Jakob hid, along with five others, there was no cover for any Boers who lost their ponies, so the razor-sharp lances were free to pick them off at will as they ran screaming across the veld. Some of the commando did manage to escape on their ponies, and these closed ranks with De Groot; their rapid fire from the saddle diverted the English cavalry from destroying trapped men like Van Doorn, but nothing could stop the butchery of the Venloo men.

At last the victorious lancers withdrew, having lost only a handful of their men; but when ashen-faced Van Doorn inspected the blood-stained veld he found more than seventy Boers slain, most with more than six deep gashes in their bodies; one young fellow caught in the full path of the first and third charges had been punctured eighteen times. When De Groot saw this lad—the one who had dared to dance with Sybilla, who had kissed Johanna van Doorn in the barn—and witnessed the obscene manner in which he had been stabbed, he stood over his young fighter and swore an oath: 'I will destroy the English cavalry.'

He got his first chance during the ensuing battle for Ladysmith. Having learned his lesson, he used the best scouts available: Micah Nxumalo and two other blacks, who reported accurately the movements of the English cavalry. He moved his commando as close to the lancers' position as he could, praying that they would accept the bait he was about to throw before them: 'They'll never catch us in the open again. But let the swine think they can eat us up like they did before.'

Like an old and practiced spider, he spun his web. On five successive days he changed his guard an hour before dusk, instructing his men to walk from their posts slowly, as if weary from the November heat. Replacements were to arrive tardily and to appear listless. Six men or seven were to be visible between the tents, and there was to be desultory movement. Everything was to look like a poorly managed Boer camp, and for five days absolutely nothing happened. So he prolonged the drill, inventing new pieces of activity which would help create the illusion, and on the eleventh day the English cavalry came out again, with nearly two hundred men.

The roles given the forward actors were perilous indeed, for the thundering cavalry was allowed right into the heart of the encampment, with enough Boers running distraught to maintain the illusion, and these must be adroit enough to escape death from the stabbing lances. Two failed, and with great cries of triumph, the cavalrymen hacked them to death.

But when the sortie had passed through the camp, it found itself enfiladed not only by the survivors of the Venloo Commando but also by one hundred burghers from the Carolina contingent borrowed for this occasion, and from those grim Boers came a withering crossfire, aimed not at the lancers but at their horses. And as the beasts went down or ran wild in fury, Boer marksmen calmly shot any surviving cavalrymen. Only those who surrendered instantly were spared, and not all of them.

The Englishmen who made it through the fusillade regrouped at the far end of the camp and wanted to speed back to save their grounded comrades, and some daring horsemen tried, but when they were mowed down by concentrated rifle fire, their companions realized that this day's battle was over. In a wide sweep they galloped away from the laager, returning to Ladysmith a sadly depleted force.

There was other bad news for the English. After the fall of Dundee, many thousands of Boer horsemen had been released to join the assault on Ladysmith, and when the English infantry marched out to give battle, they were sorely thrashed, the Boers capturing more than nine hundred prisoners. This meant that henceforth the troops in the town must stay on the defensive. The English could hold on, but they could not swing over to the attack.

It was a notable victory for the Boers, but at the moment of triumph a fatal weakness manifested itself: the Boer generals began squabbling among themselves. Paulus de Groot, epitome of the daring commando leader, repeated his request to ignore stalemated Ladysmith and gallop south in wide, swinging raids, dashing right into Durban before reinforcements could be landed, but other commandants, who were frightened at the idea of leaving a redoubt in English hands, insisted that brash De Groot stay with them, help them mount a siege, and gradually wear away the English defenders.

'We must strike while we're free!' De Groot pleaded.

'Paulus,' the old commandant-general said, 'if God extends a finger to us in this great victory, we mustn't grab for His entire hand. He would not like it if you galloped off to Durban.' De Groot was ordered to remain, to dig in, and passively watch the English in Ladysmith.

That night he met with his veldkornets. 'I am sorely worried. Commandos were born to move, we should be galloping south.' When no one spoke, tears came to his eyes. 'I can see us roaring into Durban. Taking the port. Throwing the English back into the sea.' Still no one spoke. 'Once we let them land, they'll be like bulldogs. They'll never let go.' The Venloo men knew he was right, but they had their orders and there was nothing they could say, and again tears trickled down his beard. 'We sit here tonight, losing the war.'

Then came exhilarating news which assured the Boers that victory was still within their grasp: Boers on all the other fronts had won stunning victories, which encouraged De Groot to urge once more a dash to the sea that would end the war. This time permission was granted, but he was forestalled by precisely what he had feared: thousands of English troops had sailed into Durban harbor and were already entraining for the north. This mighty force would quickly lift the siege of Ladysmith and go on to destroy the Boers.

The preponderance of power would rapidly become so overwhelming—five, sometimes ten well-armed professional soldiers against one fighting Boer, ten heavy guns to one—that the Anglo-Boer War should have ended well before Christmas. In this opinion all the foreign military experts concurred.

It was the custom in these years for any army in the field to invite uniformed observers from friendly nations to march with it, observe its performance, and report to their own headquarters the quality of this army's fighting men. German officers rode with the Boers, and French and Russian and some South Americans, while the same nations sent other officers to report on the English.

At the end of 1899 these cautious experts concluded that despite initial Boer victories, the English on the Natal front would rather quickly lift the siege of Ladysmith and then, in an orderly fashion, bring in so many troops through Durban that victory was assured. But in early 1900, after an opportunity to assess the remarkable general London had dispatched to do the job, they became confused.

Said the German observer in his cable to Berlin: 'With this man the English will be lucky to win in four years.'

But the French major wired in code to Paris: 'He's the type who, gives the enemy much trouble, the traditional English bulldog who holds on with every muscle in his body.'

Wrote the Russian: 'If this man is what the English War Office considers a general, I suggest you terminate our proposals for a military treaty with England.'

But the American reported: 'Do not underestimate him. He's the type of general who holds the British Empire together. The Boers will defeat him six times in a row, then realize with dismay that he has won the seventh, and final, battle.'

Sir Redvers Buller, scion of the noble family that had given King Henry VIII two of his queens, Anne Boleyn and Catherine Howard, was sixty years old, something over two hundred and forty pounds in weight, and chairbound at headquarters for the past eleven years. His appointment as commander-in-chief of the English effort in South Africa had been bitterly opposed by one faction in the War Office and the cabinet, somewhat tepidly supported by another faction that wanted a no-nonsense man in the field. He himself, when he heard of his impending selection, wanted to avoid it, judging himself to be inadequate, for he had never commanded a full army, but in the end he had accepted on the sensible grounds cited by many another man called to assume major responsibilities: 'I'm as good as any of the others.'

Prior to embarking on his great adventure, he had the bad luck to make an observation which would haunt him: 'I doubt I shall have to do much fighting against the Boers in the field. My only fear is that everything may be ended before I get there.'

But as his ship neared Cape Town, a passing vessel moved close, and without stopping, hung out a huge blackboard with alarming news about the confusion on the Natal front, so that when Buller reached Africa he was a much-sobered man, determined to do his bulldog best.

The troopship put into Cape Town about an hour after dusk on 30 October 1899, in a driving rain. Since this was too late for a gala entrance, the passengers slept fitfully while those ashore prepared to greet the man they relied on to protect them from the rampaging Boers.

Early next morning Cape Town was aflutter with excitement, thousands of citizens having gathered at the docks to greet their hero. Gangways threaded with ribbons led to the ship's deck, where a monstrous cinematograph was being worked by four men in cloth caps: the arrival of the great man would be recorded in motion pictures. Bands played, little girls carried flowers, every government official was present, and a bishop offered prayer.

Precisely at nine in the morning trumpets sounded, drums rolled, and Sir Redvers Buller stepped forth to command the war effort in Africa. He was of medium height, with an enormous belly, and had a strange head which once seen could never be forgotten. It was shaped like an eggplant, heavy and triple-chinned at the bottom, rising almost to a point at the top. His small eyes almost touched at the bridge of a very large nose, which guarded a huge, bushy mustache that smothered his weak upper lip. As if he sought to accentuate the odd shape of his head, he favored a small, tight military hat with a long visor that obscured his vision.

When he spoke, his one conspicuous asset manifested itself: his voice rumbled with deep, masculine authority, but what it said was rarely understood, for a rambunctious horse had kicked out his front teeth. An irreverent Capetowner, startled by Buller's appearance, whispered, 'He looks like a distressed walrus,' but a reserve officer who knew Buller's record for extreme bravery replied, 'Sir, you are wrong. He looks like John Bull.'

General Buller proceeded directly to Government House, where he was briefed on the shocking prospects facing the English forces, for as the local officer explained: 'We are threatened on two fronts. On the west our troops are besieged at Mafeking and the diamond town of Kimberley. On the east they can't break out of Ladysmith. And we hear rumors that the Cape Afrikaners are about to rise in rebellion.'

So instead of occupying a relaxed position in Cape Town and directing his subordinate generals to dash this way and that, subduing the obstreperous Boers, Buller was faced with the awesome necessity of splitting his army into two parts and taking field command of one of them. 'I'll need time to study this,' he said, and forthwith he established his headquarters in a small house on a side street; for his living quarters he chose rooms in the Mount Nelson Hotel, and early one morning a tall, handsome man in a newly purchased uniform of major in the local corps knocked on his door.

To provide Buller with maximum support, Her Majesty's government in Cape Town had scurried about to find some young man with strong business experience to serve as economic liaison, and upon the advice of several older men, Frank Saltwood was chosen.

The men who selected him for this important post advised: 'You must find out as much about Buller as you can. Always helpful to know how a man's mind works.' For the past two weeks Frank had been doing just that, and like the military observers at the front, he was getting conflicting reports.

'Most important,' an English official said, 'he's of noble lineage. Duke of Norfolk, and all that. True gentleman, but of the rough sort.'

An English military man said, 'Enjoys the absolute confidence of the General Staff. Good Old Buller, they call him. He's welcomed at court, and Queen Victoria rather dotes on him.'

But it was a South African of Dutch-Huguenot descent who contributed the first important bit of information: 'Never forget that against the Zulu in 1879 he won the Victoria Cross. Bravery beyond description. Just set his jaw and walked right through enemy fire to rescue a group of wounded men. A man of extreme bravery. Proved it again in Egypt.'

The encomiums continued, explaining why he had been selected and constructing the portrait of the classic English general, and it was not until the third or fourth day that nagging details began to surface. One enlisted English soldier told Saltwood, 'You must remember, for the past eleven years it's been mostly chair duty for that one.'

Another soldier who had seen Buller at the War Office in London contributed: 'He's past sixty, I think, and gotten frightfully fat. Must have weighed eighteen stone when I saw him.'

A major newly arrived said, 'Only hearsay, but I believe the Staff was sharply divided about accepting him. Some wanted younger, harder drivers like Kitchener or Allenby. Others wanted trusted older men like Lord Roberts. There was grave suspicion that Buller might not be up to the challenge.'

'Then why was he chosen?' Saltwood asked, scribbling rapidly to keep up with the flow of words.

'It was the general impression,' the newcomer said, 'that he was a good fellow who deserved a shot at high command.' He coughed, then added, 'He's never led an army, you know.'

'Why would they give such a man so important a job?'

'Well, he had been around a long time and it was his turn.'

A young Englishman who knew considerable about his country's military system, and who was obviously perplexed by the appointment of Buller, said reflectively, 'It just occurred to me. Take all the leading generals assigned to this campaign. Not one has ever led his troops against an enemy that wore shoes.'

This extraordinary statement produced a thoughtful silence, broken by Saltwood, who asked, pen still in hand, 'What do you mean?'

'They've fought barefooted Afghans, and barefooted Egyptians, and barefooted Sindi. "Shoulder-to-shoulder, men, and drive the pagan blighters back to the hills." I know nothing about the Boers, but I believe they wear shoes.'

'They do,' a South African conceded. 'But essentially they're a rabble. Buller should have no trouble with them.'

'But a rabble with shoes,' the young Englishman warned.

It was an older English officer who gave Saltwood the most helpful information: 'I knew him in England, after his days of glory in the field. He had only two objectives. Build the best army possible. Do everything to protect the welfare of the troops. I'm told in recent letters that he wasn't the unanimous choice of either the War Office or the cabinet, but he was a good choice. He had many Boers in his unit when he fought out here against the Zulu. He'll respect them.'

It was with this body of conflicting opinions that Frank Saltwood approached Buller's room that October morning, and before he had been with the general two minutes, he realized that all his research had been useless. Frank's major problem was understanding what the general was saying, for he had trouble pronouncing words because of his missing teeth, and those he did say were often lost in his mustache. Frank wondered if he had heard the opening words correctly.

'Glad to have you, young fellow. What I mean . . . hhmmph . . . you're to fetch me an iron tub.'

'Did you say iron tub, sir?'

'What I mean, if I have to go to the front meself. Man must have his bath, what?'

'You mean a tub to carry with you, sir?'

'Yes, damnit, what I mean, a man can't go dirty on bivouac, can he?'

He also wanted a mobile kitchen so large that it would require an entire wagon and eight mules. He wanted a feather bed with extra blankets: 'Don't want the cold to impede us, do we, hhmmph?' After a whole morning of this, in which Saltwood jotted down enough items to fill a small store, the general asked abruptly, 'How far to Stellenbosch?'

'The train might get you there and back in a day. But there are no troops, enemy or . . .'

'Damn. Well, you know, in London and all that.'

Saltwood was quite lost until Buller mumbled, 'Trianon, you know. One of the really good wines of the world. I shall want fifty dozen of their best sparkling wine.'

'That would be six hundred bottles, sir.'

'Six hundred is what I want.'

That would require an extra wagon and eight more horses, but when Frank demurred a second time, Buller raged at him, showing the force which had made him a general to be feared: 'Damnit, man, this is a campaign, don't you know? Out in the field. Months on end, perhaps. Man wants his comforts.'

Saltwood was to find that this phrase had specific meanings for Buller, because by the close of the second day he had encouraged his staff to fill the empty rooms at the Mount Nelson with the choicest free ladies of Cape Town, and with them on the scene, there was considerable revelry. On the third day Saltwood said, 'Sir, the officers want to consult with you. You're aware, I presume, that the fighting is not going well?'

Saltwood was astonished by what happened next; it was as if a magician had waved a military wand, transforming this big, bumbling man into a tough-minded soldier. Buller stiffened, and with the riding crop he kept in his quarters, indicated a top-secret binder: 'I have me orders. Before I left London the wizards planned me entire campaign. Spelled out everything I was to do.' He rapped the folder twice, not arrogantly, but in a gesture of dismissal: 'And every plan they made was wrong. It doesn't apply, not with those damned Boers . . . My word, they can move fast, those Boers.'

'What are you going to do, sir?'

Buller rose, moved about his suite, then stopped and stared out the window at the confusing land he was supposed to conquer. Turning abruptly to face his new assistant, he said, 'Prepare to spend a long time in the field. I've got to do exactly the opposite of what they order.' He shoved the War Office directives aside. 'I'm splitting me troops. Half to Kimberley to rescue them up there. You and I will be going to Ladysmith.'

He made this bold move to inspire the troops, but as a member of the clique opposed to him said, 'He did inspire the troops, but the wrong ones.' And in London a wag circulated the rumor that the Boer high command had issued an order: 'Anyone who shoots General Buller will be court-martialed. He's our strongest weapon.'

Frank Saltwood, watching closely every move he made, believed at first that the critics and the comics were correct. Redvers Buller was an ass.

The Tugela River is that lovely stream which marked the southern limit of King Shaka's Zululand, and along which Piet Retief's people had waited while he and his men marched to their death at Dingane's Kraal. When these waiting women and children were slaughtered a few days later, their blood ran into the Tugela. Now, at a small hill far upstream, Spion Kop (Lookout Hill), General Redvers Buller was about to conduct a campaign which suggested that the German observer had been correct when he added to his first report: 'When you first meet Buller you instinctively like him. A real soldier. But when you study what he actually does in battle, you shudder.'

The town of Ladysmith was still under siege. Resolute Englishmen, lacking food, medicine, fire power, horses and sleep, protected the town against encircling forces. All England, which received telegrams direct from the town, wanted these brave defenders rescued, so when General Buller joined his massive army below the Tugela, he found himself less than fifteen miles from Ladysmith, with overwhelming superiority, twenty-one thousand against forty-five hundred, and he dispatched an unfortunate heliographed message to the besieged troops: 'Will rescue you within five days.'

There were two difficulties: he had to cross the river, and once that was done, his men would have to run a gauntlet through a chain of small hills. As the German observer reported later: 'He might have accomplished either of these tasks if faced alone, but to require him to meet both of them at once posed a problem so complex that he seemed quite unable to grapple with it.'

Buller sat on the south side of the Tugela for five days, pondering the difficulties, finally telling Saltwood, 'A frontal attack would be quite impossible. Never break through there, eh, Frank? We face a long, hard fight.'

'You said in England that it would be over before you got here.'

'Would have been, if the other chaps had done their job. Now we've got to mop up.'

He worked night after night, going over and over his plans, but after he had swilled most of a bottle of Trianon, his eyes, already almost touching at the corners, seemed to come together, at which times he would drift away from battlefield problems and discourse on his theories of parade-ground military combat: 'Keep the shoulders touching, move forward in line, don't fire too soon, and the ruddy bastards will never stand up against an English march.'

'With the Boers, it's mostly cavalry, sir,' Saltwood reminded him.

'Don't like the cavalry. Never know where the devils will be going next. Give me foot soldiers every time.'

Sometimes late at night, when he was well under, he would grow sentimental: 'Worst thing ever happened to the English soldier, they put him in this damned olive-drab. Said it made him less a target. I say it killed his spirit. In Egypt you had six hundred gallant lads in bright red, marching in the sun. By gad, it struck terror, that's what it did. It struck terror.'

He never referred to his own bravery, which had been considerable, in all theaters of war, but if someone pressed him about his V.C., he would say, 'There's a job to be done, you press forward. No need to give a man medals. That's his job.'

After all his sound deliberations on the folly of a frontal assault on a river and a chain of hills, General Buller changed his mind on the eve of battle and elected to do precisely that. 'We'll roll back the Boers and lift the siege of Ladysmith,' he told Saltwood triumphantly, and as if the deed were done, he sent another heliogram assuring the defenders that he would be there within five days—with plenty of food.

With a shockingly inadequate map of the area and incomplete scouting sorties, he threw his men against the Boers, who stayed north of the river and picked them off in isolated batches. His fifteen-pounders, inspirited by the idea of the daring dash into the face of an enemy, rashly moved far ahead of their supporting infantry and were isolated. Rescue attempts failed and the guns were captured by the enemy, a loss of more than half the army's field artillery. By nightfall one hundred and forty English soldiers were killed, to the Boer's forty, and more than a thousand were wounded or missing. In dismay and confusion, General Buller ordered his first retreat from the Tugela and afterward dispatched one of the more shameful telegrams of military history.

Ordering the heliographer to his tent, he scribbled a message, which Saltwood begged him not to send: 'It will dash the hopes of the Ladysmith defenders, sir.'

'They're soldiers. They've got to know the worst.'

'But let it come upon them slowly, I beg you. Not from their own commander-in-chief.'

'Send the message!' Buller stormed, as if he were driven to prove himself an ass before the entire world, and it was sent, from an addled commander to a very brave man striving to defend a difficult position:

> It appears that I cannot relieve Ladysmith for another month, and even then, only by means of a protracted siege operation. I need time to fortify myself below the Tugela. When I'm in position I suggest you burn your ciphers, destroy your guns, fire away your ammunition, and make the best terms possible with the Boers.

A commanding general had advised one of his bravest subordinates to surrender while there was still a fighting chance to hold on. Buller himself, after a lengthy effort to pull his troops together, tried to ford the Tugela again and wound up in a second confused retreat. In desperation he told Saltwood, 'There must be a way to cross that river. I'll think of something.'

It was imperative that he do so, for the general commanding the defenses at Ladysmith had refused to surrender, and it was obligatory that Buller try once more to rescue him. Instead, in his report to London he complained that he had been repulsed at the Tugela because the Boers outnumbered him: 'They had eighty thousand in the field against me.' To this, London replied acidly: 'Suggest you check population of total Boer republics, men, women and children.'

The rebuff infuriated Buller: 'Damnit, Saltwood, back there they don't know these Boers. What I tried to tell them is that we're not fighting an army. We're fighting a nation. Men, women and children.'

With Buller ensnared, General de Groot sought permission to lead his commando on a wide sweep east of Ladysmith and deep into Natal: 'We can chop up the English supply lines.'

Permission was refused, and some of the finest horsemen in the world were held stationary to fight as unneeded foot soldiers. At the two battles of the Tugela they had conducted themselves with dignity, fighting from trenches and behind boulders, but slowly their numbers were eroding. From the original two hundred and sixty-nine, they had lost one hundred, and the waiting so irritated those remaining that more had simply gone home, leaving the commando a mere one hundred and fifty-one. De Groot was aware that unless they soon enjoyed some kind of success, even that number must diminish, and then he would be in serious trouble.

Therefore, when Christmas came, with all Boer troops still inactive, ten more Venloo men growled, 'To hell with this,' and returned home to tend their farms. De Groot was now reduced to one hundred and forty-one disconsolate men, but he was enormously encouraged when three young fellows of a different commando reported one day with the simple statement: 'Our fathers fought with you at Majuba. We'd like to join you.' It would be additions like these that would keep De Groot's commando up to strength for the major battles that lay ahead.

General Buller had been as humiliated as any general in history. His heliogram advising Ladysmith to surrender because he could think of no quick way to rescue it had been circulated to the cabinet, causing such a scandal that the War Office had to take action, and they had deprived him of the supreme command, handing it to an extraordinary man, Lord Roberts of Kandahar, approaching seventy, the hero of Afghanistan, five feet four inches tall, one hundred and twenty-three pounds in weight and blind in one eye. His chief-of-staff would be Lord Kitchener of Khartoum, and it was agreed that these two would really fight the Boers, while Good Old Buller could be left off to one side, wrestling with the Tugela River, which he had now failed twice to cross.

To compound his problems, the War Office had given him as second in command a general whom he positively detested and to whom he preferred not to speak. For Sir Charles Warren, nearing sixty, this would have to be his last command, and unless he performed with some brilliance, he could hope for no further honors, which probably did not worry him, for he had other loves, especially archaeology and the secrets of Jerusalem. He had also made an abortive run for Parliament and a more successful one for head of the London constabulary, a post he held for three years, losing it when he failed to uncover the mystery of the century: the identity of Jack the Ripper. Quietly he moved back to the army, and when war broke out he reminded everyone that he had seen much service in South Africa, had helped solve the ticklish question of who owned the diamond mines, and 'knew a thing or two about the Boers.'

Warren despised Buller, holding him to be an ass, but it was nevertheless essential that he keep close to the old general because Warren carried in his pocket a most dangerous piece of paper: it was called 'a

Dormant Commission,' and it stated that if anything should happen to Buller, or if he should fall apart, as seemed likely, Warren was to assume command. Consequently, it was in Warren's interest to see that Buller did fail.

Relieved of responsibility for the other fronts in South Africa, General Buller was free to direct all his attention to the Tugela River, and as he rode back and forth along its southern shore, pondering how best to reach the northern, he began to see that his previous attempts had been doomed because he had been heading straight for Ladysmith along roads which had to be heavily defended. What he would do would be to dash far to the west, outflank the Boers, and swing into Ladysmith in a leftward charge. With Warren's troops he again had more than twenty thousand first-class men to face a Boer force of less than eight thousand. But he had Sir Charles Warren breathing down his neck, and he still had to cross the Tugela.

A flanking movement like this required speed and deception; unfortunately, Buller surrendered both those advantages by entrusting the most important part of the campaign to the 'ex-policeman,' as he contemptuously called Warren. Sending the difficult and unreliable Warren off to the left, he moved his own sybaritic tent some twenty miles upstream, and when his feather bed and iron bathtub were in position, he astonished Saltwood and his other aides by scouting the opposite shore with his French telescope.

He did this by lying flat on his back and propping his scope on his enormous belly and toes, moving it slowly through whatever arc his position permitted, and shouting his observations to Saltwood. By now, newspapers throughout the world knew that 'General Buller is once more thinking about crossing the Tugela.'

What he saw when he lay prostrate looking through his toes were three hills perched menacingly behind the north shore of the Tugela: Hill One, nearest at hand; Hill Two in the middle; Hill Three well to the west. The plan was for Warren to move far west of Hill Three and cut the Boer line, if he ever got his land-armada across the river, with his innumerable wagons and fifteen thousand trek-oxen; this incredible train was fifteen miles long and required two days to pass a spot, even when moving sharply. Buller would then make a drive for Hill One and join up with Warren, opening the pathway to Ladysmith. A tremendous amount of staff work was done to prepare the English forces for these carefully planned moves.

At Warren's crossing point, four huge wood-fueled steam tractors had been meneuvered into position, and as they huffed and puffed, belching fire, wagons were pulled across small crevices while engineers sought low spots in the river at which pontoon bridges might be built. They isolated three such spots, and their officers chose each one in turn, abandoning it as soon as any difficulty arose. The delay was intolerable.

Saltwood had found it a memorable experience to watch these two elderly generals, Buller and Warren, go about their planning of this crucial battle, for it became apparent that in their extreme jealousy, neither was backing up the other, and each was holding his choice cards tight to his chest without permitting his colleague to see them. One of Buller's most ambitious young assistants told Frank, 'We're going to witness three great battles. Us against the Boers. Buller against Warren. And Warren against Buller.'

'Dreadful way to run a war.'

'Ah, but the last two battles will be well matched, because our two generals are of equal intelligence, somewhat higher than a mule but markedly lower than a good bird dog.'

'Buller told me yesterday we'd be ready to strike tomorrow.'

'It won't happen. General Warren has this curious fixation that armies should be allowed to get into position and face each other for three or four days. Get the feel of contest.'

'We've been trying to get the feel of it for two months now,' Frank said. 'Those poor devils in Ladysmith.'

'They've nothing to worry about. Buller heliographed them again yesterday that he'd be there within five days.'

'Any chance?' Frank asked.

'If Warren punches west through the Boer line, I'm sure we can make it. But if he swings over to Hill Two in the middle, we'll be in deep trouble.'

'Would he do such a thing?'

'With these two generals, anything can happen.'

'Tonight we should pray,' Saltwood said, and he did.

It did not help. For days Warren plodded along until Buller, who had watched helplessly since giving the man an independent command, could no longer contain his anger. Riding over to Warren's headquarters, he said gruffly, 'For God's sake, move!'

'There are thousands of Boers out there waiting.'

'There were only ten hundred when you started.'

'I've decided to go for Hill Two,' Warren said.

The young officer had been correct in his fears that these two generals would dissipate their great opportunity: the 'ex-policeman' was swinging to his right to club the Boers on Spion Kop. With incomplete orders to the troops involved, the vast plans were scrapped and whole battalions were ordered to march right when they had planned to go left. What seemed incredible then, and even more so now, they were to attack a sizable hill that no one had scouted and for which only the roughest maps existed. This error could easily have been corrected had General Buller authorized his balloonist to go aloft, for the man was a skilled observer and from twelve hundred feet, his optimum operating level, could have informed the generals of exactly what lay ahead. Buller did not hold with balloons and other such nonsense, so this invaluable tool was not used; the troops would march up Spion Kop with no concept of where they were going or what they might face when they got there.

What was worse—much worse, as it turned out—General Warren kept his headquarters far to the west, which would have been reasonable had the drive continued in that direction, while General Buller kept his far to the east, removed from everything. When Major Saltwood protested this wide separation of the two headquarters—seven miles with crude communications—Buller growled through his enormous mustache, 'It's his show. He's in charge of the troops.'

'But you're the commander-in-chief, sir.'

'Never meddle with another man's fight.'

'But it's your battle, sir.'

'It's Warren's day. He's got the finest English troops to win the battle.'

Frank wanted to cry, 'Then God save the empire.' But he did not. He rode the seven miles to General Warren's headquarters, where he arrived in time to witness an incomprehensible performance.

Warren had in his command a brilliant, headstrong cavalry leader named Lord Dundonald, a charismatic type whom the older generals distrusted, and when this fiery chap, leading fifteen hundred of the finest mounted troops, was set loose on the left flank, he launched a glorious charge which quite neutralized Hill Three and gained access to an unpatrolled road along which Warren's infantry could advance directly into Ladysmith. By this daring and gallant maneuver he opened the way to an English victory, and the younger officers were cheering when Frank reached their headquarters: 'Dundonald's done it! He said he would.'

But then Warren sprang into action. Gray with fury, he stormed into the room where the younger men were cheering and cried, 'Bring that damned fool back here. We need cavalry to protect our oxen. Let him keep a few men on his damned road, but I want the rest back here in camp!' and on the spot he deputized Major Saltwood and two others to ride posthaste after the cavalry and bring them back. 'Damned young fellows! Put them on a horse, they think they know everything.'

Saltwood, not being a member of General Warren's force, was not afraid to confront him: 'Sir, I believe Lord Dundonald should be allowed to hold the road, and we should rush men to ensure he keeps it.'

'He'll come back here, and he'll obey my orders. My God, I'll take his horsemen away from him. Insubordination.'

So Frank Saltwood had the miserable task of riding west to inform the gallant young Lord Dundonald that he was to pull back the bulk of his men. On this day Dundonald had beaten off a series of Boer patrols in savage encounters; he had won a notable victory; but now he must retreat. The burghers would win this segment of the battle without having fired a shot!

On the night of 23 January 1900 General Warren sent his men up the south face of Spion Kop; they were led by a major-general, but he was fifty-five years old, had weak legs and did not take easily to steep places, so that he had to be shoved up them by his troops. Poor man, he was soon dying from a shell fragment.

What ensued must have been orchestrated by some mad genius, because both Warren and Buller, from their separate headquarters, appointed different replacements to the vacant major-general's slot. Unfortunately, communications collapsed and no one knew who was in charge. There were, as a consequence, two British officers conducting the fight, each unaware of the other and assuming that he was in supreme command.

Two additional officers were sent in to take charge, one by Buller, one by Warren, and once again each assumed that he was in sole command. One way or another, the hill now contained four commanders leading nineteen hundred of the empire's finest, while another eighteen thousand were kept in reserve; they would be sorely needed as the terrible struggle developed, but no one would command them to march.

In grandeur General Buller sat in his tent like a sulking Achilles, out of contact with the progress of the battle and doing nothing to sort out the mess his 'ex-policeman' was getting his men into. 'It's Warren's fight,' he insisted when Saltwood galloped back from the other general's camp, begging for clarifications.

On the other hand, Buller was not loath to intervene whenever a particularly brilliant idea occurred to him, and he issued commands that would have bewildered generals as quick-minded as Hannibal and Napoleon. As for Warren, he was a fool who moved at a snail's pace, fighting a night battle on a hill he did not comprehend. Not once did he move to Spion Kop; not once did he try to see for himself the dreadful slaughter occurring there.

He issued some twenty crucial orders, half to one of his commanders on the hill, half to others battling toward it. A German observer watching this amazing battle said, 'The English army is composed of ordinary soldiers who are lions of bravery led by officers who are asses of stupidity.' And he said this before the two generals had an opportunity to display their true talents.

General de Groot chafed. Much against his counsel, his truncated commando was being held in reserve behind Spion Kop. 'We'll throw you in at the crucial moment,' he was told, but two more of his men, seeking action, had slipped away.

The scene behind the hill was extraordinary. Row after row of sleek Boer ponies stood with their halters tied to trees or rocks while their masters fought on foot up the steep hill. Some five hundred wagons huddled at a distance, field ambulances and Red Cross units outspanned among them, their oxen peacefully grazing. Near them waited the wives who had accompanied their husbands, and in one tent Sybilla de Groot tended such men as were dragged to her impromptu hospital ward. Other women helped their servants do the cooking, and from time to time everyone would stop to listen to the raging battle which was taking place less than a quarter of a mile from where they worked.

When, toward noon, General de Groot walked back through the dust to talk with his wife, the women learned that whereas the English troops had captured the top of the hill, they had placed their trench so poorly that the Boers had a good chance of taking it away from them. 'Will there be many dead?' Sybilla asked.

'A great many,' the old man said.

'Will you be going up?'

'Soon as they set us free.'

'Be careful, Paulus,' she said as he shuffled back to the hill.

It was men of the Carolina Commando, from the small town east of Venloo, who won the honors for bravery this day. They were led by Commandant Henrik Prinsloo and a short, stocky veldkornet named Christoffel Steyn, almost as thick through the belly as he was tall; when Steyn ran forward, rolling from side to side, men muttered, 'If he can do it, I can do it.' What he did was run straight through a heavy barrage to the top of Hill Three, a kopje opposite the summit of Spion Kop, where he positioned his men behind rocks so that they could fire directly into the side openings of the English trenches. This fat fellow, who had never fought before, could not believe that the highly trained English officers opposing him could have allowed him to occupy this fatal hill, but he accepted his luck and ordered his men to increase their fire into the exposed English ranks.

Whole trenches were wiped out, not a single man surviving, and of ten dead soldiers, nine had been shot not through the front of their bodies, but through the side of the head. Christoffel Steyn's men had made the difference, but they did so from a hill they should never have been able to occupy for as long as they did.

Why the ragged line of burghers was permitted to hold the strategic kopje was one of the disgraceful incidents of this battle. While eighteen thousand crack troops still remained in reserve, powerless to aid their brothers dying in such numbers on Spion Kop, a commander of the King's Royal Rifles, on his own initiative, dispatched his two finest battalions, ordering them to rush another hill opposite to the one held by Steyn. If they were successful, they could drive Steyn out with gunfire, and thus save the men on Spion Kop.

It was an impossible ascent, almost straight up, in heat of day, with Boers firing down at them from above, but these brave men, goaded by their energetic officers, somehow made it to the top, drew much of the fire away from their exposed comrades, and began to batter the Carolina burghers. It was a triumph of courage and grit, giving the English their first victory of the day.

Saltwood, witnessing the triumph, hastened to inform General Buller, but when this confused leader heard that a commander of troops had acted on his own, and had, furthermore, split his men into two groups, he fell into a fury and began to heckle his commander. At this moment a message reached Buller, warning that the Boers were in such firm control that if the King's Royal Rifles tried to cross over to Spion Kop, they would be annihilated.

'Bring them back down!' Buller fumed.

'Sir!' Saltwood objected. 'They've performed a miracle. Let them stay.'

'They should never have been split into groups.'

The commander, seeing his general in such confusion, lost all confidence in the daring action and signaled his men to climb down: 'Get off the hill! Come back immediately!' At first the men refused to believe that such a stupid order could have been issued, and one colonel refused to obey it. 'Damn them all,' he shouted, whereupon a Boer bullet struck him below the heart, killing him instantly. The retreat began.

Night fell as the beleaguered soldiers on Spion Kop watched with dismay as the King's Royal Rifles abandoned the neighboring hill. For a few more hours the officers on Spion Kop held their positions, but finally one of the finest commanders signaled a retreat. This heroic man, Colonel Thorneycroft, had been breveted general in the midst of the battle; he weighed about twenty stone—two hundred and eighty pounds —most of it hard muscle, and he was afraid of nothing. Only his courage had kept the trenches in English hands, despite the awful slaughter, but now he lost his nerve.

He led his brave men down the hill, conceding defeat, just as one of the other commanders was climbing up with fresh troops, hoping for victory. They passed in silence.

When the new commander reached the crest of Spion Kop, in darkness, he found an amazing situation: the Boers, who had faced tremendous fire that day, had decided, half an hour before General Thorneycroft began to evacuate troops down the hill, that Spion Kop could not be taken. The constant pressure of the English gunners had been more than even these Boers could absorb, and they had deserted the hill. They knew they were defeated.

In other words, two heroic armies who had fought as bravely as men could fight, had decided within fifteen minutes of each other that the day was lost. Their two retreats occupied the same moments. After deaths innumerable, Spion Kop was deserted.

The Englishman climbing up as Thorneycroft went down was the first to discover this; he was another of the four in command that tangled day, and now he had a chance to save the day for the English. All he had to do was rush back down the hill, signal his superior, General Warren, and convince him to send more troops scurrying back to the summit. Full victory rested in the hands of the English if only this officer could contact General Warren.

This could not be done. The officer framed an excellent message, calling for quick reinforcements to occupy the abandoned hill and explaining how victory was assured, but when he summoned the signalman and told him to use his night lantern to flash the good word to General Warren's headquarters, the man said, 'I have no paraffin.'

'Try the wick. It may burn. Even for one minute.'

The signalman lit his wick. It did not even sputter. For want of a thimbleful of kerosene, the fateful message was not sent. The Battle of Spion Kop was lost.

While those futile efforts were being made to get English soldiers back onto Spion Kop, on the northern side of the hill a few of the defeated Boers consulted at two in the morning concerning their fate, and as an occasional rifle shot echoed from some distant place where soldiers were nervous, they whispered in the darkness, 'General de Groot, what did you think of the battle? Could we have won?'

'I wasn't allowed in the battle. They never called for our reserve.'

'Our losses were heavy, General. But not like the English. Did you hear about the Carolina Commando? They had a clear shot, right down the English trenches. They killed everybody.'

It was another young fellow, only a boy, really, who asked the question that saved the day for the Boers: 'I was on the eastern hill when the English crawled up and took it. Why did they go back down?'

In the darkness General de Groot asked, 'You saw them go down?'

'Yes. They were very brave. One officer . . .'

'But they went back down?'

'Yes, they drove us off the hill. We lost sixteen, seventeen men. Jack Kloppers standing beside me. Right through the forehead.'

De Groot took the lad by his shoulders, pulling him into the flickering light of a small fire. 'You say they held the hill, then abandoned it?'

'Yes. Yes. I covered Jack Kloppers with a blanket and I went back to the summit. They went down and we didn't even fire at them.'

For some minutes General de Groot stood in silence, looking up at Spion Kop. Finally he said in a very low voice, 'Son, I think you and I should go back up that hill. I think that maybe God has been holding me in reserve for this moment.' He asked for volunteers, and Jakob van Doorn, of course, stepped forward.

So the three tired Boers, at two-thirty on that dark, forlorn morning, set out to climb the hill where so many had died. In front, walking faster than the others, was Paulus de Groot in top hat and frock coat.

Behind him came the lad who had occasioned this expedition, and behind, puffing heavily, came Jakob van Doorn, who had been quite content to have his commando held in reserve: death terrified him.

They climbed slowly, for there was no moon, and from time to time they trod on the face of some fallen comrade. When they approached the crest, where the fighting had been most hazardous, they stepped on many bodies, and then the old general, his hat still in place, rose upon the horizon in a position which would have been fatal had English troops been on the hill. Slowly the other two joined him, and like scouts reconnoitering some dismal field of death, they moved forward, coming to the trench where the English lads lay stacked, bullets through the sides of their heads, and all the way to the other edge of the plateau, where they could look down upon the silent camp of the enemy.

Running back to the center of the silent battlefield, where he assured himself that this miracle had taken place, Paulus de Groot removed his hat, placed it over his heart, and kneeled in the bloody dust: 'Almighty God of the Boers, You have brought us victory, and we didn't know it. Almighty God of the Boers . . . dear faithful God of the Boers . . .'

The sky was brightening when he straightened up and walked to the edge of the hill to alert his comrades below: 'Boers! Boers!'

In their bivouac the commandos had watched as sun began to break, uncertain as to what they might have to face this day from that bloody embattled mount.

An incredible sight greeted them. On the summit, outlined against the sky, stood an old man, the victor of Majuba nineteen years before, waving his top hat triumphantly. General Paulus de Groot had captured Spion Kop.

There had been at the hill that twenty-fourth day of January 1900 three young men of radically different character; no one of the three saw the other two, but each would live to play an outstanding role in the future history of his particular country.

The oldest was a Boer officer, only thirty-seven, on whom fell the burden of rallying his troops when all seemed lost and sustaining them when the leadership of the older generals proved defective. Had some young English colonel of comparable ability managed to insert himself in place of his own wavering and slow-witted generals, that side would probably have won this crucial battle; fortune dictated that it would be the Boers who would act intelligently. This splendid military genius was Louis Botha, who would become the first Boer prime minister of the new nation that would emerge from this battle. At Spion Kop young Botha, who ended the day in overall command, became convinced that Boer and Englishman would do better if they worked together. In the rage of battle he knew that this internecine warfare was senseless, and that unless the two white races coalesced in their common interests and humanity, South Africa must be torn apart. He became the great conciliator, the prudent counselor, the head of state, and few names in the history of his country would stand higher.

The youngest of the men was a rowdy newspaperman whom nobody could discipline. Reporter for a London paper, he wrote penetrating, irreverent accounts of men like Warren, so that proper military men shuddered when he approached. He was then tallish and slim, and spoke with a lisp that caused merriment among the sturdier types. He had not done well in school, had avoided university altogether, and was thought of as pretty much a freak. Because of carelessness, he had already been captured once by the Boers but had escaped through sheer brazenness. There was a kind of price on his head, not to be taken seriously, perhaps, but had he been captured at Spion Kop, things might have been rather sticky. In spite of this, he climbed three times to the crest of the hill, where he was revolted by the confusion and inefficiency. He was Winston Churchill, twenty-five years old, already the author of several fine books and desperately hungry to get into Parliament. A brief fourteen years after this day on Spion Kop, young Churchill would find himself in the middle of a much greater war, and in the war cabinet, and in charge of naval operations. At Gallipoli he would interfere in military matters so disgracefully that he would ensure the tragic defeat of a major English operation, so that his name became synonymous with civilian incompetence. On Spion Kop that day he had learned a lesson from defeat, for when the battle was dismally lost, General Buller at last took complete charge, and in rallying his men he was superb, a stubborn man with iron courage who stared into the face of catastrophe and assured his troops: 'We shall win this war.' And his men were willing to support him. Of Buller, Churchill wrote: 'It's the love and admiration of Tommy Atkins that fortifies him.' In 1941 this lesson in bulldog tenacity would lead Winston Churchill to immortality.

The third young man was a curious type; scrawny, short, spindly-legged, very dark of countenance, with even darker hair, he served that day as an ambulance runner. If Louis Botha had seen him, he would

have ignored him as an unwelcomed immigrant; had Winston Churchill
seen him foraging among the dead to ascertain if even one man still survived, he would have dismissed him as inconsequential. Born in India,
he had surveyed that impoverished land and decided that it held no
promise for young lawyers, so he had eagerly emigrated to South
Africa, where he fully intended to spend the remainder of his life. His
name was Mohandas Karamchand Gandhi, volunteer stretcher bearer to
the English forces. Aware that the ruling castes, Boer and Briton, held
all Indians in disdain, he had persuaded his fellow Hindus in Durban to
volunteer for the war's most dangerous service to prove their worth; on
this day he had escaped death a score of times, and two of his associates
had been killed. On Spion Kop, Mohandas Gandhi learned that warfare
was unutterably stupid, that it solved no problems, and that when the
dead were collected and the medals distributed, the warring parties still
faced their insoluble problems. How much better had they avoided violent discourse and taken resort to peaceful non-resistance.

There was a fourth man on Spion Kop that day, or rather that night,
but no one paid him any attention, and he did not rise in later years to
lead his nation, but on this encrusted battlefield he did learn the first
and only of his great lessons. When General de Groot, at two-thirty in
the morning of the day following the battle, climbed back up Spion
Kop, there were two men with him, the young fellow who alerted the
move and Jakob van Doorn, his constant companion. There was a
fourth man, but since he was black he didn't count. He was Micah
Nxumalo, who would never be far from the old general in the days of
this war. He did not have to participate, and he had no gun to defend
himself; he merely tagged along because he loved the old general and
had served him in various capacities. He could tend horses, scavenge
for food, help the women, serve as scout when conditions grew tense,
and tend the sick commandos. On Spion Kop, Micah Nxumalo began to
develop a great truth which he would later quietly pass along to his people. As he moved through that fiery day, seeing the troops who seemed
so numerous, he noticed that taken altogether, they numbered far fewer
than his Zulu tribe, or the Xhosa, or the Swazi, or the Basuto, or the
Bechuana, or the Matabele. He saw that the English and the Boers were
playing tremendous games, but that when the battles were finished they
would be brothers, a few white men set down amidst a vast congregation of blacks: When the games are ended and the mighty guns are silenced, the real struggle will begin, and it will not be Englishman

against Boer. It will be white man against black, and in the end we shall triumph.

For the duration of the present episode Nxumalo would continue with the Boers; they were his proven friends; and he hoped they would win this time. But he was struck by the fact that an equal number of blacks served with the English, hoping, no doubt, that they would win.

When the disaster of Spion Kop was ended, with the land-armada once again south of the Tugela, and the fifteen thousand trek-oxen pulling the massive wagons back to where they started, Frank Saltwood had to evaluate the performance, which he had witnessed mainly at Buller's elbow: He had rotten luck. Having that Warren thrust upon him. What a dunderhead! The battle could have been won four different ways, and he rejected them all. But then the question arose: I wonder why Buller didn't discharge him? Buller was in command.

The more he thought about this the more he realized that as a South African not reared in the English military tradition, he could not appreciate the reticence one general would have in ever bringing criticism upon another: They're a fraternity of aging warriors, each supporting the other, each attentive to the traditions of the service. Losing a battle is far less important than losing relative position in the hierarchy.

But even Saltwood had to admit that not all the blame could be thrown on Warren; Buller, too, had participated in the gross errors: He gave Warren command, then intervened a score of times. After all, it was my man Buller who heckled the commander of the King's Royal Rifles until those brave men were ordered to retreat.

When he had lined up in his mind all the pros and cons, one fact persisted: Buller's foot soldiers consider him the best general they ever served under. I've asked a score of them. Always the same answer: 'I'd go anywhere with Old Buller. He looks after his men.' And now Saltwood realized that many of the horrendous decisions he saw Buller make were done to preserve lives. He might drink too much Trianon sparkling, and as one correspondent wrote, he did eat gargantuan meals; but where human life was concerned, he was Spartan. 'Train them hard,' he had told Saltwood. 'Drive them hard. But bring them back in good order.' When Frank asked about this, the old man said, 'Most important fact of war? Keep your army in existence. Lose the battle, but keep your eye on winning the war.'

But everyone in Buller's command had to be aware of the attacks

being made upon their general by the experts in Europe. London newspapers began calling him 'The Ferryman of the Tugela.' In Parliament
he was known as 'Sir Reverse Buller.' After the last debacle he
humphed and mumbled, 'By gad, they're splendid troops. Retreated
without losing one gun carriage.' To which Saltwood said, 'They should
do it well, sir. They've had plenty of rehearsal.' General Buller looked
at him with his tiny pinched eyes and laughed. 'Yes, yes. What I mean,
yes. They are great troops.'

He sent another smashing heliogram to the besieged heroes at
Ladysmith, assuring them that he would rescue them within five days,
and with fortitude he crossed the Tugela yet again, only to get a shocking bloody nose which sent him reeling back across that pitiful stream
once more. In Ladysmith the rations were diminishing, and at the end
of twelve weeks Buller was no closer to the town than when he started.
Still he had the gall to heliograph yet again that he would succor the
town at any moment now.

In view of the growing criticism, Saltwood sometimes wondered
why the British authorities allowed him to retain command. There was
one reason, tragic and accidental. In Buller's first attempt to cross the
Tugela, that masterpiece of ineptitude, a gallant young officer volunteered to rescue some heavy guns that were about to be lost to the
Boers. He was killed, and he happened to be the son of Lord Roberts,
who would shortly become Buller's superior. Now, lest Roberts appear
vengeful over a death for which Buller was in no way responsible, he
remained silent, when otherwise he would have recommended his removal.

A more subtle explanation was given to some French and German
observers one night by a young English officer: 'The War Office wants
generals like Buller. They're never comfortable with uncertain types like
Kitchener and Allenby. Buller is steady, which they like, and not too
clever, which they prefer. As a young man he obeyed orders and
plunged ahead. You should have seen him, they tell me, wading into
Egyptians. Very forceful. They like it that he can't speak clearly, that
he harrumphs all over the place. That's how a proper general should
behave. Look at Raglan and Cardigan at Balaklava.'

'But why in God's name don't they dismiss him when his deficiencies become known?' the German asked.

'Ah! That's why we're English. That's why you'll never understand
us. Who appointed Buller? The establishment. The older generals. The
older politicians. Probably some of the archbishops had a hand, if the

truth were known. They like him. They trust him. He's one of them. Good family, you know.'

'But he's destroying the army,' the Frenchman protested.

'The army! What's the army? The important thing is that men like Buller be protected. He is England, not some damn-fool lieutenant who got his legs blown off.'

'In Germany he wouldn't last a week.'

'In England he'll last forever.'

'You speak as if you love the old fool.'

'I do,' the young man confessed. 'He's a doddering ass, and I love him. Because most of the people at home I love are just like him, and somehow they always do the right thing. You watch, when the decisive battle of this war is fought, Buller will be there, pushing his way ahead, just as he did with the Egyptians.'

'I wish to God he were forty years younger,' the German said.

'Why?'

'Because when our war against England comes, and it will, I would like him to be in command.'

'He will be,' the young man said. 'Under a different name. And beware of him.'

As he spoke, he tacked onto the bulletin board a notice from Lord Roberts on the other front; it referred to some of his associate officers in the South African war: Douglas Haig, John French, Julian Byng, Edmund Allenby, Ian Hamilton. They would be the General Bullers whom the Germans would have to face.

With these confused judgments rattling in his head, Major Saltwood watched with pride as General Buller finally figured a way to cross the Tugela, and that night he wrote to Maud, who was busy organizing charities for the wives of Cape men serving with the English forces:

> It was damned brilliant, really. Old Buller moved his heavy guns, we get them from the navy, you know, put them on his flank and laid down a hellish barrage, right ahead of our advancing troops. Like a fiery broom he swept away the Boers. So at least we're across this damned river, but I cannot bring my pen to say, 'We'll lift the siege of Ladysmith in five days.' We've said that too many times before. But soon we shall be there.

On 28 February 1900, ninety-five days after he assigned himself the task of relieving Ladysmith, the siege was lifted. Three memorable incidents marked the stirring occasion.

Lord Dundonald, always eager for acclaim, dispatched a unit of his cavalry to be first into town. He followed, and in his company was Winston Churchill, almost a full day ahead of General Buller.

Later, when the general's more pompous entrance was made, he got his maps mixed up and marched to the wrong gate; the heroic defenders, military and civil, were waiting on the opposite side of town, and when it was pointed out to him that since he and his men were fresh, and on well-rested horses, it might be gracious if he rode to the other side, he said, 'I enter here,' and the multitude had to hurry across town to greet him.

And finally, when the defeated Boers were in retreat, some of the cavalrymen saw a chance to chase and destroy. When they started from the town, some of the men who had withstood the siege wanted to join, but could not: 'We have no horses. We ate them.'

'Where are those cavalrymen going?' Buller asked Saltwood.

'Pursuing the enemy.'

'Pursue an enemy who's been honorably defeated? Good God, call our men back. Give the poor devils decent time to lick their wounds.'

'Sir, we've been chasing those damned Boers for months. This is our chance to eliminate them.'

From beneath his tight little hat General Buller stared at his South African aide. 'Sir, you have none of the instincts of a gentleman.' When Frank tried to protest, Buller put his heavy arm about his shoulder. 'Son, if we lose honor in warfare, we lose everything.' And he canceled the pursuit.

General de Groot was bewildered. For more than four months his commando had been abused and misused, and he could do nothing about it. Instead of riding hard and fast in a strike-and-hide tactic, at which his horsemen would have excelled, he had been held in rein and used in assault efforts. It occurred to him, as he sat with Sybilla after the defeat at Ladysmith, that almost never in these four months had his pony been at a gallop, and rarely a trot.

'You know, Sybilla, we're losing men all the time. Our burghers won't tolerate this sort of thing.'

'They'll come back, when your kind of fighting begins.'

'You can't have a commando with nine men.'

Then shocking news from the western front reminded them of the harsh possibilities of this war: General Cronje, an obstinate man who believed that the best defense against English arms was a laager, had surrendered.

'What could he have been thinking of?' De Groot asked Jakob. 'With four thousand men, you and I could take Durban.'

'It's a different war over there. General Roberts is in a hurry. He's no Buller.'

This doleful news, coinciding with Ladysmith, generated a vast depression among the retreating Boers, so that the Venloo Commando was reduced to one hundred and twenty, and when the time came to hand out assignments, those in charge looked at De Groot with pained tolerance: 'What can you do, Paulus, with so few?'

'We can attack the cavalry installation,' he replied with that bitter animosity he held for the English lancers.

'They'd slaughter you!'

'We wouldn't take them head-on.' He was so persuasive that permission was granted for what could only be a suicide attempt, except that he had no intention of allowing it to become so.

He would take his men, including, of course, Van Doorn, and they would move quietly across the Orange Free State to where Generals Roberts and Kitchener held their troops after their big victory over Cronje, and they would ride daringly close to the cavalry cantonment, trusting the natural confusion of a large assembly of horses to mask their approach. They would then dismount, wait till three in the morning, when attention was always at a minimum, sweep in, disrupt the horses, and fight any personnel that might be afoot. In the confusion they would run to their ponies and be off due north, in a direction which the English would not anticipate, because such a move would carry them directly into English lines. De Groot had a plan for what would follow.

'Sounds possible,' Van Doorn said.

'You wouldn't want a force much bigger than ours,' De Groot said enthusiastically.

'We'll need expert scouting.'

'I've thought of that. We've got to know exactly where the English troops are. That's where Micah comes in.'

Micah proved himself a good scout, always moving with caution. One morning he haltered his pony far beyond English lines while he slipped around sentries, entering boldly the small town upon which the

British were centered. Moving freely, he estimated the size and character of the forces, making shrewd guesses as to the length of time they expected to remain in this favorable location.

He stayed in town two days, losing himself within the black population, several of whom guessed his identity; they did not betray him because they were indifferent as to which side won, and if he was to be well rewarded for his mission, they were pleased.

When he regained his pony, satisfied that he knew fairly well the disposition of the army men, he rode south and toward the west to where the cavalry were billeted, and now he faced a much more difficult problem. Again tying his pony at a distant spot, he set out on foot to approach the camp, but this time there was no small town into which he could infiltrate, masking himself among the blacks. He had to move from hillock to hillock, running always the risk that a sortie from the barracks would sweep out across the veld on some practice mission and find him spying upon them.

So he moved with extreme caution until he came within some two hundred yards of the lines where the mounts, big Argentinian horses, were tied. There were more than he had ever seen before, a massive command. The Boers are in trouble, he thought as he studied the fall of the ground, but General de Groot knows what he's doing.

He had doubts about his own wisdom when a contingent of young men left their tents, sauntered over to their horses, and casually mounted. After tightening straps, they waited for the arrival of their officer, who came at last on a striking red horse much larger than the others. What a fine animal, Micah thought as he watched what had to be a development of considerable danger.

'Heh!' he heard the young officer cry, and the forty-six troops lined up behind him. Using his bare right hand instead of the saber which he kept at his side, he indicated the direction his sortie was to make, and Micah saw with dismay that it would be headed in his general direction. He flattened himself between two rocks that provided some cover.

A bugle sounded and the men came forth. They rode to within thirty yards of where he hid, not one of them looking right or left; since this was a practice session, they felt no need to stay alert, but suddenly they stopped, looked in his direction, and burst into laughter. For one awful moment he thought they were preparing to lance him as a fixed target, but then he heard at some distance a slight scratching sound. Three little meerkats had come out of their burrows to look at the horsemen, and when one of the men made a lunge at them, they scampered. One of the men shouted, 'Bravo, Simmons. Stick three little Boers like that and there'll be a medal in it for you.'

When they continued their canter they headed right into the area where Micah had left his pony, and he expected at any moment to hear a 'Halloo!' There was no cry, and after a long while they galloped back to their camp. He breathed deeply when he saw that they had no pony with them.

Because of his careful scouting he was able to inform General de Groot precisely as to the nature of the two bodies of men: 'The soldiers will be there for many days. The cavalry horses stand at the edge of the veld, the men's tents behind them. They expect an attack from the other side, where the Boers are supposed to be.'

The Venloo Commando did not form a line as they set out on their mission; they straggled over the veld in positions from which each man could dash forward or retreat according to his own judgment. They were engaged in a perilous effort and knew that maximum mobility would be essential. Slowly they covered the neutral ground, then tensed as they approached the land that held the two English contingents. Finally they reached a spot some six hundred yards from the cavalry camp, and here they dismounted.

'Guard the horses,' General de Groot told his blacks, and they were left behind; that is, all stayed with the horses except Micah Nxumalo, who crept forward with the commando to guide his general to where the enemy horses rested.

It was now dusk. Keeping low, they stooped and scurried from rock to rock across the veld, zigzagging their way till they were close upon the English encampment. They would hold these positions for at least six hours during this fine summer night, during which they must not talk or smoke. Insects attacked and there was a good deal of scratching, but in general the men remained silent.

Stars appeared, and the moon, and in the distance a hyena grumbled, then laughed. Familiar constellations climbed to their apex and began their leisurely descent, and over the camp silence reigned. At midnight some cavalrymen came out of a mess tent, stood talking for a while, and bade each other a good rest as they separated.

'Sssst,' De Groot signaled, and his six followers crept forward. They were on a mission which disturbed some of them, for the butchery they contemplated went against the grain of farmers, but a chain of recent defeats had impressed upon them that they were engaged in a struggle which would not end in truce; one side or the other was going to be totally defeated, and it had better not be the Boers, for the penalties they would pay in lost freedom and even the loss of their republics would be terrifying. They must do what had to be done.

So as they approached the encampment, De Groot touched those nearest him, saying nothing but indicating that he expected them to perform their tasks. Some of the men brushed his hand with theirs; others simply nodded in the darkness. When they were within ten yards of the horse corral, he leaped forward boldly and his men followed.

Three of them knocked down barriers and turned hundreds of horses loose. Others grabbed the bridles of seven big horses saddled for emergencies and led them outside. General de Groot and Jakob moved methodically to the line where the officers' choice mounts were kept and shot them methodically, one after another, killing them in most cases, immobilizing them permanently in others.

There was no panic, no hurry when bugles began to sound, only the piling of inflammables and the striking of matches. Before any English cavalryman could get to the stores, they were ablaze and dark figures were riding away. What infuriated the Englishmen as they rushed onto the scene, powerless to retaliate, for their horses were gone, was that in the light from leaping flames they could see Boers on horseback, galloping among the free horses and shooting them down.

'M'God!' one young officer cried. 'They're shooting the horses!' In rage he began firing at the retreating Boers, and although everyone knew that the invaders could not be reached, the entire cavalry contingent blazed away at them, firing and cursing as they watched their great steeds go down. When dawn came, both the Englishmen and the Boers realized that the remainder of this war was going to be excessively ugly.

'An inhuman act,' General Kitchener cried when he saw the dead horses. 'No civilized man would do such a thing.'

He had no right to be sensitive about what civilized men would do or not do; in the fiery battle that had led to the surrender of General Cronje and his four thousand Boers, a critical moment had come when the English line seemed to be wavering. It could be stabilized only by some drastic action which would command the attention and respect of all. Kitchener had seen the solution.

'Cavalry, charge up the center, and even if you do not reach the Boer laager, blaze away at them.'

'Sir,' the Scottish commander of the horsemen protested, 'that would be suicidal.'

Kitchener stiffened. He knew that by ordinary standards the order was insane, but this vast battle was not ordinary. 'I command you to charge the laager.'

The Scotsman saluted briskly. 'Very well, sir.' He realized that if he disobeyed, he would be court-martialed and perhaps shot, but he also knew that if he obeyed, two hundred of his best men would be slain. He solved the problem in a heroic way. Turning to the brigade, he said, 'Retire twenty paces and regroup.' To his four officers he said, 'Return to camp and fetch us more ammunition.' When all were safely behind him, he turned to face the distant enemy and started riding slowly toward the laager, as ordered.

On and on he came, far ahead of his men, riding on a tall white horse that stepped forward with stately caution. Suddenly he spurred his horse and ranged forward, closing upon the enemy guns, well hidden behind bulwarks, and it became apparent to both the English and the Boers what he was doing. He was obeying orders. He had been told to charge, and he was about to charge, but his obedience did not mean that he had to carry his men to their death. There was a hush, and then he whipped out his sword, tilting it at the proper angle, and as his handsome animal leaped forward he bellowed, 'Charge!'

Boers, watching him gallop into the muzzle of their guns, could not bring themselves to fire, but one burgher who had read Sir Walter Scott understood the traditions of chivalry and knew that from such a charge there would be no retreat, nor any place in English life after such insubordination. 'Fire!' this man shouted, but no one responded. 'Fire,' he cried again, 'we must help him,' but once more there was awed silence. But when the rider was almost to the guns, the burghers opened fire at him, and he fell dead.

For General Kitchener to order a Scottish officer and his men to certain death was warfare, and as a consequence of such discipline, he had been enabled to destroy General Cronje; but for Paulus de Groot to kill two hundred Argentine horses was, in Kitchener's words: 'A show of barbarism, an inhuman act of madness outside the rules of civilized warfare.'

From now on, the war would be marked by many inhuman acts, but it would depend upon which side was speaking as to where the inhumanity lay. The English attitude was well summarized by General Kitchener: 'Damnit all, stands to reason, what I mean. Why don't they dress in khaki, like a proper army, so you can see them, and get down off those damned ponies and fight like men? What's all this hitting a man and then running away—are they cowards, or what? The damned Wogs fought better than these fellows. The lot of them need a proper hiding.'

General Roberts, a more temperate man, objected to three things about the Boers: 'They don't obey their commanders, so it's impossible to make a truce with them. They lack discipline, so you never know what they're apt to do next. And I don't like to bring this up, but they are careless, very careless indeed about the use of the white flag.' When asked by a correspondent from a Paris newspaper what he meant by this, he sought to avoid controversy and remained silent, but when others pressed him, with their pencils ready, he said bluntly, 'They approach you with the flag. Lull you. Then drop it and are back in the battle.'

'Certainly not, sir.'

'I saw it with my own eyes. I've had various reports. Couldn't believe them. After all, these are decent human beings. But at the Battle of Driefontein, I watched as they did it.'

What Kitchener objected to, and most strenuously, was the Boer habit of ransacking the bodies of dead English soldiers and appropriating articles of needed clothing: 'The ghouls appear in our khaki. At fifty paces can't tell they're enemy. That's breaking the rules of civilized warfare.'

The English leaders made a great fuss over these rules of civilized warfare; they felt that an enemy should behave much like the barefoot Indians and Egyptians: stand in line with their rusty guns; wait as the phalanx of red-coated battalions marched at them; fire; run when the cavalry charged; surrender and go back to their land when the war was declared over. It was disturbing to think that men of European heritage would fight the way the Boers did, with trickery, speed, and the nasty habit of dissolving back into the landscape instead of surrendering. And the fact that these Boers were well supplied with the best German Mausers and French Martini-Henri rifles was distressing.

But the Boers, too, had their grievances. Like General de Groot, they felt it to be inhuman and far beyond the principles of civilized warfare for men to sit astride big horses—like those from the farms of America and the Argentine—and to ride them in among the commandos, cutting and slashing as they came. Hundreds of Boers, who started with no more than sullen resentment against the English, grew to detest them because of the cavalry charges, and when De Groot and his men destroyed the Argentine horses they applauded.

Even worse they deplored the English habit of firing their guns at two hundred yards, and then a hundred, and then fifty, and finally charging in with bayonets, a weapon the Boers never used. 'To come at a man with cold steel,' De Groot said, 'that's inhuman.' Many an Englishman who should have been captured and led away to safe imprisonment lost his life because he fought with a bayonet, for Christian men did not do that.

Between the combatants a kind of chivalry did exist, based on real respect: the English were redoubtable foes, willing to absorb tremendous losses; the Boers were often willing to go up against unbelievable odds, and many of the most unusual gestures of courtesy were extended by these rude farmers. But on two points of difference they were adamant, and when the English refused to concede on these, a deep bitterness was engendered, with each side actually flogging and shooting prisoners captured from the other.

The deepest difference, perhaps, concerned black troops; each side used African scouts, but increasingly those with the English turned up with arms, whereupon word would flash through the countryside: 'The English are arming the Kaffirs.' This was intolerable, for no matter how desperately the two white armies fought each other, in the backs of their minds the real enemy was the black man watching from the side.

English commanders were aware of Boer feelings on this point, but that did not prevent them from enlisting and arming Coloured units from the Cape, and for this the Boers would never forgive them.

Besides, for the English to use these Coloureds only deepened the Boers' resentment of the fact that so few Afrikaners from the Cape volunteered to help. Many still hoped for a massive rebellion against the English in the two colonies, Cape and Natal, but no more than thirteen thousand crossed over. What was especially galling, thousands of Cape citizens of Dutch ancestry joined men of English descent in colonial regiments which fought in British armies against the Boers. Many in the north would die hating their brothers in the south for this treachery.

The other Boer grievance was less complex. Because of their stern religiosity, they tried to avoid any activity on Sundays, and once during a protracted engagement, when General de Groot had his men at Sunday prayer, their guns silent, one of the Venloo men rushed into the service, shouting, 'They're playing cricket!'

De Groot stalked to a vantage point and looked through his glass at the green field upon which the English officers were having a merry game. He was appalled at this sacrilege and ordered a heliographer to send a message commanding the game to halt, this being the Sabbath. When the English signaled back the score, 'Eighty-seven for three wickets,' he fell into a dark fury and ran breathlessly to a large gun.

'Fire on them!' When the Creusot monster was loaded and aimed he cautioned: 'But not too close.' The shell landed well off the cricket field and killed no one. Phlegmatically the officers continued their game, so a second shell had to be launched, and this came so close that the young men flew helter-skelter. When white-flagged emissaries came to protest the breaking of a tacit truce, De Groot replied, 'On Sundays you are to pray like us, not play at cricket like heathens.'

This matter of religion always perplexed De Groot and Van Doorn. They knew they were men dedicated to God and were convinced that He looked after them with special regard; they also knew that since the English were indifferent to the Bible, God must despise them, yet there were contradictions, as De Groot pointed out in a report to the council:

> I cannot understand it. The English have what they call a chaplain attached to every unit, and braver men I have never seen. To aid a fallen comrade or give last prayers to a dying man, they will cross open areas of gunfire with such fortitude that our men sometimes cheer them in admiration. But we Boers, who live and die under a special covenant with God, have some predikants who jump if even a pistol shot goes off. Our spiritual welfare was being looked after by Predikants Nel and Maartins, but not for long. As soon as the first gun fired, both these dominees quickly found that commando life was not for them. No member of my commando felt their loss, as we provide our own prayers.

One bitter point was never discussed in public; it appeared in no news dispatches from the front, but it caused the harshest animosities, as General de Groot learned one morning when his commando captured six Englishmen. The young officer, a blond lad from Oriel College with his first commission, protested grievously: 'Sir, why do you Boers stoop so low as to use dumdum bullets?'

De Groot did not change his expression. 'Did we use them?'

'Yes! Yes!' the young man cried in near-hysteria. 'Chalmers was struck in the jaw. Should have been merely a nasty wound. Dumdum expands, makes a mess of his head. Atkins hit in the abdomen. Normally might pull through. Dumdum opens up his whole belly.' When De Groot made no response, the young fellow shouted, 'It's monstrous, Meneer.'

Quietly De Groot nodded to Van Doorn: 'Hand him three.' And from a special pouch Jakob produced three dumdum bullets, tossing them into the young man's lap. The Englishman studied them and blanched. In consternation he looked at De Groot and asked, 'Is this correct, Meneer? Our own Woolwich Arsenal?'

'Tell him where we got them,' De Groot said, and Van Doorn said, 'You heard about our raid against the cavalry? The seven big horses we kept? Those bullets you hold came from this pouch, found attached to one of the saddles.'

The young man apologized: 'They were intended for the Afghan frontier. Not for civilized warfare.'

In the autumn of 1900 such incidents receded in importance, for the massive strength of the English began to tell. They now had about two hundred fifty thousand men in the field against a maximum of sixty-three thousand Boers, and there was no way that the few, however gallant, could continue to hold off the many. With bold yet carefully prepared strikes, Generals Roberts and Kitchener rolled their choicest troops across the veld to Johannesburg and Pretoria. Town after town fell to the Tommies, and on the seventeenth of May even the tiny settlement at Mafeking was relieved at the end of a siege which had lasted interminably. General Robert Baden-Powell, who had used his scouting tactics to keep the town alive, was hailed throughout the world as a proper hero, and his manly deportment gave the English troops added courage as they headed for Johannesburg, which they captured on 31 May 1900.

Now came that most popular of all war songs, and in many ways the best, 'We're Marching to Pretoria.' Thousands of men chanted this as they closed in upon the Boer capital, and their triumphant voices could be heard as a last railway train left Pretoria on its solemn way down the line that led to Lourenço Marques in Moçambique. This was the only line the Boers still controlled, and in Car 17 that gloomy day rode Oom Paul Kruger in desperate flight.

It took the English only five days to capture Pretoria; it fell on 5 June 1900, and the great Anglo-Boer War was almost over. There was such joy in England that the police feared rioting, and families which still had sons in Africa—and there were many of them—wept openly to know that their boys would now be coming home.

There was a little mopping up to be done. General Roberts did not want to leave for London until the last railway line was in his hands, for that would mean that any further resistance, even from guerrilla units like Paulus de Groot's dwindling commando, would be impossible. Like the good soldier he was, the little one-eyed genius refrained from announcing victory until President Kruger was driven completely out of South Africa, and to achieve this, he proposed that he and Kitchener march east along the railway while General Buller came up from the south to close the final pincers.

There are in existence some fifty telegrams in which Roberts from the north begged Buller in the south to speed up his approach, and to each the Ferryman of the Tugela replied with faultless logic, explaining why he could not move a whit faster. When Roberts sent an English colonel to find out what in the world was restraining this warrior, it fell to Major Saltwood to escort him, and as the two officers inspected General Buller's operations, Frank became even more aware of the considerable change that had taken place in his estimate of Buller.

For example, the visitor exploded at the number of wagons in the train, saying, 'My God! We're in the closing stages of a war. He ought to abandon four-fifths of these and gallop north to help us.'

'Now wait!' Saltwood replied defensively. 'Buller moves slowly, but I've observed that he accomplishes his missions with minimal losses of men. No general protects his troops the way this old man does.'

'But at what cost? He refuses to take chances.'

'I used to think so, too. But watching him in action—'

'What action? Know what they're calling him at headquarters? Sitting Bull.' The colonel laughed heartily at the mess-room joke.

Saltwood stiffened. 'Sir, we have a dozen funny names for the old fellow. But do you know what his men call him? John Bull.'

The colonel was not impressed, but when he challenged Buller about his excessive wagons, all he got was a harrumph: 'Damn me, man, troops can't march forward with empty bellies.'

'General Roberts says you think too much about your men.'

'No general ever lost a battle because he defended his men.'

'When you began this campaign,' the colonel pointed out ungraciously, 'you promised it would be over by Christmas. That was last Christmas, sir.'

Buller showed no resentment. Squinting his tight little eyes beneath the brooding visor, he said simply, 'Damn-fool statement. Made it before I'd met the Boers in battle. They're formidable, sir, and if Roberts thinks . . .' The rest of his rebuttal was lost in his monstrous mustache.

The formal meeting accomplished nothing, but when Buller withdrew, mumbling to himself, Saltwood remained with the colonel. 'In our march north I've seen a remarkable man at work. Victory after victory, with almost no casualties. He seems to have an uncanny sense of what his men can do, where they should strike.'

'At Spion Kop he was a disaster.'

'At Spion Kop he relied upon General Warren. Now he relies on himself.'

'Are you defending Sir Reverse?'

'I am. He's no Roberts, flying off all over the place. He's no Kitchener, blustering into cannon fire. He's an elderly general with a smart sense of warfare and a devotion to his men.'

Buller proved this in an embarrassing way, for in the hearing of the visiting colonel he said, 'Saltwood, we're facing the final push. Go down to Trianon and fetch me five hundred of their best sparkling. It may not be champagne, but it does taste good at the end of a long march. And fetch some beer for the men.'

When the two junior officers were alone, the visitor said, 'He never took a long march in his life.'

'I can assure you of one thing,' Saltwood said. 'On the day of victory, Old Buller will be the one marching in. Not fast, mind you. But very steady.' And when the sneering colonel had departed, Frank realized to his amazement that he had grown to love the Ferryman of the Tugela, for Redvers Buller, with his squinting eyes and eggplant head and telescope between his toes, knew what war was, how it should be fought, and how it could be won.

When he reached the Trianon vineyards to commandeer the best part of their bottling, Saltwood found that his wife had come east from Cape Town to share a few days with him, and from her he learned that the war had taken a dramatic turn, about which he had heard nothing.

Maud was worried: 'Frank, do you think General Roberts is justified in this move?'

'It's brilliant. Two armies concentrating on the last railroad the Boers have. It'll end the war.'

'I don't mean the railroad. I mean the scorched earth.' He would always remember that she was incredibly beautiful as she first uttered these words: the sunlight of Trianon fell on her auburn hair, outlining the wondrous curls and twists she used for controlling it, and her eyes glowed with that intensity she had shown when first he met her. War and decisions were forgotten as he leaned over to kiss her, but after a kind of routine compliance she returned to her concern.

'Yes, he's given orders to the burghers: "Lay down your arms or we will burn your farms and devastate your fields. If you fight, you will starve."' She took a deep breath. 'Really, Frank, is that decent warfare?'

'Well, they're a difficult enemy. You scotch them here, they break out there. I hadn't heard of the new order . . .'

She produced a copy, signed by General Roberts, and he saw that she had reported it correctly. 'Looks sensible to me. We've defeated them, you know—totally defeated them—and these regulations apply only to the scattered remnants.'

'But they sound so barbaric. They don't sound like my England at all. They sound like Genghis Khan.'

'These are the mopping-up days of the war, Maud. We're gleaning the last sheaves.'

'Then why are you here buying wine for your stupid general?'

'Maud, he's not stupid. He's a man who knows exactly what he's doing, although I didn't use to think so.'

'But why the wine?'

Her chin tilted forward, and the hardness which she could command when confronted by stupidity showed itself. Frank became irritated by her questioning and blurted out: 'Because he likes to have an orderly mess, even in wartime. And he does so because he's the nephew of a great duke, who gives him the money to spend as he sees fit. He sees fit to buy champagne, that's why.'

It was a silly answer and he realized this as soon as the words were spoken. 'It's been a long, trying year,' he said. 'But I've grown fond of Old Buller, and you'd be ashamed of me if I deserted him now.'

'I'm sorry if I spoke harshly,' she said with such sweet innocence that he had to embrace her, but even as he kissed her, she returned to her concern: 'Is General Buller burning farms?'

'He could never do that. He fights armies, not women and children.'

'But it's an order. From Roberts.'

Frank laughed. 'I've learned one splendid lesson from Buller. If a stupid order comes down, ignore it.'

'But is he burning farms?'

'Darling, he's a wonderful, bumbling old fool, who has more sense of warfare than all the others. He'll fight this war his way, with good food, and sparkling Trianon, and plenty of rest for his men. And do you know what? In the end he'll win.'

On his side of the battle lines, General de Groot was encountering difficulty. Despite an occasional dashing sortie like his attack on the English cavalry, he was so stuck in routine that more of his commando had left him to affiliate with larger units engaged in the serious efforts of the war. The Venloo Commando now consisted of the general himself and ninety horsemen, plus their blacks. To keep it any longer in existence was ridiculous, and one afternoon the council told him so.

Standing before his men in his double-breasted frock coat—tattered and ruined, its silver buttons gone—and his tall top hat, he was a forlorn figure, a fat old man of sixty-eight whom the world had passed by. 'Commandant-general says we must join Tobias Brand's commando.'

'We're ninety men!' Van Doorn protested. 'We can still fight as a unit.'

'No. We must obey orders. Our commando is no more.'

'But it would be humiliating—to take orders from someone else, after you've been a general.'

'Not to me. I don't care where I fight.' He summoned Sybilla, and in the presence of his men, said, 'Old lady, they tell me I must surrender my command and fight under Tobias Brand.'

'He's a good man,' she said. 'I'll fetch the wagon.'

But when they rode over to Brand's camp, with Van Doorn sharing the wagon, the younger general said, 'You understand who's in command?' And De Groot said, 'You are, Tobias.'

Now Brand objected to having Sybilla along, for she was much older than the women in his commando, but Paulus pleaded: 'This beaten wagon is her only home. We have fought side by side for sixty years.' So she resumed her position at the rear of a column, this one commanded by a stranger. On hot days when she could shoot an antelope she would make biltong for the long treks that she knew lay ahead.

Anyone who looked even casually at the map of South Africa could see what the strategy of the English forces had to be, and De Groot listened as the combat generals explained what they must do to keep the

Boer republics alive: 'The railroad to Lourenço Marques is our only link with the world outside. It must be kept open. We've already lost it east of Pretoria, but we dare not lose this part.' A brief flick of the finger indicated all that remained: only the area between Middleburg and the Portuguese border, including the two remarkable villages of Waterval-Boven (Above-the-Waterfall) and Waterval-Onder (Under-the-Waterfall), for here in the space of a few miles the whole face of Africa changed.

The Elands River, coming down off the high plateau, cut a deep gorge through soft rock, creating a beautiful tumbling waterfall from which the villages took their names, but this was not the spectacular character of the place. Waterval-Boven, at the edge of the high plateau, was a typical veld settlement, with harsh landscape, wide stretches of almost barren land and a forbidding aspect. Then came the plunging drop, and at Waterval-Onder one was in the lush lowlands, with high humidity, twisting vines and a richness of grass and tree that was startling.

In the winter of 1900, when the Transvaal republic was falling apart, the two Watervals became the focus of world attention, for to the high one came Oom Paul Kruger, seventy-five years old, stooped and weary, a president losing his country. From his railway carriages, he tried to hold his nation together, wincing when he learned that districts upon which he had depended were gone. He had not wanted to leave Pretoria and was especially grieved at being forced to abandon his old wife, but here he was near the end of the railway line.

Men leading the commandos came to see him and spoke reverently of his accomplishments in the past: 'Oom Paul, we're near the park you set aside for the animals. The lions and giraffes send you thanks.'

'Little help you voracious men gave me in arguing for the park. All you wanted to do was shoot elephants for their tusks.'

When General de Groot came by to pay his respects, Kruger said, 'I hear you're keeping Sybilla with you. Splendid idea, Paulus. Boer women thrive on battle.'

'You and I are the only ones left who were in the Great Trek,' Paulus said, and tears came into his eyes as he recalled those days.

'Wasn't Mzilikazi a fearful enemy?' Kruger asked. 'He fought us all day, killing and slaying, then prayed with the English missionaries all night, telling them how his heart bled for his people.' The weary president shook his head, then added, 'I must say, I've never cared much for missionaries. How can the Bible produce such a bad lot?'

'They use a different Bible,' De Groot said.

Kruger slapped his leg. 'I agree, Paulus. The Bible in English, it doesn't sound the same. They do something to it.'

'What will you do, Oom Paul, if the English come down the railway line?'

'They want me to go to Europe. To stir up the nations. Find allies for us in our struggle.'

As the two old Pauls spoke, a cadre of officers came to the railway coach to inform them of disturbing news: 'We're taking you down to Waterval-Onder. Safer down there.'

At the new headquarters, De Groot was assigned the pleasant job of serving as a kind of liaison between the Boers up on the veld and President Kruger sitting in a small white house down among the tropical growth, where the air was soft and warm. But within days news of the war grew ominous: 'Oom Paul, General Roberts is coming at us along the railway line. General Buller moves up from the south.' And then Paul Kruger demonstrated just how deeply he believed in the covenant his people had made with the Lord.

'De Groot, I want you to help me draft a last message to your Venloo burghers,' he said, and laboriously, but with a kind of grandeur in their hearts, the two old men, veterans of the Great Trek to freedom, lined out the message, parts of which would be memorized by the Venloo men to whom it was read:

> Burghers, in all ages the Craven Beast has had the power to persecute Christ. Today, when God's nation put here by Him to defend the Word is assailed by His enemies, every man who loves God must rise to defend Him. The time is at hand when God's people are to be tried in fire, and those who are true to the faith and fight on in the name of the Lord shall be received in Heaven and enter into everlasting Glory. To those who talk of surrender I say that is a falling away from God. To those who are forced to lay down their arms and take an oath I say, 'Go in again at the first opportunity and continue fighting.' And to all I say that we fight on the side of God, and He will surely protect us. Read this message to officers and burghers at every opportunity.

When General de Groot took the message up to be copied and circulated, he learned that Waterval-Boven was in peril from approaching English forces. When he returned to Oom Paul's little house, he stood for some moments among the trees, looking through the window at the bearded man who was about to lose the republic he had worked so diligently to bring into being, and tears started to his eyes, but he fought them back: Nou is nie de die tyd, De Groot! (Now is not the time.)

Entering the room Kruger used as his office, he said brusquely, 'Oom Paul, you've got to go. A ship will meet you at Lourenço Marques.'

'I cannot go,' the old man said, but he went.

In doing so, he created a profound moral problem for Boer historians. They would find it impossible to say flatly that in time of deepest crisis their president had fled his country, abandoning it to the enemy. They would devise all sorts of explanations, all kinds of justifications: 'He went to enlist allies. He went to represent us in foreign capitals. He took our gold to safekeeping. We sent him away, he didn't go.' But the fact would always remain that history was replete with examples of other beleaguered leaders who had refused to quit their native lands in time of crisis—so many, that it had become the honorable tradition. When William the Norman invaded England, Harold the Saxon felt it incumbent upon him to resist, and he did, to the death. When the Muslims invaded Spain, the Spanish king held fast, and from a cave battled back. When Pizarro sacked the Inca empire, the Inca did not flee; and when Cortez attacked Mexico, Montezuma stayed to defend his land. Even in South African history, when Colonel Gordon surrendered Cape Town to the invading English, he felt it necessary in the tradition of military honor to commit suicide, which he did; and when Marthinus Steyn, president of the Orange Free State faced utter defeat, he sent the English a telegram: 'We shall never surrender!' and he fought on with his commandos. It would be difficult to find another major example in which the elected ruler of a country abandoned it, and his old wife, and his trek companions, but Oom Paul Kruger did, and the explanations he gave while wandering futilely from court to court in Europe sounded hollow.

For his strange behavior there might be political justification; an effort did have to be made to keep his nation alive, and help from Europe might have been the only practical solution. But it is impossible to conjure up any explanation as to why an old man like this would abandon his wife of many years. When word reached him in Europe that she had died back in Pretoria, he wept.

* * *

Boer intelligence, which was usually good because of a more intimate knowledge of the battle terrain, saw clearly what the English generals were up to: 'Roberts marches east along the railway line. Kitchener reinforces his rear. That's the approach we must protect.'

'What about Buller moving up from the south?'

'He never gets anywhere on time. You can forget that approach.'

So near Bergendal Farm the Boers fortified a big red hill upon which the security of their entire line depended. If that hill was captured, English cannon could destroy the Boer lines, and the war would be over.

It was a formidable target, sloping sides leading up to a plateau about three acres in size and covered with huge scattered boulders, like an untidy playground of giants. It was held by one of the stoutest of the Boer units—a group of Johannesburg policemen, the toughest in the nation, who were prepared to die.

With his bumbling instinct for seeing simple solutions to complex problems, General Buller, arriving belatedly as the battle loomed, saw that the big red hill formed the hinge of the Boer forces, and that if it fell, the entire enemy position must collapse. 'It looks like Spion Kop,' he said as his heavy guns swung into position. 'But this time I'll be in charge.' So while Lords Roberts and Kitchener approached from the west with copybook tactics, Buller thundered ahead on his own and invested the hill.

This time his tactics were impeccable, and while Roberts and Kitchener stared with mouths agape, his horde of naval guns blasted the hill with lyddite for three awful hours, blowing entire boulders apart. Then his men stormed the redoubt, slew most of the Johannesburg policemen, and fractured the Boer lines.

It was the last pitched battle of the war, and when it was over, Buller wrote to his wife: 'Here I am, as happy as a pig . . . Today I have a very nice telegram from the Queen . . . I defeated the army . . . while Lord Roberts' army, which had got there before me, had missed the chance and had to sit looking on. What a beast I am!'

Redvers Buller had won the war.

In London there were fantastic celebrations. The old queen, fresh from her Sixtieth Jubilee, decided on her own that her personal friend, Lord Roberts, had been responsible for the victory. She insisted that he be elevated to the rank of earl, admitted into the Order of the Garter and promoted to commander-in-chief. As Field Marshal Lord Roberts, he received from a grateful nation a vast estate and a cash gift of

£100,000, a huge fortune in those days. He had brought the war to an end, and England rejoiced.

But General Buller was not forgotten. As soon as the war ended he was whisked aboard ship and hustled to England, where he was given a prestigious job in the military and a score of resounding state dinners, in which one city after another handed him ornate silver testimonials in the form of old-style Roman marshal's batons inscribed with the roster of his victories: 'Conqueror of the Tugela, Relief of Ladysmith, Hero of the High Veld.' His picture in tight little battle cap appeared everywhere, and it was agreed that he was perhaps the finest fighting general that England had ever produced.

Of course, some years later, when the facts of Spion Kop surfaced, all hell broke loose, and generals in the military establishment hounded him, charging him with lack of leadership. He was dragged before boards of inquiry, where his testimony was not inspiring. These attacks by envious rivals seemed not to worry him, for he surrendered none of the public acclaim which he adored, and to his home in the country came a constant queue of men who had fought under him in South Africa to assure him that he was the finest general they had ever known. As one conscripted soldier told the press: 'When you fought under Buller, things went slower, but you did eat well.'

On the morning that Lord Roberts knelt before his sovereign to become an earl and a Knight of the Garter, a group of tired flop-hatted Boers met secretly at a farm west of Pretoria. Louis Botha was present, Koos de la Rey the brilliant improvisator and Paulus de Groot the bulldog, and a brilliant young fellow all ice and steel, Jan Christian Smuts.

They had no settled government, no railway line to the outside world, no guaranteed arms supply, no replacement of horses, no system of conscription to fill their ranks, and no money. They were as defeated a group of men as military history provided; they had been mauled and chased almost off the continent, but there was not one among them prepared to put his hands up.

'The situation is this,' Louis Botha said. 'Lord Kitchener has two hundred thousand men in arms right now. And he can get two hundred thousand more. We have maybe twenty thousand burghers in the field. That's twenty-to-one against us, plus their ships, their heavy guns, the support of their empire. But what we have is knowledge of this land and determination.'

For some hours the discussion continued, and there was still not a leader there who was not ready to continue the conflict perpetually against the English. They drafted plans which only a fool would have accepted, and they applauded the daring. When someone said, 'The sensible thing to do is attack Cape Town; that will encourage the Cape Dutch to join at last,' four different commandants volunteered to undertake this incredible mission.

'The bulk of Kitchener's force will have to play policeman,' Botha predicted. 'He'll need a hundred thousand, maybe two hundred thousand, just to hold on to what they think they've got.'

On and on went the wild discussion, until a listener might have thought that these were victors planning their next campaign, and as they talked and encouraged one another, the tremendous determination of these Boers manifested itself: 'Our women will be with us. Our children will find a way to help.'

Paulus de Groot took no part in formulating these soaring plans, but they were confirmed when he jammed on his worn top hat, fastened his coat with the two safety pins that had replaced the lost silver buttons, and said, 'The battles are over. Now the war begins.'

It began with an action that reverberated around the world. It would have been a remarkable adventure had General de Groot done it alone, but it so happened that two newspapermen, a Frenchman and an American, hearing of the dissolution of the commandos now that the war was over, sought out old De Groot, thinking that he would provide a colorful story: the old veteran of the Great Trek who had fought first as a general, finally as a mere private. Also, since he had long ago been one of the heroes at Majuba, his return to civil life would be interesting to older readers.

But when they found De Groot and asked their first battery of questions about the impending surrender, he looked at them in amazement. 'Can you men ride horses?'

'We can.'

'Are you afraid of bullets?'

'Like everyone.'

'Good, because I don't like heroes. Ride with me and see how we surrender.'

He had regrouped with ninety men, mostly from the old Venloo Commando, but including sixteen older burghers from other districts who had little to go back to and wanted a chance to twist old Kitchener's tail. They had fine ponies and, of course, the usual complement of black retainers. They also had two wagons carrying three of the wives, and when the reporters saw Sybilla de Groot, in her sixties, they gasped.

'What's she doing here?'

'I don't go to war without my wife.'

'But the war's over.'

'Only the preliminaries.'

When the newspapermen finally grasped De Groot's plan of action, they were shocked both at the boldness and at the fact that a man nearly seventy should have concocted it.

'We want to give old Kitchener a signal that his war is still under way. He thinks he took over to receive salutes and break down the camps. He has a dreadful task ahead of him, and we want you to tell him so.'

'If you do what you threaten,' the Frenchman said admiringly, 'he won't need us to tell him.'

What De Groot proposed was to swing far west of Pretoria and Johannesburg, drop down some twenty-two miles below the latter city, and cut the railway line to Cape Town. Then, when English troops were everywhere, to gallop north as he had done before, right into the heart of their strength in Johannesburg district, there to cut the line again. Then, after a forty-six-mile gallop south, to strike the line again far from the first blow. Three nights, three directions, three strikes. It was confusing even to listen to; for an English general basking in victory it would be appalling.

Far out in the veld they left the two wagons and the spare ponies. As they prepared to ride in for their insane adventure, old De Groot took off his hat, kissed his wife, and told her, 'One day, old woman . . . one day it will end.'

Casually, the Boers and the two correspondents rode east, calculating so exactly that at two in the morning, when guards were sleepy, they would have time in which to blow up the Johannesburg–Cape Town railway. They accomplished this with dispatch—a wild, violent eruption filling the night—then galloped at breakneck speed right toward the heart of Johannesburg, taking cover just before dawn.

All that day they watched English troops hustling back and forth, 'In rather a panic,' De Groot said.

At dusk they stayed where they were, but well before midnight De

Groot, Van Doorn and Micah again led a dozen burghers up to the railway, lugging a huge supply of dynamite, which they fastened to the rails, detonating it from a distance. The explosion ripped the entire rail system apart, but before the debris settled, the Venloo Commando was galloping south over back roads to their third appointment. Again they spent daylight hours watching the frustrated troops, and once more at nightfall they resumed their riding. This time they galloped till almost dawn, when De Groot said, 'They won't expect us this far south.' Calling upon his same team, he had one hundred yards of rail mined, and when the early dawn was shaken with the vast outburst, throwing lengths of rail high in the air, the Boers retreated out over the veld, then far north to where Sybilla waited with the wagons.

The American reporter wrote a story which covered front pages in all states: WAR IS JUST STARTING SAYS DE GROOT. He was so factual and outlined the daring Boer strategy with such detail that the reader had to be impressed. When the report reached England a shudder passed through the nation, with editors asking soberly: WAS CELEBRATION PREMATURE?

But it was the French report that captured the world's imagination, for it told of Sybilla waiting in the veld, of Paulus taking off his top hat before kissing her, of the unbelievable daring in riding right into English strength, and of the coolness with which De Groot and his men handled their dynamite. What caused the story to be remembered, however, was the happy phrase the Frenchman coined to describe De Groot and his mission: AVENGER OF THE VELD. It sounded better in French (*Vengeur du Veld*), but even in English it was telling, and its effect was reinforced by something that General de Groot had whispered on one of the night rides. 'He told me,' read the report, 'that now that the gaudy battles are over, the real war begins. Having seen him in action for three Scheherazade Nights, I can believe it.'

Now the old man faced a different problem. All the adventurers wanted to join him, and the name Venloo Commando flashed across the world. It struck in the north. It appeared out of the mist in the far reaches of the Orange Free State. Newspapers fought desperately to catch photographs of Sybilla de Groot driving her old wagon, or of her husband standing beside her with his tall hat in his hand.

He had ninety men, then a hundred and fifteen, and finally the maximum he felt he could handle, with Van Doorn's help: two hundred and twenty. They were the best riders, men who could load and fire at a gallop, and they had no reason to halt anywhere, for they could not return to their homes.

When Kitchener found to his grim dismay that the Boers did not intend to surrender, as a defeated rabble should, he became distraught and issued orders that the farms of dissident commando members be burned to the ground, their fields ravaged and their livestock driven away: 'They may fight, but they won't feed.'

Before he left South Africa, Lord Roberts had applied this scorched-earth policy selectively, putting to the torch only those farms known to be collaborating with the commandos, but by the time Major Frank Saltwood was transferred from Buller's defunct command to Kitchener's, the practice had spread. 'I really don't think it will have much bearing upon the burghers,' Saltwood warned when he studied the figures, but Kitchener was adamant, and for the first time Saltwood saw the steel in this man's fiber. Clean-shaven except for a distinctive mustache, trim, rigid, accepting no nonsense from anyone, he seemed the right man for the unpleasant task of cleaning up the few recalcitrant rebels like old Paulus de Groot.

'Shall we burn his farm?' an English aide asked, and before Kitchener could reply, Saltwood volunteered: 'That would be a mistake, sir. Already the man's a hero. Simply create more sympathy.' When these prudent words were spoken, Lord Kitchener stared at his South African liaison, trying to assess him: Is this man to be trusted to put England's interest first, or is he infected with local patriotism? This time, however, what he says makes sense.

'Do not burn the De Groot farm,' Kitchener ordered, and for the moment it was spared, but when the wily old man continued to strike at unforeseen places, making fools of the English, Kitchener became coldly furious, and although he did not yet burn De Groot's farm, he ordered a wide swath of desolation on either side of the railway leading to Lourenço Marques. As soon as this was done, the Venloo Commando swept in and cut the railway in four places, to the intense delight of the French correspondent who accompanied the raid.

This was important, because the press of the world, especially the cartoonists, turned savagely against Great Britain, lampooning both her and Kitchener as murderers and bullies. Hardly a day passed that the influential papers in Amsterdam, Berlin and New York did not crucify Kitchener, showing him as a tyrant burning the food needed for starving Boer women and children. When one of the noble lord's English aides saw a selection of the worst cartoons, he grumbled, 'Damned few of those great fat Dutch women are starving.' But the corrosive propaganda continued, until it appeared that the entire world was opposed to England's performance in South Africa, as indeed it was, save for countries like Canada, Australia and New Zealand, which retained legal ties to the mother country.

The hero in this ceaseless barrage of pro-Boer propaganda had to be General de Groot—*Vengeur du Veld* and a cartoonist's delight. He was an old man in a frock coat and top hat, and he was accompanied by a woman whose stately demeanor under all circumstances had won the admiration of all newsmen. Together they formed an irresistible pair, especially when an American photographer caught them holding hands beside their battered wagon. In London a brazen Cockney paperboy bought himself a stack of white envelopes, labeled them PORTRAIT OF GENERAL DE GROOT and sold them for sixpence. When the purchaser opened the envelope to find nothing, the cheeky lad cried, to the delight of those in on the joke, 'Damn me, Guv'nor, 'e got away again!'

Who was chasing De Groot in these eight frustrating months of 1901? Instead of the troops going home at Christmas, 1900, as Lord Roberts had said they would, some two hundred thousand had to stay on. To them, at one time or another, were added another two hundred forty-eight thousand, not all of whom were in the field at one time. De Groot had two hundred twenty men, but of course there were other equally insolent commandos operating; however, the disparity between forces was both enormous and enraging. The vast numbers of English troops ought to have been able to catch the commandos, but they didn't; old De Groot and his wife ambled their way right through the traps set to catch them.

At one point when the summer heat was most unkind to the imported troops unaccustomed to the highveld, the following units, among many others, were striving to catch the Venloo Commando: from England, the Coldstream Guards; from Scotland, the Argyll and Sutherland Highlanders; from Ireland, the heroic Royal Inniskilling Fusiliers; from Wales, the Royal Welsh Fusiliers; from Canada, Lord Strathcona's Horse; from Australia, the Imperial Bushmen; from New Zealand, the Rough Riders; from Tasmania, the Mobile Artillery; from India, Lumsden's Horse; from Ceylon, the Mounted Infantry; from Burma, the Mounted Rifles; from Gibraltar, the 1st Manchesters; from Mauritius, the King's Own Yorkshire Light Infantry; from Egypt, the 1st Royal Fusiliers; and from Crete, the 2nd Rifle Brigade.

Earlier in the war the Boers, too, had help from outside. Adventurers from all nations, believing themselves to be fighting for liberty against aggression, had flocked to South Africa, and one important French colonel died in their ranks. There was an Irish regiment always eager to take a thrust at the English; a German and a Hollander contingent. Most tragic was a volunteer unit composed of one hundred and twenty-one idealistic Scandinavians, mostly Norwegian; in one of the earliest battles of the war almost the entire force was exterminated.

Such events were brilliantly reported, especially in the English press, for in addition to Winston Churchill, Rudyard Kipling came out to write about the conflict, championing the English cause in prose and verse; Edgar Wallace was a frenetic legman; Conan Doyle was afire with patriotism; H. W. Nevinson showed patrician restraint, and Richard Harding Davis the opposite; Banjo Patterson, who would become Australia's Poet Laureate with 'Waltzing Matilda,' did excellent reporting; and in the closing days quiet John Buchan looked things over. A strange assortment of visitors filtered in as observers; Prince Kuhio, heir to the throne of Hawaii, appeared one day, and as the scion of a family always strongly pro-English, was invited to the front, where he pulled the lanyard of a big gun, firing his blast at the hidden Boers.

In August 1901 English pressure became so powerful that the Boer command decreed that wives must no longer ride with their husbands, and on a bleak hillside Paulus de Groot had to inform his companion since childhood that she must leave. She did not want to go; that mean farm at Vrymeer was much less attractive to her than riding with her husband into battle. She had no fear of war's rigors; she wanted to share all things with Paulus, even though she suspected that sudden death or slow disillusion must be their fate. When Paulus remained firm, she became disconsolate.

'You are my life,' she said.

'It's the others. They made the decision. You must go home.'

'Where you are is home.'

'The rides will grow more difficult. The lines tighter.'

Thinking that this might be the last time she would ever see him, she knew that she must not cry. Instead she broke into an infectious chuckle. 'Remember when we were married? After the last battle with the Zulu? And the dominee said in a loud voice, "Does any man know why this man and woman should not be wed?"'

'Good God, what a moment!' the general cried, and then he, too, laughed.

'And Balthazar Bronk, always a troublemaker for other people, shouted that the marriage was forbidden. That we had been raised as brother and sister.'

They stood silent on the dark veld, and then she took his hand and whispered, 'You were never my brother, Paulus. After that night at Blaauwkrantz, I loved you always. And I always will.'

De Groot tried to speak, but no words came.

'Get sleep when you can,' she said, and they walked to the old wagon. He kissed her and helped her up, and she started up the hill.

Paulus remained holding his hat as she climbed to the crest. He did not expect her to look back, nor did she, but when she was gone, he prayed: Almighty God, forget the battles for a while and look after that woman.

When De Groot saw the first one, he shuddered. It was Lord Kitchener's invention for ending the guerrilla war. It was perched beside a vulnerable stretch of railway track, a device of admirable simplicity. It was made of corrugated iron and looked like one of those circular Spanish barns called silos, except that it was squatter. It consisted of two iron cylinders, one fitted inside the other, with enough room inside to house armed patrolmen. In the narrow space between the two cylinders rocks and debris had been jammed to give both protection and insulation. The top was enclosed by a conical roof, so that from a distance the contraption resembled a heavy, blunt cigar jammed into the earth.

Since the new device was obviously lethal and intended to halt the depredations of commandos, De Groot wanted to know as much about them as possible, and a man from the Carolina Commando, who had seen one after it had been blown up by a large force of dynamite, told all the burghers, 'Very difficult to destroy. Manned by seven soldiers. Three little beds. Place to cook. And some have telephones to the next blockhouse.'

As the commando looked down the tracks they had expected to dynamite, they saw six more of the blockhouses, cheap to build, easy to erect, and effective in breaking the open veld into manageable units out of which a mounted commando would have difficulty in moving.

'Look!' Jakob cried, and at the far end of the line of blockhouses, soldiers were stringing barbed wire from one house to the next. 'Kitchener's building a fence across Africa.'

This was correct. Goaded by ridicule, the commander had given orders that the railway system be protected by these new-style blockhouses, and when the first hundred proved successful, he called for eight thousand more, some of them built of stone. Once a commando found itself driven against one of the fortified barriers, its retreat could be so cut off that capture seemed inevitable.

Not for Paulus de Groot. When he was trapped the first time, in southern Transvaal, there was no escape; barbed wire flourished everywhere, but the English troops still had to find him. At the darkest moment he told Van Doorn, 'No army in the world ever found a way to keep all its enlisted men awake. Somewhere there's a blockhouse sound asleep.' He sent Micah to test the line for a weak spot, but when the Zulu scout crawled back he reported: 'All manned. All awake.'

'Try again,' De Groot growled, and this time the scout isolated one iron fort in which all seven men seemed to be asleep. With a swiftness that amazed some of the commandos, De Groot, Van Doorn and Nxumalo crept up to the house, worked their way under the barbed wire, and rushed the loopholes four feet above the ground, pouring in a deadly fire, killing all the occupants. Within minutes the Venloo Commando were cutting the wires that had restrained them, and after they had regained the open veld, one newspaperman quoted De Groot: 'Lord Blockhead's little toy houses cause us no worry.'

When cartoons across the world showed the noble lord playing with blocks while old General de Groot slipped away behind him, an enraged headquarters in Pretoria commanded: 'That man must be brought in.'

Regiments from eleven nations applied pressure, and once again the old man was trapped within a barbed-wire hedge, with Canadians, Irishmen, Australians and Welshmen closing in. This time he adopted a simple device: rounding up all available cattle from unburned farms, he stampeded them toward a spot between two blockhouses, and as the frightened animals piled up against the barbed wire, they simply carried it away, while the Venloo Commando swept off to freedom yet again.

This time the cartoonists were merciless: 'LIKE ULYSSES . . .' And they showed De Groot and his men tied to the bellies of the steers as they galloped past a sleeping Polyphemus who looked exactly like Lord Kitchener.

'All of them!' he thundered. 'I want all of them thrown into camps.' So his men moved out to corral every woman and child belonging to the fighting Boers. They would be herded into camps of concentration, to keep them from feeding and supporting their menfolk. It was pointed out to Kitchener that there were already more than fifty thousand refugees in camps, many there at the behest of Boers themselves, for they had been unable to survive on farms without their men. 'I don't care if there are fifty thousand more!' stormed Kitchener.

When the drive against the commando-homesteads was well under way, and the Boer territories further denuded of women and farms and cattle, leaving only smoking ruins, Kitchener began to see good results. Three commandants, unable to survive against starvation and barbed wire, voluntarily surrendered, but before doing so their top men crept away to join up with General de Groot, whose forces now reached their maximum: four hundred and thirty hardened men, a hundred extra ponies and fifty blacks. This would be the final army, led by an old man approaching seventy.

Pleased with the apparent effectiveness of the concentration camp, Lord Kitchener summoned Major Saltwood one morning and gave him an order: 'Burn Vrymeer and herd the women into the camp at Chrissie Meer.'

'Are you sure you want to do this, sir?'

'I am,' the steely-eyed general said, 'and I deem it best if you lead the men, rather than an Englishman.'

'I think of myself as an Englishman, sir, and I don't relish assignments like this.'

'I consider you a local, Saltwood. It'll look better.'

So with a mixed detachment of seventy, including troops from various colonies, Saltwood rode east on the Lourenço Marques train, disembarked his horses at Waterval-Boven, and rode slowly south toward the lake—a journey he had taken in happier times. When he reached Venloo and saw the heavy price it had paid in this war, all windows shattered, a feeling of despair came over him, and he remembered what Maud had said that day at Trianon: 'Seems more like Genghis Khan.'

Then he turned west on the pleasant rural road leading to the lake, and when he crested the hill he could see the two farms at which he had once been so happy and so well received. It pained him to think that these good people had later considered him to be a spy, but he supposed, upon reflection, that he had been, in a general way of speaking. He did not want to go on, but when the men behind began to rein up near him he sighed and headed for the rickety buildings of the De Groot farm. 'Not much lost if they burn,' a Welshman said.

Sybilla was in the kitchen, and when she saw the troops she knew what to expect. Without saying a word, she packed a few belongings, reached for her sunbonnet, and appeared on the stoep. 'General Kitchener's orders,' a soldier said. 'Men, set the fires.'

In a way the flames were merciful; they were erasing farm buildings that had long since served their day, and removing them was an act of good husbandry, but as the fire spread, Saltwood became aware of voices behind him, and turning, saw the four Van Doorn children: the girls Anna, Sannah and Johanna, and the handsome little boy Detlev.

'Sir, sir! What are you doing?' one of the girls screamed.

At this moment Major Saltwood chanced to look down from his horse and catch the eye of the oldest girl, Johanna, twenty-one years old, and he saw in her such hatred that he almost shuddered, yet with this fierce animosity she was also studying him, as if she had seen him before. She did not seem to remember, for which he was grateful.

'I suppose you'll burn ours, too,' she said through teeth that were almost clenched. 'My father rides with the general.'

'Be gentle with the old woman,' Saltwood shouted at his men as Sybilla was placed in a wagon. 'Gather the children.' The three youngest were lifted up by soldiers and deposited beside her as the troop wheeled its horses and made its way to the Van Doorn farm—with Johanna walking grimly through the dust.

This was no outmoded collection of shacks. It was one of the stoutest farms in eastern Transvaal, a place of stone buildings and excellent rondavels for its blacks. To burn this would be to destroy the heart of a rich agricultural district. 'Burn it!' Saltwood said, but before the torch could be applied to the wooden parts that would ignite, a woman appeared at the kitchen door.

'What are you doing?' she demanded.

'Lord Kitchener's orders, ma'am. You're to get in the wagon.'

'That I will not do,' Sara van Doorn said, and when the Australians guarding the wagon relaxed their attention Johanna ran to join her mother. Together the two women blocked the entrance to the house.

'Remove them!' Saltwood commanded, and a detachment of Irish cavalrymen grabbed at the women, but they broke away and dashed into the house. When soldiers forced them out, the women carried in their arms the chief treasures of the Van Doorn family: Mevrou van Doorn held the brassbound Bible; Johanna, the ceramic pot in which her father made his bread pudding.

A good fire was now burning in the shed, and one of the soldiers tried to snatch the book, intending to throw it in, but Mevrou van Doorn struggled to retain possession, and there was a scuffle until Saltwood saw what was happening. 'Good God, man. That's a Bible. Stand off.' He was too late, however, to protect the pot that Johanna held, for a brutish soldier brought the butt of his gun around in a circle, caught the pot, and smashed it. When the dozen pieces tumbled to the boards of the stoep, it was apparent that a clever person with the right glue could reassemble the precious old thing, and Johanna stooped to gather some of the pieces, but this enraged the soldier, who brushed her aside and ground the remaining fragments under his boot.

'Stand back, you fool!' Saltwood cried, but as he did so he looked into the eyes of this embittered girl, and she remembered who he was: 'Mother! He's the spy.'

From her wagon, Sybilla looked out to inspect the man in charge of this destruction, and she, too, recognized him: 'The spy!' The twin girls, peering from beneath the canvas, saw who he was and they joined the lamentation: 'The spy! He's Saltwood the spy.'

When Frank dismounted to reassure the two Van Doorn women on the stoep, Johanna spat in his face: 'They should have hanged you.'

'They should have hanged you!' the twins shouted, and Detlev, finding sticks in the wagon, started throwing them at their betrayer. Meanwhile, the fires raged.

It was only thirty-eight miles from Vrymeer to the cluster of large lakes which the English called Chrissie Meer. Here the concentration camp had been established, but in that distance Major Saltwood's column had collected five additional wagons filled with women and children from farms en route. Since all buildings had been burned, the women were sooty and weeping as they turned the last corner; then they looked with awe at their destination. Their camp lay at the edge of one of the loveliest lakes in Africa: a surface shimmering in sunlight, hills rising softly from the shore, flowers in beds, and a hint of animals hiding in the glens. Saltwood said to a member of the Welsh Fusiliers, 'If you must have a prison camp . . . the clean air . . . the sunlight . . .' In months ahead when the name of this camp echoed with shame, he would concede that it was at least a place of physical beauty. To it he delivered Sybilla de Groot, Sara van Doorn and the four Van Doorn children, but as he did so he noticed by sheerest accident a tent in which three young children lay sleeping, he thought; on closer inspection he saw that they were awake, too emaciated to respond when he spoke to them.

Rushing to the commandant's office, a doctor from the English Midlands, he cried, 'Sir, those children in the tent at the bottom of Row Eighteen. Sir, those children are starving.'

'There is no starvation here,' the doctor said sternly, as if reporting on his hospital to a village committee of inspection.

'But those children! Legs like matchsticks!'

'We are all like matchsticks,' the doctor cried, his voice suddenly rising almost to a scream, as if his earlier composure had been tenuous. 'And do you know why?' He uttered a string of obscenities Saltwood had not heard for years; they were not used at officers' headquarters. 'It's your goddamned Lord Kitchener, that's who it is. Go back and tell him what you saw.'

'I can't leave my women here . . .'

'You're right, Colonel . . . What's your name?'

'Saltwood, and I'm a major.'

'English?'

'I'm from the Cape. And I'd appreciate your telling me where to take these women.'

'Where? Yes, where?'

'Doctor, lower your voice. You sound demented.'

'I am demented!' the little man screamed in a Lancashire dialect. 'I am demented with shame.'

With a sudden swipe of his right arm, Saltwood knocked the agitated man against a wall, then pulled him up and sat him at his desk. 'Now tell me without bellowing—what's the matter?'

'Typhoid's the matter. Measles are the matter. And dysentery, dysentery's the matter.' He broke down and sobbed so pitifully that Saltwood had to cover his own face in compassion.

'Tell me in an orderly way,' he said, touching the doctor's shoulder. 'I can see it's horrible, but what can we do?'

The doctor jabbed at his eyes, rumpled through some papers, found a report, and covered it with his hands for a moment. 'We're at the end of the supply line here, Colonel. Headquarters can't send us enough food. But the diet would sustain life, except for the incessant illness.' And here he repeated his litany of death: 'Typhoid, measles, dysentery. We could fight any one, but a body already weakened by stringent diet, it hasn't the strength. These figures tell our story.' And he shoved the paper forward. 'Deaths per thousand, months of February, March, seven hundred and eighty-three.'

'My God!' Saltwood cried.

'Those were the bad months. Chrissie Meer's average is usually less than three hundred.'

'But even so, that's one in three.'

'Yes,' the doctor said. 'Of the thirty-seven women and children you delivered today, maybe fifteen, maybe twenty will be dead at the end of six months, if dysentery runs wild again, if the food supply weakens.'

'Doctor, you are in very sore condition yourself. I think I should take you back to Pretoria.'

A nurse heard this proposal and stepped forward, an extremely gaunt woman. 'Dr. Higgins controls his feelings most of the time. We all try to. And when we get fresh vegetables or meat from the countryside, we keep many people alive. But without medicines . . .' She shrugged her shoulders. 'Dr. Higgins is a very strong man, spiritually. He does what he can.'

'What do you need?' Saltwood asked.

She hesitated, looked at Dr. Higgins, and saw that she would get no help there. He had withdrawn from the discussion. 'We need everything. Hospital beds. Medicines. We have no toilet paper. Dysentery runs wild, and children seem to starve, as you saw. If we don't get help soon, and I mean nourishing food in better supply, all the children you brought us will be dead.'

Two nights later, when he was back in Pretoria, he found that there were no additional supplies for Chrissie Meer, at the far end of the line: no extra food, no medicines, no sanitary aids, and he could see his children, the ones he had taken to the camp, dying. Retiring to his room, with dull anguish assailing him, he wrote a love letter:

My dearest darling Maud,

I have never before addressed a letter to you like this, because I did not appreciate how desperately I love you and how much I need you. I have been to Chrissie Meer, to the big concentration camp there, and I am shattered. You must do all you can to alleviate the condition of these pitiful people. Food, blankets, medicines, trained people. Maud, spend all our savings, volunteer yourself, but for God's sake and the reputation of our people, you must do something. At this end I shall do whatever I can. An evil fog has fallen over this land, and if we do not dissipate it promptly, it will contaminate all future relationships between Englishman and Boer.

When I rode back from Chrissie Meer, I reflected on the fact that the three men who were spoilers of this land, Shaka, Rhodes, Kitchener, not one of them had a wife. I fear that men without women are capable of terrible misdeeds, and I want to apologize to you for having allowed Mr. Rhodes to delay our marriage as he did. I was as evil as he in conforming to that hateful posture, and I bless you tonight for the humanity you have brought into my life.

Your most loving husband,
Frank

When word circulated at headquarters that Maud Saltwood was creating disturbances—'Not riots, you understand, but real annoyances, questions, and all that, you know'—Lord Kitchener was enraged. It infuriated him that one of his own men should be unable to control his wife, permitting her to make a fuss over the camps, where, as he pointed out again and again, 'the women and children are much better off than they would be in their own homes.'

'Bring Saltwood in here!' he thundered. When the major stood before him he used his baton to indicate a pile of papers. 'What's all this—these reports—about your wife, Saltwood?'

'She's doing what she can to alleviate conditions—'

'Alleviate? There's nothing to alleviate.'

'Sir, with all respect, have you seen the death rate—'

'Damnit, sir, don't you be insolent with me.' The noble lord looked as if he could bite Saltwood in half, and would relish doing so. 'You sit down there, and listen to someone who knows.'

He summoned a Dr. Riddle, from London, who had just returned from a tour of the forty-odd camps. He was a cheery man, obviously well-fed, and seemed full of enthusiasm. With alacrity he took the report Lord Kitchener held out to him. 'I wrote this, you understand, Saltwood. Done on the spot.' From it he read his major conclusions:

'The Boer women and children are noticeably better off than they would be if left on their abandoned farms. They receive adequate supplies of the most healthful foods, on which they seem to prosper and if—'

'Did you get out to Chrissie Meer?' Saltwood interrupted. 'Listen to the report,' Kitchener snapped. 'I wasn't able to get that far east,' Dr. Riddle said.

> 'Whatever illness appears in the camps is due primarily to the Boer women themselves. Having been raised on farms without privies, they cannot learn to adopt the sanitary measures which alone prevent the spread of epidemics. And when illness does strike, they insist upon resorting to country measures that have not been used in civilized nations for the past sixty years. They wrap a measled child in the skin of a freshly slaughtered goat. They grub in the countryside for old herbs which they claim can reduce fever. They recite rhymes as if they were witch doctors. And they will not wash their hands.'

'I am seriously thinking of bringing criminal charges against some of these mothers,' Kitchener said with great irritation. 'They should be tried for murder. It's all their fault, you know.'

> 'So I must conclude that the English authorities are doing everything humanly possible to protect the women and children in our charge. I found them in good condition, reasonably happy, and with every probability of leaving the camps in better condition than when they entered.'

'What would your precious wife make of that?' Lord Kitchener asked, fastening his hard eyes on Saltwood.

Saltwood, having once denied his wife in the presence of a strong man, had no intention of doing so again: 'I think, sir, she would say that such a report does both you and the king an injustice.'

An explosion without specific words erupted, after which Kitchener roared, 'Are you impugning the integrity of Dr. Riddle?'

Taking a deep breath, Saltwood replied, 'I am saying that his report does not begin to cover conditions at Chrissie Meer, and, I suspect, at a lot of other installations I haven't seen.'

'But your wife has seen them?'

'Sir, the day may come when you will be eternally grateful that my wife spoke out in these bad days.'

'Bad days, damn you! We're winning along the entire front.'

'Not in the camps, sir. You run great risk of damaging your reputation because of what's happening—'

'Show him, Riddle,' Kitchener said. 'Show him the other page.'

'I'll read it,' the ebullient doctor said, not wishing this secret part of his report to fall into other hands, even temporarily:

> 'The complaint of the Boers that their women and children are dying at an excessive rate is belied by the statistics of our own forces. To date 19,381 such Boers have died in the camps, but it must be remembered that in the same period 15,849 of our soldiers have died under similar circumstances. It is not our barbarity that kills, nor starvation on the diet we provide; it is the physical nature of the camps and the hospitals, the incessant spread of dysentery and typhoid, and these strike Boer and Englishman even-handedly.'

'And what do you think of that?' Kitchener snapped, but Frank was too ashamed of the mendacity of this report to say what he thought: The English soldiers went into their hospitals wounded or already near death from disease. Most Boer women and children went in healthy. Both died, and at equal rates, but from much different causes.

'Well?' Kitchener asked. 'They're equal, aren't they?'

'In war, unarmed women and children do not equal men in uniform.'

'Get out of here! You're dismissed from my headquarters. I will not have a man around me who cannot control his own wife.' When Saltwood remained at attention, Kitchener repeated, 'Get out. You're dismissed with prejudice. You can never again serve with an English unit. You are unreliable, sir, and a disgrace to your uniform.'

In a calm such as he had not known since he began serving under General Buller, Frank Saltwood looked down at Lord Kitchener at his desk, arranging reports which proved that England was winning the war. 'Permission to speak, sir?'

'Granted—then begone.'

'If you pursue the war along these lines, you'll be remembered as the general who lost the peace.' With that he saluted, marched from the room, and headed for the Johannesburg railway. At Cape Town, hungry for the civilizing spirit of his wife, he burst into their quarters to find her gone. The maid said, 'She's out to inspect the camps, Mr. Saltwood.' When the girl left, he bowed his head and mumbled, 'Thank you, God, for showing at least one of us his duty. I mean her duty.' In the morning he would find where she was working, and join her.

When Sybilla de Groot and the Van Doorns were deposited at their concentration camp, they were assigned to a small bell tent that already contained a family of four, the two youngest of whom were near death. Sybilla, white-haired and somewhat stooped, came into the tent, saw what needed to be done, and said quietly to the Van Doorns, 'We can make do.'

She moved the cots of the dying children to where they would catch a breeze, then did what she could to encourage the women to get up and see if they could scrounge even a little extra food for the children, but she saw to her amazement that the women lacked not only the stamina to do this, but also the will. In a daze of terror she left the three youngest Van Doorns in the tent and drew Sara and Johanna out into the open, where she took each by the hand, squeezing until her own fingers hurt. 'We must not surrender. The children will live only if we live. We must never give in.' Looking alternately at her two friends, she asked them, 'Do you swear?' They swore that they would not surrender.

When the first of the two children died, in terrible emaciation caused by a combination of typhoid, dysentery and inadequate food, Sybilla tried to mask the fact from Detlev, only six years old, but he knew what death was, and said, 'The little girl is dead.'

The entire tent—that is, those who could walk—attended the funeral. Camp attendants, who seemed to be quite healthy, came down the lane between the tents, collecting bodies, and at Sybilla's they lifted up the little corpse, then reached for the other child, who lay inanimate. 'That one's not dead yet,' Detlev said, and the attendants passed on.

The attendants carted the bodies to a busy burial ground, where a carpenter from Carolina had volunteered to build rude caskets from whatever odds and ends he could scavenge. He was Hansie Bronk, descendant of that Balthazar Bronk who had protested the marriage of Sybilla and Paulus de Groot; big, round-shouldered, blessed with a rural sense of humor, he was a civilizing force, his most appreciated contribution being not his caskets, but his ability now and then to find extra meat and vegetables in the countryside.

When Detlev appeared at the burial ground, Hansie chucked him under the chin and said, 'Nou moenie siek word nie, my klein mannetjie.' (Now don't you fall sick, little man.)

This day there were four caskets, and beside their shallow graves stood Dr. Higgins holding a Bible. He despised every moment of his service in this horrible place but felt obligated to oversee all that happened, as if he were both the cause and the participant, and he strove to make the burials decent. Detlev listened as the doctor prayed.

The boy was in the tent three days later when the other little girl died, her arms like threads, and he walked with the attendants as they collected the bodies of those who had died of fever in the preceding hours. He was always present at the burials, and always Hansie Bronk told him, 'Nou moenie siek word nie, my klein mannetjie.'

His watchful eye noticed when the older of his twin sisters—Anna, who boasted of her precedence—began to waste away, but he was not prepared for what happened when he said to his mother, 'Anna needs medicine,' for Mevrou van Doorn uttered a piercing scream and started running down to the doctor's quarters—but there were no medical supplies.

'My God!' Sybilla cried, running after her, slapping her and bringing her back to the tent. 'We swore an oath, Sara. We have got to protect the children.' When food was doled out, a meager amount, the hungry women apportioned much of it to the twin, who nevertheless grew weaker each day.

'Is Anna going to die?' Detlev asked.

'Don't say that!' his mother cried, whereupon old Sybilla shook her again and made her sit down, and she became quiet.

In time Anna did die, just as Detlev had expected, and at the funeral he watched attentively as Hansie Bronk placed her thin body in one of his caskets. On this day there were four other children to be buried, and when Dr. Higgins tried to read from his Bible he could not control his voice, so Sybilla took the book and finished reading the Psalm. Detlev listened to the sound of earth pitched upon the caskets.

The death of her child had such a debilitating effect on Sara that she seemed to wilt in the intense heat like one of the flowers. At night it was extremely cold, and this sharp fluctuation aggravated whatever illnesses the internees contracted, but in Sara's case it was merely lack of will power.

One week the supply of Boer meal increased noticeably, and everyone in the tent received an extra portion, but this did little good for one of the women whose children had perished. She ate a little, smiled at Detlev, and died. At her burial he wept for the first time.

But if Lord Kitchener believed that by imprisoning the Boer women he would break the spirit of their men, he misconceived the nature of these people, for when the women were thrown together, their resolve doubled and they, even more than the men, grew determined to see this war through to victory. When four had already died in her tent, Sybilla de Groot wrote a letter, which was reprinted in hundreds of newspapers:

Chrissiesmeer, Transvaal
Christmas Day 1901

General Paulus de Groot,

Never surrender. If you have to fight on foot, one against five hundred, never surrender. Carry fire to all parts of the land, but never surrender. They think that because they have thrown us here and because they deny our children food to eat that we will urge you to stop. They miscalculate. From the bottom of our hearts we cry to you, never surrender. We send you our kisses and our love, and we pray for your victory. Run, hide, retreat, burn, dynamite, Paulus, but never surrender.

Sybilla de Groot
Sara van Doorn
and 43 others

Lord Kitchener's relentless pressure began to produce limited results. Certain weary men, contrary to their wives' pleas, did surrender. They were called contemptuously 'hands-uppers,' and in the early years of the war would have been shipped off to imprisonment in Ceylon or Napoleon's St. Helena. But now, with the war approaching an end, it was deemed economical to incarcerate them within the country; with their farms burned and their families scattered, the only reasonable solution was to add them to the concentration camps. This was a dreadful mistake, for when two of these men were billeted at Chrissie Meer, Sybilla, Sara and the other incarcerated wives marched to the doctor's office and warned him: 'Get those "hands-uppers" out of here or they'll be murdered.'

'Now wait, that's a fearful thing to say. These men—'

'Get them out of here,' the women cried in unison.

'Ladies,' the doctor said in an attempt to restore sanity. Death from disease was one thing, but planned murder was another. 'Will you listen to reason?'

'If they sleep here tonight,' Sybilla said slowly, 'I myself will murder them.'

The doctor gasped. This was not a wild phrase thrown out in the heat of protest; this was the calm threat of a resolute old woman who could be depended upon to fulfill it. 'We'll move them away,' he said, and the women departed.

That was the last gesture Sara van Doorn was able to make. She was so weakened from continued fever that one morning, on a fearfully hot day, she had not the strength to rise, and Detlev went running for Sybilla, who was always up early to see if she could add a little food to the ration. 'Ouma Sybilla,' the boy cried. 'I think Mother is going to die.'

'You're not to use that word.'

'She can't lift her head.'

'Then we must see what's the matter,' the old woman said, and she led the boy back to the tent. He was right, his mother was about to die. The long ordeal of keeping her family together without a husband, and now without proper food and medicine, had been too demanding. Her strength was gone, and even when Sybilla and Johanna pleaded with her, reminding her of her promise, she was powerless to respond, and toward noon, in the blazing heat, she expired.

Five in this tent had now died, so after the attendants took away her body they moved a new family of four in to take their places, and Detlev watched with equal interest the departure of his mother and the arrival of these four doomed women. But then he realized that he would never again see his mother, and with a half-wail he ran after her, clinging to Johanna's hand as the body was placed in one of Hansie's caskets. When Detlev sought consolation from this kindly carpenter, Hansie had to turn away, for he was weeping.

'Almighty God,' intoned the weary doctor, 'take these Thy children to Thy bosom.' He looked as if he might topple into the grave with them.

Of the four newcomers, two died quickly, and Johanna, watching her brother carefully, worried that he had now witnessed seven burials of people with whom he had shared the tent, two from his own family, and she asked Sybilla what the effect might be. 'Children can stand anything, if even one person loves them,' she said, remembering the days after Blaauwkrantz. 'You and I must love that boy, Johanna.'

'What about Sannah?' the girl asked, and the old woman said harshly, 'Death is upon her.'

And with dreadful speed it came. Her frail body, fourteen years old and at the height of its beauty, wasted so swiftly that even Sybilla, who had anticipated this, was aghast. The child was laughing wanly one day, unable to move the next.

'Oh, Sannah!' the little boy wept. 'I need you.'

'I need you, Detlev, my dear, dear brother.' Limply she extended a hand, and he sat holding it through the night, but before dawn he crept to where Sybilla slept and whispered, 'I think she's dead.'

'Oh, God,' Sybilla sighed.

'Shall I tell Johanna?'

'No, she needs her sleep.' She rose wearily, near fainting from lack of food, and went to the cot on which the dead girl lay and sat beside her, taking her lovely head in her lap. Detlev joined her, not crying, just sitting there in the dark. When he took one of her hands he could feel no flesh, only bones, and as he clasped it the hand grew cold.

'You are very dear to me, Detlev,' Sybilla whispered. 'You are my own son, the son of General de Groot, too. He and your real father, they fight for us, and in the years to come you must fight for us, too. You must remember these nights, Detlev. Never, never forget how Sannah felt in your arms this night. It is nights like this, Detlev, that make a man.'

They were sitting there when the attendants came, but when Johanna, waking tardily, saw them reach down for her beautiful sister, she started screaming 'No! No!' and it was Detlev who had to tell her that the girl was indeed dead. But this time at the grave he could no longer constrain himself, and when the attendants placed her in a box he started shivering as if this were some entirely new experience, and Sybilla took him in her arms.

With three of the Van Doorns dead, and both Johanna and Detlev obviously weaker each day, Sybilla de Groot realized that the salvation of this camp depended upon what women like her accomplished in the perilous days ahead. If they flagged in their dedication, the death of despair could sweep the camp, but if they sustained hope, and encouraged discipline and fortitude, lives of enormous value could be saved. She took as her litmus paper young Detlev: If I can save him, I can save the Boer republics.

Weak though she was, and close to her own death, she rallied the children of the camp about her. 'I am General de Groot's wife,' she told the parents, 'and while he is on commando in the field, you and I are on commando in this prison camp. I want your children.'

With indomitable force she organized a system whereby the children could receive just a little bit larger share of the daily ration. She persuaded Hansie Bronk to steal just a bit more food, then teased him about his notorious grandfather. But most of all she concentrated on the children, instructing them in the legends of their people.

'I was at Blaauwkrantz,' she told them. 'I was no older than you, Grietjie, when Dingane's men came after me. And do you know what I did?' The hollow, ghostly eyes of the children would stare at her as she acted out that night. 'My father placed me under a tree, in the darkest hours, and what do you think he told me?' And she would watch quietly as the children pondered, and always someone, enchanted by the story, would guess that her father had told her to be quiet, and she would smile at that child.

She told them of the long years she and Paulus de Groot had waged their battles, and of Majuba, where she saw the charge up the hill, and of recent Spion Kop, where a handful of Boers had beaten back the entire English army. She sang songs with the little ones, and played easy games that required no motion, for they were too weak, but always she returned to the theme of heroism and the simple things one man and one woman could accomplish: 'The battle was lost, no doubt about it, but General de Groot saw a weakness in the line and drove his men right at it, and we triumphed.'

'Were you afraid?' a girl asked.

'I am always afraid,' Sybilla said. 'I am afraid that I will not be brave, but when the test comes, we can all be brave.'

And at some point in each session she spoke directly to Detlev, whose salvation was paramount in her plans. She told him of how Boer boys were supposed to act, of how they had sometimes run at night to alert the villages, and of the joys they had known during long treks. Day after day she hammered into his soul the binding nails of patriotism, and reverence, and persistence. And each day she saw him grow physically weaker.

When Jakob heard that his wife and the twins were dead, and that his son Detlev was near death, and his farm totally destroyed, he became a somber madman, eager to support the wildest schemes of his general, and when De Groot suggested that the commando make a swift foray through English lines and down into the Cape, he was first to volunteer.

'I want no more than ninety men,' De Groot said. 'Forty extra horses and some of the best scouts. There's little chance we can return. Five hundred miles down, five hundred back.'

'What are we going to do?' one young fellow asked.

'Burn Port Elizabeth.'

The crowd cheered, and within a minute the old man had his ninety, but enthusiasm was tempered when plans showed that they would be forced to cross both the Vaal and the Orange . . . twice. Some wanted to know if that could be done, and he said sharply, 'It has to be.'

The Vaal, smaller of the two, would present most dangers, because the drifts were heavily guarded with extra blockhouses and mobile troops who patrolled it constantly; Lord Kitchener, having driven the various commandos into pockets, did not want them coalescing. During a dangerous reconnoiter Micah Nxumalo located a spot where the guard seemed to be relaxed, but as he explained to De Groot: 'That's because the riverbank there is steep. Difficult to ford.'

'We can't have everything,' De Groot said, but since he treasured his men, he wanted to see the terrain himself, so he went out with Micah and saw that what he had said was true: weak defense but perilous crossing. For a whole night the two men searched the area, concluding in the end that Micah's spot was best.

'We go!' De Groot said.

It was to be a brutal affair. Cut the barbed wires, overwhelm two blockhouses, killing all the guards, and gallop the ponies over the steep banks and into the Vaal River, trusting to luck that no mounted English patrols would be astir. They would do it at twelve thirty-five, an odd and arbitrary hour, and as it approached, the ninety whispered among themselves, 'On to Port Elizabeth,' and they laughed to think how surprised those people would be when their town was ablaze. That the odds against such a success were in the order of five thousand-to-one did not distress them.

At midnight they approached the blockhouses, each with seven soldiers, two ordinary posts among the eight thousand. At twelve-thirty no armed patrols had appeared, and at twelve thirty-five the Boers rushed forward. The wire cutters went to work, and the men reached the corrugated-iron silos before those inside could fire. All fourteen were slain before they could signal the next blockhouse in line.

But soldiers in the distant houses had detected that something was wrong, and they telephoned for help. An armed patrol in the district asked for directions and began galloping across the veld, but as they reached the threatened area, they saw only the flanks of many ponies thrashing through the dark waters. There was firing, but not to much account—and in Pretoria, Lord Kitchener was awakened with the news that General de Groot had broken loose once more.

'Do the correspondents know?'

'Everyone knows.' As Lord Kitchener had said several times, 'I'd like to shoot every damned newsman. They make these damned Boer banditti the darlings of Fleet Street.'

It was a gallop for two days, then a canter for seven through the loveliest parts of the Orange Free State. They bivouacked for some time near Thaba Nchu and listened to De Groot tell about his first great battle, when Mzilikazi's men killed his entire family: 'I was a coward hiding in the wagons of this man's father.' And he slapped Van Doorn.

They rode in a kind of dream world, with the veld stretching in all directions, never a tree in sight, only the sweeping valleys, the lovely flat-topped hills, with now and then a herd of antelope moving against the slow motion of the horsemen. Thousands of skilled soldiers were hunting for this little group, but still they rode in comparative safety, the distances were so vast. When the meerkats spied on them, De Groot called down from his pony, 'Hurry and tell Lord Kitchener you saw us. And demand more pay.' Only the sky, and the distant hills, and the gentle sweep of the barren land. 'This is earth we must keep,' De Groot told his men as they rode easily, one foot in the stirrup. 'We could ride like this forever,' Jakob said quietly to a friend. There was no war, no chase, no sudden death.

The crossing of the Orange was not especially difficult because no one dreamed that a Boer commando would try anything so preposterous as an invasion of the Cape, but when the news flashed that Paulus de Groot had forded the river between Philippolis and Colesburg, the world came to attention, and diverse reactions were voiced. Those who wished England well were disgusted that the Avenger of the Veld had been allowed to run loose yet again, while those who hoped to see England humiliated, the greater part, reveled in his escapade. It was predicted that he would head west to pick off some town like Swellendam, but instead he turned sharply east to avoid Graaff-Reinet, which would be well defended; he came at last upon his original De Groot homestead, now owned by an English family.

'Each of you, select two horses,' he told the Englishman.

'What are you going to do?'

'Take two horses and anything you especially prize. Ride to Grahamstown.'

'What are you going to do?'

'This was my farm. My family's farm. And I'm going to burn it to the ground.'

'That's insanity.'

'I'll give you thirty minutes to pick the things you want. You women, gather your personal possessions.' When the Englishman protested, he said quietly, 'That's more than your Lord Kitchener gave my wife.'

When the people were herded away, he set fire to everything, adding to the combustibles when the flames threatened to go out. When the farm was reduced to ashes, he rode to the next one and then the next. At last he told Van Doorn, 'Over that hill, if I remember. I was only a child then, and maybe I don't remember. But over that hill . . .' When they reached the top there was nothing, and De Groot said, 'I was afraid. But aren't those tracks? It'll be the next hill, maybe.'

At the top of the fourth hill Jakob van Doorn saw, for the first time in his life, the splendid farm put together by his ancestors: 'I think Mal Adriaan must have started the place. The house was built by Lodevicus the Hammer. Those additions were Tjaart's, God bless that fighting man. He'd understand.'

'When this one goes up,' De Groot said with soaring enthusiasm, 'all the Cape Boers will rally to us. It'll be a whole new war.'

'All who intend to are already riding with our commandos,' Jakob warned. 'There'll be no more.'

'Of course there will. They're patriotic . . .'

'They have money, Paulus, not patriotism. I was here, remember?'

'At this farm?'

'No, but at the Cape. They talk politics, not war.'

As the commando came down the hill, the men began to shout, and from the farm buildings numerous people appeared. 'Get ready to leave!' the Venloo men cried as they began to light their torches, but before General de Groot could give the signal, a woman in a gray linseywoolsey dress appeared at the door of the principal house.

'What do you want?' she asked as the men approached.

'I am General de Groot, of the Venloo Commando, and we are going to burn your farm.'

'I saw your wife at Chrissie Meer,' the woman said quietly. 'And aren't you Van Doorn? I saw your son and daughter.'

There was a long silence as the two men looked at this fearless woman, and finally De Groot asked, 'Are you the woman of the camps?'

'I am Maud Turner Saltwood.'

Both of the Boers spoke at once: 'The traitor?'

'The man who quit Lord Kitchener because he could not tolerate the camps.'

'You are that lady?' De Groot asked again. When she nodded, he hesitated, then wheeled his horse about and led his men, still with their flaming brands, away from the farm. He rode farther south for two days, but during that time he began to realize the futility of attempting to reach the Indian Ocean; from three directions young Boer scouts reported the presence of enemy troops, and Micah Nxumalo, who had gone in the direction of Grahamstown, said that a force of English and Cape colonials were massing there. At dawn on the third day De Groot told his commando, 'We could never get to Port Elizabeth. Let's go home.'

They left behind them a flame of glory and wonder, the commando that almost reached the sea, the men from the tiny town of Venloo who rode through the heartland of the conqueror and then turned back, untouched by the four hundred thousand who searched for them.

When Maud Saltwood returned to Chrissie Meer to complete her documentation on the concentration camps, she wanted to examine, as dispassionately as possible, the actual conditions, and she sought out Sybilla de Groot, knowing her to be a sensible woman. But she found her so emaciated from dysentery that she wondered how she could stand, let alone converse intelligently.

'Was Frank Saltwood a spy?' the old woman asked.

'We've never discussed it.'

'We know that Lord Kitchener's a monster.'

'He's not a monster. He's a foolish, bullheaded man who has no heart. Now we must get you some medicine.'

'There is none,' the old woman said, and she was right. The English could bring into this tight area four hundred and forty-eight thousand soldiers, but they could not find space in their ships for the extra medicines and food needed to save emaciated women and children. They could import a hundred thousand horses for their cavalry, but not three cows for their concentration camps. Guns bigger than houses they could haul in, but no hospital equipment. It was insane; it was horrifying; and in her news reports Maud Saltwood said so.

'That woman should be shot' was Lord Kitchener's sober evaluation of the affair. Many members of Parliament felt the same way, and her husband's cousin, Sir Victor, kept a low profile, for she had besmirched his name. But on she went, one woman exposing to the world the monstrous wrong of these camps. In Cape Town many English families stopped speaking to her husband, while others commiserated with him over his wife's misconduct, not realizing that he supported her enthusiastically. His income, which she spent lavishly, kept alive some three hundred women who would otherwise have perished, and for this he would be forever grateful to his vigorous wife.

While Kitchener raged, Maud quietly continued interrogating women at Chrissie Meer, spending much time in the associated camp where blacks were being held. There she talked with women of Micah Nxumalo's family, and they were suffering as sorely as the whites.

'Why we here?' one woman asked plaintively, showing her thin arms.

'Isn't your father fighting with the Boers?' Maud asked.

'Your husband fight with English. They throw you in jail?'

Her most fruitful discussions were with Sybilla de Groot, for the old woman sensed that she would soon die and was eager to have her views spread before the world: 'Like many wrong things, it was all wrong. There should have been no camps.'

'Some say,' Maud argued, 'that the camps were good for you women. They gave you security.'

If Sybilla had been strong, she would have raged and stomped about the little bell tent; she was so weak she had to remain seated, but she did point to the entrance: 'Through there we have carried eight dead. Detlev counts them for me. What kind of security is that?'

But when Maud asked about sanitary conditions, the old woman did make certain concessions: 'We were farm families, far from towns. We didn't have privies like they say we must. We didn't have these new medicines. In the free veld we were never sick. In these tents, these dirty barracks, we die. Eight of us, and soon me.' She rocked back and forth, tears streaming from her eyes. 'That's why I say it was wrong from the beginning. It was all wrong.'

'Did you get enough to eat?' Maud asked.

Sybilla held out her arms for inspection. 'You don't get enough. You grow weak. So you get sick. Then, no matter how much you eat, it does no good.' She pointed to the field not far from her tent where women and children, driven mad by dysentery, were squatting and wrenching their insides. 'It's all wrong,' she said.

Desperately Maud wanted to keep this great woman alive, as a symbol of the fact that English women, at least, would do everything in their power to save a Boer woman, even though she was the wife of their country's principal aggravator. She failed.

In April 1902, when the imperial armies were at last closing in upon Paulus de Groot, pinning him against the barbed-wire fences but never catching him, Detlev woke early one morning to find his Ouma Sybilla gasping. Since it was a clear autumn day, with the air somewhat fresher than usual, he knew the old woman was in distress, and he wanted to awaken Johanna, but his sister was deep in sleep, exhausted in the cool morning air, so he went to Sybilla's cot alone.

'Are you awake?'

'I hoped you'd come.' She turned her head weakly, and when he looked at her arms, thin as the reeds beside their lake, he realized that she was powerless to move. 'Fetch Johanna.'

'She's still asleep.'

'Let her rest.'

'Are you all right, Ouma?'

'I'm resting, too.'

'Shall I sit with you?'

'Oh, I would like that.' She lay quietly, his hand in hers. Then she showed renewed vitality and clutched him tighter. 'They say the war's almost over, Detlev. For you it's just beginning. Never forget these days. Never forget that it was the English who did these things. You must fight, fight.'

He wanted to say that he had no horse, but she continued: 'Detlev, you may never see the general again. Remember, he did not surrender. Even when they came at him from all sides . . .'

She seemed to fall asleep, then awakened with a start. 'Whether she's sleeping or not, I must speak to Johanna.' When he roused his sister, the old woman said brusquely, 'Now you go out and play.' He walked slowly from the tent, but there was no play. There were more than seventy young children in the camp that morning, but there was no play. They sat in the sun and breathed deeply, as if they had strength only for that.

On her deathbed Sybilla admonished Johanna: 'If I die before noon, tell no one. That way you can get my ration for today. And,

Johanna, it's now up to you to see that Detlev survives. Women are stronger than men. You must keep him alive so he can carry on the fight. Even if you must starve yourself, keep him alive. Never surrender.'

This effort exhausted her, and she was near death, but suddenly her entire face became animated, not only her eyes. Clutching at Johanna, she gasped, 'And if they bring "hands-uppers" into this camp, kill them. Find long needles and kill them. In this camp heroes lived, not "hands-uppers."'

She was dead. Johanna called Detlev because she knew her brother loved this old woman, and he understood when she pledged him to secrecy. They sat all morning on her bed, talking to her, and got her ration, and when the attendants finally came to take her away, Detlev did not cry; many children in this camp never cried. But toward evening, when Johanna was apportioning the stolen ration, something happened that he would never forget: years later, generations later, he would remember that instant. Johanna broke the food into two equal pieces, weighed them in her two frail hands, then took from one and added to the other, making it much bigger. 'This is yours,' she said, and she handed him the larger share.

When the remaining Boer generals met to consider what they must do in the face of the overwhelming pressure brought against them by Lord Kitchener, they realized that in order to have an orderly discussion they must somehow muzzle Paulus de Groot. They knew that he would bellow 'No surrender,' and they were willing to have him say this once, to clear his conscience, but they did not want him repeating it every ten minutes to the detriment of sensible evaluations.

'We are not defeated,' one of the younger men said. 'The English have lost six thousand men killed. Sixteen thousand more dead in their hospitals. Twenty-three thousand more or less seriously wounded.'

'What have our losses been?' an older man asked.

'Maybe five thousand killed, but they were our finest.'

'How many children have died in the camps?' the old man asked.

'Twenty thousand.' From the rear of the room a man sighed. It was Jakob van Doorn, there to support his general.

'More than all the men on both sides, we have lost our children.'

'There was nothing we could do about it,' a young general said.

'There's something we can do about it now,' another man said. 'We can surrender.'

This was the word that De Groot was waiting for. Quietly he said, 'We shall never surrender. We can carry this fight for another six years.'

'We can indeed,' one of the younger generals said. 'But can our children?' And the debate continued.

On a day in late April an event occurred at the Chrissie Meer camp which worsened, even more, English-Boer relations. As Detlev van Doorn was about to eat a spoonful of meal, his sister Johanna rushed into the tent and knocked the bowl away.

'Don't touch it!' she screamed.

He was so ravenous that he automatically fell to the floor, grabbing for the mealies, but again she cried, 'Don't touch it!' and although her own body was wasting away with hunger, she ground the food into the dust.

'Johanna!' he pleaded, bewildered by her action.

'They've mixed ground glass in our food. Mrs. Pretorius ate some and died.'

There were sixteen good medical reasons why Mrs. Pretorius should have died that day, and the seventeenth was most forceful of all: typhoid. But the prisoners began to believe that she had died from eating powdered glass, and no amount of logical persuasion could convince them otherwise. Thus the hideous legend festered and spread.

The little doctor, whose voice so often rose to a scream in this charnel house, came out to the women to swear upon his sacred honor that the English would never do anything like that. He himself ate the pap. Would eat another dishful right now, taken from anywhere. 'The English,' he insisted, 'do not put ground glass in people's food.'

'Kitchener would!' a woman cried, and all his efforts were fruitless. As Johanna told her hungry brother that night, 'Always remember, Detlev. When we were starving the English tried to kill us with ground glass in the mealies.'

At the final meeting of the generals it was agreed that Paulus de Groot be kept away. They had heard his speech on bitter-ending; they respected his heroism; but the time had come when further resistance was futile. The Boers were ready to surrender.

After the painful decision was reached, they sent the young lawyer Jan Christian Smuts to inform the old man. Smuts, having been a courageous commando leader himself and one of the youngest, carried good credentials, and when he appeared, De Groot could guess his mission: 'It's all over, Paulus. You can go home.'

'I would like to fight once more, Jan Christian.'

'So would we all. But the children . . .'

'The children most of all would understand.'

'You must go home.'

'Let me have my Venloo men and we'll go.'

'No.' Smuts laughed. 'None of that, old man. We've sent the Venloo men on ahead. We couldn't trust you.'

'Can I be at the surrender? I'd like to smash that Kitchener.'

'No, it's best if you go home.'

'Perhaps so,' the old man said, and without farewells he called for Van Doorn, and together they sought out Micah Nxumalo, and the three veterans headed north. When they reached the crest from which they could first see the lake, they looked down at the awful desolation of what had been their homes. Of De Groot's farm, there were no signs except the charred stumps of the buildings, not six inches above the ground. Of Vrymeer, only the shells of the structures built by Tjaart van Doorn were visible. Of the place where Micah Nxumalo's huts had stood, only the base of the rondavels remained.

The two white men did not speak. Sybilla was dead, and Sara, and the twins. Johanna was lost somewhere, and Jakob prayed that the boy Detlev was with her. When he turned to look toward the direction of the concentration camp, as if to find the children, he saw the matched peaks of Sannie's Tits and they reminded him of the twins, those precious girls. He dropped his head. He had not the courage to go down the hill to that ruined farm, those vanished hopes.

General de Groot tugged at his arm: 'Come, Jakob, much work to be done.' And as the ponies moved forward, the old warrior said with clenched determination, 'We lost the battles. We lost the war. Now we must win in other ways.'

XI.
Education
of a Puritan

THE education of Detlev van Doorn began on the day he came over the hill with his sister from the concentration camp at Chrissie Meer and saw the devastation of his home. His father and old General de Groot were waiting in the ruins, and after the briefest greetings they led him to a grassy slope where Nxumalo's five huts had stood. There he saw, sticking up from the earth at regular intervals, four wooden tombstones bearing in ill-formed letters the names: SYBILLA DE GROOT, SARA VAN DOORN, SANNAH, ANNA.

'Never forget,' the general said. 'These women were murdered by the English, who fed them powdered glass.'

Detlev was seven, a little boy with the pinched features of an old man and the cautious wisdom of someone in his forties. 'They were buried in the camp. They can't be here.'

'Their tombstones,' De Groot said. 'For remembrance.'

'Those aren't stones,' Detlev said.

'Later, when we have a farm again,' his father said. 'We'll have proper stones.'

'Wood or stone,' De Groot said, 'you must never forget.'

'Where shall we stay?' Johanna asked.

'We've fixed up the old wagon,' her father said, and he led his children to that frail relic in which his father, Tjaart van Doorn, had taken his family across the Drakensberg, then north of the Limpopo, and finally back to Vrymeer. Van Doorn and the general had locked the big wheels and used boards to form a kind of shelter on the wagon bed, but it clearly could not hold a young woman like Johanna, a boy and two grown men. When De Groot saw her look of perplexity, he laughed. 'You two sleep up here. We two down below.' And she saw that under the wagon body, her father had arranged boards on the ground, where he and the old man would make their beds.

On the first wintry night that the four spent together—no pillows, no blankets—Jakob awakened at dawn, and in the dim light saw over his head, carved into the heavy wood of the frame, the rubric TC–43 and he wondered what it signified. When De Groot awakened, Jakob asked, 'What do you suppose this means?' The old general squinted his eyes, studied the marks, and remained silent, as though brooding over something. Finally he grumbled, 'One of the only two decent Englishmen I ever knew. Thomas Carleton built this wagon and he and Richard Salt-wood gave it to your father. Yes, gave it.' He reflected on the enormity of having taken refuge under an English wagon, then added, 'I rode two thousand miles in this wagon . . . walking beside it most of the way.'

Detlev, who was already awake, called down from above, 'How could you ride and walk at the same time?'

Reaching into the wagon, General de Groot pulled the boy out and tossed him in the air. When he set him on the ground he said, 'You do what you have to do. Once I helped carry this wagon down the Drakensberg.'

'What will you do, sleeping down there, if it rains?' Detlev asked.

'I won't let it rain,' De Groot promised, and during the four weeks it took to assemble a kind of roof over one room of the ruined farmhouse, it did not.

In the second week they stopped work when Detlev cried, 'People coming!' Across the veld they saw a distant file walking toward them, and ominously Jakob reached for his gun. 'Kaffirs,' he said, indicating that his son must stand behind him.

In the chaos after the war, bands of homeless hungry blacks had started raiding Boer farms in the district, stealing what they could find and roughing up any farmer who tried to protest, but there was nothing to fear from this company, for Detlev shouted, 'It's Micah!'

At the sight of only three Van Doorns and one De Groot, tears began to roll from Micah's eyes, for he knew that the absence of the others could mean only one thing, for he, too, was returning from a camp, one for blacks, in which his family and friends had been interned, and of his four wives, only two had survived; of nine children, only three were left.

The suffering of these black Boers would go unrecorded. Even Maud Turner Saltwood, who had done so much for Boer women and children, had to admit, in a final report, that the situation of the black internees had been without hope: 'Beyond affording a little relief to the sick in the few camps I visited, we were able to do nothing.' More than one hundred thousand blacks and Coloureds had been herded behind barbed wire; how many came out alive would never be known.

When De Groot learned of Nxumalo's heavy loss he was overwhelmed. In a gesture from the heart he held out his arms to his saddle companion and embraced him: 'Kaffirtjie, as true as there's a God in heaven we'll not forget what they did to both of us. Stay close and one day we'll ride again.'

Nxumalo nodded.

'This what's left of your family?' the general asked, and when Nxumalo nodded again, the old man took a step back to survey the land where the handsome rondavels had once stood. 'We must all start over. But this time, by God, they'll not be able to burn down what we build.'

So Nxumalo and his people returned to their security at Vrymeer, and he sketched in the ruins how his women must build the new huts. Early next morning he led the men who'd accompanied him from the camp to the Van Doorns' farmhouse, where they all started work. They did not ask what the arrangement would be for their employment. They just carried on as before.

The Van Doorns were surprised at the end of the first month when the old general informed them that since they now had protection from the weather, he would like to start rebuilding his farm. 'But you're to live with us,' Johanna protested with great warmth.

'No, I want a place of my own.'

'Who will cook? How will you live?'

The answer came from one of Nxumalo's wives. 'He is old,' she said. 'He needs help. We go to his place.' And Micah agreed that the woman and a young girl must accompany the old warrior to his shattered home.

Utilizing the foundation of what at best had been a miserable house, they put together what could only be called a hartebeest hut, a pitiful affair with a flap-door and no windows. One morning as Jakob surveyed the astonishing place he thought: In our barbarism we retreat many centuries. A hundred years ago our people lived better than this. Two hundred years ago they surely built better huts.

Could he have gone back to the year when Mal Adriaan, Dikkop and Swarts lived here beside the lake, he would have found them in simpler but better quarters than these, and certainly in the days of the first Nxumalo the village and fine rondavels that stood here were superior to what the old man occupied. The centuries pass, Jakob thought, and men stay about where they were.

The rains were coming late this year, producing a drought so severe that many farmers in the area, faced by the necessity to rebuild and also to fight dust, were giving up and moving to Johannesburg, where they could at least find some kind of employment in the mines. 'I don't like this,' the general complained when he heard that four families had pulled up stakes and headed for the city. 'Boers are farmers. Our name says that. We don't do well in cities. The damned mines, they're for the Englishmen and Hoggenheimer.'

'Who's Hoggenheimer?' Detlev asked.

'The Jew who owns the mines,' and he produced a newspaper which had been circulated avidly from farm to farm. It contained two biting cartoons by a persuasive artist named Boonzaaier, showing a bloated Jew, fingers bejeweled, vest enclosing a gigantic belly, cigar at an angle, wearing a derby while gorging on the food for which starving Boers pleaded in vain. That was Hoggenheimer, and on him was thrown the blame for everything ill that was happening in the conquered republics.

'If you ever run away to Johannesburg,' the old man said, 'you'll meet Hoggenheimer.'

The old general came over to the Van Doorn farm quite often, riding his pony, wearing his frock coat and sometimes his top hat. He came not for food or companionship, but to supervise the education of young Detlev: 'You must remember that your great-grandfather, one of the finest men who ever lived, was dragged to an English court, where a Kaffir was allowed to bring testimony against him . . .' Night after night he reviewed with Detlev the vast wrongs done by the English at Slagter's Nek and at Chrissiesmeer, where they put ground glass in the meal. 'Never trust an Englishman,' De Groot reiterated. 'They've stolen your country.'

'But Mrs. Saltwood was English,' Detlev said. 'She brought the food that kept us alive.'

De Groot, remembering how he had confronted Mrs. Saltwood on the stoep at De Kraal, would concede only that 'some few English ladies, yes, they had hearts.' But having granted this, he would proceed with the litany: Slagter's Nek . . . Kitchener . . . glass in the meal.

The education was fiercely effective and achieved precisely what De Groot intended. 'Detlev, your father and I fought our battles, and we lost. You will fight other battles, and you will win.'

'I can shoot straight.'

'Every Boer boy can shoot straight,' and he would digress to tell the boy of how his men, always outnumbered, would hide behind rocks and pick off Englishmen one by one: 'Ten bullets, you ought to get at least eight Englishmen.'

'I could shoot an Englishman,' Detlev insisted, whereupon the old man clasped him tight and whispered, 'Pray God you never have to. You'll win your battles in more clever ways.'

'How?'

De Groot tapped the little boy on the forehead: 'By learning. By becoming clever.'

And that was to be the foundation of Detlev's formal education, which began one day when there rode up to the farm a remarkable man: tall, thin, with very big hands that he used awkwardly and knees that protruded from his heavy trousers. He had yellowish hair, not at all becoming a man of his size, and one of the kindest faces Detlev had ever seen. He told the Van Doorns, 'My name is Amberson, Jonathan Amberson, and I've been sent by the new government to open a school at Venloo. I should be most happy to see your son in my classes.'

'He can't ride into Venloo every day,' Jakob protested.

'Nor shall he. Mrs. Scheltema will be running a hostel—'

'Are you English?' Johanna broke in.

'Of course. It's the new school, the new government.'

'We wouldn't want any English here,' she said bitterly.

'But—'

'Out. Get out of this house and off this farm.' Detlev, watching everything, feared that she might strike the tall stranger, who bowed, backed down off the stoep, and departed.

When General de Groot heard of this some days later, he became quite agitated: 'No, no! Not that way at all.'

'He was English,' Johanna snapped. 'Do you think we want our boy to learn English ways—'

'That's exactly what we want.' And for the first time young Detlev heard the strategy of his life spelled out—and he comprehended every word.

'The problem is this,' the old man said, while Detlev sat on his knee. 'The English know how to run the world. They understand banks and newspapers and schools. They are very capable people . . . in everything but war. And do you know why, Detlev?'

'At the camp, Dr. Higgins cried a lot.'

'Who was Dr. Higgins?'

'The man who was supposed to keep us alive. When we died, he often cried. Men don't do that.'

'Answer my question. "Why are the English so clever and we Boers so dumb?" '

'My father isn't dumb,' Detlev said quickly. 'And you're not dumb, Oupa.'

'I mean in books and banks and things like that.'

'I don't know.'

'The English are clever because they know things we don't.'

'What things?' Detlev asked, all attention.

'Books. Figures. Big ideas.' These words landed like Krupp shells in the little kitchen. No one spoke, and Detlev looked at his three elders, each of whom nodded. He would never forget this heavy moment.

'So what you are to do, my young clever one, is go to the English school and find out everything they know.' When Detlev nodded, the old man continued: 'You are to be the brightest boy that teacher has ever met. You are to learn everything.'

'Why?' the somber little boy asked.

'Because when you know as much as they do, you can declare a new kind of war against the English.' The old man's hands began to tremble. 'You are the generation that will win this country back. You will win the war that your father and I lost.'

General de Groot felt so strongly about this that he personally led Detlev in to Venloo, and he was impressed by the efforts taken to improve the old house that now served as schoolroom and hostel, and by the care with which Mr. Amberson had arranged things. There were books, and slates, and pictures on the wall . . . When he saw the florid portrait in color of King Edward VII he turned away.

'We are honored to have with us this morning,' Amberson said in hesitant Dutch, 'a great hero of this country, General Paulus de Groot, the hero of Majuba, the Avenger of the Veld. We never did catch you, did we, General?'

De Groot was astounded by such words coming from an Englishman, and when the nineteen children applauded he dropped Detlev's hand and retreated.

At the end of the second week, when De Groot returned to fetch Detlev, he asked no questions on the short ride to the farm, but that evening when supper was ended, the three adults sat the boy in a chair, faced him, and asked, 'What happened?'

He liked school and especially he liked Mr. Amberson, who was patient with his young scholars. 'He explains everything,' Detlev said enthusiastically, 'but sometimes I can't understand his words.'

'Does he teach in Dutch?' Johanna asked.

'Of course. We don't know any English.'

'What does he teach you?'

'That King Edward is now our king . . .'

Johanna stomped out of the room.

'Does he teach you how to figure?' De Groot asked.

'Oh, yes!' And with some enthusiasm the little boy began to recite the two-times table, but in English.

'What are you saying?' De Groot cried.

'Two-times,' the boy replied.

'But in what language?' the old man roared.

'In English. Mr. Amberson says that after he learns our language and we learn his, all classes will be in English.'

De Groot was so agitated that he began pacing about, but after a while he calmed down and lifted the boy up, sitting him on his knee. 'Of course. You must learn English as fast as you can. Every week you must learn more English, because that's how they conduct their affairs.'

But at the half-year mark, when General de Groot went to fetch Detlev, he found the boy quite distraught but unwilling to talk, so on the way back to the farm he did no probing, but when they were assembled that night Detlev suddenly burst into tears. 'What is it?' Johanna asked with great solicitude. She allowed the old general to mastermind the lad's education, but she felt responsible for his safekeeping, and when he wept in this manner she knew that something most serious had occurred, for he was a boy who did not cry.

'What is it, Detlev?'

'I had to wear the dunce's cap.'

He knew the word only in English, and when the three demanded further explanation, he fashioned with his hands the long, thin paper hat he had been required to wear four times that week.

'What for?' the general exploded.

'Because I used Dutch words.'

'You what . . .'

'Yes. New rules. Any boy or girl who speaks Dutch instead of English must stand in the corner, with the tall hat and a sign which says "I spoke Dutch today." '

'But Mr. Amberson himself speaks Dutch. You said so.'

'Not any more. He said we'd been in class half a year now and must never again speak Dutch.'

'That monster!' Johanna snapped. She was twenty-three, a fierce, hard-working young woman, and if this schoolmaster was mistreating her brother, she would teach him a lesson.

'No,' Detlev said quietly through his tears. 'He is not a bad man. He is very kind, and he helps me with my numbers. But he says that our country is now English—the war decided that—and we must forget we were ever Dutch.'

'Good God!' Johanna cried, but to her surprise it was General de Groot who pacified her.

'We must remember that this is still war,' the old man said, and he took from his pocket a newspaper containing a new set of Hoggenheimer cartoons, proving that the Jews were stealing the country. It carried also a statement by the English high commissioner, which unknowingly outlined the nature of the insidious battle the Boers now faced:

> If ten years hence there are three men of British race to two of Dutch, this country will be safe and prosperous. If there are three of Dutch and two of British, we shall have perpetual difficulty.

Coldly, De Groot explained the next level of strategies: 'The English are doing everything they can to bring in more of their people. Bring them in and drown us in a wave of English books, English plays, English education.'

'But you said you wanted me to learn English,' Detlev said.

'I do. Detlev, I want you to learn all of everything. Whenever he offers you a new English word, take it and say to yourself, "This is a knife I shall use against you." '

'When?'

'Every day of your life from now on. When you are twelve, use your knowledge against the English boys that age. At eighteen, use it against the young men in college. At thirty, against the Hoggenheimers in Johannesburg. At fifty, against the government people in Pretoria. And when you're an old man like me, keep using it. The enemy is the English, and they can be destroyed only by cleverness.'

Johanna, deeply angered by the psychological abuse heaped on Detlev by the dunce's cap and the degrading sign, wanted to ride right in to Venloo and confront Mr. Amberson, but the old general had more to say: 'Accept English in your mind, but keep Dutch in your heart. For if a conqueror once makes you accept his language, he makes you his slave. We were defeated . . .'

He had never voiced that admission before. He had said, 'We've lost the battles. We've lost the war.' But he had never conceded that he had been defeated. Now, as he uttered the terrible words, he rose from his chair and stamped about the little kitchen. 'We have been defeated— your father, I, Oom Paul, General de la Rey, General Smuts . . .' He stopped speaking, for the words were grinding in his throat. Then with a great roar he cried, 'But the next war we shall win. The war for ideas. You and I will see the day when Dutch is the only language in this land —the only one that counts. There will be no English spoken where men of power assemble.' Towering over Detlev, he pointed a long finger at him: 'And you will be responsible.'

Johanna felt her own responsibility, and early Monday morning when the time came for General de Groot to take the boy back to school, she surprised him by saying sternly, 'I take him today.'

She arrived at the school half an hour early and found that Mr. Amberson was there, arranging his materials. The first thing she saw, waiting in the corner, was the dunce's cap and the elegantly lettered sign: I SPOKE DUTCH TODAY. Walking directly to them, she said, 'Why would you dare use these?'

'I use the cap every day. For numbers missed, for words misspelled.'

'But this?' she demanded, shaking the sign at him.

'It's half a year now, Miss van Doorn. The children must begin seriously to learn the language under which they will live for the rest of their lives.'

'It won't be English, Mr. Amberson.'

He was astonished by this statement, for it had never occurred to him that Dutch could persist in competition with the victors' language, but he surprised both Johanna and Detlev by the gentlemanly manner in which he reacted. 'Sit down,' he said graciously, and when she elaborated her complaint, he listened attentively, endeavoring to catch the full meaning of her words, for she would speak only in the language of her people, the vital adaptation of Dutch by generations of her ancestors.

'There is something else we must take into account,' he said courteously, as if reasoning with a child. 'I'm told that the Dutch you do speak—in these parts, and throughout the country—I'm told it really isn't very good Dutch and should not be perpetuated.'

'Who told you that?'

'Mr. Op t'Hooft, who comes from Amsterdam and works in the education department.'

'Another Hollander! Damn them all, they come out here, take a job and then lord it over us.'

'But Mr. Op t'Hooft intends taking out citizenship. He prefers it here.'

'We don't want him.' The mention of another Hollander who was riding roughshod over the local Boers enraged Johanna and sidetracked her from her main complaint.

'Miss van Doorn, I'm sure President Kruger's government didn't want to hire so many Hollanders, but it had to, because your people out on these farms . . .' He felt that he was getting into deep water, and tried again: 'The Boers were simply wonderful at warfare, maybe the best free fighters on earth. My brother fought against General de Groot, you know. King's Own Royal Rifles, you know.' Johanna stared at him as if he were an imbecile, and he ended lamely, 'You Boers refuse to learn business procedures, so President Kruger had to invite the Hollanders in to run the government. Absolutely essential.'

'They can go home now,' she said tartly. And then she changed the subject: 'Mr. Amberson, I wish you would not again hang that sign about my brother's neck.'

'He must stop speaking Dutch in class, really he must.'

'Why? If this is to be a Dutch country?'

'Ah, but it's to be English.' He hesitated. 'The language, that is.'

They had reached an impasse, and when she returned to the farm she sought out the general, asking him if he thought the Dutch spoken by the people of Venloo was as corrupted as Mr. Op t'Hooft, whoever he was, seemed to think.

'Yes. We have a different language now. Our own. Your father and mine fashioned it. Simpler and better.'

'Should we allow the Hollanders who run everything to stay on?'

'Kick them all out. They despise us, and God knows, we despise them. Just because they can speak like Amsterdamers, they think they're lords and ladies. I say, "Kick their asses out."' He apologized for his rough speech, then repeated it.

But any worry over the insolent Hollanders, most of whom were going home anyway, since they deplored the barbaric level of society they had to suffer in towns like Pretoria and Bloemfontein, vanished when the real menace showed itself. Word of this disastrous decision had reached Venloo, and when Detlev came home from school he astonished his elders by announcing, 'They're bringing in sixty thousand Chinese workmen.'

'What?' the general shouted.

'Yes. The mine owners say that since the war they can't get any more Kaffirs, so ships are sailing into Durban with Chinese.'

'Who is doing this?' the old man bellowed, but despite his fevered questioning he could find no rational answers, so he decided to take the little money he had and ride the train in to Johannesburg and see for himself what the crisis amounted to.

'You're to come with me,' he said to Detlev, and when the boy protested that he must report to school, the general said, 'More important that you see the enemy,' and he rode with the boy to Waterval-Boven, where they caught the train.

It was a stunning adventure for Detlev—travelers eating their meals while they sped westward, the sweep of the veld, the farms struggling back into production, and on the far horizon the first sight of a major city. De Groot was welcomed wherever he went, both by his former Boer cronies and by the English, who held him in high regard for his heroic conduct in two wars. From his acquaintances he learned that yes, the government was in the process of importing sixty thousand Chinese to work the mines, and he also heard disturbing rumors about the behavior of these coolies.

The government and the Englishmen who ran the mines seriously believed that it was possible to import sixty thousand vigorous young men, all of them under thirty, and have them work deep in the gold mines—without their wanting any recreation, or association with women, or any kind of reasonable relaxation for a period of ten or twenty years. When the young men began to gamble, the Dutch Reformed Church was horrified. When they began to form liaisons with black or Coloured or lowly white women, the predikants screamed from their pulpits that God would scourge this land if that were permitted. And when some enraged coolie actually killed another, Englishmen and

Boers alike claimed that this proved the Chinese were a gang of animals.

Nothing that the government would do in the first decade after the English victory would so excite the Boers as this importation of Chinese, and when Paulus de Groot actually saw the yellow men going down into the mines he experienced an anger that would not be assuaged. In fact, he was so outraged that when he returned to his quarters in the city, a Boer friend, who shared his emotion, suggested that they go see General Koos de la Rey, who had tormented the English for three years during the late war. When Detlev met this famous man, not so tall as General de Groot but gentler of face, he realized that he was seeing a significant part of his nation's history, and when later General Christiaan Beyers joined them, Detlev saw a grand triumvirate.

They discussed how they might force the government to rescind the law which allowed the importation of the Chinese. 'More important,' De la Rey said, 'is how we kick those already here out of the country.' It was agreed that everyone must work for the repatriation of the Chinese, but then talk turned to an even more serious point.

'I am disgusted with the mistakes this government is making,' De Groot said bluntly. 'Do you know what they're doing with our children? Tell them, Detlev . . . about the dunce's cap.' When the little boy did, the generals listened soberly, but then De Groot said, 'The sign. Tell them about the sign.' When this humiliating incident was related, they shook their heads, and after a long while De Groot said quietly, 'One of these days we will all be riding again. Against the English, for they do not know how to govern.'

Neither of the other generals responded to this, but De Groot repeated his prophecy: 'You will be back in the saddle, both of you. And do you know why? Because Germany is stirring. Germany is on the march, and sooner or later we'll see an expeditionary force landing in South-West Africa. What'll they do? They'll march this way and consolidate with their colony in East Africa. And what do we do? We join them. And in that moment we kick the English out of here forever.'

Detlev would remember that somber moment: De Groot, De la Rey, Beyers looking ahead to the wild twists and turns of war, and he suspected that each man hoped that when Germany began to play a vital role in Africa, all decent men would side with her against the hated English.

'If it were to happen,' General Beyers asked carefully, 'would the others join us?'

De Groot was sure that the great hero De Wet would support Germany, and so would others. 'The man we'd have to fear is that young upstart Jan Christian.'

'Who is he?' Detlev broke in.

'Smuts,' De Groot said. 'A brave general, but I despise his politics.'

After this informal meeting, De Groot walked the boy around Johannesburg, pointing to the large buildings dominated by the English business leaders. When they came to one group of important offices he made Detlev stand there and read off all the names of the lawyers, the insurance men, the business negotiators, and when the boy reached FRANK SALTWOOD, AGENT, he said, 'That was the spy who burned our farms. Never forget.' And once more the boy symbolized the contradictions in which nations and people find themselves, for he said, 'Mrs. Saltwood saved my life.'

The most important lesson General de Groot taught Detlev came not from what he said but from what he did. When the English government released the captured Boers who had been interned in distant places like Ceylon, Bermuda and St. Helena, from the latter island came a great hulking man, taller than De Groot, on whose sloping shoulders rested a heavy burden. He was General Pieter Cronje, who in 1900 had surrendered at Paardeberg his entire army of nearly four thousand troops, the most disastrous loss in the war.

A photographer had happened to catch a stunning shot of the surrender, from which an artist working for the *Illustrated London News* made a most effective sepia wash, which eventually was seen throughout the world, becoming the traditional depiction of Boer-English relationships. There came Cronje, looking six feet seven, in rumpled field trousers, vest, coat and overcoat, bearded, dirty, and wearing a huge broad-brimmed hat. Waiting for him stood little Lord Roberts, one-eyed, one hundred and thirty pounds, bristling mustache, all spit-and-polish boots and leatherwork, jaunty expeditionary cap at a sharp angle. 'The Giant Surrendering to the Midget' the picture was sometimes called.

The copy which General de Groot kept on the wall of his house showed signs of having been spat upon; it was also punctured where the old man had thrown a fork at it. This version was titled 'Cronje Meets His Master,' and when De Groot explained its significance to Detlev he said, 'A man should rather die with six bullets in his belly than face such a moment. Don't ever surrender.'

Detlev was surprised, therefore, when he looked up one morning at the farm and saw the gigantic figure of General Cronje waiting on the stoep. It could be no one else, and when the deep voice rumbled, 'Waar is die generaal?' Detlev replied, 'He lives at the house.' He led Cronje to De Groot's place and was present when the two generals met. They did not embrace in the French manner, but stood respectfully apart, inclining their heads slightly out of mutual respect.

'Come in, Cronje,' De Groot said, ushering him into the sparsely furnished room. 'How was St. Helena?'

'Napoleon died there. I didn't.'

'What happened at Paardeberg?'

The general seated himself uneasily on an upended box and shrugged his shoulders. 'From babyhood we were taught "When you face trouble, go into laager." I faced trouble, Kitchener hammering at me like a madman, Roberts waiting. So I went into laager, but the old rules no longer applied. Not when they had cannon to rim the laager and blow its insides to bits.'

'Now, that's curious,' De Groot said. 'My family lost its life against Mzilikazi because it didn't go into laager. You lost everything because you did.'

'Times change.' He shook his head, then got down to business. 'Paulus, you're living like a pig. Things aren't good for me, either. But we both have a chance to earn a lot of money.'

'How?'

'Have you ever heard of St. Louis? The American city?'

'No.'

'I'm told it's important, bigger than Cape Town.'

'What's it got to do with us?' De Groot asked suspiciously.

'They're having a large World's Fair. Biggest of its kind.'

'Yes?'

'They've seen the drawing of me and Lord Roberts. They've sent a man here, untold funds. He wants me to collect a small commando of Boers who can ride well and shoot from the saddle. Blanks, of course. They'll have American soldiers dressed like Englishmen, and in a big arena you and I will come in riding and shooting. There'll be a mock fight, and then there'll be a tableau.'

'A what?'

'Everybody stops . . . dead still. And the audience sees that it's a representation of my surrender to Lord Roberts.'

De Groot simply sat there, arms folded, legs spread apart, staring at his old companion. Cronje had helped storm Majuba back in 1881. He was a verified hero, but he was also the man who had behaved poorly at Paardeberg. If such a tragic twist in fortune had been forced upon De Groot, he would have shot his brains out. Cronje was proposing to go to St. Louis, wherever that was, and ride his pony into an arena firing blank cartridges, and then surrender again, twice a day, six days a week, to Lord Roberts.

Slowly the old man rose, indicating that Cronje must do the same. Sternly he edged the huge warrior to the hut doorway, where he said, 'Piet, dear comrade, as you can see, I need the money. But there's never been a time in my life when I fired blank cartridges, and I'm too old to learn.'

Cronje had no trouble in conscripting other fine horsemen, who went to St. Louis and put on an exhibition that dazzled the locals, improving considerably their estimation of Boers. But whenever the band stopped dramatically, and two small cannon roared, and the lights came on, General Cronje stepped forward in the costume he had worn in the photograph and surrendered to a taut little major on detached duty from Fort Sill who wore a fake mustache and a replica of an English uniform.

When photographs of this tableau filtered back to South Africa, they caused anguish, but in St. Louis the approval was so marked that Cronje's contracted salary was raised. General de Groot found one of these photographs and tacked it to the wall, beside the original version.

'Remarkable,' he told Detlev when the boy first compared the two. 'How could they get the surrender so accurate?' Detlev was afraid the old man was going to tear the wall apart, so strained became the muscles on his neck, but all he did was tap the two pictures gently, as if they were of value. 'Never surrender, Detlev,' he said. 'Not even in play.'

The people at Vrymeer were so obviously concerned about Detlev's education that Mr. Amberson fell into the habit of riding out from Venloo now and then to report on their boy's progress, and as he sat in the kitchen at the farm, Detlev noticed two things about him. Unlike the hefty Boer farmers of the area, this thin young man could sit in a chair, twist his left leg over his right knee, and then hook his left toe under his right ankle, as if he were made of rubber. Detlev could imitate this, but none of the chubby larger boys could, and certainly none of the elders. Also, Mr. Amberson was interested in everything, and that was why Vrymeer acquired an additional beauty which made it somewhat different from the other farms.

'They have a new system now,' he said with some excitement. 'They come from Australia, mostly.'

'What does?' the general asked suspiciously. He did not like Mr. Amberson, but Detlev noticed that he appeared whenever the tall Englishman visited, because he enjoyed arguing with him.

'The trees. The government are importing millions of trees to spruce up the veld.'

'Who pays for them?'

'I think they're free. Eucalypts, I believe, and something they call wattle.'

'Free?'

'Yes, but you must plant them. That's only fair.'

Mr. Amberson used that phrase a good deal, for he saw many things in life that could be adjudicated easily on that principle: 'It's only fair.'

'Is it fair for you to make our boys learn English?' De Groot asked, as usual.

'I've learned Dutch.' He coughed modestly. 'Such as it is. I do this out of respect. But Detlev must learn English for a better reason. Because the world runs on English, that's why.'

On this basic point he would make no concessions. English was the language of the great world, and provincial Boers stuck off in their corner must learn it, if they presumed to participate in world affairs. On all else he was conciliatory, granting that the Boers probably won the war through their obstinate heroism and conceding that Dutch cooking was much better than English. He was really rather a likable chap, and when he sat with his legs twisted in knots, rocking back and forth on his haunches, arguing abstruse points, he lent a touch of congeniality and culture to what was otherwise a dull existence.

The farm was in good condition now. With help from Nxumalo's people, all buildings were roofed; the Herefords were maturing; the wool clip was coming in at a satisfactory level; and the black farmworkers had gouged out two small lakes, or catchments, below the big lake, so that on sunny days the three bodies of water shone like a necklace of jewels. Detlev was especially pleased with them, for he saw that by this device the water that came down from the hills behind the farm was used three times—four, really: 'It runs past the house as a stream, then builds our big lake, then goes on to make the two smaller ones for the cattle.'

It was to the north shores of these attractive lakes that Mr. Amberson brought the thousand saplings when they arrived at Durban from Australia. They were, as he predicted, mostly eucalypts, those shaggy-barked wonderful trees whose leaves when crushed had a minty odor. But he also delivered some two hundred wattles, the bushlike trees whose golden flowers would adorn the landscape.

'That many trees is a monstrous task,' he warned the men, and to help them with the planting he excused his entire school one Thursday and Friday, bringing all the boys out to work by the lakes. 'Practical learning' he termed it, and he worked hardest of all, dashing here and there to satisfy himself that the trees were in line. The only charge to the Van Doorns for this unusual service was a barbecue for the lads, and it was after the boys and their teacher had returned to Venloo that Detlev first voiced his suspicion. The two older men were sitting in the kitchen while Johanna cleaned up, and when she left the room, Detlev said quietly, 'I think Mr. Amberson is in love with Johanna.'

'What did you say?'

'He comes here to argue with you, General de Groot, but he really comes to be with Johanna.' He mimicked the way in which the Englishman pronounced her name, not Yo-hon-na, like a Boer, but Jo-hann-a, in the English manner.

This news was so frightening that General de Groot whispered 'Shhhhhh' lest Johanna hear that they were discussing her indiscretion, and when she returned to the kitchen six eyes studied her cautiously. When she left again, De Groot snorted: 'Unthinkable! A Boer girl in love with an English . . .'

'I didn't say that,' Detlev protested. 'I said he was in love with her.'

'A fine girl like Johanna,' the general said. 'She'd never do a thing like that.' He uttered the words with such contempt that he might have been speaking of prostitution.

'She is twenty-six,' Jakob said thoughtfully. 'She's a precious girl and ought to be finding herself a man.'

'You need her here,' De Groot said, meaning that he needed her.

'She mustn't wait much longer, though,' Jakob said. 'But I agree I don't want an Englishman in my family.'

Everything these three male spies saw in the next weeks confirmed their suspicion that Johanna van Doorn was falling in love with an Englishman, and one weekend when he appeared at the farm to inspect the young eucalypts, General de Groot bearded him: 'Young man, did you come here to see the trees, or did you come to see Johanna?'

Mr. Amberson blanched, then turned bright red. 'Well, I . . .'

'It would be better if you didn't come here any more.' When the young man started to defend himself, Jakob entered the discussion: 'Yes, it would be better if you stayed away.'

'But . . .'

'Starting now,' the general said firmly, and the two men remained at Amberson's side, edging him toward his horse. The general said, 'We don't want an Englishman making up to one of our girls. Now get!' And he slapped the horse, sending the long-legged teacher back toward Venloo.

At lunch, when it appeared that Mr. Amberson would not be joining the family, Johanna asked why, and the general said bluntly, 'We don't want him fooling around with a decent Boer girl.'

Johanna blushed, but did not retreat. 'Did you send him away?'

'We did,' the general snapped.

'Who are you to send people away, General de Groot? You're a guest here.'

'I am the protector of this house,' he said firmly.

'I don't want your protection.' She wanted to cry. Badly she wanted to weep, for there were no young men in Venloo, and Mr. Amberson had proved himself to be a generous, understanding human being. The war was over; the camps were over; and she felt a great urge to get on with life, to start a farm of her own with children of her own, and if no one else came along, she was prepared to marry an Englishman, repulsive though it seemed.

But the three men in her family would not allow it. Detlev spoke for them all when he said, 'Johanna, you can wait.'

This observation surprised her. 'But you like him best of all. You brought him here.'

'As a teacher,' the boy said. 'Yes, he is a fine teacher.'

'Unthinkable,' General de Groot pronounced as the final verdict, and Mr. Amberson was seen at Vrymeer no more.

At school he betrayed not a single indication of his disappointment; if anything, he treated Detlev with added consideration, which was natural, since this boy was one of the best. In numbers and history and clear handwriting he received good marks, and Mr. Amberson gave him much encouragement, stopping by Mrs. Scheltema's sometimes at night to assign him further tasks so that he could excel.

What he did to sublimate his rather strong feelings toward Johanna revolutionized Venloo; it would not be the same after that summer. The metamorphosis started slowly, with his bringing an ovoid football to the school and telling the bigger boys, 'You must play rugby. And one day, even though you come from this small town, you may be famous like Paul Roos.'

Up to then the Boers of this little community knew little of the vigorous game that was sweeping the country. Before the war they had heard of the visits of teams from England, first in 1891, when the visitors won every match, and again in 1896. But it had remained an exotic game played principally in the Cape.

Through rugby Mr. Amberson endeared himself to the locals. Day after day he went onto the playing field, in boots, knee-length socks, short pants and jersey, to go up against the strongest boys in his school. They would race up and down the area, bend down in scrums, and play till they were exhausted. 'My word,' he often said as the games ended, 'that was a good effort. Boys, you're becoming first rate, absolutely world class.'

Older men in the community ridiculed the schoolmaster: 'He's a man among boys and a boy among men.' But when he suggested that the older youths, those now out of school, also form a team, he assured them that he was prepared to play with them, and now the entire male population of the town came out to watch the gladiatorial games.

He was remarkable, a tall, somewhat frail fellow who showed no fear of slamming into the biggest and toughest of the local Boers. Some boy would break loose with the ball and be on his way to a score when Amberson would detach himself from the pack, fly across the field, and tackle the brute with bone-crunching force, knocking the ball loose, then scrambling to his feet and running with it himself until some mighty Boer brought him down.

At the end of a game he would sit on the sidelines, panting, his body bruised, his mouth showing flecks of blood, and the hefty men would come by and slap him on the shoulder and say, 'You know how.' And he would reply, 'It was a mighty game.'

His principal interest, however, remained the boys in his school, and he was delighted when Detlev showed signs of becoming a first-class stand-off halfback, the capable lad who received the ball from the scrum half and passed it along to the speedier backs.

He had a natural aptitude for the game, and while he did not love it with the passion Mr. Amberson exhibited, he did appreciate the fellowship, considering it an attribute to a good life. This was helpful, because South Africa was in the process of becoming one of the world's fanatic sports centers, and if a boy like Detlev ever made a national team, his future would be assured.

It was this mania for sports which made it necessary for Frank Saltwood to issue an edict which went far in determining the social structure of his country. Like all Englishmen, he was dotty about games and served as chairman of the board governing cricket. He was a good player himself, having been a sometime member of the Oxford eleven, and in South Africa, had dedicated his spare time and surplus funds to encourage the game. Whenever a team was chosen to play visitors from Scotland and Wales, he was apt to serve as manager of the tour, ensuring that his men comported themselves within the grand traditions. He was insistent on this: 'Cricket is the game of gentlemen, and its rules apply even more to life than to the playing field. I like to see men extremely energetic, but within the set rules.'

This posed a dilemma in the postwar years when the great clubs of England extended an invitation to their former enemies to come home and play a set of gala matches; more than anything else, this would make the peace treaty a conclusive fact to families who had lost sons in the war. But a serious problem arose, in the person of Abu Bakr Fazool, a Coloured Muslim gentleman from Cape Town who was probably the best bowler in the world. When C. Aubrey Smith, himself a stalwart bowler and future motion picture star, captained his cricket team on a tour of South Africa, he said of Fazool, 'Has the fastest riser I've ever seen. Much better at the tricky stuff than I am.' He promised Fazool that if the latter ever came to England, he'd find a place for him on one of the county teams.

So now the question was: Should Abu Bakr be a member of the team visiting England? And at first it was assumed throughout South Africa that he should. Local enthusiasts predicted that he would mow down the English batters; but gradually people in rural areas began deploring the possibility that a Coloured might represent South Africa abroad, and articles appeared in the better papers, asking: 'Have the board really sorted this thing out?'

The burden fell squarely on Frank Saltwood, and had he stood before his board and said, 'We would appear stupid before the world if we omitted Abu Bakr,' they would have agreed, but after he had studied the matter from all angles, he became cautious and gave the board members craven advice:

'It is acknowledged here and abroad that Abu Bakr Fazool is perhaps the best bowler alive today. As C. Aubrey Smith said at the end of his successful tour, "That young man is ready for county cricket right now." So we would be doing our side, and the mother country, a favor by including him. I am enthusiastic about doing so. But we must consider carefully certain objections to such an act. The scars of our recent war are slowly healing, thanks to the good conscience of both sides, and it would be almost criminal to do anything at this early date which would reopen those scars. Our Boer brethren have certain clear-cut traditions about handling their Coloured and Kaffir neighbors, and it would ill-behoove us to offend those traditions. Such consideration would dictate that we not take Fazool to England with us.

'A more serious aspect, in the long run, is "What kind of impression do we wish to make upon the mother country when our team takes the field?" I know that dark-skinned Indians have played at Lords with distinction, but all England knows that India contains Indians, and it would be ridiculous if none appeared. In the same way very dark West Indians have represented the Caribbean colonies, but again that is the color of those colonies. With South Africa it is different. It is important that we present ourselves to the mother country in garb as like hers as possible. This is a white man's country and always will be. Our welfare depends upon the good opinion the mother country holds of us, and when our team appears on its sacred pitches, it would be better if it represented what we want to be: England's white colony, safe, secure, well-educated, loyal to European tradition, and to be trusted. I am afraid the appearance of Abu Bakr Fazool among our players would not enhance that image.'

Had Frank Saltwood in that moment of great, though unrecognized, crisis come out in favor of sending Fazool to England, and had the gifted athlete performed as might be expected, a whole pattern of acceptance might have been launched. There were other Coloured cricket players

who could have made those touring teams, and when their white colleagues observed how well they played and with what ease they fitted
into mother country festivities, an attitude of approval would have been
generated throughout South Africa; and if gifted blacks had been
trained for the rugby teams, smashing their opponents about in the
scrums and running like antelope for scores, the nation would have seen
that they were little different from the Boers and the Englishmen who
played beside them.

But time was not ripe for such acceptance. Frank Saltwood convinced his board and kept Fazool off the team. He did not appear in
England to take his place beside the fabulous bowlers from India, the
immortal batsmen from Australia. He continued to play in the darker
neighborhoods of Cape Town, and as the rules against interracial competition stiffened, he quit the game altogether. He could often be seen at
the docks, in the fish market, tallying not runs but the daily catch of
snoek.

Often in the biographies of important women and men one comes
across the phrase: 'Like a burst of light, the idea which would animate
her life came upon her.' In the case of Detlev van Doorn this simile was
literally true. A flash of light struck him, and the course of his life was
set.

It happened because of a packet of powdered jellies imported from
France. When General de Groot and her father forbade Johanna to see
Mr. Amberson, she was left with little to do and began to occupy her
spare time with knitting and embroidery. The arrival at the Venloo
store of the imported powders excited her, and swiftly she presented her
men with acidy orange and lemon desserts. They liked them, and asked
for more, so she returned to the store and purchased the large-size
packets, and when she reached home she found that she now had some
six or seven different flavors. She experimented with each, and the men
found them so tasty that they encouraged her to continue.

She was a resourceful young woman, nearing thirty now, and one
day as she was pouring the jelly into her glasses it occurred to her that
if she poured only a small portion into each glass, allowing it to harden,
she could then pour on top of it another jelly of a different color, and
repeat the process until she had a multilayered glass which would be
not only quite tasty but also attractive to look at.

On her first tries she failed, because she poured the succeeding colors while they were too hot and thus melted any that had already firmed and cooled. Being a provident woman, she mixed the mangled jellies into one mélange and decided to try again later, but when the mixture hardened and she served it to her men, Detlev protested: 'This doesn't look right and it doesn't taste right.' She offered no explanation, but did agree with him. That experiment had failed.

Next time, however, when the first jelly was well firmed, and she made the next flavor, she allowed it to cool almost to point of hardening, then poured it in, and her plan succeeded. Indeed, it produced a result much finer than even she had anticipated; it was really quite handsome, for with artistic taste she had placed the black currant layer at the bottom, the light brown apple atop it, then the reds, and finally the orange and the light lemon. The glasses were almost works of art.

When Detlev came into the kitchen they were perched on a window ledge, with one well off by itself, and when rays of sunlight struck that glass, the layers scintillated, each color showing to maximum advantage, throwing delightful patterns of black, brown, crimson, orange and lemon on the opposite wall, and in that moment Detlev understood the grand design of life.

'Look!' he cried, bringing the general and his father into the room. 'How each color keeps to itself. It doesn't muddy the other. It shines like a diamond.' And with one finger he outlined the nature of humanity as God had ordained it: 'Here at the bottom the black. Then the lighter brown. Then here the Indian . . .' Already he had translated the colors into racial groupings. 'Up here the Englishman, he's orange. And on top of them all, the Afrikaner, clear and . . .'

'You are a Boer!' De Groot said.

'They keep telling us at school we're not Boers any longer. We're not fighting anybody . . .'

'We're always fighting the English,' De Groot said. 'In your lifetime we will never stop.'

Detlev returned to the jellies: 'Each color in its own level. Order. Neatness.' He had found the guiding secret of life. 'We're Afrikaners, that nice clean color on top.'

'That's the way it should be,' De Groot said, and that week he launched his campaign to get rid of Mr. Amberson as the Venloo teacher. He had learned to like the Englishman and told him so openly, but he also felt that the time had come for the education of Boer boys . . . 'Afrikaner boys deserve Afrikaner men to teach them.' He liked this Afrikaner business. It bespoke the true heritage of his people. They were not Englishmen, and God knows they were not Dutch. They were men and women of Africa, and the word carried crisp meaning.

Mr. Amberson reacted as one would expect: 'I think you have a legitimate concern, General de Groot. Besides, you should be bringing up a generation of your own teachers. I've been offered two appointments to the English schools in Grahamstown. My rugby training, you know.'

Even when public meetings were convened to discuss the necessity of dismissing him, he continued with rugby games, striving in his final weeks to instill his boys with the abiding principles of sportsmanship: 'Don't crybaby . . . A tooth can be replaced . . . Be gallant when you win and extend your hand to the man who played opposite you . . . Fight to the very last second, then give a cheer for the goodness of the game . . . Be manly . . . If the other man is bigger, you be more clever . . . The goal is to win . . . Always you must win . . . You must drive for that score . . . But there are rules you dare not break in trying to score . . . Be manly . . .'

In the grand exhibition prior to his departure he was about as capable as a stand-off halfback could be, diving straight into the biggest bully on the town team and being knocked so silly that when he got the ball he ran in the wrong direction. In his farewell speech he paid resounding tribute to General de Groot: 'Just as this noble captain led his men through every difficulty, so our team has fought against all the odds presented by bigger schools and heavier opponents. To General de Groot I give my fullest admiration. He is the spirit of Venloo. To my boys I give the eternal challenge. Be manly.'

It was the consensus that this small town had been lucky in having this scrawny Englishman in the period of transition. He had helped make boys into men, Boers into Afrikaners, and former enemies into relaxed allies.

The week after he departed, the new schoolmaster appeared, a young man of much different stamp. He was Piet Krause, graduate of the new college at Potchefstroom, which would become the most Afrikaner of the universities, and he let it be known on his first day that the nonsense about instruction in English was ended. To the delight of the local farmers, this tense, crop-headed young fellow announced: 'The spirit of a nation is expressed in its language. This nation is destined to be Afrikaner. Therefore, its language must be Afrikaans.' This was the first time that word had been used in Venloo, and when he saw the confusion on the faces before him, he explained: 'Just as we have created a new people in this cauldron, steeped in Slagter's Nek, Blood River and

Majuba, so we are building a new language, simpler than the old, cleaner, easier to use. It's our language now, and with it we shall conquer. One day we shall give thanks for this victory, using our own Bible in our language, the Afrikaans Bible.'

General de Groot applauded all but the last sentence; he was not sure that the Bible should be in any language other than Dutch: 'That's the way God handed it down to us. Those are the words He used when He spoke to us. He gave us our covenant in Dutch, and we should keep it that way.'

He and others like him raised such a howl about printing the Bible in anything but pristine Dutch that the project was dropped, nationally, but not in Venloo. Krause rode out from Venloo to meet with the Vrymeer people, and told them, 'We must eliminate all areas in which we are subservient. No more English, except what the law demands. No more Dutch. All the damned Hollanders thrown on a ship and sent back to Amsterdam. We are Afrikaners, and whether General de Groot likes it or not, one of these days we'll have our own Bible.'

He spoke with such force, and in defense of a program so needed in this community, that Johanna van Doorn listened with growing joy. This was what she believed. Her liking for Mr. Amberson had been physical only; spiritually she had been repelled by his Englishness. But here was a fiery young man whose eye was on the future, the only future that made any sense for South Africa.

She resumed taking Detlev to school on Monday mornings, arriving even earlier than she had in those first tender days with Mr. Amberson, and she came with a firmness Detlev had not seen before. Her eyes glowed as she supported the new teacher in all he attempted, and three times she invited him to Vrymeer for long discussions and good boboties. 'I think Mr. Krause has lost the battle,' Detlev joked one night after the schoolteacher had left for Venloo. Johanna, disregarding his teasing, said nothing, and during Krause's next visit at the lake, Detlev himself fell under the spell of this dynamic man.

'What we must have in this country,' he cried with expanding excitement, 'is a system of order. Indians, Coloureds, blacks, all in their proper place, all obedient to the wise laws we pass. And I don't want Englishmen passing them, either. I want Afrikaners in all positions of decision.' When Detlev heard these words he realized that Mr. Krause, starting from his own experiences, had discovered the principle which he, Detlev, had seen in the glass of jellies. They both believed in discipline and the ascendancy of the Afrikaner Volk.

'What was that?' General de Groot asked when Detlev first used the phrase in the kitchen.

'Mr. Krause uses it all the time. It means the People, the secret force of the Race that makes us different from the English or the Kaffir.'

'I like that word,' De Groot said, and soon he was speaking about the mission of the Afrikaner Volk.

Detlev was not surprised when at the end of only five weeks Mr. Krause came nervously to the kitchen to inform the men: 'Johanna and I seek to marry. I know she's four years older, but we love each other. We have work to do, and I ask your permission.' It was granted—by the general, by her father, and most enthusiastically by her brother.

The wedding ceremony was performed by a newcomer to the community, a man who added much to the quality of Venloo. He was the Reverend Barend Brongersma, a graduate of Stellenbosch, the prestigious university of the Cape, and a most excellent young man. He was thirty-one when he took over the Venloo church, tallish, well proportioned, with very black hair and deep-set eyes to match. His outstanding characteristic was a resonant voice which he had carefully cultivated so that it could range downward from a high, impassioned plea to a thundering middle accusation to a solid reassuring affirmation. It was obvious, when one heard him preach, that he gave much thought to his sermons and that he was a young man who would surely go far in the management of the South African church. He spoke with great conviction, outlining his arguments so that anyone could follow, and buttressing them so firmly that everyone had to agree. He was as fine a predikant as the Dutch Reformed Church offered in this period, and his stay in Venloo would be limited, for he would be needed in some larger community.

He was married to a woman much like himself: solid good looks, eager, a winning smile, and unafraid to say what she thought. They made an impressive couple, and the three men at Vrymeer were pleased to have them in Venloo.

It was customary now to speak of three men at the farm, because Detlev was growing into such a hefty young fellow that he was assigned a position in the forward line at rugby, where his weight and more than ordinary strength would prove an advantage. Several times his father had said, 'Detlev, you're built just like your grandfather Tjaart. He was a strong man.' There had been a photograph of the old man, with belt and suspenders, tight-trimmed beard from ear to chin, flat black hat, staring straight ahead; it had gone in the flames, but Detlev could remember it and hoped that one day he would look the same.

Venloo had now fallen solidly into place as the prototype of a small Afrikaner community: it had in General de Groot its hero of past wars; in Piet Krause, a fiery teacher who wanted to remold the world; in Dominee Brongersma, a charismatic predikant who could both instruct and censure; and in Detlev van Doorn, the typical young lad of promise. At times it seemed that all the forces of this community conspired to make this boy more intelligent, more dedicated.

At the moment his brother-in-law, Piet Krause, had the greatest influence, for Detlev tended to see society through this vibrant young man's eyes. Once, coming over the hill, Piet stopped their carriage, looked ahead at the broken farm occupied by General de Groot, and began to rant: 'Never forget that scene, Detlev! A man who led us in battle living like the swine, forgotten, unloved, a castaway.'

'He wants to live that way,' Detlev explained. 'Every year Father asks him to move in with us. He says he likes the old place, the old ways.'

'But look at him, a great hero forgotten.' When the teacher spoke like this to De Groot, the old man laughed. 'Detlev's right. I like it this way. You should have seen how we lived on the trek.' He told of his family on that last evening when he elected to stay with the Van Doorns, and thus escaped being killed by Mzilikazi's men. 'Halt the wagon. Spread some blankets. Draw a canvas out from the wagon. Three poles to form a kind of tent. Go to sleep, and have your throats cut before morning. That's how we lived.'

'General,' Krause said with brimming emotion, 'Johanna and I want you to come in town and live with us.'

'Oh, no! You two would be arguing with me all the time. I'm happy where I am. If I get hungry, I come over to Jakob, here.'

The Vrymeer farm, with no white woman in attendance now that Johanna was married, faced problems which were solved when Micah Nxumalo and two of his wives moved back from the old general's place. This did not leave De Groot bereft, for two younger black women looked after him. Five rondavels existed again at Vrymeer, looking much as they had for the past fifty years, and they were occupied by some twenty blacks, half of whom had drifted up from Zululand. They worked at the farm, but it was Nxumalo who remained in charge.

With Van Doorn's encouragement he had patiently coaxed a herd of blesbok, more than sixty of them, to lodge permanently beside the three lakes. A stranger coming to the farm would see these handsome animals, white blazes gleaming in sunlight, and think that they had wandered in from the veld, but as day waned and they stayed fairly close to the house, he would realize that they lived here. How beautiful Vrymeer was, with the blesbok and the fattening Herefords and the eucalypts attaining enough height to form tall hedges, and sunlight falling across the lakes.

Four or five times a year Van Doorn harvested one or two of the older blesbok, turning the meat over to Nxumalo's wives for making biltong, and this seemed to help the herd rather than hurt it. Van Doorn usually shot unwanted bucks, but with such care that the other members of the herd scarcely knew that a shot had been fired. Certainly he never stampeded them, for he loved these beasts and felt that they helped tie him and De Groot more tightly to the soil of their ancestors. Nxumalo felt the same.

Piet Krause saw it as his duty to keep the farm and the town of Venloo at the center of Transvaal activity; he forced everyone to follow with careful attention everything that happened, and was always ready to explain its significance. On the memorable day in 1910 when the four disparate colonies—the English Cape and Natal, the Afrikaner Orange Free State and Transvaal—were united by the Act of Union into one nation, with its own governor-general, prime minister and parliament, Krause exulted: 'Now we're set on our own course. What we accomplish is up to us. Think of it, boys! Someone in this school may be a future prime minister of a country that is totally free.' He looked at each of the boys, endeavoring to inspire them, but he was thinking of himself.

'We're not totally free,' one bright lad said cautiously. 'We're still a union which owes allegiance to the king.' Seeing his teacher frown, he added, 'We're part of the British Empire.'

'Don't use that word!' Krause stormed. 'We have no quarrel with Britain. Do we fight against Scotland or Wales or Ireland? Not at all. Our fight is with England.' And from then on, his students used only that word.

'Will we always owe allegiance to the king?' the same boy asked.

'That will change,' Krause said firmly, but for the moment he was not prepared to explore details. However, on his next visit to the farm, Detlev recalled that brief exchange and asked, 'Do you think we will break away from England?' and to his surprise, Krause did not respond, but Johanna did. With a fierceness Detlev had not seen before, she orated: 'We shall never be free until we do break away. We must have our own flag, our own anthem, our own president, and not some be-damned Englishman like Governor-General Gladstone making believe he's our king.' On and on she went, outlining a program whereby the Afrikaners would take over control of the nation, as free men and women: 'In Pretoria only Afrikaans will be spoken, only Afrikaners will hold positions of power.'

'Will the English allow this?' Detlev asked.

'We will find ways to make them allow it,' Johanna said, at which General de Groot applauded.

'There will be ways,' he agreed, slapping Detlev on the knee. 'And this young fellow will discover what they are.'

In private conversations Johanna Krause was always the one who gave fiery direction, but in public, as in any good Afrikaner family, she allowed her husband to take the lead, and one morning in school he ex-cited his pupils by announcing, 'I want everyone who can do so to bring his parents and his wagon, and we'll ride up to Waterval-Boven to see a magnificent sight.' He would not tell them what, but when he insisted that General de Groot come along, the old man predicted: 'He wants you to see where President Kruger ruled this country in the last days,' and when they reached that revered spot, De Groot lectured the chil-dren: 'The great man lived on these railroad tracks, in Car Number 17, first up here above the waterfall, then down below in the little house next to the hotel. And you must remember one thing,' he warned them in a voice quivering with anger, 'no matter what lies the English news-papers print, Oom Paul Kruger did not run away with half a million pounds in gold. It left Pretoria somehow, but he never took it.'

It was neither the waterfall nor the lost gold that had attracted Piet Krause. His attention was reserved for the clock, and at three he as-sembled everyone at the railway station.

'We're about to witness a glorious moment in our national history,' he said, and when the train from Pretoria appeared around a bend he and his wife led the children in wild applause, though what they were clapping for, the students did not know.

Piet had arranged with the stationmaster that the train would halt for six minutes, but when the first three customary carriages drifted slowly past, showing no special passengers, General de Groot told Det-lev, 'I don't understand.' But now fifteen roofless cattle trucks creaked to a halt, allowing the amazed schoolchildren to stare into the yellow faces of seven hundred Chinese coolies. They were the last contingent of workers imported from Shanghai in 1904. All were being expelled from the country, and when this train slid down the grade to Moçambique, South Africa would be cleared of this menace.

'Out they go!' Piet Krause exulted as the wagons stood in the sun. 'A fearful wrong is being corrected.'

The Chinese, bewildered when they left Canton years ago, bewildered by their treatment in the mines, and now bewildered by this enforced exodus, looked out impassively at the boys they had never understood and the grownups they had never known. One schoolboy picked up a stone and threw it at the hateful exportees, but Piet Krause halted that: 'No abuse. Just cheer when the train starts.' And when it did, and the trucks moved again, everyone applauded, for a heavy burden was being removed from the homeland. 'Die Volk,' said Krause, 'is nou skoon!' (The Volk has been purified.)

When the boys returned to their school, Krause said, 'Our next task is to repatriate all the Indians. Gerrit, what does *repatriate* mean?'

'To send back a person to where he belongs.'

'That's right. Every person on earth has a place where he belongs. He should stay there. We've sent the Chinese back to China. We must send the Indians back to India. And the English should go back to England. This is the land of the Afrikaner.'

'What about the Kaffirs?'

'They belong here. They're as much a part of Africa as we are. But they're inferior. They know nothing. It's our responsibility to protect them, and explain to them how they must obey our laws. The Kaffirs will always be with us, and we must treat them with respect, but also with firmness.'

Whenever Detlev heard such preachments he thought of that glass of layered jellies, each color in its proper place, each clearly demarked from the other, and as he recalled that moment of revelation, he remembered the earlier day, when Johanna's experiment had not worked and she had mixed all the jellies together. That result had been pleasing neither to the eye nor to the taste: It was a jumble without character and I didn't like it. But when it was done right, look what happened! It was beautiful to see, and when you dipped your spoon in, each layer had its proper taste. The orange was the way orange should be, the lemon on top tasted right, and even the currant on the bottom preserved its real flavor. That's the way races should be.

Not long after the disappearance of the Chinese, Piet Krause invited three of his best students to accompany him to an important meeting near Johannesburg: 'You are to hear the one man in this country who knows what he's doing.'

It was General J. B. M. Hertzog, a hero during the Boer War, a brilliant lawyer afterward. He was not overpowering, like old General de Groot, for he was only of medium height and weight. He was a handsome man, with a close-clipped mustache and neatly parted hair. He wore steel-rimmed glasses and a business suit, and spoke softly as he offered a justification of his recent behavior:

'I said that South Africa must be for South Africans, and I make no apology. By South Africans, I mean those persons whether of Dutch or English heritage who have committed their lives to this country, and who do not think fondly of some place else as "home." [He spoke this word derisively.]

'I said that I wanted my country to be ruled by men who are totally South African at heart, and I make no apology. By this I mean that we should be governed only by men who understand this land and its language, who are working for its welfare and not for the welfare of some empire. [Here there was both applause and boos.]

'I have been accused of wanting to make the Afrikaner baas in this country, and I confess to the charge. I certainly don't want some newcomer who knows nothing of the land or the language or the religion to be my baas. I want South Africa to be ruled by South Africans.

'I have been accused of not being willing to conciliate, and I confess to that charge also. On what principle should I conciliate, and whom? I have done no man any wrong, others have done me wrong by invading my country, and I await conciliation from them. If conciliation means that Dutch-speaking South Africans must always make concessions to English-speaking South Africans, I say that we are not ripe for conciliation, and I refuse to sacrifice the future of one child of the true South Africa on that altar.

'I have been accused of putting the interests of South Africa ahead of those of the empire, and to this accusation I most gladly plead guilty. I will always place the interests of my country first, for unless we are strong, and good and able to govern ourselves, we shall be no use to the empire or anyone else. [At this Krause and many others applauded.]

'Finally, I have been asked by many in authority to dissociate myself from the striking statement made some months ago by a great hero of our country, General Paulus de Groot of the Venloo Commando. He said, while standing on a pile of manure at his farm, "I would rather be here on this dunghill with my people than in the palaces of empire." I say the same. This is my country, such as it is. This is the country of those who love South Africa. [Here Krause led wild cheering.] First, foremost and always.'

Detlev had never before heard such a speech, so rational, so carefully organized, and with such a constant appeal to the crowd's emotions. 'He must be the finest mind in South Africa,' he whispered to Piet Krause when the cheering stopped.

'He is. He will lead us to freedom.'

'What does he think about the Act of Union?'

'What I think. That it should be used intelligently as a weapon to attain our freedom.'

'Does he agree with you about the Kaffirs?'

'Absolutely. South Africa must always be a place of white supremacy.' Detlev had not heard this phrase before. 'We shall assume fatherly responsibility for the Kaffirs, who will never be able to govern themselves. But we must rule them, for they are children and we must tell them what to do.'

In these days, when Piet Krause was promoting such ideas, no one noticed that Micah Nxumalo was sometimes away from Vrymeer for the better part of a week. His wives were so capable that they kept things moving forward in his absence, assuring Jakob that their husband was over at General de Groot's, and telling the latter that he was working the far fields.

He would actually be on his way to Waterval-Boven to catch a train to Johannesburg, where he ducked down alleys to a ramshackle building. For these trips he wore an old dark suit which Van Doorn had given him, shoes, a white shirt with high collar, a four-in-hand tie and a stiff felt hat made in England. He was in his forties, and except for his good clothes, in no way conspicuous. Of medium height and weight, he looked like any of the blacks who worked in Johannesburg offices.

The dozen blacks who met with him in secret one night in 1912 looked the same. 'This is Reverend John Dube,' a man explained, introducing him to the persuasive chairman of the African National Congress.

'This is Solomon Plaatje. He served with the English forces during the siege of Mafeking.' Nxumalo nodded toward the famous newspaperman and said, 'I served with the Boers at Ladysmith.' Whereupon Plaatje, a small, nervous man, laughed. 'Two rather ugly affairs.'

Of the other ten, all men as prominent in black circles as Dube and Plaatje, Micah noticed that each spoke English with beautiful ease and pronunciation. Plaatje, of course, had worked for the *London Times,* so that his mastery was not remarkable, but it was curious that some of the others had acquired such fluency. Nxumalo had only the most meager vocabulary and felt himself at a disadvantage, but not when the discussions started, for by listening to General de Groot and especially young Piet Krause, he had acquired a solid comprehension of what the new laws signified.

Plaatje was speaking: 'We are in the position Thomas Jefferson was in in 1774, prior to the revolution. By that I mean, we must utilize all the legal processes open to us to protect our position and to gain such advantage as we can.' Those were the exact words he spoke, and when others took the floor, they referred in comparable phrases to conditions in England, France and Germany.

They were bitterly opposed to the sections in the Act of Union which denied Coloureds and blacks the right to vote in three of the four provinces; only in the Cape was such voting allowed. There was strong feeling that this provision must be attacked, but as one of the men pointed out: 'Keeping us off the rolls was one of the principal clauses in the peace treaty that ended the war. It is defended not only here in South Africa but also in London. We are stuck with it, I am afraid.'

Talk then turned to a new bill which these men saw as a serious step backward in relations between the races; the Natives Land Act established the principle that some lands were reserved for the blacks, some for the whites, and that the law itself protected and ensured this division. 'The land should be for us all,' Plaatje argued, and others joined in so forcefully that it was unanimously agreed that a delegation of five be appointed to travel to London to present to the king their plea for protection. 'We cannot look to the Afrikaner for fair treatment,' one of these men argued, 'because his custom and his church deny that we have rights—'

'Now wait!' another interrupted. 'They recognize our rights. Even Hertzog does that. What they want to do is restrict them.'

The first speaker ignored this interruption; in the crowded little room with inadequate light he reasoned: 'So we must depend upon England and the liberal opinion there. We must keep constant pressure on them to accord us the same privileges they grant native-born New Zealanders and Australians.'

'In the long run,' one man predicted, 'the English of this country will prove no different from the Afrikaners.'

When the rules were spelled out for the conduct of the commission to the king, the members wanted to hear from Nxumalo about conditions on the frontier, those little Afrikaner towns where the ideas which would later sweep the cities germinated, and now he spoke, slowly, while the others listened. He had not their command of English, and more than half of them would not have difficulty in understanding his Zulu had he used it; none wanted him to speak Afrikaans, even though he was proficient in it, and they too.

'We have a new teacher, very forceful. Took his boys to see the expulsion of the Chinese. Some came home wanting to expel the blacks, too. But he calmed them down. Took another group to hear General Hertzog. They came home wild-eyed with patriotism. They want to fight the English again. General de Groot encourages them. He says war must come. He speaks of Germany a good deal. He is in contact with other generals, and they may cause trouble one day.'

He spoke of many things, displaying an uncanny understanding of what was motivating the sturdy Afrikaners in the Venloo district, but it was when he came to matters of real importance that he showed his sensitive awareness of probable trends: 'The young schoolteacher is like the general; he wants to go to war now. But his ideas come from his wife. She is four years older. Was in the camp at Chrissiesmeer. She is strong, wanted to marry an Englishman but her family wouldn't allow it. She makes no senseless challenges. She thinks.

'But the true power in Venloo is the new predikant. Very good man. Has a strong mind like yours, Plaatje. Preaches careful sermons, very logical. He has an orderly view of what is going to happen and takes no risks. When I drive the people to church, I stand outside and listen.

Powerful voice. Good man. But he is totally against us. He uses the Bible to club us. And in the long run he will be more dangerous to us than anyone you have mentioned.'

'What can he do to hurt us in Venloo?'

'Soon his voice will be heard throughout the land. He is like Jan Christian Smuts. To see him is to know that he will one day command.'

The other men took notice of the name, Barend Brongersma, of Stellenbosch.

In 1913 Detlev received the first letter that had ever been addressed to him specifically, and it came in such form that it overwhelmed him, as well it might, for his response would go far in determining a major part of his life. It came from a committee of women in Bloemfontein, and said:

> We have erected a noble monument in remembrance of the Boer women and children who perished in the infamous concentration camps of our Second Freedom War. Since you were in a camp and lost a mother and two sisters, and since your teacher Mr. Krause has given us your name as an able scholar, we deem it proper for you to join us at the dedication of a monument that will stand forever as a reminder of your mother's heroism and the cruel deaths of your sisters.

The letter went on to say that he would be one of a group of twelve survivors of the camps, six girls, six boys, who would stand at attention as the monument was dedicated. He was eighteen that year; the others would be younger.

Bursting with pride, he showed the letter to Mr. Krause, who said, 'It is proper for the Volk to honor its past. This is a profound honor, and I trust you will conduct yourself appropriately.' He added that he would not have recommended Detlev had he not been sure of the boy's loyalty and patriotism. Detlev walked several inches taller when he carried the letter out to Vrymeer, where General de Groot explained that Detlev would be standing as surrogate for all the young heroes who died in the camps: 'You escaped the ground glass in the meal. They didn't.'

For the first time Detlev traveled on a train alone. He carried with him four books of South African history, which he read so assiduously that when he paused for a bite to eat, a young man traveling to Cape Town asked, 'What preoccupies you?'

'I am reading about the English settlement of Grahamstown. That's where my family lived in the old days.'

'That was a bad period,' the young man said in fluent Afrikaans. 'If we hadn't allowed those extra Englishmen ashore, they wouldn't have been able to steal our country from us.'

'One of the Englishmen, man named Saltwood . . .'

'One of the worst. Do you know anything about that infamous family? They rob this country blind. Offices in the cities, stealing Afrikaner money.'

'Mrs. Saltwood saved my life, I think.'

'She was all right. That I grant. But every family has to have one decent member. Her husband, you know. The big sportsman. Cricket and tennis. He was one of Cecil Rhodes' worst young men. Horrible spy, and all that.'

After a long and confused tirade, he asked Detlev where he was going, and when he learned about the dedication of the Vrouemonument his manner changed completely: 'Wonderlik, wonderlik! And you're to stand there representing us all! How ennobling! Oh, I do wish I could go with you!'

'Why?'

The young man, who had been so authoritative only a moment ago, could not reply. His eyes filled with tears, and when he tried to speak he choked. He blew his nose, looked out the window at the highveld, glowing in the sun, and tried again to speak. Finally he surrendered and wept for some moments. Then he muttered, 'My mother. My brother. All my sisters. They died at Standerton.'

When he recovered he told Detlev about the last days, when food was scarce: 'There was an English hospital nearby. Their troops wounded or knocked down by the enteric. I was sure they must have food, so I sneaked out of our camp and crept along to theirs, but they were dying too. It was a horrible war, Detlev.'

He spoke with such an unusual mix of deep feeling and wide knowledge that Detlev deemed him the appropriate person to answer a nagging question: 'You don't believe those stories about ground glass in the meal, do you?'

'Absolute rot. I just told you, the English died the same way we did.' Abruptly he asked, 'Detlev, what a curious name. What's it mean?'

'German. Along the Rhine. My mother was a very beautiful woman who had a German uncle or something.'

'Detlev! It's not a Dutch name, you know.'

'I said it was German.'

'Why do you keep it?'

'You keep the name God gave you. Look at General Hertzog. Nobody more Afrikaner than he . . .'

'Now, there's a man, not so?'

'Do you know his name? No? Well, it's James Barry Hertzog, that's what it is.'

'He ought to change it. With his ideas, he ought to change it.'

'It's the name God gave him.'

'It isn't at all. Some damn-fool English name, that's what it is.'

The young man seemed to have so many positive ideas that Detlev wanted to know what he was doing on the train to Cape Town. 'I'm going down to work in Parliament. I'm to be a clerk of some sort, and one day I'll be head of a ministry, telling you farmers what to do.'

'How did you get the job? How old are you?'

'I'm twenty-one, and the country is hungry for bright young men who can speak Afrikaans and English. You might say that I am needed in Cape Town.' He said his name was Michael van Tonder and that one day he would be as famous as Jan Christian Smuts, but Detlev never heard of him again.

At Bloemfontein he was met by a committee of women wearing sashes; they were in charge of the ceremonies and had brought with them bold sashes for the twelve young survivors of the camps to wear. Across each was lettered in red: CONCENTRATION CAMP SURVIVOR, and when Detlev was handed his the woman said, 'Wait here. We have to find a girl coming down from Carolina. Her father was a hero of that commando and her mother and two brothers died in the camp at Standerton.'

So he stood alone on the platform, his sash across his chest, while the committee searched for the girl; and when they found her, they placed a ribbon on her, too, bearing the same words but in blue. She was introduced as Maria Steyn of Carolina. 'We're neighbors,' Detlev said and she nodded.

For three days they were together, young people caught up in the tormented memories of the camps and proud of the performances of their mothers and their siblings struck down by disease and hunger, and especially their fathers, who had served in the great commandos. 'My father,' Maria said, 'is Christoffel Steyn. Of the Carolina Commando. Many said they were the finest unit in the war.'

'We all know Christoffel Steyn and Spion Kop. My father rode with General de Groot in the Venloo Commando. They didn't accomplish much at first.'

'Oh, but they were heroic! That dash down to Port Elizabeth.'

'That didn't accomplish much, either, from what they tell me.'

'But such willingness!'

At the dedication they stood facing each other, Maria with the young women, Detlev with the young men, and he noticed that when the solemn words of remembrance were spoken, she had tears in her eyes as he did in his.

'I wouldn't want to do that again,' she said, but then they were taken to a church where a very old predikant delivered a marvelous oration, preaching forgiveness and the love which Jesus Christ extended to all his children:

> 'And I would say to you young people who bear across your bosoms the sash that tells us that you were in the camps, that Jesus Christ personally saw to it that you were saved so that you might bear witness to the forgiveness that marks our new nation.'

This was followed by a sermon of a much different stripe, for at the conclusion of his prayer he announced that one of the most brilliant of Stellenbosch's recent ministerial candidates had been asked to speak of the new South Africa that would be erected upon the spirit of the Vrouemonument. It was Barend Brongersma, who spoke in a deep, controlled voice of the dedication 'which we the living must accept from the hands of those dead':

> 'Not a day dare go by without our remembering the heroic dead, the loving wives who would see their husbands no more, the beautiful children who were destined to cruel death before they could welcome their fathers home from defeat.
>
> 'Yes, it was defeat, but from such defeat great nations have risen in the past, and a great one will rise today if you have the courage to ensure it. You must build on the crucifixion of your loved ones. You must take to your hearts the covenant your forefathers

received from the Lord. You must ensure and send forward the convictions of the devout people who formed this nation . . .'

His voice rose to a powerful thunder as he challenged every individual in that audience to do some good thing for her or his nation so that the martyrs represented by the Vrouemonument should not have died in vain. Detlev, looking across the aisle to where the young women sat, saw that Maria was sobbing, and he felt his own throat choke with patriotic emotion, so forceful had been the peroration of the predikant from Venloo.

During the final session on a vibrant spring day Detlev found himself with Maria constantly, under various circumstances, and while eating a hearty breakfast provided for the young people or walking to a church service with her in central Bloemfontein, he had an opportunity to study her closely, as he did with all people who interested him. She was three years younger than he, but mature for her fifteen years. She was a heavy girl, not beautiful, and even though she had lovely blond hair, which she might have dressed in some attractive way, she ignored it, pulling it back tightly in the old fashion. None of her features was distinctive, each being marked by a certain rural grossness, and she moved with no special grace. She was not a lumpy peasant type, not at all, for she had a quickness of mind which showed itself constantly; she was, indeed, much like Johanna Krause, and since Johanna had served as Detlev's mother, he had a predilection toward that type of woman. But the essential characteristic of this girl, which even Detlev was old enough to perceive, was the gravity of her deportment. She was a serious young woman in all the best meanings of that word, and any young man who came into contact with her at an emotional level would have to be impressed by her moral solidity. She was not a person forced by the tragedy of the camps into a premature adulthood, worn and withered; she was naturally adult.

Therefore, when the young couple walked to the Vrouemonument for the farewell picnic they walked together, their conversation falling into the pattern of grave thoughts. 'How were you chosen for the honor?' Detlev asked as they strolled across the grassy mound. 'I mean, I know about your father. We learned about him in school. I mean, who chose you?'

'I think it must have been the dominee.'

'In my case it was the schoolteacher. He's married to my sister, you know.'

'I was not aware of that.' She spoke cautiously and in a somewhat old-fashioned way.

'What do you propose doing after we return?' Anyone talking with Maria Steyn found himself quickly falling into her stately patterns.

'I shall continue to read. And work on rebuilding the farm. My father remarried, did I tell you?'

'No.' He reflected on this, then said, 'I wish mine had. I think Father has been very lonely.'

'War alters people,' she said. 'Perhaps he had no further need of a wife.'

'All men need wives.' He said this with such speed that he felt embarrassed. He had not yet touched Maria, not even by any accident, other than shaking hands one time at the railway station, and he was deeply impelled to take her hand now, but as they turned a corner in the path they came upon another young pair who were kissing rather ardently and bumping into each other, and, as Detlev later expressed it to himself, 'perhaps doing other things even more awful,' so that he and Maria backed away in deep confusion. The lively eroticism of the other couple did not, as it might have done with another pair, inspire them to kiss, too; it shocked them; and they returned to the monument, in whose grim shadow they finished their conversation. They were, in other words, both puritans of an especially tenacious character: Huguenots imbued with the living spirit of John Calvin and the intellectual and moral torments that come with that persuasion. But they were also lusty Dutch peasants, close to the soil, and had they once kissed there on the mound, they would have expanded with happy love. The moment gone, they talked, reverently.

'Detlev,' Maria said. 'That's a curious name.' When he explained its German origin, she said with some force, 'But if you're to be an Afrikaner, working on the things your brother-in-law . . . What was his name?'

'Piet Krause.'

'Now, that's a proper Afrikaner name. You should have one too. Detleef, that's what it ought to be, here in a new land.'

'Do you like it as Detleef?'

'I do. It sounds proper and responsible.'

Whenever their conversation might have taken a lighter tone, the shadow of the monument fell across them, and they would study its well-carved figures and envision once more the episodes of the camps, or they would look up at the monitory obelisk rising one hundred and thirteen feet above them, summoning them back to serious matters.

'If the Germans should arrive from the west and the east, would you join with them?'

'Is there reason to believe . . .'

'Oh, yes! My father is sure there will be war in Europe, and that the Germans will mass their forces in South-West Africa and Tanganyika and come toward us like pincers.' She hesitated. 'You'd join them, of course?'

Detlev didn't know what to say. He'd heard such rumors frequently in recent years, when things seemed to be going badly in Europe, but he had never believed that Germany would actually strike at South Africa. If she did, he would leap to her support, of course, because any enemy of England's had to be a friend of his, but he was not prepared to commit himself openly.

'My father will be the first to join them,' Maria said. 'We pray that they will come soon to liberate us.' Detlev understood this enthusiasm but still remained silent. 'It would be rather wonderful, you know, to be a free country again,' she said, 'under our own rulers, with a strong Germany on either side to protect us.'

When Detlev made no response, she changed the subject: 'Will you make your name Afrikaans?'

'I've been thinking about that. I don't much like it the way it is.'

'Detleef,' she repeated. 'I like that.'

'Done!' he said. 'I prefer all things Afrikaans. I am now Detleef van Doorn.' He was sorely tempted to take her hand, or even to kiss her to mark the solemnity of his rechristening, but the mournfulness of the monument prevented this, and they spent the rest of that meaningful day talking of sober subjects.

When he returned home he found himself something of a hero, for he was invited to speak at various communities, telling of the splendid monument which memorialized their hardships in the camps. He was asked to come even to Carolina, an invitation he accepted eagerly, since it enabled him to renew acquaintance with Maria Steyn and to meet her father. When in his talk he alluded gracefully to the heroic performance of Christoffel Steyn and the Carolina men, everyone applauded.

After his speech he shared supper with the Steyns, and in later years he remembered this affair as one of the most important in his life. It had nothing to do with Maria, and was a silly thing, really, but as he watched Mrs. Steyn, almost as plump as her husband, moving easily about the kitchen and displaying her love for her family, it occurred to him that she was a second wife, not a first, and he wondered if his childhood would not have been happier had his father married again. He saw Mrs. Steyn as the epitome of what a loving Afrikaner woman could be, and it was important that he see this.

When he returned to his own home he was struck by its bleakness, and he felt depressed, but his thoughts were diverted by a series of mysterious incidents. Unidentified horsemen arrived at Vrymeer asking where General de Groot lived, and when they were told, they galloped off into the darkness. Excitement was caused by the appearance of an automobile containing three serious-looking men who wanted to consult with the general, and one afternoon Maria Steyn's fat little father appeared on the stoep, asking to talk not only with General de Groot but also with Jakob. Van Doorn was now sixty-nine years old, white-haired and somewhat stooped, but still mentally alert, and after the meeting ended he was obviously disturbed.

One evening in midwinter, 1914, when supper was over, he pushed back his plate and looked at his son. He said nothing, reflected for some moments, then stalked from the room, and Detleef could hear him walking back and forth across the stoep. Much later he returned to the kitchen and said brusquely, as if his thoughts had suddenly clarified, 'Son, England has declared war unrightfully against Germany. We must all make decisions. Let's go see De Groot.'

In the moonlight they walked to the other farm, where they found the old general in bed, a weary man past eighty, very thin, his long white beard rimming his sunken face. He had not been eating well, and it looked as if his sheets had not been changed for weeks, or even months, but the fire in his eyes had not abated. 'Have you heard the glorious news?' he cried in weakened accents. 'We have a chance to fight England again!'

'We come asking your advice, Paulus.'

'Only one thing to do. Take this country into the war on the side of Germany. Only that way can we win our freedom.'

'But won't Smuts try to make us fight in the English armies?'

General de Groot got out of bed and began to stride about his little room. 'There's the man we have to fear. That damned Jan Christian Smuts. He will try to make us fight on the wrong side, because he loves everything English. Uniforms. Medals. The king. People bowing to him. I wish I could shoot him tonight. Save us all a lot of trouble.'

They talked long about the strategies they must follow to assure that South Africa joined this war beside Germany, and what great steps they would take when German victory set them free of the bondage in which they were convinced they languished. Toward dawn De Groot said, 'By tonight I'll have the commando assembled again, and if they'll take me as their leader, we'll ride out to battle once more.' And from a pile of clothes in a corner he found his frock coat and top hat, donned them, and rode off toward Venloo to start training his men.

In the last weeks of August, when the big guns were firing salvos across wide fronts in Europe, the schoolteacher Piet Krause was marshaling public opinion in Venloo, and he was most persuasive: 'There is no reason on God's green earth why we Afrikaners should fight on the side of England against Germany, the land of our brothers, to whom we have always looked for deliverance. We must tell Jan Christian Smuts that he cannot bludgeon us into this war on the wrong side.' Constantly he harped on this theme, convincing most of the Afrikaners in his region that they must join with the Germans. In a show of hands in his classroom he found that some fifty-two boys out of sixty would volunteer for war against England. 'Wonderful! It proves that the spirit of the great commandos is not dead.'

'What will you do, Mr. Krause?' one of the boys asked.

'What could any self-respecting man do? I shall ride with the commando.'

Detleef, hearing this response, thought: They all speak of riding their horses with the commando. This time it'll be automobiles, and trucks, and the government will have them. He alone among his friends was apprehensive about the outcome. He considered Jan Christian Smuts a clever man who would defend the imperial cause effectively; but despite his caution, he knew that if the Afrikaners did not rebel now, they might never win their freedom. When Mr. Krause asked, 'You, Detleef, what will you do?' he responded promptly, 'I shall fight in defense of South Africa.'

'Which South Africa?'

'The Afrikaner homeland my father fought for.'

'Good, good.'

Now the night visitors to General de Groot increased in number, and Detleef came to know the great heroes of his people: General de Wet, General de la Rey, General Beyers, tough Manie Maritz, big as an ox, ferocious as a leopard. But the hero who impressed him most was Christoffel Steyn, who showed himself to be a man of iron courage and sober judgment. Said he during one meeting with De Groot: 'The tides of history run tempestuously. This has always been a storm-tossed land, and where the currents will sweep us now, we cannot foresee. But to stand on shore and watch others breast them would be disgraceful. De Groot, you have the Venloo Commando in excellent condition. Visit the others. Get them ready. And when the time comes, you must lead your horsemen into battle. This time we shall regain our freedom.'

From that strong position Steyn never retreated. When others wavered, pointing out the considerable advantages the government forces would have, he persisted on one steady course, freedom, and he expected all about him to do the same. But Detleef noticed that even in his most stubborn moments, he sought guidance from General de Groot and insisted upon the old man's approval and allegiance, as if he knew that he himself lacked the leadership qualities to head a revolution, whereas De Groot had them in marked degree.

'Keep your eye on Smuts,' the old man warned. 'Christoffel, you will succeed or fail insofar as you can outsmart Slim Jannie.' When De Groot used *slim* he did not intend the English word, although Jan Christian was that—slim and tall and handsome—but rather the Afrikaans word pronounced the same way: clever, shrewd, sly, not to be trusted, devious, tricky, deceitful, treacherous. It was a wonderful word, used often in connection with Smuts, whom no republican-minded Afrikaner could trust. 'Be careful, Christoffel, of that Slim Jannie.'

It was sound advice, for Smuts, perhaps the keenest brain that South Africa had ever produced, was convinced that the destiny of this country had to lie with England, and stood ready to repel any German invader from the outside or discipline any German sympathizer who sought to operate secretly on the inside. Supporting him were English-speaking South Africans and many like-minded Afrikaners who were eager to forget the past and wanted to unite the two white tribes of the land. Paulus de Groot was shrewd when he perceived that the battle of his commandos would be not against England, but against Slim Jannie. It would be a precarious revolution and he said so.

But he was impatient to lead it. He fed his Basuto pony extra rations, oiled his rifle, and consulted constantly with leaders of the other commandos. He was in Venloo church that Sunday morning, tall and straight for all to see, when Predikant Brongersma delivered his famous sermon on patriotism:

'The Bible is replete with instances in which men were called to defend their nations, in which they rode forth to protect the principles upon which their homeland existed. The Israelites in particular had to protect themselves against Assyrians, Medes, Persians, Egyptians and Philistines, and whenever they fought in accordance with God's principles, they were victorious. When they raised their own false banners, they were defeated.

'What words appear on the banner of God? Justice, fortitude, obedience, charity to the defeated enemy, reverence, prayer, and above all, sacred respect for the covenant under which our nation exists. If we, in moments of crisis, can comport ourselves in harmony with those commands, then we can be assured that we fight on God's side. But if we are arrogant, or seek what belongs to others, or are cruel, or behave without respect for the covenant, then we must surely earn defeat.

'How can a man discern, in time of crisis, whether he is in harmony with God's commands? Only by searching his own heart and comparing his proposed behavior with instructions he has learned in the Bible. And only by subjecting himself to that comparison constantly. It is in the Bible that we find our instructions.'

After the sermon, when De Groot asked him point-blank if he would be riding with the commandos, the predikant said that his duty lay with the community, to help guide it regardless of the outcome. 'Then you are afraid we'll lose?' De Groot asked.

'I am,' Brongersma said.

'You mean our cause is unjust?'

'I mean, General, that I have heard you say a dozen times, "We have lost the battles. We have lost the war. Now we shall win in other ways." You were right when you said that. But now, at the first chance, you go back to the battles. Why?'

'If a bugle sounds against the English, who can stay home?' As he asked this, the old warrior stared straight into the eyes of the predikant, recalling the dismal fact that in the great moments of his life—the trek, the frontier, the battles—his church had never supported him. He did not expect it to now.

The first two weeks of September 1914 were a hectic and dazzling experience: Paulus de Groot dispatched emissaries to the other commandos, advising them that he expected them to rise as soon as the great generals declared themselves in favor of Germany; Christoffel Steyn assembled seventy-two men out of a possible ninety, each ready to mount his pony and ride forth; Piet Krause had already put away his books and was eager to fight; Jakob van Doorn, at seventy, had purchased an automobile; and his son Detleef, at nineteen, was up in the hills behind Vrymeer, practicing with a Mauser.

Beginning on Friday, September 12, De Groot convened a series of leader-meetings attended by a secret agent of the German armed forces in South-West Africa, who assured the locals that all was in readiness. The uprising was to start on Tuesday, September 16; wild Manie Maritz would lead his commando across the border into German territory; General Beyers would resign his position with the government after releasing a fiery condemnation of Smuts; and General de Groot would summon the men in the northeastern Transvaal. Pretoria would be taken, the government would be captured; and German power would reach from the Atlantic on the west to the Indian Ocean at Tanganyika. Combined with victory in Europe, this would herald the dawn of Germanic hegemony, in which Afrikaner nationalism would dominate southern Africa, under German guidance.

On the night of Sunday, September 14, Detleef van Doorn rode slowly eastward to Venloo, where his brother-in-law, Piet Krause, had assembled twenty-two men of the local commando. They rode through the starry night to a meeting point where others were gathering for the uprising; when morning came and he saw the masses of men willing to fight once more for a republican South Africa, his excitement soared and he cried to Krause, 'Nothing can stop us now!' He gained additional reassurance when he found that these men were to be led by Christoffel Steyn.

And then the blows of misfortune began to fall. As Barend Brongersma had foreseen, God was not with these Afrikaners this time. The general on whom they depended most to lead them, Koos de la Rey, a fine and brilliant man, had the horrible misfortune to be riding out of Johannesburg to convene his segment of the rebellion when a policeman, suspecting that the speeding car might contain a team of gangsters who had committed many depredations, including murder of policemen, fired a shot at the Daimler's tire. It should never have hit the car, but it ricocheted off a rock, smashed into the head of De la Rey and killed him. Sometime later, capable General Beyers, who might have taken the dead man's place, tried to flee across the Vaal River and was drowned. Tough Manie Maritz was neutralized across the border, and even brave General de Wet, noblest of the lot, was surrounded and forced to surrender.

Slim Jannie Smuts made not a single mistake. When the rebellion appeared to be powerful, he did not panic; instead, he called up loyal Afrikaner troops to confront their defiant brothers, keeping the English section of the nation out of the fight. And when the rebellion began to fizzle, he did not exult. He simply maintained one pressure after another, and in the end, found himself victorious on every front: the German invading force from South-West Africa was beaten back; the Germans in Tanganyika were immobilized; and within the country only Paulus de Groot and Christoffel Steyn held out against him, pinned down, as in 1902, in a wee corner of the Transvaal.

'We must fight to the death,' De Groot told his men, and if any showed an inclination to despair, young firebrands like Piet Krause disciplined them, saying, 'In Europe, Germany is winning everywhere. Victory will still be ours.'

But then they were crushed by the most devastating blow of all. One night in November 1914, after a tiring ride across the highveld, General de Groot said to Jakob and Detleef, who had ridden with him, 'I feel tired.' A bed was made for the old man, the first he had slept in for the past ten days, and he began to breathe heavily. He said a most curious thing: 'I would like to see my Basuto.' So the little horse was brought to where he lay. Sixteen, eighteen, fifty . . . how many of these wonderful beasts had he ridden and out of how many traps? He tried to pat the munching animal, but fell back, too exhausted to complete the effort.

'Take him away,' Jakob told his son, but the old man protested: 'Leave him with me.' Toward midnight he rallied somewhat and told Christoffel, 'Lead the men toward Waterval-Boven. We always fought well there.' In some bewilderment he looked at Jakob and could not remember who he was, but then he saw Detleef, who had been so kind: 'Are you Detleef with the new name?'

'I am.' The old man tried to speak, fell back, and died. Born in 1832, he had witnessed eight decades of fire and hope, defeat and victory.

With his death, the last commando more or less dissolved. Christoffel Steyn made a valiant effort to hold the men together, and Piet Krause threatened to shoot any who deserted, but finally, even men like Jakob and Detleef drifted away, for as Van Doorn told his son-in-law, 'Piet, it's time to get back to the farm.'

'No!' the young schoolteacher pleaded. 'One more battle, just one big victory, and the Germans will come storming up from Moçambique to save us.'

'There are no Germans in Moçambique,' Jakob said, but Krause was so determined to pursue this logic that he maneuvered the men into a position from which they could not escape without giving battle, and in this fight Jakob van Doorn caught a burst of .303 bullets right between the eyes. Little of his head was left to be buried with the shattered trunk, and after prayers were said at his improvised graveside, Detleef said, 'Piet, I think we'd better go home.'

It was fortunate they did, for the very next day government troops surrounded the remnants of the commando and arrested Christoffel Steyn.

Then began the worst agony of this abortive affair, for Jan Christian Smuts discovered that Christoffel, in the years of peace following the end of the Boer War, had accepted a position in the South African army which he had never resigned. Technically he was a traitor, and while hundreds of other rebels had been dealt with leniently, Smuts was determined to prosecute charges against this officer. On an awful day in December 1914 a court-martial condemned Steyn to be executed. From the Afrikaner community, including many who had not supported the rebellion, came a cry of protest, voicing respect and admiration for this brave man who had conducted himself with such integrity during the forays of the Carolina Commando. But Smuts would not listen.

Piet Krause led a delegation of schoolteachers to Pretoria to plead for Christoffel's life, and Reverend Brongersma preached four tremendous sermons, two in Johannesburg, begging the government to show clemency, but to no avail. Only a few days before Christmas, Steyn was taken before a firing squad in Pretoria Central Prison, where he sang an old Dutch hymn: 'When we enter the Valley of Death we leave our friends behind us.' As the soldiers took up firing positions he refused a blindfold and continued singing until the bullets silenced him.

Detleef was torn apart by this tragic culmination of the rebellion: De Groot dead on the battlefield; Jakob buried in strange soil; Christoffel, of them all the most chivalrous, executed on a summer's morning; his own life shattered. That night he wrote to Maria, the rebel's daughter:

I fought alongside your father. I saw him at his noblest and his
memory will always abide with me. He was executed most un-
fairly, and if I ever see that Slim Jan Christian Smuts, I will put a
bullet through his brain, if he has one, which I doubt.

She, being a prudent young woman, showed the letter to no one, for she
realized that if it were seen by the police, the young man she loved
might be in serious trouble. She folded it carefully and placed it with
mementos of her father: a handkerchief worn at Spion Kop, his car-
tridge belt, a book of Psalms in Old Dutch that he had carried with him
in all his Boer War battles.

Christoffel Steyn was dead, but his memory would be kept alive not
only by his daughter but also by a whole people longing for heroes.
Slim Jannie Smuts had created a martyr out of this little commando and
left a burning wound in the soul of Afrikanerdom. It would flame
alongside the charred memories of Slagter's Nek, Blaauwkrantz and
Chrissiesmeer—a bitter legacy upon which the sacred history of a nation
would be built.

Detleef would surely have married Maria Steyn not long afterward, except that Reverend Brongersma came to the farm with news that carried
him off to wholly new adventures in education: 'I have the most exciting development to discuss with you, Detleef. Some time ago I wrote to
a group of professors at Stellenbosch, telling them two things: that you
were good at studies and unusually good at rugby. They want you to
come there to pursue your studies.'

'What studies?'

'I would say philosophy and the sciences. And it would please me
greatly if you found it in your heart to enter the ministry. You have a
strong character, Detleef, and I think you could be of notable service to
the Lord.'

'But who will tend the farm?'

'Piet Krause and Johanna. I've spoken to them.'

'He can't live here and teach in Venloo.'

'Recent events have spoiled him, Detleef. He no longer wants to be a
teacher.'

'He won't be very good at farming.'

'No, but he'll look after the place till you get back. And then we'll
see what happens.' He paused and rubbed his chin. 'You know, Piet is a

remarkable man. He could move in any direction if God ever shows him the right one.' He laughed. 'You have found your path.'

'And what is it?'

'To get an education. To serve God and your society.'

It was a long journey in miles from Vrymeer to Stellenbosch, a much greater one in mental and moral significance, for this quiet town with tall trees and white buildings had become a beautiful and seductive educational center like Cambridge in England, or Siena in Italy, or Princeton in America, a town set apart to remind citizens of how splendid colleges and libraries and museums could be. It was an Afrikaans-speaking place, heavily tinged with religious fervor, but also imbued with an intense speculation about the nature of politics in South Africa, and its professors were some of the most astute men in the nation.

At first Detleef was merely a big, bumbling oaf from the country, forced to compete with the sharper minds of lads who had matured in places like Pretoria, Bloemfontein and Cape Town, but when he settled down in the home of a clergyman's widow and navigated his first term of advanced trigonometry, beginning philosophy and the history of Holland in the golden century, all of which he fumbled rather badly, he found his sea legs, as it were, and proceeded firmly into his second set of courses, in which he began to display the solid learning he had mastered in the good school at Venloo.

He was especially attracted by his older professors, those men of learning, some from the university at Leiden, some from Oxford, who saw their nation as it actually was, a mix of cultures striving to achieve a central tendency, and he found to his astonishment that two of the classes he enjoyed most were taught by Englishmen, in English. But he appreciated them as he might an especially provocative class in Latin; these men were dealing in historic materials that were long since dead, and if they did so brilliantly, they did so nevertheless with a sense of the mortuary, and he knew it.

The men who exerted the deepest influence were the younger professors who discussed contemporary values, the future of South Africa, its current crises. There were no courses in such subjects, but the better professors knew how to slip relevant teaching into their lectures. In 1916, for example, there was much discussion of how the war in Europe would terminate, with some professors still convinced that Germany would win, but conceding that her victory would not mean much constructively to South Africa, which would face a new set of problems. One man warned: 'I cannot see Germany surrendering Lourenço Marques to us when she conquers it from Portugal. It will be her port, not ours, and indeed, she may drive a harder bargain for its use than the Portuguese did.' Hardly a day passed but what some challenging idea was extruded, sometimes painfully, always cautiously, and his mind expanded with this new aspect of learning.

Living in the house of a predikant's widow, and buttressed by constant pressure from Reverend Brongersma back in Venloo, it was natural that Detleef should fall into the orbit of the professors of religion, and they quickly saw in this able young man a likely prospect for the pulpit. He was inherently devout and well informed on Biblical matters; both his father and the old general had taught him from the time-scarred Bible, and the predikants of Venloo had been a virile lot, preaching a durable version of the Old Testament, while Barend Brongersma had introduced him to the subtleties of the New, so that by the end of his first year it was generally assumed that he would be heading for the ministry.

As had been the case for the past hundred years, one of the most influential voices in the Dutch Reformed clergy at Stellenbosch was a Scotsman, a devotee of John Knox named Alexander McKinnon, whose ancestors had been Dutch-speaking Afrikaners since 1813. It was he who introduced Detleef to the persuasive teachings of the conservative prime minister of Holland, Abraham Kuyper, who had promulgated new theories on the relationship between church and state. It was from McKinnon that Detleef first gleaned an appreciation of the fact that South Africa might soon have to evolve new patterns for contacts between the races. On this subject McKinnon was most conservative, going back to a strong Calvinism to support his contention that races, like people, were foreordained to either salvation or damnation: 'Obviously, the Bantu are the children of Ham, as the Bible explains.' Detleef noticed that like most cultured people these days, he avoided the pejorative word *Kaffir,* using instead the curious word *Bantu,* which more accurately was the name of a language, not that of a tribe or nation. 'Obviously, the Bantu as a group cannot be among the elect, although individual Bantu can become highly educated and just as favored of God as the finest Afrikaner. Individuals can be saved, but the race as a whole is certainly condemned.'

But in the latter part of his first year at Stellenbosch all such matters faded into insignificance, for the university discovered that in Detleef they had a natural-born rugby player, and in a nation increasingly mad about sports, this attribute superseded all others. He was a thick-necked block of granite, tested in real battle, and extremely quick in adjusting to the movements of the enemy. He played forward, and in the scrum his shoulders disrupted the opposition, breaking holes in their line, while his feet were unusually nimble at hooking the ball or sending it forward. He was a stubborn chunk of aggression who could absorb punishment without flinching, and as such, he was invaluable.

The Stellenbosch fifteen were known as the Maties because of their strong sense of fraternity; they were a formidable combination, capable of playing the best regional teams, but their special delight came in defeating the Ikeys of Cape Town, so-called because that university admitted a goodly number of Jews, who were not exactly welcomed at Stellenbosch. Any Maties-Ikeys game was apt to be exciting, and in the first one Detleef played, he excelled. From then on he was accepted as a member of the Afrikaner group that specialized in sports, and by virtue of this he traveled to many parts of the country, playing against the men who would later occupy positions of leadership, for in South Africa there was no passport to preferment more effective than membership on the Stellenbosch rugby team.

These were the years when the game was dominated by one sensational family, the Morkels, and sometimes Detleef would go up against a team that fielded six players with that name, or seven. Twenty-two Morkels were playing in this decade: brothers, cousins, unrelated solitaries, all of them stout lads. Detleef knew it was going to be a strong game whenever he bent over in the scrum and found himself facing two or three of these rugged types. Once, the four biggest men facing him in the tight confrontations were Morkels, and he left that game, as he told his coach, 'as if I had slipped by accident into a threshing machine.' He was not surprised when an entrepreneur announced plans to invade Europe with a team composed only of Morkels; it would be formidable.

It was as a rugby player that Detleef finished his first year at Stellenbosch, and it was principally because of this reputation that he attracted the attention of the Van Doorns who operated the famous vineyards at Trianon. One afternoon, to the house in which he boarded, a Bantu came bearing an invitation to Detleef van Doorn to take dinner that evening with his Trianon cousins. It was the day after a game in which five horrible Morkels had run up and down his spine, so he was not exactly lively, but he had heard so much about Trianon that he accepted, and rode out to the winery.

Like many before him, he gaped when he approached the western entrance and saw for the first time those enchanting arms reaching out

and the pristine façade of the main house waiting to welcome him. The
war years had been good to Trianon; General Buller had paid top prices
for its premier wine and other officers did the same for the lesser
blends, so that the Van Doorns had sold their entire pressings for European prices without having had to pay freightage to get the bottles to
that market. In all respects the place had been improved, and now
looked pretty much as it would through the twentieth century.

On the stoep, resting on one of the tiled benches built two centuries
earlier by Paul de Pré, waited Coenraad van Doorn, head of the establishment, who had extended a similar welcome to Jakob in 1899, on the
eve of the Boer War. He was heavier now, a man in his late forties, and
his manner was even more affable, for life had been exceedingly good.
He loved sports and was proud to have a member of his family, even
one so remotely associated as Detleef, playing well at Stellenbosch.

'So this is the hero I've been reading about, the Matie who sweeps
them aside!' Extending both hands, he drew Detleef up to the stoep and
in through the front door. In the wide hallway between the rooms
Detleef saw for the first time the Van Doorn daughter, Clara, nineteen
years old and so pretty she caused him to gasp. Her face was beautifully
oval, with cheekbones just a bit too wide, and framed by carefully
brushed amber hair worn in a kind of Dutch-boy bob. She smiled
warmly as she stepped forward to greet her distant cousin, and said,
'We are so happy to see such a rugby player in our home.'

At dinner her two older brothers, Dirk and Gerrit, who had by now
graduated from Stellenbosch, asked a barrage of questions about the
university and their chances of beating the Ikeys again, and the evening
proved to be one of the most pleasant Detleef had ever spent. It was
fortunate that it was occurring at the end of his first year, because by
now his success at rugby had transformed him from an awkward country lad into a self-confident university man, quiet-spoken and interesting. When talk turned to the war in Europe, he repeated some of the
things he had heard in class, predicting a German victory in Europe but
no significant change in the countries bordering South Africa.

'What I feel precisely,' the older Van Doorn said, and as Clara
walked with Detleef to the automobile that would take him back to his
lodgings she said, 'You've been learning something at the university.
Come back and share your knowledge with us.' He started to protest
that he really knew very little, but she halted him: 'No! My brothers
went to Stellenbosch and they learned precious little.' It was as if she

rode in the car with him back to town, so vivid was his recollection of her lovely bearing.

He spent two weeks trying to invent some excuse for returning to Trianon, and then one night the driver was there again with a note: 'Dr. Pretorius of Paarl is coming to dinner and would like to meet you. Clara.' It was the beginning of a thrilling experience, for Pretorius was active on a committee agitating to have Afrikaans accepted as the legal equivalent of Dutch and he was excitable about the matter: 'Acts of Parliament must be printed in Afrikaans. Our major newspapers should convert to it immediately. I've been speaking with our leading clergymen. I want our Bible to be in our language.'

'Are they ready for that?'

'No. In that quarter I receive much opposition. But consider. For three centuries in the late Middle Ages people spoke one language and read their Bible in Latin. That had to change.'

'The Catholic church still conducts its Masses in Latin.'

'That will change, too. The day will come when your daughter here is married by a predikant reading the service from an Afrikaans Bible.'

'You think so soon?' Mrs. van Doorn asked. 'I'm afraid you'll be an old maid, Clara, if you wait for that.' Clara did not blush, but Detleef did.

After one agitated flight of speech, Dr. Pretorius looked about the room as though to command close attention, then said in a softer voice, 'I want to speed the acceptance of our true language because it can become the chief agency in uniting the Afrikaners of this land and inspiring them to wrest the government from the English.'

'We have the numbers already,' Coenraad pointed out.

'But without a central soul, numbers are nothing. And what is the soul of a people? Its language. With Afrikaans we can capture this nation.'

At a subsequent meeting, at which he especially wanted Detleef to be present, Pretorius faced up to the accusation, launched by Coenraad, that Afrikaans was a second-class peasant language: 'Exactly, and that's why its vitality is assured. It will be precisely like English. And why is that language so effective?'

Each listener offered some reason: 'No declension of nouns.' 'Few subjunctive verbs.' 'Strict word order, which assures meaning.' 'A lot of quick short words to indicate case.' 'A simplified spelling.'

Clara said, 'And if English spots a good word in another language, it takes it . . . with no apologies.'

At each idea, Dr. Pretorius nodded approvingly, then asked permission to read from the work of a distinguished Danish scholar who was exploring this subject: 'He is Dr. Otto Jespersen, world-famous authority, and he says, "The English language is signalized by order and consistency . . . Simplification is the rule." And here he makes a point which relates specifically to our new Afrikaans: "Whenever I think of English and compare it with other languages, it seems to me positively and expressly *masculine*. It is the language of a grown-up man and has very little childish or feminine about it." '

He asked Clara to pass out slips of paper, and when they all had pencils he directed them to write this sentence in English: *We ourselves often took our dogs with us*. 'Four pronouns to express the first person plural. Now see what happens when we write the same sentence in Afrikaans: *Ons onsself het dikwelf ons honde saam met ons geneem*. One word—*ons*—to convey all those meanings.'

'But isn't the English more precise?'

'It is indeed. Just as the Latin forms *agricola*, by the farmer, *agricolae*, to the farmer, are more precise than *the farmer*. But we refuse to bother with such niceties. Prepositions are so much simpler. One word for *farmer*. Sixty prepositions to define relationships.'

From another pocket he produced a handful of sheets on which verses from Matthew, Chapter 6, had been printed in English:

9. Our Father which art in heaven, Hallowed be thy name.
10. Thy kingdom come. Thy will be done in earth, as it is in heaven.
11. Give us this day our daily bread.
12. And forgive us our debts, as we forgive our debtors.

He pointed out how relatively simple this was, and how direct. He then asked the Van Doorns to study other sheets of paper, where the same verses appeared in the Old Dutch of their 1630 Amsterdam Bible.

9. Onse Vader die daer zijt inde Hemelen: uwen name worde geheylicht.
10. Drijckje kome. Uwen wille ghejchiede op der Aerden gelijck inden Hemel.
11. Gheeft ons heden ons daghelijcks broodt.
12. Ende vergheeft ons onse schulden. Gelijch wy oock vergheven onsen schuldenaren.

He read this aloud twice, stressing the beauty of the flowing Dutch they had learned as children and still used when reciting their prayers. He obviously cherished the rhythms of this version, but indicated that it would be better when translated into Afrikaans, of which he gave a sample:

9. Onse Vader wat in die hemele is, laat u Naam geheilig word;
10. laat u konindryk kom; lat u wil geskied, soos in de hemel net so op die aarde;
11. gee ons vandag ons daaglikse brood;
12. en vergeef ons ons skulde, soos ons ook ons skuldenaars vergewe . . .

'Ah!' he cried triumphantly. 'How excellent!' And he went over the new translation, line by line, indicating its superiority: 'See how much simpler the Afrikaans is, how purified of old encrustations. This is to be the language of the future, believe me.'

When the two older Van Doorns protested that they did not want their Bible tampered with, he said bluntly, 'The generation that is forty years old when the change comes will know an agony of the soul. After that we will be a new people.' When Coenraad tried to voice another doubt, he said abruptly, 'Remember, if John Calvin were alive today, he would be using a Bible in Afrikaans.'

Detleef, back in his room, balanced the two versions of a word he loved: The old *Nachtmaal* becomes the new *Nagmaal*. I don't like it. The mystery of *night* is lost. And for the first time he sensed that many great good things of ancient virtue might be lost during a normal lifetime: the women he had loved so much in the concentration camp, the sturdy virtues of General de Groot. He stared at the night and could not sleep, but as dawn broke he thought: It's my duty to save the good old things.

While Detleef was enjoying these varied experiences, the young men of the Saltwood families were pursuing their studies in a much grimmer classroom. Near the city of Amiens and east of the great battle site of St. Quentin was a hunting preserve known as d'Ellville Wood, and both the Allies and the Germans realized that this grove of trees would prove crucial in the tremendous Battle of the Somme.

The German high command issued the order, 'D'Ellville shall be taken, regardless of cost,' at exactly the time when the Allied command said, 'The wood must he held at any cost.' A titanic battle to the death had become inescapable.

On 14 July 1916 Colonel Frank Saltwood, fifty-six years old and one of the first volunteers in his country's expeditionary force, received orders to take and hold d'Ellville Wood. In his command were four of his nephews—Hilary and Roger of the Cape Town Saltwoods, Max and Timothy of De Kraal—and they, too, had volunteered early.

Throughout four unbroken days the two armies battled, calling upon every great gun in the area until the trenches shuddered from explosives. Without any rest or hot food, the five Saltwoods defended their terrain heroically, with Colonel Frank moving from spot to spot to encourage his nephews.

On the second day Hilary was shot through the head. On the third day young Max led a valiant charge, which was annihilated. And on the last day Colonel Frank, rushing to an endangered point, was struck full in the face by seven German bullets, and with his death the South African position was doomed.

But into his place leaped Roger, who at twenty years old assumed command of the battle. He would have led his men to defeat had not Timothy gone totally berserk, as heroic young men sometimes will, and held off a platoon of Germans, killing most of them. And now the two cousins, surrounded by innumerable dead, including three Saltwoods, rallied the South Africans. Ignoring the hailstorm of German shells, grimly preparing for the next attack, they staffed the command post and defended the woods which they had occupied at such fearful cost and held so tenaciously.

When the South Africans were finally relieved on the fifth day of battle Roger Saltwood, as senior in command, reported: 'We took 3,150 men into the wood five days ago. We are marching 143 out.'

Delville Wood, as the battle became known in English, represented perhaps the high spot in human courage during this war. The South African volunteers had given new meaning to the word *heroism,* but the cost could not even be calculated by critics who were not there. In the pompous tradition of the time, British headquarters issued a statement that was supposed to compensate for the terrible losses, as if this had been a kind of rugby game: 'In the capture of Delville Wood the gallantry, the perseverance and determination of the South African Brigade deserve the highest commendation.'

This suicidal action had been devised and ordered by Sir Douglas Haig, one of the young generals who had learned their trade with Redvers Buller during the Boer War. Unfortunately, few of them had acquired his concern for the fighting man.

The two surviving Saltwoods, Roger of Cape Town and Timothy the V.C. from De Kraal, managed leaves together. They spent them at Sentinels with their Salisbury cousins, and as they sat beside the River Avon and looked across at the timeless cathedral, it was Timothy who told the local Saltwoods, 'We did lose three of us, yes. But it was only what we should have done for England.'

At Stellenbosch, as the war in Europe stumbled to an end, there was considerable commotion. One of the university's most promising recent graduates was announced as offering a series of four lectures on the moral bases upon which any government of the country must rest. Detleef was especially interested in the event because the speaker was Reverend Barend Brongersma, his own predikant. He invited Clara to hear the lectures with him, and her parents asked to come along, as did one of her brothers.

At Brongersma's request, the assemblies were held not at the university but in the largest of the local churches, and all seats were taken. Brongersma was now thirty-seven, at the threshold of his powers and the apex of his appearance. He was tall, slim, with a head of dark hair, and he appeared modern in every way as opposed to the older Dutch and Scottish theologians who normally occupied podiums at the university. He was different from them, too, in that he did not address himself to abstruse philosophical problems, but to the down-to-earth difficulties a politician met in running a proper government. His voice was equal to the task; Dutch Reformed congregations appreciated a predikant who could storm and thunder, and he could.

He was certainly not a coward. At the opening of his first lecture he said that the future of this nation depended upon the way it managed its relationships with the various racial groups, and so that his listeners would know what he was talking about, he invited them to write down the figures he was about to recite: 'They deal with the actual and projected populations of this country.' And he gave these data:

THE UNION OF SOUTH AFRICA

Group	Actual Population	1950 Estimate	2000 Estimate
Afrikaner	800,000	2,700,000	4,500,000
English-speaking	400,000	900,000	1,500,000
Coloured	525,000	1,200,000	4,200,000
Indian	150,000	366,000	1,250,000
Bantu	4,100,000	8,600,000	33,000,000

Without comment on the relative strengths of the five groups, he launched into a review of the positions the Dutch Reformed Church had taken on the matter of race during the past two and a half centuries, reminding his listeners of things they might have forgotten:

'Under Jan van Riebeeck, whites and blacks worshipped together, which was sensible because there was no alternative. In the frontier churches at Stellenbosch and Swellendam, similar conditions prevailed.

'Problems arose with the rite of communion, many whites not wishing to drink from the same cup that blacks used, but various ways were devised to get around this, and in general, worship continued to include both white and black. At mission stations especially this was the custom, with whites being invited to attend churches that were primarily black.

'But at the Synod of 1857 pressure was exerted to change this, and a curious solution was proposed. The leaders of our church confirmed that Jesus Christ intended his people to worship as one, and this was to be preferred, "but as a concession to the prejudice and weakness of a few, it is recommended that the church serve one or more tables to the European members after the non-white members have been served." It was further recommended that whereas it would be healthy and in accordance with Gospel for all to worship together, "if the weakness of some requires that the groups be separated, the congregation from the heathen should enjoy its privilege in a separate building and a separate institution."

'So in certain districts separate church organizations were established whose members worshipped in separate church buildings, and in time this custom became universal. It was found that most white church members preferred to worship only with other whites, on the sensible ground that health could thus be protected and the dangers of miscegenation avoided.

'As a result of such pressures, a policy developed of having separate church buildings and church organizations for each of the various racial groups, and this lent strength to the Christian movement, for the Coloured and Bantu now had churches of their own which they could operate according to their own tastes, yet all were united in the brotherhood of Christ.'

He said much more, of course, in this historical lecture, but he left the impression that the Christian church was one and undivided, that the Coloured and Bantu preferred to have their own church off to one side, and that the present division of the church into its various components was something ordained by God, approved by Jesus, and eminently workable in a plural society. He certainly did not apologize, and would have been astounded had anyone asked him to do so.

'That man is an asset to any community,' Coenraad van Doorn said when he assembled his family and Detleef at Trianon. 'He speaks with a clarity one seldom hears.'

'He told me things I didn't know,' Clara said. She looked as if she had been crying, and Detleef asked what had happened.

Her mother answered, 'The awful deaths in Europe. Clara has many friends there, you know.'

Detleef said, 'I didn't know there were very many Afrikaners fighting in that silly war.'

'There are,' Clara snapped, 'and it's not silly.'

'Any men we have there are certainly fighting on the wrong side. Germany's bound to win, and a good thing, too.'

Mr. van Doorn intervened to quash a difficult subject: 'I wonder what Brongersma will tell us next time?'

'He said in passing that it would deal with the New Testament,' Clara's brother said.

'Good. None of us know that section of the Bible well enough.'

'The Old Testament is sufficient, really,' Detleef said, and again the atmosphere chilled, but when it came time for him to say goodnight, Clara volunteered to walk with him to the car, took his hand and squeezed it. 'You mustn't be so contentious, Detleef. A living room isn't a rugby field.'

'But if a man has beliefs . . .'

'All men have beliefs. And sometimes they adhere to theirs as firmly as you do to yours.'

'But if theirs are wrong . . .'

'You feel obligated to correct them?'

'Of course.'

To his astonishment she leaned over and kissed him. 'I'm glad you're strong, Detleef. You're going to need it.'

He was trembling, and clutched her hand. 'I don't want to be obstinate, but . . . well . . . even Reverend Brongersma can be wrong sometimes.'

'For example?'

'Well, I felt he was apologetic about the way our church separates into white, Coloured, black. But that's what God intended. Even the whites separate. Afrikaans for the true believers. English for the others.'

'Detleef, how can you say that?' When he looked blank in the pale light, indicating that he had no concept of what she was talking about, she said, 'The Afrikaners and the English as being different religiously.'

'Well, they are!' he said forcefully. 'They believe quite differently from us. They don't pin their faith on John Calvin. They're almost Catholic, if you ask me.' He trembled again, this time from the terrible force of his convictions. 'And surely God entered into no covenant with them.'

To this extraordinary body of belief, Clara had no comment; her family had developed under quite a different body of faith and had often gone to the Church of England for services when that was more convenient. But now it was time for Detleef to return to the university, and as he held her hand he asked shyly, 'May I kiss you goodnight?' but she deftly pulled away.

'No, no! When I kiss you that's one thing, but when you kiss me that's another.' And before he knew what was happening, she touched him lightly with another kiss and skipped away.

Reverend Brongersma's second lecture was a revelation to Detleef and a surprise to others who thought they knew the Bible. It dealt almost exclusively with the teachings of the New Testament and the nature of

Christ's church on earth. It was highly theological, but also intensely practical to those Afrikaners who sensed that with a German victory in Europe, and perhaps in Africa, relationships were bound to be different from what they had been in the past. The audience sat in deep, religious silence as he spoke with that fluid breadth of concepts which would characterize this series:

> 'I told you last time that the orderly development of our church from the days of Van Riebeeck to the present was a good thing, approved by God and consonant with the teachings of Jesus Christ, and that we must always be proud of the high mission of our church. But since it exists in the bosom of Christ, it behooves us to know what exactly He said about our responsibilities and conduct.'

With this he launched into a patient hour-and-a-half analysis of New Testament teachings, drawing upon the soaring texts in which Christ set forth the essence of his thought. He said, when introducing the focal passage from Matthew, 'If we live in a land with divided populations, almost every question we face will pose special problems which other more homogeneous nations can evade. We cannot, and how we solve these problems of race will determine the character of our existence.' He then read the passage:

> 'Master, which is the great commandment in the law? Jesus said unto him, Thou shalt love the Lord thy God with all thy heart, and with all thy soul, and with all thy mind. This is the first and great commandment. And the second is like unto it, Thou shalt love thy neighbour as thyself. On these two commandments hang all the law and the prophets.'

He cited so many passages in Christ's teaching bearing on this issue that Coenraad whispered to Clara and Detleef, who sat together, 'He sounds like an LMS missionary,' and none could discern what he might be driving at:

> 'For as we have many members in one body, and all members have not the same office: so we, being many, are one body in Christ, and every one members one of another.'

And if anyone felt reluctant to accept this teaching, he threw at them a text which emphasized the message. It came from Colossians:

> 'Where there is neither Greek nor Jew, circumcision nor uncir-cumcision, Barbarian, Scythian, bond nor free: but Christ is all, and in all.'

This led him to what he warned was the key text of his entire series, the noble passage on which a God-fearing nation should build its patterns. It came from Ephesians and summarized, he said, the whole teaching of Jesus:

> 'There is one body, and one Spirit . . . one Lord, one faith, one baptism, one God and Father of all, who is above all, and through all, and in you all.

'The spirit of Jesus Christ resides in the bosom of every man and woman and child living in this nation,' he said in rising voice to indicate the conclusion of this lecture. 'It takes no cognizance of white or black, of Indian or Coloured, of woman or man, and certainly it does not dis-tinguish between Englishman and Afrikaner. We are all one in Jesus. He loves us equally, He cares for us evenly.'

There was some restiveness in the audience at this revolutionary doctrine, for members felt that whereas these precepts did undoubtedly occur in the New Testament, their application was a more delicate mat-ter than Reverend Brongersma appreciated. When he concluded with the stern warning that Christianity required its adherents to apply these fundamental strictures in their private and public lives, and especially in the organization of their societies and nations, there was actually a rum-ble of disapproval, but he stalked from the podium without taking cog-nizance of it.

That night there were no hearty invitations for him to join suppers at Stellenbosch homes, and the Coenraad van Doorns were so agitated that they did not even invite Detleef to Trianon; before they parted Mr. van Doorn said, 'Your predikant hasn't learned much up north,' and Detleef, without endeavoring to defend him, admitted, 'It all sounded so woolly. I like more order in society than that,' and even Clara, who had liked parts of the lecture, grumbled, 'He doesn't seem to understand his audience. We face real problems in this country, and he talks mealie pap.'

But Barend Brongersma did not graduate from Stellenbosch with honors because he was stupid. He had intended his long second lecture to create the effect it did because he wanted it to serve as preparation for what he knew would be one of the most important performances of his life, and when he stepped boldly to the podium for the third lecture he quickly told his audience why:

'Tonight I am addressing the young men who in the years to come will govern this nation. Look about you, I pray. The lad sitting next to you may be your prime minister one day. That fellow over there will preach in the mother church at Cape Town. You will be chancellor of this university, and you will be ambassador of our independent country to Paris. It is important that you think about the future, that you ponder the nature of a free society.

'Jesus addressed himself to this grave problem, and so did St. Paul, and in the New Testament they provide us with guidance. To govern well, we must govern justly, and to govern justly, we must govern wisely. What does Jesus tell us to do?'

Before he cited the relevant texts, he asked his audience a series of blistering hypothetical questions, until everyone present was aroused, leaning forward to catch what solutions he was about to propose. Then, with low voice and gentle patience, he began to unfold the teaching of Jesus, and the text he chose was so recondite and arbitrary that someone not from South Africa would have been at a loss to understand its application, but he claimed it to be the very foundation of the law, the most vital text in the entire Testament, insofar as the governance of nations was concerned. It came from the second chapter of Acts:

'And when the day of Pentecost was fully come, they were all with one accord in one place. And suddenly there came a sound from heaven as of a rushing mighty wind, and it filled all the house where they were sitting . . . And they were all filled with the Holy Ghost, and began to speak with other tongues, as the spirit gave them utterance . . . every man heard them speak in his own language.'

What could be profound about that? How could the policy of a nation be built upon such an esoteric base? As he elucidated the text, it became clear: God created all men as brothers, but he quickly divided them into distinctive groups, each man to his own kind, each nation separate and off to itself, and here he thundered forth that wondrous sequence of names appearing in this all-important chapter:

> 'Parthians, and Medes, and Elamites, and the dwellers in Mesopotamia, and in Judea, and Cappadocia, in Pontus, and Asia, Phrygia, and Pamphylia, in Egypt, and in parts of Libya about Cyrene, and strangers of Rome, Jews and proselytes, Cretes and Arabians, we do hear them speak . . .'

He explained that God willed this diversity and applauded the strangeness that existed among nations. He wanted tribes to be different, to retain their distinctive qualities, and Brongersma suggested that if South Africa had been in existence when Acts, Chapter 2, was delivered, the litany might have ended thus:

> 'Afrikaners and Englishmen, Coloureds and Asians, Xhosa and Zulu, all spake in their own tongues.'

Detleef snapped bolt upright, for these local names were recited in the exact order he had seen them that morning when sunlight struck the glass of jellies. His world was in order; the races were distinct and they were separated, each in its proper place. He heard the remainder of this remarkable oration in a kind of majestic stupor; this was a confirmation that would last a lifetime, and others in the audience that evening would say the same when they governed this nation, as Brongersma had predicted they would: 'One lecture unfolded the future for me.' Brongersma now cited some fifteen pertinent texts, one of the most powerful coming from another chapter in Acts:

> 'God that made the world and all things therein . . . hath made of one blood all nations of men for to dwell on all the face of the earth, and hath determined the times before appointed, and the bounds of their habitation; that they should seek the Lord . . . and find him, though he be not far from every one of us.'

From this passage he derived the principle that God wanted each race to have its own boundaries and not to trespass on the territory of others; this applied both to physical boundaries, such as where people lived, and to mental, so that each race retained its own customs and laws. He then pointed out that religion asked all groups to accept the limitations placed upon them, especially people in the lower ones:

> 'As the Lord hath called every one, so let him walk . . . Let every man abide in the same calling wherein he was called. Art thou called being a servant? care not for it: but if thou mayest be made free, use it rather. For he that is called in the Lord, being a servant, is the Lord's freeman: likewise also he that is called, being free, is Christ's servant.'

And then he came to the crucial issue: 'Are all groups equal in the eyes of God?' He reminded his listeners of what he had said in Lecture Two, that unquestionably all men were brothers, but he went on to say that not all brothers stand equal in the sight of God. On this the New Testament was most specific; there were good nations and bad nations:

> 'When the Son of man shall come . . . then shall he sit upon the throne of his glory: and before him shall be gathered all nations: and he shall separate them one from another, as a shepherd divideth his sheep from the goats: and he shall set the sheep on his right hand, but the goats on the left. Then shall the King say unto them on his right hand, Come, ye blessed of my Father, inherit the kingdom . . . then shall he say also unto them on the left hand, Depart from me, ye cursed, into everlasting fire . . .'

He ended superbly, looking with flashing eye at his listeners, as if to challenge each one personally: 'In the time of judgment, which is now, will Jesus Christ set our nation on His right hand among the sheep, or throw us on His left side, among the goats? For the nature of our society we must look to the Old Testament, which I shall do in my concluding lecture.'

That night the audience was ecstatic as it left the church, for listeners could be sure that the Afrikaner nation was saved, while the English and the Bantu were probably lost. More than a dozen families wanted Brongersma to come with them to share supper, but he elected to go with the Van Doorns, and it was then that he saw the dangerous waters into which his young friend Detleef from Vrymeer was heading. He said nothing that night, but he wondered what good could come from this country boy's falling so blindly in love with a young woman who obviously lived in a much different world, and thought in much different ways. Detleef had said nothing about his deep affection for Clara, nor did he need to.

In his last lecture, like a healing balm, the predikant soothed all spiritual strains by reverting to the marvelous texts of the Old Testament, reminding his Afrikaners of who they were and the special obligations they owed God. He started by assuring them that in the Calvinistic sense they were among the elect, for God had specifically said so:

> 'Now therefore, if ye will obey my voice indeed, and keep my covenant, then ye shall be a peculiar treasure unto me above all people: for all the earth is mine.

'If you are a peculiar treasure, what follows?' he asked, and in the thundering passage from Leviticus he provided the answer:

> 'But I have said unto you, Ye shall inherit their land, and I will give it unto you to possess it, a land that floweth with milk and honey: I am the Lord your God, which have separated you from other people.

'It is right that you should be separated, for you have special tasks to perform'—and he elucidated them: 'To rule justly. To be fair to all men. To love your neighbor as yourself.' On and on he went, instructing the future rulers of the country as to how they must behave when they assumed power. 'I tell you these rules, young men,' he cried in his most powerful voice, grasping his lapels with two hands and leaning far forward, 'because God is most specific as to how he will punish you if you ignore his teaching,' and he set forth the unmistaken call for obedience:

> 'If ye forsake the Lord, and serve strange gods, then he will turn and do you hurt, and consume you, after that he hath done you good.'

He concluded this lecture and his series with a crisp twenty minutes of what this all meant to the governance of a church, and specifically the Dutch Reformed Church of South Africa. He dealt briskly with the most trying problems, brushing them away as if adherence to basic principles eliminated difficulties. When he came to the question as to whether it was proper for the white church to prevent blacks from worshipping side by side with them, he cried, 'Certainly it is proper. What does Deuteronomy say? "When the Most High divided to the nations their inheritance, when he separated the sons of Adam, he set the bounds of the people." Almost the last words of the Old Testament, the final verse of Zechariah, address this problem: "And in that day there shall be no more the Canaanite in the house of the Lord of hosts." We are separate. We are wonderful each in our way. God has assigned us our proper places and our proper tasks. Let us live accordingly. But I would close with these words of Jesus Christ which launched these talks: "Thou shalt love the Lord thy God. Thou shalt love thy neighbour as thyself. On these two commandments hang all the law and the prophets."'

In these four lectures, among the most important ever delivered at Stellenbosch, Brongersma spelled out the dilemma facing any theocracy: How does one organize a society so as to attain the order of the Old Testament and the freedom of the New? Detleef van Doorn, whose advanced education started with these lectures, heard only the first half of that question.

When the speculative and philosophical aspects of Detleef's education fell into place, thanks to that penetrating series of lectures by Barend Brongersma, and when his position at the university was securely established because of his excellence as a rugby player—at Stellenbosch that would always be determinative—he felt that it was time to start thinking seriously about a wife. He was twenty-three now, much older than the Voortrekkers when they married, and his thoughts turned to two young women.

He had not seen much of Maria Steyn, for she had remained on her family farm at Carolina. With her mother dead in the camp, and her father shot as a traitor, she had to assume heavy responsibilities and was able to travel little. She had never visited the university, and from the nature of Detleef's few letters she deduced that they were growing further and further apart; she pondered most carefully how best to reveal through the post her continued affection for him, but she found no womanly way to do this. She simply could not write: 'I love you deeply. Please come and rescue me from this prison of the spirit.' But that is what she felt, and as the years passed and she realized that she would never want to marry anyone but him, she experienced all the anxieties an uncertain young woman of twenty could feel. Desperately she awaited his letters, weighing each phrase to detect hidden meanings, but she found little to console her. Morning after morning she awakened at the farm, dreading the possibility that on this day she would learn that he had married someone else.

Far in the back of his mind, Detleef sensed that this must be the situation, and he sometimes admitted that in a proper world he would long since have been married to this stalwart girl he had liked so much that spring in Bloemfontein; whenever he mailed her a letter he visualized her as a married woman in church, or attending her duties, or caring for children. He never thought of her as beautiful, which she was not, but as some fine, solid human being for whom he had a steady affection.

But with Clara! That was different. For one thing, she was here in Stellenbosch, not in some distant Transvaal country town. She was alive with information, awake to changes occurring in the countryside. Her family had a new car, imported from America, and in it she loved to tour over the mountains to Fransch Hoek, where the Huguenots had clustered, or down to Somerset West, where the fine houses were. She was one of the first to learn that the war had ended in Europe, not with a German victory, as many had supposed, but with a smashing Allied triumph. For her own reasons, this gave her considerable satisfaction, but she did not annoy her father or her brothers by expressing this preference.

During the victory celebrations, in which the English settlers around the Cape were downright obnoxious, Detleef confided to her his disappointment: 'It would have been much better had the Germans won. They would have brought order to Europe.'

'And here, too, I suppose?' When he realized that she was goading him, he said no more, but when church services were held at the university to give thanks for the cessation of battle, he stayed away.

He began his serious courtship of Clara at Christmas time, 1918, spending most of his pocket money on a present for her. After considerable reflection he decided upon a small, fine leatherbound Bible published in Amsterdam, in which he wrote, facing the page on which their marriage and their children would be recorded: *To Clara, the best of the Van Doorns.*

She was embarrassed by the gift and wanted to return it, deeming it most inappropriate, but her father would not permit this: 'He gave it to you as a sincere expression. Accept it on that basis.'

'If I do,' she said, 'it can only mislead him.'

'That's the risk we all take when we give or accept things,' he said, and that night at supper he said to Detleef, 'I cannot imagine a finer gift.'

As the year drew to an end, Detleef became quite tense, rehearsing how he could best make his declaration to this exciting girl: I surely have the money to support a wife. Even Piet Krause, who doesn't farm very well, is showing a profit at Vrymeer. I have an education, so I can talk with her. I'm accorded a certain respect because of rugby. And I'm a good Christian.

But then he would in honesty list his deficiencies, and they seemed to weigh down the balances, but nevertheless, he decided to plunge ahead. However, there was to be no New Year's celebration, at least not with the Trianon Van Doorns, for they all drove in to Cape Town to greet a troopship that arrived on the last day of the year. It brought back to South Africa those gallant men who had volunteered to fight for king and country, and among them were some forty soldiers who had fought at Delville Wood.

As they came down the ramps, led by Timothy Saltwood, V.C., there was a curious silence. Most men and women in the crowd, English and Afrikaner alike, were overcome with emotion: but a few Afrikaners were, like Detleef, silent because of perplexity. These men were heroes, unquestionably, but they had fought on the wrong side. Then a wave of sentiment swept over the crowd as the men actually landed on home soil, and cheers deafened the Van Doorns as they applauded the men.

When the party returned to Trianon, with the tidy buildings appearing more secure than ever, there were celebrations, to which Detleef was not invited, but on the third of January, 1919, he bicycled out to the vineyards, prepared to make his formal proposal: I'll speak to Coenraad first, and then Clara's mother, and when I have their permission, I'll go to Clara herself. But as he pedaled his way down the long lane, he saw at the end of the little houses on the left a young woman who looked much like Clara kissing rather ardently a young man in military uniform. In great confusion he rode on, staring ahead, but from the corner of his eye he saw the woman break away when she noticed him, then move quickly back for another kiss.

'It's you!' Coenraad cried happily from the stoep. 'Come in, Detleef. It's a real celebration. Timothy Saltwood's home, covered with medals.'

'Is he in uniform?'

'Of course.'

When Clara and young Saltwood came into the hallway, Detleef felt weak, for the officer was a handsome fellow, lean, bemedaled, eager. 'This is Timothy Saltwood, of De Kraal,' Clara said. 'He tells me your family used to own his farm.'

'Long ago,' Detleef mumbled, and as soon as he could manage it, he whispered to Clara, 'Can I speak with you?'

'Of course! What?' She must have guessed what he was about to ask, but she gave him no help, standing firm in the middle of the room.

'I mean, can we talk . . . alone?'

'Of course,' she said brightly, leading him into her father's office.

'Clara,' he said. 'I gave you the Bible . . . I mean . . .'

'What is it?' she asked.

'I want to marry you.'

She placed her fingers on his lips: 'Don't, Detleef.'

'To ask you to marry me,' he muttered.

'Detleef, I'm so sorry. I'm going to marry Timothy.'

He gasped. 'But he's an Englishman!'

'He's a very brave young man.' When Detleef tried to speak, she placed her hand over his mouth and said firmly, 'If you do care for me, come out now and behave like a gentleman.'

'I am not a gentleman,' he said harshly, pushing her hand down. 'I'm not some fancy Englishman.' He looked at her in anger, and said accusingly, 'You knew this all the time. You let me make a fool of myself.' He fumbled for words and said a most stupid thing: 'You let me give you that Bible.'

'I think,' she said with asperity, 'that you had better take your damned Bible back,' and she hurried from the room.

He was aghast that a young woman he loved should use such a word in such a connection, and when she flounced back into the office, thrusting the Bible into his hands, he dumbly accepted it, then watched as she recovered it, opened it, and ripped out the page on which he had written his dedication. 'Give it to someone else,' she said sternly, and with that she left him.

For some minutes he stood there, holding the maimed book. He did not know what to do. He heard voices in the house, people talking gaily as if nothing embarrassing had happened, and then he made up his mind. Stalking from the room, looking at no one, he went out the front door for the last time in his life, and marched to his bicycle. Holding the Bible first in his right hand, then in his left, he pedaled down the long driveway, then jammed the book under his belt and went back to Stellenbosch.

Two days later Coenraad van Doorn came to see him, and said quietly, 'Detleef, things like this happen to everyone. My wife and I want you to attend the wedding. Clara wants it, for she considers you her good friend.'

With a hatred that burned his throat, Detleef said, 'All you English-lovers will be driven from power.'

Coenraad was a man who had worked hard to keep his vineyards solvent through war and peace, and to him such talk was shameful, for Afrikaners could prosper best if they cooperated with the English who had made South Africa their home, and he for one was pleased that his daughter was forming an alliance with one of the strongest English-speaking South African families. He wanted such conciliation to be repeated across the country, and since it was imperative that young Afrikaner men appreciate this, he swallowed the rebuke and begged Detleef to reconsider: 'Lad, don't you see that sometimes a gap can be too wide for ordinary measures to bridge? You saw Christoffel Steyn shot because he sided with Germany. The Saltwoods saw their men slain at Delville Wood because they sided with England. Such wounds can only be healed by men of good will—like you and me.'

'I hope England perishes.'

Coenraad would accept no more. With contempt he snapped, 'Detleef, you're a tight-minded fool. Get out and see the world. I'll have no more of you.'

As Detleef might have guessed, the Van Doorn–Saltwood wedding did not take place in Stellenbosch. It was performed with high ceremony and lavish celebration in the English cathedral in Cape Town.

Like many a young man before him, Detleef found vengeance in sports. He played rugby with a fury that astounded older men, throwing himself about with special abandon when pitted against teams like Somerset West, which had a more than average proportion of English players. Against the Ikeys he played like a wild man, for he suspected that somehow the Jews were involved in his loss of Clara. In fact, he played so magnificently that several newspapers predicted that when South African rugby teams resumed touring England and France, he would have to be included: 'Pound for pound, he may be the best forward playing today.'

At the same time he did well in his studies, and there was renewed interest in having him transfer to divinity school. Indeed, Reverend

Brongersma himself came down to Stellenbosch to talk with him, but not on that subject. In fact, for the first half-hour of their conversation Detleef could not fathom what the visit was about.

'Your brother-in-law Piet is no farmer, Detleef. You must come back and take over, because he wants to find other employment.'

'He's not paying much attention to the farm?'

'You're not to worry.' He coughed, then said in an entirely different voice, 'What you should worry about, Detleef, is finding yourself a wife.' Before the bewildered young man could respond, Brongersma said hurriedly, 'Detleef, I have great affection for you. No boy from Vrymeer has ever shown more promise. I've heard about you and Clara van Doorn. I could see it happening when I gave my lectures. You've behaved miserably, Detleef. Like a damned fool, if you'll forgive me that word. But you have been a damned fool, and I'm ashamed of you.'

It was a blast Detleef had not expected. On the rugby field he had been knocked about by the biggest—mouth cut, eyes blackened—but the dominee's words were blows to his pride, and he gasped.

'There's a fine young woman in Carolina who is wasting her life for love of you. Maria Steyn, daughter of heroes, a heroine herself. For God's sake, Detleef, open your eyes. It was never intended that you marry Clara van Doorn. It would have been wrong. It would have ruined your life to have beat your head against that wall. And all the time you had a sweet, good woman waiting for you, and you were too blind to see.'

After a long silence Detleef asked weakly, 'Did she send you?'

'I heard about her, and I came on my own, as your friend.' When Detleef made no comment, the predikant asked in a low voice, 'Detleef, shall we pray?' And on his knees beside the young man for whom he had such high hopes, he talked with God about the extreme difficulty men face when they want to lead a Christian life.

The wedding was to be held in the Dutch Reformed church at Carolina, where numerous Steyns from the region gathered to honor Christoffel's memory. At the strong suggestion of Reverend Brongersma, Maria's predikant was asked to perform the ceremony, but on the evening before the wedding Detleef went to the church in Venloo and said, 'Reverend Brongersma, I wouldn't feel properly married unless you helped,' and when the pastor said that he would drive Detleef down to the wedding, the young man fumbled with a package and asked hesitantly, 'Dominee, tell me. I paid a lot of money for this Bible. Could I give it to Maria?'

Brongersma took the book, opened the cover, and saw that a page was missing; it required no cleverness to deduce what had happened. He thought for a moment, then asked gently, 'Don't you think that a bright girl like Maria might guess about Clara?'

'Yes, I suppose she would,' he said dejectedly.

'I'll tell you what we'll do, Detleef. I've always wanted a leather-bound Bible. I'll trade this for a new one of mine.' And next day Brongersma printed in firm clear letters on the page reserved for family records:

DETLEEF VAN DOORN–MARIA STEYN
Kinders van ons helde. Getroud 14 Maart 1919
(Children of our heroes. Married 14 March 1919)

And then Detleef was thrown out into the world, just as the Trianon Van Doorns had advised: the committee that selected rugby players for a team which would tour New Zealand chose him to be one of the principal forwards, and Venloo expanded with more pride than it would have done had he been elected general of the armies. For a small town to provide a Springbok was a glory that rarely came.

A Springbok was any athlete of world class who wore the green blazer with its golden springbok emblem while representing South Africa against another nation. A cricketer could be a Springbok, so could an Olympic runner, and as such they were entitled to full honors; but it was generally understood that only a rugby Springbok was a true immortal. This was especially true in 1921, because the New Zealand All-Blacks, so called because of their ominous uniforms, were regarded as the finest team that had ever played the game, and it was agreed that the winner of the forthcoming matches would be world champions.

Detleef was twenty-six that year, the father of a boy, the master of a growing farm. When his picture appeared in the city papers, it showed a stocky farmer, feet wide apart, rope around his ample stomach as a belt, and with absolutely no neck. The line from the bottom of his ear to the break of his shoulder was straight and unbroken, and when he posed next to his heaviest pair of oxen, he resembled them.

The problem of who would tend the farm while he was absent was conveniently solved: when Piet Krause left Venloo he had expected to find work quickly in Johannesburg, but these were hard times, and at one industry after another he was rebuffed. Chastened, he was glad to accept Detleef's offer of a free home and meals for himself and Johanna: 'But only during the rugby tour. I know I can find work in Johannesburg. This nation needs men like me.'

When Detleef, accompanied by five of the horrible Morkels, stepped ashore at Auckland, he was like some gape-eyed child, for the people of New Zealand were immersed in frenzy over this championship series. The South Africans were allowed to warm up, of course, against regional teams, and in the first match Detleef discovered what he was going to be up against. When he hooked arms in the scrum, he looked into the face of a gigantic New Zealander with the sloping shoulders and quick moves of a true athlete; he was Tom Heeney, soon to fight Gene Tunney for the boxing championship of the world, and when he slammed into Detleef, the latter felt his knees jump backward. In the afternoons to come, he would face Heeney often.

When the regional warm-ups were finished, the two nations played a series of three games, the first on the southern island at Dunedin, the last two on the northern island, at Auckland and Wellington. Detleef would never forget that opening game: 'When we lined up for the photographers to take pictures, I was like a little boy. I had to go to the bathroom. So I went and was almost late for the whistle. I remember nothing about the first half, except that I kept bumping into some very strong men. We ended the half ahead by five-to-nothing.' Whenever he spoke to audiences about that game he stopped at this point, laughed and said, 'But I certainly remember the second half. New Zealanders kept running up and down my spine. The crowd kept roaring. The ball kept slipping away, and at the end of the game New Zealand won thirteen-to-five.'

But he was blooded. Like an animal that has gone up against a lion and escaped with its life, he knew what fear was; he understood the meaning of pressure and became indifferent to the roar of the crowd. Before the opening of the second game he gathered the five Morkels on his team and said, 'We show them no mercy.' It was an epic struggle, tied at five-all until the gang of Morkels made superhuman plays to eke out a 9–5 victory. 'That night,' Detleef often said in later years, 'was the high point of my life. Nothing could ever excel that victory over New Zealand.'

The third and deciding game should never have taken place, for the field was so water-soaked and the rain so incessant that play resembled swimming more than rugby. The score was a frustrating 0–0, but the last seconds were a kind of majestic triumph for Detleef; a huge New Zealander broke away for what seemed the game-winning score, except that Van Doorn made a diving tackle that slowed him down. Boy Morkel rushed up to help hold him, whereupon six New Zealanders piled on. In the tangle and mud, Detleef's leg twisted, then broke. His rugby days were ended, but as he was carried off the field, refusing to surrender to the pain, he was able to tell Tom Heeney, 'Well, you didn't beat us,' and the Hard Rock from Down Under laughed and said, 'We nearly did.'

In the ensuing years Detleef was remembered wherever he went as 'the man who saved the day in New Zealand.' He treasured his green jacket with the emblazoned antelope and kept it on a special hanger in his wardrobe, taking it out occasionally for some sporting event. It became a sacred object, replacing the ceramic crock in which the men of his family had long made their bread puddings.

XII.
Achievement of a Puritan

WHEN Detleef limped home on crutches in 1921 and saw how ineptly Piet Krause had managed Vrymeer during the rugby matches in New Zealand, he was tempted to show his disgust, but Maria calmed him by pointing out: 'Piet kept worrying about Johannesburg. Don't blame him for what he overlooked here.'

Krause had found—or more accurately, Johanna had found for him —a minor job as labor advisor to the government. He specialized in gold-mine problems, and when he returned to Venloo for a visit, Detleef, seeing the excitement with which he attacked his new duties, forgave him: 'You were never meant to be a farmer, Piet. Tell me, why do we hear so many rumbles from your city?'

That was all Piet needed. In wild bursts of words, interrupted by Johanna with her own interpretations, he explained why the burgeoning city had become the focus of the country: 'It's there the real battles are being fought. Our excursions up north, where General de Groot died and you and I took part, they were nothing. Echoes of the nineteenth century. But in Johannesburg . . .'

'Who's fighting?'

'The Afrikaner. He's fighting for his soul.'

He insisted that Detleef come back with him to witness the struggle of the white Afrikaner workman against the English mine owner, the Hoggenheimer financier, and especially the Bantu worker, but Detleef said that until he could move without crutches that would be impossible. However, he did want to understand the gold mines and promised that he would read whatever Piet mailed him in preparation for his later visit.

Johanna made the selection, and what she sent was startling. One gang of workers wanted to establish a soviet in which laboring men would take control of the mines, overthrow the government, and establish a Communist dictatorship in harmony with Russia. One group of mine owners wanted to fire all white workers and use only Bantu to work the gold, but when Maria read the literature more carefully, she pointed out: 'That's not what the owners said, Detleef. That's what their enemies said they said.' But then he received other mailings which proved that many owners wanted to cut back the number of white workers and increase the number of black.

From a distance, the city seemed such a jungle of competing forces that Detleef was actually eager to get there, and as soon as his leg mended he informed Johanna that he was ready. She advised him that if he caught a train at Waterval-Boven they would meet him at the railway station in central Johannesburg, and when they did they led him into a miasma of urban horror.

His education up to that moment, except for Chrissiesmeer, had been romantic: old generals fighting lost battles, gallant young men on the playing fields of New Zealand, sentimental remembrances of the Vrouemonument, unrequited love. Now his realistic instruction was to begin; he experienced it first in the section of Johannesburg called Vrededorp, where thousands of rural Afrikaners, driven off their farms by rinderpest and drought, had collected. They stopped at a small house occupied by a family named Troxel: tall, gaunt husband who should have been back on the open veld; scrawny wife with flat, sagging breasts; unkempt children, their faces drawn with hunger. In that dwelling there was little hope.

'Will you take us to other homes?' Piet asked, and Troxel led them to much worse hovels, whose occupants were desolate. After talking with these forlorn people, Detleef felt sick at the stomach, not figuratively but actually, almost to the point of vomiting. 'We've got to do something, Piet. These people are starving.'

'Tomorrow we'll see what lies behind the starving,' Piet said, and on this day he took Detleef to a workers' hall, where there was much agitation about new rules which the Chamber of Mines had promulgated.

'They're cutting back the proportion of white workers,' an agitator explained. When Detleef asked what this signified, the man screamed, 'Extermination, that's what it means. Extermination of the white Afrikaner,' and he explained that tradition in the gold fields had been that for every eight Bantu diggers, there had to be one white man. 'Now they want to make it ten blacks to one white. We can't accept that. It would cost too many Afrikaners their jobs.'

A stronghold of the strikers was Fordsburg, a working-class district near Vrededorp, and here Detleef was taken to an inconspicuous shed in which the future soviet was being planned. Here rabid Afrikaners met with Cornish miners imported to do the basic work down deep and three fiery Englishmen who were determined to take South Africa into the Communist orbit: 'There'll be blood this time! Are you with us?' When Detleef said he didn't work the mines, but was a farmer, four excited Afrikaners surrounded him, demanding to know why he did not bring food into the city to feed his starving compatriots.

That night he could not sleep, seeing the pinched faces bearing in upon him, for he knew what starvation was, and when on the third day Piet took him back to Vrededorp to talk quietly with Troxel and the other Afrikaner families, and he heard their pitiful tales of perished hopes on the farms, the doleful trek to the city, the cruel exploitation in the mines, and the endless struggle to maintain their rights against the pressure of the blacks, his earlier sickness returned, and abruptly he informed Piet and Johanna that he was going home. When they accused him of rejecting his own people, he assured them: 'I'll be back.'

And he was, with a convoy of three large wagons bringing all the spare food he had been able to collect in Venloo. He drove the lead wagon, Micah Nxumalo the second, and Micah's son, Moses, the third. They brought the food into the center of Vrededorp and started to distribute it, but they occasioned such a disturbance that a riot would surely have ensued had not the Communist workers swept in, taken charge, and told the hungry miners that this food came from their committee.

This second visit had one by-product neither Detleef nor Piet had intended; Micah, left in charge of the three empty wagons, drove them out to a different section of Johannesburg where his people clustered. It was called Sophiatown, and when Micah came back to tell Detleef where he had been, Van Doorn decided to go with him to see how urban blacks lived.

Sophiatown had come into existence some two decades earlier, planned as a suburb for whites but spurned by them when a sewage works was located nearby. It was only four and a half miles from the center of Johannesburg, and the owner of the land had to do something with it, so he started renting and selling land to the blacks who were pouring in from the countryside to fill jobs in the postwar industrial boom.

For Detleef it was a journey into hell, for Sophiatown had no proper streets, few proper houses and no proper water supply. It was a mélange of prostitutes, tsotsis, and decent mothers trying to maintain a home against phenomenal odds while their husbands worked ten and twelve hours for a daily wage of twenty pennies.

When Detleef looked at Sophiatown he saw a festering sore, dark and malignant, threatening to spread over a clean white city. It reached dangerously toward Afrikaner communities, as if it intended to engulf them. He was shocked to learn that blacks could actually own land here, which meant that they could stay permanently. 'A hideous sore,' he muttered to himself. 'It must be removed.'

This conclusion was intensified when he saw the home Nxumalo's relatives occupied. The Magubanes had a house with walls of real wood and a secure watertight roof made of paraffin tins. One of the Magubanes told him, 'Yes, when our people get the money they will make a lovely place of Sophiatown. Just like the homes of the rich people in Parktown.'

'Where do your people work?' Detleef asked.

'Offices, factories. And if the new rules come for the mines, thousands of our people back in the kraals will be eager for jobs. Fifty thousand, a hundred thousand if you need them.'

So Detleef left Sophiatown with the certain knowledge that the blacks would insist upon improving their lot, but he saw that this would be possible only at the expense of the white Afrikaners already trapped in poverty. He found that Troxel and the other white miners were willing to express themselves quite forcefully: 'We want this to be a white nation run by whites and not a black nation run by blacks.' Detleef could not imagine the huddled blacks of Sophiatown running anything; they would be lucky if they survived. His sympathies lay with the white miners, and when the callous owners announced even more stringent rules which might cost four thousand additional white men their jobs, he knew there would have to be a strike, although he himself did not want to support any moves which might turn this country into a soviet.

When the strike began, he knew he ought to hurry back to the safety of Vrymeer, but he was hypnotized by the intricacy of the struggle and curious to see how it turned out. So Piet Krause, whose job made it logical for him to stay on the scene in Vrededorp, asked the Troxels whether he and Detleef could board with them during the trouble, and the destitute Afrikaners were eager to have paying guests.

This was a battle much more fundamental than the pro-German rebellion of 1914. Miners were fighting for survival; owners were fighting for financial control; and the government, led by Jan Christian Smuts, was fighting for continuation of an orderly society. The hatred Krause and Van Doorn felt for Smuts clouded their vision of what was right, and they tended to cheer for whatever group opposed him.

It was real combat. Detleef turned a corner and saw sixteen civilians mowed down by machine-gun fire. A government building was dynamited and fourteen soldiers were killed. Police were gunned down, and on one awful day airplanes flew over the city, dropping bombs on concentrations of miners.

The death toll was fifty, then a hundred, then a hundred and fifty, with food running low and arson becoming common. There was talk of shutting off water, and children in the streets were slain by stray bullets.

'Why are Afrikaners fighting Afrikaners?' Detleef asked in anguish, and Troxel growled, 'Because we Afrikaners want to keep this nation white.' He was a brave man, and when General Smuts in total frustration warned that heavy artillery would shell the heart of Vrededorp at eleven the next morning, he refused to move his family. 'Shells matter nothing,' he muttered, but when they began to fall, monstrous things intended for shattering forts, he quivered. Detleef, comforting the Troxel children, could not believe that his government was doing this, and as the dreadful concussions continued he thought: This is insanity. There must be a more sensible way.

In the midst of the barrage, Troxel left his shelter and ran directly across the open square where the shells were falling. He was heading for strike headquarters, and when he returned through the smoldering debris he was weeping: 'They committed suicide!'

'Who?' Detleef asked.

'Our leaders. The Englishman, the other. Pistol shots through the head.'

The armed rebellion was over, with the competition between the very poor Afrikaners in Vrededorp and the totally poor blacks in Sophiatown no closer to settlement than when the strike began. Only one poverty-stricken Afrikaner came out of the affair better than when he went in: after the fighting, when Nxumalo reassembled the three wagons for the trip back to Vrymeer, and Detleef saw them standing empty, he impulsively ran to the Troxel house and said, 'Come with me. This town is no place for an Afrikaner.' And on the spur of the moment he and Piet Krause threw into one wagon the pitiful collection of goods this family had accumulated after ten hard years in the city; it did not begin to fill it.

'They can use the De Groot place,' Detleef said as the bewildered cavalcade started eastward. He had seen Johannesburg and was appalled.

One Sunday, Detleef received the distinct impression in church that Reverend Brongersma was preaching directly to him, not in the long ordinary passages of the sermon, but whenever something of special import had to be said. Then Brongersma would stare in his direction, sometimes looking at others in his vicinity but again and again coming back to Detleef to make his points.

He said nothing about this to Maria and even doubted if she had been aware of it, but when on two following Sundays the same thing happened, he asked casually on Monday night, 'Did you notice anything strange in church yesterday?'

'No, except that Reverend Brongersma seemed to be preaching to you more than anyone else.'

'You noticed it?' When she nodded, he said, 'Did you not see it on the past Sundays?' and she said that she had. 'Why didn't you speak?' he asked, and she said, 'I thought that perhaps you had done something wrong and would tell me at such time as you deemed best.' In some anger he asked her what she thought he had done wrong, and she laughed.

'Detleef, I only said *perhaps*. You're not the kind of man who does wrong things. And if you have done something, it couldn't be very big.'

'There you go. What have I done?'

'Detleef, I only said *if*.'

But he was troubled, and every time his brother-in-law visited the farm and asked probing questions, Detleef became even more irritated, especially since the dominee continued preaching at him.

He was about to confront his two tormentors when Piet said abruptly one day, 'Detleef. Can you come to a special meeting tonight?' Hoping that the mystery would be revealed, he said quickly, 'Yes,' and that evening he was taken to a house he had never taken much notice of before, where the owner, a man named Frykenius, sat waiting, with Reverend Brongersma standing by a table.

'Sit down, Detleef,' Frykenius said. 'We want to ask you some questions.'

'What have I done?'

'Nothing, except being a good citizen. We want to find out how good.'

'I've done nothing wrong!' Detleef protested, and this was ignored.

'Tell me,' Frykenius said. 'In the rebellion against the war in Europe, would you have fought on, even though your father was killed?'

'I would have fought the English forever.'

'Do you speak Afrikaans in your home?'

'Nothing else.'

'Do you insist that your children speak it?'

'I allow them to speak no English.'

On and on came the questions, covering all aspects of what might be called his political, emotional and patriotic life. At the end his three interrogators asked him to step out in the yard, and while he looked at the glorious stars of the Southern Cross, they whispered among themselves. After about fifteen minutes Piet Krause came out and said with obvious pleasure, 'Detleef, please come in!'

When he entered the room, both Frykenius and Brongersma rose to greet him: 'Detleef. You are one of us.' When he asked what this signified, Frykenius said, 'Sit down, Brother.' And when he was in his chair the three men, speaking alternately, informed him that a powerful and secret band of brothers, a Broederbond, had been quietly operating for the past five years, accomplishing much good. After the most careful investigation of his credentials by men in Pretoria, he was being offered a chance to join.

'Are you members?' he asked.

Frykenius said, 'I helped start it.' This seemed strange to Detleef, for he could recall no instance in which this quiet man had ever played a major role in anything; he knew that he attended church, but was not even an elder. He had heard that he had ridden with the Venloo Commando but had accomplished nothing of note. He ran the butcher shop in town, but obviously never made much money. And he never spoke in public. But it was clear that he was now in command.

'Reverend Brongersma has belonged almost from the first,' Frykenius said, 'and Piet here, one of our best, has been with us for three years.'

'What would I be supposed to do?'

'Advance the Afrikaner,' Frykenius said.

'I already try to do that. But how?'

Piet was eager to explain, but was interrupted by Frykenius: 'I already know the answers to these two questions, but we must have sworn statements. "Have you ever been divorced?" No. That's good. "Is your wife English?" No again. You're eligible.'

'Morally, we're very strict,' Piet said.

Satisfied that Detleef had committed no serious breaches, the three men placed before him a program of simple integrity: 'Whatever you do, from this moment till you die, must work toward making the Afrikaner supreme in this country. In politics you must elect men who will carry us away from English domination.'

'That I would like,' Detleef said.

'In education you must insist that every teacher become an agent for the supremacy of Afrikaans. They must teach our national history in the patterns we provide.'

'In the armed forces,' Krause said excitedly, 'we must remove every English officer. In government we've got to clean out the English office-holders.'

'But it's in the spiritual realm,' Brongersma said, 'that we must do our hardest work. Cultural societies. Work groups. Festivals. Patriotic gatherings. If there is to be a speaker, it must be one of us.'

'You saw the fighting in Johannesburg,' Frykenius said. 'Jan Christian Smuts using Afrikaner soldiers to fight Afrikaner workmen. That must never again be allowed.'

'Can we drive Slim Jannie from office?' Detleef asked.

'We must,' Frykenius said. 'Are you with us?' When Detleef nodded, as enthusiastically as if he were going to war with General de Groot or to a rugby game against New Zealand, Frykenius in his dry, unemotional voice administered the oath of the Broederbond, and Detleef swore to uphold its secrecy, advance its purposes, and live each moment of his life so as to achieve the dominance of the Afrikaner. That night he rode home with a greater sense of mission than he had ever before experienced. The other war that General de Groot had so often referred to was under way and he had enlisted for life.

In the weeks that followed, Detleef developed an enormous respect for his brother-in-law. He was no longer the somewhat flighty schoolteacher or the man who had quit the Vrymeer farm after discarding responsibility; instead, Piet Krause showed himself as a fine strategist. Frykenius was a staunch administrator and Brongersma a source of the spiritual strength which such a movement needed, but Krause was downright brilliant: 'Let us look honestly at the condition of the two groups. The English are educated; we aren't. The English control the money; we don't. The English are in command of the armed forces; we hold no high appointments. The English know how to manage; we don't. And above all, the English are supported by an entire empire; we stand alone.'

When Frykenius protested that the Afrikaners had strengths, too, Krause brushed him aside, and Detleef noticed that whereas Frykenius issued operational commands, which Piet obeyed, in the field of ideas Piet accepted guidance from no one. 'Yes, we have strengths,' he agreed impatiently, 'but not the ones you think.'

And he outlined a program of daring character: 'We can't take control of business away from the English. They're too clever to allow that. And we can't dictate in politics yet. But I can see two areas which employ a lot of people where we can dominate. Trains and schools. From now on, every trainman who is hired must be an Afrikaner. Every schoolteacher, too.' He explained that if the Broederbond could control the railway union, it would have a solid base from which to operate; and if it controlled the teachers, it could monitor what the young were being taught: 'Out of a hundred boys leaving school, ninety would be potential Broederbond members.'

'No, our membership must always be restricted,' Frykenius said, and when Detleef was taken to meet with cells in other areas, he found that this was true. Of a hundred members, thirty were schoolteachers, thirty were predikants, and the other forty were mostly farmers of solid position in their communities. There were, of course, no members who were bankers, lawyers or elected officials, for few Afrikaners had yet attained such positions.

After three years of the most exciting participation, Detleef saw with satisfaction that every teacher appointed in a vast area had been an Afrikaner, and eleven of the best had been permitted to join the Broederbond. Of a hundred new employees of the railway system, all had been Afrikaners. There had been musical exhibitions arranged by the Bond, art displays, barbecues, lecture series and sports events. Whenever an Afrikaner in rural South Africa stepped out of his house, he fell unwittingly under the influence of the Broederbond, but it was the new proposal offered by Piet Krause to a plenary session in Pretoria that moved the Bond onto an even more effective level:

> 'We have won the railways and have triumphed in the battle of the schoolroom, but in business and politics we have accomplished nothing. I cannot yet see how we can gain any victories in politics, but I do see clearly how we can gain effective control of business. We Afrikaners are not yet smart enough to run the insurance companies and the big banks. That will require time and education. Let the English continue to control the businesses which appear on the stock market. What we'll do is control the stock market. And how do we do that? We become the officials who make the rules, who supervise the operations, who stay in the background as watchdogs.'

He launched an ingenious program aimed at filling every available administrative position with Afrikaners: 'Of course, the Englishmen will continue to occupy the flashy front offices. We'll take the unseen jobs, none of them attractive or well paid. And once we have Afrikaners inserted in the system, we'll promote them quietly, until they attain positions of real power.

'Then do you see what will happen? The insurance company will still be owned by Englishmen. But our people will pass the little rules by which they operate. And in time we will control everything—not own it, control it.'

He preached that an essential factor in such a strategy was the proliferation of minor administrative jobs: 'Where one man is needed, let us appoint three. If an old office falters, let us establish two new ones, staffed always with our people. Jobs, jobs, jobs. Whether they're needed or not, create more jobs because they must pay for them. And always in the legislation creating them insert the phrase "The occupant must be bilingual." With Afrikaans we will strangle them to death.'

As a consequence of this policy, South Africa would become one of the most overly administered governments on earth, and gradually, because of the bilingual requirement, this plethora of officeholders became predominantly Afrikaner. Piet Krause had shown far-seeing wisdom: the English insurance company did continue to make money, but it operated under rules promulgated by Afrikaner functionaries, who drafted these rules in accordance with the wishes of the unseen Broederbond.

* * *

While cells of the Broederbond in all parts of South Africa were convening secretly to determine the future character of their nation, awakening young black men were meeting, also in secret, to decide what patterns should be followed when they attained the leadership to which they felt entitled.

Micah Nxumalo was not a great man, but he had always associated with great men, and that was almost as good. Paulus de Groot, Christoffel Steyn, the various Boer generals during the war—he had worked with them all. Usually they had not been aware of him, but in his quiet way he had been intensely aware of them, and had learned from them lessons which would have amazed them had they known the depth of his perception.

He was bewildered by white men. They lived surrounded by blacks, but made no effort to understand them or to profit from the association. The whites were outnumbered in many areas forty-to-one, but they continued living as if they alone possessed the landscape and always would. He watched them making decisions which had to be against their own best interests, and doing so only to maintain control over the larger number of blacks who surrounded them.

For example, Micah was astounded that the two white tribes, Boer and English, should have fought each other so viciously for so long, when at any time each could have achieved everything that came out of the peace treaty and at one-fiftieth of the cost. For him the insanity of their behavior was epitomized by the Battle of Spion Kop, in which he had played a major role. 'I tell you, Moses,' he said to his son, 'one side marched up to the top of the hill, then the other side marched up, then one side marched down, then the other side marched down. Then, long after midnight, General de Groot and I walked up, and we captured it. And three days later it didn't make a bit of difference who held it, but hundreds of white men lay dead and wounded.'

He saw also that it made very little difference, really, which side won: 'We fought for the Boers, Moses. They were good people and we could trust them, men like Jakob from this farm, and the old general. But when it was over, we got no thanks. They made laws against us just the same. And don't you ever believe that the Kaffirs who fought on the English side came off any better. Because the English abandoned them as soon as peace came. "We will never desert you," they promised in 1899 when they needed black help, but at the peace treaty they forgot about our rights. And now they're just as eager as the Afrikaners to hold us down.'

Micah, who could not read or write, could formulate such sophisticated analyses because he had for many years been quietly associating with that remarkable group of black leaders who moved through the countryside talking about actual living conditions, legislation and civic rights. These few men were well educated, some in England, one or two in the black colleges of America, and some of them had even visited the Parliament in London with petitions drawing attention to the worsening conditions in South Africa. 'It would be improper for England to interfere with the internal relations of a dominion,' they were always told, and helplessly they watched the deterioration.

These men, who would be the leaders of their race in coming years, first brought Nxumalo's attention to the problem of the poor white Afrikaner, the numerous people like the Troxels, who had been driven off their inherited farms by drought and rinderpest and who had taken refuge in Johannesburg. 'I assure you,' Sol Plaatje said at one meeting, 'in their hovels they live worse than the blacks do in Sophiatown. Every law that holds us down, holds them down too. In a sensible world the Troxels would combine with us to improve everyone's condition, but they stay off to themselves, the poorest of the poor, and we stay off to ourselves, the dispossessed.'

What perplexed these leaders was the contradictory policy of the white government: 'They spend enormous sums to bring in white settlers from Russia and Germany and Poland, when they have right on their doorsteps better labor and cheaper, which they refuse to use.' John Dube, in one of these meetings, offered the statement which Nxumalo would always remember: 'The worst thing a nation can do to itself is to cultivate and maintain a supply of cheap labor. When salaries are kept down, money stops circulating, taxes bring in diminished funds, and everybody loses. The white man thinks he's hurting us when he keeps our wages low. Actually, he's hurting himself.'

At one meeting a young Swazi who had studied in London said, 'In our worst industries, the white man earns sixteen times as much as the black man doing the same kind of work. Now, I don't mean the same work. As you know, certain jobs have been defined by law as too complicated or pivotal for a black man to master. Such jobs must be held by whites only. What I mean is that whites and blacks work together, the whites doing the so-called critical work, which a schoolboy could learn in fifteen minutes, the blacks doing the manual labor, which the white could do more efficiently because he's usually better fed and stronger.

Taking all industries, the white worker gets nine times the wage of a black, and they propose to build a sensible society on that basis!'

Nxumalo understood such reasoning; he would never have elucidated such thoughts himself, but when others did he approved. However, on one point he was as obtuse as the white man: when he contemplated the long future of South Africa he could not visualize any logical place for the Coloureds. The white man had stated in a hundred different laws and regulations that the Coloureds were not white; the blacks knew intuitively they could never be black. Almost never was the problem discussed; once Plaatje said after returning from London, 'The white men, if they had any sense, would embrace the Coloureds instead of importing white immigrants at great expense.'

'Should we embrace them?' Nxumalo asked.

Plaatje thought a long time, then said, 'I think not. They want to do what they call "moving up to whitehood" and would never be satisfied with doing what they would call "falling back to Kaffir status." Why distract our attention by bothering with them, when we can argue directly with the whites?'

It was from such discussions that Micah Nxumalo acquired his obsession: 'One day our boy Moses will attend the college at Fort Hare.' To that end he terminated his own practical education; no longer would he waste his few rand by attending the secret meetings in Johannesburg. That money would be saved for the boy. He went to the Van Doorns, asking them to help toward the fees Moses would have to pay, but Detleef growled, 'He needs no further schooling, he has a job here,' and the meager funds that Micah could accumulate were inadequate for so bold a venture, and the dream of sending a black lad from Vrymeer to college vanished.

But not the dream of learning: 'What you must do, Moses, is read the books that educated men read. You must associate with men who have traveled to America and Europe, and you must listen to what they say. Most of all, son, you must get off this farm. You were not meant to be a peasant.'

Using some of the money he had saved, he returned to his friends in Johannesburg and asked them for books that would start his gifted son on the right track. They gave him one book by Marcus Garvey, the American black; two books by Plaatje on the South African condition; one by George Bernard Shaw; and a splendid volume on the golden age of the Dutch Republic. As he was about to depart, the young Swazi who had recited the figures on comparative wages at the earlier meeting, had an afterthought: 'What might do him the most good—this novel about Java.'

'What is Java?'

'It used to control South Africa.'

'Why should he read about that?'

'Because you never know, Mr. Nxumalo, what will ignite a boy's mind.' And he handed over a Dutch novel, *Max Havelaar,* by a man who had been a civil servant in Java in the 1800s; he wrote under the name of Multatuli, Latin for Many Sorrows, and although he spoke only of conditions in Java, everything he said applied to South Africa.

The five scholarly books Micah brought back to Vrymeer were helpful, but *Max Havelaar* sharpened the mind of Moses Nxumalo. He was in his twenties when he read it, bewildered by the flood of ideas that had been coming at him from his own observations, the canny wisdom of his father and the lessons from the serious books; the novel tied these scattered concepts together in a way that was almost magical. It was poorly written, really, forcing upon the reader more instruction about plantation life in Java than he needed, but in the end it left a residue of emotion and moral commitment that would otherwise have been unobtainable. After an absence of two hundred years, the power of Java had returned to South Africa.

When he finished the six books, Moses told his father, 'I want to try it in Johannesburg.'

'You should,' his father said. 'And I suppose you know that the chances are good that you'll be dead before the end of the year.'

'I've heard.' In *Max Havelaar* a young Javanese much like Moses had gone to his Johannesburg and died with a belly full of bullets. As in the past, Java was instructing South Africa.

So in the mid 1930s Moses Nxumalo of Vrymeer went quietly away from the farm and into the city, a journey of ninety-nine miles in physical distance, an incalculable distance spiritually.

He sought out his cousin, Jefferson Magubane, somewhat older than he was, and found him living in Sophiatown, and on the first night he was there, police came hammering on the rickety door, demanding to see all documents. By a miracle of timing, Jefferson managed to slip Moses into an alley leading to the communal privy, and there he hid while the others presented their papers for inspection. Although his sheltered life at Vrymeer had not prepared him for this indignity, his experiences with Max Havelaar had, and he thought how strange it was that he, whose ancestors had lived on this land for a thousand years, should be restricted by incomers as to where and how he could travel.

Next morning Jefferson, who had not been distressed by the police visit, for that was a common occurrence, said brightly, 'Moses, I think we can get you the proper passes.' And he took his cousin some miles out toward the country to a large suburban house called New Sarum. There, deferentially, he went to the back door and informed the black maid who tended it that he had brought her a first-class houseboy. With nudges and winks he instructed Moses in making proper responses, with the result that a black man was summoned, who led the applicant through the kitchen to a kind of office where a white husband and wife waited. They introduced themselves as Mr. and Mrs. Noel Saltwood, whereupon Mrs. Saltwood, a tall, fine-looking English woman, asked him a series of questions, using English, Afrikaans and Zulu interchangeably.

'Can you read and write?' she asked. When he nodded, she asked him where he lived; he panicked, not knowing what to say, but she perceived this and said quickly, 'I know you have no papers. Jefferson told us. We'll arrange for your passbook.' She spoke as if she were a conspirator.

'I'm from Vrymeer.'

'I don't know that. Is it a small place?'

'It's near Venloo.'

'Ah, yes. The Venloo Commando. Who doesn't know about that!' She looked at her husband approvingly, and Moses wondered if he should volunteer further information, but his quandary was solved by Laura Saltwood. 'Did you know, perchance . . . No, you'd have been too young. But a very brave man came from Venloo. General de Groot.'

'My father rode with him. I used to live with him.'

Both the Saltwoods gasped, and they spent the next fifteen minutes asking about his father's experiences on commando, after which Mrs. Saltwood said, 'Noel, we really must put someone to the job of compiling the record of the black commandos. On both sides. Their stories must be incredible, and they'll be lost if we don't do something.'

Then she became strictly business: 'We'll get you your papers, Moses, but you must work here faithfully, because if you don't, back you'll go to the farm. Is that understood?'

'Yes, Baas.'

'We don't use baas here. I'm ma'am, he's mister.'

His pleasure at the prospect of both a job and the papers to prove it was diminished that night when he sat with Jefferson in the cramped room the Magubanes called home and heard the sound of running feet, then screams, then ugly grunts and more screams.

When he rose to intercede in whatever was happening, his aunt Mpela raised her hand and stopped him. 'It's the tsotsis,' she said, and before she could lower her hand, there came the long terrible scream of a woman, then the echo of runners retreating.

In the morning the police came, tardily, indifferently: 'Another Three Star killing.' They ordered a cart to haul the corpse away, and after they had departed and Moses had inspected the blood, he asked what a Three Star killing was.

'The tsotsis carry knives made in England. Three stars on the handle.'

'How do I avoid them?' Moses asked.

'Play the coward. They run in gangs, and if you see them coming, get out. Do anything—hide, run, stand behind a woman—but get out of their way.'

'Don't the police . . .'

'The police say, "The tsotsis do our work for us." You see, Moses, they kill only Bantu.'

'Does this happen often?'

'All the time,' Jefferson said.

So whenever Moses detected these youthful murderers, pimps, scavengers, thieves, dagga-peddlers and bullies in the area, he quietly disappeared. He was eager to keep himself safe because of the consuming interest he had in the things that Jefferson was doing: the political meetings, the long discussions with knowledgeable men and women. He was enchanted to find that one black woman, a handsome person older than he, had actually been to America and won a college degree; she was Gloria Mbeke, a bold and forceful speaker, and although he was too shy to approach her directly, he did frequent her discussions, listening attentively as she outlined her principles:

'The one thing we can be certain of is that if we endeavor to confront our oppressors with any kind of force, they will not hesitate to mow us down with their machine guns. That realization must be the foundation of our policy.

'When Enoch Mgijima encouraged his Israelites, following their own interpretation of the Bible, to claim land at Bulhoek, the police warned him once to move them off. They warned him twice, then they opened fire on people who carried not even sticks. One hundred and sixty-three dead, one hundred and twenty-nine wounded for life.

'When a remnant of Hottentots in the deserts of South-West Africa a few years ago wanted to continue hunting while the government wanted them to work on farms at almost no pay, what did the government do? They placed a huge tax on dogs, and when the Hottentots refused to pay, they sent in airplanes that bombed them as they ran across the veld. One hundred and fifteen killed, three hundred wounded for life.

'Our policy must be the policy of Mahatma Gandhi, who originated it when he lived among us. Passive resistance, legal pressure, and the constant education of our young people.'

At another meeting he heard Miss Mbeke say something which influenced him deeply. She returned to the slaughter of the Israelites at Bulhoek:

'There are two lessons to be learned from this. The white police will never hesitate to shoot us down if they don't like what we're doing. But also, we blacks get ourselves into trouble when we listen to messianic leaders. Remember how Nongqause led thousands of Xhosa to commit suicide in 1857? You agree now that that was insane. But how did Enoch Mgijima get his hypnotic hold on his Israelites? When Halley's Comet passed overhead in 1910, leaving a long trail of star dust, he said it was a message from God to him.

'Do not believe outside messages. Many of the gold miners who were shot down during the strike in Johannesburg had been listening to leaders just like Nongqause and Mgijima, except that their revelations came from Moscow. Communism will not save us in South Africa. The silly teachings of Marcus Garvey in America will not save us. We will save ourselves.'

Thirty minutes after hearing this constructive speech, as he and Jefferson were drifting home through the alleys of Sophiatown, discussing Miss Mbeke's theses, they were suddenly attacked by a gang of sixteen tsotsis wielding Three Star knives. 'Give us your money!' the tsotsis screamed as if demented, and quickly Jefferson did so, but Moses hesitated, and in that flash of a second, the knives came at him. It was a miracle that he was not killed, for even after he had fallen, horribly cut, the inflamed young men kicked at him viciously, and would surely have finished him off had not Jefferson yelled at the top of his voice, 'Police! Over here!' There were no police, but the tsotsis dared not take the risk.

Many had heard the fracas, but none would help. Behind closed doors they thought: In the morning they'll come and clean it up. It's not our affair.

So Jefferson took his cousin home, where his aunt Mpela was always prepared for such an event. She washed the wounds, borrowing from a neighbor a vial of concentrated iodine, which caused Moses to faint, and when she satisfied herself that no arteries had been cut, she went to bed and advised her son to do the same.

In the days of his recuperation, Moses had an opportunity to evaluate the experiences which had been cascading down upon him. He saw the farm at Vrymeer as a system whereby white employers were able to control black peasants with wages preposterously low. Essentially goodhearted men like General de Groot had never in their lives considered that what they were enforcing was Old Testament slavery, and had they been advised of this, they would not have understood what was wrong. He saw Detleef van Doorn as doing practically the same thing but from sanctimonious motivations, and he found that he had little regard for his father's employer. He realized that Van Doorn's associates might force him at any time to return to the gentle slavery at Vrymeer.

He was impressed by the generosity of the Saltwoods and hoped that he might be able to continue working for them, but he had little faith that they would stand by him when the confrontations that Miss Mbeke foresaw came to pass. The English were excellent people, but too concerned with pleasing others.

Sophiatown was no worse in his eyes than Vrededorp: in both places he found strong, honest men fighting to uplift their people and give them hope. Again and again he was struck by this parallel between poor Afrikaners and poor blacks: both groups grappling for roots in an alien city, both sharing poverty and dispossession. He constantly hoped, like old Micah, that blacks and Afrikaners alike would escape their wretchedness. But even as he perceived these relationships he had a terrible fear that what Miss Mbeke said was right: 'The victory of the poor Afrikaner will be at the expense of the blacks.'

Of the young black intellectuals he had listened to, he found to his surprise that he valued most not Miss Mbeke, who was so fluent in both speech and idea, but the young Swazi who had been to London and who had studied economics. He talked sense. Again and again he laid out the limits of a problem and indicated how it could be solved. It was he who uttered the sentences that influenced Moses most deeply: 'In South Africa last year thousands of black men and women were arrested because they moved about with improper documentation in a country which they own as much as the white man.' And 'Sometimes it seems that we have more black children in jail than in school.'

It was not long after he recovered from his stab wounds that the permanent wounding of Moses Nxumalo began. One morning he was stopped by police on Eloff Street, Johannesburg's glittering shopping avenue, and his documents were demanded: 'I see you haven't paid your annual tax of one pound. You must come with me.'

With sixteen more black tax-dodgers he was hustled into a police van, but he never got to jail. He was taken instead to a vacant lot, where a different policeman snarled, 'Now, you damned Kaffirs, you listen. Tomorrow you go before the magistrate, he'll give you jail, three months. You know what it's like in there.'

'Yes, Baas.'

'But I'm willing to give you a chance.'

'Yes, Baas.'

'That truck you see over there belongs to a farmer from Hemelsdorp. He needs strong men who can work well. You sign a two-month contract with him, I'll forget about the magistrate, you can forget about jail.'

Moses and most of the others chose Hemelsdorp, Village of Heaven, but the farm to which they were headed lay not in heaven. For twelve hours a day they toiled in the fields; at night they were thrown into a stinking cattle shed, where they lay awake listening to two of their crew who had pneumonia. One morning the older of the pair was dead.

At the end of one fearful month Moses tried to run away, but was captured in the hills beyond Hemelsdorp and dragged back to the farm.

'Miserable Kaffir bastard!' the farmer screamed. 'Time you learned a lesson.'

The punishment was administered by two of the black overseers, who stripped Moses and bound him about a forty-four-gallon drum. With the rest of the workers forced to watch, he was thrashed with sjamboks till he fainted.

Two days later he was sent back to the fields, but on the first night, when others were asleep, he made another dash for freedom. A black overseer spotted him, but before the man could raise an alarm, Moses knocked him to the ground. When the overseer tried to rise, Moses smashed him in the temple with a large rock, then fled.

For six months he hid in lands along the Limpopo River, then crossed over into Rhodesia, following an ancient route which took him to the Zimbabwe ruins, but he did not tarry there. For two years he worked as kitchen 'boy' in a Bulawayo hotel, and he was at his job one day when a man from Vrymeer found him: 'Your father died last Christmas.'

Moses waited till the end of the month, took his pay and journeyed south, for he was now head of the Nxumalos, and his place was with his people. He slipped in quietly, said nothing to the Van Doorns, who hadn't even noticed his absence, but his family saw the scars on his back. Within a few weeks he was the acknowledged boss boy, and any dream of a more meaningful life vanished.

He said little as he went about his work, but sometimes when he was alone he would look across the veld and swear: 'If I have a son, he will go to college at Fort Hare, and get started right.' This hope compensated for the pain he felt at his own failure.

The Saltwoods made efforts to trace Moses, but when he stayed away for months they supposed that he had merely gone back to his kraal. 'You can never trust a native,' a neighbor said. 'You do everything in the world for a boy like your Moses, and when your back's turned, he steals you blind. How much did he take?'

'I rather think something terrible happened to him,' Laura said. 'He was so willing, so keen to please.'

'No doubt the tsotsis got him.'

'Could be,' Mrs. Saltwood said, but for a long time she continued to wonder about Moses Nxumalo.

In the heady atmosphere of Johannesburg, when the grand strategies of the Broederbond showed their initial signs of succeeding, Piet Krause was thinking one day about the opportunities that would present themselves for a patriotic outburst in 1938, the hundredth anniversary of the Battle of Blood River, the culminating event of the Great Trek.

'We must think of something,' he told Johanna as they came home from a meeting of schoolteachers, 'that will stir up the nation and remind the Afrikaners of their heritage.' They discussed a master rally at the site of Blood River, but that location was so far removed from major centers of population that only a devoted few would be able to attend. They thought of a celebration at Blaauwkrantz, but since that lay in Natal, which was notoriously pro-English, they quickly dropped it.

In fact, they could think of nothing original, and then one morning Johanna read that a committee of Afrikaners was considering the erection of a massive monument on a hilltop outside Pretoria, a memorial to Blood River and the covenant that was entered into on that sacred day. This excited Piet, and the couple talked of inviting huge numbers of people, even from Cape Town, to the dedication of this proposed monument, and when they saw a sketch of how the building might look —a splendid, blunt affair reminiscent of the structures at Great Zimbabwe—they became positively dedicated to the task of making this a historic affair.

Johanna said, 'We must see that all parts of the nation cooperate, all the Afrikaner parts, that is,' and she began to construct patterns for the celebration. As a woman, she was of course not allowed to participate in the Broederbond, but since her husband talked everything over with her and respected her opinions, it was easy for her to feed her ideas through him. She suggested a convocation of religious leaders from all over the world, but discarded this when Piet pointed out that she would have to invite the Pope and certain rabbis. 'What we could do,' she countered, 'is ask the leaders of the Dutch and German churches to join with us.'

On and on went the planning, and then one day Piet suggested the best thing of all: 'What might be a splendid idea—we could see if any of the old ox wagons still existed. There'll be plenty of oxen. Why not build replicas of the old wagons, we have their dimensions, and have two or three of them travel from Graaff-Reinet to the monument. People could dress in the old style—men could let their beards grow like Piet Retief and Gert Maritz . . .'

For two days the Krauses imagined this cavalcade winding north over the old route, and then Johanna proposed a brilliant concept: 'Piet! Not a cavalcade. Five or six separate wagons. Each starting from a major point. Detouring slowly to every small town en route. And all converging on Pretoria on December 16. Every Afrikaner in the nation would have to be there.'

It was this plan which Piet Krause presented to the Broederbond leadership, and he was astonished to find that several prominent members of the railway cultural society had proposed an identical program, except that they visualized only two ox wagons starting from Cape Town. The advantages of Piet's scheme of five or six were recognized and he was assigned the task of organizing the 1938 trek.

'It can be,' Reverend Brongersma predicted to an English newspaper, 'a great outpouring of the Afrikaner spirit. It can at once both unite and ignite.' To a reporter he said, 'It will rejuvenate Afrikaner politics as nothing else could do. I expect wonders from this trek.' In private he added that if sufficient spirit were generated, the Afrikaners might at last succeed in taking South Africa out of its present Union status, making it republican. To any Afrikaner who asked, he said, 'That is the goal we seek,' and if they asked further whether this would mean an exodus or expulsion from the British Empire, he replied, 'Not necessarily. England might like us better as completely equal partners.'

There was, however, one question which he never answered frankly. One night Piet Krause, flushed with his success in launching the wagons, asked, 'Dominee, this time will we join Germany when war comes?' Brongersma did not like to discuss this ticklish situation, for he saw much in contemporary Germany which bothered him. In 1914, like many intelligent Afrikaners, he had felt strongly that his country's future lay with Kaiser Wilhelm's Germany; the latter had good leadership, power, intellectual force and a strong Lutheran tradition. In retrospect he still believed that it would have been better for the world had Imperial Germany won and imposed her version of peace on troubled areas, but he certainly did not believe that about Adolf Hitler's Germany. He saw too much that disturbed, for if in his great series of lectures at Stellenbosch he had educated the young leaders of his nation, he had also educated himself. He believed every word he spoke in those four carefully reasoned discourses, and believed it even more now. South Africa was a Christian country. It endeavored to combine the best of the Old Testament and the New. It believed in justice for all peoples, and if it insisted upon the separation of races, that was only because God had done the same, and he believed that his country managed its separation with firmness and justice. He did not like what Hitler was doing and felt that he would have to oppose an intrusion of his concepts into South Africa.

'Will we join Germany this time, Dominee?' Piet repeated.

'I pray the whole world can avoid war,' he replied.

* * *

In early 1938 Detleef astounded the committee supervising the trek by announcing that he had found on his farm the only surviving ox wagon that had been used by one of the important leaders of the 1838 period, and when it was dragged forth, the wagon he had slept in during the weeks following the end of the Boer War, carpenters said that whereas it was obviously in ruins, it could easily be restored, and they set about doing so. For weeks various newspapers printed photographs showing the progress of rehabilitation, and when the rubric TC–43 was uncovered, correspondents in Grahamstown were able to state what it signified, and recalled the generosity of the English settlers of that period toward a man they trusted. Because of where the wagon had originated, it was proposed that it start its journey to Pretoria from Grahamstown, but Detleef would not permit this; he wanted his wagon to have no contact with Englishmen, so it started from Graaff-Reinet.

The journey north, in those winter days of August 1938, began on a high emotional pitch, with the central square of Graaff-Reinet looking much as it had during the historic Nachtmaals: tents pitched, women in sunbonnets, children playing, men in beards and suspenders. As the wagon moved slowly forward, a tremendous visual remembrance of heroic days, people came from fifty miles to see it pass, its sixteen sturdy oxen walking slowly, as their ancestors had done a century ago.

The *Tjaart van Doorn* did not go to Bloemfontein, for another wagon was starting from there, but it did move east through the historic sites: Thaba Nchu, Vegkop, the site on the Vaal where the De Groot family was assassinated, then east through the concentration-camp towns of Standerton and Chrissie Meer. In early December it headed, west to Carolina, where the members of Christoffel Steyn's family paid it honor, and then on to Venloo, where descendants of the commando of Paulus de Groot formed an honor guard. When it reached Waterval-Boven, from which Oom Paul Kruger had left for his exile, the emotional strain was intense, and thousands prayed along the roadside as it passed. This was a wagon in which women and men of stature had risked their lives and fortunes in the building of a nation, and to see it move so slowly, with such strain and with so cramped a space for survival, brought tears.

On December 13 the *Tjaart van Doorn* slowly approached the vast field at the foot of the mound on which the future monument was to stand, and when Detleef and Maria, in their 1838 costumes, saw the throng that awaited them, they stopped the wagon and bowed their heads. What had started as a topic of conversation had expanded to a mighty outpouring of the Voortrekker spirit. Two days before the event, more than eighty thousand Afrikaners camped at the site, and that night Detleef led his wagon into a simulated laager with six others. The oxen were turned loose to graze, as in the old days, and children brought thorn bushes to weave among the wheels to keep away the Zulu. When the moon rose late, and the silhouettes of the wagons stood against the dark horizon, men wakened their families to witness the sight, and improvised choirs chanted the Psalms in Afrikaans.

On December 17 Piet Krause rode among the wagons already in position, assuring the men that all was in order; the two major wagons from Pretoria and Cape Town would arrive next morning. By now the crowd approached a hundred thousand—families camping on the slopes, as in the old days—and friendships that had languished for years were renewed with pledges to maintain them.

On this day rumors began to circulate: 'The mayor of Benoni will not be allowed to participate. He's Jewish. They've told the general not to appear. He's English. Best news of all, Jan Christian Smuts will not be coming. They want nothing of him in this celebration. He's more English than he is Afrikaner. No speeches in English will be allowed tomorrow.' Piet Krause, the originator of most of these rumors, had personally decreed that what would be the major monument in South Africa must be a purely Afrikaner affair.

On December 18 some two hundred thousand people gathered on the hill south of Pretoria to consecrate the spot on which their monument would rise. If, despite everything they had heard, General Smuts and other Afrikaner supporters of the government did appear, the occasion would become an affair of state, and 'God Save the King' would have to be played, but Piet Krause openly avowed that if the band played one note of that anthem, he and a gang of toughs would smash every instrument. Aware of the bitterness of the issue, Smuts prudently stayed away, and to the joy of the Afrikaners only 'Die Stem van Suid-Afrika' (The Call of South Africa) was played, and many swore that it would soon be the official anthem of the Afrikaner republic when the new nation came into being.

The orations in Afrikaans, one delivered by Reverend Brongersma, were dignified but charged with heavy implications. Hardly any words of historic evocation could be spoken without producing cheers from the massed throng, and when symbol-words like Slagter's Nek, Black

Circuit and Christoffel Steyn were uttered, the crowd cheered automatically. When heroes were recalled—Pretorius, Retief, De Groot—the crowd yelled till it was hoarse, and as the day waned and the leaders realized how far beyond their expectations their success had been, it began to penetrate to all involved that something more than a celebration had occurred here this day. 'This is the opening gun of our campaign to break away from England altogether,' Piet Krause cried in an ecstasy of patriotism.

He became so mesmerized by that assembly of two hundred thousand Afrikaners that it was not long before he began to have visions of a vast national uprising, and to discover how this could be orchestrated, he slipped down to Cape Town, boarded a ship for England and quietly crossed to Germany, where he quickly made contact with Nazi leaders.

He was overwhelmed by what he saw. At a tremendous rally in the stadium used by the 1936 Olympics he realized how amateurish the Voortrekker thing had really been. 'We had all those people in one place,' he told his Nazi guide, 'and did nothing with them. They went away with the same thoughts they had when they came. Next time it must be different.'

He was so intelligent, and appeared to be so highly placed in South African politics, that the men about to launch a total war in Europe were captivated by the possibilities he offered: 'Could you arrange an uprising against the English government—if war happened to come to Europe?'

'Look at what we did in 1914, without help or guidance from you,' he reminded them. When they admitted that they were ignorant of that affair, he told them of the courageous effort made by men like Paulus de Groot and Jakob van Doorn, who devoted their lives to the struggle for freedom. 'Van Doorn was my father-in-law. De Groot you've heard of, naturally.' They hadn't, so he dropped that subject.

'But what can you do this time?' they asked.

'I give you my solemn promise that Jan Christian Smuts will not dare call for mobilization. No one would report.'

'The police?'

'They'll fight for Germany.' Recklessly he promised everything, implying that he spoke for all segments of the population. If he did not convince them of his interpretations of South African politics, he did persuade them to invest a modest amount in a potential subversion of that government. They granted the funds on the sensible basis of disrupting the English power at all points, provided the cost proved not too high; they never expected the southern tip of Africa to become a German enclave, but they could reasonably hope for enough disruption to impede the war effort.

With these assurances, Piet Krause, who spoke miserable German, went to Nuremberg for one of the frenzied rallies of mid-1939, when the leadership knew that war was inevitable, though the people did not. The stadium was filled with ecstatic young men who would shortly die in Greece and Italy and Russia and the North Atlantic and in the skies above England. He heard eleven preliminary speeches, pounding into him the need to exterminate Jews and cleanse the bloodstream. He appreciated the enormous appeal of the word Volk and decided to increase its use in South Africa. But when the lesser orators were finished, Herr Goebbels appeared, and after him, Adolf Hitler, the man who would save the world.

Piet Krause stood enthralled as Hitler unfolded his plan for regeneration, and each word he said applied to conditions in South Africa, so far as Piet was concerned. He was hypnotized by Hitler's force, his clear logic; and when the wild cheering died, he still stood there, trying to determine how best he could assist this man in bringing the same kind of order and enthusiasm to South Africa.

That night, in his Nuremberg room, he drafted the blood oath which he would administer to all who later joined him in his enterprise:

> In the presence of Almighty God and on the sacred blood of the Volk, I swear that my higher authority will find me obediently faithful and eager to obey in secret any command given me. I shall fight constantly for the victory of National Socialism, because I know that democracy has become like an old shoe which must be thrown away.
>
> > If I advance, follow me!
> > If I retreat, shoot me!
> > If I die, avenge me!
> > So help me God!

When he reached home in midsummer, 1939, his wife could see that he had undergone some thunderclap experience, for he was not the man she had known before. When he confided the responsibilities that had been placed upon him, she knew that she must assume responsibility for the family, since he would be preoccupied with a score of duties. He started with the police, talking quietly against the local custom of conscripting the whole force into the armed services: 'Don't let them make you go to war. If Jan Christian Smuts wants you to fight his battles in England, don't permit it. This time England must lose, and when that happens, you and men like you will be in command.'

He was also active with young Afrikaners: 'Do not allow the government to force you into uniform. And for the love of God, don't volunteer. When the Germans recapture South-West Africa, there'll be a place for you in a real army.'

He asked certain trusted clergymen to preach against participation in this impending war, and he did effective work among the unions. He talked with schoolteachers, advising them what to say to their pupils, and when war did come, in September of that year, Smuts found himself unable to order conscription, or to move policemen bodily into the armed forces, or to argue young men into volunteering. In fact, when Smuts sought to take his country into the conflict on the side of England, he was strongly opposed by those who insisted that it remain neutral. At the final moment South Africa joined the Allies by a vote of only 80–67.

'He is taking us onto the wrong side,' the principal members of the Broederbond cried in dismay, and some of the future leaders of the nation went into detention camps rather than fight against Germany. Piet Krause, escaping police attention, swung into violent action, organizing disruptive squads, which secretly attacked military installations, power lines and even military training camps. Men loyal to the Allies, especially young Afrikaners seen as traitors to the Volk, were assaulted and some were killed.

The government was in pitiful shape to fight a war. It dared not call for nationwide conscription, and those soldiers and policemen who volunteered to serve outside the country were required to wear orange swatches, which distinguished them from others who announced that they would not fight abroad; this presumably divided the men into heroes and cowards. But there was a disadvantage in such a system; Piet Krause's young hoodlums who were against the war could easily spot the men with swatches who were willing to fight for the Allies, and it became fashionable to beat such soldiers up, killing them on occasion.

Piet and his wife did whatever they could to exacerbate such situations, and in the heady days of Nazi victories on all fronts, they received a cryptic message from Berlin: 'Meet Wyk Slotemaker Mafeking.' He was a minor South African actor who had appeared in several

German films, absorbing propaganda as he worked, and when Piet encountered him at a ramshackle hotel he whispered, 'I have weapons, fifteen thousand American dollars, and plans to assassinate Smuts.'

'The hour is at hand!' Piet exulted.

It was a sorely divided South Africa that tried to prosecute this war. Johanna van Doorn and her sister-in-law Maria prayed daily for a German victory and hoped that it would be of such magnitude that England would be crushed forever. Detleef agreed with them in principle, but had reservations about Adolf Hitler and real doubts as to whether South Africa would gain much from a German victory in Africa.

The Saltwoods of New Sarum, led by Maud Turner Saltwood, now a feisty sixty-nine, were totally supportive of the Allied cause and were overjoyed when the United States joined in. Her daughter-in-law, Laura Saltwood, Noel's wife, organized canteens to help England and was distraught when some of them were vandalized by Piet Krause's storm troopers.

The Saltwoods of De Kraal and the Van Doorns of Trianon faced difficulties in determining their allegiances, for Timothy Saltwood, V.C., was married to Clara van Doorn, a stalwart Afrikaner. Like many similar families, they prayed quietly that the war would end and did not parade their emotions.

The Nxumalos were perplexed. As a family that had always been loyal to General de Groot, they at first favored a German victory, but when the African National Congress pointed out that Herr Hitler thought even less of blacks than he did of Jews, they realized that in his moment of victory they were going to be in trouble, so gradually they transferred their moral support to the English. They were astounded as they watched contending elements within the white population fight each other, and slowly they realized that the Afrikaners would win, here in South Africa if not in Europe, and that when they did, they were going to be very harsh with the blacks. Old Micah, at the end of a long, wild life of fighting great battles without weapons—Majuba, Spion Kop, the raid into the Cape—had sadly assured his family: 'Whoever wins, we lose.'

The heaviest burden of moral decision fell upon Reverend Brongersma; as the son of a family that had provided five commandos in the Boer War, he was staunchly pro-Afrikaner and his whole sympathy had to be with their nationalist and republican aspirations. His lectures at Stellenbosch had not dealt with this aspect of South African life; he had avoided the issue lest he give offense to the English half of his community. But on balance, and looking at the entire world as he was permitted to understand it, he could not see that England had ever exhibited any great moral superiority. Their record in India and South Africa did not impress him, and he suspected that most of what was commendable in the United States stemmed from its non-English immigrants. So he would be quite content to see a German victory—except for the fact that no Christian could remain blind to the awful excesses of Hitlerism. The Nazis had perpetrated crimes against the family, the church, the youth of the nation, and certainly against the Jews. Sitting alone in his study, his tall body hunched over at times, at other times thrown far back as he propped his legs on his desk, he wrestled with this problem: Nazism, using the most exalted impulses of the human race, seems to release the lowest urges of the human animal. Leave Germany out of it. There must be millions of people in America who would gladly staff a Nazi prison. God knows we could find them here in South Africa. And one of the ugliest, I am afraid, is my good friend Piet Krause. Like a dog, he grabs hold of one idea, gnaws at it, worries it, and allows it to obsess him.

He felt that in common decency, but also for the good name of the Broederbond, which did not sponsor such behavior, he must talk with Piet, but when he tried to reason with him, he found the former school-teacher glassy-eyed with dreams, and in the end he dismissed him as hopeless. But after the disappointing session he did consult with Frykenius, who was still Piet's superior in the brotherhood, and implored him to summon Krause back to Venloo, where together they might knock some sense into him. This Frykenius agreed to do, because he, too, was worried by the excesses Piet was engineering.

Krause, as an obedient member of the Broederbond, came down from Johannesburg, but as soon as he saw that Reverend Brongersma was with Frykenius he bristled: 'Dominee, we do not seek your counsel.'

'Piet,' Frykenius said, 'sit down.'

But even after the two older men had spread before him their analysis of the harm he was doing, he refused to accept their rebuke: 'Have you two any idea of the great forces set in motion by the ox wagons? This country is seething with patriotism.'

'Don't use anything as precious as patriotism for a wrong purpose,' Brongersma cautioned.

'Dominee, there's to be a great uprising!'

When he heard these words the predikant sat back, his hands folded in his lap. He knew that what Piet had just said was true: there was going to be a tremendous uprising of the Afrikaner spirit, so vast that it would sweep Jan Christian Smuts and his English ways right out of office and keep them out forever, so vast that every aspect of life in the country would be modified. Because of the spirit generated by the ox wagons, the Afrikaner was on the verge of victories which only the idealist had dreamed of. South Africa would quit the empire. No more would bands play 'God Save the King,' no more would Englishmen sit in the cabinet. The Afrikaner nation would be free to solve its racial difficulties in its own just way. And strife would end.

'Piet,' the predikant said softly, 'you've won your victory. Don't contaminate it with violence.'

'Dominee, the real victory is just beginning! Herr Hitler is about to sweep the English from the seas. America can do nothing, he'll sink their ships. His principles will rule this land.'

When Frykenius tried to soften this tirade, Piet cried, 'You men have a choice you must make in a hurry. Are you for the revolution that's breaking, or against it?'

'Piet,' Frykenius reasoned, 'you know what the aims of the Broederbond have always been. Of course we're for an Afrikaner triumph. But not on your violent terms. The rioting in the streets, that's got to stop.'

Piet drew back as if dissociating himself from the timid approach of the Bond. 'You men in the Broederbond. I see your kind in Pretoria and Johannesburg all the time. You're like a pretty girl who gives a boy a kiss, three kisses, a dozen, then runs away when he wants to get down to business. Well, I'm getting down to business. I have work to do, and I doubt that we'll be meeting any more.'

In a frenzy he dashed out and went to Vrymeer, burst into the kitchen and presented Detleef with an ultimatum: 'Either you join us this night or you miss your chance to lead the nation when we triumph.' When Detleef asked for details, Piet thrust a typed card into his hand, crying excitedly, 'Take this oath. Now. And tonight you ride with us . . . if we get instructions from Berlin.' Before Detleef could respond to such a commitment, Piet said with urgency, 'I must use your radio,' and through the shortwave screeching he listened to Radio Zeesen:

'Good evening, dear and loyal friends in South Africa. This is your favorite program, By Kampfuur en Ketel [By Campfire and Kettle]. Today our glorious Führer has enjoyed victories on all fronts. The decadent democracies cringe and crumble. [Here came a series of coded instructions, at which Piet Krause leaped with excitement.] Trusted friends in South Africa . . .'

Neither he nor Detleef heard the final words, for Piet snapped off the radio and asked bluntly, 'Well, Brother, do you join our revolution?' and faced with that moment of decision, Detleef finally concluded that he distrusted Adolf Hitler and doubted his ultimate victory.

'I can't accept such an oath,' he said.

'Heroes can,' Piet said, and he was off.

He drove recklessly from Venloo to Waterval-Boven, where he picked up two conspirators who had taken the oath, then west to Pretoria, where Wyk Slotemaker, the one-time actor eager to assassinate Smuts, joined them, then down to an army base south of Johannesburg, where they were scheduled to blow up a major ammunition dump. When the actor saw the intricacy of the barbed wire, he drew back, and this also deterred the other two, but Piet, inflamed with memories of Nuremberg and Berlin, and visualizing the same kind of glory breaking over South Africa, crept forward alone, dynamite strapped to his back.

His careless use of wire clippers activated a warning bell in the guardrooms, and seven sharpshooters streamed out as huge searchlights flashed on. An Afrikaner from Carolina who had volunteered for Smuts' army drew a bead on the dark figure creeping toward the ammunition, and fired. His bullet struck the package on Piet's back, detonating it and blowing him to shreds, but even so, Krause gained a limited victory, for he had reached a spot so close to the dump that his explosion ignited combustibles—and through the long night shattering concussions threw flames far into the sky.

In 1946, when Detleef and Maria van Doorn were once more peaceful farmers at Vrymeer, they were visited by his sister Johanna, a widow with a minor job in Johannesburg. She came with a proposal from a group of persons much interested in the welfare of the nation, and although Detleef was suspicious of almost anything she did these days, he had to listen, for whenever he met with her his first impression was of that evening in the camp at Chrissiesmeer when she apportioned the food delivered to the dead Ouma Sybilla, and weighed it in her pale hands, giving him the larger share. He was alive today because of her courage and generosity.

'Detleef, and this concerns you too, Maria. In business the English are proving much more clever than we suspected. We've made almost no headway in penetrating their offices of power. We just don't have enough trained young men. Damnit all, our best people go down to Stellenbosch, and what do they study? Religion, of which we have far too much. Philosophy, which is of use to no one. Some history. Some literature. A little science. What we need is accountants and bankers and managers.'

'I certainly have no capacity in those fields,' Detleef protested.

'Of course you don't. Because you wasted your time at Stellenbosch. Playing rugby.'

'Wait a minute! Don't you say anything against rugby.' When she had railed against religion a few moments before, he had remained silent, but he could not do so if she spoke against rugby.

'Forget that. We've decided that what we must do is place men like you who can speak good English . . . Well, what I mean is . . . you must take one of the permanent secretaryships with the committees in Parliament.'

'That pays nothing!'

'Of course it doesn't. That's the point. We slip you in there. Nobody notices because no Englishman would want the job. And you serve there twenty-five or thirty years . . .'

'I'm already fifty-one.'

'So you serve twenty years. In time you make enormous inroads. It's you who will be drafting the laws. And we will gain by indirection what we can't win head-on.'

She had with her a list of some forty inconspicuous vacancies, not one of which would be mentioned in the newspapers when it was filled: a series of jobs which might have tempted a boy out of high school, but not Detleef. They were mostly in agencies of the government dealing with financial or business affairs, in which he felt no competence, but as he was returning the paper to her, his eye fell upon one line, off to itself, relating to an office so small it provided only one vacancy: Commission on Racial Affairs. Idly he said, 'Now, if a man had to accept an assignment . . .'

'Which?' she pounced.

'That one.'

'A man could do much good there, Detleef.'

'No! No!' He dismissed the invitation absolutely and would say no more about it, so dutifully she gathered her papers, smiled at Maria, and left.

Three days later Mr. Frykenius summoned him to Venloo. The two Broederbonders had grown so close since the deplorable death of their mutual friend, Piet Krause, that they attacked any subject without formalities: 'Detleef, they want you to take the position with the Commission on Racial Affairs.'

'I can't leave the farm.'

'But you can. The Troxels can manage, and you and Maria can divide your time between Pretoria and Cape Town.'

'Really, I can hardly . . .'

'So many times have you and I discussed what to do with the Bantu and the Coloureds. Here's a chance to put our principles into operation.'

'I don't want to leave Vrymeer . . .'

'Detleef, you and I have only a limited number of years remaining. Let's spend them on things important.' When Van Doorn hesitated, the butcher said, 'Remember when you told me about your vision for this country? The sun striking the glass of jellies. Each on its own level, clean and separated? Now you have an opportunity to achieve that dream.'

'I shall have to speak with Maria.'

'Detleef, on crucial matters, leave the women to themselves.'

'But how did you hear about this job? Surely it was my sister Johanna who told you.'

'I never speak with women. This came as an order from Pretoria.'

Detleef smiled and thought: But who told Pretoria to send the order? It had to have been Johanna, and he remembered the debt he owed her: She broke the rations in half, then added to one portion and gave it to me. She kept me alive. She helped form my beliefs.

'So the problem we have is of our own making,' Frykenius was explaining. 'In order to get the little jobs in government, we insisted that every employee must be bilingual. It worked. We got all of them because the English wouldn't bother to learn Afrikaans. But now the big jobs are opening up and we damned Afrikaners have too few bright people who can speak English well. We'll get them when our universities get going. But right now we must depend on people like you.'

When Detleef remained silent, the butcher said, 'I have written this letter for you, accepting the assignment. Sign it.' And he pushed forward the document that would ultimately make Detleef van Doorn one of the most influential men in the nation.

Because there had been fierce antagonisms among cities when the Union government was established in 1910, each insisting that it be the capital, Detleef's new position required him to maintain three homes: the permanent farm at Vrymeer, a six-month home in Cape Town, and a year-round pair of rooms in a Pretoria hotel. Fortunately, he had the funds for such extravagance.

The reasons for this proliferation were complex. The contest for the capital had been solved rather neatly: Pretoria housed all executive operations; Cape Town hosted the Parliament; and Bloemfontein had the Appellate Court. Financial and business interests, although not forming a recognized branch of government, more or less ran the country from Johannesburg, which left poor Natal with nothing except a semi-tropical climate and breathtaking views of the Indian Ocean.

As a consequence, the South African government resembled the Indian, which during hot months moved entirely from steaming Delhi to cool Simla in the Himalayas. During the half year that Parliament was in session most of the executive branch boarded trains and went down to Cape Town, and during the other half, parliamentary offices moved up to Pretoria.

The Commission on Racial Affairs was in those years a trivial Cape Town operation dealing mostly with housing; it was chaired by an elected member of Parliament and staffed by officeholders of little distinction. There was a secretary, an Englishman who had held the position for twenty routine years, and a pettifogging assistant of equal service whose resignation because of failing eyesight had created the opening which Detleef was filling. His salary was £900 a year, scarcely enough to live on if one had to move back and forth between the cities.

In 1946 the commission had so little work to do that Detleef slipped into place with no notice of his appointment appearing in any newspaper, but in early 1947 an event occurred which projected him into permanent attention; after that, whatever his commission did attracted notice.

In that year Jan Christian Smuts, as filled with honors as a man could be—Prime Minister of South Africa, Field Marshal of the British Empire, Chancellor-elect of Cambridge University, sponsor of the United Nations and co-drafter of the noble preamble to its charter—

decided that to cap his career and at the same time increase his chances for reelection, he would invite the King and Queen of England to visit their dominion; and he had the happy idea of asking them to bring along their two charming daughters. All four accepted, and when they landed at Cape Town there was an outpouring of loyalty to the royal family by all but a determined group of Afrikaners who were working assiduously to take South Africa out of the empire.

Detleef became involved in the royal tour when his prize bull, a gigantic beast called Oom Paul, won the blue ribbon at the Rand Agricultural Show. This meant that Vrymeer could charge sharply increased fees for Oom Paul's services, and Detleef was delighted.

But then he found that to receive his blue ribbon, he must accept it from the hands of King George VI, who would be attending the Rand show, and this infuriated him. As Maria said bitterly, 'My father was executed by soldiers of the king. Your father was shot by his soldiers. How could you accept a prize from his bloodstained hands?'

'It was soldiers of King George V,' Detleef corrected, but this was unfortunate, because Maria said, 'The English killed most of your family at Chrissiesmeer.'

The word inflamed him: 'Chrissiesmeer! Do you know how they spell it on their maps? Chrissie Meer. They're even stealing our names from us.'

'Detleef, you cannot accept a prize from that man.'

Painfully aware of the money he was sacrificing, Detleef stormed down to the cattle pens and told his manager, Troxel, 'Take Oom Paul home.'

'But the blue ribbon!'

'I will accept no prize from the hands of a bloodstained king.'

A newsman heard the fracas and recognized Detleef as a former rugby great. Sensing a great story, he shouted for his cameraman, who was photographing sheep. When the man ran over, he quickly grasped the situation and dragooned Detleef into posing beside his champion. At that moment Oom Paul, irritated by the commotion, assumed a sneer almost as contemptuous as Detleef's. The scene was frozen on film: an honest Afrikaner and his bull defying the empire.

As the 1948 election neared, the stately English homes in Johannesburg suburbs glowed with color portraits of the royal family standing with Jan Smuts, while the Afrikaner homes displayed the shot of Detleef standing with Oom Paul. When the agricultural attaché from the American embassy visited eastern Transvaal to check crops, he listened for two days to the scathing accusations lodged against Smuts, then broke into laughter. 'You people feel about him the way my father in Iowa feels about Roosevelt. Smuts won the war for you, and now you want to kick him out. Roosevelt won the war for us, and men like my father wanted to hang him.'

The voting took place on 26 May 1948, and that evening the Van Doorns invited to their Vrymeer home their sister Johanna, Mr. Frykenius and their dominee, Reverend Brongersma. As a cool autumn night descended over the lakes, the five people sensed that this could be a day of majestic change. The king and queen were going to be banished. Slim Jannie Smuts' party would be tossed out. The days of smug Englishmen like the Saltwoods were numbered. And those wavering Afrikaner families, like the Van Doorns of Trianon, half Dutch, half English, would be forced to make up their minds and nail their colors aloft for others to see.

Frykenius spoke: 'I see a tremendous nationalism assuming power in this country tonight. Smuts? Forget him. The king? He'll be gone in ten years. The English language? Now it falls to second place. Tonight we take revenge for Slagter's Nek and the concentration camps. I pray we have the energy to capitalize on the victory we're about to win.'

When the first returns came in they were from strongly English areas, and Smuts' tenure as prime minister seemed to be secure, but as the night wore on, startling upsets were reported, with men who had been in internment camps during the war because of their pro-Hitler stance winning astounding victories. When it became clear that Daniel Malan's National party was winning, Detleef began to cheer, and said to his sister, 'I wish Piet Krause were here to see this night. All he dreamed of we're getting, and without one rifle shot.'

Toward two in the morning, when neighbors dropped by to share sandwiches and coffee, the really glorious news reached them: 'Jan Christian Smuts has lost even his own seat at Standerton. The field marshal leaves the field of battle.'

'Thank God!' Maria Steyn van Doorn cried, and she knelt. Johanna joined her, and the two women prayed in thankfulness that they had seen the fall of this man who, they believed, had hurt them so grievously.

When they rose, Frykenius turned to Brongersma and asked, 'Dominee, would you lead us in prayer? This is a night to be remembered.' And the tall man, who would shortly leave Venloo to occupy the pulpit in the leading Pretoria church, asked his four listeners to pray with him:

'Almagtige God, ons dank U. From 1795 when the Dutch first
lost their colony at the Cape, through vicissitudes untold, we have
fought to establish a just society in this land. In those troubled
years You extended a covenant to us, and we have been faithful.
Tonight You bring us great victory, and our only prayer is that
we may prove worthy of it. Help us to build here a nation in
Your image.'

Fervently the others cried 'Amen,' and that very afternoon Detleef and
Maria headed for Cape Town, where with a new majority in Parliament
they would begin their arduous work of reorganizing the nation.

The first thing Detleef did was to make life so miserable for his superior, the senior secretary to the Commission on Racial Affairs, that
the only sensible thing that Englishman could do was to resign. For several weeks he tried to avoid this drastic step, trusting that the new
member of Parliament who was taking over the chairmanship would
protect him, but this man was a tough-minded farmer from the Orange
Free State, and instead of defending the aggrieved secretary, he treated
him even more contemptuously than Detleef had, and in disgust the
man quit. He left government altogether, beginning the hemorrhage that
would drain every department until the civil service at all levels became
almost totally Afrikaner-minded and -managed.

With Detleef in position, the commission was ready to tackle the
vast problems of whipping the various elements of society into shape,
and it fell to Van Doorn to draft the preliminary directives, then construct the proposed laws that would convert them into a permanent discipline. He worked endlessly for this goal, at first a faceless bureaucrat,
but as his accomplishments became known, a nationally acclaimed hero
in the movement to protect the race.

Like puritans in all countries, he started with sex. He saw that in a
decent society white men should marry only white women, Coloureds
marry Coloureds, and so on down to the Bantu, who would marry
among themselves. Whenever he thought of these matters, or discussed
them with his wife, who heartily approved of what he was trying to do,
he started at what he visualized as the top with Afrikaners, working his
way down to the Bantu, who represented the vast majority at the bottom. Afrikaners were entitled to top position because they respected
God and were faithful to the directives of John Calvin; Coloureds stood
higher than Indians for two reasons: they had some white blood and
they usually believed in Jesus Christ, and even those who didn't, ac-

cepted Muhammad, who was higher than the Hindu gods; and Bantu were at the bottom because they were black and heathen. Of course, a large proportion of them were Christian, hundreds of thousands being enrolled in their own Dutch Reformed churches, but this was a complication which he ignored.

His first proposal was simple: no white person, regardless of his or her situation, could marry a non-white. If he attempted to do so, he would be thrown in jail, and if he actually entered into such a marriage, it would be invalid.

This presented little difficulty in the Afrikaner provinces of Transvaal and the Orange Free State, but in Cape Town, where more than half the population was Coloured, it created havoc, and there was great outcry. But that very year in Durban, blacks and Indians engaged in wild communal rioting in which nearly one hundred and fifty people were slain, and Detleef could tell his people, 'See, races should be kept apart.' To those in his confidence he often spoke of his vision: the glass with the perfect separation of jellies.

In 1950 he carried this marriage ordinance to its next logical improvement: he pulled out an old immorality act of 1927, which had struggled ineffectively to deal with the matter, and gave it new teeth, so that sexual relations between persons of unequal color were criminalized; any man embracing a woman of different color would be jailed. His wife and sister approved of this law and said it would perform miracles in purifying life in the Union.

The use of this word *Union* irritated Detleef, and he wondered how soon the Afrikaner majority would officially break ties with England. When he asked his superiors about the timetable for freedom, they told him gruffly, 'One thing at a time. Get along with your own tasks.' He was diverted temporarily when at the United Nations, Madame Pandit of India launched a bitter attack on South Africa's racial policies, particularly the treatment of Indians. He was enraged that a woman should presume to speak so, and that a Hindu should so make a fool of herself by criticizing a Christian country. At his suggestion, he was given time off to draft a reply to Madame Pandit, but it was so discourteous to an ambassador of another Commonwealth nation that it was not dispatched, but for many weeks he continued to mutter to his Afrikaner friends, 'Imagine. A woman and a Hindu daring to say those things. She should be muzzled.'

When his superiors ordered him to forget India and get back to work, he produced for them four smashing proposed bills, all of which became law. As one newspaper said of this herculean output: 'Rarely in the history of the world has one nation opened its floodgates to such a torrent of legislation.' When he and Maria surveyed what they had accomplished, they could take pride in the fact that they had achieved through quiet application of their talents what their fathers had failed to attain through battle. 'Think of what we've made happen in such a short time!' Detleef said after a six-month stint in Cape Town, and like a professor he ticked off the changes.

One, he had begun to codify customs and rules forbidding contact between whites and non-whites in any public amenity. Toilets, restaurants, trolley cars, taxis, elevators, post-office windows where stamps were sold, station platforms and even park benches had to be clearly designated with large signs as to who could patronize them, and across the nation WHITES ONLY proliferated. Maria was particularly gratified by the post-office restriction: 'I would hate to stand in line behind some big Bantu, waiting for my stamps.'

Two, he had helped his cohorts in Parliament pass a Group Areas Act that would enable the government to divide the entire nation, and especially every city, into segments allocated to specific groups. Thus, the central urban areas would be cleared of any Indians or Bantu so that whites alone could live there. Huge areas now occupied by Coloureds in Cape Town would be reserved for whites only; the Coloureds would be removed to new housing tracts on the windy Cape Flats. The Bantu would be confined to vast locations outside the limits of white cities and towns, and would be allowed to stay even there only so long as they provided meaningful labor for white interests. 'With these reasonable actions,' said Van Doorn, 'the racial cleanliness which is the mark of any good society will be both defined and enforced.'

Three, he aided in drafting harsh, good laws for the suppression of Communism, making them so sweeping that almost any activity the Afrikaner majority did not approve could be punished by extremely long prison terms, often without due process of law. 'This is needed,' he assured any who questioned him, and when certain liberals, often Englishmen, pointed out that for every Communist thrown into jail without trial, sixteen non-Communists who wanted better schools or labor unions would be so penalized, he answered with a remark he had only recently heard: 'You can't make an omelet without breaking eggs.'

Four—his major achievement—he conceived the law which came closest to his heart, and in the formative stages, long before it had passed, Maria and Johanna had applauded the far-sightedness of his planning. 'What we propose,' he explained to the parliamentary members who would push the bill through, 'is that every human being residing in this country shall be listed in our records—available always to police and government—as to his or her specific racial identity.'

'What I mean,' an English member fumbled, 'if this classification is to follow a man all his life, oughtn't we to be fairly careful—'

Detleef did not let him finish: 'Sir, the utmost care will be taken. White people of the finest reputation will do the classifying, and of course we can expect a few mistakes. You know that and I know it. But when they're pointed out, and any man can challenge his classification, a committee of three responsible white persons will meet with that complainant, look at his skin color, study his background, even take testimony from his close friends and neighbors, and reclassify him upward, if the facts warrant.'

'And if the facts are unclear?'

'Then it will be better if the classification stands.'

'And what if a man you classify as white wants to be classified as Coloured?'

'Downward?' Detleef asked. The question was so preposterous that he could think of no answer, but what he did reply was interesting: 'I can see the day when a man classified tenuously as Coloured will have lived such an exemplary life and so clearly have acquired civilized habits that his community will assent to allowing him to change his classification upward to white. Everyone can aspire to upward movement, especially if his skin is on the light side.'

Because Detleef exulted over these new laws, it must not be assumed that he had much to do with their actual passage through Parliament. He never forgot that he was only a bureaucrat working out of a small Cape Town office, and many members of Parliament, especially those of the opposition parties, almost forgot that he existed, for he never appeared on the floor. But through persistent pressure and the fact that he kept his job while the members often lost theirs, he gradually acquired a leverage quite out of proportion to his position.

Even so, when the bells of Venloo marked the beginning of a new year, he knew that despite his victories, he had failed to deal with the worrisome nettle that would torment his nation into the next century, and on New Year's Day 1951 he posed the dilemma to Maria and Johanna: 'What are we going to do about the Coloureds?'

The question was most perplexing. The Bantu were clearly black, with historic areas to which presumably they belonged: the Transkei of the Xhosa, Zululand, the lands of the Tswana and the Sotho. It wasn't really as neat and tidy as that, for there were millions of Bantu living loosely throughout the nation, but it was a definable problem that could be solved.

Since the Indians kept to their crowded ghettos, mainly in Natal, they, too, could be handled logically. 'Give them a shop, restrict them, and don't allow them too many liberties' was Detleef's prescription.

But the Coloureds—what to do about them? They were not of any one clear race—white-black-Malay-Indian-Hottentot—nor of any one religion, for many were Muslim. They had no specific terrain, for they lived everywhere. And they were certainly not primitives, for most of them had the intellectual and technical capacities of whites. But they were in a sense unidentified, unspecified, and as such they could be ignored.

They were needed. In every industry, jobs went unfilled because Coloureds were not allowed to take them. In every aspect of growth there was inhibition because Coloureds were forbidden to associate equally with whites. Constantly they were restricted to lower levels of achievement when obviously they had the capacity to do much better. In these years a marvelous opportunity was lost.

All nations make mistakes, terrible miscalculations which once adopted can rarely be amended. In England it was social categories that inhibited normal development in many areas, creating animosities that festered. In India it was rigid stratification of caste, descending even to untouchability. In Japan it was the persecution of the Eta and the denigrating of the Okinawan. And in America it was the blundering incapacity to deal with blacks. In South Africa the fearful miscalculation occurred in the 1920–1960 quadridecade when the white ruling classes could have reached out and embraced the Coloureds, welcoming them into a respected partnership.

Only by following the logic of Detleef and his two women on New Year's Day 1951 can one approximate an answer to this enigma of a nation's casting aside a major treasure. Detleef opened the conversation: 'It occurs to me that we are far from solving the big problem.'

'The Bantu?' Johanna asked. She was seventy-one now, no longer employed in Johannesburg, but nevertheless a major factor in Afrikaner women's circles. 'We know very well what to do with the Bantu. Treat them justly but keep them in their place.'

'I mean the Coloureds.'

'That is a problem,' Maria agreed, and she set the tone for the discussion: 'They are the children of sin, and God must despise them.'

'They are mongrels,' Johanna said, 'and I wish we could cleanse the nation of them as we did the Chinese. Remember that day, Detleef, when you saw the last Chinese go down the cog railway to Waterval-Onder. That was a wonderful day in our history.' Longingly she thought of this, then said briskly, 'In Cape Town the other day I walked about District Six. That could be made into one of the finest sections of Cape Town, but it's crowded with Coloureds. They must all be moved out.'

'To where, Johanna? Where?'

That line of discussion ended, but the three puritans were not finished with Maria's opening statement. 'They really are children of sin,' Detleef agreed. 'They're a rebuke to God-fearing Christians, a reminder of our fathers' transgressions.'

'Not our fathers,' Maria protested. 'It was sailors from the ships that stopped here.'

Detleef and his sister nodded. The existence of the Coloureds was an affront to them, and it was a blessing, the gathering felt, that the original Dutch and Huguenot settlers had not been involved. 'It was the sailors,' Detleef repeated, and as he thought of this blot on the nation he resolved to do something about it. Accordingly, when he returned to Cape Town and the session of Parliament, he labored far into the night, week after week, trying to devise some cauterization of this ugly moral wound.

When the year was well spent he discovered one area in which he could introduce reform, but it was so controversial that it would occupy major attention for five years. In 1910, when England had engineered Union between its colonies, two clauses in the enabling legislation were entrenched—that is, they were judged so vital that they could be altered only by a vote of two-thirds of the two Houses of Parliament sitting together. Section 137 protected English and Dutch (later Afrikaans) as languages of equal legal merit; Section 35 assured the Coloureds that they would always have the right to vote in Cape Province.

Although no Coloured men could stand for Parliament—that would be repugnant—they did vote on a common roll with the whites, casting their ballots for the white candidate who would best represent their interests. In 1948 more than fifty thousand had voted, almost all for Jan Smuts' party, and in seven crucial constituencies their vote defeated the Nationalists. They were a growing power, and the vote must be taken from them.

'They pollute the political process,' Detleef warned again and again. 'This is a white man's country, and to allow those damned Coloureds to

vote dilutes our purity.' He located parliamentarians to bring onto the
floor the bills he masterminded, but trouble ensued. 'It's that miserable
Section 35,' he growled to his women. 'I'm afraid we can't muster a
two-thirds vote.' He was right. When his men carried to the floor their
bill stripping Coloureds of their voting rights, it failed to win the majority required, and it seemed as if the attempt was dead, at least for the
1951 session.

But Detleef was resourceful, and spurred by a suggestion thrown
out by his sister, he convinced his supporters in Parliament to try a daring gambit: 'Because of changes in the laws governing the British Empire, Section 35 is no longer operative. We can pass our bill with only a
simple majority.'

With excitement and joy his men did just that, and the Coloureds
were disenfranchised. But the Appellate Division of the Supreme Court,
sitting in Bloemfontein away from the pressures of the Cape, declared
the new law unconstitutional, and 1951 ended with Coloureds still allowed to vote, a most offensive situation.

Detleef would not surrender, and his next move was downright ingenious. He did not dislike Coloureds personally; he knew some of excellent reputation and wished them well. But he was galled that these
offspring of sin should have equal rights with white people, and now he
came up with a master plan: 'Maria, I think I have it! We will super-
sede the Appellate Court!'

'I shouldn't think that would be possible. It's in the constitution.'

'We'll leave it there. What we'll do is establish Parliament itself as
the "High Court of the Nation." If the two Houses, sitting together, approve a law which they themselves have passed—and it seems to me
they always would, having just passed it—then it becomes law and the
Appellate Court can say nothing in the matter.'

It was clean and simple. It passed Parliament quickly and the High
Court, composed entirely of Nationalist members, reversed the decision
of the nation's highest court of justice. With blazing speed the
Coloureds were thrown off the common rolls, and with almost equal
speed the Appellate Court annulled the whole process, pronouncing it a
mockery. So 1952 ended in another defeat.

Elections in 1953 gave the government more Afrikaner seats in Parliament, so once more Detleef shepherded his bill toward a two-thirds
majority, and once more he failed. At this point the average man would
have quit, but Detleef was so offended by those who resisted his attempts to simplify matters that he barged ahead with still new devices.

As he told Johanna and Maria after this third disappointment: 'The damned Coloureds don't seem to realize that we're doing this for their own good. It's our job as white men to study the nation and determine what's best for all, and then to pass the necessary laws.'

'They don't really need the vote,' Maria agreed. 'They can't possibly be interested in the things that concern us. They should fall back into place and be quiet.'

Johanna, feeling her life slipping away, was more bitter: 'Detleef, you must eliminate them from national life. Clear them out of the cities. Keep them off the work force. They're an affront to the nation, and if you don't keep trying to get rid of them, I'll be ashamed of you.'

'You speak as if you wanted us to ship them out, the way we did the Chinese.'

'I'd like that.'

'But don't you see, Johanna, there's no place to ship them. They have no homeland. They're the bastards of the world, and we're stuck with them.'

'Well, think of something!'

'I will. I promise you I will, but I must have time to plan.'

National attention was diverted from the Coloured question by 'Virtue Triumphant,' a rather florid statue that was placed in front of the government buildings in Pretoria. It had been carved by a promising young Afrikaner much influenced by Michelangelo and sculptors of the Quattrocento; it showed a woman of rather heroic proportions fending off lions, pythons and a politician who looked remarkably like Hoggenheimer. As with the work of many great sculptors, the woman was nude.

Many Afrikaner housewives, especially those from the Transvaal country districts, questioned the propriety of such a statue, and Johanna van Doorn, now seventy-four, came rushing down to the Cape, where Parliament was in session, to share her outrage with Detleef: 'It's immoral! There's no place in the Bible that condones naked women. St. Paul is emphatic that they must remain covered.'

'I think that refers to wearing hats in church,' Detleef said.

'If he could see this statue, he'd include it, believe me.'

She got nowhere with Detleef, but her feeling was so intense that Maria said, 'When we return to Pretoria, I must see this thing.'

'You won't like it,' Johanna predicted, and later, when the two women went to inspect the offending sculpture, Maria was even more incensed than her sister-in-law, and when she reached her rooms she penned a sharp letter to an Afrikaans newspaper:

> All Afrikaner womankind is insulted by having such a statue in such a place. It is offensive to the spirit of the Bible and treats with contempt the noble traditions of our people. Women in Afrikaner statues should wear long dresses, like the ones shown in the Vrouemonument in Bloemfontein. For them to appear naked embarrasses not only all Afrikaner women, but also most of the men. The damage it does to children is incalculable. On behalf of all Afrikaner women, I demand that either the statue be taken down or that Virtue wear a dress.

Of course, the English-language press, always eager to embarrass its Afrikaner opposition, had a frolic with Mrs. van Doorn's proposals, and cartoons appeared showing Virtue wearing a Mother Hubbard, or a chain of fig leaves, or bending over to protect herself. One especially scurrilous cartoon depicted Oom Paul Kruger as this excellent statue, completely nude except for his top hat and one rather large oak leaf.

Foreign newspapers, ever on the alert for a story that would symbolize the curious happenings in South Africa, quoted Mrs. van Doorn's strictures about art, and when, under pressure, she gave an interview about the statue, editors had a joyous time:

> 'Ninety percent of Afrikaner women feel the way I do about that horrid statue. A few spineless art critics who defend it say that Michelangelo carved such statues for the prominent plazas in Italy. All I can say is that Michelangelo may be all right for Italians, who have a very low standard of morality, but he has no place in South Africa. Besides, what was this woman doing fighting a snake with no clothes on?'

She won her battle. The matter was resolved rather neatly—by converting 'Virtue Triumphant' into a man, who fought the same enemies naked but behind a shield that protected the sensibilities.

While his wife was defending the moral purity of the nation, Detleef was laboring yet again to save its political purity, and this time, with the help of some very able parliamentarians, he came up with a totally new stratagem, which he explained to the leadership in this way: 'No more struggling with minor problems. We take this thing head-on. We need a two-thirds majority in the Senate and can't get it. Simple. Create forty-one new senators guaranteed to vote our way. And if you're still afraid that the Supreme Court might overturn the vote these new men give us . . . Simple—add six more judges pledged to vote for us.'

It was, as he assured them, a simple solution, a steamroller so monstrous that any possible opposition would be crushed, and the government proceeded. It might have gone into effect without undue publicity except that a group of Afrikaner women with a social conscience united with a similar body of English women to activate a political-action committee called the Black Sash, as heroic a group as the world at that time knew. Against the full flood of national opinion, these women opposed every unlawful and restrictive measure of their government, never hysterically, never aimlessly. They protected people who could find no other protection and kept a relentless spotlight on the irresponsible acts of their government.

Their president was a forceful woman, Laura Saltwood of New Sarum, the Johannesburg residence of this important industrial family. Born in Salisbury, near the cathedral, she had met Colonel Frank Saltwood's son Noel under memorable circumstances. As a resident of Salisbury she knew the local Saltwoods, of course, and did not like them; Sir Evelyn, a staunch conservative, made such an ass of himself in Parliament that she and her brother Wexton vowed they would run a liberal candidate against him when they were old enough. Her brother went to Cambridge University, a site she loved; whenever an opportunity presented, she went up to visit with him and his brilliant associates, and while on such a visit in 1931 she met a quiet young man from Oxford to whom she was much attracted. 'It's so nice to be with you, when the others talk so much and say so little,' she told him, and he blushed. He was Noel Saltwood, of the South African branch, and after a leisurely courtship in two of England's most enchanting towns, Cambridge and Oxford, they were married.

She had the good luck to reach Johannesburg while Maud Turner Saltwood was still alive, and from that stalwart woman, who had done so much to make South Africa habitable, she acquired the custom of direct speech and timely intervention. Like her mother-in-law, whom she revered, she was afraid of nothing: literally, she hunted lions with the same verve that she tracked down the latest restrictive laws of Detleef van Doorn. He despised her for the opposition she continually mounted against his best projects, and as for her Black Sash, he believed it should be outlawed and its members thrown into jail. He would look into this possibility after he settled with the Coloureds.

For the present he fenced with Mrs. Saltwood, who had accurately identified him as a major force behind the previous legislation and the current effort to strip the Coloureds of their vote. She spoke at meetings, gave interviews, appeared on radio whenever possible, and maintained a constant scrutiny. She was such an effective opponent, that at one strategy session held in Detleef's Pretoria home, Johanna wanted to know why a woman like that should be allowed free speech. That was a relevant question, for which Detleef had a quick answer: 'Because this country is not a dictatorship. Your husband, Johanna, had dangerous ideas, about Hitler and all that, but men like Brongersma and me drew back. We did not want Hitler then, and we don't want him now.'

Johanna began to cry, thinking that her dead husband's martyrdom was being denigrated, but Detleef consoled her: 'We're aiming at the same goals, really, but by legal means. We will perform no un-Christian act, but in the end we'll have a regulated society. Almost exactly what Piet and I talked about years ago.'

In 1956 Detleef van Doorn engineered one more assault on the Coloureds, and this time, with a vastly enlarged Senate and a Supreme Court more than doubled, the law was passed by Parliament and certified by the Court, but Detleef's sense of triumph, to which he was entitled, was diminished by the severe illness of his sister. He was with her when she heard the joyous news that Coloureds were to be thrown off the common roll, first step in their total disfranchisement: 'It is our duty, Detleef, to make decisions. We must see that they are just, but we must also see that they are enforced strictly so that we retain control. I wish our father and mother could have seen this day.' She passed into a mumbling period, then called for Maria: 'Detleef lacks will power. When the time comes, he won't want to fight to take South Africa out of the Commonwealth. Pressure him, Maria. We must be free.' And she died, never for a moment perceiving that Coloureds and blacks might also want to be free.

In the sad wake of his sister's death Detleef worked diligently on the next chain of laws which would bind the nation together. Only whites could attend the great universities. Bantu education was severely revised, taking it away from religious organizations and missionaries and placing it under the control of politicians: 'Blacks must not be troubled with subjects which they have not the brain power to comprehend, or trained for jobs which will never exist for them. They should be taught only those skills needed to enable them to support the dominant society. Instruction should be in Afrikaans, since that is to be the language of the nation of which they will form a helpful part.'

He then directed his attention to living areas, for it angered him to see attractive spots in the big cities still occupied by Bantu. In sweeping regulations, which he drafted but which appeared over the signature of others, he authorized the evacuation of such areas and gave special attention to one particular eyesore in Johannesburg—Sophiatown—where he called in the bulldozers to start leveling the place; the black occupants were sent out into locations he had set up in the countryside. These blacks, all of whom worked for white families and establishments in Johannesburg, joined the masses of workers herded together southwest of the City of Gold. High-speed railway lines soon carried nearly half a million black servants into the city at dawn, out to the countryside at dusk.

In 1957 Detleef played no part in two major decisions, but he supported the men who made them: 'God Save the Queen' was dropped as the national anthem, to be replaced by 'Die Stem van Suid-Afrika,' a fine, stirring song; and the Union Jack no longer flew as a national flag. Maria was especially gratified by these changes, for they proved to her and others that the country was at last becoming the Afrikaner republic it should always have been: 'The bad years since 1795, when the English first intruded, are almost over. I was just a little ashamed of myself for cheering when Jan Christian Smuts died, but I was glad to see him go. He betrayed the Afrikaner, and it was only just that he should have died rejected by his own people.'

And then the euphoria of the Van Doorns was shattered by an act they could not comprehend. Their son Marius, an excellent rugby player at Stellenbosch, with every promise of graduating to Springbok status, was selected to be a Rhodes scholar and offered a sumptuous grant of money to study at Oxford.

'It's reassuring to know he was eligible,' Detleef told his friends in Parliament. 'He's one of the best.'

'Will he accept?'

'Certainly not. There's talk of his being selected for the next tour of New Zealand.'

'A Springbok?' the men asked excitedly.

One man who followed sports avidly broke in: 'Detleef's too modest. I've heard rumors that they might choose Marius to captain the side.'

'Well,' the father said deprecatingly, 'he'd be a little young for that. Those New Zealanders . . .' And the rest of that day was spent reminiscing about the 1921 tour and the way Detleef had handled, or not handled, Tom Heeney, the Hard Rock from Down Under.

Maria was pleased that her son should have received such recognition from the Rhodes committee, but like her husband, she said she would be offended if he showed any signs of accepting: 'We don't need a son of ours going to Oxford . . . like some Saltwood with divided loyalty . . . living here and calling Salisbury home.'

Both the Van Doorns wrote to Marius that night, congratulating him on the honor, but telling him also that they had heard whispers of his becoming a Springbok, perhaps even the captain, but before their letters could be delivered, he appeared in Cape Town to inform them that he had accepted the scholarship and would be leaving soon for England.

Detleef was so shocked he could hardly speak: 'You're not . . . passing up a Springbok blazer . . . for a Rhodes scholarship?' When Marius nodded, Detleef cried, 'But, son! A scholarship comes every day. To be a rugger Springbok, that comes once in a lifetime.'

Marius was firm. He was twenty-one, taller than his father, and without the bull neck. He played not as a rugged forward in the scrum but as a fleet, elusive back. His intellectual brilliance, inherited mostly from his maternal grandfather, Christoffel Steyn, shone in his face, and he could not mask his delight at going to Oxford and competing with the best.

'But, Marius,' his father pleaded. 'You can learn things out of books anywhere, but if you have a real chance to captain a Springbok side— that would be immortality.'

'There's more to life than rugby,' the young man said.

'What?' Detleef demanded. 'I've done many things in my life. Seen the camps. Had the prize bull at the Rand Agricultural. Fought with De Groot and Christoffel. And watched the triumph of my people. But nothing comes close to stepping on a rugby field in New Zealand wearing the Springbok jersey. For God's sake, Marius, don't throw away that opportunity for something Cecil Rhodes devised as a trick to seduce our Afrikaner lads.'

'I can still play rugby. I'll play for Oxford.'

'You'll what?' Detleef looked at his wife in blank stupor.

'Did you say you'd play for Oxford?' Maria asked.

'Yes, if I can make the team.'

'A man who could be a Springbok . . . playing for Oxford?' Detleef choked a bit, then said, 'You realize that the way things fall, you could one day be playing against South Africa?'

'It's only a game.'

Detleef rose to his full choleric height: 'It is not a game. It's how we instilled patriotism in this nation. I would rather be captain of a Springbok team in New Zealand than prime minister.'

No argument could dissuade Marius, and when, three years later, he informed his parents by cable that he was going to marry an English girl, they wept for two days.

The marriage of Marius van Doorn, Oriel athlete and scholar, to Clare Howard was solemnized on 20 March 1960 at the home of her parents in a village northwest of Oxford. His parents were not present, for although they had been invited, they refused to set foot on English soil, and this accounted for the fact that they were at home in Pretoria the next day when South Africa was torn nearly apart by a fusillade of police bullets at Sharpeville, a black township near the Vaal River.

For the past year black indignation had swelled against the laws that placed increasingly severe restrictions on black freedoms: Albert Luthuli, soon to win the Nobel Peace Prize, had been confined to his home district for five years; African women marching in demonstrations had been baton-charged; in the Transkei and Zululand, uprisings had left dozens dead and injured.

At Sharpeville the blacks decided to try peaceful protest: they would turn in their passbooks and offer themselves for arrest, holding it to be an insult to carry such identification in their own country; some ten thousand converged on the police station. Without a warning shot to turn them back, the front line of police opened fire on the crowd. Sixty-seven were left dead and more than one hundred and eighty men, women and children were wounded.

'It was inevitable,' Detleef said when he heard the news. 'We do what is right for the country and they refuse to cooperate.' When he heard that blacks were massing in various other cities, he told Maria that any uprising must be stamped on without mercy. He was not a vicious man, but he did believe in order, and when Parliament, after due deliberation, decided that the country should be organized a certain

way, it was everyone's duty to conform: 'You cannot have Bantu deciding whether they will obey the laws or not obey them. The laws have
been passed. They must be obeyed.' It was his opinion that white agitators, especially women like Laura Saltwood, were responsible for these
disturbances, and he began pondering ways whereby people like her
could be restrained.

Detleef was sixty-five and considering retirement, but the chain of
dramatic events in 1960 convinced him that his lasting achievements
still lay ahead. Not long after Sharpeville a maniac, overwrought by the
anxieties thrust upon him by recent changes in national life, fired a re-
volver point-blank into Prime Minister Verwoerd's head. Miraculously,
that brilliant political leader survived, and this, said the Van Doorns,
proved that God wanted him preserved for noble tasks. In October,
Verwoerd accomplished one of them: he engineered a plebiscite which
authorized the government to break all relations with the English crown
and declare itself a republic.

With enormous vigor Detleef and his wife had worked at erasing all
vestiges of what they termed 'a century of English domination.' Earlier,
a series of modest changes had been made—no more knighthoods like
Sir Richard Saltwood's; Jan van Riebeeck's face on coinage instead of
king or queen; *lieutenant* changed to *veldkornet*—but now Detleef
moved among his colleagues pressuring them for the most important
change of all.

'We must eliminate the last remnant of past degradations,' he
preached. 'We must leave the British Commonwealth of Nations, for it's
only an English stratagem to keep us subservient.'

Many who heard him say this were aghast that he should carry his
obsession so far: 'When we voted to break ties with the monarchy, we
certainly did not intend to leave the Commonwealth.' To such objections he had a rigid answer: 'When you start on an honorable course,
pursue it to the end. Our end is complete freedom.' And when he came
home at night to discuss these matters with his wife, she supported him:
'They shot my father. They killed my people in the camp. We must end
every association.'

In March 1961, when the Van Doorns were at Vrymeer, the glorious news arrived. An assistant at Pretoria telephoned: 'Sir! Sir! We're
free at last. Verwoerd has taken us out of the Commonwealth!'

Detleef was cautious, so before he shared the triumph with Maria he
made two calls to confirm the news, and when he was satisfied that his
country was at last free, he did not run exultantly to his wife or start a

celebration. Instead, he left the house and walked gravely to the largest lake, where blesbok were grazing, and he looked across to where the hartebeest hut of General de Groot had stood in the bad years following the end of war, and he could hear the old warrior predicting: 'You are the generation that will win this country back. You will win the war that your father and I lost.'

Raising his fist, as he had done years ago when celebrating a rugby victory, he shouted, 'Old man! We've won! We've won!'

Detleef was retired now, with no office in either Cape Town or Pretoria to report to, and he might have rested, for the laws he had sponsored had specified proper behavior for all residents of the republic, but sloth was alien to his puritanical nature, and he began to fret over another mammoth task which he felt needed to be done: 'I could die happy, Maria, knowing that we have our great file in Pretoria showing everyone's proper racial classification. The green identity cards are good, too. But what we really need is an identification document covering a person's entire life—everything he does. He'd carry it with him at all times, so that the authorities could see exactly who he was and what he's done.'

The small booklet he devised, 4¾ x 3½ inches, was a masterpiece of sound planning. It contained forty-eight pages—which summarized a life and provided in one convenient place all kinds of helpful data. Long coded numbers indicated racial derivation, status and domicile. Space was provided for a series of photographs covering different ages and styles. Four pages were given to marriage records, with the printed assurance that if the holder was embarrassed by a proliferation of divorces, she or he could apply for a new booklet and start fresh. Included was a complete record of immunizations, allergies, blood group and any other medical information that might prove helpful to an ambulance attendant or a hospital nurse. It was also a driver's license, reserving pages 18 through 21 for police endorsements as to arrests; it was also a license to carry firearms, with four full pages to record weapons. Pages 26 through 46 were marked 'For official use,' without any clue as to purpose, but available for insertion of whatever information the authorities might in the future wish to include. The last two pages contained a voting record, and a pocket at the rear was to hold a list of all real estate owned.

Every white citizen, under Detleef's plan, was obliged to carry this document at all times. 'Now we will know who everyone is,' he said, 'and we can have an orderly state.'

He was congratulating himself one afternoon when Reverend Brongersma, white-haired and failing, stopped by to pass the time of day. He no longer preached, but he did try to follow the activities of the Broederbond; along with the church, that fellowship had been the high point of his life: 'I often think back to the vigorous days, Detleef. You and Frykenius, me and Piet Krause. That was a lively foursome. We accomplished so much.'

Then he said, almost abruptly, 'Call Maria. I want to see the girl whose life I saved.' And when stout, squat Maria came into the room, he rose and kissed her. 'I rode all the way to Stellenbosch to tell this young fellow he had to marry you, and this fine Christian home resulted. I wish I could have visited Marius before he married that English girl. Now he can never join the Broederbond . . . never play a major role in our society.'

That was regrettable. He talked of Piet, too, then said something which disturbed Detleef profoundly: 'Piet was a radical on the left, and he destroyed himself. You were a radical on the right, and you've destroyed many of our freedoms.'

'What do you mean?'

'Detleef has worked only for good,' Maria said defensively.

'I'm sure he has,' the old man said, 'but I fear he got things out of balance. The fellowship of Christ is meant to bring freedom, not restraint.'

'But society has to be disciplined,' Detleef protested. 'You know that.'

'I do. But if we read the Old Testament too grimly, we miss the lovemaking, the adventure, the wild triumphs, the dancing and the sound of flutes.' He shook his head. 'I was to blame, too. I sought a new world so forcefully I forgot the goodness in all worlds. Do you know my favorite verse in all the Bible, now that I approach death? "Word wakker, word wakker, Debora: Word wakker, word wakker, hef 'n lied aan." *Deborah, sing us a song!* You have killed the singing, Detleef.'

When he left, Maria said, 'Poor old man, his mind's wandering.'

A few moments later men rushed into the house, shouting, 'The prime minister's been assassinated!'

The Van Doorns, trembling, rushed to the radio. Detleef tuned it so nervously that he could not locate a station, so Maria took over and found the awful verification: 'Today as he was attending his duties in

the House of Parliament, our prime minister, Hendrik Verwoerd, was
stabbed to death by an assassin who approached him in the guise of a
uniformed pageboy. Three knife wounds entered the throat and chest
and he died before he could reach the hospital.'

In darkness the Van Doorns sat silent, contemplating the nemesis
that seemed at times to hang over their nation: a splendid patriot assassinated in the halls of government; foreigners making accusatory
speeches at the United Nations; blacks obstinately refusing to accept
their assigned positions; and Marius married to an English girl.

In the days that followed, Detleef's tightly organized world seemed
to fall apart, because the very laws which he had structured to defend
the state had been used to destroy its elected leader. 'It seems as if God
Himself willed this tragedy,' Detleef wailed, and in mounting fury he
shared the evidence with his wife.

'Who killed him? A man who should never have been allowed entrance into the country. A nobody from Moçambique.'

'How did he sneak in?' Maria demanded, voicing the anger of two
and a half million Afrikaners.

'You won't believe it, but four people I trained myself—immigration
officials who were supposed to check all entering aliens. The man had a
criminal record. It was in his papers and no one saw it.'

'But how could such a man get a job as messenger, right in the heart
of Parliament?'

Detleef shuddered. 'His papers specifically stated that he was half-
white, half-black. Everyone in Moçambique knew it. Our embassy knew
it. But what happens? He walks in here bold as brass, and my office
gives him an identity card stating that he was white. After that, everything was easy.'

'But why did he want to kill our prime minister?'

Van Doorn lowered his head and covered his eyes. He did not want
to answer this ugly question, but in a weak voice he confided: 'He said
he became bitter over the fact that as a man with a white card, he was
forbidden to have sexual relations with a Coloured girl he liked.'

In a sullen rage Detleef stormed about the kitchen in which his early
lessons had been learned. He could hear the voice of old General de
Groot, who had never stopped fighting. He listened to Piet Krause, who
had such a clear vision of the future. And from the corner came the
powerful voice of his sister Johanna, who had been the backbone of the
family and of the nation. He was embittered by the sardonic trick

whereby his own laws had been used against him, but he could find nothing wrong with those laws.

'What we must do,' he told his wife, 'is pass stricter laws. And then enforce them better.'

XIII.
Apartheid

THE complex fabric of old custom and new law woven by Deetleef van Doorn and his peers came to be known as *apartheid*, a classic example of the misfortune Afrikaners had in naming things. The word meant *apartness*, and did not appear in older dictionaries of the language; it was invented, and reflected their belief that God willed the races be kept separate, each progressing properly at its own speed within its own confines.

The word should have been pronounced *apart-hate*, appropriately ominous, but by foreigners it was usually *apart-hite*, which is merely ugly. Either pronunciation was unfortunate, for it connoted offensive intentions which its authors did not contemplate.

As the years progressed, so did the names used to describe apartheid: *guardianship, separate development, separate freedoms, separate amenities, indigenous development, multinational development, self-determination, plural democracy*. No matter how diligently they tried, the architects of these laws were unable to erase the first, correct name they had given their grand design.

No one could study the instrumental role played by Van Doorn in drafting these laws without being impressed by the planner's oft-repeated assertion: 'I acted from the best and most honest motives, and without personal rancor, in accordance with His will.'

He certainly wished no harm to the Coloureds, Asians and blacks whose lives he circumscribed; he often said, 'Some of my best friends are the Bantu who work on my farm,' and although it was true that he had always refused to alter the conditions under which they worked, he did constantly examine his Christian conscience when deciding what was right and wrong for them. Often he paid them higher wages than they might have got elsewhere. He insisted that he did not regard them as inherently inferior human beings, only different; he did not want to dominate them, only act as their well-intentioned guardian.

But even honest intentions sometimes create problems which the promulgator of a law could not have foreseen; apartheid became so pervasive that it dominated the lives of ordinary people from birth to death to resurrection.

AT BIRTH

The Afrikaner was never afraid to fly against the winds of history, and usually with success. Other nations had learned to utilize, and sometimes condone, the mixture of their races, with enviable results. No more beautiful people exist in the world than the languorous, able Chinese-Polynesians of the South Seas. The black-white mixture in Brazil produces offspring of extraordinary quality, while the Japanese-white children of Hawaii are exceptional in both talent and appearance. The Indian-Spanish mix in Mexico is a good one, and so is the Indian-black in Trinidad.

The Afrikaner saw the hand of God in the creation of his small nation, and was determined to isolate it from admixtures that would dilute its purity. Indeed, it was difficult to find a more homogeneous, handsome and dedicated body of people than those Afrikaners nurtured on the veld and in the valleys of the continent's southern tip. Of course, the pure Dutch strain had been infused with contributions from the gifted Huguenots who filtered in, never many in number, and with heavier contributions from the Germans, who at times actually outnumbered the Dutch. But these were peoples of roughly the same physical and mental inheritance. Additions from the English were inescapable; they came to form a large part of the white community. And it would have been impossible for the Afrikaner not to draw, too, from the Hottentot, the black and the Coloured. In pioneer days he acknowledged this, but his descendants were determined to prevent any further penetration of their white laager.

His jealous guarding of blood purity did exact a social cost, for the Coloured peoples that had arisen, here as elsewhere in the world, had to be savagely excluded from national life. Not only were they forbidden to intermingle with whites socially; they were also cut off economically, professionally, creatively, until the loss to the nation was incalculable. How much poorer the United States would have been without the contributions of persons whose light skins would cause them to be classified as Coloured in South Africa: Frederick Douglass, Ralph Bunche, Martin Luther King, O. J. Simpson, Harry Belafonte, Lena Horne, Diahann Carroll, Senator Brooke and Congressman Powell. Or how the world's creative pool would have been diminished without the work of Coloureds such as the poet Pushkin, the painter Pissaro, and the flamboyant storyteller Dumas.

South Africa silenced in the cradle all such potential contributions from its Malay-Hottentot-black-Afrikaner-English-Coloureds, and its loss was never greater than when it rejected young Heather Botha, twenty-three years old and of such a mixture. She was exotic, like a palm tree bending beside a lagoon, or a tawny pearl held in a Balinese hand. She combined the most attractive features of all the wanderers who had figured in her background: the fiery-tempered Malay slave woman who had fought her Compagnie master for nine years, then slept with his son for eleven; the Dutch sea captain who had fought storms in too many seas to give a damn about what Compagnie officials said regarding fraternization with girls of mixed breed; the Hottentot herdsman who had protected with a gun the forty-seven cattle he owned, plus the fifty-seven stolen from Compagnie herds; the black warrior who had defended himself against both Zulu and white man; the fair-faced English officer, India-bound, whispering love to a young Coloured maiden beside a brook on the slopes of Table Mountain. Heather was the child of lusty forebears, and all of them would have been proud of her, for as she said on various occasions, echoing her Dutch sea-captain ancestor, 'I don't give a damn.'

At the university in 1953 she had openly dated white men, despite warnings from the faculty that she might fall into danger and from the police that such action was criminal. It would have been difficult for her to refuse the numerous invitations she received from white students, for she was a spectacular young woman and one of the liveliest on campus. She had a rowdy laugh, a provocative manner of walking, and a smile which showed white teeth against a golden complexion.

But she was condemned. At birth she had been classified Coloured,

which meant that for the remainder of her life this would be her outstanding characteristic, outweighing her intelligence, her beauty and her
capacity to contribute to society. Where she lived, the quality of her
early education, what job she could hold, whom she could fall in love
with, and the role she could play in South African life were all sharply
proscribed. Everyone in the nation would know Heather's limits, everyone, that is, except Heather.

At twenty the police arrested the young student for 'inciting white
men to have interracial carnal intercourse or to commit an act of inde-
cency,' and rarely was a miscegenation charge more correct—she certainly was tempting, to white men or those of any other color—or more
fallacious, for it was not she who did the tempting; it was the men. On
that charge she was given three months in prison, suspended on condition that the tempting cease. She was warned that if she was again
brought before a magistrate on a charge of immorality, she would suffer
the consequences.

'I don't give a damn,' she told her fellow students after the trial, and
continued to behave with an insolence that was charming to those who
knew her, insulting to those who merely watched. She went where she
wished in Cape Town, ate wherever her crowd stopped for food, and
when late October came around she frequented the beaches reserved for
whites, where her striking figure, her sun-tanned skin and her lively
manner gained attention, if not always approval. Twice white sun-
bathers warned her that in using beaches legally reserved for their
group, she was breaking the law. She tossed her head and smiled at
them.

At Christmas vacation, which marked the height of the summer season, Heather was sunning herself at a white beach when Craig Saltwood, aged twenty, came home from Oriel College at Oxford for a visit
with his family, and it was not remarkable that he met her. They talked
about college classes, and of recent developments in South Africa. He
poured warm sand upon her legs, then gallantly brushed it off, one grain
at a time. She told him to be careful where his fingers went, and soon
they were kissing in hidden corners where the police would not see
them, and on the third afternoon young Saltwood drove her home in his
Morris Minor.

He was delighted with her parents. Simon Botha was a skilled
builder, head of his own construction company. His wife, Deborah, was
a quiet homemaker who took pride in caring for Simon and their three
children, of whom Heather was the oldest. Mrs. Botha was often to be

found in the kitchen of their home in Athlone making the boboties and sweet confections her family had always prepared with elegance. Like her daughter, she had a glowing complexion, but unlike her, she was shy.

'I often worry about Heather,' she said softly. 'Going to the white beach. She's bound to get into trouble.'

'I'm not trouble,' Craig said.

'For my daughter you are,' Mrs. Botha replied.

Then Mr. Botha talked about the letting of recent contracts to build houses in a new township, and of how white officials discriminated against Coloured artisans, awarding large constructions to certain white builders who really lacked expertise and experience. 'They won't let me build those new boxes, yet when one of the great old houses like Trianon needs attention, they call me.' He laughed. 'Then it's "Botha, can you fix that gable in the old way?" Or "Botha, we want to restore that barn built when Jan Compagnie was here. We've got to protect our cultural heritage." And who protects it? I do.'

There was much laughter in the Botha home, and many books and quite a few records by Wilhelm Fürtwangler and Arturo Toscanini, plus a shelf of His Master's Voice operas. The Bothas spoke English, but were at ease in Afrikaans, and on Sundays they worshipped at the Dutch Reformed church (Coloured) where Simon and Deborah had been married and their children confirmed.

The Korean War had just ended, and Simon spoke proudly of the South African fighter planes in the Far East, but he could not mask his disappointment when reflecting on his own four-year service during World War II. 'Jan Smuts came personally to thank our Coloured unit when it was over, and I can still see the Oubaas standing not ten feet from me, telling us we were needed back home to build a new South Africa. "God bless you all," he said. "May you prosper in peace even more than you did in these years of conflict." Fifty thousand men like me fought against Hitler. For freedom, they said. But when we got home, Smuts forgot every promise he made, and now they're even trying to take away our right to vote.'

When Heather saw how sympathetically Craig participated with her family, her response was so warm that all suspected that she might be spending the next nights with him in the Sea Point boardinghouse he was using for his vacation, but on the second night a suspicious woman in a room opposite telephoned the police to warn them that a crime was being committed in Room 318. The case was handed to two policemen, a sergeant fifty-five years old who was revolted by such duty, and a gung-ho young fellow of twenty-two from a country district who was greatly excited by the prospect of bursting into rooms where nude couples were in bed. At four-fifteen one morning, having kept the premises under observation for several nights, they crashed their way into the room, took photographs, and arrested the naked couple, the older policeman blushing with shame.

'The sheets! Don't forget the sheets!' cried the younger man as he watched Heather while she dressed, and the sergeant was forced to strip the bed and wrap the sheets in a bundle. The investigators would send the linen to a medical research institute, where highly paid technicians using ultra-modern equipment would ascertain scientifically whether miscegenation had truly occurred.

'I'm sorry for this,' the older policeman apologized as he led the lovers down the corridor and past a doorway in which a triumphant woman demonstrated her pride in having served as guardian of her nation's morals.

'You pitiful creature,' Heather said to the watchdog, and this 'act of arrogance and spite against a decent citizen' was cited against her at the trial.

'Insolent and unrepentant, even though guilty of a major crime,' the magistrate thundered at her, after which he delivered a sentence standard in these cases: 'Craig Saltwood, you come of a good family and have a respectable university record. You have clearly been influenced by alien ideas in England, and your behavior is a disgrace. The example set by you and other white men of your ilk cannot but be seen as shocking in the eyes of decent Coloured people, whose daughters must be protected against such liaisons. Three months, sentence suspended for three years' good behavior.' The magistrate glowered. 'But if you ever again consort with any woman outside your own race, you will go to jail.'

He studied Heather for a moment, balefully, then said, 'You have chosen to ignore the warning I issued at your previous appearance. I have pity for what your parents must feel as a result of this disgraceful act. But the court has no alternative. Prison, three months.'

It was assumed that the white man, feeling the sting of censure from his society, would slink off and keep his mouth shut. But Craig Saltwood was so outraged by the gross unfairness of Heather's sentence that instead of hurrying back to Oxford and forgetting his vacation escapade, he phoned his mother and asked her, 'Will you help correct a grave injustice?'

'I would like nothing better,' Laura Saltwood said.

She had already battled, with little success, for the rights of black and Coloured ex-servicemen and was appalled by the injustices that were being perpetrated under the new laws promulgated by the Nationalists since their 1948 victory. When Craig explained how he had been excused and Heather thrown into jail, she was outraged.

'Clear up one thing, Craig. Is she a prostitute?'

'Hell no! She didn't entice me, like the court said. I chased her.'

'You visited her home?'

'Had dinner with her parents. As I would with any girl I liked.'

'Isn't her father Simon Botha, who restores the old Cape Dutch houses?'

'He is.'

That was all Laura Saltwood needed. Convening the small group of women who had joined her in her efforts to protect the rights of ex-servicemen, she laid the facts before them, and they were disgusted, but when she suggested ventilating the story in the newspapers, a Mrs. van Rensburg asked her if she thought this prudent: 'Hasn't your son suffered enough publicity?'

'We Saltwoods have never worried much about that,' Laura said, and she hurried to Cape Town, where she poured out her anger to the *Argus* and the *Times*. She visited Heather's parents and told them to be of good courage, but she also advised them that if her fight to get this infamous sentence revoked was successful, Heather should leave the country.

'And go where?' Deborah Botha asked sadly.

'Canada. There they behave like human beings.'

She also visited Heather in jail, ignoring the snide remarks the authorities threw at her when she sought permission. She found Heather to be the kind of young woman a mother hopes her son will meet—attractive, strong and with a robust sense of humor. 'We'll get you out of here, Heather.'

'In three months,' the girl joked.

'I mean out of the country. You must get leave.'

'I like it here.'

'You have no future in South Africa. Elsewhere you could lead a normal life.'

'I lead a pretty normal one here.'

'In a prison cell? For loving a young man? Don't be a fool.'

Heather had only a week to ponder this advice. In that time Craig Saltwood returned to Oxford, and his mother sought out the one person she thought would listen to her, Detleef van Doorn, chairman of the Committee on Racial Affairs, architect of the new laws. He did listen to her, attentively, then patiently explained that white South Africa had to protect its racial purity against the hordes that were trying to destroy it: 'Heather Botha's sentence is appropriate to the grave damage she might have done if she gave birth to yet another Coloured child.'

'What about my son's crime?'

'She tempted him,' and he cited several instances from the Bible in which honest young Israelites were tempted by the daughters of Canaan, and when Mrs. Saltwood smiled indulgently, he reached in his desk and produced an English Bible, which contained many paper markers. Searching for the applicable one, he opened to Genesis 28:1, which he read in sonorous English: ' "Thou shalt not take a wife of the daughters of Canaan." ' Closing the Bible triumphantly, he stared at Mrs. Saltwood.

'He did not, so far as I know, intend taking Miss Botha as his wife.'

Van Doorn, like any proper puritan, was incensed by this flippancy, but after a moment's silence, he said quietly, 'Mrs. Saltwood, if you continue along the path you've chosen, you'll find yourself in great difficulty.'

'No,' she said evenly, 'I shall find myself raising merry hell wherever I can about Heather Botha's disgraceful sentencing.' Laura was a resolute woman who feared nothing, who intended her closing years to be meaningful. The contributions of her family to this nation had not been minimal, and she did not propose surrendering her moral positions to the judgment of Afrikaner Nationalists, whom she considered excessively bigoted.

Van Doorn, looking at her determined face thrust forward toward his, could imagine that he was confronting Hilary Saltwood, that first and worst of the difficult clan. Whenever the trekboers tangled with that demented missionary, they had come away scarred, and Detleef suspected that in any open contest with Laura Saltwood, he would be scarred too.

'I'll talk to the proper authorities about commuting her sentence,' he said.

'As of today?'

'I can't speak for others.' Then he dropped his voice and pleaded with his difficult visitor: 'Could we keep this a secret between the two of us?'

'We certainly shall. Detleef, I knew you were a man of common sense.'

'No, I'm a poor Boer, madam, incapable of combating you bedon-derde Saltwoods.'

Heather was set free, and six months later, on a visit to Cape Town, Laura found the young woman packing. 'I'm off to Canada,' the girl said happily, and she kissed Laura for having shown her how a free woman should behave.

She took up residence in the best of Canadian cities, Toronto, where her style and beauty attracted people of diverse qualities, including several young men captivated by her exotic appearance and spirited wit. Friends helped her locate a job as secretary to a firm with overseas connections, where her facility with languages proved an asset.

In Toronto she was prized for those qualities which at home had made her a criminal: a saucy indifference to outworn custom and an infectious acceptance of people, whatever their station. She was free to contribute to Canadian life to the extent of her capabilities, but she never became pompous or pontifical. When well-meaning travelers tried to inform her about current happenings in South Africa, she smiled graciously and said, 'I no longer give a damn what those poor sick people do to themselves down there.'

But she did care, for she never threw away a small green plastic identity card which proved she had been a South African citizen. In red letters it also informed the world that she was COLOURED-KLEURLING.

Heather Botha married a young Canadian lawyer, had three fine children and became a patron of the musical arts in Toronto. She kept the plastic card at the bottom of a drawer in her bedroom as a sober reminder of the prison from which she had escaped.

AT SCHOOL

At Venloo there developed alongside the school founded after the Anglo-Boer War by Mr. Amberson, the rugby player, a girls' school with a notable reputation for producing excellent Afrikaans-speaking graduates who did well at university. It had a patriotic tradition of which its students and teachers were proud. Said the principal, Roelf

Sterk, 'My grandfather started this school in a cattle shed back in 1913, when our people were in the years of their suffering. He had no money and his scholars had none, either, but he gathered girls from the neighborhood and told them, "We will not be able to build a free nation in which Afrikaners can live in dignity unless you future mothers master the skills practiced by the English. You must learn to figure and write and reason. You must study." I now tell you the same thing. We've won our rightful place in the government of this land, but to keep ahead of those English, we must study as never before.'

He was especially proud of the way in which two girls in Standard Two took his lectures to heart. Petra Albertyn, aged nine, and Minna van Valck, aged ten, were the kind of students teachers pray for. They were eager and attentive; they behaved themselves without being subdued; they did well in classes requiring memory, but just as well in singing and drawing; and in whatever good thing was afoot, they could be depended upon to take the lead. In addition, as if God sometimes gave certain chosen persons too much, each child was unusually attractive—Petra a handsome dark-haired girl, and Minna a striking blonde with classic Dutch features.

It was arithmetic that started the trouble. Minna, being older than Petra, excelled in most branches of study, which in no way distressed the latter, who told her parents, 'I love Minna. She's so sweet and kind.' But in arithmetic little Petra had uncanny skill; she was really quite brilliant, and her teacher, a woman from Pretoria University who recognized brains when she viewed them in action, reported: 'This girl is a precious little genius.' Obviously, she received highest marks, well ahead of her friend Minna.

This did not disturb Minna, for she told her mother, 'I don't like numbers anyway, and I'm not very good at them.'

'But you allowed Petra to excel,' Mrs. van Valck complained with some irritation. 'Have you no pride?'

'I beat her in everything else!' Minna exclaimed, but her mother suspected that something might have gone amiss at the school, and she was determined to ascertain whether or not her brilliant daughter had been improperly treated. Accordingly, she marched to the school and demanded to see the principal.

Roelf Sterk was accustomed to meeting distraught parents; in fact, he rather liked it when they thought enough of their daughters' progress to interrogate him, but he was not prepared for the harshness with which Mrs. van Valck assailed him: 'I'm convinced that Minna must have done better than this Petra, whoever she is, because I myself corrected her exercise book every night.'

'You mean, you helped her?'

'I did not say that. I said that when her work was done I checked it to be sure she understood the problems. And she never had an incorrect solution.'

'That's why she received such a high mark,' the principal explained.

'But this Petra received a higher. My daughter was penalized . . .'

'Mrs. van Valck,' the principal explained patiently, 'in Petra Albertyn we have a near-genius in arithmetic. She's extraordinary. There's no way your daughter could equal her in this one field. Remember, Mrs. van Valck, Minna got highest in all her other subjects . . .'

Mrs. van Valck was still not satisfied and demanded to see who this superior child was, so Dr. Sterk consented, hoping in this way to defuse the mother's suspicions. Since Petra, like many of the scholars in this school, lived in a town many miles away, she stayed in a dormitory, which differentiated her from other children like Minna, who stayed at home, and this aroused Mrs. van Valck's suspicions: 'Who is she? Why does she come so far to school?'

Patiently Dr. Sterk explained that more than two-thirds of his best students came from considerable distances: 'It was the same in my grandfather's day. Most of those first scholars who earned this school its reputation, well, they came here by wagon in January and never returned home till June.'

The simplest way for Mrs. van Valck to see what was happening in the school was for her to peek in the door of the classroom, but when she reached that spot from which this would have been possible, Dr. Sterk pushed open the door, interrupted the class, and announced: 'This is Minna's mother.' The students rose and bowed, whereupon Dr. Sterk pointed to a girl in the first row, saying, 'And this is Minna's good friend, Petra Albertyn.'

Later, when he testified before the Race Classification Board, he would recall: 'When Mrs. van Valck first saw Petra Albertyn her jaw dropped and she froze. I noticed it at the time but could think of no reason for this strange behavior.'

That morning in the classroom she said nothing, just stared at Petra, then hastened from the school, going straight to the magistrate's court, where she swept past clerks, burst into his room, and dropped into a chair. 'Leopold,' she said, 'there's a Coloured girl in Minna's school.'

'Not likely,' her husband, the magistrate of Venloo, said.

'Leopold, I saw her. Not ten minutes ago. If that girl isn't a Hotnot, I'm not a Potgieter.' She used her maiden name, one of the most revered in Afrikaner history, as verification of her own pure lineage.

'Mother,' her husband said quietly, 'Dr. Sterk does not allow Coloureds into his school. The law forbids it. Parents have to show their white I.D. cards before any child is accepted. Sterk and all his teachers are most circumspect in such matters. Now you go—'

'Leopold! This Coloured girl has become Minna's closest friend. Minna wanted to bring her to sleep in our home last week.'

'Are you still angry about the arithmetic grade? Forget this silly accusation, and let's go home.'

That night the Van Valcks interrogated Minna, who said, 'Well, she's darker than me. But she talks like me.'

'You mustn't say anything about this, Minna. This is an important secret, but tomorrow ask her about her parents. Where do they live? What do they do?'

So Minna became a spy, and after much interrogation, was able to report to her parents: 'Her family is all right. Her father is foreman in a garage. Her mother runs a store. She says that's where she learned to add so fast, in the store.'

This did not appease Mrs. van Valck, who arranged for her husband to visit the school so that he, too, could see the suspected child, and when he did, his jaw dropped and he would utter no further words inside the school, but when he joined his wife in their car he said, 'My God! That girl is Coloured.'

The Van Valcks stayed awake most of that night, trying to decide what decent course they must pursue. For a Coloured child to pass as white was immoral, illegal, and crucially dangerous to their daughter, since the two were not only thrown together, but had established bonds of friendship, if not downright love. A thing like this could ruin a white girl, could tarnish her for life if it became known in the community. And it was not only the Van Valck family that was endangered; any school had to be constantly protective of its reputation, and the easiest way to lose it would be for it to harbor children of the wrong color.

Toward morning the Van Valcks decided that they must place this difficult problem in the lap of Dr. Sterk, a man of demonstrated competence and a stout defender of Afrikanerdom. Indeed, many supposed that he must be the head of the local Broederbond. So after Minna was safely in her classes, they drove inconspicuously to the school and slipped in to the principal's office. 'Dr. Sterk,' Mrs. van Valck said sternly, 'we have reason to believe that Petra Albertyn is Coloured.'

He choked. 'Mevrou van Valck! That's a serious charge to make.'

'We're making it. That girl is not white.'

'Impossible.'

And then something happened that sent a chill down his spine. The two Van Valcks simply sat there, firm in their chairs, their fists clenched, staring at him. They said nothing, made no threats, just waited. Finally he coughed, then said, 'You really are serious about this.'

'We are,' Leopold van Valck said.

'You're charging Petra Albertyn with being Coloured?'

'We are.'

'You're aware of the grave consequences? To the girl? To her parents? To the school?'

'We are.'

'Let me consult with her teachers.'

'That's not necessary,' Mrs. van Valck snapped. 'You can tell by looking at her that she's trying to pass. And she's endangering our daughter.'

'I need time to consider this,' he said firmly. 'Now you return home and I'll visit you tonight, after I've spoken with my people.'

That night, at half past eight, he came to their door, accepted the coffee and biscuits they offered, and reported: 'Not one of our teachers ever suspected Petra of trying to pass. She's a splendid little girl—'

'She's Coloured,' Mrs. van Valck said firmly.

'We find absolutely no evidence—'

'Have you checked her family?'

'I do not know her family,' Dr. Sterk confessed. 'Their I.D. cards say they are white.'

'I shall visit them tomorrow,' Mrs. van Valck said. 'Can you give me their address?'

'They live at Blinkfontein.'

On Friday afternoon she drove forty-eight miles north of Venloo to a crossroads village with a single store, Albertyn Super Shop. Parking her car, she looked for the police, but there were none. She walked to the post office and asked to see the man in charge, whom she swore to silence: 'It's a most important matter, Meneer. Things are being said about those people across the road. Back in Venloo. Their child Petra is in school there.'

'What are you talking about, Mevrou?'

'What do you know of the Albertyns?' Shrugging one shoulder toward the store, she added, 'Over there . . .'

'They've lived here for—'

'Where'd they come from?'

'They've always lived here.'

Receiving no help from the postmaster, she went to the store itself, in search, she said, of Trotter's jellies. The assistant, a man suspiciously dark, said he had none, and she asked, 'Will you have some later, Mr. Albertyn?' and he replied, 'I'm not Mr. Albertyn. He works at the garage. I just help here.'

'Could I see Mr. Albertyn? Or Mrs.?'

'You can see them both. They're out back.'

When she met Petra's parents they seemed as white as any Afrikaner, but she noticed something she found most ominous: in spite of the sun, Mrs. Albertyn had no freckles.

Back home she told her husband, 'As clear as the lines in the palm of your hand, that woman's Coloured.'

'How can you be sure?'

'No freckles.'

The Van Valcks returned to the school to present their hard evidence to Dr. Sterk, who laughed nervously and said, 'Really, I can't act upon freckles.'

His use of this word angered the Van Valcks, who rose to leave. 'My husband knows what to do,' Mrs. van Valck said. 'The life of our daughter is endangered.'

'Now wait,' the principal said, inserting himself between them and the door. 'A public charge could hurt this school. It might even rebound against your daughter.'

'It's our daughter we're thinking of,' Mrs. van Valck said.

'Will you grant me two days? Please?'

'We'll grant you two months,' Leopold van Valck said generously. 'But only if you take this seriously.'

'I do. I do. I'm thinking of the great damage that might be done to the Albertyn girl if your charges are made public . . .' He tried vainly to find some good way to end this sentence, but none surfaced. 'And are found insubstantial,' he added.

This angered both the Van Valcks, but it was the wife who replied, 'They are substantial. That girl's Coloured. Now get her out of here.'

'It had better be two days,' Mr. van Valck said sternly.

That afternoon Dr. Sterk held a meeting with three of his wisest teachers, two women and one man, good Afrikaners all, and their counsel was crisp and clear: 'The Van Valcks are troublemakers, especially the mother. She raised the merry devil last year when Minna received a caution on her deportment. If she's threatening to bring public charges, she'll do it. Better get the Albertyn girl out of here quietly and forget the matter.'

'But is the girl actually Coloured?'

'No sign we've ever seen,' the arithmetic teacher said, 'but she'd better go.'

'Mrs. du Plessis, you've always told me what a splendid child Petra is.'

'I did and I love her. But in a case like this, it may be best for the child's sake if she leaves.'

The three teachers were adamant. The welfare of this important school superseded all other considerations, and whereas to suspend Petra might be heartbreaking for the girl, even the rumor that she was Coloured might have disastrous consequences for the school if circulated by determined people like the Van Valcks.

But Dr. Sterk refused to accept such advice, and next afternoon drove out to the Albertyn store, where he asked the owners to get into his car so that he might take them to some isolated spot on the veld where they could talk privately. As they drove in silence the Albertyns could only speculate on what painful thing might have happened at school: Petra had done something warranting punishment, and they were distressed, but they were also prepared to support Dr. Sterk and school discipline. Mrs. Albertyn placed her hand in her husband's and took deep breaths as the car stopped and the principal turned toward them. He looked ill-at-ease, distant, and finally he came out with it.

'Charges have been made that Petra is Coloured,' he said.

'Oh, Jesus!' Mr. Albertyn gasped.

'Most serious charges, by persons prepared to press them publicly.'

'Oh, my God!'

The anguish expressed by Mr. Albertyn was an indication of the gravity of this accusation. To make such a charge in South Africa was not like someone saying in Hungary, 'I think Lazlo's a Rumanian.' Or saying in the west of England, 'If you look into it, you'll find that Masterson is really Irish.' In normal countries such charges were matters of social judgment; in South Africa they determined life and sometimes death.

'Is there any foundation to the charge?' Dr. Sterk asked.

'None whatever,' Mr. Albertyn said, and right there the great suspicion began, for the principal noted that whereas Mr. Albertyn leaped forward to defend his family and his daughter, Mrs. Albertyn did not, and he said to himself: Why is the woman so quiet? She must be hiding something. I do believe Petra is Coloured!

At the conclusion of the interview on the veld Dr. Sterk suggested, 'I think under the circumstances you'd better take your daughter out of our school.'

'I refuse,' Mr. Albertyn cried. 'Have you any idea what it would mean to the child? Thrown out of school for doing nothing wrong?'

'I understand your sensitivities,' Dr. Sterk said with a certain unctuousness. 'But have you considered the consequences if a public charge is made? There would have to be a Race Classification inquiry. The effect on Petra . . .' He paused, not ominously, but with just the hint of a threat: 'The terrible consequences to yourselves?'

Belatedly Mrs. Albertyn spoke, and she did so with quiet force: 'Have you been thinking of the consequences, Dr. Sterk? Of persecuting a poor little child?'

These words had just the opposite effect to what she had intended. Dr. Sterk interpreted them as a challenge to his integrity, and said crisply, 'I'm always mindful of my duty, Mrs. Albertyn, to my pupils and to my nation. If you are attempting to pass into a white society, that is against the laws of our country, and a board will determine the facts.'

He took them back to their cottage, then speedily returned to Venloo, where he joined a meeting of the school committee: 'A most serious charge, not yet formalized, has been made that our child Petra Albertyn is a Coloured. Have any of you evidence bearing on this?'

Two of Petra's teachers had asked to be present and volunteered their assurances that Petra Albertyn was one of the finest— Dr. Sterk cut them off: 'We're not testifying to her quality. We're interested only in her race.' And the way in which he spoke these words conveyed the clear impression that he now considered the accusations against this child justified. This encouraged the vice-principal to say that he had been watching Petra for some time, and she not only looked suspiciously dark, but she also behaved in distinctly Coloured ways.

'What do you mean?' Dr. Sterk asked.

'The way she says certain words.'

Venloo's dominee, Reverend Classens, was a committee member, and he asked ponderously, 'Do we appreciate what we're doing here to-night? This child's entire future is at stake.'

'No one could be more sympathetic than we are, Dominee,' Dr. Sterk said. 'But if she is Coloured, then one of her parents must be Coloured, too. They can have a future among their own people. Not here in Venloo.'

'Does this mean,' the dominee asked, 'that you plan to examine every child who seems a bit dark?'

'They are examined every day. By their fellow students. By every-one who sees them. This is a Christian nation, Dominee, and we obey the law.'

'That is what I preach. But I also preach "Suffer the little children to—"'

'We don't persecute little children. But we must keep serious priori-ties in mind.'

'Such as?'

'The moral welfare of every child in this school.'

After the meeting a grim-faced Dr. Sterk went to see the Van Valcks, and reported: 'I've seen the Albertyns and there is foundation for your accusations. The vice-principal has also had his suspicions.'

'That's what we told you,' Mrs. van Valck said smugly. 'What are you going to do about it?'

'I've asked the Albertyns to remove their daughter.'

'And they refused?'

'They have.' There was a long pause, in which each of the three considered the inevitable next step, the one that would throw the com-munity into turmoil. Twice Dr. Sterk made as if to speak, then thought better of it. In a matter of such gravity the decision must be made by the people involved, and he would wait upon them.

Finally Leopold van Valck asked in a low voice, 'You want to know whether we're prepared to lodge formal charges?'

'We are,' his wife interrupted with great force. Having made the de-cision for all of them, she sat primly in her chair, hands folded, chin jut-ting out as if she were already bringing her testimony before the Race Classification Board.

Dr. Sterk felt that he was the only one in this mess who appreciated the terrible confrontation that threatened; only he foresaw the conse-quences, once this social avalanche was torn loose, and he wanted to give the Van Valcks time to consider. He said nothing, and in the si-lence Mr. van Valck might have wavered, except that his wife rose suddenly, smoothed down her dress, and said, 'Well, that's that. It is our job to inform Pretoria.'

'You're sure you want to?' Dr. Sterk asked one last time.

'We are,' she said firmly, and next morning she went early to the Venloo post office to buy a money order for £10, which she carried to her husband's office. He had been in since seven, preparing two affidavits detailing the grounds for their complaint. When she filled out the forms, she took them back to the post office and mailed them to the Director of Census in Pretoria. At home she told her husband, 'I'll be proved right. They're trying to penetrate white society. And when the verdict's in, I'll get my ten pounds back.' This deposit, the government believed, was required as an indication of good faith on the part of accusers: 'It stops malicious persons from bringing frivolous or vexatious complaints.'

A tornado broke over the school, for rumor quickly spread that Petra Albertyn was Coloured; her father was white enough, but her mother was Coloured, maybe even a Bantu, and the inquisition to which children are prone ensued. Two teachers, unusually mindful of the race laws, told the principal they did not wish to have any Coloured child in their classes, that to do so was not only illegal but also personally offensive. By midafternoon the school was polarized, a few older students and the two younger teachers defending Petra, the rest ostracizing her.

It was obvious to Dr. Sterk that such a situation could not be tolerated during the weeks it would require for a Race Classification Board to be appointed, so once more he drove out to the Albertyns', imploring them, for the welfare of their daughter, to remove her from school. Mr. Albertyn, keenly aware of what could happen to his family if his daughter was declared Coloured, was disposed to comply, but his wife said, 'No. If a cruel charge like this can be made against Petra this week, it can be made against others next week. Let's settle this once and for all.'

But next day a deputation of parents stormed Sterk's office, demanding that the girl be removed immediately. One was the wife of the sergeant at the Venloo police station, and her husband stepped forward: 'Wouldn't it be best for all if I drove Petratjie to her home?' So Petra's things were collected from the dormitory and placed in the sergeant's car. On the way to Blinkfontein he said little, but he did offer her several of his extra-strong white peppermints: 'Don't worry, Petratjie. These things always work out for the best. You'll be much happier with your own people.'

The Race Classification Board was appointed by Pretoria, for this was one of the early cases under the new regulations and it was important that precedents be established. The membership was curious: the chairman, Detleef van Doorn, the lawmaker, who had at one time or another headed every important local organization and was still head of the committee of the Paulus de Groot High School; Mr. Leopold van Valck, the magistrate, who in another country might have been disqualified as being partner to the litigation; and the Venloo dentist with the good English name of John Adams, to avoid charges that the commission was overloaded with Afrikaners judging their own special laws.

They met in one of the town's two courtrooms and spent the first days taking testimony from any interested parties: teachers who had always suspected the child, playmates who might have observed suspicious behavior, village gossips interested in the Albertyns' personal life. The intention was to learn whether their friends and others regarded them as white persons. The testimony was conclusive that they did.

But the vital evidence was taken on the third day, and the community watched grimly when a motorcar brought the Albertyns, including two older children, to be inspected visually by the three commissioners. This was all-important, for what the investigators were endeavoring to decide was whether the Albertyns as a whole were Coloured or not, and looking at them face-to-face was one of the best ways to judge.

The four Albertyns, lacking Petra, were lined up before the commissioners, who studied them minutely prior to questioning. Mr. van Valck, whose name meant *falcon,* rose from his chair behind the prosecutor's table, where the commissioners sat, and suggested that they move onto the bench used by judges 'so we can look more impressive.'

'No,' Detleef objected, 'this is a simple family matter, so let's handle it that way. Our job is to start sorting out our nation, putting everyone in his place. This wouldn't have been necessary if the English had kept people properly separated, but once those first fatal steps of intermixing occurred, the damage was done. Now we must move back to an honest base.'

Detleef van Doorn began: 'Who were your grandparents?' He placed great store on lineage.

'Have you any Coloured friends?'

'What is your minister's name? His initials?'

'Is his church exclusively for whites?'

'Are you and your husband registered as voters?'

'Have your names ever been removed from a voters' list?' Here Magistrate van Valck interposed gravely: 'Remember, you are under oath, and one false answer will put you in jail.'

'Have you ever traveled in a train for Coloured persons?'

'When you go on holiday, where do you stay? What hotel? Is it for whites?'

On and on, for three hours, the questioning went, inconclusively. The Albertyns seemed much like any other South African family, mostly Dutch, with a strong strain of German and perhaps a Huguenot ancestor far back. No English. Probably no Malay or Hottentot or Bantu.

Now the fascinating part of the investigation approached, when the commissioners actually inspected the bodies of the suspects. Each commissioner had his or her special clues for detecting Coloured blood, the result of rural superstitions. Mr. van Valck, coached by his wife, placed emphasis on freckles and ear lobes: 'White people freckle. Coloureds don't. It's as simple as that.' But when he examined the Albertyns, he found Mrs. Albertyn and one son with no freckles, Mr. Albertyn and the other son with a copious supply. 'Now, with ear lobes,' he explained to everyone in the room, 'with whites, there's an indentation. With Coloureds, there isn't.' But again the Albertyns divided two and two.

The dentist had heard that something about the half-moons at the base of fingernails furnished some clue to racial origin, but he could never remember what it was. He considered an investigation like this offensive but felt he had better go through the motions, so he carefully studied forty Albertyn fingernails, and said, 'Hmmmmmm!' The other two commissioners were relieved that he was taking his assignment seriously.

Van Doorn trusted only hair, especially on the backs of hands, where it could not be tampered with, as it often was on the head: 'Hand hair that twists in a certain way.' Eight Albertyn hands were carefully inspected, after which Detleef asked for a pencil, which relieved Mr. van Valck, since he placed considerable store in the pencil test. 'We twist the hair over the ears tightly around this pencil,' Van Doorn explained to the watchers, 'and if the subject is white, it unravels quickly when the pencil is withdrawn. With blacks, as you know, it remains crinkled.' Studying the pencil to see that the hair was properly drawn, he jerked the pencil away and watched with satisfaction as the hair responded. 'You may sit down,' he told the Albertyns.

Now came the time to investigate the little girl herself, the one who had technically committed the offense. Petra was brought into the room and told to face the interrogators, who went through the tedious business of asking her profound questions when everyone knew that it would be the physical examination that counted.

Even so, little Petra responded with answers that were innocent and sometimes charming. Yes, she understood this was a serious business. Yes, she knew that if she were indeed Coloured, she would have to go to a school with her own people. Yes, she knew that every group had its own place in South Africa so that it could be happy. In fact, she knew a great deal and demonstrated the intelligence of which her teachers had spoken, even those who wanted her expelled.

'Now, Petra, walk to the end of the room and back.' It was clear to Mr. van Valck that she walked like a Coloured.

'Now we come to the most important part.' It was Mr. van Valck speaking in a rather conciliatory voice, for he was about to impose the one inspection that some people deemed foolproof. 'Slip down your dress,' he said as gently as he could.

So the little girl, shyly but with no fierce embarrassment, dropped her dress and then her petticoat until she stood practically naked before the commissioners. Since her breasts had not yet formed, she felt no need to cover them with her hands; nervously she twined her fingers over her flat stomach. 'Drop your hands to your side, Petra, so we can see how you stand,' Detleef said, and the commissioners examined her, paying special attention to the small triangle at the base of the spine, for as Mr. van Valck had assured them: 'If that's dark, you can be sure she has Bantu blood.' Dr. Adams, ashamed of himself for participating in so ghastly a ritual, looked at the triangle and saw only the properly developing spine-tip of a little girl.

When the Albertyns, all five of them, were dismissed from the room, the commissioners excused Dr. Sterk and the two policemen and started their deliberations, and it became quickly evident that Mr. van Valck was determined to find the family Coloured, while Dr. Adams, a naturally sardonic type, would have none of it; indeed, he appeared to be contemptuous of the whole affair. The deciding vote would therefore be cast by Van Doorn, and he intended to be as just as Solomon.

'I think we should begin our deliberations with prayer,' he said in Afrikaans.

'Why?' Adams asked in English.

'Because we're about to decide the fate of a family,' Van Doorn replied.

'Seems to me it's already decided,' Adams said. 'Not a shred of evidence that family's Coloured.'

'That's what we're here to decide,' Van Doorn reminded him, and he launched into a long, fervid supplication to God, asking Him to monitor their deliberations as they endeavored in good conscience to protect the nation.

Before the voting could begin, an investigator from Detleef's office broke into the room without having been invited and handed the chairman a report: 'It's what you asked for, Mr. van Doorn.' For three weeks this man and four of Detleef's assistants in Pretoria had been scrutinizing the Albertyn past, because the government was determined that this important race-classification hearing be conducted so as to evoke maximum impact.

'Mr. van Doorn, sir,' the investigator whispered. 'I don't think you'd better let anyone see our report.'

'The other members are entitled . . .'

'It was the other members I was thinking of.'

Moving apart from Van Valck and Adams, Detleef read the document and became ashen. He was astonished that detectives could uncover so much and appalled at the possible consequences of what they had learned. The detective, seeing his dismay, whispered, 'Shall I burn the report, sir? I made only one copy.'

It was the severest moral test Detleef would ever face. His whole being urged him to quash this report, but the dignity of his office and its obligation to purify the race took precedence. If at this first hearing he smothered evidence, all subsequent ones would be suspect, and the good that such procedures might otherwise accomplish would be aborted. Wiping the sweat from his forehead, he cleared his dry throat and said, 'Gentlemen, I think we should hear a rather remarkable report. It bears directly on our case. Mr. Op t'Hooft here is an investigator from my department, and he's been looking into the heritage of the Albertyns. You may proceed, Mr. Op t'Hooft.'

The detective squared his shoulders and read a concise account of the Albertyn record:

> 'The charge that Mrs. Albertyn is Coloured is completely false. There is no blemish of any kind on her family record. The possibility that she may have had sexual intercourse with a Bantu is remote, for not only does she have an impeccable reputation, but we can find no occasion when she could have been in contact with a Bantu. Also, since her other children all look like Petra,

there would have to have been repeated acts of intercourse with the same black man, and that seems positively impossible.

'Mr. Albertyn, however, is another matter. He is contaminated doubly, and proof of the contamination is contained in a straight, unbroken, demonstrable line back to 1694 when the Coloured slave Bezel Muhammad married the Trianon spinster Petronella van Doorn.

'Bezel and Petronella had four children who carried no last name, and they might have been lost in the general Coloured population except that neighbors kept track of them, knowing them to be Van Doorns. We have found numerous families well regarded today containing the blood of Bezel and Petronella.

'In or about the year 1720 their daughter Fatima, named after Bezel's mother, became the third wife of the notorious frontier outlaw Rooi van Valck, who had four wives, one yellow, one brown, one black and one white. Fatima was the brown one, and she became the progenitress of a large unruly breed.

'One of her daughters married an early Albertyn and was thus the direct ancestor of our Henricus Albertyn. Without question, he is doubly Coloured. Without question, his daughter Petra must be so classified.

'Our investigators could not avoid remarking upon the extraordinary fact that our Petra thus becomes a lineal descendant of the original Petronella, who broke the rules of her community. Could this be an example of Divine intervention?'

When Mr. Op t'Hooft finished reading the report, he waited in some confusion as to what he should do next. He looked in vain at Chairman van Doorn for instructions, but Detleef was too shaken to act intelligently, and as for Mr. van Valck, whose redoubtable ancestor Rooi had been dragged from his stormy grave, he was in a state of shock.

Dr. Adams reached for the report, but Mr. Op t'Hooft was not sure he should deliver it to a man known to be difficult where Afrikaner matters were concerned. Dr. Adams solved this by snatching the paper and holding it aloft. 'Did you say this was the only copy?'

'Yes. Not even one carbon was made.'

'Good. I want you to watch what happens to your one copy.' Crumpling it in his left hand, Dr. Adams produced a match, scratched it across the top of the polished table, and set fire to the report. Holding it by one end, he watched the flames creep closer to his fingers, then dropped the burning paper on the table, where it vanished, leaving a scar.

'I think we should all forget this report,' Adams said. 'It can do no one in this room any good, and it could do distinguished citizens outside a great deal of harm.' When Mr. Op t'Hooft, completely bewildered, left, Adams said, 'It looks to me as if I'm the only one here who is not related to this little Coloured girl.'

Van Valck and Van Doorn glared at him, but he ignored them, saying brightly, 'I propose we declare the child white and end this farce.' He supposed that the shaken men, in order to hide their own involvement, would agree, but he underestimated Detleef's moral tenacity.

In silence the Commissioner on Racial Affairs lowered his head and pondered what to do. In his anxiety he could hear the voices of his family orating savagely on the problem of the Coloureds:

> Maria van Doorn: 'They are the children of sin, and God must despise them.'
> Johanna Krause: 'They are mongrels.'

But then he heard his own voice: 'They're . . . a reminder of our fathers' transgressions.'

He was sorely tempted to follow Dr. Adams' advice and terminate the investigation, for he knew that if the facts became public, the sins of his ancestors must surface; but to evade his responsibilities would be craven, so he decided to plow ahead.

He was about to voice his decision when he saw, shimmering in air, that decorated page of the ancient Bible on which the data of his family were inscribed, and on it in blazing letters stood that second entry, the one that was never discussed in his family: *Son Adam van Doorn born 1 November 1655.* Generations of Van Doorns had tried to ignore that cryptic passage, avoiding the question of who the boy's mother could have been. And there was the later entry: 'Petronella'—but with no statement as to whom she had married. Always the Van Doorns had suspected that they were related to Coloureds; always they had submerged this truth. Now the gossip-whispers were about to rampage, and Detleef was sick with shame.

But he *was* the Commissioner on Racial Affairs, he *was* the chairman of this Race Classification Board, with a duty to perform. In a voice scarcely more than a whisper he said, 'Clearly the child Petra has contaminated blood from both the Van Valck and the Van Doorn lines. Clearly she must be classified as Coloured.'

Van Valck shuddered: 'All along I thought it was Mrs. Albertyn who carried the fatal strain.'

'What in hell do you men mean?' Dr. Adams exploded. 'Words like *contaminated* and *fatal strain?*'

'We mean the defilement of Afrikaner blood,' Detleef whispered. 'We have all been defiled this day.'

From the moment the date 1694 was mentioned, Dr. Adams had started doing calculations and now produced his results: 'At least eight, and possibly more, generations separate the slave Bezel Muhammad from our little girl . . .'

'She's not my little girl,' Mr. van Valck interrupted. 'She's a Coloured trying to penetrate our community.'

'Eight generations would mean that back in the 1694 period she would have had no fewer than two hundred and fifty-six potential ancestors in existence. And because two of them were Coloured—'

'More,' Detleef interrupted. 'You're forgetting Rooi van Valck.'

'I was just coming to Rooi. By the way, Van Valck, from which of his wives were you descended? Don't bother to answer. Whichever it was, Petra's your cousin.'

Leopold leaped from his chair, and would have assaulted the dentist had not Van Doorn intervened. 'Gentlemen, sit down. We have a vote to take. The evidence against this girl is overwhelming. Do I hear a motion to declare her Coloured?'

'I so move,' Van Valck said firmly.

'Do I hear a second?'

Dr. Adams stared at his fingernails, trying to guess how he would be evaluated a decade from now when this movement for racial purity became a mania and some ill-spirited neighbor denounced him.

'Dr. Adams, do I hear a second?'

'Not from me.'

'Please, we must conduct this meeting in orderly fashion.'

'Then I move that you two men vote to declare your cousin Petra Albertyn white, for I am certain that she's as white as any of the three of us.'

'I second the original motion,' Detleef said, his blood raging and his mind taking note of this man Adams. He would be dealt with later. The medical commission should look into that man's credentials.

'Moved and seconded that this commission finds the girl Petra Albertyn Coloured.'

'No!' Adams called in a loud voice.

'The vote was not called for,' Detleef said, trying to control his anger. 'Now I ask for the vote.'

'Ja,' Van Valck cried. Van Doorn did the same, then looked at Dr. Adams, who was again studying his fingernails. 'And you, Adams?'

'Record it that I was ashamed in the sight of God to vote upon such a motion. That I refused to condemn your cousin Petra.' He rose and started to leave the room, but Detleef intercepted him.

'Please! It's of major importance that we start this procedure correctly. You must be seen sitting with us when we deliver our decision.'

So, reluctantly, Dr. Adams resumed his chair and watched as the Albertyns and the spectators were brought back into the room. The family was ranged neatly along one wall, and little Petra, hands primly at her side, was again asked to stand facing her judges, who looked down upon her.

'Petra Albertyn, you are Coloured.'

She made no response, but did turn slightly to see what the noise was to her left. Her mother had fainted.

The fateful decision in Petra's case launched a time of terror for the Albertyns. She was immediately dismissed from school, and when her family appealed to the courts they were turned down: 'Clearly Coloured.' In a few months the board declared Henricus Albertyn Coloured, too, so he could no longer work at the garage, since his foreman position was classified 'whites only.' Nor could he find work elsewhere; he was unemployed and would remain so for more than a year.

It was absolutely forbidden for the Albertyns to continue living where they had for the past forty years; as Coloureds they must move into some township reserved for their race, but no such group area existed in Venloo, so they decided to uproot their entire family and move down to Cape Town, where the vast majority of Coloureds lived. Because they were forced to sell their house under crisis conditions, they received £2,000 for a £4,500 investment.

When they reached Cape Town the only accommodation they could find was in a collection of three-story hovels originally designed as a transit camp for the military. It was now one of the shames of South

Africa, with multiple families crammed into each flimsy-walled apartment.

When the shattered Albertyns moved into Orchard Flats they contemplated suicide. The cleanliness of Blinkfontein was gone, the neatness of their home, the warmth of their relationships in the tiny community—all lost. In their place was filth, criminality and social hatred. That anyone should have to live in such surroundings was disgraceful, but that proven good citizens could be forced into them by a government acting in the name of God and racial purity was criminal.

Henricus Albertyn discovered how criminal one evening when he came home from his job as grease-monkey in a distant Cape Town garage. As he climbed the stairs to his third-floor room, assailed by the smell of cheap wine and urine, he racked his brain trying to devise some tactic whereby he could organize a decent life for Petra, for upon her he now fastened all his dreams.

But when he reached his door he heard sobbing, not Petra's but his wife's, and he burst into the room—to find her quivering in a corner, with a pair of long scissors, covered with blood, in her hand. For one terrible moment he suspected that something beyond words had happened to his daughter, but when he looked about in frenzy, he saw Petra seated by the lone window, reading a book. Whatever foul thing had happened, she had remained untouched.

Quickly embracing her, he asked, 'What's happened?'

'Just the skollies,' Petra said, apparently unconcerned. 'Mama stabbed them, and they ran away.'

From her corner Mrs. Albertyn said softly, 'No skollies will rape my child. We'll never surrender to this dreadful place.'

And Petra, putting aside her book, showed her father the long knitting needle she had for some days kept secreted in her dress: 'I stabbed them too. Shamilah downstairs told me how to jab at their eyes.' And without any sign of agitation she returned to her homework.

She was in school again, at a much bigger institution in nearby Athlone, staffed by a group of dedicated Coloured men and women. When her father attended a parent-teacher meeting, the chairman of the school committee, a prosperous builder named Simon Botha, sought him out: 'Albertyn, our teachers tell me that your little Petra is a near-genius. You must give thought to her future.'

'In this country what can a Coloured do?'

'You mustn't limit your horizon to this country. My daughter in Canada tells me the universities there have many bursaries. They're hungry for children like Petra. Australia, too, or even London.'

Such thoughts were beyond Albertyn's ken, but he realized that he must learn to grapple with them, for as Botha said, 'To leave a girl like Petra in this country is to commit her to death.'

Even though Venloo had been cleansed of the Albertyns, the Van Valcks could not feel victorious, for they were assailed by haunting questions. One night Leopold asked bluntly, 'Do you think that English atheist would dare to start rumors about us? I mean, about Rooi van Valck and his three dark wives?' Later he asked plaintively, 'Could I possibly be carrying contaminated blood?'

They spent much time inspecting the half-moons on his fingernails, and although these were inconclusive, Mrs. van Valck did find comfort in his many freckles. After convincing themselves that he was safely white, they relaxed and invited Principal Sterk to dinner and listened as he reported on the final outcome of their crusade to purify the community. When they heard of the area in which the Albertyns were forced to live, Mrs. van Valck said without rancor, and even with a sense of forgiving them for the trouble they had caused, 'It's only what they deserved, trying to be something better than they were.' Then she added brightly, 'Yesterday I had a letter from Pretoria. They sent me back my deposit.'

AT HOME

February 8, 1955

Greetings,

Further to my previous letter this is to advise you that my Board will provide transport free of charge for yourself, members of your household, and property belonging to you on February 9, 1955.

Will you kindly pack your belongings and be ready to load by 6 A.M. on that morning.

Attached hereto is a letter which, please, hand to your employer. It explains why you cannot be at work on February 9, 1955.

I. P. van Onselen
Secretary to the Native Resettlement Board

February 9 was the kind of crisp summer's day Johannesburg often provided, but this year it carried special significance, for the government had announced for the last time that the bulldozers were going to move; no further legal complaints would be tolerated. The first batch of blacks to be evicted from Sophiatown were to obey the secretary's letter to the last word.

Barney Patel, a clothing dealer aged forty-six, and his friend Woodrow Desai, aged fifty-nine, owner of a grocery store, had traveled from their shops in Pageview, an Indian trading and residential area in Johannesburg since the days of Paul Kruger. They were standing on a hill overlooking Sophiatown, where bulldozers were lined up, awaiting the signal. From their vantage point the two Indians were able to look down into the township which blacks had occupied for decades; fifty-seven thousand of them now lived here, some in ugly slums, many in fine houses which they owned. In a last-minute appeal that failed, an expert in housing had testified: 'Only one structure in eight is a slum that warrants complete demolition.'

It had to be admitted, however, that the slum area was an amazing collection of buildings divided into five easily recognized categories: at the bottom, cardboard walls acquired by flattening grocery boxes; next, tin walls made from hammering out paraffin cans; next, corrugated iron siding; next, actual wood to protect the walls; and finally, cinderblocks to replace everything that had served before. But whatever the building material, all the houses were jammed together along narrow streets or dark alleys, and from this assembly came not only the patient black workers of the area but also the incorrigible young tsotsis, the peddlers of dagga, as marijuana was called, the prostitutes and the horde of petty criminals.

Sophiatown was a tightly knit community, and for every tsotsi who prowled the streets, there were a dozen good youngsters; for every father who staggered home drunk to a tin shack, there were a dozen others who cared for their families and supported the churches and schools and traders. But this black township had had the poor foresight to situate itself in the heart of what would become a predominantly Afrikaner white suburb. It must now be bulldozed off the face of the earth not for the sake of honest, if somewhat overzealous, urban renewal, as might have happened in many other countries, but because it stood in the path of white aspirations.

'There must be no confusion of thinking,' a cabinet minister said. 'Sophiatown counts as a black spot on our land.' He then explained that a black spot was a place where Bantu had acquired land ownership under old laws. Under apartheid, such offensive spots had to be rubbed out. Thirteen percent of the land, traditional sites for kraals, had been set aside, and there blacks could own land. 'At Sophiatown, and spots like it that we need, their temporary sojourn in our midst is over.'

'I can't believe they're going to knock it down,' Barney Patel said as the bulldozers revved their engines.

'The paper said they start today.'

'But all the people living there?'

'Out in the country. To the new settlements.'

'You mean they'll have to travel all those miles?'

'That's not the government's problem [he pronounced it gommint]. Out they go. Gommint says they shouldn't have been here in the first place.'

A bell started ringing in a Protestant church right in the middle of the slum area, and continued for some minutes until a policeman hurried through the crowd to silence it. 'They don't want any trouble,' Patel said. 'They've banned meetings of more than twelve people.'

'They won't have any trouble,' Desai said. 'Look at the police.'

To deal with the first one hundred and fifty families ordered to abandon the homes they owned, the government had brought in two thousand policemen armed with Sten guns and assegais, backed by troop carriers, signal units and squads of military police.

When the bulldozers were ready, two men to each machine, a Resettlement Board official gave the signal, and the powerful scrapers moved forward, their blades lowered, their snouts hungry.

'I just don't believe this,' Patel said, his throat suddenly dry.

'Look!' the older man said, and they watched as the monstrous machines ripped a path through a group of shacks. A single bulldozer would wipe out an entire house, but this was no great accomplishment, for that one had been cardboard and planks.

'Look over there!' Desai cried, and as he pointed, a bulldozer chewed its way into a substantial home of wood and brick.

'That house must have been worth . . .' Patel did not finish his sentence, for the bulldozer, having attacked something it could not easily subdue, hung in the air for a moment, then slid sideways, endangering the driver but not upsetting. Angrily it backed up, sped its engine and tore back into the house, which collapsed in a cloud of dust.

'Look at the people!' Desai said softly, and the two Indians turned to the south where large groups of blacks gathered silently to watch the demolition, mindful of what was in store for them. They stood with anguish on their dark faces, their hands clenched, powerless to obstruct either the bulldozers or the officials who directed them. This black spot could not be tolerated by whites in neighboring Mayfair; it must be cleansed of its vermin and converted to higher purposes.

'There come the trucks,' Patel said as a line of vehicles moved in to carry away the residents, and while the 'dozers knocked down the unwanted houses, the trucks carted off the unwanted people, free of charge, as the letter had promised.

There were, of course, those few blacks who refused to quit their homes; these were routed out by the police but no harm was done them. From one house near where Patel and Desai stood, a team of soldiers carried away an old man who had stubbornly refused to budge. 'Come on, old grandpop, we're in a hurry!' the soldiers said in Afrikaans ('Kom, Oubaas, ons is haastig'). Almost gently they bore him to a waiting truck and sat him down among the others, and he was scarcely seated before a bulldozer eliminated the house in which his children and grandchildren had been born.

The two Indians remained on their prominence most of the morning, gripped by the drama of this vast removal and weighing the possibility that they might be next. 'Do you think they'll really knock down our houses?' Patel asked as the bulldozers ate into Sophiatown.

'Gommint policy,' Desai said. 'All Indians to get out of Johannesburg.'

'You think they'll move us miles out in the country, like they say?'

'Look, Barney. Mukerjee told me yesterday the surveyors were out there, laying out streets.'

'Who can believe Mukerjee?'

'Well, he kept warning us that one day Sophiatown would be knocked down. Then I laughed. Today I believe.'

'But blacks are different from Indians. There are so many of them. So few of us.'

'Numbers mean nothing to apartheid. It's only interested in color. Today it hates this black spot. Tomorrow it'll be a brown spot, and off we go.'

'But Kruger's gommint gave us the land we have. I own my land.'

'Yes, they put us there for what they called "sanitary" reasons. Today their grandsons will kick us out for economic reasons. Believe me, Barney, the bulldozers will come down our streets, too.'

They stood in silence, watching the destruction, marking the exodus of black families, and as they knew themselves to be powerless to protest this brutal maneuver, they thought back upon their own curious history in this fertile land.

Woodrow Desai's grandfather had been one of the three Desai brothers shipped to the sugar fields by Sir Richard Saltwood. When their contracts had been worked out, they had stayed on and were soon joined by 'passenger Indians' like the Patels, who had paid their own way to serve the rapidly growing community as shopkeepers and traders.

The Indian immigrants settled mostly in Natal, near the port of Durban, and there they proliferated: Patels, Desais, Mukerjees, Bannarjees. Unlike the Dutch before them and the Chinese, the Indian men would have nothing to do with black women, or white either, for that matter. They remained strictly aloof, and in the first forty years of their work in mine and field, few Indians married persons of another race. Woodrow's father and others moved to the Transvaal, and in the smallest towns they opened shops to which all customers were invited, but in their homes they kept to themselves, with their dishes of ghee and lamb and rice and curry. They were clean, usually law-abiding, and the other people of South Africa hated them.

'Without the little one,' Patel reflected, 'Indians would have been in even worse shape.'

The little one was a skinny lawyer with a high whining voice who emigrated to Durban in 1893. His name was Mohandas Karamchand Gandhi, intelligent enough to have made a good life for himself in South Africa had he been free to operate there. Indeed, when he arrived at age twenty-four he intended to remain, but the disadvantages which Indians suffered so irritated him that he found himself constantly at war with the authorities.

'He was a fighter,' Desai mumbled, recalling this contentious man who had defiled the entire white establishment.

'And clever too,' Patel said admiringly. 'When the Boer War was at its worst, what does he do? Organizes an Indian ambulance corps. Helps the English, even though they've been harrying him. Very brave, you know.' He chuckled to think of little Gandhi issuing orders to the white government.

'My father knew him well,' Desai said. 'But Father was much like me. Never wanted trouble. So when Gandhi started sending letters to General Smuts, like he was head of an Indian gommint, my father warned him: "You watch out, Mohandas. Gommint's going to throw you in jail." That was when he invented Satyagraha, right here in South Africa.'

'If he were watching this disgrace now, he'd do the same for the blacks as he did for us. Peaceful resistance. Just lie down in front of the bulldozers.'

'The bulldozers in India were British. They stopped. These are Afrikaner bulldozers and I don't think they'd stop. Not even for Gandhi.'

'I love him,' Patel said. 'Not for what he did in India. For what he did here.' He paused and shook his head. 'I often wonder what might have happened if he'd stayed in Durban. To help our people.'

'He'd have been shot. I don't think Afrikaners understand Satyagraha.'

The mention of shooting saddened the two Indians, for the Desai and Patel families back in Natal had suffered grievously when the Zulu, infuriated by government laws restricting them, had taken vengeance not on the whites who had passed the laws but on the Indians with whom they traded daily. For three days the tall Zulu had chased little Indians through the streets, slashing and killing, while some whites even looked on with approval, shouting at times, 'Kill 'em, Zulu!' More than fifty Indians were slain; more than seven hundred required medical attention. It was a different South Africa after that, with many whites muttering that it would have been better if the Zulu had been allowed a free hand to settle the Indian Question once and for all.

Desai, who had lost an uncle in the riots, smiled sardonically. 'Well, we had a chance to get out. Remember when gommint provided boat fare and leaving funds so that every Indian could go back to India? I think three old men accepted. Wanted to be buried in their native villages. The rest . . .'

'My father told me,' Patel said, 'that any Indian who left South Africa for India could be certified insane. This was so much better than what he had known . . .'

As the sun approached its zenith, and the blacks' houses crumbled to dust, the two Indians went soberly home to Pageview, where they stood at an intersection and stared at the rows of houses and shops occupied by their compatriots; Indians always preferred living in tight communities for mutual protection. 'Do you think they'd dare knock all this down?' Patel asked nervously. 'Five thousand people. Homes, businesses. Insurance told me ten million pounds, at least.'

Before he could answer, Cassem Mukerjee came running. He was a small nervous man, much like Gandhi in appearance, and he spoke with that agitated enthusiasm some men display when circulating bad news: 'My cousin Morarji saw the papers at his office. They're going to bull-doze this place, too. All our houses are to go. And they'll take our shops too.'

Barney Patel did not like Mukerjee, and now he shook him. 'You stop that rumoring! Your cousin knows nothing.'

'He knew they were going to bulldoze Sophiatown,' the little man said, almost gleefully. 'Are the houses gone?'

'It'll take years,' Patel snorted, but Desai wanted to know about the supposed papers: 'Did Morarji actually see anything?'

'The orders have been drafted. All Indians to be cleaned out of Johannesburg.'

'My God!' Desai said, and he leaned against the wall of a solidly built brick house, and as he stood there, sick in the sunlight, he could see the dust of the future, and thought:

> They will move the bulldozers here, and these houses of warmth and love will go down. The stone ones like mine and Barney's, they won't destroy them, but we'll be forced to sell at government price—twenty cents in the rand. The school where my children went will be razed, and all the little houses where the old people expected to live until they died. Our stores on Fourteenth Street . . . My God, I worked so hard.

> And we'll be moved far out into the country. Miles, miles from all our friends, all our customers. There'll be new houses at prices people can't afford, and new stores with no customers, and hours on the train each day, and all our money wasted on trans-portation we don't really need. And we'll be off to one side where no one can see us, and the streets we once knew will have van-ished—and for what great purpose?

Woodrow Desai decided that night to form a committee to visit Pretoria for a serious talk with the government official whose office was respon-sible for planning the future of the Indian community. He took Barney Patel with him, but not Morarji Mukerjee, who was something of an alarmist. Patiently they explained the folly of such an evacuation, point-ing out that it would accomplish not one single economic advantage, but the official assigned the task of dealing with them cut them off: 'We aren't really talking about economics, are we? We're talking about instilling some order in the community. Each group secure in its own place.'

'But if you put all of us in this so-called Lenasia so far out into the country . . .'

'That's for your protection. All the Indians in one spot.'

'But so far out. We'll waste hours and rand every day.'

'My dear friends,' the official, a Natal-born Englishman, said with warmth but also with a certain stiffness, 'our country has no finer citizens than you Indians. We wouldn't dream of doing anything to your disadvantage. But we must bring order into our lives. Pageview is intended for whites. Look at the map!' And he showed them how where they lived and traded intruded into areas that could better be used for whites.

'And you can have nice new shops out there,' he assured them, waving his hand in some vague direction. 'You'll like it better when it happens.' He paused. 'We're doing this for your own good,' he said. And before they could reply they were out on the street.

'I wish Mohandas Gandhi were here again,' Patel growled. 'He'd know how to stop this.'

AT WORK

The Golden Reef Mines southwest of Johannesburg needed a constant supply of black workers to man the deepest shafts where blasting of the face rock occurred. From all over southern Africa planes and trains and buses brought almost illiterate black men to the compounds within which they would live for the six to eighteen months of their contract. Critics of the labor system likened these compounds to harsh prisons in which the blacks were incarcerated; management spoke of them as well-run dormitories in which the laborers lived infinitely better than they did at home.

There was one clue to the truth of these contrasting claims: black men in the bush of Moçambique, Malawi, Rhodesia, Lesotho and Vwarda fought for a chance to work at the Golden Reef, and for good reason. Though the wage was trivial, it was much more than they could get in their home villages; the food was better; there was more of it; beds were covered with good blankets; and doctors provided health care. Black nationalists in surrounding countries would publicly inveigh against South Africa but privately see to it that planes which came flying into their airstrips were loaded with workers, for only in this way could some of the economies be kept afloat. Black families also encouraged their men to fly to the Golden Reef for the sensible reason that a good percentage of a man's wages was paid only when he returned home, and his wife and children could temporarily escape their poverty.

When blacks from thirty or forty different tribes, speaking radically different languages and dialects, had to work together, it was necessary to construct some simple language they could all understand. Fanakalo was the ingenious solution. The word came from pidgin Zulu and meant roughly 'do it like this,' and the lingua franca it represented was a marvelous mélange of Bantu, English, Afrikaans and Portuguese. It consisted mostly of nouns, with a few essential verbs, some profanity for adjectival emphasis and a great many gestures. One linguist who tried to analyze it said, 'You don't speak Fanakalo. You dance it while shouting.'

Few things in the world worked better, for a tribesman could master simple instructions in three days: 'This here wrench, fanakalo.' (You do it like this.) And once learned, it served as a magical passkey to all the levels of the mine, so that a man from Malawi speaking a unique dialect could work deep in the shaft beside one from Vwarda speaking his. One white supervisor asked an associate what the workers on his shift meant when they referred to 'Idonki ngo football jersey,' and the second man said, 'Simple. They mean *zebra*.'

A miner could renew his contract again and again, but it was found better to have him return home after a long stint in the mines, see his family back in his home village, and return rested up. These returnees usually spoke well of the Golden Reef, especially the food. Once when Vwarda's representative at the United Nations was addressing the Security Council and asking for sanctions against South Africa, the government was filling six planes with Vwarda men who wanted to get back to work.

Not all the black mine hands came from foreign countries; the Golden Reef, along with sister mines, maintained a vast network of some forty recruiters who were engaged only in the enlisting of South African blacks, who comprised a third of the mines' work force. One such recruiter came to Venloo, set up his table, and counseled with young blacks from that area. Since jobs were scarce, he was able to sign up a score of workers, among them Jonathan Nxumalo, oldest son of Moses, who had been so long associated with the Van Doorns.

Jonathan was a bright lad of twenty, eager to see something more of the world than the restricted view available to a farm hand at Vrymeer, but as soon as he passed through into the Golden Reef compound, where five thousand other black men lived, sixteen to a room, he heard the gates slam behind him—and realized that he had gained not freedom but a new kind of restriction. To learn Fanakalo became essential.

It took the white overseers only a few weeks to promote Jonathan as the best of this gang, and they designated him to work at the face, more than ten thousand feet down the rocky shaft. This paid more money, but it demanded more intense work in a constant temperature of 114° F. Water to cool the body and salt to protect it became almost as important as the gigantic jackhammer drill Jonathan handled, and when the long shift ended and the men from below shot up in the elevator they had the self-satisfaction of knowing that they had completed one of the world's hardest jobs.

White men shared the heat and the danger. No black was ever assigned a job more treacherous than what the white overseer was willing to do, so that a kind of camaraderie developed among the teams, with each white boss settling upon one or two superior blacks on whom he could rely. Jonathan became an aide to Roger Coetzee, an ambitious Afrikaner who loved the mines and would one day become the big boss.

Jonathan's job was an exciting one. At the start of each shift he entered the cage with the rest of his gang, bolted the doors, and dropped a sickening ten thousand feet straight down. Occasionally some visitor from Johannesburg or overseas would want to inspect how the men worked, and then the cage was lowered at a much slower rate, which irritated Nxumalo, for he had grown to like that awful drop; it was a badge of his profession. He could take it, whereas a stranger could not.

Below, he would meet up with Coetzee, who came down only with other white miners; the two men and their helpers walked about one mile hunched over, their heads protected by hard hats, which bumped against jagged rocks, their bodies exuding perspiration. After a long drink of water and some salt pills, they followed a narrower tunnel, in which the noise became shattering. Now they were approaching the face of the gold-bearing rock, and here huge pneumatic drills were sending steel probes far into the rock, prior to the placement of the next charges of dynamite.

It was hellish work. Jonathan would creep into the working hole feet first, lying on his back and never able to sit erect. When he reached the drilling machine, a heavy instrument with cross-bar handles and stirrups for the feet, he would adjust himself, check the electrical lines, then jam his feet into the stirrups and deftly point the six-foot diamond-tipped drill at the spot to be dynamited. Then, taking a deep breath, which always stimulated him, he would squirm about for a comfortable position, thrust his feet forward, and flick the switch. With incredible power and noise, the water-cooled jackhammer drill would eat into the rock, throwing spray and slush until Jonathan looked like a white man.

When the hole was drilled, Nxumalo would squirm back out and signal to Coetzee that all was ready. The Afrikaner would then replace Nxumalo in the cramped tunnel and fix the dynamite, the cap and the connecting wires. Whistles would blow. Sirens would whine. And all men would retreat from this area as Coetzee plunged the detonator, exploding the charge and breaking away the next burden of gold-bearing rock.

When the dust settled and it seemed probable that no last rocks would tumble down from the new ceiling, Jonathan Nxumalo and Roger Coetzee would creep back into the tunnel and start calculating how long it would take for the ore to be hauled away from the stope face to the breaker and then to the refinery. It was hard work, dust-filled and exciting, and the men deep below developed respect for each other's capacities. Of course, when they left the danger area to go aloft, their lives changed radically. Coetzee could jump into his car and drive where he wished; Nxumalo was restricted to the compound, where all needs were provided by the company.

He was not exactly a prisoner. During any eighteen-month contract, workers were allowed into Johannesburg six times, but only in a group, with some white like Coetzee holding the passes of thirty-six workmen. Should one want to break away from the ensemble, he could risk it, but he would then find himself with no pass, and since spot checks for pass inspection were quite common, sooner or later he would be detected and packed off to jail.

Several times, however, Jonathan did receive, through Coetzee's intervention, a special pass allowing him to visit a Vrymeer friend who, with sheer duplicity, had contrived to land a job in Johannesburg without proper papers. 'What I did,' he confided, 'was to grab on to this white family that had to have help. They protected me.' He added, 'Of course, since we're both breaking the law they pay me less than proper wages. But I don't complain.'

'You like Johannesburg?' Jonathan asked.

'Good food. Work not too hard. And look at these clothes.'

Jonathan was so enticed by city life that he tried on other visits to find an illegal job, to no avail. During the final moments of one leave he pleaded for more information as to how he should proceed, and his friend asked, 'You know anybody important might help you get a pass?'

'My father works for Detleef van Doorn.'

'You crazy? He's the one behind these laws. He's no friend. He's your worst enemy.'

Back at the mine, Jonathan asked Coetzee if he could help, but he said firmly, 'You're a mine worker now. You'll never be able to change because we need you.' And when Jonathan inquired at the pass office about getting an endorsement that would enable him to work in Johannesburg, the official snapped, 'You have mine papers. You'll never have anything else.'

Since he was sentenced to the underground, as it were, he decided to strive for the best job possible, but here again he was forestalled: 'You're qualified for drilling. Wasteful to try you anywhere else.'

Back in his quarters, Jonathan talked with men from Malawi and Vwarda: 'I'm going to apply for a job like Coetzee's. I know all he knows, or any of the other white bosses who work our deep shafts.' But in cautious Fanakalo the black workers warned him not even to whisper such a possibility: 'That job whites only. No matter how stupid, they smarter than you. No black ever be boss.'

Coetzee must have suspected Jonathan's concern, for one day as they crept out of the tunnel he volunteered: 'You could do my work, Nxumalo, but the law is rigid. No black must ever hold a job in which he might give orders to a white.' Before Jonathan could comment he reminded him of the Golden Reef work rules, which stipulated that dynamite placers had to be white. No black could ever aspire to that job, for the intelligence required to tamp dynamite into a hole drilled by a black was entirely beyond the capacity of non-whites. The fact that black workmen throughout the rest of the world easily performed that function was ignored; in South Africa they could never learn enough to do it properly.

Sometimes the white bosses didn't do it properly, either. One terribly hot and dust-choked day Roger Coetzee placed his dynamite carelessly, and Jonathan Nxumalo started to point this out, but before he could persuade Coetzee to correct it, the charge went off and an unplanned leaf of ceiling rock fell, trapping the Afrikaner behind a mass of rubble. The rock did not fall directly on him, or he would have been crushed. A sliding fragment did break his leg. He was trapped in a pitch-black, airless, waterless crevice with the temperature at 114° F. It was imperative that air and water pipes be got to him in a hurry, and with no white bosses in the vicinity, the task of doing it fell to Nxumalo. He probed through the fallen rock, lifted aside the chunks that he could handle, and called for other blacks to help with the bigger slabs. Within a few minutes white rescuers appeared on the scene, and proceeded exactly as Nxumalo had planned it. They succeeded in breaking Coetzee free, and from his hospital bed he asked to see Jonathan, who was ushered in by nurses who resented his being in the white hospital.

Coetzee was lucky to be alive, for there was no more deadly work in South Africa than that performed by men like him and Nxumalo. Each year more than six hundred men died in the gold mines—nineteen thousand in thirty years—and more than ninety percent were black.

'I know it was you that got me out,' Coetzee said, and before Nxumalo could say anything, he added graciously, 'And you were about to warn me not to do it that way.' He grinned and extended his hand. 'I wish I had a cousin in Johannesburg who needed a houseboy.'

No such luck. With Coetzee hospitalized, Nxumalo's shift got another boss, a tough Afrikaner who despised blacks. Once, when he saw Jonathan resting after a particularly stiff spell at the face, he growled at him, 'You work-shy idle black bastard.' Another day, when Nxumalo suggested approaching the face from a different angle, the boss yelled, 'No lip from you, you cheeky Kaffir bastard.'

Since Nxumalo's contract had only five more weeks to run, he tolerated the new man's insults, and when the compound manager said, at the termination of his eighteen months, 'I hope you'll sign on again,' he was noncommittal, but he was satisfied that he wanted no more of the Golden Reef. What he would do, he didn't know.

AT DEATH

Old Bloke, who delivered lawyers' letters at the Cheston Building in Johannesburg, was only fifty-four years old, but his life had been so demanding that he looked older than he was. His name was Bloke Ngqika, and in his early years he had worked at heavy labor in industry, where he had acquired numerous skills that could have been utilized in several advanced positions, but since he was a black he was prohibited from taking any of them.

After an accident in a tool-making foundry, which left him with a shuffle, he was extremely lucky to land a job delivering important papers by hand. It paid little, and the hours it took to commute to work and back home were intolerable, but he dared not quit because of a peculiar law which was severely enforced: it was possible for a black to qualify for a legal pass to remain in Johannesburg and permission to occupy a house in Soweto, but to do so he had to work for one employer only for a period of ten years. If he quit or was fired, he lost the endorsement in his pass book, lost his house and his right to remain in Johannesburg. He was like a medieval serf, bound perpetually not to the land, as the serf had been, but to a specific job. This meant, obviously, that his employer could pay him scant wages, and he was powerless to protest, for if he were fired, he would lose not only his job but his entire pattern of living. As his employer often reminded him, 'Bloke, it isn't only wages I'm paying you. It's your house, your pass, the permission for your wife to be here too. Mind your step.'

He did not mind his step one blustery August day when he stepped off a curb in Commissioner Street into the path of a truck, not immediately in the path, for the driver might have avoided him had he been attentive. As it was, the truck hit him hard, and the last words he heard before he fainted were the familiar ones: 'Bloody stupid Kaffir.'

He did not have to die. He could have been saved, except that the first ambulance on the scene was marked WHITES ONLY, and of course it could not help. It did radio for a NON-WHITE; however, Old Bloke lay on the sidewalk for nearly half an hour before the proper ambulance arrived, and on arrival at the non-white casualty ward of Jo'burg hospital he was certified dead.

The anguish that showed on his face just before he fainted was not caused, as some thought, by extreme pain; nor was it resentfulness at the muttered cursing of the truckdriver, for he got that all the time. It was his instant realization of what his death might mean to Miriam, his wife of more than thirty years. In a flash he saw her patient acceptance of the hardships thrown her way, the years of separation, the hard work of rearing children alone. Whole decades had passed with only brief visits from her husband; she could not join him, apartheid laws forbade that. So she had lived a meager life in one part of South Africa, he in another, and when Bloke at last gained the right that enabled her to live with him, she was so grateful that she advised him to accept any injustice regarding hours and wages: 'We got each other at last. You do the work, we say nothin'.'

On the third day after the funeral, Miriam was summoned to the

office of Pieter Grobbelaar, director of the subdivision in Soweto where
the Ngqika home was located. He informed her that since she was no
longer married to a workingman with a legal right to remain in Soweto,
she had become what the law called 'a superfluous appendage,' and as
such, lost all right to remain in Johannesburg. He used the language
well and outlined the steps of her expulsion.

'You can stay here to collect your things, but then you must leave
for Soetgrond.'

'I've never been there. I don't even know where it is.'

'But you're a Xhosa. Your papers say that.'

'But I was born in Bloemfontein. I never been in Xhosa country.'

'The law says that you are now a temporary sojourner . . .'

At least ten times that first day Mr. Grobbelaar used the phrase 'the
law says.' On every point raised by Mrs. Ngqika the law had anticipated
her. Did she want to hold on to a house which she and her husband had
occupied for ten years and had improved significantly? Mr. Grobbelaar
could cite a law which said that the widow of a man lost all her rights
when her husband died. Did she want to stay for six months in order to
find some alternative place to stay? Mr. Grobbelaar could quote a law
which said that he could order her to clear out within seventy-two
hours. Did she want permission to take with her the new kitchen sink
which Bloke had given her last Christmas? Mr. Grobbelaar had a law
which said anything attached to the walls of government-owned property had to be left behind.

The first interview had miserable results. When she left Mr. Grobbelaar with his pile of papers, Mrs. Ngqika wept for two hours, then sent
a young boy into Johannesburg to find her son, who had a 'location in
the sky,' that is, quarters atop the apartment block in which he worked
as cleaner. When this young fellow heard that his mother was being dispossessed and shipped off to a country location which she had never
seen, he hurried out to Soweto.

'Mom, they can't send you to a place like Soetgrond. That's just a
bunch of shacks in the veld.'

'Super says I got to go.'

'To hell with Super. I won't let you go.'

'He told me to come back to his office next week. You talk with
him?'

And there was the difficulty. Her son's right to stay in Johannesburg, where he had not been born, depended upon his remaining invisible to the law. Were he to complain to Super, his papers would be in-

spected, the police would be summoned, and he, too, would be banished to Soetgrond. He was powerless to help his mother.

'Mom, there ain't nothing I can do,' and he was off to his location in the sky. If he could somehow hang on for ten years, he might earn a pass permitting him to remain in the area.

On the second visit Mr. Grobbelaar was as patient and as understanding as he had been on the first. He listened quietly to each of Mrs. Ngqika's frantic requests, then leafed through his gray canvas notebook till he found the relevant law and quoted it. He never raised his voice, and spoke not in Afrikaans, which she might not understand, but in English. He merely leafed through his papers and produced the law. When she got home she felt weak, and now she had only three weeks before she must quit this place into which she had poured so much of herself.

She was not being evicted because Bloke had been careless with his money; he had even gone to Super to ask if he could buy their little home, but the law book was explicit: 'No non-white may own land in Soweto.' And since Johannesburg non-whites were forbidden to live anywhere but Soweto, home ownership was impossible. As Mr. Grobbelaar explained: 'Bloke, you are allowed to remain here only so long as you do meaningful work to help the whites. And your wife is welcome only so long as your pass remains valid.'

That evening a group of black ladies met in Miriam Ngqika's kitchen to console her and to bid her farewell, and there was an awesomeness about the gathering, for each of these women knew that when their husbands died, they, too, would be exiled to some distant black spot which they had never seen and with which they had no affiliation whatever except by dictate of the new laws.

There was, however, in the group a schoolteacher who said, 'The Black Sash ladies have been asking us to find a case which they could fight. I think this is it.'

'I don't want to fight,' Miriam said quietly.

'But we got to fight,' the teacher said, and she warned the black women that it could become ugly and that reputations could be injured. 'Is there any scandal in your family?' the teacher asked, and the women stayed late at night, reviewing Miriam Ngqika's history, and it was blameless.

Early next morning the schoolteacher reported to the Black Sash society, and it happened that Mrs. Laura Saltwood was in attendance at a meeting of the national board, and when she heard the facts in the Ngqika case she exclaimed, 'Just what we've been waiting for!'

The committee agreed that Bloke Ngqika's fine record would be an asset in protesting this eviction, and the respectable manner in which he and his wife had lived would also help. Miriam Ngqika had an admirable reputation in the township, and it was assumed that Superintendent Grobbelaar would not be able to testify adversely against her.

He didn't. He listened carefully as Mrs. Saltwood made her plea, then in good English explained that the law . . . Here he turned the leaves to the applicable law: 'Mrs. Ngqika was always well behaved . . .' He sounded like an elementary-school teacher reporting on some infant; in fact, he was saying that he approved of the conduct of a woman fifteen years older than himself: 'She was neat, didn't drink, and I had no occasion to reprimand her.'

'Then why can't she stay?'

'Because all the Bantu are temporary sojourners, in a sense. She has become a superfluous appendage and must go.'

For an hour Superintendent Grobbelaar patiently glossed the laws, patiently explained that when a non-white family ceased to be useful to the white community, it must get out.

'But she's never been to Soetgrond,' Mrs. Saltwood protested.

'That may be so, but the law says that we must begin to get those non-useful people back to their own homelands.'

'Johannesburg is now her homeland.'

'Not any more.'

Mrs. Saltwood became almost offensive in her pressure for a humane concession, but Grobbelaar never lost his temper. When Mrs. Saltwood cried in moral outrage, 'Can't you see, Mr. Grobbelaar, that this is a great human tragedy?' he replied gently and with no bitterness, 'Mrs. Saltwood, every decision I have to make, week after week, involves what to the people concerned seems a great human tragedy. But we're trying to get our society sorted out.'

'At what human cost!'

'The cost may seem excessive to you, now. But when we have everyone in his place, you'll see that this is going to be a splendid country.'

With a wave of her arm she asked, 'Are you going to evict a million people here in Soweto?'

Superintendent Grobbelaar smiled. 'You English always exaggerate. It's five hundred and fifty thousand.'

'You don't count the illegals?'

'They will be dealt with.'

'You're going to evict them all?'

'Certainly not. Those who are essential to the operation of our businesses and industries will be allowed to remain. The rest? Yes, we'll evict them all. They'll have their own cities in their homelands.'

'How many black servants does Mrs. Grobbelaar have?'

'Two, if that's relevant.'

'You'll allow those two to stay?'

'Of course. They're essential.'

'Mr. Grobbelaar, can't you see that if you evict the blacks, Johannesburg will collapse?'

'We'll keep the ones we need.'

'But not the wives? Nor the children?'

'We want to avoid the clutter. They'll stay behind in the homelands.'

'Is there no appeal I can make in this matter?'

'Mrs. Ngqika is what the law calls a temporary sojourner, and she must go.'

He would make no concession. Never raising his voice or showing any irritation, he rebuffed every suggestion this difficult woman made, but when she was gone his face went livid and he roared at his assistant, 'I want three men to look into every aspect of that Ngqika woman's record. I'm going to teach that pair a lesson.' And forthwith he phoned a friend in the Security Branch: 'I suggest you take a close look at this Laura Saltwood. She consorts with Kaffirs.'

In the case of Mrs. Saltwood, secret police in various cities turned up only the facts that had appeared in newspapers. For some years she had been a thorn, defending non-whites against the just application of the new laws, but she had always acted in the open, so that no reasonable charge could be made against her.

'We'll keep close watch on her,' the Security Branch assured the Johannesburg police. 'One of these days she'll trip.'

In the Ngqika case something was found; a black living in Soweto informed the police that Miriam had a son occupying a location in the sky, but when they went to the address given they found that living there was an official of the government, whose wife protested that Miriam's son was the best and strongest cleaner she had ever employed and his continuance in the job was essential, so he was allowed to stay in Johannesburg, for the time being.

On a night in the third week, the last that Miriam Ngqika would spend in the house she had possessed for more than ten years but which she had not been allowed to own, the black women met in prayer and consolation. Afrikaners believed and tried to indoctrinate foreigners with the thesis that blacks of South Africa could never coalesce because they were tribal, with one group hating the other, but on this sad night Miriam's kitchen housed Xhosa, Zulu, Pondo, Sotho, Tswana and Shona. True, they were sometimes suspicious of one another, the way a respectable Episcopalian worries about a hard-shell Baptist, or the way a Catholic looks askance at a Jew, and sometimes that mistrust flared into faction fights, but that they were engaged in mortal combat was preposterous. These women shared a common destiny, and they knew it.

But as the night wore on, a remarkable event occurred. The school-teacher who had enlisted the futile aid of the Black Sash crept through the streets leading a white woman, whose presence in Soweto was illegal and whose willingness to come at night was downright revolutionary. 'This is Mrs. Saltwood,' the teacher said. 'You've heard of her.'

The women had, especially the Shona woman who had been paid by Superintendent Grobbelaar to attend this meeting; she would report this criminal act, and the dossier on Mrs. Saltwood would note that at last this dangerous English woman had stepped across the boundary line from open defiance to criminal conspiracy.

What did the conspiracy consist of? Mrs. Saltwood told the black women, 'There are women all over the world who are fighting to stop such injustices. We've lost this battle, and Mrs. Ngqika will have to go this time, but . . .' Suddenly her stalwart manner vanished and she came close to tears, but she controlled herself, thinking: Tonight they need no white woman's tears. In a low voice she said, 'Miriam, we shall pray for you. In our hearts you will always have a home, even if they take this one . . .' Now she was almost crying, but she bit her lip and sat silent, the black women taking no notice of her emotional reactions.

In the morning Superintendent Grobbelaar appeared with a govern-ment truck, and Miriam's possessions were thrown into the back. Grobbelaar checked to be sure she did not take the kitchen sink, which was now government property, and at ten o'clock the truck pulled away, with Mrs. Ngqika and two other dispossessed women sitting atop their goods.

When the truck reached the Johannesburg railway station, the driver was surprised to see Mrs. Laura Saltwood waiting to accompany Mrs. Ngqika to her new home. She would, of course, have to travel in the WHITES ONLY coach, but there was nothing to prevent her watching over the dispossessed woman; if Mrs. Saltwood wanted to waste train fare to cry over one black woman no longer needed by the white community, that was permitted; but the driver did make note of the fact, and when he reported it to the superintendent, Grobbelaar had this latest evidence of rebellion forwarded to the secret police.

It was a tedious trip south; in the rude third-class compartments provided by the South African Railways for their black customers, women from various towns, whose husbands had died, were heading for homelands they had never seen. Young men who had tried to establish themselves in cities like Pretoria and Johannesburg were being sent back into their Bantustans. Most pitiful, in many respects, were the young married women who had wanted to live with their husbands in a real home, but who had been sent away; their husbands would work in Johannesburg for six or eight or ten years without their wives. In the end they might get legal papers; they might not.

'What is so wrong,' one young woman with a college education obtained in the black nation of Lesotho said, 'is that in Alexandra the government will build a six-story building for black men working in the city, and a mile away, surrounded by a high fence, another six-story building for black women, and they honestly believe that they can keep those men locked up at night in their building and the women locked up in their building, with no communion between them. And this is supposed to continue forever. Men and women aged twenty are to live like bees in these cells, without love between them, in a temporary sojourn that could be prolonged for forty years.'

Late on the second day the train reached a small station—Hilary Siding—in eastern Cape Province, and there the women destined for Soetgrond were ordered into trucks. Mrs. Saltwood was determined to stay with Miriam, but a white policeman said that that was impossible, and he refused to allow her to ride on the government truck. So she watched in angry silence as Miriam's few belongings were thrown on the ground. Then she phoned the Saltwoods at De Kraal to borrow one of their cars, and when it arrived, she drove with Miriam sitting beside her.

They followed the route of the truck to its miserable destination, and shuddered as they saw how bleak the area was. Soetgrond became even more forbidding as rain began to fall and darkness deepened, with the car sliding this way and that in the glassy mud.

They came at last to a village, some two hundred flimsy houses recently erected on eroded land, without a tree, without one square of grass or garden. There was a store, lit with kerosene lamps, and the beginning of two roads, mostly mud. Evacuees who had been moved down during the preceding year gathered to greet the newcomers and give them such encouragement as was possible. A government official took note of names, and when he came to Mrs. Ngqika he said, 'You have Lot Two-four-three.'

'Where's that?' Mrs. Saltwood asked.

It was now evening, and the official pointed down one of the dark and muddy roads. 'Down there. You'll find a placard.'

'Is there anyone to help us with these things?' she asked.

'Help?' The official laughed. 'You carry your own. Down there.'

So the two women, one black, one white, lifted the bundles and started down the almost impassable road. In some of the shacks lights shone, and this helped them to pick their way, but in others there was nothing, forcing Laura and Miriam to stumble about. They found shack Two-three-nine, then Two-four-zero, and Laura said, 'It can't be far.' But at Two-four-one the shacks stopped. Beyond, there lay only darkness and mud.

'We must be on the wrong road,' Laura said, and they went to the last house and inquired as to where Lot Two-four-three was, and an old man said in Xhosa, 'Just down there.' And he pointed to open space.

'What did he say?' Laura asked, and Miriam said, 'My lot is down there.'

'But there's no house!' Laura exclaimed.

In the gloom the two women stared at the vacant lot, and again Laura was tempted to turn back and ask for clarification, but a faded cardboard tacked to a leaning stick said clearly: Lot Two-four-three.

Good God! This was it. This woman who had worked so hard for so many years, this woman who had reared her children and educated them, who had mended her husband's clothes so that he could hold his precious job, received this as her reward.

'There really must be some mistake,' Laura said brightly. 'I'll ask.' And leaving Miriam, she trudged back to the official at the truck. He laughed again and said, 'That's how they all started. They got their lot and made something of it.'

'But where's she to sleep?'

'That's her problem.'

'No,' Laura said quietly. 'It's my problem, and it's yours.'

'Lady, get in your car and go home. These people find a way.'

She wanted to argue with him, but he turned his back and left. Standing in the drizzle, she thought: It is his problem. Government has plans to move three million eight hundred thousand people. One in six. In America that would be forty million people uprooted from good homes and moved to bad. And tonight I'm responsible for one of them.

Slowly, refusing to cry in her anguish, she trudged back through the mud, unable to believe that what she was experiencing could occur in a civilized society. A sovereign state, in the latter half of the twentieth century, believed that this was a solution to a problem involving human beings. In the muddy darkness, with soft rain slanting at her, she could visualize Superintendent Grobbelaar leafing through his canvas-backed book, finding the applicable law. It would be there, and it would be enforced.

'We'll sleep in my car,' Laura said softly when she joined Miriam. In the rain the women wept.

In a valley not far to the north, on an eroded hillside, stood two stone cairns marking the graves of Mal Adriaan, who talked with hyenas, and Seena van Doorn, lusty daughter of old Rooi van Valck. Close by was the grave of Lodevicus the Hammer, to whom God had sent two faithful wives. Those Afrikaner pioneers had paid a terrible price for a foothold in this land, and they had done it in order to be free. In sentencing Miriam Ngqika to this awful place, their descendants had become prisoners of their own restrictive laws.

AT RESURRECTION

Despite the deprivations imposed by apartheid, the blacks of South Africa never lost their courage. They dreamed of a resurrection when they would again be free, and it is important to differentiate between the character of this dream prior to 1975 and after. The crucial change can be perceived in the contrasting lives of two men from the Vrymeer area: Daniel Nxumalo, grandson of Micah who had ridden with General de Groot and served the Van Doorns for so many years; and Matthew Magubane, whose parents worked on a farm near Venloo.

As a child Daniel Nxumalo showed such promise that as soon as possible he went not to the mines, like his brother Jonathan, but to the black college at Fort Hare. Since 1911 this institution had grown from little more than a high school to a full-fledged university with a faculty like no other in all Africa, composed of informed blacks who glimpsed the possibility of an awakening among their people. 'Teach as if the destiny of a free South Africa depended upon you alone' was the whispered motto of these teachers, and each devised tricks of speech and emphasis to signal to their wiser students: 'The police won't let me say what I ought to say next, but ask yourselves if Napoleon ever destroyed the national aspirations of any land he temporarily conquered?' A clever student at Fort Hare learned that what happened in the rest of the world might also happen in South Africa.

It was in a class in world history that Daniel first caught these signals. A woman professor who had never impressed him one way or other was teaching about the Norman Conquest of England; the curriculum was heavily loaded with developments in Holland and England rather than with pertinent events in South African life. She was explaining how Frenchmen had stormed across the Channel to impose their rule on the Saxon peasants of England, and Nxumalo was dozing.

She spoke in a singsong voice, reciting meaningless dates and genealogies, and then without a cue of any kind she stood quite still before the class and began to tell in her own words what it had been like in one small Saxon village when the conquerors arrived, and she used such vivid images and so many parallels to the trekboer invasion of frontier villages that all students became attentive. No papers rustled as she spoke on and on, treating of Saxon women with babies who could no longer own a cow for milk, and of the marching of Norman soldiers, and of the payment of taxes, until at the end she just stood there, tears streaming down her dark cheeks, not moving a muscle of her body as her voice continued with overwhelming passion the story of alien occupancy and lost freedoms.

For three months there was no other day like that, but its harrowing into the students' lives was deep and fertile, and word passed among the beds in the dormitory that this woman knew. She also knew that if she said anything specific relating to the condition of blacks in South Africa she would be spirited away by BOSS (Bureau of State Security) and perhaps never be seen again. Therefore, she had to convey her inner convictions without ever spelling them out, educating her pupils while keeping clear of BOSS. She played an intricate game, knowing that her history classes waited tensely for the next revealing lecture.

It came some fourteen weeks after she spoke of the subjugation of the Saxons. She was dealing with the difficult times America faced in

1861, when the nation was ripped apart by civil war, and meticulously she avoided the question of slavery or brutality, focusing instead on the movement of the battles, as was required in schools at that time. But when she came to the end of the war, she began to speak of what it meant to the blacks in one small town in South Carolina, and again she seemed to go into a trance and stood quite rigid as she imagined the impact of freedom on a community that had been so long in bondage, and she aroused in her students such wild visions of a different pattern of life that her small classroom became like a bomb, fused and eager to explode.

No young black, listening to her that day, could fail to comprehend her message, and among her students was one put there by BOSS, and this girl reported secretly to the police the subversion her teacher was practicing. There was no third lecture, because officials appeared, took the teacher away, and questioned her for three days before she was released. That was only the opening salvo of their harassing, and before the term's end she vanished. Her students were convinced she'd been sent to Robben Island; the fact was, she had fled the country on a forged exit permit and was teaching at the university in Nairobi, where she did not have to use Norman and Saxon as evasions for trekboer and Xhosa.

From this incident Daniel Nxumalo derived two generalizations which would determine his life pattern: It is imperative for me to learn what is happening to blacks elsewhere in the world, but I must do it so that I never attract the attention of BOSS. The first generalization was easier to carry out than the second, for as he learned more and more about Africa and Europe, he moved ever closer to the danger line.

BOSS was a semi-secret agency with power to arrest and detain without warrants of any kind. Any black or Coloured or Indian or even white who did anything that might conceivably endanger society could be investigated, and if shown to be a threat to apartheid, imprisoned on Robben Island, a speck of rocky land in Table Bay with a fine view of Table Mountain. Because of its mysteriousness, the legend grew that it was a hellhole. 'It makes Devil's Island look like a *fête champêtre*,' a French journalist wrote, but he was wrong. It was merely a strongly guarded prison for political dissidents, and was much more lenient than Alcatraz or even the best jails in Russia.

Blacks were sent there with shocking frequency, and there they stayed for having promoted the concept that their people should be freed from serfdom . . . or for having imported machine guns from

Moçambique. Some were Communist revolutionaries, but too often that label had been pasted onto men who merely sought to be the Martin Luther King or Vernon Jordan of South Africa. Had Andrew Young been a citizen of the Transvaal, he would more likely have ended up on Robben Island than as an ambassador in the United Nations.

It was not easy for an involved black scholar to stay clear of BOSS, and by the time Daniel Nxumalo left Fort Hare he had entered their notebooks in four instances: (1) at a student gathering, as reported by the same spy who had turned in the history professor, he had given a rather pointed talk when someone mentioned Brazil; if he had said nothing, the topic in itself would have alerted suspicions, because Brazil had a mainly black population, but he reviewed a book by the Brazilian professor Gilberto Freyre, *The Masters and the Slaves,* which contained ominous parallels to South Africa; (2) at a mock United Nations convention he was assigned the role of Gromyko; he hadn't sought it, but someone had to be the Russian, so he accepted, and as a good student, studied Gromyko's life and opinion; his speech was quite Slavic; (3) at a cricket match in Port Elizabeth he was noted as having cheered not for the South African team but for England; (4) on several occasions he was observed singing the Freedom Hymn, popular with students, 'with more than necessary enthusiasm.'

At the end of his student days at Fort Hare it seemed pretty clear that eventually Daniel Nxumalo would be sent to Robben Island, but when he reported to Witwatersrand University to take his master's degree in sociology he fell in with quite a different kind of professor, a white man trained in England who summoned him to his office one day and roared at him, 'You damned fool! Keep your mouth shut. How can you exercise any leverage if you're in jail? Your task is to learn. Make yourself the brightest black in South Africa, then teach others.'

The professor was careful to avoid stating specifically the end purpose of such education and never explicated his ideas of revolutionary change through superior knowledge, for this would project him also into BOSS territory, but he did defuse Nxumalo's exhibitionism, converting him into a solid, knowing scholar.

The days at Wits were like the rich summer days of February in a good year; the enthusiasms of spring were gone, but the fruition of the ripening season was at hand. Daniel met students from all over the country, and professors of extraordinary brilliance from all over the world. Many of the students were Jewish, a group he had not known before, and their keen analysis of things he took for granted enlightened him; he was particularly impressed by the way many Wits students ridiculed apartheid, defying the segregation laws in private and infuriating the more conservative citizens of Jo'burg by lining the sides of Jan Smuts Avenue outside the university and waving at them, as they streamed home from work, amusing placards of an abusive nature.

But his real education came not from Wits, where he acquired an M.A., but from a university unique to South Africa and one of its most commendable inventions. The University of South Africa had no campus, no buildings, no classrooms in the sense of a regular university. Its campus was merely a post-office address in Pretoria and a faculty of learned men and women capable of supervising students throughout the republic. By mail Nxumalo registered for his doctoral studies and by mail he conducted them. He rarely met his professors, posting them each week the results of his study. He worked in silence, spending large sums on books published in London and New York, and if he lacked the advantage of arguing with students in dormitories, he achieved a comparable intellectual stimulus when his professor wrote: 'Interesting, but apparently you haven't read what Philip Tobias says on this subject. Can you dismiss Peter Garlake's theory on Great Zimbabwe?' In fact, he read rather more widely than young men his age at Stanford or the Sorbonne.

UNISA enabled any bright young man or woman in even the most remote village to acquire an advanced degree, and from government's point of view this produced two desirable results: South Africa was becoming one of the most capable nations on earth; and the lack of a central campus prevented potentially rebellious students from congregating at one spot, where ideas offensive to the proponents of apartheid might germinate. It also avoided the problems that would arise when the government ordered other universities like Wits and Cape Town to segregate.

At the conclusion of his doctorate-by-mail, Daniel Nxumalo, having utilized the system to maximum advantage, was an educated man with a burning determination to effect revolutionary change in his birthplace, and a firm resolve to escape entanglement with BOSS. Few men graduating that year from universities like Harvard or Oxford were undertaking a more difficult, tightrope assignment, but unexpected assistance from Matthew Magubane enabled him to fulfill it.

In his early years this Matthew had showed little promise—a bull-necked boy who resented discipline—and his education might well have ended at fourteen, except that his father knew the Nxumalos and asked young Daniel, already studying for his doctorate, to talk with his son.

Nxumalo found the boy quite difficult and was about to conclude that further education would be wasted, when the boy said suddenly and with great arrogance, 'Man don't have to go to college like you did to get what you want.'

'And what do I want?'

'Change things. I can tell by your face.'

'And you want to change things, too?' When the boy just sat there, refusing to answer, Nxumalo wanted to shake him as if he were a stubborn child, but he repressed the urge and said quietly, 'Matthew, to achieve what you want, you, too, must have an education.'

'Why?'

'Because I can see that you want to lead others. And you can't do this unless you know at least as much as they do.'

He arranged for Matthew's entrance to the black high school at Thaba Nchu, erected on the very site which Tjaart van Doorn and his Voortrekkers had occupied when they were seeking their freedom. There, like Nxumalo before him, he fell under the spell of an inspired woman teacher who kept on her desk a wood-carved motto: TEACH THIS DAY AS NEVER BEFORE. She was convinced that a revolution in values was under way across all of Africa; the Portuguese had been driven from Moçambique and Angola; South-West Africa would soon be black-governed; and great Rhodesia was crumbling. She never ranted about these vast changes, merely kept on the wall behind her as she lectured a large map of the area with three changes indicated by paste-on alterations: South-West Africa became Namibia; Rhodesia was Zimbabwe; and the fine port city of Lourenço Marques was now Maputo. Day after day her students saw those signals.

'You will be with me only for a brief time,' she told them. 'I must arouse enough enthusiasm to last your lifetime.' And she did, and underlying it all was a visible commitment to revolutionary change. On no student was her impact greater than on Matthew Magubane, whose marks never exceeded a low average but whose fiery convictions surged to an apex.

Magubane expressed himself not in sports, for he was awkward, nor was he much good in debating, which required an adroit mind. What captured him, sweeping his soul, was music. He had a resonant bass voice, unusual in a high school student, and an innate sense of how to use it to advantage. He sang alone; he sang in the quartet; and best of all, he sang in the school chorus. Four times a year the South African

Railways offered black high schools concessions so that soccer teams and choruses could travel to various parts of the republic for competition with other black schools, and these safaris awakened Matthew to the possibilities of his country. He saw the rich ranching lands of the north, the Indian character of Durban, the majesty of the Cape. While other boys roughhoused in the S.A.R. coach, he stayed at the window staring at the endlessness of the barren Karroo, taking its brutal quality to heart, and with this awareness of the land he had inherited, even though it was not now his, he began to appreciate what Daniel Nxumalo had told him—that to accomplish anything in South Africa, he had to learn. In his final year he won the English and history prizes.

Magubane and Nxumalo arrived at the University of Zululand the same April, the first as a stocky fellow with the kind of hairdo that infuriated whites, the second as a gracile young man with a three-piece suit and neat haircut. They maintained a cool distance until the first term had almost ended; then Nxumalo went to the younger man's quarters, missed him, and left a note: *I would be pleased to see you in my room at five, Daniel Nxumalo.*

When Magubane in his rough clothes reached there, he found two upperclassmen seated on the floor, accompanied by three girl students, all drinking sweetish tea and discussing Gunnar Myrdal. It was a disconcerting experience, with Magubane conspicuously out of place but appreciative of the fact that Professor Nxumalo still retained an interest in him.

He did not want to become like the polished young men sitting on the floor; he was more at home with radical students who met around back tables at the café, and it was through association with them that he fell afoul of BOSS. It had started on a train excursion to Durban when Matthew led a gang of noisy students in a selection of revolutionary songs:

'There's a sun in the east
Rising, rising.
There's a moon in the west
Falling, falling.
I follow the sun, no matter how bright.
There goes the moon, down into night.
Oh, glorious sun!'

Police officials went to the university following this exhibition, for there were always spies, and the administrators asked Professor Nxumalo to warn young Magubane of the dangerous path he was pursuing, singing songs like that and encouraging others to join him.

When they were alone Daniel turned to Matthew: 'You're heading for trouble. You must pause and take a deep breath.'

'There can be no more pausing,' Matthew said.

'What do you intend?' Nxumalo asked evenly, not wanting to hear the response.

'I think many like me will have to go into exile. Into Moçambique.'

'No!' Daniel cried. 'That is not the way.'

'We'll go into Moçambique and get guns, the way the blacks in Moçambique went into Tanzania and got their guns.'

'South Africa will not be Moçambique. The Portuguese did not have the will to defend themselves. The Afrikaners do.'

'Then we will have to shoot the Afrikaners.'

'Believe me, they will shoot you down.'

'The first ten thousand, the second. But others will keep coming.'

'You expect to be in the first ten thousand?'

'I'd be ashamed not to be.'

They spoke in Zulu, and the phrases young Magubane used echoed the great periods of Zulu history; they were words from a past century applied to the one that was coming. He visualized himself as marching in an impi that dared not turn back, even though it faced certain annihilation. 'The others will keep coming,' Matthew said. He would not be among those others, and the victories they won would be unknown to him, for he would be dead, but they would be his victories, too.

Teacher and pupil ended this painful exchange centuries apart but with strong admiration each for the other, and when Professor Nxumalo discussed Magubane with the administration, he used empty and non-committal phrases: 'I came away convinced that Matthew Magubane saw the error of his ways . . . There is no reason why he cannot return to what he was at Thaba Nchu . . . I see a bright future for this young man, for his commitment will match his grades . . .'

Before the end of the second term, Magubane was picked up by BOSS operatives and transferred to a police interrogation center in remote Hemelsdorp, where many infamous inquisitions had been conducted and where Jurgen Krause, grandson of Piet Krause, was determined to stamp out even the slightest signs of black insurgency.

He was a six-foot-three, broad-shouldered blond Afrikaner with a generous smile and powerful fists. As soon as the door closed behind

Magubane, and the northern officers were gone, Krause said to his assistant, Sergeant Krog, 'Bring him here.'

With a mighty sweep of his right arm, Krog struck Magubane from behind, knocking him forward, and as the black stumbled toward Krause's desk, the latter swung his right fist with full power and smashed Matthew in the face. As the boy fell, both Krause and Krog leaped at him, punching and kicking until he fainted.

A security investigation anywhere in South Africa was a solemn affair; over the years some fifty men had fallen carelessly from eight-story buildings, strung themselves up with public-works blankets and died, but in Hemelsdorp, investigation was an art, and here such mistakes were avoided. When Magubane revived, his face wet with the water tossed over him, he found himself facing Sergeant Krog, who held an electric cattle prod.

'Undress,' Krog said.

When Magubane hesitated, the sergeant summoned two minor assistants, who ripped Matthew's clothes away, and as soon as he stood naked, Krog applied the prod to his testicles, watching with satisfaction as Matthew leaped and jumped to avoid the torture. When he ran into a corner, bending to protect his genitals, Krog jammed the end of the prod into his anus, applying such a heavy charge of electricity that the student fainted.

Year after year one black in four throughout the general population was arrested for some trivial offense or other, and it was fortunate for them that not all police were as determined and sadistic as the team of Krause and Krog. Their like could be found in most countries; Russia, East Germany, Iran, Argentina, Brazil, all had such interrogators. But the majority of South African policemen tried to be law-abiding officers of justice; Krause and Krog were officers of terror.

For three days Magubane was punched and kicked and tormented. He did get fed and he was allowed to go to the bathroom and drink as he required, but the torture was incessant. At the end of four days the only charge against him was 'You cheeky Kaffir bastard,' a phrase leveled against any black who had progressed as far as high school or who refused to behave deferentially. It was a terrifying charge, because almost invariably it was accompanied by some brutal punishment, so that the words actually meant 'Take that, you cheeky Kaffir bastard,' the *that* being a smash to the mouth or a prod with an electric probe.

Matthew had been told, on the playing grounds at Thaba Nchu, that 'white police officers are preoccupied with black genitals,' but in his innocence he could not conceive what this meant. Now he was learning, for Krause and Krog relished having him stand before them naked so they could jab his private parts with the electric tip, and once, as they prepared to do so, Matthew broke into laughter. He was recalling what he had heard a black man say after being released: 'They put so much electricity into me I was afraid I'd light up like a bulb.'

Matthew's laughter so infuriated Krause that he and Krog kicked him unconscious, and when he revived, still naked in the cold room, he heard the first serious charge against him. The officers were singing in cracked and unharmonious voice the freedom song:

> 'There's a sun in the east
>   Rising, rising.
> There's a moon in the west
>   Falling, falling.'

The words were familiar, as Matthew came out of his daze, but not the tune, and he looked with pity at the two officers, for they were singing their own dirge and could not find the melody.

'What do you mean, "a sun in the east"?'

'Nothing, Boer.' A smash to the side of the head.

'Don't you mean Moçambique?'

'No, Boer.' Another smash behind the ear.

'Don't you mean the swine who have fled this country into Moçambique?'

'No, Boer.' Another smash.

'I suggest, Magubane, that you mean the terrorists with guns over there.'

'No, Boer.' This time he was jabbed so hard with the electric prod that he danced in the air, arms and legs in all directions.

'Running to Moçambique, are you?'

He was too numb to respond, so they jabbed him for almost two minutes, after which he fainted.

When he revived, too weak to stand erect, they propped him against a wall, and he felt blood oozing from his nose. He was positive that this had not occurred when he was conscious; they must have been kicking him while he lay on the floor, and had moved parts of his body to see if anything had been broken by their heavy boots.

'And what, pray tell, Mr. Magubane, is "falling, falling"?'

'Nothing, Boer.' More punishment.

'Stand up, you cheeky Kaffir bastard. Now you tell us what you mean by "falling, falling." I put it to you, Magubane. You mean that South Africa is falling, don't you?'

There was more punishment, the flailing out of worried men, and Matthew realized that he was being tortured so furiously because he had been overheard singing a song whose words the police could not interpret.

'All right, you cheeky bastard, you sing the song for us.' Krause began in his monotone to chant the words, joined quickly by Krog, whose efforts augmented the dissonance. 'Sing!' Krog screamed, and slowly, with deep powerful tones, Magubane picked up the song, lending it significance and beauty:

> 'I follow the sun, no matter how bright.
> There goes the moon, down out of sight.'

Krog, reading from a typed copy of the song, detected Magubane's change in words and halted the singing.

'You changed the words!'

'There are many verses,' Magubane said.

On the seventh day he heard the second serious charge: 'People say you're a black-consciousness activist.'

'I am for black power, yes.' Smash to the jaw.

'You're a Bantu, a stupid goddamned Kaffir Bantu, with no power at all!'

'Yes, Boer, I am an African.' Fist in the mouth.

Afrikaners like Marius van Doorn, the son of Detleef, looked forward to the day when there was one citizenship in South Africa; he felt himself to be a man of Africa—an African—and he did not want that honorable word applied only to blacks. But other Afrikaners were infuriated if any black claimed to be an African, as Magubane was doing, for they sensed a grave danger: the black was seeking outside help from his brothers in powerful black nations like Nigeria.

'Now, Mr. Magubane, I want you to explain what makes you think you're an African.' Prod with the electric tip. 'Dance if you wish, but go on with your explanation.' More prodding.

'I'm a native of Africa, as you are. We're both Africans.' Smash to the face. 'I'm willing to accept you, and you must accept me.'

'You cheeky bastard!' And the fury of the two officers at being linked in a brotherhood stemming from a common terrain was ungovernable.

Next morning Magubane awakened convinced that on this day Officers Krause and Krog intended killing him. He was mistaken. BOSS was never so callous as to plan a murder; all it sought was to intimidate potential troublemakers. 'Trimming the hedge,' Krause called it. 'When a cheeky Kaffir starts to stick his head up, like a wild branch in a hedge, what's the sensible thing to do? Knock it back.' This prevented trouble later on, so BOSS developed the system of bringing any black who was beginning to exhibit leadership into custody, kick him around a bit, and set him free. The danger was that after nine or ten days of interrogation the black man might be beyond freedom: 'Case No. 51. Verdict. Death while trying to escape.'

And this might have been Magubane's end except for the work of two men outside the jail who had never met Magubane. The first was André Malan, white, twenty-nine, and a reporter for the *Durban Gazette*. He was a courageous chap dedicated to the high quality of South African journalism and suspicious of why so many Hemelsdorp investigations ended in fatal attempts at escape.

On the day of Matthew Magubane's arrest two black men had slipped into Malan's office and expressed a premonition that the young man was exactly the kind of black who would prove so intractable that Jurgen Krause would be tempted to forget what the regulations said about avoiding undue pressure. 'Watch what happens,' the blacks warned.

So André Malan began writing articles about the detention of Magubane, and he asked the police to issue reports of the young man's well-being. In fact, he created so much pressure that officials became irritated and decided to apply one of their laws against him.

There was a law in South Africa which said that BOSS could invade the quarters of any writer at any time without a warrant, and if they found any notes or materials or photographs which *might* be used to write an article which *might* be offensive to the government, that writer could be detained indefinitely without any charges being brought against him.

On the morning of the eighth day one of Malan's two black informants ran to his apartment, shouting, 'Get rid of your papers!'

As a newsman who had watched three of his colleagues imprisoned by BOSS, he required no additional explanation; he destroyed the few papers he had allowed to accumulate, even those not relating to Matthew Magubane, then hastily scanned his bookshelves to see if any of the thousands of books banned by the government were there. Reasonably assured, he waited.

The BOSS crew did appear. They did ransack his quarters. And they did find one book published by the World Council of Churches in Geneva, and it was this which justified them in putting him in jail, on no charges, with no warrant, and with no right of self-defense.

News coverage of Matthew Magubane ended. The police were free to continue their probing of his life and beliefs as they wished, except that on a farm near Vrymeer the rebellious young black Jonathan Nxumalo, unemployed now but once a worker at the Golden Reef Mines, had been following in the newspapers the running record of Magubane's detention. Now he heard of Malan's arrest and deduced that Magubane was about to be murdered. Convening four friends, he took an informal vote: 'How many say we try to rescue Magubane?' All five voted yes. 'And then flee to Moçambique?' This time only four voted, the man who refrained explaining, 'My mother . . .'

'No explanations necessary. Tomorrow night we could all be dead.'

'Or on the way to Moçambique.'

Jonathan then cleared his throat and said, tentatively, 'My brother's home on vacation from university. I think we should have his advice.' Someone was dispatched to fetch the professor, and when he stood at the entrance to the small room in which they met, he realized that the men inside represented a conspiracy. To take even one step into that room would make him a part of the criminal movement, with the possibility of a lifetime in prison, or even death. His whole inclination was to turn and run, but the liveliness of their faces made that impossible. These were the young men he had been training, and now they were about to train him. He joined them.

'We're going to storm the jail at Hemelsdorp,' his brother said.

'I supposed that might be it.'

'We've a cache of guns smuggled in from Moçambique.'

'I wish you could do it without guns.'

'This is the year of the gun,' Jonathan said. 'If we get to Moçambique, what do you think we should do?'

If he had left the room even at this point he might have avoided incrimination, but like other blacks across the nation he felt a growing sense of the future. 'I would not storm the police station. You could all get killed.' As soon as he uttered these words he knew they were irrelevant; these men were prepared to die.

'About Moçambique,' his brother repeated.

'I can't go with you. My job is to teach young men at the university.'

'Daniel,' his brother cried. 'We don't want you to come. Men like you . . . stay here to build. Men like us . . . get out so we can tear down.'

Professor Nxumalo felt old and out of place; he was alarmed at where his teaching had led, but he was also profoundly excited by the challenge. 'When you reach Moçambique—and you will, I know you will—you've got to consolidate. Make no move till you can rely upon help from all the frontiers. Namibia, Zimbabwe, Botswana, Vwarda, and especially Moçambique. Then move subtly, a push here, a retreat there. In a dozen years, with help from Russia, East Germany and Cuba, the monolith will crumble.'

'We give it the first push tomorrow,' Jonathan said, embracing his brother. And when the professor was gone, he handed out the guns.

By separate routes the five young men journeyed to Hemelsdorp, having agreed to rush the detention center at one in the afternoon, when lesser policemen, like Krog, would be at lunch and their superiors, like Krause, so well-fed as to be lethargic. Jonathan's men would be armed, a fact which almost guaranteed their execution if apprehended.

Quietly they converged on the barracks, waited an interminable five minutes in position, then without any kind of juvenile exhibitionism, walked resolutely into the headquarters, took possession of the desk and the hallways, and hurriedly searched the rooms till they found Magubane.

'What's happening?' he asked through swollen lips.

'Off to Moçambique!'

As they ran from the barracks without having fired a round, the young man who had to care for his mother headed north, where he would function underground. The others concealed their guns and went into exile.

One of the most gratifying days in Van Doorn's life occurred on 16 December 1966, when he was invited to deliver the main speech at the Day of the Covenant celebrations at the new housing development that had arisen, under his direction, on the site from which the black township of Sophiatown had been bulldozed. The area had been renamed Triomf and was now occupied by white Afrikaner families who kept their little houses neat and their flower beds flourishing.

But as Detleef drove along the clean wide streets that had replaced the slum alleys he said somewhat sourly to his white chauffeur, 'I'll wager most people in those houses have no idea what the new name means.'

His chauffeur said quickly, 'But we know what a triumph it was, don't we?'

Van Doorn showed his appreciation for this support, then said, 'Sophiatown was a national disgrace. Crime, poverty, young tsotsis running wild.'

'A white man would be afraid to go there after dark,' the chauffeur agreed.

'Tell me frankly, isn't our new Triomf a hundred times better?'

Like any impartial judge, the chauffeur had to admit the new suburb was not only better, but was also inhabited by people of a much higher status: 'You did a wonderful thing here, Mr. van Doorn.'

Inspired by such approbation, Detleef showed real enthusiasm as he approached the podium in the church hall. Among the other dignitaries on the platform were four ancient men, oudstryders (old fighters), veterans of the Boer War, who nodded approvingly as he lambasted the enemies of the nation. In many ways his speech was a summation of his vision regarding the future of the Volk:

'Our beloved Voortrekkers, Retief, Pretorius and Uys, who answered the summons to freedom, saved this nation when it faced mortal danger. With pride I add my own grandfather, Tjaart van Doorn, who helped in handing to us the precious gem that is South Africa. They gave us more—their vision of God's will as it guides the destiny of the Afrikaner nation . . .

'Never forget, this is the land of the Afrikaner, paid for with our blood and held through our faith. When the father of this nation, Jan van Riebeeck, first set foot on this soil in 1652 he found it empty, absolutely empty, of any Xhosa or Zulu, who had not then reached south of the Limpopo. Oh, there were a few Bushmen and Hottentot who died tragically from smallpox and other diseases. But this land was empty and we took it . . .

'To protect what God gave us in His covenant we have fought and won great battles, and we shall forever be ready to move back into laager to resist any onslaught against us. This we must do, because we were placed here by God to do His work . . .

'But let us be always mindful that there are vicious forces arrayed against us, eager to break the spirit of our small proud people who sparkle like a diamond among the nations of the earth. These bitter enemies refuse to see the wisdom of what we are trying to accomplish here. Who are these enemies? The anti-Afrikaner establishment. The priest establishment. The English establishment. The press establishment. The wealthy liberalists who still grudge us our glorious national victory in 1948 . . .

'When we occupied this empty land, we were a pitiful few, devout Christians unable to stem the entrance of Xhosa and Zulu into our country. Now that they are here, it is our duty to guide and discipline and govern them. When the English ruled, the blacks were like cattle moving over all the land, grazing here, grazing there, destroying the rich veld. We put a stop to that. We put them back in the kraal. And now we move them from places like the old Sophiatown to new quarters of their own . . .

'But we are told today that civilization means equality and that the Kaffir [his first use of this word] must be raised up and given a free share of everything the Afrikaner worked and died for. I have nothing against the black man. I have deep sympathy for his backwardness, but I do not want him as my brother. [Laughter from the audience] And I certainly do not want to hear him prate about "Africa for the Africans." This part of Africa is for the Afrikaners, and no one else . . . [This occasioned wild applause, and Detleef took a drink of water; he was sweating now and very red in the face; his voice shook with emotion.]

'I am the first to admit that the Kaffir has a place in this country, and our new laws will help him keep to it. We will never allow him to dictate: "White man do this," or "White man do that," for if we do he'll take our head. I say to the Kaffir and the brown man, "Out of the kindness of our hearts, out of our deep study of Divine Providence, we will chart a path for you along which you can find happiness and peace . . ." [More applause and cheering]

'My final message on this sacred day commemorating the death of our heroes in Dingane's Kraal is to our young people. Sons and daughters! Be physically and spiritually prepared for the assaults our enemies will make. Protect your identity as we protected your language. When I was a child they stuck a dunce cap on my head because I spoke Dutch. I fought back. You, too, will have to fight, as these veterans behind me fought. Allow no terrorist regiments on your soil, no Communist propaganda, no liberalist weakness, no Anglican bishops spreading lies. And when you fight, know that you are doing God's will, for he ordained that you should be here . . .

'If you are steadfast, you will triumph, as we triumphed over poverty and slums when we bulldozed Sophiatown to make way for this splendid development you see today with its white houses and neat gardens. In the darkest days of war Oom Paul Kruger said, "I tell you God says this nation will survive. Most certainly the Lord will triumph." Today, young people, look about you. This is the hour of Afrikaner triumph.'

As he moved away from the podium, he felt a pain in his chest; he swayed unsteadily, but reached his chair and sat down. Other speakers followed, with one confining himself to 'Triomf over Sophiatown,' but it never occurred to anyone present to ask what it was that they had triumphed over when they erased this black spot. Over the old women who had worked in white homes for fifty years and hoped for a refuge in which to die? Over young black children who had begun to learn in Father Huddleston's missions? Over sturdy black workmen who had long manned essential jobs in Johannesburg and who now had to travel many miles to work each morning and back at night? Over the clergymen who had protested the immorality of bulldozing serviceable homes so that favored whites could be spared the sight of black neighbors? Over the good white women, English and Dutch, of the Black Sash who had tried to protect the rights of black mothers and their children? Over the attempts at reconciliation, which should have prevailed in South Africa and didn't? Over what had Van Doorn's system triumphed, except the forces of reason?

The pains assailed Detleef again, accompanied this time by a heaviness in the chest which he had to recognize as serious. To the Boer War veteran next him he whispered, 'Damnation! Just as we were getting things truly sorted out.'

He was whisked to a private ward in the Johannesburg General Hospital, and his family was summoned from Vrymeer. When they assembled at his bed and heard his labored breathing they waited for

Marius to speak, but Detleef did not want to hear from that one. He distrusted his son, and as older people often will, leaped a generation and extended his shaking hands toward his granddaughter, flaxen-haired Susanna. 'Come closer, Sannie,' he whispered, and when he kissed her hands, a gesture most inappropriate from him, the others realized that death must be near. Marius left the room to call Vrymeer, asking that two things precious to the old man be brought in at once.

'Sannie,' the dying man said, 'you must always do the thing that is right for your country.' This had been the dictate of his life: the honest move, the just act. He felt that the determination of what was just and honest had best be left to the judgment of men like himself, who were above greed or vanity and who acted solely in the interests of society.

'You're inheriting a noble country,' he told the girl. 'Now that people have been told their place and can rely on just laws to help them keep it.' He noticed that Marius had reentered the room and was wincing at this summary, but he could not understand why. He could not conceive that a son of his might ask, 'Who assigned the places? Can such allocations be made without consultation with those who are being assigned?' Detleef was convinced that since well-intentioned men, attentive to God's teachings, had made these decisions, to question them endangered the republic. He could not believe that his son would peck like a raven at a fabric so justly woven.

As the afternoon wore on he again began to visualize the enemies who had endangered his land; immortal adversaries, they ranged themselves along the wall waiting for him to die. First were the blacks, who threatened to engulf the nation, cursed offspring of Dingane and stained, like him, with treachery. No! No! First there were the English. Always there were the English enemies, with their clever ways, their superiority of language and class. Two thousand years from now, when Great Pretoria lay crumbled in dust, you could be sure that some Englishman had knocked down the stones. They were the permanent enemy, and he was about to cry out that he still hated them when his mind cleared and he said boldly to everyone in the room, 'I have never hated anyone. I have acted only from a sense of justice.'

He did not hate the English—he pitied them, with their lost empire and their doomed superiorities. Nor did he hate the Indians, either; they were a sad lot huddling in their stores. It was regrettable that they had not been expelled, as the Chinese were; then he smiled, for the vision of Mahatma Gandhi flashed across his mind. 'We got rid of that one,' he said. Nor did he hate the Jews, even though they had stolen the diamond mines and the gold. 'They contaminate our land. We should have expelled them, too.'

'Who?' his wife asked, but before he could respond, there was a commotion in the hall. An official of some kind, you could tell that from his voice, was warning someone: 'You can't go in there. Blacks are not allowed on these floors.'

Marius hurried into the hallway, offered explanations, and soon brought into the sickroom Moses Nxumalo, who carried in his arms the great brassbound Bible. It was impossible to determine which of these gifts from the country pleased the dying man most. He loved old Moses, who had shared so many of the important moments of his life, and he cherished the sacred Bible which contained the record of that life, reaching back through the generations to the young sailor who had planted this Holy Book, actually and figuratively, on South African soil.

He held out his hands to both the black and the Bible.

'I'm so glad you came,' he said weakly.

'I've been weeping for you,' Moses said. 'But now my eyes are cured, seeing you again.' They spoke of old days, of meaningful adventures, and it was impossible for the black to acknowledge that it was this white who had done so much to hedge in his sons, who had promulgated so many laws to restrict and emasculate them. Detleef was merely the good master, and to see him so near death was bitterness.

It was the Bible that brought Detleef back to reality, and he began thumbing its heavy pages, printed so long ago in Amsterdam, its heavy Gothic letters setting for all time the course of right and wrong. It was inconceivable that God had delivered these words in anything but Dutch . . .

He stopped. Not even at the doorway to death could he forgive one insidious enemy who fought both South Africa and God: the infamous World Council of Churches, which refused to see that what Van Doorn and his helpers had done was right and openly made cash contributions to murderous revolutionaries. 'How can they ignore the good things we've done?'

'Who ignores us?' Marius asked.

'Why do they all persecute us?' he whimpered.

And he began to recite the sufferings of the Boers: 'The Black Circuit. Slagter's Nek. Blaauwkrantz. Dingane's Kraal. The Jameson Raid. Chrissiesmeer Camp.' Bitterly he repeated that infamous name: 'Chrissiesmeer!' Then: 'Where's Sannie?'

Impatiently he gestured Moses and Marius aside and reached toward his granddaughter. When he saw her bright face outlined against the stark-white walls he whispered, 'Sannie, never forget what they did to us at Chrissiesmeer.'

Mention of that dreadful place so enraged him that blood drained from his brain and he passed into a strange kind of coma: He saw his bed ringed not with members of his family but with the timeless enemies of the Volk: Hilary Saltwood siding with the Xhosa. The man from America giving orders to the hangman at Slagter's Nek. Dingane giving his bloodstained signal. Cecil Rhodes, implacable foe. Teacher Amberson making him wear the sign: I SPOKE DUTCH TODAY. The Jew Hoggenheimer, who had monopolized the mines. The Catholics who had sought to destroy his Martin Luther church. Officials from the United Nations talking sanctions. Was ever a nation so beset by enemies? And among the shadowy figures he saw his own son, who had chosen a scholarship at contaminating Oxford rather than a captaincy of the Springboks. Enemies all.

Then blood returned to his fevered brain and a light seemed to enter the room, illuminating past and future. He rose on his arm and began shouting, 'Laager toe, broers— Draw the wagons into a circle!

'Sannie, tell the drivers to draw . . .' He fell back, breathing heavily, and reached for old Moses: 'Warn your sons—everyone must hold to his assigned place . . .'

When it became apparent that he was dead, Marius leaned down to kiss the embattled face, then covered it with a blanket. Closing the old Bible, he said, 'Lucky man. He won't have to watch the consequences of his handiwork.'

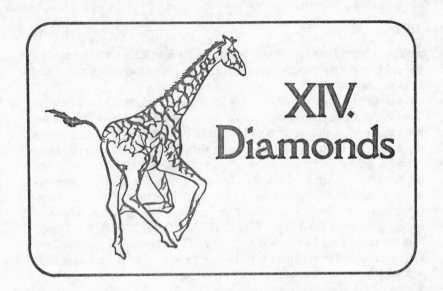

XIV.
Diamonds

ON three hundred and fifty-five days a year you could smell Pik Prinsloo at a distance of twenty feet. One old prospector who had worked the diamond diggings with him said, 'Pik takes a wash once a year. Twenty-fourth of December. Says it covers him three ways. Christmas, New Year's and the heat of summer. So for about ten days he's tolerable, but come the middle of January, then it's the same old Pik.'

Had he been married, his wife would probably have made him bathe, but he lived with a slatternly sister in a gypsy-type tin-walled house-wagon drawn by eight donkeys. He was seventy-one years old, toothless, bearded, stooped, with rheumy eyes and matted hair; he wore a flimsy undershirt, sagging pants, untied shoes with no socks and an oil-stained khaki hat. He had been haunting diamond fields since the age of ten.

He lived on canned foods, bits of meat and such mealie-pap as his slovenly sister bothered to make; his house-wagon was such a disgrace that other diamond hunters said, 'Even the bush lice won't go in.' Yet he lived in a kind of odoriferous glory, because on six mornings a week, year after fading year, he wakened with the conviction that on this day his luck was bound to change: 'Today I find that diamond as big as a fist.' After a swig of lukewarm coffee two or three days old, he would shuffle out the door of his house-wagon, stand in the dust, scratch himself under both arms and shout, 'Kom nou! Waar is die diamante?' And he would almost run to the spot where his five sieves waited and his pick and shovel rested against a tree. He was perpetually convinced that a day would come when he would find his diamond.

He had little cause for optimism. As a boy of fourteen he had been the main support of one of those marginal Afrikaner farms, and on this waterless land he had been expected to sustain himself and his sister. Four dreadful drought-ridden years passed as they fought to grub existence from the inhospitable acres, always urged on by their predikant, who cited various parables relevant to their condition. One Sunday, after returning from prayers for rain to a noontime meal of pumpkin and mealies, Pik and his sister concluded that God did not intend them to struggle with land to which He sent no water, so they abandoned the farm and acquired the house-wagon and eight mules.

In 1926, as a youth of eighteen, he searched for alluvial diamonds on the Lichtenburg diggings, following a tributary of the Vaal, and there he found his first profitable gem: a flawed stone of just under four carats for which he received the intoxicating sum of £47. That night he announced himself as a diamond digger: 'Pik Prinsloo, diamonds.'

His luck had not held. For five desolate years he trudged the Lichtenburg diggings without turning up another diamond of any size. He found chips. He found trivial stones of less than half a carat. But the diamond as big as a fist eluded him, as did those as big as the tip of his little finger, and in 1932 he experienced the indignity of having to quit the diamond fields to test his fortune in the eastern Transvaal gold fields, but even when he did pan a few payable nuggets he derived little satisfaction from them. He was a diamond man; the lure of those beautiful gems tantalized him, so back he went with his spinster sister, his mules and his sieves to probe the smaller streams of the north.

He had no luck whatever, and 1937 found him on the emerald fields near Gravelotte, at the western border of the Kruger National Park. Sometimes at night, sitting in his house-wagon in some lonely spot, he would hear the lions and hyenas, but unlike the other diggers, he never ventured into the park to see the great beasts. 'I'm a diamond man,' he growled. 'I oughtn't to be here at all. A bucketful of emeralds isn't worth one good diamond, and some day . . .'

No matter where he went, or how his fortunes decayed, he had one treasure which differentiated him from most other men, and on the rare occasions when he left his sister to join the other diggers in some rural bar and strangers would intrude, he would be apt to place upon the counter a small flat object wrapped in dirty canvas and say ominously, 'Look in there and you'll see who I am.' And the stranger would rather gingerly unfold the canvas and find therein a Digger's Certificate, printed by the government in 1926, which stated that Pik Prinsloo, of Kroonstad in the Orange Free State, was a licensed digger. And on the back, in variously colored inks, stood the record of his having renewed this precious license each following year, at a fee of five shillings.

'I'm a diamond man,' Pik explained, and if anyone pointed out that he was working emeralds, he would apologize: 'Right now I'm gathering capital, because I got me eye on a stream up north . . .' He would hesitate, turn his rheumy eyes upon the stranger, and ask, 'Would you maybe want to back me? I know where there's diamonds for certain.'

In this way, in the summer of 1977, Pik found his fifth partner, a commercial traveler from Johannesburg who had always wanted to participate in the diamond madness. They had met in a bar, and when Pik displayed his Digger's Certificate with its endless renewals, the man said, 'I been looking for a fellow just like you. How much do you need?'

In the excited discussion which ensued, the Johannesburg man had the good sense to ask, 'By the way, has anyone else staked you? I mean, would there be outstanding claims ahead of mine?'

For Pik Prinsloo to lie about his diamond business was impossible: 'I owe four men ahead of you.' Then, grabbing the stranger's arm, he added quickly, 'But they was long ago. Maybe twenty years.'

The Johannesburg man drew back, looked at the old digger, and hesitated. But then he saw that wizened face, the lips without teeth, so that nose and chin almost met, the torn undershirt, the sockless feet and the deep fire burning inside the watery eyes, and he knew that if he intended gambling on some self-deceived diamond man, this was the kind he had been seeking.

'How much would you need to move north?' he asked quietly.

Without hesitation, for he had been calculating such problems for fifty years, Pik replied, 'Three hundred and fifty rand.'

'You have it,' the man said, and that was how in the New Year of 1978, Prinsloo and his nagging sister drove their donkeys north to the Swartstroom, parked their house-wagon in a field some miles north of Sannie's Tits, and started their prospecting.

Old Pik had been attracted to this particular stream by signs he had seen many years before, the harbingers of diamonds: agates and flecks of reddish garnet mixed in with ilmenite, the jet-black rock which had first been identified and named at the Ilmen Mountains in Russia. The more he studied the stream in those days, the more convinced he had become that it must be diamantiferous. 'The bantoms are heavy and black,' he told his sister in their filthy wagon. 'There's got to be diamonds here.'

'If there was,' she grumbled, 'somebody else would've noticed.'

'Maybe somebody else wasn't as smart as me,' he said, but when weeks passed without a find, she insisted that he head south to sites which had been proclaimed.

Now he still had more than three hundred rand, enough, counting his state pension, to live on for three years at the frugal rate at which he and his sister ate. One huge can of baked beans, the top knocked off by a dulled opener, a pot of mealie meal and some scraggy mutton would suffice for three days, bent forks scraping over the tin plates. 'Ek sê vir jou, Netje. [I'm telling you, Netje.] There's diamonds this time, and I'm the one to find the damned thing.'

Jamming his beaten hat with its torn wide brim onto his uncombed head, he hunched up his shoulders as if marching to war, and went forth to probe the Swartstroom.

Fortunately, the level of the stream was low, so that he could concentrate on the meanders of this remnant of the mighty rivers which had cut away the earth. He worked only the inside of the bends, for there the water slowed and dropped whatever heavy objects it might be carrying. If there were diamonds, they would be hiding here, so day after day he dug the gravel and passed it through his sieves. When he eliminated the larger rocks, which he inspected fleetingly, he was left with a residue which might conceivably hide a diamond, and this he sieved carefully, with much water and a poetic, drifting motion that swirled the gravel about in such a way as to gravitate the heavier bantom to the bottom and into the center. Thus, when he flipped the sieve over onto a flat surface, any diamond would be on top, in the center.

On a hot morning in January 1978 he carried his sieve to the shaded area where he always did his inspecting, flipped it, and with a curious knifelike scraper, which he had been using for more than forty years, sorted the agates, certain that on this lucky day he was destined to find a diamond. None appeared. Had one been in the rubble it would have shone so brilliantly in the shadows that he would have spotted it within seconds, but none did. Instead he saw something which pleased him mightily, so that he ran from his pan to call his sister: 'Netje! Look at what we have!'

In her felt slippers and faded cotton dress she came grumbling from the house-wagon, picking her way along the rocky footpath to the stream, where she studied the mess left by the sorting and snorted, 'Gemors, man. Nothing!'

'The little ones!' Pik cried with bursting excitement.

She looked at the little ones and saw nothing, at which her exasperated brother shouted, 'The little red ones! They're garnets!'

Beside them she saw the ilmenite, too, glistening black, and then even she had to concede that this stream was worth searching.

January and February, the sweating months, were spent probing the inner banks where the water slowed, and although not a single diamond chip was found, garnet and ilmenite continued to show in faint traces, signs as positive as if someone had posted a notice: DIAMONDS HIDING HERE.

So he kept searching, and then one morning in October, after he had gobbled two spoonfuls of cold pap, he shuffled out, heart high and trousers dragging, to a new bend in the Swartstroom, and on the first panning, when he flipped the gravel, there in the middle of the small mound rested a shimmering gem larger than the end of his thumb.

There could be no mistake about it, for although the stone lay in shadow it glimmered like a light in darkness, vibrating even through the film of muddy deposit that clouded it. It was a diamond, the biggest old Pik had ever found in fifty-two years of searching, and he was so stunned by his discovery that when he tried to shout for Netje, no sound came from his throat.

And that was good, because as soon as he hefted the diamond, and cleaned it, and studied it in sunlight, seeing that it had pentagon-shaped faces and what appeared to be a good color, he realized that he must keep his find secret until such time as he had explored the vicinity. But this posed a problem. South African diamond law was bitterly severe where possession of uncut gems was concerned; and the most reviled profession a man could follow was I.D.B.—illegal diamond buyer.

The finding of even the smallest diamond became an act encased in legal paperwork. Within twenty-four hours Pik had, by law, to enter his diamond in his personal register, stating its site of finding, its approximate weight and likely value. Then within three days he must carry his diamond to some police station and register it, and he could not simply report that he had found such-and-such a stone of such-and-such weight; he must show it to them physically, and allow them to describe and weigh it. These details would be entered in both his register and the police record, and stamped. And as soon as that was done, the world would be informed that Pik Prinsloo had found a diamond stream, and hungry men would flood the place.

Pik was familiar with this procedure; indeed, he had often dreamed of chaperoning a real diamond through the intricate process, but now that he had control of one, he sought to protect himself. He wanted four or five days to inspect this bend on the chance that it contained a parcel of equal gems, but to delay involved illegality, and he had seen too many men go to jail for ignoring the strict rules.

What to do? He sat for some time with the diamond in his cupped hands, convincing himself that it was as fine a stone as he had first believed: Hell, this one'll bring two thousand rand! The thought staggered him, so he studied the stone again. It was a good one and it really could bring as much as two thousand rand: God Almagtig! We're rich! Trembling, he spit on the diamond, polished it, and was sitting with it in the sun when he became aware that a drop of moisture had fallen upon it. He was sweating, and it was then that he buried the diamond beneath a well-marked rock and returned feverishly to the stream.

He dug and sieved and gravitated all that day, but found nothing. At dusk he returned to the house-wagon, tethered the mules, and came in to supper. 'Why you so nervous?' his sister asked, and he said his head ached. But when he got up twice during the night to stand barefooted outside the door, staring toward the rock where his diamond lay, his canny sister whispered as he came back in, 'You found one, didn't you?' And he could not repress his surging excitement.

In mumbles that came rushing forth through his toothless gums, he told her of his legendary find: 'Bigger than my thumb. Fine color, fine color. Netje, this one could bring two thousand rand.'

'Don't be a damned fool,' she growled.

'It could. Honestly it could. When you see it . . .'

'So you hid it under a rock?'

'I want to search the stream.'

'You want to go to jail. You enter it in the book, proper. You take it to the police.'

'I got to protect myself.'

But she was adamant, and as soon as enough light showed in the east for them to see, she marched to the rock, and when the diamond was placed in her hands, and its true weight and color were evident, tears came to her eyes. 'It's a real diamond,' she conceded, but the concept of two thousand rand was beyond her.

In the house-wagon it was she who took down Pik's register and in an almost illiterate scrawl wrote: 'Swartstroom, by the three acacias, 11 October 1978, about five carats, color good. Maybe two thousand rand.' That afternoon she and Pik walked six miles to the nearest police station to register their find.

Once the diamond was legally registered, it became Pik Prinsloo's property, to dispose of as he wished, but only through established channels. If he allowed this stone to fall into the hands of some I.D.B., both he and the buyer would go to jail; he must take it personally to the diamond market at Boskuil, two hundred and sixty miles to the west. The trip could be made by train—four hours to Johannesburg, five more to Boskuil—but old Pik felt that with such an impressive stone, he ought to travel by private auto, so with great difficulty, because he hated telephones, he called his backer in Johannesburg: 'We got the biggest diamond in my life. Let's go to Boskuil and sell it for two thousand rand.'

The man said he could break free late Friday afternoon— 'Stop right there!' Pik shouted. 'We got to be in Boskuil Friday morning. Only day the buyers come.'

So early Thursday his backer came for him and they got in the car and started for a location which had no equal in the world: a remote farm lost in the barren lands south of Johannesburg, where by tradition diamond buyers from all over the nation clustered in a collection of rough corrugated-iron shacks to see what the local adventurers might have found. The trip was not easy, for whenever Pik and his diamond left one magisterial jurisdiction to enter a new, he had to be prepared to produce his registration papers so that the authorities could trace this one diamond across the country and be assured that it made its way into the hands of a licensed buyer. And when Pik reached the jurisdiction in which it was to be sold, he must register it anew.

The halts were tedious enough, but this October day was turning out to be one of the hottest of the new spring season, so that the car steamed inside, and Pik's habit of not bathing now became a penetrating problem.

The Johannesburg man tried opening his window, then Pik's, then all the windows, but even this flow of fresh air failed to alleviate the awful smell, and the man began to wonder if even a five-carat diamond was worth the torment. But at last they came to Boskuil farm, at about the same time as the evening train which brought the buyers for the Friday market. Office Number One had for some years been occupied by

H. Steyn, Licensed Diamond Dealer of excellent reputation, and early Friday morning Mr. Steyn, a small, knowing man dressed in a dark suit, posted his certificate on the outer door, donned cuff guards, and placed his German-made six-power loupe on the table upon which his elbows rested.

First man in line was Pik Prinsloo, grubby khaki shirt, sagging trousers, hat with broken brim. For fifty-two years the diamond merchants had known this fellow, a splinter diamond here, a fragment there, and always the promise that one of these days . . . No buyer had ever handed old Pik more than three hundred rand at a time, and on this meager flow of capital he had survived.

H. Steyn, seeing the old fellow approach, assumed that once again Pik had found himself a quarter-carat stone worth a few pounds, but when he noticed that the smelly old man was trembling, and there was a wild light in his eye, he realized that this day was special. And when Pik's backer started to enter the shack, Steyn noticed how the prospector waved him back: 'You stay outside. This is my job.' There was some muffled conversation, at the end of which the old man screamed, 'Of course I'll tell you how much, and if I don't, Mr. Steyn will. Now get out!'

'You have a stone?' Mr. Steyn asked.

Pik's hands shook, but after an awkward moment he produced a matchbox, which he slid open with difficulty, and placed upon the table a diamond large enough to make H. Steyn cough. 'You have your papers for this?' he asked.

'Papers?' old Pik shouted. 'You're damn right I got papers.' There was more fumbling, and when the familiar documents were spread before Mr. Steyn he pretended to read them, using this as an excuse for finding time to run through a series of hasty, silent calculations: Goodness, that looks to be at least five carats! It's makable. Possibly a brilliant. Can't see any big flaws. What's the color? Might even be an ice-white. Probably cut down to about one-point-four carats. I could sell this to Tel Aviv for maybe ten thousand dollars. They could sell it to New York for fifteen thousand. Ultimate buyer, as much as twenty-eight thousand dollars. So I could afford to pay him fifteen hundred dollars a carat or seventy-five hundred in all. But that would be shaving it a little close. Best I ought to go would be fourteen hundred dollars a carat, or seven thousand in all. I'll offer him thirteen fifty a carat, or sixty-seven fifty in all. Like all diamond buyers, he did his calculations in dollars, since America was the ultimate market, but since he had to pay in rand, he knew immediately what the exchange would be. It took $1.16 to purchase one rand, so that the final price of $6,750 worked out to about R5,800, and that was the figure he kept in mind as he prepared to speak.

While H. Steyn was completing his calculations, old Pik was pursuing his: It's a good stone. It's worth two thousand rand. And I saw his eyes light up when I placed it on the desk. Damn, I will ask two-five. Look at that diamond. He doesn't see a diamond that good in a month. It could even go for two-six. Damn, I'll go for two-six.

H. Steyn cherished his reputation as dean of diamond buyers, 'the man who never cheated anyone,' but did not feel that in order to sustain his good name he had to pay exorbitant prices. He had found it most effective to state an honest price, just a fraction less than some hungry buyer might offer, and then to adjust it slightly upward if he really wanted the stone.

The more he studied this one, the more he wanted it. This could be a fine stone, he said to himself. The color might turn out to be much better than I think. It won't cut to more than one-point-four carats, but when it's done, it could be an exciting diamond.

'Pik,' he said in the low voice he used in such negotiations, 'I won't fool around. You've got yourself a very good stone. I'm going to offer you top price. Five thousand, eight hundred rand.'

Pik stood silent. Mustering all his strength, he was able to keep from gasping or staggering backward. His head bent forward, so that Steyn could see only the broken rim of his big hat, and it was very still. Finally Pik gained control of himself, and in what he assumed was a normal voice he asked, 'Of course, that's an open offer?'

Now Steyn had to control himself, not from trembling but from laughing. Here was a man in his seventies, never had a real diamond in his possession before, would probably earn more from this one than he had from all his fragments in the past twenty years. And he was haggling. But Steyn enjoyed such men and wished them well, so if old Pik wanted to haggle, he'd go along.

'Wait a minute!' he said with a show of irritation. 'I make you a firm offer of fifty-eight hundred now. I am not making you an open offer, allowing you to go up and down the row, seeing if you can engineer a bid a little higher. I'm warning you right now you won't. So don't come back here at nightfall and tell me, "I'll take your fifty-eight hundred, Mr. Steyn," because at nightfall that offer don't stand. You accept it right now, or I withdraw it.'

Pik said nothing. Steyn's offer was almost triple what he had realistically expected, more than double his most sanguine hope, and desperately he wanted to accept it, pay off his five backers, and take Netje enough to live on for the rest of their lives. But as a diamond man he also wanted to play the whole game, to go from shack to shack, displaying his incredible find, to hear the other men whispering, 'Prinsloo's got himself a diamond,' and he would not be cheated of this exercise, not even by an offer of great wealth.

'Got to see what the others say,' he muttered, closing his matchbox and heading for the door.

H. Steyn rose to accompany him. Ignoring the horrendous smell that radiated like a halo, he threw his arm about the old man's shoulders, and said, 'I'm sorry to lose that stone, Pik. It's a good one. Don't let them cheat you.'

'Don't intend to,' Pik said.

By midafternoon the backer from Johannesburg was weary of the charade: 'Damn it, Pik, you got three good bids. Take one of them and let's get out of here.'

But Prinsloo was enjoying himself as never before. To walk into a real buyer's shack, to open the matchbox, to watch the buyer as he studied the find in disbelief, to hear the tentative offers, and then the real bid. Buyer Number Five had offered five thousand, nine hundred, and kept it an open bid: 'I'd like to get that stone, Pik. Come back, because I know you won't find any higher.'

At the seventh shack, Adams and Feinstein, the bid went to six thousand rand even, and this, too, was open. 'Six thousand rand!' Pik reported to his backer. 'God Almighty, that's more money than you earned in your whole life.'

'We're taking it, I hope.'

'Nope.'

The Johannesburg man exploded, did some cursing, then listened, amazed, as Pik said, 'All my life I dreamed of walking in to H. Steyn's and selling him a diamond. A real diamond.' So against the protests of his partner, the old man went back and told Steyn, 'I got me a bid of six thousand even. Would you consider going along with it?'

Without hesitation Steyn said, 'No.' But when the old man's face turned gray, he added, 'I made you an honest offer, Pik. But let me see the color again.'

With a rush old Pik produced the matchbox, fumbled awkwardly, and placed the stone once more upon the table. With a show of studious professionalism Steyn picked up his loupe, took the diamond in his left fingers, and studied it carefully. No detectable flaws. A color perhaps one grade higher than he had judged at first. The stone cut from this raw diamond might sell in America for . . . Who knows what the Harry Winston people could get for such a stone—$32,000?

Slowly Steyn put down the loupe, shoving the lovely diamond back toward the old man. 'Best I can do, Pik. Fifty-nine fifty.'

'Sold!' Pik cried with exultation. But when he reached the car his partner berated him: 'You damned fool! Adams and Feinstein offered you six thousand. Cash in hand. What in hell are you doing?'

'I want to act like a gentleman,' Pik said. 'I like to deal with them. You should know that. When you offered to back me, there in the bar—did I haggle over terms?' The Johannesburg man made no reply, so Pik finished: 'Tomorrow you and me find the others. Give them their share. Then we divide a fortune.'

'If you're going to be rich,' the partner said, 'would you consider taking a bath?' Pik said nothing. He was imagining the look on Netje's face when he told her that he had walked right into H. Steyn's office and demanded six thousand rand . . . and almost got it.

News of the Swartstroom find flashed across South Africa, and before nightfall was known in Tel Aviv, Amsterdam and New York. It alerted geologists at the Anglo-American offices on Main Street in Johannesburg, and especially the officials at Amalgamated Mines in Pretoria.

'This is our chance,' the president told the executive board that convened in special session on Saturday morning. 'What do we know about the Swartstroom?'

His men knew a great deal: 'Little stream flowing into Moçambique. Researched many times. Negative. It does lie in the general vicinity of the Premier Mine, but doesn't seem to be connected in any way. No logical pipe areas near it, and remember that it's cut off from Premier by those low mountains.'

'You think Prinsloo's find was an accidental?'

'No find is ever accidental, if it's been honestly reported.'

'What do we know about Prinsloo?'

'For over fifty years he's always prospected the possible streams. Never wasted his time where there were no signals.'

'What signals could he have seen?'

'Damned if I know. I've been up and down that stream six times. Never even saw garnets.'

'Well, he saw something. And we'd better go back.'

There was much discussion as to whom to send, and the geologist who made the earlier six explorations eagerly wanted another crack at it, but the president said, 'There's that American who's being expelled from our mines in Vwarda. Isn't he exceptionally good?'

When the young man's file was produced, the man from personnel summarized it rapidly: 'Born Ypsilanti 1948. University of Michigan. Graduate work at Colorado School of Mines in Golden. Worked at Broken Hill in Australia. Supervisor at Mount Isa. We offered him a job on the strong recommendation of all his professors and superiors. He worked at our place in Sierra Leone, then to Botswana, and finally as field manager in Vwarda.'

'His expulsion from Vwarda?' the president asked. 'Did it reflect on him. Morally, I mean?'

'Certainly not from our end. He did a splendid job for us.'

'I mean, was there a public scandal? Would we be hurt if . . .'

'Sir,' the personnel man said in a tired voice, 'it was the usual. I have the whole nonsense, too damned dismal to repeat. After independence he was kept on at our mines. When Richardson was fired on that trumped-up currency charge he became chief. Did a first-class job for us and for Vwarda. One of the few white men accepted by the new regime. But one day a committee went to the prime minister and accused him of racism. And he was expelled.'

'Is he racist? These southern Americans, you know.'

'I think Michigan is in the north. When Richardson was kicked out, the government insisted upon placing in all the second echelons Vwardians who could scarcely read or write. But they were cousins of the prime minister. So one day, when the entire operation threatened to collapse, our man fired them all. Said he had to have someone in command who could manage without coming to work at eleven in the morning in a Mercedes-Benz.'

'And those men,' the chairman suggested, 'formed the committee that charged him with racism.'

'The same,' the personnel man said.

'What's our chap's name again?'

'Philip Saltwood.'

'Related to that Saltwood woman who keeps provoking the government?'

'Not likely.'

'We can't afford to go looking for scandal, you know.'

'This Saltwood's an American.'

He was summoned from Zambia, to which he had fled after his expulsion from Vwarda, and he arrived one morning at the Swartstroom driving a white Toyota with the gold monogram AMAL. He was followed by two other white cars bearing the famous letters, and then by two white trucks carrying five workmen each. A team of eighteen would now work every bend of this little stream, for it was imperative that the industry know whether a new source of alluvial diamonds had been found, and if so, where the master pipe might be hiding that produced them. It would be Philip Saltwood's responsibility to answer these questions, and he had seventeen assistants and twelve months in which to do it.

When he first arrived at the Swartstroom that sunny November morning in 1978 he seemed ideally suited for the task. A theoretical geologist well trained in America and Australia, he had acquired broad experience in the oil fields of the former country and the gold mines of the latter. In recent years his specialty had become diamonds, as a result of his intensive work in places like Sierra Leone, Botswana and Vwarda, and he brought to his present task a considerable knowledge.

He was thirty years old, bright, hard-working, and because of his American-Australian diet, much more solid than the average South African Saltwood. He had always known vaguely that his family stemmed from Salisbury in England, with a major branch in South Africa, but none of his relatives had ever made contact with either branch.

He was divorced from an Australian girl, and since they had had no children, there were no lingering emotional ties. They had met while he was working at Broken Hill and had courted while chasing brumbies across the Outback. They had spent their honeymoon on the skislopes in New Zealand, and as long as Philip worked Down Under they were a happy pair.

But when he was sent back to America, she could not adjust. The oil fields of Oklahoma had broken her spirit, and prospecting in central Wyoming had proved intolerable, so one afternoon she fled those barren regions in a Quantas plane to Australia, informing Philip of her departure only when she reached the safety of civilized Sydney. There she obtained a divorce on the grounds that he had deserted her, and sometimes he could scarcely remember her name.

He established his camp quickly and with stern authority: 'At the beginning we work three weeks unbroken, then a week off. Spend that week as you will, but come back sober. Workday starts forty minutes after sunrise, so get up early and hit the chow line. Good on you.' His speech was an amalgam of Texan, Australian and African diamond field; his manner, international-mine-field. He was a bold man determined to whip this crew and this rivulet into shape, and when he surveyed the six white tents in which he and his men would live for the following months, he took satisfaction in the secure way they had been pegged to the ground and the orderly manner in which they lined up. He knew of no other way to work.

There was great excitement in surrounding towns like Venloo when it was learned that Amalgamated Mines was making a serious probe of the Swartstroom, and curious businessmen kept trying to discover whether any further diamonds had been uncovered: 'They work from sunrise to sundown, and they got all kinds of machinery. They've an American in charge, and he drives them.'

'But did they find any diamonds?'

'Not from what I hear. That stream's been worked before, you know. Back in the thirties, I been told. They found nothing then, either.'

But old Pik Prinsloo had found his diamond, now reported to have been eleven carats in size. 'Yes, but sometimes I wonder. He's a canny old coot. You suppose he salted it?'

Why and from where would a seventy-one-year-old man salt a trivial little Transvaal stream? From time to time Saltwood would hear rumors that he was hauling his house-wagon to some new site, but none of the workmen had ever actually seen the filthy old fellow. They attended their power-driven scoops, their mechanized gravitators as they moved methodically from one bend in the stream to the next, finding nothing.

'Hell,' a long-time Amalgamated field man growled, 'we aren't even finding garnet or ilmenite.'

And then, in late November, Pik Prinsloo, working on his own at an unpromising site, came up with a find that was in some ways more exciting than his first: at locations well separated he uncovered two diamond chips, the largest only one-tenth of a carat, both together worth only seventy rand. The significance of this find was that it confirmed the fact that the Swartstroom was indeed diamantiferous.

Saltwood's men, working at the Amalgamated camp, were even more pleased by this unexpected find than was old Pik, and although the week of their vacation was upon them, they agreed to work straight through and delay their off-time till December. For the first six days they found nothing, then, on Saturday, they produced a third chip, about one-eighth of a carat, so small the layman would barely have noticed it, and they telephoned the stirring news to Pretoria. They had confirmed a new diamond site.

Philip Saltwood spent his week of vacation in the small town of Venloo eating good food at the neat hotel run by a Jewish couple, and since on Sundays there was absolutely nothing to do there, he attended the morning service at the Dutch Reformed church, where he caught his first glimpse of the real South Africa.

He wandered in a few minutes after the service had started, and by good fortune the congregation was singing a hymn he had grown to love, popular in both Australia and America. It was Martin Luther's *'Ein Feste Burg Ist Unser Gott,'* and although it was being sung in Afrikaans, its noble message was the same in any language, and he bellowed his version in English. As he did so, he became aware that a most lovely Afrikaner girl, her hair in Saxon braids, was laughing at him. Turning his head quickly, he caught her eye, and she blushed and buried her face in her hymnal. But since she knew this greatest of the Afrikaans hymns by heart, she soon looked up, and he saw the golden face that would haunt him during the remaining months of his dig. It was squarish, characteristically Dutch, with broad forehead, blue eyes, generous lips and pronounced chin. She was not a tall girl, but she gave the impression of being extremely solid, like some tidy Cape Dutch farmhouse nestled against the berg. She was dressed in white, so that her flaxen hair and golden complexion shone to good advantage, and in no way could she discipline her mischievous smile.

He ended Luther's rousing hymn, this battle cry of a new religion, with his voice in full power, then sat so that he could watch the girl with the Saxon braids, but before long his attention was drawn to the pulpit, raised high above the congregation, from which a young predikant with brilliant forcefulness had begun to deliver his sermon, leaning down in his black robes to castigate, implore, inspirit, deride, cajole, threaten and bless.

I haven't heard preaching like that since the Holy Rollers in the Oklahoma oil fields, Saltwood said to himself, and for the moment he forgot the girl as he tried to follow what the predikant was saying. He knew only such Afrikaans as an engineer would acquire in a mining camp, but this was sufficient for him to pick out the main ideas: Joshua was on a hilltop looking down at Jericho, facing a great obligation placed upon him by the Lord, and the people of this congregation, every man, woman and child, stood this morning upon a similar hilltop staring down at his or her obligation.

The theme of the sermon was powerful, but it was the delivery that overwhelmed Saltwood: This isn't your basic Episcopalian homily. This is by-God religion. That man's the best I ever heard.

And then he saw something which had escaped him at first. In a special section of pews at the right hand of the predikant sat a group of older men, solemn-faced and rigid, each dressed in somber black with white shirt and gleaming white tie, and each word that the young predikant uttered seemed to be recorded mentally by these thirty men, who nodded when they approved what he said, or sat grimly silent when they did not. Because they were seated well below the pulpit, which was hung suspended from the ceiling of the church, they had to raise their faces to see the predikant, so that they looked like a group from some Ghirlandaio fresco in Florence or the figures from a dark terracotta casting by one of the Della Robbias.

To the left of the preacher, in a similar collection of pews, sat a much younger group of men, also dressed in funereal black with the same type of white shirt and white tie. They, too, followed the predikant with intense interest, but their special function did not become clear until toward the end of the service, when they rose en masse, moved to the foot of the pulpit, and took heavy wooden plates in which to gather the collection. As the choir sang, the young men moved briskly along the aisles, and when Saltwood saw how big they were he thought: I'd hate to tackle that gang on a rugger field. He smiled, then looked at the older men: Or try to pass a law that they didn't approve of.

The service ended with a brief, sweet prayer of consolation and reconciliation, and when Saltwood started for the exit he concluded: This could be the finest church service I've ever attended. He sensed that it had been a community affair, a gathering of like-minded persons who sincerely sought the message their predikant had to offer, and whose voices were raised in unison to give thanks to God for once more having demonstrated His benevolence and concern.

He was thinking in this manner when he felt his arm taken by a firm grasp, after which a strong voice asked, 'Aren't you Philip Saltwood, from the diggings?'

'I am,' he said, and turned to see a stalwart man in his forties, obviously Afrikaner, although why Philip thought so he could not have explained. The man smiled the warm greeting which Afrikaners always extended to strangers visiting their churches.

'I'm Marius van Doorn. We live just west of here, and we'd be honored if you'd take dinner with us.' With this the speaker reached back, clasped the arm of his wife and brought her forward, and she, in turn, reached for the hand of her daughter, and Saltwood saw to his delight that this was the girl with the Saxon braids who had been laughing at him.

'This is my daughter Sannie,' the man said.

'Susanna van Doorn,' her mother explained, and they headed for Vrymeer.

The original invitation had been for one dinner, after church, on one Sunday afternoon. It was extended to drop-in meals whenever Saltwood could detach himself from the diamond explorations, and whenever he drove the few miles from Venloo to Vrymeer and came over that last hill, his heart beat faster to see the white-faced blesbok grazing quietly. They seemed like unicorns of legend attending the lovely young woman waiting in the farmhouse.

Because of the shape of the Van Doorn house and the way the road twisted, visitors were attracted automatically to the kitchen stoep, as if aware that here life centered. The front door was rarely used, and this was understandable, for at the Van Doorns', the family usually gathered in the big, inviting rear room. It contained a long plank table, two comfortable carver chairs, one for the master, the other for any honored guest, and nine sturdy chairs of lesser dignity. Against one wall stood shelves of Ball jars containing canned fruits and vegetables; opposite was a collection of old copperware. There was a big glass container, too, but only rarely did a guest learn of its contents: all that remained of the old brown-and-gold Dutch crock that had been in the Van Doorn family for generations. At the far end of the kitchen an electric range had long since replaced the old coal-eating monster, but the servants who had tended that area were still present: an older Nxumalo woman and two young girls. Most of all, the kitchen exuded a sense of warmth and home, as if here innumerable meals had been eaten, vivid topics discussed.

Sannie did not try to mask her pleasure in having the American geologist as an unannounced suitor; when he came to the farm she ran to the stoep to greet him, extending her two hands and bringing him into the kitchen, where hot coffee and cold beer were waiting. By the end of his second month at the dig he had begun to think of Vrymeer as his headquarters; he even took his telephone calls there. It was a constantly rewarding experience, for not only was Sannie a charming young woman, but her parents were helpful and instructive. Mrs. van Doorn was English and represented the thinking of that large segment of the population, but her husband was a true Afrikaner, and from him Philip derived his insights into the thinking of the men who directed the country. Debate in the Van Doorn kitchen was apt to be heated and prolonged, and as Saltwood listened to the conflicting points of view he realized that he was sharing a privileged introduction to South African life: the Afrikaner view; the English view; and in Sannie's bold opinions, the view of the new breed who represented the best of the two older stocks.

Like all visitors, Philip was astounded by the freedom with which the citizens of South Africa discussed their problems. The expression of ideas and the exploration of alternatives were totally free, and what was not said in the kitchen debates was spelled out in the very good English-language newspapers. This was no dictatorship, like Idi Amin's Uganda or Franco's Spain; within fifteen minutes of meeting the average Afrikaner family, a stranger was sure to be asked: 'Mr. Saltwood, do you think we can escape armed revolution?' or 'Have you ever heard anything more stupid than what our prime minister proposed yesterday?' What with his intense work at the diggings, where he was in contact with all types of South Africans, and his discussions at Vrymeer, Philip was learning much about this country.

But of course his real purpose in visiting the farm was not to gain an education; he was falling in love with Sannie van Doorn, and he had reason to believe that she was most seriously interested in him. In the third month, with her parents' obvious consent, she accepted his invitation to visit the diamond claims, and then to drive over to Kruger National Park, where they would spend two days watching the great animals.

At the diamond camp she asked, 'Philip, what is it you're doing?'

He showed her where they had found traces of diamond, and when she saw how minute the specks were she gasped: 'Why, they're not worth anything!' And he said, 'They're pointers, and diamond experts all over the world are thrilled that we've found them.'

'Pointing to what?' she asked, whereupon he honored her with a graduate seminar on diamonds. She understood only the highlights, but when he reinforced his lecture with a rough diagram, she grasped what he was up to.

'This is the Swartstroom, the little river we're exploring. It's yielded diamonds, so we know they exist. Our problem is "Where did they come from?" They didn't originate in this stream, that we know. It merely carried them here. But from where? This branch of the river is Krokodilspruit. After we finish here, we'll look there. Maybe they were carried down that stream. We'll look everywhere.'

'What for?'

'The pipe. My life is spent looking for the pipe.'

'And what's that?'

'About a billion years ago, give or take a million or two, one hundred and twenty miles straight down, somewhere near here, a kind of subterranean cave or area developed. We know its characteristics completely: twelve hundred degrees Celsius, pressure sixty-two thousand times greater than here at the surface. In that environment, and there alone, carbon transmutes into diamonds. In some circumstances down there this carbon becomes coal; in others, graphite. In ours it becomes diamonds.'

'But what's the pipe?'

'The diamonds form in a kind of blue clay, and when everything is just right, that clay, carrying its diamonds with it, roars upward through one hundred and twenty miles of intervening material and bursts loose, something like a volcano.'

'I still don't know what the pipe is.'

'The channel it leaves on its upward journey. Lined with that blue clay and sometimes diamonds. We call the blue clay kimberlite, after Kimberley. And my job is to find that pipe, lined with kimberlite, carrying diamonds.'

'Where do you think it might be?' Sannie asked, and he said, 'For this year I torment myself with only two questions: "Will Sannie van Doorn marry me?" and "Where in hell is the pipe that produced these diamond fragments?"'

'Where could it be?'

Returning to the diagram, he said, 'You can see that it can't be down at Chrissie Meer. Those mountains would prevent this river from coming this way. That region up there is too far north. It can't be over at Vrymeer, because those two little hills . . .' He paused in some embarrassment.

'You mean Sannie's Tits?' she asked demurely.

'You damned Afrikaners are very careless with words. We better get over to Kruger Park.'

At the close of their first long day with the animals they stopped at a camping site, whose manager asked routinely, 'One rondavel?' and Sannie said promptly, 'Two, if you please.'

So that night they slept apart, but on the second day of viewing animals they came upon a glade where giraffes were resting in shadows, some seventy of them, and two were in the courting mood. It was an extraordinary sight, these tall, ungainly animals, preserved by some freak of nature from ages past, standing under trees facing each other and twining their necks in the most lovely, slow, poetic way, as if they were weaving dreams. It was their love dance, unmatched in nature.

As they watched, Sannie moved closer, until at the conclusion of the giraffes' exquisite performance the human beings were duplicating the animals, touching and kissing and moving apart, then rushing together again. That night when they approached the same camping ground, it was Sannie who suggested: 'Let's drive to the other one. It'll be less embarrassing.' And when they reached the alternate and the caretaker asked, 'One rondavel?' she said, 'Yes.'

In succeeding weeks Sannie and Philip took excursions to various sites in eastern Transvaal—north to Waterval-Boven to see the cog railway, south to Chrissiesmeer to see the site of the concentration camp—and on one weekend they drove to Pretoria to see the capital, and the rugged beauty of this veld city was a surprise. Philip was excited by the imposing statue of Oom Paul Kruger in the center of town, with four handsome statues of burghers ready to ride forth on commando.

'It's heroic—the way a patriotic statue should be,' he exclaimed.

'Wait till you see the Voortrekker Monument!' she cried, pleased that he was respectful of her treasures. And again she was right. This great, brooding pile atop its mountain, this amazing echo of Great Zimbabwe, was such a perfect evocation of the Afrikaner spirit that he was almost afraid to enter. 'Do they allow Englishmen in here?'

'They're not welcome,' she joked, 'but I'll tell them you're my Afrikaner cousin from Ceylon.' When they went inside and Philip saw the fiercely patriotic bas-reliefs depicting Blood River and the other victories of the Afrikaner tribe, he was struck by the strangeness of a nation's having as its principal monument a memorial in which only a small segment of its population would feel welcomed. There were no blacks here, no Englishmen at ease, only Afrikaners reveling in their hard-won victories.

'How many people are there in South Africa?' he asked as they sat on stone benches in the lower crypt.

'About thirty-one million, all told.'

'And how many Afrikaners?'

'Let's say three million maximum.'

'Less than one-tenth of the total. Doesn't it seem odd to you, Sannie, to have your major national monument restricted to one-tenth of the population?'

'It's not restricted. On certain days, at certain times, blacks are allowed in.'

'Would they want to come? A monument dedicated to their defeat?'

She drew away from him for a moment, then said stiffly, 'We're a nation in laager and we cannot deny our past. It's from the scenes in this building that we derive our strength.'

From this vast, awesome structure they went back to the residential areas of the city, and it was here that Philip received his major shock, because whole avenues and scores of broad streets, reaching as far as he could see, were lined with jacaranda trees bursting with purple, not hundreds of them but thousands upon thousands, until the entire city seemed a bed of flowers. He had never seen anything to compare with this explosion of purple elegance, and when they slipped into bed that night he whispered, 'You're a blend of monument and jacaranda—fierce durability and soft elegance.' When she said nothing, snuggling closer to be kissed, he asked, 'Shall we be married?' but then she drew away, for she was not yet prepared to make such a commitment.

Wherever they went on their brief excursions she provided him with new revelations of her country. After they had visited some dozen little towns, each with its statue of some minor Boer War general, they returned to Pretoria, where she took him to the fine figure of General Louis Botha in front of the government buildings. Behind it stood a somber, handsome memorial to the 2,683 South African soldiers who had lost their lives in a single battle.

'Wasn't Delville Wood, back in 1916, the most important battle your troops ever engaged in?' Philip asked.

'Perhaps,' she said grudgingly.

'All those men lost . . .'

'It was the wrong war, fought on the wrong continent, by the wrong troops.' After reflecting upon this curt dismissal, she added, 'It was an English affair that played no part in our history, an incident well forgotten.'

He was struck by the exposed beauty of South Africa, the endless veld, the treeless reaches of landscape, the wonderful little flat-topped hills, the enclaves with elephants, and white rhinoceros, and eland, and the great blazing sky. 'Your roads, you know, are much better than those in the United States,' he told her once as they were driving across a far stretch of veld on a roadway that contained not a ripple.

Most of all he liked the little towns with their public squares, their low white-walled buildings and their jacaranda trees. He became familiar with a dozen other blossoming trees whose names he did not know: 'This is a land of flowers!' And of all those he saw, better even than the jacarandas, he liked the protea: 'You must have a hundred varieties!'

'More, I think.'

They were able to take these excursions because of his schedule at the dig: three weeks of dawn to dusk, then a week off, and once when he was entitled to a break she said, 'We have a remarkable village which you really must see,' and when he took out his map she said, 'You will find it as Tulbagh, but we like to call it by its old name, Church-Street-in-the-Land-of-Waveren.'

'What a delightful name!' and they drove two days to an enclave among tall hills where in a closed valley stood this remarkable thoroughfare, as beautiful as any in the world. It had been founded as early as 1700, one long street with a church at one end, a parsonage about half a mile away, and some fifteen houses connecting the two. As the centuries passed, the low houses seemed to settle close to the ground, and the place might have been remembered only as a fading echo of past times, except that on 29 September 1969 an earthquake shattered the area, knocking down some of the dwellings and damaging all of them.

'What happened,' Sannie explained, 'was that some energetic men and women, Father among them, got together and said, "This is a chance to rebuild the street as it was in 1750," and believe it or not, Philip, that's just what they did.'

When they approached the village, Philip saw a church of stubborn beauty and in the distance a stately parsonage, but what captivated him was the row of stark-white houses, all cheap adornment erased, standing pristine as they had two centuries earlier. It was as if a magician had waved a wand and restored patterns of living long since vanished. They stayed that night in one of the houses, whose proper owners were distressed at the idea of Sannie's traveling with a man to whom she was not married: 'What would your grandmother Maria Steyn have said?' The wife had clippings of Maria's famous altercation over the nude statue in Pretoria, and Philip guffawed at some of the statements the old lady had made: 'If the Israelites could destroy the statues of a golden ass, we women of South Africa can destroy this statue of a naked woman.' She had also told one newspaper: 'A naked man is not much better than a naked woman, but he's easier to fix.'

'Times change,' Sannie said, but the woman would not allow the couple to share the same bedroom. Late at night, in the darkness, Philip tried to reach Sannie's room, only to find that buckets had been placed across the hallway. He made a terrific clatter, at which the man of the house came out with a flashlight to be sure he returned to his own quarters.

As soon as breakfast was over and they were driving north, he said, 'Sannie, we've got to get married. I can find a good job almost anywhere in the world, and I need you.' But again she held him off.

He supposed that this was because she loved her own country too much to leave it, and he had to admit that it was magnificent in a great, brutal way, unlike any he had previously seen, but an observant traveler had to spot three grievous problems which warranted attention: 'Sannie, as a geologist I see one hell of a lot of your country is desert, and according to old maps, it seems to be spreading eastward.'

'You're right,' she conceded.

And whether in the countryside or in the small towns, he became increasingly aware that whites and blacks occupied two radically different worlds. The separation was constant, universal and severely enforced. Philip was by no means a liberal; as a practical engineer, he knew that separation was sometimes advisable: 'I was never much for interracial dating. I observed that the men in my class at college who dated girls of other races—Chicanos or blacks or Orientals—they were all alike. Aloof, bad complexions, and wrote letters to the editor advocating the abolishment of fraternities.'

'Here it would be intolerable,' she agreed.

'But I've also noticed that countries which support a cheap supply of labor always impoverish themselves.'

'We're certainly not impoverished,' she protested.

'In many ways you are. You ought to pay your blacks high wages, then tax them like hell to provide public services. That's the path to civilization.'

'Philip! They'd not be worth a penny more than they're paid.'

'Wrong.' He became quite excited on this point. 'I've worked in three different black nations. With all kinds of black workers. And whenever we had in our cadre a black from South Africa, especially a Zulu or a Xhosa, he was invariably the best in the work force. If blacks with much less experience can rule Moçambique and Vwarda and Zambia, yours could certainly run this country.' It was a startling statement, which she did not wish to discuss.

The third sad discovery came always at night. They would have had a fine dinner with friends she knew from one past experience or other; the conversation would have been lively, ranging over politics and economics; the food would have been superb and the local wines even better; and then, as they were about to depart, Philip would see on the mantel over the fireplace three handsome photographs of young people Sannie's age.

'I didn't know you had children.'

'Yes!' And if the family was of English derivation, or Jewish, or enlightened Afrikaner, either the mother or father would say, 'That's Victor, he's in Australia. Helen is married to a fine young man in Canada. And that's Freddie, he's at the London School of Economics.'

They were gone. They were gone to the far continents. They would never return to South Africa, for the pressures were too great, the possibilities too forbidding.

When the young lovers returned from one such trip Mrs. van Doorn asked unobtrusively if she could speak with Philip, and when she had him alone she said forthrightly, 'You must not lose your heart to Sannie. The Troxel boys will soon be back from the frontier, and then things will be different.'

'Who are the Troxel boys?'

'Their families own the old De Groot farm. Their parents, that is.'

'Those people who live on the far side of the lake?'

'Yes. Marius' father brought them here from Johannesburg over fifty years ago. Wonderfully sturdy people.'

'And they have two young men, Sannie's age?'

'Yes. They're cousins. On military service just now, but they'll be back, and things will be different.'

'Sannie's said nothing.'

'I think she has, Philip. Didn't you ask to marry her?'

'Twice.'

'Why do you think she hesitated?'

'Had she some arrangement with one of the boys?'

'With both, I think. Point is, when they left she hadn't made up her mind between them. But she will, Philip. She's Afrikaner to the core and will marry an Afrikaner. Of that I'm convinced.'

'I'm not,' he said with laughter that softened the disagreement.

'Nor should you be. But remember my warning. Don't take this too seriously, because, I assure you, Sannie doesn't.'

He was prevented from brooding about his courtship when his obligations at Swartstroom suddenly intensified. His men had come upon a reach where the stream took a pronounced turn to the left, producing a bend where diamonds ought to have been deposited had any ever existed in this territory.

The crew found what it was looking for, two tiny bits of diamond, glistening so pure in sunlight they seemed to create a radiance all the way to Pretoria, Antwerp and New York, where word circulated that 'Amalgamated Mines may have something at Swartstroom.' The two tiny fragments were worth about four rand, enough to pay one black worker for one day's effort, but they had the power to inflame men's imaginations, for when taken in conjunction with Pik Prinsloo's earlier find, they confirmed that at some time far distant this little stream had been diamantiferous. Saltwood's problem was to isolate the ancient source, but so far he could find no signs of it.

A helicopter was flown in to take him aloft so that he might inspect contiguous areas, but this disclosed nothing, and he had to revert to time-tested procedures of following the little stream. He discovered no more diamond chips, but in reality he needed no more. Those he had found proved that somewhere in this vicinity there had been a source of diamonds, and in time he, or someone like him, would uncover it.

So he was kept at the dig and for some weeks found no opportunity to visit with Sannie, but his spare time was not wasted, for an unusual young man came to visit him, and through this accidental meeting he was about to behold rather more of South Africa than the average foreign geologist would ordinarily have seen.

His visitor was Daniel Nxumalo, a black of about Saltwood's age; he spoke the precise English of one who had been educated in a colonial college by itinerant scholars from Dublin or London, and he was

on a curious mission: 'Mr. Philip Saltwood? I'm Daniel Nxumalo, associate professor—as you would call me in America—at Fort Hare. I was
advised to come see you.'

'By whom?' Saltwood had the prejudices of a typical Texas engineer: he would hire anyone, but he had an instinctive distrust of any
black who spoke in complete sentences.

'The people in Venloo. They told me you were interested in all
things South African.'

'How would they know?'

'They've seen you in church. They listen.'

'What was it you wanted?'

'Because you've seen so much of Africa, Mr. Saltwood, I thought it
would be courteous if I showed you the real part—our portion, that is.'

With this rather condescending introduction, Daniel Nxumalo,
home on vacation from his duties at the university, began to take his
American guest to little enclaves in eastern Transvaal occupied by
blacks who, like his own predecessors, had fled the Mfecane of King
Shaka and Mzilikazi. They had survived for the past century and a half
in various settings, some attached to white farms like Vrymeer, some
living by themselves in hidden valleys. Quite a few clustered about the
environs of rural towns like Carolina and Ermelo, but all had made sensible adjustment, and Philip was surprised at the substantial goods some
of them had accumulated.

'But under the new laws,' Nxumalo said, 'we must move ourselves
to one of our Bantustans . . . By the way, ever met any Xhosa?'

'Had two of them working for me in Vwarda. Spoke with clicks.'

'In some ways they're more fortunate than the Zulu; in other ways,
not.'

'I'm amazed to hear a Zulu confess that anyone is better.'

'I didn't say better.' Nxumalo laughed. 'I said "more fortunate."'
When he grinned, his teeth were extremely white and his eyes glistened.

'Let me guess,' Saltwood said, for he was growing to like this somewhat cheeky fellow. 'It's something the white man did to the Xhosa and
you, something very unfair to the Zulu.'

'You're perceptive, Mr. Saltwood. The Afrikaners have given the
Xhosa a beautiful territory, compact and arable. The Transkei. And
next to it another cohesive tract, the Ciskei. In that land the Xhosa have
a fighting chance to build something good. But what did they give the
Zulu? Fifty, a hundred unconnected fragments of land. They call it
kwaZulu, and it's supposed to be a homeland for all the Zulu. But it's

really a collection of junk. They want us to occupy that broken territory.'

'In time it'll coalesce, if the idea's a good one.'

'The idea's bad and the land's bad, because all the good parts have been preempted by white men.'

'I should think that could be changed.'

'You haven't lived here very long.' He altered his tone completely. Up to now he had been a college professor, outlining a general problem; now he became a human being, lamenting a wrong done him personally: 'In pursuit of their policy, Mr. Saltwood, they insist that we Zulu, who have made good lives in places like Vrymeer and Venloo, pick up all we have, leave all our friends and our ways of life, and move off to one of the fragmented sections of their kwaZulu.'

'I thought you said it was your Bantustan.'

'We don't want it. It was never our idea.'

'You're to be evacuated?'

'Yes, as if a plague had struck our land. As if locusts had eaten our little fields and we had to move on.'

When Saltwood argued that Nxumalo must be telling only part of the story, the professor agreed, heartily: 'I am indeed. And the reason I came to see you is that I wondered if you would like to see the other part.'

'I certainly would.' Philip Saltwood operated on the principle that governed many young scientists these days as they worked about the world: whether they were American or Russian, Chinese or Australian, they wanted to know what was happening in the lands which employed them at the moment, and often they moved far from their basic tasks, investigating possibilities that at the moment seemed remote but which, at some future date, might become all-important.

With Nxumalo as guide, Philip drove west to Johannesburg, where they toured inconspicuously up and down the handsome main streets of that thriving American-style city. Since it was four in the afternoon, the business areas were jammed with people, and half of them black. They were laborers, and messengers, clerks and minor officials, shoppers and dawdlers, and they could all have been in Detroit or Houston. 'Look at them,' Nxumalo said with some pride. 'They keep the wheels of this city spinning.'

At quarter to five he directed Philip to the area around the central railway station, and in the ensuing hour Saltwood saw something that was so shocking as to be unbelievable: from all parts of central Johannesburg streams of black men and women converged, more than half a million of them crowding to leave the city before sunset, after which it would be unlawful to be there. Like swarms of grasshoppers leaving a ruined field, the workers of Johannesburg hastened to that endless belt of steel that ran perpetually out of the city at sunset and back in at sunrise. It was a movement of people of such magnitude that he knew nothing with which to compare it.

At the end of the hour he thought: When I look at those streams of black people I see all the occupations of a major city. You have street sweepers and young men with briefcases. Sheep butchers and young women who work as doctors' assistants. There are draymen and junior executives. And they are all being expelled.

'Are you game to see where they're going?' Nxumalo asked, as if he could read Philip's mind.

'It's forbidden, isn't it?'

'Yes, it's against the law for whites, but it can be done.'

It was the kind of challenge a peripatetic geologist often faced: Strangers are not allowed in that temple, it's sacred to Shiva. Or, You're not permitted in that corner of Afghanistan, too close to the Russian border.

But always the daring ones went, and now Philip Saltwood was on his way to a clandestine visit to Soweto, a nonexistent city of at least one and a half million black people. South Western Townships was its official title, the first two letters of each word having been taken to form the acronym.

As they drove the twelve miles to it, with trains rushing past in orderly procession, each laden with workers, some clinging to the doors, Nxumalo said, 'It's the same problem as the little one we saw at Venloo. The Afrikaners honestly believe that no black people live in their all-white cities. They believe that we work there briefly during daylight hours, then vanish. Soweto up ahead does not exist officially. The million and a half people who live there, fifty percent of them illegally, are not really there. They're supposed to sleep there temporarily while they work in the city, but if they lose their jobs, they're obligated to move back to their Bantustans, which most of them have never seen.'

When Philip started to respond to this macabre fairy tale of the city twice as large as Boston that did not exist, Nxumalo grinned and jabbed him in the arm. 'I'll wager you didn't notice the most important fact about that exodus at the railway station.'

'As a matter of fact, I did. I saw that the crush contained all kinds of workers, from street sweepers to college professors.'

Nxumalo laughed. 'You failed your examination. The significant fact was that almost everyone carried a package of some kind. You see, because Soweto doesn't exist, and because it's seen as only temporary, ephemeral . . . Well, what's logical? It has no stores. No real ones, that is. They're not allowed, because they don't fit into the white man's plan. Everything except a few minor commodities must be purchased from white-owned stores in Johannesburg. Soweto is not a city. It's a dormitory.'

Saltwood's first impression was arbitrary and in a sense preposterous: 'Christ! Look at all those churches. I never heard of one of them before.' At frequent spots in areas that contained nothing but row upon row of uniformly dismal blockhouses, a flagstaff would display a torn ensign indicating that this building was the Church of Zion, or the Church of the Holy Will, or the Xangu Church, or simply the home of a holy man who had direct contact with God.

'After the beer hall,' Nxumalo explained, 'it's the best racket in Soweto. Maybe four thousand different churches preaching God-knows-what.' But now they were opposite a huge wire-enclosed shed, devoid of any charm whatever, where hundreds of workingmen sat at long bare tables guzzling weak Kaffir beer. That word was officially outlawed now, and if a white man called a black a Kaffir he could be charged with common assault, but the name for the beer persisted. It was a pernicious drink, strong enough to be expensive, weak enough to prevent a man from becoming dangerously drunk.

'The beer hall is the greatest anti-revolutionary instrument in Africa,' Nxumalo said, but even as he spoke, a force of much different character swept past, a gang of tsotsis running to some rendezvous that could involve theft, or rape, or one of the thousand murders each year, fifty percent unsolved because the victims were black.

Out of the vast miasma of this forsaken city, this purgatory that was not hell, for the houses were livable, nor heaven, for there was no ease or hope, Nxumalo led Saltwood to the small dark house that was the focus of this visit. Inside the curtained kitchen sat nine men in a kind of ring, into whose center Philip was thrust: 'This is my friend, Philip Saltwood, the American geologist who is highly respected by his workmen at Swartstroom. He is completing his education.' The men acknowledged him briefly, then turned to Nxumalo and started to press him with questions.

'What do you hear from Jonathan?' one asked, and Philip had no way of guessing who Jonathan might be.

'Nothing.'

'Any news at all from Moçambique?'

'From this side we know that the frontier patrols are penetrating into Moçambique every week. They must be doing damage.'

'Is your brother still alive?'

'I hear nothing from Jonathan.'

Philip judged that Nxumalo hedged on his reply, perhaps because he did not want to say anything incriminating in the presence of a white witness.

They discussed the situation on each of the other frontiers, where apparently they had men from Soweto in position among the rebels, and in no segment of the extensive border did their people seem to be accomplishing much. But when Philip analyzed what actually had been said, he realized that verbally at least these men were not plotters against the government; they were simply discussing events along the frontier, exactly as the white people at Vrymeer followed these affairs, but from a much different point of interest.

The talk was broad in scope and free in manner. These men were teachers, a clergyman, businessmen of sorts, and they were concerned about the directions their nation was taking. They were deeply worried about the forthcoming American presidential election and wondered whether Andrew Young would regain his position of power in a new administration. They were particularly interested in one aspect of American life. 'What accounts for your ambivalence?' a teacher asked. 'Your big newspapers are against apartheid, so is President Carter, so is Andy Young, but ninety-eight percent of the Americans who visit our country approve of it. Almost every American who comes here goes home convinced that Afrikaners are doing the right thing.'

'It's simple,' Philip said. 'What Americans come here? It's far away, you know, and very expensive. Businessmen come on company accounts. Rich travelers. Engineers. And they're all wealthy and conservative. They like what they see. They approve of apartheid, really, and would like to see it introduced in America.'

'You're an engineer. You're not a conservative.'

'On many things I am. I'm sure as hell no liberal.'

'But on apartheid?'

'I'm against it because I don't think it works.'

'Do you find the world turning conservative? Canada? England? Maybe America?'

'I do.'

Late in the evening they got down to cases, and now Nxumalo moved to the fore: 'I've been pondering what we might do to inspirit our people. To send a signal to the men in Moçambique that we're still with them. And it seems to me that the most effective single thing, under present conditions, is to organize a day of remembrance for our dead children who were gunned down in Soweto in 1976.'

'That has merit.'

'I would propose that on June 16 this year we have a national day of mourning. No disturbances, just some kind of visual remembrance.'

'Would that antagonize government?' a short man asked.

'Anything we do antagonizes government.'

'I mean, to the point of retaliation?'

Nxumalo sat silent. This was a penetrating question, for the tactic of committees like this had to be protest up to the edge of the precipice at which Afrikaner guns began to fire, as they had at Sharpeville, in Soweto and at a score of other sites. Judiciously he said, 'If the white man can make a national holiday of Blood River, where he slaughtered thousands of us Zulu, we can remember Soweto '76. I say let's go ahead.'

It was agreed, and when Saltwood left the meeting, and slipped out of Soweto, he was aware that his new friend Daniel Nxumalo had entered upon dangerous ground, but he had no idea that by this simple gesture of irritating the government the young educator would place himself in mortal jeopardy.

When Philip returned to Vrymeer he found his life much altered, for the Troxel boys were back from border duty and were out of uniform. One sight of them warned Saltwood that he was in trouble, for they were a handsome pair, with the fine looks and open smiles of the true Afrikaner. Frikkie was twenty-five, about six feet three, slim, easy in his movements and with a rather serious mien. When Mr. van Doorn introduced him he said, 'Frik's a rugby halfback and one of the best.'

Jopie was different. Well under six feet, he was built like a Roman wall, one massive building block set down upon another. He was broad, in all respects. He had a wide face and very wide mouth from which massive square teeth showed. His shoulders and hips were enormous, for although he was much shorter than Frikkie, he was also much heavier, but what startled Philip was the fact that Jopie had no neck. As with many of the historic rugby forwards, Fanie Louw and Frik du Preez among them, Jopie Troxel's head was set square upon his shoulders, giving his body a battering-ram quality which he used to powerful effect, but in no way was he a gross or insensitive person, and he had in the middle of his chin a deep dimple which quivered when he laughed. His humor was robust, and it was obvious that Sannie van Doorn appreciated it.

Her father had introduced Frikkie; she took charge of Jopie: 'This is my dear friend, who wears his hair forward, like Julius Caesar, and that isn't the only thing forward about him.' With a massive right hand Jopie grabbed Philip's and said, 'Did Jimmy Carter and Andy Young send you over here to tell us how to run our country?"

Philip stiffened. 'I came to find diamonds.'

'Finding any?'

'No. You damned people keep everything hidden.'

'We'd better,' Jopie said, 'or you and the English would steal it.'

'How was the border?' Marius asked, aware that these three young men were behaving like bulls caught up in the heat of spring. He suspected that daughter Sannie was about to experience a difficult spell.

Frikkie dropped into a chair and accepted the beer that Sannie brought. 'It's rotten work. You patrol fifteen days in the bush and see maybe one terrorist. Ta-ta-ta-ta. He's gone, but you know there's a dozen back there somewhere.'

'But we're holding our own?'

'Definitely. There's this Kaffir from here, this Jonathan Nxumalo. He issues a threat now and then on Radio Maputo, as you know. Going to storm Johannesburg. But he's damned sure to stay clear of our patrols.'

'You mean there was real fighting?' Sannie asked.

'Whenever the black bastards gave us a chance,' Jopie said.

'How long were you at the border?' Philip asked, and Jopie looked at his cousin to check whether this was privileged information.

'Six months. It's our obligation.'

'We certainly missed you on the team,' Marius said, hoping to change the conversation, but Philip asked, 'How long can this go on? I mean, with so many young men taken out of productive work?'

'You ask two questions which only an American would ask,' Frikkie said sharply. 'How long? As if everything had to be completed in a hurry. We can guard our borders for the next hundred years. And is it productive? No, it isn't, in the sense of making things at a factory. But what could possibly be more productive than protecting one's country?'

'That subject is closed,' Marius said. 'Now tell me, how soon can you men get back into shape for the big matches facing us?'

'On the border,' Jopie said, 'you're always in shape. I could play Saturday.'

'Do you mean that?'

'Me, too,' Frikkie said, and when Philip looked at the young commandos he knew that they were telling the truth.

The game was against a team from Bloemfontein, and when the Troxels ran onto the field the crowd cheered wildly, for newspapers had hinted at their exploits at the frontier. They displayed the poetic abandon for which they had been famous, but they lost, rather badly, as a matter of fact, 23–9. They did have a great time and in the drinking bouts after the game they smashed a few windows.

When they returned to Vrymeer, there was serious talk as to what they might be doing in the future, and as Philip listened he learned to his surprise that they were suited only for farming. Frikkie had been to the university at Potchefstroom but had learned nothing of practical value, nor much of anything else, while Jopie had shown no interest in going beyond high school. Their two families, offshoots of the Troxels whom Detleef van Doorn had rescued from the slums of Vrededorp, had not acquired much land, so that both boys could not look forward to farming their own fields, but they were capable, and Marius suggested, to Philip's dismay, that they think seriously of assuming responsibility for the extensive acres at Vrymeer. Logically, this would imply that one of them should marry the Van Doorn daughter, and this each was eager to do.

Sannie's intentions were not entirely clear. She was more than fond of her American geologist; her excursions with him had been instructive to her, too, and some of the nights in Kruger Park rondavels or country hotels had been rapturous. He was by no means an improbable suitor, for many South African girls of her generation had breathed sighs of salvation when their marriages carried them away from this turbulent cauldron; she had personal friends who proposed to spend the rest of their lives in places like Toronto and the University of Southern California, and those who wrote spoke often of homesickness for the veld, but more often of the freedom they enjoyed in their adopted homes. She could be happy in Texas and at times had a positive longing to see it.

Also, she might be tempted to emigrate with Saltwood because she was sometimes painfully reminded of her mixed heritage. Her father had sprung from impeccable Afrikaner roots but had gone whoring after a Rhodes scholarship, and in so doing, had acquired an English wife. This killed his eligibility for membership in the Broederbond, nor had he been selected an elder in the local church. Mrs. van Doorn was openly pro-English, but Sannie felt no attachment whatever to England and had refused two opportunities to spend vacations there.

As she matured, she found herself becoming more and more an Afrikaner. She understood why Frikkie and Jopie were willing to serve on the border, and she shared their love of this land. She had known these young men all her life, had played with them as a child, and felt she could be happy with either of them on this enchanting farm with its tumbling lakes and wild blesbok. Which of the cousins she preferred she could not say, for up to now she had never been required to choose between them.

There was one further complication. She was almost in love with Philip Saltwood. Intuitively she sensed that he was a finer-grained human being than the Troxel boys, a man who was going to take life seriously. Besides, she had enjoyed sharing a bed with him. For the time being she postponed divisions, trusting that things would sort themselves out.

They were in the kitchen drinking beer and telling Van der Merwe stories. Frikkie said, 'Van der Merwe and two rascals from Krugersdorp went to Paris to hold up a bank. But on the way to the job, Van der Merwe dropped the dynamite and the three were arrested. All of them sentenced to the guillotine. But when the knife came thundering down on the first man, it stuck and he was miraculously spared. French law declared him free. So the second man was strapped down, and again the knife came roaring down and again it jammed. He was set free. Now came Van der Merwe's turn, and he was so curious about what had happened that he looked up as they laid him on the plank, and just as the executioner was about to pull the lever that released the knife, Van der Merwe shouts, "Hold everything! I see what's wrong with this crazy machine!"'

Jopie said, 'Van der Merwe, as you know, always had a low opinion of Englishmen, and one day he watched in disgust as three of them spent more than two hours digging a hole for a fence post and setting it in the ground. "Lazy bastards! Two hours for a job like that. I could do that by myself in fifteen minutes, you give me nine Kaffirs."'

'Jopie!' Sannie warned. 'Government says we're not to call them Kaffirs any longer. The legal word now is Plural.'

Frikkie said, 'You know what Van der Merwe calls a Bushman rock painting? Under the new law, that is. "A rural plural mural."'

Jopie said, 'You know what Van der Merwe says to a Kaffir holding a machine gun? "Good morning, Baas."'

Frikkie said, 'Van der Merwe had a flagpole lying on the ground. He propped it in its hole, got a ladder and a tape measure and tried to climb up to measure it, but the flagpole fell down. Twice again he propped it up and tried to climb it. Finally a Kaffir said, "Baas, why don't you measure it when it's on the ground?" and Van der Merwe said, "Stupid Kaffir, I want to know its height, not its width."'

Jopie said, 'Speaking of width. Air France sent out its top pilot to see if Van der Merwe was ready to fly to Paris and London. Van der Merwe made one of the greatest landings in aviation history—his 747 touched down at the front edge of the tarmac . . . screamed to a braking stop, its front wheels three inches from the other end of the landing surface. "Absolutely *magnifique!*" the Air France inspector said. "This man is ready for any airport in the world. But tell me, why does South Africa make its runways so short?" "I can't explain it," Van der Merwe said. "And look at the crazy thing. It's almost five miles wide."'

Koos van der Merwe was the prototypical Afrikaner boob on whom all jokes about rural stupidity and childlike simplicity were hung. Everyone had his favorite, so that a session like this could run for hours, with an endless chain of hilarious insights into the stolid Afrikaner mind. It was interesting, Philip thought, that most of the jokes were told by Afrikaners themselves, and not by Englishmen, although he had discovered, from several such affairs, that any really ugly jokes were usually told by the latter.

After Frikkie, Jopie and Sannie had each reeled off half a dozen stories, some of them very rough on their fellow Afrikaners, they turned to Philip and asked him what his favorite was. 'I rather fancy one I heard at the diggings. "What do the numbers 1066, 1492 and 1812 have in common?"' When Sannie pointed out that they were dates important in history, Philip replied, 'Wrong. They're adjoining rooms in Van der Merwe's motel.' Then he asked, 'Why do you tell such jokes?' and each of the three had a sensible explanation. Frikkie felt that any people who were essentially rural took refuge in two kinds of comedy:

'Barnyard-sexual, and the Afrikaners have some very funny stories in that style, and country-bumpkin. In the first we're laughing at the dominee and the domination of the church. In the second we're laughing at ourselves. You hear the same jokes in each category, I'm quite sure, in rural Germany . . . or Norway.'

Jopie had quite another theory: 'We know that the Englishmen laugh at us. So we beat them to the punch and do it better.'

Sannie thought otherwise: 'We do it out of affection. Every one of us has in his family somewhere a Koos van der Merwe. He never comes exactly into focus. But we love him just the same. How many pieces in Van der Merwe's jigsaw puzzle? Two.'

When Sannie said this, Jopie broke into wild laughter, quite out of proportion to the merits of the joke. Frikkie looked at him and asked, 'Have you gone bonkers?'

'No! I just happened to think of something terribly funny.' When the other three turned to stare at him, he said, 'I was in Pretoria when Andy Young and two of his assistants from the State Department were there making speeches and giving interviews about the rights of blacks in South Africa. And I burst into laughter.'

'Why?' Saltwood asked defensively. 'Sometimes Young makes sense.'

'Granted. But not that day. Because it suddenly occurred to me, when I had a chance to look at him, to see him . . . You know, he's not black at all. Neither of his two aides were black. I've never seen a black American. Everyone who comes here is Coloured.' Here he broke into convulsive laughter, and after a moment Frikkie joined him. The two athletes punched each other and almost gagged on their merriment.

'I don't get it,' Philip said.

'Don't you see?' Sannie explained as her two suitors tried to control their raucous behavior. 'If Andy Young and your other black leaders in America lived in South Africa, and if they got their way—one-man, one-vote—and the blacks took over, the very first people to be done in would be Andy Young and his gang.'

'Now wait!' Philip snapped. As a loyal American, he felt obligated to defend President Carter and former Ambassador Young when they were attacked, which in South Africa was almost daily. 'I don't approve of Andy when he shoots from the hip, but on basic African policy he makes sense.'

'How could he?' Frikkie asked. 'One-man, one-vote?'

'I mean his view of the continent as a whole. There are three million

Afrikaners at most. Three hundred million blacks at least. Should we support you few against so many?'

'Of course you should, since our interests are the same as your interests,' Frikkie said.

'But what was your point about Young being in danger?'

'My dear stupid American,' Frikkie said, winking at Jopie. 'Don't you know that Zulu, Xhosa, Fingo, Pondo—all of them—dislike Coloureds even more than they dislike whites?'

'Why?'

'Because they feel that when decisions are made, Coloureds will side with whites. They're seen as traitors to the black cause.'

Jopie broke in: 'You may have heard. When the blacks rioted at Paarl. Quite a few dead. The Coloureds didn't raise a finger to help. Believe me, Philip, when the crunch comes, Andy Young would be in a lot more danger than me. The blacks know they'll need men like me to help organize their new world. But they'll have no place whatever for Andy Young and his light-skinned Coloureds.'

Frikkie became quite serious: 'We've watched this in many former English colonies. When the natives assume power, they ostracize the lightskins . . . if they don't slaughter them. The reason's simple. "If we must do business with people other than ourselves, let's do it with the best of the lot, the real white people." The Coloureds in this land—how many of them? Three million, perhaps. They have no future except with us. So if your Ambassador Young wishes to help his kind, he better come to Jopie and me and say, "Afrikaners, save me!" because the blacks will do him in.'

Jopie broke the tension by tickling Sannie under the chin as she finished her beer. 'You know, I don't believe I've ever seen an American black. I wonder if anyone in South Africa ever has. We made a big to-do over Arthur Ashe, and the rock musicians, and what not. But when the crunch comes, everyone like them will be dead. Because there'll be no place for those cats in the new South Africa.'

Sannie said, 'Would you like a Van der Merwe cocktail? Perrier and water?'

It was language, which tyrannizes us all, that converted Laura Saltwood into a major criminal. It began accidentally during a trip home to England; she had stopped at a store in Salisbury and the shopkeeper had said, 'I can't deliver it today, Mrs. Saltwood. My temp didn't report.'

'Your what?'

'My temp. The boy who comes in occasionally.'

On her way back to Sentinels she used a footpath through the cathedral grounds, and as she glanced about her she thought: How we English do corrupt our language. Mr. Dixon has a temp. I go to the hairdresser's for a perm. My cousin leaves the telly, goes to the fridge to get herself a snack of meat and veg. How awful.

In succeeding days she paid extra attention to what was being said around her, and heard such words as *perks* for perquisites, *grungey* for objectionable, *grotty* for distasteful, and what was probably the ugliest verbal invention of all time, *brolly* for umbrella.

When she spoke about this debasement with her cousin she noticed approvingly the precise English pattern of Lady Ellen's speech: 'Mustn't be put off by the odd bit of verbal invention, must we?'

'I was thinking of how the Dutch language deteriorated at the Cape. Became quite debased, you know.'

'I shouldn't wonder if they'd done a good thing, Laura. Mark you, languages change. You say the Afrikaners blotted their copybook. I say they've kept up with the times, and a good thing, too.'

'But there's a grandeur about language. I don't like to see it cheapened.'

'The odd bit of improvement never hurt any language. I relish some of the changes the Americans have made. *Mortician*'s a delightful word. *Custodian*'s much higher-toned than *janitor*. Not to worry about a few modifications.'

'It offends me to see signs in my dress shop which say, "Wear U get tru value," and in Afrikaans, "U is welkom." I may sound chauvinistic, but they seem silly.'

Since Lady Ellen knew nothing of Afrikaans, Laura dropped the subject, but three nights later when they drove north to see the Oxford Players do *King Lear* at Stonehenge, and the great monoliths glowed somberly in the night shadows, she surrendered to the glories of Shakespeare and actually trembled when the old king, huddling against the darkest pillars, shared his pity with those less fortunate:

> 'Poor naked wretches, wheresoe'er you are,
> That bide the pelting of this pitiless storm,
> How shall your houseless heads and unfed sides,
> Your loop'd and window'd raggedness, defend you
> From seasons such as these?'

It seemed to her that words could not be more glorious, and later, when the young man tried to frighten the crazy blind Earl of Gloster by describing the cliff and the workman climbing perilously down its face, she sighed with the terrible power of the words:

> 'How fearful
> And dizzy 'tis to cast one's eyes so low!
> The crows and choughs that wing the midway air
> Show scarce so gross as beetles: half way down
> Hangs one that gathers samphire—dreadful trade!
> Methinks he seems no bigger than his head . . .'

Unaware of the dangerous path she was treading, she sat there in the shadow of Stonehenge and gave herself over to the magic of great-fashioned words hurled into the night and became drunk on them, and when old Lear at the end confessed his weakness, she had tears in her eyes from suffering with him:

> 'I am a very foolish fond old man,
> Fourscore and upward, not an hour more nor less;
> And, to deal plainly,
> I fear I am not in my perfect mind.'

Three days later, still mesmerized by words, she borrowed Lady Ellen's Austin and drove by herself to Cambridge, where as a young woman of twenty she had enjoyed such flawless hours with her older brother, Wexton.

Parking the car in a municipal lot, she walked along King's Parade, ignoring the noble chapel of King's College, for she wanted to see again the austere entrance to Clare College, which her brother had attended. Walking as if in a dream, she entered the old surroundings which had housed scholars since 1326 and stood for a long time recalling ruefully those long spring days when she had visited Wexton here. How mercurial they were, how filled with surging ideas. Shaking her head in mournful recollection, she left Clare, nodding her head as she remembered the excellent education her brother had obtained here: You were one of the brilliant lads, Wexton. Oh, God, how I miss you.

She walked aimlessly south till she reached the gatehouse to King's College, where almost against her will she entered that stately court where Wexton had encountered the temptations he could not resist. She intended hastening through, wanting to see the Backs, where she and her brother's friends had enjoyed so many hours, but she was diverted to the right toward that grandest of England's self-contained chapels, King's, with its glorious arches reaching to heaven, its ornate choir reminding one of kings and princes. It had been spoiled somewhat since she first knew it by the installation of one of the best canvases Peter Paul Rubens ever painted, a gigantic adoration of the Magi worth millions of whatever currency might be in vogue: Damn, that's a fine painting, maybe the best he ever did. But it doesn't belong here.

She sat in one of the choir stalls, envisioning the days long ago when she and Wexton had come here with his friends to hear evensong: Those damned friends. Those accursed friends. Oh, Wexton, all life's a falling away, a dismal falling away, but why did you . . .

Tears came to her eyes and for some moments she wept, refusing to use a handkerchief, for these were not handkerchief tears. Pressing her fingers to her cheeks, she wiped the tears away, then left the chapel to walk slowly down one of the major sights of England and perhaps Europe, that expanse of green grass hemmed in by the walls of Clare, the chapel and King's. The buildings were admirably suited to each other, but it was the long sweep down to the River Cam and the Backs beyond that gave the place its nobility. Here she had been sitting on the grass one evening during the Mays—that week of frivolity which falls in June—when Noel Saltwood, from Oriel College at Oxford, drifted by in a boat with Cambridge friends he was visiting. They had met, fallen in love, and pledged a marriage which she had never once regretted. Life in Noel's South Africa had been rather primitive, and good conversation lagged, but often he encouraged her to get back to Salisbury, and from there to the theaters in London, with occasional excursions to Cambridge, and that had sustained her.

'Oh, Wexton, why in God's name did you do it?'

'Pardon, ma'am, but did you call?' It was a short little man wearing a rather long overcoat although the day was warmish, the kind of odd attendant one found everywhere.

'No. No. I was just thinking.' The man moved closer to assure himself that she was all right, then passed on. As he left she thought: I was indeed thinking. Of years gone, and of evenings on this grass when I first met Noel and his fine, unaffected approach to life. He listened like a country oaf to everything that Wexton and his clever friends and that brilliant young tutor said so glibly. And as he walked me back to my digs he said bluntly, 'I think your brother and his cronies are half-daft.'

'Don't you dare say a thing like that.'

'The way he ridicules everything. Don't you ever listen to him?'

So under Noel's tutelage she did listen, and Wexton and his friends, and especially the tutor, did ridicule everything. They despised Australia. They considered South Africa a blight. And they positively excoriated the United States. They also put George Bernard Shaw in his place, and John Galsworthy was beneath their contempt.

It was only then, spurred by Noel's sharp analysis, that she realized that her brother had fallen captive to a clique that idolized the young tutor, and in later years she watched with horror as they landed fine jobs in government, accelerated to positions of importance, then scurried off to Russia with high state secrets. Three of them, including Wexton, were living there now in lifelong exile. Two others had ended up in American jails, and one had committed suicide to avoid a treason trial. No one identified the tutor who had enlisted them, and so many others, in the revolution which was to eliminate excrescences like Australia, South Africa and America.

Oh, Wexton, I would travel to Leningrad on my knees if I could see you again! Once more she broke into tears, thinking of the dazzling manner in which this group of young brilliants had used the English language, and of the pitfalls into which it had led them. With them cleverness was four-fifths of the battle, she said to herself. Remember when one of them dismissed all of South Africa with a joke, even though he knew I was engaged to a South African: 'We had sense enough to let America win her war against us and got rid of that bad apple. We had to win our damned war against the Boers, and we're stuck with that atrocity.'

When she dropped her head in her hands, displaying an anguish that all could see, the little man in the long coat hurried back: 'Ma'am, I say, are you all right?' She was so preoccupied with her grief that she did not see another man, in a dark suit, who watched her from a far bend of the River Cam.

Very slowly she drove back to Salisbury, experiencing a vague presentiment that this might be the last journey she would ever make to Cambridge, or to England either: I'm old now. I should be visiting here as a dignified old lady coming to see my brother to talk about old times. But he's in Leningrad. God, he must be homesick.

When she tried to decipher how he had been seduced into committing his mortal sin—the betrayal of his nation and his peers—she began to think of the role words play in life: Our family was so keen on word games. Wexton and I played them incessantly. I think I first came to suspect him when he cheated one day. Altered the meaning of a word in order to win. At Cambridge he altered the meanings of the great words and ended a traitor. Back in Salisbury, walking within the shadow of the cathedral, she thought: Integrity in words protects integrity in life. If the word is corrupted, everything that stems from it will be evil. And this made her ponder word usage in South Africa, and it was then that she made her decision.

Immediately after she deplaned at Johannesburg she telephoned her son: 'Yes, tonight. I want you and Susan and the children over here at once.' When they arrived she took her son aside and said bluntly, 'Craig, I thought you were wasting your talents when you took science at Oxford. Now I thank God you did.'

'What are you prating about?'

'Your salvation. I want you to cable Washington tonight. Tell them that you've accepted the NASA position. Go to America. And take your family with you . . . forever. But first you must visit Salisbury—make arrangements for Timothy's college.'

'But why? You've always said you love it here.'

'I do, and that's why you must go.'

'To what purpose?'

'To get out of here. I'll put aside funds for Timothy's fees at Oriel, and Sir Martin can find him something in England when he graduates.'

Mrs. Saltwood asked her son to call in his wife and children, and when they were formally seated before her she said, cryptically, 'Very ugly things are going to happen in this country. They're beyond our control—beyond the control of any sensible people. If there was a chance that you could modify them, I'd want you to stay. I will.'

'We can't leave you here, Mother,' Craig's wife said earnestly.

'I'm expendable. You're not. I've had my life, you haven't—and it would be crazy to try to spend it in this insane atmosphere.'

'What makes you so agitated?'

'I went to a performance of *King Lear* at Stonehenge. I heard majestic words. And I dare no longer turn my back.'

'Mother, you're not making sense.'

'All you need to know, Craig, is that after the first of June it will not be wise for any Saltwood to be living in South Africa.'

'What happens on the first of June?'

'I go bowling. I go bowling in Cape Town with the Lady Anne Barnard Club, and I want you to be safely home in Salisbury.'

She would say no more. She bought four tickets on South African Airways: 'They have the best planes, you know, and the best pilots, too.' And she spent many hours at the Johannesburg offices of the Black Sash, discussing events with the ladies who were endeavoring to alleviate the tragedy and hardship engendered by enforcement of apartheid. She also sent four urgent letters to Sir Martin Saltwood at Sentinels, explaining the necessity for sending Timothy to England and asking him to watch over the boy. Finally she wrote to the principal of a black high school in the Transvaal, assuring him that she would speak at his school, as requested. After that she spent her spare time with the sonnets of Shakespeare, until a chain of those unequaled lines echoed in her head, building an eclectic sonnet of their own:

> When to the sessions of sweet silent thought
> I all alone beweep my outcast state
> Bare ruined choirs, where late the sweet birds sang
> Roses have thorns, and silver fountains mud
> Like as the waves make towards the pebbled shore
> When yellow leaves, or none, or few, do hang
> Not mine own fears, nor the prophetic soul
> Of the wide world dreaming on things to come.

At times the sheer beauty of the words overcame her, and she felt that men and women give their lives for many good and noble causes, but none more sacred than the keeping alive of words that thunder and sing and console, and it was to such a mission that she now dedicated herself.

When word reached Vrymeer that Craig Saltwood and his family were leaving, the Van Doorns were startled, for this was only the latest in that flood of talent that was pouring out of South Africa. 'Craig must be out of his mind,' Marius stormed. 'Good job here. Sound prospects.'

'And a clear view of the track ahead,' his wife agreed.

Philip Saltwood had dropped by to see Sannie, but she was out with the Troxel boys, and Marius put the question to him: 'Would you be frightened out of South Africa today?'

'I'd want to stay. But that's because I like crisis situations.'

'You imply that if you were Craig, you might leave.'

'I might. I doubt a non-Afrikaner has much future here. I'd probably go back to where I was wanted.'

'You damned foreigners,' Marius growled.

'I'm staying,' his very English wife said. 'But of course, my life is here. Sannie and the rest.'

'Are you also saying that if you were Craig, you'd take the chicken and run?' her husband asked.

'I would, for the reasons Philip has just cited. It's not pleasant, Marius, living where you're not welcome—'

'Rubbish. All my friends adore you.'

'And half our Jewish acquaintances have sent their children out of the country. Never coming back. And we know many English who are doing the same.'

Marius adopted a philosophical view: 'Every organism ought to cleanse itself now and then. The brains we lose will be replaced locally.'

'But if you Afrikaners despise speculative thinking because it might turn radical, how can the gaps be filled?' she asked. 'Have you heard what Afrikaner professors and ministers are teaching these days? Not much leadership there.'

'It'll come,' Philip interposed. 'I see some very bright young engineers.'

'One thing does worry me,' Marius said reflectively. 'Of all the places in the world I've seen, the one that impressed me most was Princeton, New Jersey. When I was there Einstein was in residence, and John von Neumann, and Lise Meitner was visiting. All the brilliant scientists that Europe had lost in the 1930s. They were the ones who paved the way for the atomic bomb. Fermi, the others. And when the urgent need came in World War II, the Germans looked around for their help and they were gone. I wonder if we're alienating similar talent.'

But when Frikkie and Jopie arrived with Sannie, they put things back into perspective. 'To hell with all English fugitives,' Jopie said. 'They fight for nothing these days. Won't even play us in rugby.' But as soon as he said this he remembered that Mrs. van Doorn was English: 'I don't mean you.'

Frikkie said brightly, 'Let the Jews and the English hands-uppers clutter up Harvard and Yale. We have work to do here which they would never stomach. And we're going to do it.'

When the time came for the Craig Saltwoods to leave the country, Philip announced that he'd like to drive to Jan Smuts Airport to see them off, for this would give him a chance to meet Laura Saltwood, of whom several local people had spoken with regard. However, the journey was a hundred miles, and he might not have gone had he not received a surprising telegram from Craig Saltwood, whom he had never met: IMPERATIVE I SEE YOU JAN SMUTS AIRPORT PRIOR MY DEPARTURE.

Frikkie and Jopie volunteered to drive, because they knew that Sannie enjoyed seeing the 747s even if she wasn't flying in them, so as a foursome they drove across southern Transvaal, roaring into the airport well ahead of takeoff. They found Craig Saltwood anxiously looking for his American cousin. When Frikkie identified the Englishman, the three Afrikaners withdrew, leaving the cousins alone. Then Craig said, startling Philip even more, 'I know we're practically strangers, but . . . Philip, would you please watch over my mother. I'm sure she's up to something dramatic and I'm damned if I can learn what.'

Philip was at a loss for words. Stunned by the request, he finally said, weakly, 'I can't very well watch over her from Venloo.'

'I don't mean that. You can never stop my mother from doing what she wants.'

'What do you mean?'

'I think she's going to fall afoul of the law. Everything she says and does strengthens the impression.'

'Then why are you leaving?'

'Because she insists. Says things here are bound to go to hell— Here she comes.'

Laura Saltwood was sixty-seven that day, tall, white-haired, thin as in her youth, and clear-eyed. She was quite content to see her family leaving 'for a better climate,' as she phrased it, and she did not intend showing tears as they departed. She was somewhat disconcerted to meet Philip, for his unexpected presence made the departure one degree more grave than she had intended; however, she greeted him cordially and asked him to join them in the lounge to await the plane's takeoff.

'I have these friends with me,' he apologized, and when he called them over she widened her conversation to include them, using Afrikaans when introductions were made. The situation was strained, for the Craig Saltwoods were embarrassed at leaving the country, while Frikkie and Jopie were obviously disgusted with them for doing so.

Now the plane was wheeled into position, a modified version of the standard 747, shortened so it could fly non-stop to London, since South African planes were not allowed to refuel anywhere in black Africa. An all-white flight crew took their places in a land that was eighty percent non-white, and after formal goodbyes another family left the country, its children never to return to the land which had nurtured them and which sorely needed whatever contributions they might have made.

Jopie said as the plane soared off, 'The English—last to land, first to flee.' And Frikkie said, 'A wise farmer weeds out his weak mealies.' They made no attempt to hide their bitterness.

They might have been even more upset had they chanced to see at a far edge of the airport an unscheduled Boeing to which a sequence of small automobiles reported during the space of about an hour. No announcements were made over the loudspeakers regarding this plane; no uniformed stewardesses flourished through the airport, heralding it. Quietly it filled with passengers, quietly it taxied to the far end of the runway, and without notice of any kind it took off, circled, and flew directly westward on a very long flight to South America. It contained one hundred and eighty businessmen and farmers, most of them Afrikaners, who were going with their wives to visit Rio de Janeiro and São Paulo to investigate farmlands of the interior against the day when they might wish to quit South Africa for a new frontier. Of these passengers, forty-three families would like Brazil so much that they would make arrangements to purchase vast *fincas,* holding them in reserve for the day when they might be needed. The others would make their decisions later. As for the secret plane, after an appropriate rest it would load up with Afrikaner and English doctors and fly them to Australia to register with that country's medical association, so as to ensure a refuge . . . when the crunch came.

On May 30 Laura Saltwood appeared at the black school in the Transvaal to find that publicity regarding her visit had encouraged some thirty or forty black principals and school officials to drive substantial distances to hear her. They knew her to be a remarkable woman, a quiet worker in a score of worthy causes. She had the reputation for both good sense and fearlessness, and they knew she would not have come so far unless she had something pertinent to say.

Although she had written her speech in detail, suspecting that it might be the most important she would ever deliver, and perhaps the last, she did not refer to notes but spoke extemporaneously. She announced her subject as *Language,* one of the most mercurial topics in the world, and eased the apprehensions of the older conservatives by praising Afrikaans:

'As you know from the Old Testament, South Africa and Israel have much in common, especially their determination in creating and establishing a new language. Israel went back to ancient Hebrew. South Africa went to classical Dutch, adding a wonderful assembly of new words, new spellings, and new arrangements.

'Don't let anyone ridicule Afrikaans, just because it uses compact constructions. The greatness of English is that it simplified High German, made it more attainable, knocked out the silly declensions. A German purist would have every right to scorn English as a bastardization, just as Dutchmen scorn Afrikaans as a cheapening of their language. That's unfair. Two centuries from now Afrikaans may be a major language and Dutch may have disappeared, because Afrikaans speaks to simple needs, and therefore creates its own vitality.'

The more volatile younger teachers were disappointed by the conciliatory approach, and one history teacher whispered, 'She could be the spokesman for the Africaner universities.' But then she launched into the heart of her message:

'Before Soweto 1976 the black children of South Africa were advised that since their future lay in this country, they should adopt as their second language not English but Afrikaans. And they were ordered to use Afrikaans as the medium of instruction in half their subjects, when they clearly preferred to use English in all. They were right to demand English. To deny them that language would be a most grievous deprivation. [Here several teachers applauded.]

'English is a universal language, a lingua franca in all parts of the world. Airlines fly by English. Scholarly reports from all countries are circulated in English. To have this language is to have a key to the world's economies.

'English also has a literature probably richer than that of any other language, because in English you have not only the immortal contributions of Milton and Shakespeare, Dickens and Jane

Austen, but you also have contributions made by people like Ernest Hemingway from America, Patrick White from Australia and William Butler Yeats from Ireland. To surrender English when you have a chance to acquire it is like throwing away the key to a treasury.

'Learn Afrikaans to help you in your daily life in this country, but learn English to help you live in the whole world. The conqueror who makes me learn his language makes me a slave. The edict that makes me learn a language spoken by only a few people puts me in a cage. The teacher who enables me to learn the lingua franca of the entire world sets me free. If you learn Afrikaans, you will be able to read a few fine books; if you learn English, you will be able to read the greatest body of learning and literature in the world.'

The principals applauded; the teachers cheered; the students went out and marched with banners. The police looked diligently for Mrs. Saltwood, but she had traveled by back routes to her home in Johannesburg; the next day she flew to Cape Town with a friend who served with her on the board of the Black Sash. What was more important, they made arrangements to bowl together on the Lady Anne Barnard team.

On June 1 Laura Saltwood rose at seven, read from the little book of Shakespeare's sonnets which she kept with her, and after a spare breakfast in her friend's kitchen, dressed in her bowls uniform: white stockings, white shoes with pale blue trim, white dress with heavy braided piping, white sweater with the Lady Anne Barnard colors on the pocket, and a stiff white straw hat with Barnard streamers. A selected group of women, most of them Church of England, had proudly worn this uniform for the past eighty years, and now twelve of them journeyed by different ways to the bowling green in the park, where they were to meet the distinguished Ladies of the Castle. During much of South African history this team had enrolled titled members.

Most of the players were in position when Laura arrived; some were much older than she; most were in their fifties. They were a handsome group of women, sun-tanned, each in proper uniform, each keen on the game which they had played for decades. The Ladies of the Castle could be easily differentiated from Laura's team: they wore brown shoes with very heavy rubber soles, and their hats had wide brims, down in front, up in back, with ribbons that hung neatly from the left side. It was obvious that they intended to win.

No one, either from the Barnards or the Castles, spoke to Mrs. Saltwood in any way other than their normal greeting on a June morning when the air was brisk and the sides of the playing field rimmed with beds of late-autumn flowers, but their tenseness indicated that this was not an ordinary day.

Laura was paired with the best bowler on the Barnards, Mrs. Grimsby, a stern-faced woman who intimidated her opponents by wearing on her dress a band of six medals she had won in international competitions. She was formidable, and shook Laura's hand firmly when they met: 'We'll have at them, yes?'

'It's our turn to win,' Laura said.

The teams bowled in sets of four, two opponents at one end of the rink facing two at the other. Today Laura would be bowling against Mrs. Phelps-Jones, who consistently beat her, but she felt that with Mrs. Grimsby at the other end, they just might pull off a surprise victory.

Laura won the right to send down the target bowl, the jack, which she did with some skill, landing it almost exactly the right distance from the backstop, but a little too much to the right. Since other foursomes would be playing at the same time on adjoining rinks, it was customary to move the jack into the center of the lane, at the distance set, and when this was done, the game began.

Laura and Mrs. Phelps-Jones were each to bowl four balls, Laura's marked with a small blue triangle inset into the wood, her opponent's with a green circle. A small mat was spread to protect the grass where the bowlers would be standing throughout the game, and on it Laura took two firm steps, swinging her right arm at the same time and delivering a ball with a decided spin. She launched it far to the left of her target, but since it was not perfectly round and since she had been careful to start it on its largest axis, it gradually twisted itself to the right, ending up not too far from the jack.

Mrs. Phelps-Jones was not daunted. Taking over the mat, she swung her first bowl well to the right, watching with satisfaction as it cut a large parabola toward the left, ending closer to the jack than Laura's. At the end of this first head, Mrs. Phelps-Jones scored one point, for her first ball rested closer than any that Laura could send down, but Laura escaped disaster because one of her bowls was better than her opponent's second closest.

Now it was Mrs. Grimsby's turn, and she was a terror. Sending her wood right-to-left, she seemed to have implanted a magnet in the jack, for it drew her wood to it, and at the end of that head she had scored a cheering three. The game continued close through the twenty-one heads, with Mrs. Grimsby scoring the points that Laura failed to make. It was a splendid competition, with all four ladies delighted by the closeness.

It was Mrs. Grimsby who first saw them. She had delivered a smashing wood, sharp right-to-left, that knocked away two of her opponent's bowls, and when she looked up, they were standing off to one side, two men in dark suits watching the game, saying nothing.

Mrs. Grimsby's opponent saw them next, then all the women on the far ends of the rinks. No one spoke, but gradually their changed expressions alerted the women, whose backs were to the men. Finally Mrs. Phelps-Jones said matter-of-factly, 'Laura, I think they've come.'

Mrs. Saltwood did not look up. She was checking the position of the balls sent to their end by Mrs. Grimsby and her opponent, and she said, 'I think Esther has two, do you agree?'

Mrs. Phelps-Jones bent over to inspect and said, 'Two, right.'

The game continued, as the men intended it should, and although Laura did poorly, the remarkable bowling of Mrs. Grimsby enabled their side to win 25–21, but as Laura knelt to recover the bowls, she saw that Mrs. Phelps-Jones was weeping, and when she moved down the rink to congratulate Mrs. Grimsby, she found that she, too, was crying.

It was Mrs. Grimsby's opponent who spoke: 'Laura, you were the dearest woman in the teams. May I kiss you?'

Tears streaming down their faces, the women gave her their farewells, aware that they would probably never again compete with this fiery, wonderful woman. When they were finished, the two men moved forward, stood facing Mrs. Saltwood, and said quietly, 'Laura Saltwood, you are banned.'

She sat in her house, alone. For the next five years she must never be seen in the presence of more than one other person. She could attend no public meeting of any kind, nor address any gathering of even three, nor publish anything, nor consult with anyone except her doctor, her dentist and her lawyer, but not even them in unison.

No mention of her could be made in the public press; no quotation could ever appear in print of anything she had ever done or said or written or thought. She could not receive money from abroad, or appear on radio or television. If she went into town, she must never appear with more than one other person, and if friends stopped to talk with her, she was obliged to turn them aside.

It was because she had anticipated this imprisonment that she had sent her son and his family out of the country, for as a banned woman she would not have been free to meet with them or to travel with them on vacations of any kind, and she did not want them to share such painful limitations.

When anyone visited her, she had to leave her door open so that police or even strangers could satisfy themselves that she was not conducting a meeting, and if more than one person came to her house, with spying neighbors knowing that they were there, she had to provide chairs for the extras so that they could sit outside and be seen as not participating in the visit.

Since she would never be told what charges had been brought against her, there was no way to defend herself against the banning or clear herself once it had been imposed. Some eighty or ninety minor officials had the right to recommend to higher authorities the names of those they disliked, but the victims would never know who the accusers were or what had provoked them. In Laura's case heavy emphasis was placed on the report from the secret operations maintained by the South African government in London:

> Our agent 18-52 followed Mrs. Saltwood to Cambridge University, where her brother Wexton enrolled in the Communist Party prior to his escape to Moscow, and here she visited his old college Clare, from which she went to the banks of the River Cam at King's College, where a courier in a long coat approached her once, went to a telephone, and approached her a second time with messages not heard.

Only certain types of citizens were apt to be banned: newspapermen, writers, clergymen who strayed from the dictates of the Dutch Reformed Church, women who agitated, and of course any black who showed signs of potential leadership. The good thing about banning, from the government's point of view, was that it involved no prolonged court case, no publicity, and no obnoxious statements by the accused in their defense. It was clean, effective and final.

On the third night of her banning, Laura Saltwood was not surprised when at four in the morning a bomb exploded outside her door. When the government designated a person like Mrs. Saltwood as objectionable, she became a free target for every hoodlum in the neighborhood, and the police did little to discourage the rabble from bombing and firing the homes of banned persons. In recent years six hundred and seventeen such bombings and attacks had been made, and never once did the police track down the culprits. Always the authorities said, 'The bombing was despicable. Every effort is being made to identify those responsible.' In some of the cases, including Mrs. Saltwood's, fragments of the bomb contained serial numbers comparable to those issued to the police, but the best detectives in the country could not track down the perpetrators. They could trace a lone fountain pen sent into the country by a church in Geneva and know every person who handled it before it found its way to some black scholar, but they could not track down a bomb whose serial number indicated its place of manufacture, its designation, and who had signed for its receipt.

Of the previous attacks, many had resulted in disastrous fires, several had maimed and two had killed, but no suspect had ever even been listed, let alone arrested. In Mrs. Saltwood's case, the bomb destroyed a door and left a heavy fire-stain on the woodwork, but that was all. What the next one would do she could not know, but there would surely be a next one, which the police would investigate and the officials in Pretoria deplore.

The harshest aspect of Laura Saltwood's banning was that on the morning of the day when her five years expired, the same two men could appear at her door and say quietly, 'Laura Saltwood, you are banned for five more years,' and after that, there could be another five, and another.

That was why the members of the Lady Anne Barnard Club wept as they bade her goodbye that first day of June. They expected never to see her free again.

In his discussions with young Afrikaners, both at the fossicking and at Vrymeer, Saltwood was disturbed by the cavalier manner in which they dismissed world opinion. The United Nations would pass a resolution condemning South Africa for its racial policies, or its treatment of Indians, and the Troxel boys would laugh: 'What can they do about it? They need our minerals. To hell with them.' Newspapers in London and

New York would print bitter editorials, and the young geologists working with Philip would sneer: 'What can England and the United States do? They've got to rely on us as bulwarks against Communism, so the bleeding hearts can bloody well drop dead.'

No outsider could talk with these vital young people without becoming convinced that they intended using military force to defend their way of life and were prepared to use their guns against either outside threats or internal ones. 'Let their armies step one foot across our borders,' Frikkie said, 'and we'll blow their heads off.'

Jopie made a much different point: 'If this Jonathan Nxumalo or any of his kind try to infiltrate us from Moçambique, we'll shoot them the moment they step on our soil. And we'll shoot any Kaffir inside our country who raises a finger to help them.'

'You sound like the Götterdämmerung Commando,' Saltwood said one Sunday afternoon at the farm.

'What's that?' Jopie asked.

'A German myth. The gods have loused everything up, hideously, so they go into laager, and to solve their problems, they burn down all of heaven.'

'I volunteer for that commando,' Jopie said.

'I, too,' said Sannie.

'You mean you would risk destroying the whole structure of South Africa to prolong your advantage?'

This was the kind of rhetorical question that would have been effective among university students in Paris or Berlin. At Vrymeer it evoked from Frikkie an answer which simply stunned Saltwood: 'No American could understand our situation. You have a problem with your blacks which you solve in ways harmonious to your history. But what you do bears no relationship to us. Because God placed us here to do His work. He put us here to serve as a bulwark of Christian civilization. We must stay.'

Philip gasped. In the United States, Frikkie and Jopie would be professional football players, and he could not conceive of a pair of athletes from the Dallas Cowboys or the Denver Broncos citing God as the sponsor of their political behavior. 'Do you believe what you just said?' he asked, and Sannie replied, 'We were placed here to do God's will, and we shall do it.' When Philip tried to question her, she interrupted: 'If Frikkie and Jopie were to be killed in the first battle, I'd take up their guns.'

'To do what?'

'To preserve our Christian way of life.'

'You would go out to your rondavels and shoot the Nxumalos?'

'I certainly would.' And almost imperceptibly she moved toward the cousins.

Silence fell in the kitchen. This was the first intimation that she had decided to cast her lot with the Troxels and against the American intruder, and Saltwood decided it was futile to speak further. Which of the cousins she would ultimately prefer was not discernible, but it was clear that she had enlisted in their Götterdämmerung Commando.

Later, when he was alone with her, he dared to reopen the difficult subject, but at the first tentative question she made her position clear: 'Philip, we're a small group of white people on the edge of a hostile black continent. God placed us here for a specific purpose and gave us a commission. I assure you that we will all perish before we prove false to that obligation.'

'Sannie, it seems to me you're overpowered by the attitude of Frikkie and Jopie. What do your parents think?'

'What Mother thinks isn't relevant, she's English. But if you want to ask Father . . .'

They went to Marius in his study, a room lined with books he had used at Oxford and others he had imported from London and New York through the years. 'In my father's day,' he said, 'this room contained one book, that old Bible. Now I can't even read the Dutch.'

'We've been having a sharp argument, Father. Philip accuses the cousins and me of being members of a Götterdämmerung Commando. Burning South Africa down to save it.'

'He's correct about your attitudes now. But as you grow older . . .'

'I'll grow more convinced. I have no patience . . .'

'Not now, but when you face the real alternatives.'

'What are they?'

Marius leaned back. For some time now he had been worried about Sannie's growing militarism; she behaved as if she thought a machine gun answered all questions. But he also wondered about his own attitudes; had his years at Oxford and his marriage to an Englishwoman contaminated him? Well he remembered his father's telling him what Dominee Brongersma had said about his marriage to a non-Afrikaner: 'Now he can never join the Broederbond . . . never play a major role in our society.' Brongersma had been right. No man who had chosen Oxford above the captaincy of the Springboks, and an English wife over a loyal Afrikaner, could be other than an outcast from the governing cadre; he had never been taken into the confidences of anyone seriously connected with government and had existed in a kind of limbo, neither Afrikaner nor English. He once said of himself, 'I'm like an Afrikaner Coloured,' and having admitted this, he realized that his daughter Sannie, who seemed bent on becoming pure Afrikaner, would hold anything he said in suspicion.

'I've been pondering this question constantly,' he said slowly. 'I've had to evaluate the things Father did in his long years on the Race Commission. And I've come to the conclusion that Afrikaners like Frikkie and Jopie will never change.'

'Hooray for them!' Sannie cried.

'And at her own request I must place my daughter in their camp.'

'Which is where I want to be.'

'So, Philip, I would be most happy, and so would my wife, if you married this girl and took her away with you.' He was speaking gravely, almost sorrowfully. 'I see no happy future for her here. Like the gifted children of so many families we know, she must make her home in Montreal or Melbourne.'

'Leave me out of it,' Sannie said abruptly. 'I can fend for myself. What future do you see for the country?'

'With the fall of Moçambique to black forces—Namibia, Zambia, Vwarda and Rhodesia—can we logically suppose that we can hold out indefinitely against . . .'

'I can,' Sannie said. 'So can Frikkie and Jopie and all loyal Afrikaners.'

'For your lifetimes, perhaps. Or for as long as your guns can find bullets. But in the long run, beyond our petty personal interests . . .'

He was hesitant about sharing his apocalyptic view with a foreigner who had no vested interest in the country, or even with his daughter, who might be alienated by it. But like all South Africans, he was eager to talk about the future, so he carried on: 'I think the blacks, like the Nxumalo brothers—Jonathan in Moçambique, Daniel at the university—will be willing in their moment of triumph . . .'

'You think they'll triumph?' Sannie asked contemptuously.

'Or their sons, who will be much like them,' her father said.

'My sons will shoot them down,' she said.

'Then their grandsons. History has time . . . It can wait.'

'For what?' Saltwood asked eagerly.

'As I was saying, I think the black victors will be generous. They'll want us to stay. God knows, their brothers haven't made much of the countries they now control. They'll realize they need us.'

'You really believe that?' Sannie asked.

'Without question. The black leadership in this country has been the most patient on earth, the most understanding. It's been a miracle of compassion and tolerance, and I think it will continue in that vein.'

'Then where's the trouble?' Philip asked.

'With us. With Sannie and Frikkie and Jopie. We won't be able to accept the change. We'll ride the Götterdämmerung Commando, as you predict, but we'll grow sickened of it, even if the rest of the world doesn't intervene. And then . . .'

Here he showed himself truly reluctant to spell out his vision, and neither his daughter nor his American guest could possibly have foreseen what he was about to say: 'At that moment of crisis the Afrikaner and his English supporters, of whom my wife will be one, will go into perpetual laager. With the full connivance and even assistance of the new black rulers, we'll retreat to the western half of the Orange Free State and Cape Province west of Grahamstown. We'll keep the diamond mines at Kimberley, but surrender the gold fields at Johannesburg. That city and Pretoria will be turned over to the new black government, and in our compressed little area we will build our Afrikanerstan. The tables will be reversed. When we were in power we tried to concentrate all the blacks into little areas, while we held the vast open spaces and the good cities. In the future they'll hold the open spaces and the good cities, and we'll be compressed.'

'What will happen to the Coloureds?' Philip asked. 'They'll all be with you—in Afrikanerstan?' And Marius van Doorn gave the same answer his people had been giving for the past three hundred years: 'We'll deal with that knotty problem later.'

When Philip and Sannie, much sobered by her father's predictions, repeated them to the Troxels, the cousins guffawed, and Jopie said, 'When they try to capture Pretoria, they'll find us in the trenches at the monument, and they better be prepared to die.'

'Father said the real tests will come with your grandsons. They'll be smart enough to—'

'If one of my grandsons talks like your father, I'll beat him to a jelly.'

Frikkie sought to face the problem more philosophically: 'There was no one on this land when we arrived. God gave it to us. We found a primitive paradise and converted it into a great nation.'

'Just a minute!' Philip protested. 'I'm sure I read that natives greeted your ships when they arrived at the Cape.'

'There was no one here,' Jopie insisted. 'I heard Sannie's grandfather state this in a public meeting.'

This evidence so startled Philip that he asked Marius to join them to clarify the facts. 'Jopie says he heard your father . . .'

'On several occasions,' Frikkie added.

'. . . state that when the Dutch arrived at the Cape, they found the place completely empty.'

Marius laughed. 'My father was fond of claiming this in his orations. It was a basic tenet of his religion—still is for the average Afrikaner.'

'See, there were no people here!' Jopie cried triumphantly.

'Detleef was right, according to his definitions. There were no Englishmen, no Spaniards, no Portuguese. And certainly no blacks.'

'We took over a virgin land,' Frikkie said quietly.

'Not exactly. There were many little brown people. Bushmen, Hottentots.'

'They don't count,' Jopie protested. 'They weren't human.'

'They did die out,' Frikkie said. 'Diseases took them. And a few returned to the desert, and pretty soon they'll die, too.'

'Like we said,' Jopie concluded, looking fiercely at Philip, 'the place was empty. God called us here to perform a task on His behalf.'

The Troxel arrogance was somewhat shaken by two events which occurred not in South Africa but abroad, and when Philip saw how the cousins reacted, and the young men working for him, he thought: Maybe the outside world is beginning to penetrate, after all.

The first jolt came from a most unlikely source. Reverend Paulus van den Berghe, moderator of a group of French and Dutch Calvinists, came to South Africa to ascertain whether the rupture which had separated the mother church in Holland and the Afrikaners' church in South Africa could be repaired, and in the course of his investigations he asked permission to meet with the son of one of its principal architects. Marius, always eager for foreign contacts, agreed to have the distinguished theologian spend some days at Vrymeer, where in the gentlest manner Van den Berghe interrogated not only Marius, but also Frikkie and Jopie and then Daniel Nxumalo, home on vacation.

At the end of four days Van den Berghe knew something of conditions at Venloo from both the white and black points of view, and at the final session, to which Philip was invited and Nxumalo, too, he voiced a few of his tentative conclusions:

'What do you suppose the two biggest surprises were for me? Meeting two rugby players of international status and seeing for myself what sterling young men they are. I wish you good luck, Troxels, with your forthcoming games in Australia and New Zealand. The second big surprise was to find that I was on the farm once occupied, or shared, by Paulus de Groot, who was my hero when I was a lad. I was born the year he died, and how often I heard my parents talk about the heroic Dutchman—to us, Boers were always Dutchmen—who held at bay four hundred thousand Englishmen. It was a moment of deep affection when I was allowed to place flowers on his grave.

'As to the purposes of my visit, it must be obvious that clergymen like me in The Netherlands and France are disturbed by the course your Dutch Reformed Church has been taking since you Afrikaners assumed control of the nation in 1948. It has become a handmaiden not of a religion, nor of the republic, but of a particular political party, and that's always regrettable. A church should be the handmaiden of Jesus Christ first, the entire society second, and to align it on the side of faction is dangerous.

'Concerning its preachments regarding apartheid, it would be improper for me to voice my personal judgments before the whole commission has had a chance to evaluate and temper them. But I must confess that I leave your country with a heavy heart. I had not realized you had grown so far apart from us. It will now be the duty of all to conciliate our differences.'

When he was gone, Frikkie said with ill-masked fury, 'This land has always been cursed by missionaries. That man's an agent of the World Council of Churches and I should have shot him for a spy.'

'Oh, Frik!' Mrs. van Doorn protested.

'I mean it. What did the foreign churches do in Rhodesia? They gave money to terrorists. And how did they spend it? Killing women and children and missionaries. Is that Christianity?'

Jopie joined in: 'You watch what he writes when he gets back to

Holland!' And the Troxels were right, for when the commission's report appeared, it was a devastating attack on the South African church:

> With mounting sorrow your committee must report that our Afrikaner brothers in the white Dutch Reformed Church of South Africa have strayed so far and so willfully from the path of Christian morality as evidenced in the preachings of Jesus Christ and St. Paul that reunion now between our church and theirs would be inadvisable and unproductive. Your committee therefore recommends unanimously that the present severance of affiliations be maintained until such time as the Dutch Reformed Church of South Africa manifests a Christian concern in ending its support of the system of repression known as *apartheid*.

Saltwood was surprised at the fury with which the Troxels reacted to this censure: 'We're the polecats of the world, and damnit, if they come at us, we'll squirt in their eyes.' Sannie agreed, and even though Saltwood cautioned the young people that they could not indefinitely ignore world opinion, Frikkie responded, 'We can if it's wrong.' Philip then asked if young men like him and Jopie ever admitted that anything was wrong with South Africa, and they replied together, 'No.' And Jopie added, 'We've worked out a decent, fair system of handling the races in our society. The laws have been passed, and they must be obeyed.'

'But in most countries,' Philip said, thinking of the drastic readjustments in America in recent years, 'provision is made for reassessment. A law tends to be applicable for only about ten or twenty years. The laws your grandfather passed, Sannie—'

'He didn't pass them. He proposed them.'

'Haven't they served their day? Shouldn't they be repealed?'

'Repealed?' the Troxel boys echoed. 'They should be strengthened!'

'You see, Saltwood,' Frikkie explained, 'we know the blacks. They're wild veld creatures like the antelope, and we won't allow them to be spoiled by modern ideas, no matter what the Dutch churchmen advise.'

Jopie was more blunt: 'To hell with the Dutch churchmen. They're today's missionaries.' And at this, Sannie grasped the hands of her young men and started a dance, chanting an improvised song:

> 'To hell with the missionaries!
> To hell with the men of Holland!
> To hell with all who interfere!'

Marius, hearing the clamor, came from his study, and Sannie danced up to him: 'We're consigning the missionaries to hell.'

'That was done long ago,' Marius said, and when he joined the young people in a beer, Saltwood asked, 'How do you see the church problem?' and after some reflection he replied, 'When I accepted my Rhodes scholarship instead of playing rugby for the Springboks against New Zealand, I knew I was sacrificing a lot.' He smiled at the Troxels. 'These lads go against New Zealand next month. It'll be the great adventure of your lives.'

'Apparently you have regrets.'

'One you'd never expect. When I returned home with an English wife, I couldn't be a member of the Broederbond, but who cared? What did hurt was that I was denied the right to be a full member of the Dutch Reformed Church. I've never been an elder, you know.'

'Does that matter?' Saltwood asked.

'Grievously. I truly believe that our church is the most effective on earth today. It has spirit, meaning, force. It obeys the word of God and endeavors prayerfully to implement it. A real church.'

'But its support of apartheid? Surely . . .'

Marius rose and went to the refrigerator for another beer. 'Churches go through cycles. In America, if I understand correctly, your Catholic church is riding rampant on birth control and abortion. That's temporary, a fashion of the moment. It has very little to do with the ongoing operation of the church. Same with our church and apartheid. It's a problem for the 1980s. Fifty years from now it will all be settled.'

'So you support your church in all it does?' Philip asked.

'I do, because it's the moral force of South Africa. It's forever.'

'And in the meantime,' Jopie cried, 'to hell with the visitors from Holland.'

'And the World Council of Churches!' Sannie cried, resuming their dance.

A few days later Saltwood observed his arrogant young Afrikaners knocked flat by a much different kind of foreign intervention. He was alone in the Van Doorn kitchen, waiting for Sannie, when her father and Jopie burst into the room, looking ghastly. Without speaking, they fiddled with the radio, located a Pretoria station, and listened as the awful news was reported: 'There is an unconfirmed report out of Auckland that the governments of Australia and New Zealand will be forced to cancel the scheduled tour of those countries by a rugby team from South Africa.'

'Good God!' Marius said, looking at Jopie as if the latter's arms had been amputated. 'That would mean you wouldn't get your Springbok blazer.'

'Wait, wait! This can't be serious.'

But it was. A different newscaster announced in tremulous Afrikaans, his voice near breaking: 'We have nothing definite yet, but governments of Australia and New Zealand have explained that rioting in the streets protesting the tours have made cancellation advisable.'

'Have you heard?' Frikkie bellowed as he rushed into the kitchen. 'Tour's been canceled.'

'Not officially,' Jopie said, his hands sweating.

Then came the appalling bulletin: 'It is now confirmed that the Springbok tour of Australia and New Zealand has been canceled.'

Marius fell into a chair, staring pitifully at the brothers. 'It's like you said, Jopie. The world thinks we're skunks.'

The three rugby players huddled at the radio, shaken by the urgent bulletins that flooded the air, and when the ugly story was fully verified, Saltwood was amazed by the violence of the men's reactions.

'It's criminal!' Marius shouted. 'Using sport as a weapon of confrontation. A game's a game, and politics should have nothing to do with it.'

'I'll teach them politics,' Jopie thundered. 'I'll fly to New Zealand and break those protestors in half, one by one.'

'It's not the ordinary citizens,' Marius said. 'It's the damned press.'

'The press in all countries should be muzzled,' Frikkie stormed, but at this moment the minister of sports came on the radio to console the nation, and he was bidding them be of good spirit despite the shattering blow, when Sannie burst into the kitchen, weeping. 'Oh, Jopie! Oh, dear Frikkie! They've stolen your glorious tour from you!' She ran to the cousins and kissed them; Jopie gulped so deeply that Philip feared he might burst into tears, but instead he went about the room, knocking his fist against doorjambs.

Then came more shocking news: 'In New Zealand the agitation against our Springboks was led by a South African citizen, one Fred Stabler, who himself used to play rugby for Rhodes University in Grahamstown. This agitator has moved through both North Island and South, spreading the poison about what he calls apartheid, and he raised such a virulent storm that the New Zealand government had to intervene and order the tour to be canceled. In Australia, at least, it was native-borns who led the agitation. In New Zealand it was one of our own.'

Gloom settled over the Van Doorn kitchen as the Afrikaners real-

ized the full impact of this decision. A generation of fine young athletes
would never know whether they could match courage with the ferocious
All-Blacks. The great good feelings that welled up when a touring side
ran onto the field against New Zealand would be lost. It was important
when a South African tennis player was barred from competing in
world tennis, a thing to be deplored, but when a whole rugby team was
denied an opportunity to win the green blazer, it was a national scandal,
and men of all stripe were finally driven to wonder if perchance their
nation was on the wrong track.

This self-exploration was intensified next day when newspapers carried full reports from New Zealand, and one Auckland paper, long a
defender of South African teams, editorialized:

> Through the years this newspaper had prided itself on being a
> champion of restraint in dealing with the thorny problem of
> South African rugby. In 1960, when our Maoris were threatened
> with expulsion because their skins were not white, we apologized
> for the backward attitudes of a nation grappling with a serious
> problem. In 1965, when in the heat of one of our grandest vic-
> tories Prime Minister Verwoerd announced that henceforth no
> New Zealand team containing Maoris would ever again be wel-
> comed in South Africa, we discounted his threat as one given in
> despair over the unexpectedly poor showing of his Springboks.
> And in 1976, when all the world condemned us for sending the
> All-Blacks to perform in a country so ridden with racial hatred,
> we supported the tour. And even when the refereeing proved dis-
> gracefully one-sided, we argued that any All-Black–Springbok
> championship series was worth the effort, and we urged our boys
> and our nation to enjoy it.
>
> But we can no longer see anything to be gained by allowing sport,
> however noble its intentions, to be used to shore up a racist re-
> gime. Belatedly, and with the saddest possible regret, we support
> Government's decision that this tour must not be allowed to pro-
> ceed. There are some things in this world bigger than an All-
> Black–Springbok match, and humanity among brothers is one
> of them.

Jopie Troxel folded the paper and shoved it over to Sannie. There was
so much he wanted to say, but he would not trust himself to speak.

They don't understand us, he thought. They accuse us of things we've never done. All we want is to maintain an orderly society, and they protest.

While Sannie and Frikkie prepared sandwiches and beer, he sat staring at his knuckles and brooding. The United Nations had condemned South Africa, but that was a bunch of dark-skinned third nations flexing their feeble muscles, and could be disregarded. The World Council of Churches had condemned apartheid, but they were a gang of radicals. The French-Dutch Commission had spoken harshly, but they were vexed because South Africa did not follow supinely in their missionary-socialist trail. But when Australia and New Zealand canceled a rugby tour, the heart and spirit of the nation were endangered.

'Why can't they try to understand us?' Jopie cried. Sannie and Frikkie kept cutting sandwiches.

A few days later Saltwood was introduced to a South African game even more brutal than rugby, if that was possible. Daniel Nxumalo came casually to Swartstroom and asked, 'You free tonight?'

'Let me phone Sannie.' But when the call went through, Mrs. van Doorn said that her daughter had gone to Pretoria with the Troxel boys, and Philip visualized them moving as a threesome beneath the jacaranda trees. 'I'm free.'

By roundabout paths Nxumalo led Philip to a shack where three tall blacks waited: 'This is my brother Jonathan. This is my cousin Matthew Magubane. This is a new recruit, Abel Tubakwa.'

Philip gasped. A thousand police were searching for Jonathan and Matthew; indeed, the Troxel boys had been on the border primarily to pursue these two into Moçambique, yet here they were, boldly in the same hills as those who were hunting them. 'They were in Soweto last night,' Daniel said, 'and they go north tomorrow. Or at least that's what they told me.' The conspirators laughed.

'We suggested the meeting,' Jonathan said in Afrikaans.

'Why?' Philip asked.

'So that you could tell the Americans, when you go home, that we are far from defeated.'

'I may not go home.'

'You should. In a few years this could be an ugly country.'

Magubane interrupted: 'Marry the girl and get her out of here. All the bright young whites are leaving.' He spoke in such rapid Afrikaans that Saltwood failed to catch his full meaning, so Abel Tubakwa interpreted in fine English.

'How do you see the future?' Philip asked in English, and after that the men used this language.

Jonathan was obviously the tactician: 'If they caught us tonight, we'd all be shot. But they won't catch us. We move about pretty much as we wish.'

'Terrorism?'

'We don't call it that. Sporadic attacks. Harassment. Ridicule. War of nerves.'

'To what purpose?'

'To remind them always that we're serious. That we will never again go away and lie down like good dogs and not growl.'

'Will that accomplish anything?'

'It will gnaw at their minds. Saltwood, you've seen the enlightened Afrikaners. These people are not stupid. They know that accommodation must be made. I think they're ready to accept us now, on some radically new basis. Not total equality, not yet. And not one-man, one-vote. But a true partnership.'

'Look at what's happening in Pretoria right now,' Daniel said excitedly. 'They've built this new theater. With public funds. I understand it's as good as anything in Berlin or the one in Minneapolis.'

'I've been reading the stories,' Philip said. 'Public funds, and then they state that only whites will be admitted.'

Jonathan slammed the table. 'They doing that again?'

'Yes,' his brother said, 'but there's been this great outcry. From all parts of the public. People you'd never expect have stepped forward to demand that the theater be made available to everyone.'

'Goddamn!' Jonathan cried, and Magubane rose and walked agitatedly about the room. It was the situation they had fought against for the past three years. 'We no longer want crumbs from the master's table,' Jonathan said. 'We don't want a slice of bread. We don't want the loaf. We want the whole damned bakery. And we want it now.'

'We're not part of their society,' Magubane said sardonically. 'We would not appreciate Shakespeare or Goethe.' He kicked at the chair he had just vacated. 'I can recite whole pages of *Othello,* but I can never see it performed.'

Jonathan burst into laughter. 'Magubane, you ass. *Othello* is not really welcomed in South Africa. He's black, man. He's black, or didn't you know?'

Magubane brushed his chin as if embarrassed by his ignorance, then stood by the door, his right hand across his chest—'I am a Moor of Venice!'—and declaimed:

'Had it pleased heaven
To try me with affliction; had they rained
All kinds of sores, and shames, on my bare head;
Steeped me in poverty to the very lips,
Given to captivity me and my utmost hopes,
I should have found in some part of my soul
A drop of patience . . .'

He quit his oratory and said quietly, 'We have that "drop of patience," but only for so long.'

'What I was trying to say,' Daniel Nxumalo continued, 'was that right now in Pretoria booths have been set up in many spots. White people, women mostly, manage them . . .'

'For what purpose?' Jonathan asked.

'They're collecting signatures, petitioning the authorities to allow non-whites to attend performances in the new theater. And I understand the response has been overwhelmingly in favor.'

'Well,' Jonathan admitted grudgingly, 'change does come. Slow—but inevitable.' He rocked back and forth, then asked, 'Dan, do you think I'll ever be free to come back here and live like an ordinary workman?'

'Yes. Without the slightest hesitation I say yes. There's change in the air. Good things are happening, and I honestly believe we can attain our goals.'

'I don't,' Jonathan replied. 'Not without armed revolution, which will probably not come till I'm an old man.'

'You see yourself living a life of exile?' Philip asked.

'Yes. Magubane here will never see his birthplace free. Tubakwa, when you join us over the border you will never come home.'

'What will you do?' Philip asked.

'Maintain pressure. Goad the Afrikaners into taking an open Hitler stance until the world has to intervene.'

'If the government offered you amnesty—'

'We would reject it,' Magubane broke in. 'This is war to the finish. The evil tricks of these people must be ended.'

'But Frikkie and Jopie, the two rugby players. They say almost the same thing. War to the finish. To preserve the kind of government God willed them to have.'

Jonathan started to make a cynical denouncement, but Magubane cut him off, saying to Philip, 'That's why I advise you to marry the girl and get out of here. You Americans proved in Vietnam you had no stomach for the long fight. The Troxels do. And we do. This war will last forty years, and it can only increase in severity and barbarity. That's why the airplanes are filled with those young people leaving. That's why you should go.'

Philip turned to Daniel Nxumalo. 'But you think there's still hope?'

'I do! The people signing those petitions in Pretoria are proof.'

But when Philip reached his camp he found his workmen excited by a news flash from the capital. Rural Afrikaners calling themselves the Avengers of the Veld had stormed into Pretoria, dynamited the kiosks in which the theater petitions were being signed, and burned the rubble, threatening to donder the women if they persisted in this unpatriotic effort to mix the races. The spokesman for the Avengers explained: 'God has forbidden us to accept Canaanites in our midst, and if this effort continues, we shall have to burn down the theater.'

When Sannie and the Troxel boys returned home, they were elated.

Philip wasted much of his leisure time at the diggings trying to fathom why—above all else—the men at Vrymeer were so devastated by the cancellation of the New Zealand tour. He reached no conclusion, but one morning he was summoned to Pretoria for an evaluation meeting with Amalgamated Mines. The principal officers convened at the Burgers Park Hotel, and as they sat in the lounge with drinks, Philip saw coming through the door a man whose face was vaguely familiar. 'Who's that?' he whispered to one of his superiors.

'That's the minister of finance,' the Johannesburg man said without taking further notice, but apparently there was some kind of governmental meeting, for within a few minutes the new prime minister came bustling in. He had been in office such a short time that Philip only vaguely recognized him. 'Is that who I think it is?' he whispered.

'Yes, that's the prime minister.' And again no one moved.

A little while later an extraordinary man walked past them. It seemed to Philip that one of the Drakensberg Mountains had come to Pretoria, for the man was gigantic, not in height, although he was quite tall, but in the girth of his body, the enormous spread of hips, the lower

jaw that jutted at least four inches farther than normal. He had black
hair and great dark eyes.

'Who's . . .' Philip started.

'My God!' the chairman of Amalgamated cried. 'That's Frik du
Preez!' At this, all the businessmen stood up and nodded at the great
Springbok who had played in more international matches than any
other South African. Like an Alp wading across the Mediterranean, he
moved majestically through the lobby to enter the dining room, and everyone in Saltwood's party marked his progress.

'That was Frik du Preez,' the chairman repeated.

'I think my family had some doings with the Cape Town Du
Preezes,' Saltwood said, and at this news all the men regarded him with
additional respect.

The most revealing incident concerning rugby occurred one morning
at the camp when Philip received a day-old Pretoria newspaper, across
the front of which appeared four excellent photographs depicting one
continuous play in Saturday's game against Monument. The left-hand
picture showed Frikkie Troxel being savagely tackled by a Monument
brute named Spyker Swanepoel, who was using what American football
called 'the clothesline tackle,' in which a man with the ball running full
speed east is grabbed about the neck by a bigger man running full speed
west. In this photograph it looked as if Frikkie was about to lose his
head.

Shot two showed him flat on the ground, unconscious, ball flopping
away, while Spyker Swanepoel delivered a savage, heavily booted kick
with full force right at his temple. It was a blow which would have
killed a mere human being, but rugby players were something beyond
that.

Shot three was the precious one. Frikkie lay almost dead, spread-
eagled. The triumphant Spyker was striding away. And up behind him
could be seen Jopie Troxel, leaping off his left foot, his right fist swinging forward with terrifying force and striking Spyker so fiercely that it
was clear that his jaw jumped sideways three inches.

Shot four was total bedlam. Frikkie lay dead, or almost so. Spyker
Swanepoel lay unconscious, his jaw awry in such a way as to impart a
beatific smile. And seven Monument men, engulfing Jopie, were knocking him to the ground and kicking him. In other parts of the photograph
some half-dozen major fistfights were taking place, with one Venloo
man neatly kneeing his opponent in the crotch. The series was entitled
SPIRITED PLAY AT LOFTUS VERSFELD.

When Frikkie regained consciousness in the hospital, sports reporters wanted to know how he felt about the game, and he said, 'We
should've won.'

'You did,' they told him.

'Hooray!' He tried to get out of bed, but could not control his
movements and fell back.

'Did you know that Spyker kicked you?'

'What if he did?'

'Did you see the papers?'

'I haven't even seen daylight.' They showed him the four photographs, and he spent some time on the first one. 'That Spyker made a
strong tackle, didn't he?'

'But the kick?'

'Jopie took care of that,' he said, pointing to the ferocious blow in
the third shot. Then he studied the last picture: 'I'm down. Spyker's
down. Jopie's going down. I'm glad we won.'

The kick to the head had temporarily deranged the mechanisms
which enable a human being to maintain equilibrium; it was as if someone had set in motion a gyroscope which held to one course, no matter
what the lateral pressures. Frikkie would start walking in a given direction, and when the time came to make a turn, he would continue
straight ahead, sometimes going right into a wall.

The doctors were more alarmed than he. 'I'll get it back into control,' he said, and added that he fully intended to play in Saturday's
fixture against a team from the Orange Free State, but by midweek it
was quite clear that he would not even be out of the hospital. It was
then that Sannie began attending him regularly, and as she observed the
straightforward manner in which he accepted his punishment, and the
determined way he went about recovering, she felt increasingly that he
represented the best in South Africa. Was there a job to do on the Moçambique border? He would go do it. Was there a tackle to be made?
He would make it. Did the government require some new approach to
old problems? He was the man to effectuate it. He was direct, un-
complicated and trustworthy.

She was at his side when Spyker Swanepoel came to visit, his jaw
wired back into place. 'That was a strong tackle, Spyker' was all Frik
said.

'You still got ringing in your ears?'

'Something's out of balance. It'll fall into place.'

'What you need, Frikkie, I've seen it a dozen times. A little sharp exercise and a dop of brandy.'

'I think so, too,' and he allowed big Spyker to pull him to his feet, steady him, give him a drink, and then run him right at the farthest wall.

'Whoa!' Spyker cried, and back they came the other way.

'That feels great!' Frikkie said. 'Let's go out in the hall.'

'Frikkie!' Sannie protested, but she could not stop these two great hulks, and out into the hall they went. She watched as they started down the long passageway, running and dodging as if they were on a rugby field. 'Hey! Hey!' Spyker grunted, shouting encouragement, and soon he was in the lead, allowing Frikkie to run by himself, but as before, the internal gyroscope prevented Frik from making a turn and he ran right into the end wall.

'Jesus Christ!' Spyker bellowed through wired teeth. 'Don't run into the goddamned wall.'

'What in the world?' the matron in charge of the floor cried as she saw two huge men coming back down the hall, Spyker in front, Frikkie dodging along behind and going great until he again plowed into the wall.

'We've got to work on it,' Spyker said as he led Frikkie back to bed. 'How do you feel?'

'That damned wall . . .'

By now the hospital staff had crowded into the room, and the head doctor was upbraiding Sannie for allowing such a dangerous situation. 'You should have stopped them,' he blustered.

'Have you ever tried to stop them?' and when Spyker was led away, and she was alone with Frikkie, she went to the door and locked it. 'You're all right,' she said, returning to the bed, where she took his hands and pulled him to her. 'You're a little weak on turns to the left, but who cares?'

And as she slipped into bed with him she whispered, 'As soon as you can walk straight, we're getting married.'

'I'm playing next Saturday,' he announced, and it must have been the therapy she provided, because on Friday morning he left the hospital, on Saturday he sat with her watching his team play, and the next Saturday he was on the field against Natal. It was during the celebration following that game, which he played like a ghost looking for a lost glen, that Sannie announced that she was going to marry him.

Jopie poured champagne over his rival, then kissed the bride-to-be and said, 'I always suspected he'd be the one.' But when Philip Saltwood heard the news, he dashed in from the diggings to beg Sannie to reconsider.

'I did,' she said. 'In the hospital. I love you, Philip, and will never forget how good life with you could have been. But Frikkie is South Africa. And so am I.'

When Sannie van Doorn, firmly and finally, rejected Philip Saltwood's offer of marriage and indicated that either of the Troxel boys would have been accepted ahead of him, he slipped into a profound melancholy, unable to force his tangled values into sensible patterns. He felt discarded not only as a suitor but also as a human being; for some years now he had been working in suspension, not attached to any specific country, or enterprise, or woman. He was a man in limbo, and the growing affection he had felt for Sannie was caused partly by her unusual attractiveness, partly by her promise of being a solid anchor for his drifting boat. He liked her and he liked her country; its challenges did not frighten him, for he would enjoy participating in its violent development.

Even without Sannie he wanted to stay on, so he directed all his energies to an even more frantic search for the hidden source of the diamonds, and one day while looking at the map he saw that he should investigate the headwaters of Krokodilspruit, a minor tributary to the Swartstroom, and when he consulted the managers in Pretoria, they agreed. Since Daniel Nxumalo was acquainted with that lonely terrain, he was invited along. What made the trip memorable was that as they left the dirt road and walked quietly along the stream, they came upon a small valley encompassed by low hills, and there for the first time in his life Philip saw a herd of eland, some thirty majestic beasts, golden tan in color, with white blazes across the back and on the legs. They were so much bigger than the antelope he had seen in places like Wyoming and Colorado that he gasped and held out his right arm to halt Nxumalo's movement, but this was unnecessary, for no one who loved the veld of Africa ever took such a herd casually.

'Look at the dewlaps!' Philip whispered—certain of the bucks showed massive appendages to their chests that swayed gently as they walked.

For perhaps ten minutes the two men stood motionless, watching these noble beasts, dark glowing in sunlight, symbols of the Africa that had always mystified both strangers and those who knew it well. In every respect these were notable animals, for they were not of gigantic size like huge elephants, nor threatening like the rhinoceros, nor ethereal like the flamingos, nor utilitarian like the horse, nor repellent like the black mamba snake. They were among the regal beasts of the world.

'Jesus, they are beautiful,' Philip said, and then for reasons he could not have explained he started running toward them, shouting and waving his arms as if to dissolve this vision. At first only those at the rear were aware of him, but when they started leisurely to move on up the banks of the Krokodilspruit, the others realized that something untoward was occurring, and they, too, began moving off, until at last the entire herd was in motion, not frantically and not in leaping bounds, but with a dignity befitting their exalted place in the animal kingdom.

When Philip continued his running, they disdainfully acknowledged that something must be done to protect themselves from whatever danger he represented, so they ambled easily away from the spruit and into a sparse collection of low trees, where mysteriously their brown colors and white patches blended so perfectly with the shadows that they became invisible.

'They've disappeared!' Philip said, but when Nxumalo joined him the black could see colors which the white could not, and he pointed out the various large bucks who trailed behind protecting the herd, and when Nxumalo affirmed that they were still there, Philip could see them. It required the eyes of Africa to see Africa.

Daniel was so favorably impressed by Saltwood's enthusiastic response to the eland that when their exploration of the Krokodilspruit was completed, he studied the white man as if judging whether he could be trusted, then said abruptly, 'Saltwood, there's something I'd like to share with you.'

'What?'

'Something exceedingly precious. A surprise,' and he directed Philip to drive along narrow, unpaved roads. On the long ride the two talked seriously of matters to which they had merely alluded in previous sessions. Nxumalo was thirty that summer, Saltwood a year older, and he spoke first.

'When you court a girl in a strange land, seriously, I mean . . .'

'I know what you mean. I could see.'

'Well, it jolts you down to hard-rock common sense. Seeing those eland hiding off in a valley had the same effect. Christ, Nxumalo, what's going to happen to this land?'

'It has its own force, you know. The great revolving of the earth.

The inescapable numbers of people. There are limits beyond which we can't go. And there are directions in which we must go.'

'Are you a fatalist?'

'No, a determinist.'

'A Marxist?'

'No, but in certain analyses Marx does make sense. Just as Frantz Fanon does. Or Thomas Jefferson.'

'What do you see happening?'

'Would I share my vision with a white man?' When Philip looked at him in astonishment, Nxumalo said prophetically, 'Must I not take into account the possibility that I will be arrested one of these days and that you will be required under oath to report what I said to you one summer morning as we rode to see the rhinoceros?'

Philip sat silent, acknowledging the heavy truth of what this man was saying: with a black, everything of day and night, of work and relaxation was subject to interrogation, with death and life hanging in the arbitrary balance. He was under no such constraints, not in his own country or in any other he visited, and that was the terrible, inescapable difference between being a white man in America and a black man in South Africa.

'Can you not imagine the prosecutor hammering at you: "Why in the world, Mr. Saltwood, were you going with this suspect black to see a rhinoceros?" except that he would call it *renoster*. And what could you say?'

Philip did not try to answer; instead he asked, 'What will be the future of the Coloureds?'

'Why do you ask such a question?'

'Because Frikkie and Jopie warned that once you blacks took control, the Coloureds were finished.'

'Frikkie and Jopie are right. There'll be no place for them. They had their chance to work with us, but stupidly they clung to the hope that one day the whites would accept them. They wanted to move up to catch the whites rather than down to work with us, and their decision was fatal.'

'Could it be corrected?'

'I think not, but maybe they will be given another chance to save themselves.'

'The Indians?'

'Who in Africa has ever solved the problem of the Indians? In Malawi, in Uganda, in Burundi—out! They've tossed them out. I could see something like Viet . . .' He stopped. He was confiding too much. Recently he had visualized crowded boats leaving the Natal coast burdened with Indians expelled from the country. England would no longer have them. No African nation would permit them entrance. Madagascar would fire upon the ships if they attempted to land there. And certainly homeland India would refuse them, for it already contained three bodies for each available space.

'How's your brother in Moçambique?'

That was another question that had better not be answered.

'Do you see any permanent place for the white man?'

'For the true Afrikaner, yes. He belongs to Africa and can learn to live with us. For the others, I'm afraid not. They'll never commit themselves to our soil.'

'What language will you be using?'

'Now, there we are.' He rapped his knuckles against the car door and blew out a heavy breath. 'It ought to be Afrikaans, really. That's a splendid, functional language. Most of my friends speak it, even though they don't like it. I'll tell you what Afrikaans is. Do you know Fanakalo, the made-up language of the mines? Afrikaans is the gentleman's Fanakalo.'

'Then you'll drop English?'

Nxumalo abruptly changed the subject: 'Did you follow the case of Mrs. Saltwood down in Johannesburg? She must be a distant relative of yours.'

'She is. Afrikaners who despise her behavior keep reminding me of it.'

'Accept her, Philip. Embrace her. She's one of God's rare women.'

Fleetingly, Philip thought of Craig Saltwood's request, and felt a twinge of guilt. 'But she's banned, isn't she?'

'She's sitting in silence at the foot of God.' He bowed his head for a moment, then said briskly, 'When our student group met the other day in Bloemfontein, black students, that is, we spoke nine different languages. Zulu, Xhosa, Swazi, Sotho, Tswana, Fingo, Pondo, Venda and Tonga. In self-defense we had to use English as the functional language.'

'Why didn't you use Afrikaans?'

'Could anyone use Afrikaans to discuss freedom?'

'Afrikaners do. They would die to preserve their freedom.'

'Isn't it curious?' Nxumalo cried. 'From the first day the Dutch landed at the Cape they struggled for freedom. Their whole history, as they teach it to us, was a ceaseless battle to be free. Yet when we say, "As major inhabitants of this land, we blacks would like to be free," they look at us with horror, call us Communists, and grab their guns to shoot us down.'

For some minutes they drove in silence over the veld, where tiny flowers in myriad colors looked like magical gems shining in the dust. 'Philip,' Nxumalo repeated, 'have you looked into the Laura Saltwood banning? Do you know why the government pounced on her?'

'No. All I saw was a formal announcement, then nothing.'

'That's what banning is—"then nothing." She advised blacks to cling to English and not permit the government to force Afrikaans upon us.' He paused, then laughed. 'You see, that's where the dilemma stands. Afrikaans could be a useful language for us. You know, I suppose, that it's the basic language for the Coloured, too? They helped invent it, and most of them speak it.'

'Sounds confused.'

'It is, philologically, historically, socially and politically.'

'Which will win, Afrikaans or English?'

'Contests between languages are always settled by poets. Most Coloured poets write in Afrikaans, and very movingly. But what black poet would care to do so?'

They now rode along a ridge from which vistas were immense, and to the south Philip saw a small conical mountain, and it was to this that Nxumalo directed him: 'There's only a small path. If many people knew of this, the place might have to be cordoned off. This is treasure, you know.'

After a brief climb the men came to a small flat area, bounded on one side by a large overhanging rock. At first Philip assumed he was being taken to a rude cave with some archaeological significance, but he found no signs of a dig, nor any potsherds to indicate that one had ever taken place. Then, gradually, he saw on the sloping wall the distinct outline of a rhinoceros, very large, with flecks of color still marking its hide fifteen thousand years after its completion. Aridity and remoteness had protected this masterpiece, so that it looked not significantly different from what it had been originally.

Philip leaned against a rock and studied the amazing work. As one familiar with engineering, he could appreciate the exquisite manner in which the long-dead artist, Gao of the Bushmen, had used so few lines to accomplish so much: 'Look at that! One unbroken line from mouth to tail! Look how he does the whole rear ham with one sweep! This was worth the trip.'

Pushing some rocks together, he formed a kind of chair on which he could sit and view this wonderful rhinoceros, and once or twice he broke into laughter. 'Hey! Hey! Rhino! Look at him gallop!' But then, after nearly an hour of looking, he covered his face with his hands, as if he wished to see the wall afresh, with no preconceptions.

'This is amazing, Daniel. I mean . . .'

In awe he studied this other vision of Africa: the timeless beauty galloping out of dark caves, the unknown wonders of the dark human soul, the sweep of line that captivated the senses, the overpowering sensation of being in the presence of vanished people who had come this way.

'Run, you sonofabitch—run, or they'll get you!' He bowed his head again and thought of Sannie, and the placid lakes at Vrymeer, and of Daniel Nxumalo's terrifying words: 'Must I not take into account the possibility . . . that you will be required under oath to report what I said one summer morning . . .' Africa was rather a bigger bite than one could chew.

When they left the rhinoceros still galloping across his timeless veld, Philip wandered around the side of the rise and saw to his astonishment that just a little distance to the west lay the buildings and lakes of the Van Doorn farm at Vrymeer. Nxumalo chuckled. 'That's why I brought you by the little roads. Yes, we're on one of Sannie's Tits.'

'Why didn't they tell me?'

'We Zulu keep it to ourselves. It's our rhinoceros. The Van Doorns are in Africa, but they aren't of it.'

Nxumalo's high praise for Laura Saltwood created in Philip a burning desire to visit the woman he had only glimpsed at the airport, and whose son had asked that he 'watch over' her. He had been remiss, but nothing he could have done would have altered what happened to her. He suspected that she might be something of a rhinoceros herself.

He sought permission from Pretoria to travel to Johannesburg on what he claimed was personal business, South Africa having infected him to the extent that he deemed it prudent not to confide that he intended speaking with a banned person.

When he reached her house he saw that it had been recently damaged by fire, for the façade was scarred; when he knocked, he heard a scurry of feet. Looking this way and that, he saw that he was being followed by a policeman, who was taking notes from across the street, and then the door opened.

Pointing to the scarred area, the white-haired woman said, simply, 'Bomb. This time they set the house afire. I'm sure they hoped it would burn me out, but as Louis Bromfield said in his good novel about India, "The rains came."'

'You mean this was a bomb?'

'Third in a row. Once you're banned, hoodlum patriots feel it's their obligation to bomb you or shoot you, or whatnot. Government encourages them.'

'Surely not!'

Mrs. Saltwood had made no move toward inviting him to come into the house, and he supposed this was because of the damage it had suffered, but she disabused him: 'Actually, they do little harm, the bombs. Scare hell out of one, but that's secondary to the greater indignity of banning.' She coughed and said, 'I'm going to meet with you out here, Philip, because the policeman over there must be assured that I'm meeting with only one person. That's my allocation, you know.'

She led him to a small lawn with a table and two chairs. 'We used to have four. Tea in the better afternoons. But we'll not have four again.' For the first time her voice trembled. 'Now, if you'll excuse me for just a moment.'

When she went back into the house, Philip felt an overpowering urge to confuse the watching policeman, so he rose as if in deep thought, walked to where the most recent bomb had struck, and took out a piece of paper. To his disgust he could find no pencil or pen, so he made believe he was taking copious notes on the damage, stepping back now and then to assess it. From the corner of his eye he could see that the policeman was becoming agitated, so he tucked away the paper and pretended to take out a camera, as though he were about to photograph the fire damage. This brought the policeman running.

'You can't do that, sir!' he cried in heavily accented English.

'I wasn't doing anything,' Philip said, showing his empty hands.

'You was taking a picture. That's forbidden, you know, at a banned site.'

'No, sir,' Philip said with great deference. 'I'm an architect. I was just taking proportions,' and he framed a box with his thumbs and fingers.

'That's permitted,' the policeman said.

'What's going on out here?' Laura asked as she appeared in the doorway with a silver tray containing tea things.

'I'm terribly sorry,' Philip apologized, more to the policeman than to Laura. 'I was stupid. This good man feared I had a camera. I am sorry, sir.' To Laura he whispered, 'I did it on purpose to throw him a scare.'

'I say, that's jolly! But we mustn't appear to be laughing. He has the power to be very unpleasant if he wishes.'

'Why the furor about the photograph?'

'When I'm banned, my house is banned. The evidence that it's being bombed is banned.' Abruptly she halted that chain of complaints and invited Philip to sit with her, and when he saw the exquisite silver service—tray, teapot, creamer, sugar, small tray for biscuits, little receptacle for marmalade, butter tray, spoons, little forks for the lemon—he almost burst into tears. It bespoke the long heritage of his people, and for the first time in his life he felt like an Englishman.

'Now tell me,' she said brightly, 'how did a decent Saltwood ever get to an outlaw place like America?' She laughed.

'As far as I can tell, there was a renegade brother far back. You English are wonderful in producing renegade brothers.'

'Woods are full of them.'

'So about the time your branch came out here, our branch, and a very lowly one it must have been, came to America. Massachusetts, Ohio, Indiana, Michigan. If you can visualize the map, they're stations west. My family was always on the move.'

'The sheriff?'

'I think so. I continued the tradition. Colorado, Texas.'

'You're a real American. Tell me, have you ever visited Salisbury? The old cathedral town west of London? No? Well, you must. The Saltwoods have a very ancient house there, with the tiles upside down or something. Quite wonderful, you know, with a river at the doorstep and a cathedral across the meadow.'

'This silverware . . .'

'A wedding gift in Salisbury, many years ago. My husband and I named this house New Sarum after the little hill where the members of Parliament used to be elected. Do you know about that? Well, we'll talk about that later. We liked to entertain and had plenty of servants. In the old days white people in this country always seemed to have plenty of servants. And my vanity was to have five complete tea services in silver.'

'Why?'

'Because in the morning we liked to serve our guests tea in bed. At seven o'clock sharp, bare feet came down the hall. Five servants, five tea services. Knock on the door, "Tea, Baas," and there was your tea.' Delicately she ticked off the silver pieces: 'Tea in this, hot water in this, toast in its silver rack, sugar, cream, lemon, one sweet biscuit.' Suddenly she rose and went inside the house, returning after a brief moment with four silver teapots, which she added to the tray.

'These were my only vanity. I wanted to remember Salisbury and tea in the shadow of the cathedral, and these enabled me to do so. But I also wanted to put away childish things and engage myself in Africa. So I helped found the Black Sash, and I spoke as I did, and now I'm banned. For life, I judge.'

Philip dared not speak. Staring at the five glistening teapots, he felt a chaos of thoughts rush through his brain, but there were none he cared to verbalize. Finally he asked, 'How do you keep these damned things so highly polished?'

She answered in a curious way: 'Do you know what I miss most? Not the meetings, where people say the same things over and over. And not the friendships, really, for people like you come by often. But I do miss the bowls. That's a wonderful game for relaxation—the proper uniform, you know, the lovely green grass. I miss that.'

'I don't follow you.'

'I can't bowl any more, of course, so whenever the urge strikes me, I polish my silver. Again and again I polish it. Everyone who comes here gets a cup of tea. It's compulsive, really, because I want to use a different pot each day. This one, then this one, then this one.'

Philip got up and walked away to hide his emotion, and of course Laura knew why he had done so. 'One must do something to keep occupied,' she said gaily. 'One can't read Solzhenitsyn week after week.'

'Good God! What are these?'

'Bullet holes,' she said matter-of-factly. 'At night sometimes they shoot at me.'

He wiped his forehead and sat down. 'What I'd really like,' he said, trying to sound casual, 'is another cup of tea . . . from that one,' and he pointed to one of the highly polished pots.

'That can be arranged,' she said, and with an elegant sweep of her hands she emptied the tea from the filled pot into the waiting one, then graciously poured Philip a cup. 'But I shall have my cup from this pot,' and once more she transferred the tea.

The policeman took notes.

'What's going to happen, Mrs. Saltwood?'

'Laura. We're cousins, you know.'

'How do you see things?'

'For me, a continuation of this until I die. For the country I see some hope. And do you know why? Because every decent and sensible man and woman in this nation knows that changes will have to be made. The Afrikaners who pass these horrible laws are not stupid people. They know this is a last gasp. Our blacks are among the most brilliant in Africa. They know time and pressure are on their side. There is enormous wisdom in this land, and one prays it will be granted the necessary time to manifest itself.'

'Will it? Moçambique, Zimbabwe, Vwarda, Zambia, Namibia pressing in from all directions?'

'The machine gun will guarantee reasonable time, I think. When you return to America assure your people that Afrikaners will use their machine guns if forced to do so. This is not Rhodesia, where retreat became epidemic. This is South Africa, where the gun rules.'

'That sounds rather hopeless.'

'Not at all!' She suggested that they utilize the final two teapots, pouring the cooling tea rapidly from one to the other, to the total bewilderment of the policeman. 'What I mean is, the machine guns will be used to buy time, probably through the remainder of this century. But with every moment gained, more wisdom is gained, too. And the day will come when the bright lads from Stellenbosch and Potchefstroom will lead the way in conciliation.'

'Can they do so soon enough?'

'The other great asset we have is the stability of our Zulu and Xhosa. They're the most patient, wonderful people on this earth. They make me humble, they have behaved so well for so long. Beside them I'm an uncivilized boor, and I think they can wait, intelligently, till the sick white man sorts things out.'

'Sick?'

Laura Saltwood pointed to herself, to the watching policeman, to the closed-in yard, to the bombed front of her house. 'Would any society invent banning if it wasn't sick?'

This seemed to be the period for Philip's intensive course in African realities, for when he returned to his hotel an urgent telegram was awaiting him from his superiors in Pretoria: FAVORABLE UPHEAVAL VWARDA. PROCEED IMMEDIATELY TEMPORARY DUTY KATOMBE TO PROTECT OUR INTERESTS. ANTICIPATE TWO MONTHS ABSENCE VRYMEER. INSTRUCTIONS AWAIT YOU THERE. PETERSEN. He caught a plane which took him to Zambia, where a smaller one belonging to the Vwardan government was waiting. Two other Anglo-Saxons who had once worked in that republic were aboard, and they informed him of the revolutionary decision President M'Bele had made last Friday: 'He informed London, Geneva and the United Nations that his country was plunging into chaos—industrial, financial—and he was inviting back at full pay plus bonuses some five hundred foreign technicians, mostly English, who had been in charge of technical details at one time or other during the past decade. I'm to head the distribution of flour.'

'Why?'

'You see, I was run out of the country three years ago. Pretty much like you, Saltwood, if I understand your case. My Vwardan understudy accused me of racism because I yelled at him one day. And why did I yell? Because he was supposed to watch the granary levels throughout the country, and he had allowed those in districts occupied by tribes other than his own to dwindle to zero. I really chewed him out and was expelled.'

'What happened when you left?'

'He became chief of grain procurement, and damned if he didn't continue to let his rival tribes starve.'

The other man had previously been in charge of Jeep and Land Rover procurement and had established a spare-parts replacement system based upon knowing calculations of what happened to vehicles in a primitive country. After drawing up a table of shrewd estimates, he proposed a law which would forbid the importation of any more Jeeps or Land Rovers until stockpiles of spare parts had been accumulated and stored in nine scattered warehouses, from which they would be efficiently distributed to broken-down vehicles that would otherwise stand useless.

'But a nephew of the president had the monopoly for importing Jeeps, and he demanded that he be allowed to bring in as many as he wanted, and to hell with spare parts. So what have they been doing? Cannibalizing perfectly good Jeeps to get a generator here or a differential there. The rest of the Jeep stands rusting, but the president's nephew doesn't give a damn.'

When their plane landed at Katombe they were hustled to a bright new hotel built with Swedish capital, where more than four hundred technical experts were herded together to hear an address by President M'Bele. He spoke with such eminent good sense that even men like Saltwood, who had legitimate grudges against him because of his earlier treatment, applauded, for it was quite obvious that he and they now had identical interests; they were men of Africa:

'Gentlemen, from the bottom of my heart I am most pleased to see you here. You are men of great experience in running aspects of our society. You are all men who performed well in the past and whom I can trust to perform equally well in the future. If I suspected for one moment that I could not rely upon you, I would not have called on you for help.

'We do need your help. The productive wheels of this nation are grinding to a halt. And why? Not because we haven't the brains to keep them going. And not because we are lazy or indifferent. The reason is simple. It takes time and long apprenticeship before anyone can master the skills necessary to keep a complex machine functioning. Our people, good-hearted though they may be, lack that long know-how, as the Americans term it. You men have it, and therefore we need you.

'Take bread. The citizens of many of our towns are close to rebellion because they have no bread. We have the money for it. Bread appears in our budget. And we have the grain. What do you suppose is holding us back? No one remembered to order yeast. No one purchased replacements for baking tins that wore out. And the damned flour is stored in the wrong places. How many bakers and grain experts are there in this room? Gentlemen, get working before nightfall.

'One vastly important thing which I know you will understand and remember as you go about your resumed duties. Vwarda has not changed its attitude toward racial equality one percent. We are not inviting you back because you are superior whites. We are asking you to help us because you are well trained in fields where we are not. We will not tolerate any racial-supremacy nonsense, and if you abuse our people, you will have to go. We are a black nation and proud to be so.

'But I promise you this. Our judges, our committees and my staff will not listen to wild charges of race discrimination. I know the injustices that occurred with some of you in the past, and they will not be repeated. It is more important that we get our bakeries functioning again than that my son-in-law drive a Mercedes from one plant to the other.'

Saltwood was shipped back to the mines he had once supervised, and when he reached them he was pleased to see that no chaos had resulted from his absence. Dynamite was being handled properly, with safeguards observed, and the lifts that shot workers down and up the deep shafts at incredible speeds were in order. Where the trouble lay was in planning, the subtle shifting of work forces and the movement of ores to logical locations. At the end of a week he reported to President M'Bele:

> The mines, when I reached them, were ninety-five-percent effective in their basic techniques. Your workmen were performing their jobs skillfully and responsibly, and Cornish miners could have done no better. There were, as you know, grave errors in scheduling. We require eight or nine men of broad grasp and firm decision. These are hard to come by in Vwarda, or America.

He found one young fellow who showed signs of catching on; he had acquired skills by working in the gold mines of Johannesburg. He asked the young man if he had any acquaintances who had shared that experience, and four were brought forward. Two had learned nothing in South Africa, but the other two were clever like the first, and around this cadre he began to build his staff. Fortunately, he found one older man who had had three years at the London School of Economics, and just as factories in South Bend, Indiana, profited by having young men from such provocative schools, so the mines in Vwarda began to function better when he assumed partial control.

Ultimate control remained in the hands of President M'Bele's son-in-law, who had been mainly responsible for Saltwood's firing in 1978. He was a much-changed man; having taken his mines almost to the point of bankruptcy, he now knew that he was not free to make decisions on narrow, tribal lines. He was scared, for he enjoyed his Mercedes and welcomed any guidance that would enable him to keep it. This time he listened when Philip outlined the need for a world view: 'You must know what Japan is doing with her metallurgy, and what Russia is up to. You've got to watch the markets, and you don't need a computer to do it. Your aim must be constant flow. Keep all parts in balance.'

At the end of his two months he was able to recommend a Belgian engineer with wide experience in Katanga Province over in Zaire: 'He's a knowing man. Works well with black nations. And he's better informed on your problems than I am.' When President M'Bele implored Philip to stay on till the Belgian was properly indoctrinated, he saw the sense of this and agreed to extend his stay, but only for three weeks.

When these passed, and he was confident that the Belgian was qualified, he sought permission to fly back to Johannesburg, but when the plane landed he was prevented from going directly to his job at Venloo by three BOSS officers. 'You must come with us,' they said, and he was whisked off to a small room at the airport.

'This in no way endangers you, Mr. Saltwood. We know why you were called to Vwarda and how competently you did your job there. We must interrogate you about an important trial and would prefer that no one talk with you.'

'Whose trial?'

'Daniel Nxumalo. High treason.'

The Terrorism Act of 1967, based on careful preliminary work supervised by Detleef van Doorn the year he died, was both wonderfully vague and terrifyingly specific. It was vague because it forbade any act or attempted act which in any way embarrassed the state. Almost any behavior which protested apartheid could be so construed, and the bases of proof were also extremely vague. What was specific? The minimum penalty the court could impose: five years, most likely on Robben Island. The maximum: death.

Twelve kinds of behavior fell under the ban, and of these the government conceded that nine did not apply in Nxumalo's case. He had not interfered with the police; he intimidated no one; he did not cripple production; he did not lead any insurrection; he did not advocate cooperation with any foreign government; he had caused no bodily injury; nor had he brought financial loss to the state, or endangered its essential services, or obstructed its land, sea or air traffic. On those counts he was patently innocent and the indictment ignored them.

But on three other counts most threatening to the security of the state he was presumably guilty: first, he had agitated blacks by asking disturbing questions, so was accused of promoting disorder; second, by reminding blacks of past grievances, he had encouraged hostility between races; third, in various ways he had embarrassed the government. And for these offenses he must be tried, and if found guilty, sent to prison or hanged.

Philip learned that the trial would be conducted in Pretoria by a crusty old judge, Herman Broodryk, who had a record of handling such cases covering more than two decades. Prior to his appointment to the bench in 1958, he had been a brilliant advocate who gained favorable attention in the 1940s by defending Afrikaner radicals charged with attempting to sabotage Jan Christiaan Smuts' efforts to take the country into the war on the side of England. He was a personal friend of all the recent prime ministers, and Philip thought it disturbing that a man with such credentials should sit in this case; but an Amalgamated Mines lawyer told him, 'The South African higher judiciary is above reproach. We can be proud of two liberties—judges like Broodryk and our free press.'

And then Philip made an even more startling discovery: 'Is it true that Justice Broodryk will hear the case alone . . . without a jury?' And again his lawyer friend defended the system: 'One of the best things we've done, abolish the jury system. What chance would Nxumalo have against a jury of twelve white men and women? I leave to your imagination what would happen in the circuit court at Venloo, for instance, if a black appeared on a charge of molesting a white farmer's daughter. With an all-white jury!'

Daniel Nxumalo was to be defended by Mr. Simon Kaplan, a Johannesburg advocate well experienced in fighting the battles of blacks who had offended the mores of apartheid. The accusations of terroristic activity would be presented by Mr. Martin Scheepers, a specialist in the Terrorism Act; nineteen times he had prosecuted such cases, winning fourteen and sending a total of eighty-seven men and women to prison. In three recent cases involving armed insurgency, he had won the death sentence.

In England, in America and in most Western nations a judge could spend a lifetime on the bench without ever sentencing a man to death; year after year in South Africa some eighty people went to the gallows, more than in the rest of the Western world put together. When Saltwood asked about this, the Amalgamated lawyer said, 'Most of them are black. Murderers, rapists. We are forced to do this to maintain order. There's four million of us, twenty million of them.'

The courtroom was packed when Judge Broodryk took his seat. He was a large man, with heavy, bushy eyebrows, pendulous cheeks and a fearsome manner, but as the trial proceeded Philip would find him patient, attentive and considerate. When a judge had no jury to contend with, he had to be judicial, uncovering facts and judging character, for on him alone would rest the decision of innocence or guilt, death or life. In his years of mining experience Philip had attended trials in several African countries, and in none had he found a wiser judge.

Broodryk extended every courtesy to Nxumalo, listening with obvious attention whenever he spoke. In his opening address Advocate Scheepers spread before the court the essentials of his case against Daniel:

'The state will prove that it was this man who conceived the idea of having the blacks of this nation gather in large numbers to observe the anniversary of what he called Soweto '76. What was this but a device to engender bad relations between the races? The evidence will show that in a manner calculated to be provocative and conducive to disorder he organized such a gathering in Bloemfontein and harangued it. And why, pray, did Mr. Nxumalo choose to hold this meeting in Bloemfontein? Because he knew it to be the most loyal of our cities, where what he had to say would create the most inflammatory reaction.

'It is on another charge that he will be found most guilty. His every act is carefully premeditated to bring embarrassment upon our government. He appeals to the basest emotions of our cruelest critics in London and New York. He makes crude appeals to agencies like the World Council of Churches, and we will show that his acts and intentions are such as to bring discredit upon us, arguing as he does that our laws are unjust and our system of apartheid unfair. He is an evil man whose activities must be halted.'

Thus was set the tone for the clash between Nxumalo and Scheepers, a bitter division between two able men that flared on the first morning of the trial when Nxumalo began his careful campaign to place the grievances of his people on the record:

DEFENDANT NXUMALO: Only in recent years have our people begun to discover themselves, to seek an identity different from the one the white man says we must wear. We are in the position the Afrikaner was before he crawled out from under English domination, and we respect his struggle for his *volksidentiteit*. But from this reasoning I conclude that if the Afrikaner is free to celebrate his victory over Dingane at Blood River, we blacks ought to be free to recall the powerful events that shook Soweto in June 1976.

STATE ADVOCATE SCHEEPERS: What events did you have in mind?

NXUMALO: The deaths of our children who protested apartheid.

SCHEEPERS: Mr. Nxumalo, those schoolchildren rioted in the streets, burned down buildings, killed innocent civilians, and challenged just authority. You see that as equivalent to a battle fought between two armies?

NXUMALO: I agree that the circumstances are not the same—well, not entirely—but the end result, my people were left with anger and sorrow.

SCHEEPERS: And you wanted to use that anger to generate disorder?

DEFENSE COUNSEL KAPLAN: I must object to the way my learned friend phrases that.

SCHEEPERS: That anger and sorrow were at the basis of your wanting to celebrate Soweto '76 as a remembrance day?

NXUMALO: I believe we owe a great deal to those children. They showed us that change in this country must come from within. That we must make a stand against a system we abhor.

SCHEEPERS: You presume to speak for all blacks?

NXUMALO: Someone must. We have been silent for too long.

SCHEEPERS: In celebrating our great victory over Dingane, we Afrikaner people observe a solemn Day of the Covenant in which we pray for peace, not disorder; for unity, not chaos. Were those your aims in sponsoring Soweto '76?

NXUMALO: We also want peace and unity for all. And prayers for the children who fell at Soweto, victims of the unjust system which deprives them of a right to citizenship in the land of their birth.

JUDGE BROODRYK: Mr. Nxumalo, this court is not here to debate what happened at Soweto in 1976. We cannot decide whether the students were victims of injustice or not. Confine your answers to Mr. Scheeper's questions.

NXUMALO: My Lord, the Afrikaner in his schools, his churches, his celebrations of the Day of the Covenant is reminded by his teachers, his ministers and his political leaders of Slagter's Nek, of ground glass in the mealies, the execution of Christoffel Steyn. With deepest respect I submit that such constant remembrance of blood that flowed in the past engenders bad feeling between the races.

BROODRYK: Mr. Nxumalo, the Afrikaner and the Englishman are of the same race, so what you charge could not possibly take place. We are concerned only with the delicate balance between the white and black races in this country and the danger of fostering ill-will between them. By your irresponsible speeches, for example.

NXUMALO: I do not believe that the black people of this country can be denied the right to remember the Slagter's Nek of their history. I mean Sharpeville and Soweto '76. Until we find our own dignity and identity, we can never be free.

SCHEEPERS: What would have to happen, Mr. Nxumalo, for you to consider yourself a free man?

NXUMALO: Apartheid would have to end. Blacks would have to have a proper voice in running this country.

SCHEEPERS: Ah! You mean one-man, one-vote?

NXUMALO: Yes, I suppose I do.

SCHEEPERS: Do you think that by encouraging bitterness among your people, by waving Soweto '76 at them, you'll get your vote?

NXUMALO: A man has a right, surely, to remember ugly things that have happened to him. To us the dead children of Soweto were heroes.

SCHEEPERS: It's impossible to follow your reasoning. Those young people were undisciplined rioters. They were led by professional agitators.

NXUMALO: I must beg to contradict. The young black boys of Soweto were rather similar to the young Boer lads who fought the English in 1899. They took up arms against their oppressors, the English.

SCHEEPERS: Ah-ha! So you do advocate that young blacks take up arms against the Afrikaner? Against the legal government?

KAPLAN: My Lord, my client said nothing of the sort. I must object most strenuously to my learned friend's attempt to misconstrue the evidence.

BROODRYK: Sustained. Mr. Nxumalo, I can appreciate some of the points you are making, but it seems to me there is a danger that if your inflammatory remarks are constantly thrust before the public, a revolutionary climate will be fostered throughout this country.

NXUMALO: Yes, there is such a danger, my Lord.

BROODRYK: Then should you not pursue your objectives through a more peaceful method? By negotiation rather than violence?

NXUMALO: Most certainly that would be preferable.

BROODRYK: Then you agree that by working through established channels, and there are many, mass upheaval could be averted?

At this point the judge was so reasonable and conciliatory that Salt-wood, listening carefully to every nuance, felt certain that if Nxumalo reciprocated, Judge Broodryk would be eager to find him guilty only to a limited degree, and his life would be spared, for everyone in the court-room knew that Nxumalo had performed no overt act of real revolu-tion. But to Saltwood's dismay, his friend refused the olive branch the judge had extended. Indeed, his rejection of Broodryk's invitation was cold and total.

NXUMALO: Your Honor, we cannot accept the status quo because we had no voice in establishing it. We will never accept it, for this is our land, too, and we of this generation cannot abdicate the rights of our children still to be born. We are opposed to apartheid now and forever.

BROODRYK: But people may not oppose it, Mr. Nxumalo, with ac-tions that contravene the law of the land. They may not engage in acts of terrorism to upset what the government has patiently and justly or-dained.

NXUMALO: Not justly, my Lord.

KAPLAN: What he means, my Lord—

BROODRYK: I know what he means. Let him continue.

NXUMALO: I stand before this court accused of terroristic activities. Every day in South Africa acts of terrorism are committed against my people through the harsh application of laws not justly ordained. To me it was an act of terror to banish an old woman to a resettlement camp. It is an act of terror to starve a young mind hungry for learning. It is an act of terror to force apart a man and woman who love each other. It is an act of terror to say to a black man born on this land, 'You cannot live here because white people want the land.' Or to tell that same man he cannot go to a town where he can earn a decent living for his family.

BROODRYK (*with great patience*): I am waiting for your point, Mr. Nxumalo.

NXUMALO: I will state it honestly, my Lord. We deny that the laws of apartheid are just or that this is a just society. We see it as a society with only one ambition—to maintain white supremacy.

BROODRYK: But that is the acknowledged goal of this society. If you have a solution that is better for all, this court would like to hear it.

NXUMALO: We might start with justice for the majority of people living here.

BROODRYK: And the minorities, who also deserve protection?

NXUMALO: A minority with machine guns can always protect itself.

Judge Broodryk was meticulous in according Daniel every opportunity to defend himself, and although some of the young professor's answers must have infuriated him, he betrayed nothing, and Saltwood saw that Nxumalo was going out of his way to antagonize the judge. What the young man's strategy was, Philip could not discern, and the trial proceeded.

Prosecutor Scheepers now turned his attention to two curious aspects of the case, returning to them again and again during the four days he interrogated the young teacher.

SCHEEPERS: Where did you first hear the phrases Black Power and Black Consciousness?

NXUMALO: I can't say. They were in the air.

SCHEEPERS: Could I put it to you that you heard them from Communist agitators? Men infiltrated here to agitate the unthinking blacks?

NXUMALO: Blacks do not need Communists to agitate them. Apartheid does that every day.

SCHEEPERS: But what does the phrase mean—Black Power? Doesn't this necessitate blacks opposing whites? Like your older rallying cry 'Africa for the Africans?'

NXUMALO: There's nothing subversive about that. You're a man of Africa. My counsel is a man of Africa. The learned judge—

BROODRYK: I will assign myself.

SCHEEPERS: If we are all Africans, why the emphasis on the power of black Africans?

NXUMALO: As I explained before, our people must develop pride in themselves—Black Consciousness. And if you force me—Black Power. We cannot negotiate with whites from a position of inferiority.

SCHEEPERS: I see your Black Power only as an agency with which to confront whites and embarrass this government.

NXUMALO: In the eyes of the civilized world, this government embarrasses itself.

BROODRYK (sternly): No flippancy, young man.

NXUMALO: The protests sounding around the world against this trial are not flippant. They are very real, and one day—

BROODRYK: No revolutionary threats will be tolerated. Mr. Kaplan, advise your client to mind his tongue.

KAPLAN: Believe me, my Lord, my client utters his words without any coaching from me.

BROODRYK: I believe you, Counsel, for this court has always found you to be a prudent, loyal and patriotic man. But you must warn your client that he damages his case by engaging in revolutionary threats.

This court is not impressed by what happens 'around the world,' as he says. For some decades this nation has been endeavoring to act in accordance with God's dictates and not the yammerings of the discredited World Council of Churches.

After this resounding statement Judge Broodryk declared recess, during which Saltwood endeavored to talk with Nxumalo. No outsider was permitted to approach the prisoner lest the latter receive coaching, which was what Philip sought to offer, for he had seen signs that Broodryk wanted to avoid a severe sentence, if only Nxumalo would admit minor guilt and appeal for clemency. He suspected that for arcane reasons of his own Nxumalo would refuse to act humbly; this became evident when the prosecutor attacked him on language.

SCHEEPERS: May I put it to you, Mr. Nxumalo, that you borrowed your ideas about language from Laura Saltwood? It was her preaching, wasn't it, that encouraged you to advise your students not to accept any instruction in Afrikaans?

NXUMALO: With your permission, respected sir, there are two errors in your question.

SCHEEPERS: And what are they?

NXUMALO: I gave my advice long before Mrs. Saltwood was banned. And nothing in my advice was antagonistic to Afrikaans. What I said was, 'Learn English first, for it is the language of international communication.'

SCHEEPERS: But why should a Bantu . . . Excuse me, m'Lord. Why should a black child whose life is to be spent in South Africa bother with international communication?

NXUMALO: Because it will be our international associations—I don't mean international committees, I mean the contacts we establish with people overseas—that will go far in determining the nature of our future government.

SCHEEPERS: You mean, of course, Communist Russia?

NXUMALO: I mean the civilized world. We cannot speak to them in Afrikaans, because nobody out in the world understands that language.

BROODRYK: You seem determined to insult this nation, Mr. Nxumalo. First you ridicule our most sacred holiday. Now you ridicule our language.

NXUMALO: I said merely the truth. That it is not used anywhere outside this small country.

BROODRYK: You consider South Africa a small nation? In comparison with Belgium, say?

NXUMALO: In comparison with Brazil and Indonesia. In comparison to the rest of Africa.

SCHEEPERS: When you advised your students not to study Afrikaans—

NXUMALO: I never advised that, sir.

SCHEEPERS: May I read from a transcript of your speech at Bloemfontein:

> 'Our program must be to insist that basic instruction be given in English, for then our young people will be able to communicate with the entire world and not only with a few bigoted Afrikaners stuck away in their little corner.'

Are those not inflammable words, Mr. Nxumalo? Are they not an incitement to the blacks to ignore the laws of this land?

KAPLAN: Your Worship, I wish you would direct learned Counsel to read the next sentences of his police report.

SCHEEPERS: I've read everything I have, and I assure you that it is—

KAPLAN: Your Worship, I happen to have the full text, and with your permission may I read a few additional sentences? I think you will find them instructive:

> 'I want every student to learn Afrikaans, for it is an excellent medium for conducting our affairs in this country. I speak Afrikaans, use it all the time, to my great profit, but when I do speak it I can communicate with less than three million. When I speak English, I communicate with the entire world.'

SCHEEPERS: Why would a black child in Venloo wish to communicate with the entire world?

NXUMALO: Because we are citizens of the entire world.

SCHEEPERS: But repeatedly we find evidence that you call yourself African. Is not your claim—

NXUMALO: I am a citizen of Venloo, which makes me a citizen of eastern Transvaal. That gives me citizenship in South Africa—

SCHEEPERS: Not South Africa. You're Zulu, I believe. You belong to kwaZulu, the Bantustan of the Zulu.

NXUMALO: I was born at the farm Vrymeer. I have taught in the University of Zululand, but Vrymeer is my home.

SCHEEPERS: Nevertheless, you are a citizen of kwaZulu and must eventually make your residence there. That is the law.

NXUMALO: So as a citizen of South Africa—

SCHEEPERS: M'Lord, I protest this insulting behavior.

BROODRYK: Let him make his point.

NXUMALO: As a citizen of South Africa, I automatically become a citizen of Africa the continent, and as a citizen of Africa, I am obligated to behave as a citizen of the world.

SCHEEPERS: With allegiance to Communist Russia.

NXUMALO: With allegiance to the total human race. It is because I want to share ideas with them that I advocate the learning of English.

SCHEEPERS: Then our language is not good enough for you?

NXUMALO: I speak your language, and it is certainly good enough for communication with Pretoria and Cape Town. But, your Honor, it is not understood in Paris or Madrid or Rio de Janeiro, and on certain occasions we require to speak with them, also.

As the trial droned on, with only such flimsy evidence as might have been appropriate in a public school if some obstreperous scholar had misbehaved, Saltwood began to realize that in this courtroom the real culprit was never mentioned. Daniel Nxumalo was being prosecuted not for what he had done but because his brother Jonathan in Moçambique was a thorn. Since Prosecutor Scheepers never charged 'You are guilty, Daniel Nxumalo, because your brother is a revolutionary,' Philip had to assume that the state had no proof of complicity; and because Judge Broodryk did not thunder 'We are going to imprison you, Daniel Nxumalo, because we can't get at your brother,' Philip supposed that the state wished this aspect of their case to be smothered. But that Daniel was being attacked because of Jonathan, there could be no doubt.

And that raised a fascinating point, which Philip contemplated many times as the trial progressed: Daniel did receive Jonathan in his house in Venloo. He did conspire with him, in a manner of speaking. Is he not guilty—if one accepts South African law? And when that rhetorical question had to be answered affirmatively, an even more perplexing one presented itself: I was there that night. I was at the clandestine meeting in Soweto. Am I not also guilty of conspiracy? When he first acknowledged this question, he was looking at Judge Broodryk, and it occurred to him with horror that on the facts, the judge would be justified in sentencing him, Philip, to imprisonment. Thus, at unexpected moments, the visitor to South Africa found the realities being driven home, and it was as a condemned man that Saltwood listened to the final two days of a trial in which he had subtly become a co-defendant.

This sense of unspecified doom intensified when Mr. and Mrs. Frikkie Troxel, accompanied by their cousin Jopie, entered the courtroom to hear the concluding testimony against their neighbor, the son of Moses Nxumalo. Arrival of these two distinguished athletes caused approving smiles, and Judge Broodryk welcomed them to this court. They sat not with Philip but across from him, indicating that they opposed his alien, socialist views, and this allowed him to see their undisguised satisfaction whenever the state made a telling point against the black man who threatened their comfortable way of life. They loved their freedom, those three Troxels, and were prepared to lay down their lives to preserve it, no doubt about it. What they refused to understand was that Daniel Nxumalo might feel the same way about his freedom.

It was deplorable, Philip thought, that these three fine white people should know so little about the Nxumalo family with whom they had shared their farms; had they reached out to form a partnership with Daniel and his brother Jonathan, they could have built a powerful force, able to lead their section of the country into better understandings and more logical arrangements, but they had remained enemies. Worse, they had remained strangers. Now they listened intently as Nxumalo was interrogated on his politics:

SCHEEPERS: Let us return to that provocative phrase 'Black Power.' Doesn't that mean black supremacy and the expulsion of whites?

NXUMALO: You seem to have a complete file on me, Mr. Scheepers. Nowhere in it will you find a word I have ever said advocating the expulsion at any time in the future of all white men. In the society I visualize, you white men will be needed, most urgently needed. Twenty years from now when—

KAPLAN: I must warn my client against completing that statement.

BROODRYK: I am most eager to hear what awaits us twenty years from now.

NXUMALO: Twenty years from now, when blacks have the vote, not one-man, one-vote, perhaps, but some reasonable concession for the moment, I would expect Prosecutor Scheepers to be serving exactly as he is serving now, and Defense Counsel Kaplan to be defending some business client—

BROODRYK: And the judge?

NXUMALO: I would expect the judge in this court to be black. (*Laughter*)

BROODRYK: I thought so.

NXUMALO: By that time, your Honor, you might well be in the Appeal Court, you and three black judges. (*More laughter*)

BROODRYK: You, as dictator, would appoint me?

NXUMALO: A consortium of the people, white and black, would want the best judges they could get.

BROODRYK: 'A consortium of the people?' That's Communism, isn't it?

NXUMALO: No, your Honor, that's democracy.

BROODRYK: Sounds more like dictatorship.

NXUMALO: No, we have a dictatorship now.

BROODRYK (*in towering rage*): I cannot allow you to denigrate this government.

NXUMALO: I meant no offense, your Honor. I was merely speaking the truth. In the great election of 1948 that threw Jan Christian Smuts out of office and brought your party in, that was against the wishes of white people. You might say you engineered a takeover, like the Communists in Czechoslovakia.

SCHEEPERS: That's a lie. We won that election fair and square.

NXUMALO: No, the record must be kept straight. You won seventy-nine seats in Parliament to seventy-one.

SCHEEPERS: A majority of eight, as I said.

NXUMALO: But in the popular vote you lost by a substantial majority. Something like six hundred thousand against you and four hundred thousand for. Many white people did not want your brand of government.

SCHEEPERS: How could that—

NXUMALO: You know very well. The white vote in this nation is heavily weighted in favor of the farmer, heavily skewed against urban dwellers. A farmer's vote may count as much as thirty-five percent more than a city dweller's.

SCHEEPERS: And rightly so. The virtue of a nation resides in its farmers. The rot that destroys a nation thrives in the cities.

NXUMALO: Then we blacks, who are mostly farmers, ought to have a larger vote than anyone.

SCHEEPERS: We're talking of civilized voters.

And there it ended, with Daniel Nxumalo having offended the judge, the prosecutor, his own advocate and most of the public. Even Philip Saltwood had to concede that he was guilty as hell—but of what? No overt act of treason had been proved; he had been in contact with no foreign power. He had said certain things which college professors and students around the world were saying, except in Russia and Uganda. He had organized a day of remembrance for the dead of Soweto. He had spoken in favor of English as the major language for students. He had used the phrases Black Power and Black Consciousness. And he had done certain things which might embarrass the government, which tried to hide the worst effects of apartheid.

For these trivial offenses he must be imprisoned?

Pursuing this line of thought, Saltwood then had to admit that his friend was guilty of two additional crimes which were not trivial: he had visited with revolutionaries in Soweto; he had provided refuge for his renegade brother. But these had not been discussed in court. The final, damning evidence was that Nxumalo had consulted with black leaders—and this was tantamount to conniving with an alien nation. Also, Nxumalo had advanced the disgraceful argument that when blacks honored Soweto they were doing only what whites did when they honored the Day of the Covenant. That was blasphemy; and in a theocracy, a mortal sin.

It was essential for the protection of the state that Nxumalo be severely punished, perhaps even hanged, but when the court convened in dreadful silence and the time came for Judge Broodryk, creature of the system, to defend the system, he surprised his listeners by intoning:

'Prisoner Daniel Nxumalo, this court finds you guilty on all counts as charged. You have, whenever an opportunity arose, sought to endanger the security of this state by furthering the aims of revolutionary groups plotting to overthrow the government of this republic. The court has listened with patience to your pleas about Black Consciousness and identity, but the good people of this nation have evolved an intricate system which ensures fairness for all. It is defined in sensible laws which you must obey, and for a man of your education to subvert them is criminal. The maximum sentence laid down by the Terrorism Act is death, but in your deportment during this trial I have seen repeated evidences of a superior mind and a solid character, and in this world that counts for something. I sentence you to ten years' imprisonment.'

So Daniel Nxumalo, thirty years old, whose only real crime was that he had spoken in terms used by people like Jean Jacques Rousseau, Abraham Lincoln and Winston Churchill, was sentenced to a decade on Robben Island.

He was not frightened by the prospect of imprisonment because he suspected that it would not be long before reason would prevail in his land; even if he were banned for five years after his release, he knew that a time would come before the end of this century when he and black men like him would know real freedom. At that time he would occupy a privileged position because of his martyrdom—as the prisoners Nehru, Mussolini, De Valera, Vorster, Kenyatta, Lenin, Hitler and Gandhi had done before him. He would use his time in prison as they had used theirs: to perfect his theories of government, coming out a much stronger man than when he went in. Nations tend to be governed by men who have been forced by adversity to clarify their thought; those who have enjoyed unbroken smooth sailing are often too lazy to speculate on how to manage their ship in storms.

In the military prison at Chrissie Meer, Detleef van Doorn had begun his education in restrictive puritanism; in the political prison on Robben Island, Daniel Nxumalo would undergo his apprenticeship in the strategies of freedom.

When Philip Saltwood landed his job with Amalgamated Mines he promised his favorite professor, Gideon Vandenberg of the University of Michigan, that he would not form any hard conclusions about South Africa until he had worked there a full year, but that when he had done so, he would report to Vandenberg. The professor was a member of that distinguished family which produced Senator Arthur Vandenberg and General Hoyt Vandenberg; he spent his summers in Holland, Michigan, tulip capital of America, and was a kind of professional Dutchman. Just as the senator had presented himself to the electorate as an incorruptible Dutchman, conservative but prudent, so Gideon yearly offered a course in 'The Golden Age of Holland, 1560–1690,' in which he extolled those creative pressures which had made this minute country one of the masters of the world, possessors of Java and Cape Town. He needed to know what was happening in the latter and had commissioned Saltwood to tell him:

Dear Professor Vandenberg,

One of the best bits of advice you ever gave me was to wait a year before reaching any conclusions about South Africa. Ten years would be a better study period. But I've worked diligently with Afrikaners, Englishmen and lots of blacks. I've also been in all parts of the nation. And I've reestablished contact with the local Saltwoods, whom our branch last knew in 1810. I offer you these tentative speculations.

South Africa must be one of the most beautiful lands on earth, surpassed in my experience only by New Zealand. All thinking must start from this. It's a land worth keeping. For whites it also has one of the highest standards of living in the world, and if people in Europe and America knew how grand the daily existence was, they'd all emigrate. Compared to the upper South African white, rich people in Texas and Oregon live like serfs. If you taught here, at your salary, you'd have four servants, a life of ease, and all the amenities. The South African way of life is worth preserving (for whites) and even worth fighting for. I have never lived so well.

For urban blacks the standard of living is also higher than I have seen in Nigeria, Zambia and Vwarda, and much higher, I'm told, than in any of the surrounding black countries, which is why hundreds of thousands of blacks in those countries would like to emigrate to South Africa. Personal freedoms, of course, are another matter, and much of what you hear in a liberal university like Michigan is true.

The people of South Africa perplex me. Even cursory investigation proves that what we call an Afrikaner is rarely of pure Dutch descent. The mix seems to be Dutch ancestry thirty-five percent, German a hefty thirty, Huguenot twenty, English five, other European five, and a submerged and denied five percent due to early miscegenation with slaves from Madagascar, Angola, Java, Ceylon and lots of Malays, with a liberal salting of brown Hottentots. But apparently one drop of Dutch blood supersedes all other European strains and can even mask black infusions, if they occurred long enough ago. A man who is demonstrably seven-eighths German, Huguenot and English will say proudly, 'My ancestors were Dutch.'

But in recent times the process seems to have been reversed, for now one drop of black blood contaminates ninety-nine percent of white blood, which accounts for the steady rise of the Coloured population. You could live here a thousand years, Dr. Vandenberg, and never understand this problem. The Coloureds, who should be the natural allies of the pure-white man—if ever there were a pure anything—are kept in limbo without any fixed place in society. The Afrikaner language evolved in large part because of contributions from the various languages spoken by the

Coloureds, as did many of the social customs and habits, like the Afrikaner's love of spicy foods. Anyone with training in history, like you, would have to conclude that one of the saddest mistakes the Afrikaners made was to divorce themselves from people of great ability who are in effect their half brothers—these Coloureds.

Such argument would infuriate the Afrikaner, who is absolutely convinced by his historians, his teachers and his predikants that the white-slave mixture was the consequence exclusively of sailors and soldiers roistering into Cape Town on shore leave, and that no self-respecting Dutchman ever touched a slave girl. A naughty lad at Witwatersrand University has calculated that to achieve the amount of infusion that obviously occurred, every soldier and sailor would have had to come ashore with his trousers half down, go to work immediately, and not stop till the bo's'n blew his whistle to summon them back to the ship.

A phenomenon that you with your Dutch background might anticipate, but which I certainly didn't, is the Afrikaner's unshakable belief that God personally has ordained his state and its traditions. I cannot tell you how shocked I was in discussing a management problem the other day with two university graduates and hearing them tell me, 'But God wants us to do it that way. He entered into a covenant with us for that purpose.' Any prime minister taking office assures the people that he will keep the nation on the course outlined by God. Students in school are taught that God devised apartheid, and I even heard a rugby enthusiast say that God engineered South Africa's victories, because He wanted His chosen people to triumph. Any outsider who minimizes the influence of this belief in South African politics misses the core of the problem. Of the four dozen Afrikaners I know well, forty-seven honestly believe that God has directed them to stay on this land, run it exactly as they are now running it, and defend it against blacks and Communism. I have never known an American to be so sure that God personally looked after American interests, which of course He does.

Like most Americans, I know little about religion, but here one cannot ignore it, it dominates government and gives sanction to whatever the ruling political party decides. Aren't Presbyterians Calvinists, too? I don't remember them behaving like this at home. The Dutch Calvinists, you know, have rejected the South African church, and recently a famous theologian from Holland came out here to try to mend fences. I attended a thoughtful lecture he gave in which he said that John Calvin was firm on this matter of government, and he quoted from Calvin himself, something to the effect that all men are certainly subject to the magistrates that rule over them, but only insofar as the magistrates obey the basic rules of God. If they do otherwise, the citizens should not pay them any regard, nor be overawed by the dignity they possess as governors. The visitor didn't go so far as to call for revolution, but he sure did call for new evaluations of government policy.

As a matter of fact, every sensible Afrikaner, Englishman and black I have met knows that great changes must be made, and they know what changes. But some eighty-five percent of the rural Afrikaner population would rather die than accept even one of those changes, and they are assured by their reactionary leaders, lay and cleric, that they are right. The tragedy is that the philosophers of all sides are prepared to make those changes now, but they will not be made, and ten years from now, when they are grudgingly conceded at the point of a gun, they won't be enough. In every conversation I have I hear comparisons made with Rhodesia. Ten years ago the whites there should have made certain concessions, but they refused. When they became more than willing to make them, the time for accepting that modest change was past.

Seems to me there are four alternatives. First, peaceful, gradual change to a modern multi-racial state. The die-hard whites say they will never accept this. Second, black revolution sweeping the whites from power and perhaps from Africa altogether. The blacks don't appear to be capable of this, yet. Third, continued white domination, with more and more repressive measures as surrounding black nations achieve the power to support infiltration guerrilla forces. The present nation becomes a white laager defending itself from black Africa. Most of my workmen, white and black, think this is what will happen, and that the whites can get away with it for the remainder of this century. But if they persist in rejecting the Coloureds, forcing them into alliance with the blacks, the whites will endanger what chance they have. In the short run, at least, events will be strongly affected by what the Coloureds do.

The fourth alternative shocked me, but since it was proposed by the finest mind I've met here, black or white, Afrikaner or English, I must take it seriously. He suspects that things are moving so swiftly that the Afrikaner will not be able to hold his country

against a combination of outside pressure and inside urban warfare, and that if he tries, the land will go down in terrible revolution. He advocates that white men, all of them, retreat voluntarily
into the old Cape Province, there to establish a real republic in
which Afrikaner, Englishman and Coloured work together as full
partners. I was really jolted when he drew the outlines for me on
a map. Pretoria and Johannesburg would be surrendered, as
would Durban. Port Elizabeth and Grahamstown would be retained, as would Kimberley and Bloemfontein. This beautiful, rational area would be as big as Texas. It would be ruled by those
whites who refused to cooperate with the black government of
the north, plus the many Coloureds. Safe on the southern tip of
Africa, they would become a new Hong Kong. When I asked if
the triumphant blacks would permit such a withdrawal and con-
solidation, he said something profound, which I want you to discuss with your students and all who are interested in Africa. I'll
try to give it in his words:

'If the black men in Africa refuse, as they seem to have done
elsewhere, to allow any reasonable partnership for indigenous
whites, the result would be harmful to Africa but disastrous to
the United States, because your country is in the throes of accepting and defining justice for its black minority. If it sees a black
majority in Africa denying comparable justice to whites in countries that they dominate and slaughtering them on television, the
backlash could be frightening.'

I said that he was asking blacks to define their behavior as a majority before they attained an equality, and he said, 'That's when
the definitions should be made.'

Which of these four scenarios do I subscribe to? I've had pretty
good luck as an engineer working on the principle that if I'm
smart enough to see something, the people intimately involved
must have seen it too. If every sensible man knows what concessions ought to be made right now, my constant hope is that they'll
be made. Therefore, I incline toward the first solution: peaceful,
accelerated change leading to a nation in which all men and
women vote and in which the black majority safeguards a place
for white participants—whom they might not like—because they
are needed, just as today the Afrikaner accepts as a partner the
English-speaker whose ancestors he opposed so bitterly.

I'm going to ignore the die-hard machine-gun type of Afrikaner
who shouts, 'Over my dead body.' The Afrikaner leaders I've met

are at least as prudent as the American politicians I know, and more so. I'm going to put my faith in them. And I want to make one point clear, which is never ventilated in the South African press. The blacks of South Africa are as capable as any people with whom I've worked. Wherever I've supervised a mine, I was relieved to find some South African black to take charge, because he was sure to be clever and hard-working and informed. If blacks inferior to him can run Zambia and Tanzania and Vwarda, however awkwardly they may do so at the moment, he can surely run South Africa. As a matter of fact, a grand coalition of black capacity, Coloured adaptability, English skill and Afrikaner force could forge a nation that would be one of the most powerful on earth, situated in one of the best settings, and with a way of life that most other people would envy. This is what I hope for.

If, as some fear, any rational solution becomes impossible because the stubborn Afrikaner refuses to yield any of his prerogatives, then I see great pressures along all the borders, encouraged and sometimes engineered by Communist-bloc countries, incipient and real civil war within those borders, with the Afrikaner able to defend himself for the rest of this century, after which other pressures which we cannot now foresee will alter the picture radically. On one thing I have been convinced. The young Afrikaners I know will use their guns. They will go forth fighting, to defend a way of life which God Himself has ordained and which, for them, is one of the best on this earth. They will not hesitate to slaughter, because God Himself assured the Israelites, after whom they pattern themselves, 'One man of you shall chase a thousand: for the Lord your God, he it is that fighteth for you, as he hath promised you.' More frighteningly: 'And they utterly destroyed all that was in the city, both man and woman, young and old, and ox, and sheep, and ass, with the edge of the sword.'

The major impediment to rational solution is Afrikaner stubbornness, but a contributory one is the regrettable division within the white community. Smashing Afrikaner triumphs at the polls have meant that they can ignore the other sections of the community and throw them out of all official positions. There are no Englishmen in the cabinet, or at the head of major police units or the armed services. I asked a leading Afrikaner whether the nation he foresaw would have any place for Englishmen, and he said bluntly, 'Not really.' Then he remembered that I had English relatives here and he conceded, 'Well, if they quit running back to England every time there's trouble, we might find a place for them, and even trust them when the crunch comes.'

The key phrase in every serious discussion is *'when the crunch comes.'* Everyone expects it to come. Super-patriots argue that when it does, the English will somehow chicken out. Everyone is convinced that when it comes, only the Afrikaner will prove reliable. And what is this mysterious *crunch?* The armed rebellion of the blacks.

You must not conclude from what I've just said that the English-speaking South African is much different from the Afrikaner. In fact, he profits equally from the present situation and might be even more reluctant than the Afrikaner to surrender his servants and his prerogatives. My English foreman confided the other day, 'Sure I talk liberal, and I vote liberal, but on election night, when the tally's announced, I'm damned relieved the Afrikaners have won again. They'll know how to handle affairs when the crunch comes.'

I hate to say this to a professor of history, and a very good one, but South Africa is a land cruelly wounded by its constant recollection of things past. At certain points the English did behave poorly; this is never allowed to be forgotten. At every memorial the same time-worn litany of incidents must be recited. Hatreds become enshrined as the most vital components of the national mythos, and no one is ever permitted to forget, or turn his attention to more creative tasks. I remember that day you told us what Santayana had said: 'Those who forget history are condemned to repeat it.' Well, those who remember it obsessively are poisoned by it.

After my third long trip through the country, friends at the mine asked what my most lasting impression had been, and I said, 'Just once I'd like to enter some South African town and see a statue to someone who wrote a book, painted a picture or composed a song.' I was weary of those dreadful monuments to minor generals who had fought battles involving thirty-eight men. It's as if our country were festooned with statues of Francis Marion, Pierre Beauregard and James Van Fleet. I'm sure they were meritorious fellows worthy of remembrance, but they would form a fragile base for constructing a national hagiography.

As for my final guess, if the Götterdämmerung Afrikaners do use their blazing guns to protect themselves for the rest of this century, I think they can get away with it. But any hope of later rec-

onciliation would prove impossible. I would expect them, sometime around 2010, to retreat under pressure to the Cape Province
enclave, there to become the Israel of Africa, surrounded not by
Arabs but by blacks. I cannot see them leaving Africa, nor
should they. They have no other homes. They have lived here
much longer than most American families have lived in the
United States.

You have probably detected that I write with more fervor than
ever I dared exhibit in your class. The reason is simple. I fell in
love with an adorable Afrikaner girl, much prettier than those
professional models who appear in wooden shoes on your Holland, Michigan, postcards, and through her I saw the best of
Afrikanerdom, which I liked much better than I did my own English strain. I saw them as excellent people trying to find their way.
Alas, she married the other guy, the one with the machine gun at
the ready, and I find myself speculating on what her future will
be. I am desolate of spirit.

Philip Saltwood

He was indeed desolate. He had come to South Africa to find diamonds,
and had found none. He had tried to marry a beautiful girl, and had
failed. Most nagging of all, he had tried to comprehend a land with
which his family had many ties, but had finished his tour as ignorant of
its real construction as when he started.

He did not know why Frikkie and Jopie were so determined to settle questions with their machine guns, nor could he guess how much
longer Nxumalo would be willing to make concessions. Indians, Coloureds, Zulu, Xhosa, Afrikaners—he was puzzled by them all, and especially by Craig Saltwood, who had accepted exile. Had he been Craig,
he would not have fled.

Yet he was leaving. His work was ending on a cascade of falling
notes, like a music box that has run down; his only reasonable next step
was toward the exit. He packed his gear at the camp, notified Pretoria
that all accounts with the workmen would be cleaned up as of Saturday,
and made inquiries about flights back to New York, where a group of
oil men wished to talk with him about problems in Texas.

By Wednesday he had things in order, with clean-up jobs assigned
to all men still on the payroll. He talked with each about plans, about
his wife and children. By now the blacks trusted him and were willing
to explain their uncertainties: 'Maybe a job here. Maybe we go to Zim-

babwe to help get their mines working again.' They were wonderfully
resilient men, these Zulu and Xhosa, and he felt that regardless of how
badly the black and white leaders messed things up, these technicians
would keep their proficiencies ready to serve whatever type of government emerged. They did not seem sorry to see him go, but they did respect the high standard of his work as they had witnessed it. He knew
his job.

The white workers usually knew what they were going to do next;
like the blacks, they were not sorry to see the American go. He had
never really fitted in, never quite understood the reasons why they had
to keep the blacks in their place.

'Don't mess with any gangsters,' they warned him.

'Tell Jimmy Carter we're desperately awaiting his next words of advice.'

'If you see Andy Young, up his bucket.'

They were a competent, rowdy lot and he would be pleased to work
with them anywhere, anytime, but they did not represent the South
Africa he had grown to love. That was centered on Vrymeer, and when
the camp was fairly well secured he drove over the hills to Venloo and
then out to the farm nestling beside the lake. When he came down the
approach and saw once more that enticing cluster of buildings, the five
rondavels, the step-lakes and the herd of blesbok, he stopped his car,
studied the relationship of each item to the others, and thought: This is
paradise, chopped out of rock, and rich even in time of drought.

He noticed that several months of dry weather had lowered the level
of the lake considerably, so that the rather steep flanks were visible, one
layer after another of seemingly different kinds of rock: More likely all
the same rock, but stained different colors by different exposures to
water and air. He was about to formulate additional thoughts when a
large group of flamingos rose from the far end of the lake, wheeled
about in breathtaking patterns for several minutes, then landed delicately on one of the smaller lakes, annoying a flock of guinea fowl that
had been pecking at the sand nearby. Whatever thoughts he might have
had about the lake vanished, so he drove down to the yard, parked the
car, and shouted, 'Marius!'

Before he could reach the house Van Doorn was at the door, laughing uproariously and waving a newspaper. 'Philip! I'm so glad you arrived. This is so good it must be shared.'

'What have the Americans done now?'

'No fear. This is Afrikanerdom at its best,' and he dragged Saltwood into the main room, where the first thing Philip saw was a colored photograph of Sannie in her wedding dress. Quickly he turned away, but as he did so he caught Marius looking at him, so he asked casually, 'How's she doing?'

'Fine. Frikkie has a job with government. Everyone has a job with government.'

'What's the hilarity?'

'The drought.'

'I fail to see the humor. Things look rather barren out there.'

'Not here. Up north at Blinkfontein.'

'Let me see,' Philip said in total confusion as he reached for the newspaper.

'No, you must read the background story first. I have it here somewhere,' and Marius held on to the paper which had caused his mirth while rummaging through a pile by the window. 'Here it is.'

When Philip took the old paper he had no doubt as to which story had caused the merriment, for the first page was dominated by a carefully posed half-page photograph of a man completely nude, accompanied by the headline: NUDIST IDENTIFIED AS CAUSE OF DROUGHT. The straight-faced story explained that Mrs. Leopold van Valck, chairlady of the Blinkfontein Moral Action Committee, speaking on behalf of her forty-three members, had determined that the prolonged drought which had so harmfully affected her area was caused by God's anger at a man named Victor Victoria, who invited couples, not always married, to his farm near Blinkfontein to engage in nude sunbathing. Mrs. van Valck believed that if Mr. Victoria was allowed to continue his nude bathing, God would continue to afflict Blinkfontein, so her committee was handing down an ultimatum: 'Get some clothes on or face the consequences.' She did not indicate what these consequences were, but implied that they would not be pleasant. On the other hand, if Mr. Victoria would consent to get dressed, she assured him and the other citizens of Blinkfontein that rain would fall fairly soon, in accordance with II Chronicles, Chapter 7, verse 14:

> If my people . . . shall humble themselves, and pray . . . and turn from their wicked ways; then will I hear from heaven, and will forgive their sin, and will heal their land.

She concluded, 'So it's up to you, Mr. Victoria. Put on your clothes and bring us rain.'

Philip passed the paper back with a sigh. 'We have crazies in our country, too. And you ought to see what happens in Texas.'

'That's not the point!' Marius cried, slapping the later paper into Saltwood's hand, and there on the front page was another photograph of Mr. Victor Victoria, fully dressed, accompanied by the headline: NUDISTS DRESS, HEAVENS BLESS. On the afternoon of the morning on which Mr. Victor Victoria's guests put their clothes back on, a torrential rain arrived, not only ending the drought but also washing away two small bridges. Mrs. van Valck, chairlady of the Blinkfontein Moral Action Committee, was quoted as having said, in the midst of the storm, 'Mr. Victoria is a good neighbor. He pays his bills. And he listened to reason.' There was a second photograph of Mr. Victoria, fully clothed, at one of the washed-out bridges, with the caption: I MUST HAVE WORN TOO MUCH.

'Perfect ending for my visit.'

'Are you really leaving?'

'Reluctantly.'

'Amalgamated would certainly find you a job, the price of gold being what it is and diamonds doing so well.'

'Yes, but . . .' He indicated the photograph of Van Doorn's daughter.

'I know at least two dozen girls in Pretoria as pretty as Sannie.'

'But not Sannie. If things had worked out differently . . .'

He was standing at the big window, looking off toward the lake and the striations left around its sides by the drought. 'If it rained up in Blinkfontein, it'll be moving down this way within the next couple of days. Your lake should fill again.'

'Always has. Looks to me as if it's been there a thousand years, maybe a million.'

'Things here are very old,' Saltwood said perfunctorily. Then he stopped, turned, and faced his friend. 'What did you say?'

'I said it looked to me . . . Well, I know nothing about these things, but I've always thought the lake had been here for thousands or even millions of years.'

Grabbing Marius by the arm, Philip ran toward the lake, and when they stood at its edge, he said, 'Suppose this lake has existed for eons. Why did it settle—here in this declivity?'

'Why not?'

'The only explanation would be that it filled some natural dip in the earth. And what caused that dip? The mouth of an old pipe.' He knelt down, pecked at the striations with no purpose, for they could reveal nothing, then rose and cried, 'Marius! What I've been searching for could be right here.' And he turned eastward toward the spot where old Pik Prinsloo had found his diamonds, far beyond the intervening hills, and with a sweep of hand obliterated the hills, for he supposed correctly that they had erupted millions of years later than the formation of this lake.

With the hills gone, he could visualize the river that had carried the diamonds downstream; it had come from the west, probably, along this chain of little lakes, and it had flowed eastward right over the roots of those hills, and it had not turned northward, along the path of the river that now existed, but always eastward in a logical direction, bearing the diamonds with it.

'Marius!' he cried. 'I think I've found it.'

'What?'

'The pipe that produced those diamonds. I've spent a year searching in the wrong direction.'

'You think it might be here?'

'I'm convinced of it. Not because of anything I've seen here today, but because I've exhausted all other possibilities.'

The words had a heavy impact on Van Doorn, for he saw his country in the process of exhausting *its* various possibilities before it came to grips with the towering one that threatened its existence. But as with Saltwood and the diamonds, preliminary exploration required time and the cauterizing of old animosities. If Philip had spent a futile year searching for his diamonds, South Africa could afford ten or twenty searching for its solution:

Let's say ten years' toying with the idea of a total, military-style repression, then maybe five with some kind of neo-fascism, then another five in a retreat to sanity, and then perhaps another ten in fumbling attempts at a shared democracy. Hell, time moves in vast cycles, but this whole thing could be solved in my lifetime. In my white-hair period I could see a splendid society here. We wouldn't have to scuttle down to the Cape enclave. Black and white, Coloured and Indian could participate equally.

'Marius, are you listening?'

'What?'

'I said I'd like to drill one more experimental hole. Over there at the margin of your lake.'

'For what?'

'I'm convinced I'll find kimberlite. Maybe five hundred feet down, through the detritus.'

Detritus, that's the word. The awful accumulation of wrong decisions, improper turns. You scrape away the excrescences of history—the hangings at Slagter's Nek, the awfulness of the prison camps, the sins we've committed with apartheid—and maybe you get down to the bedrock of human society, where diamonds hide. God of my fathers, how I wish we could bring in the psychological drills and probe down to bedrock.

'So, I have your permission?'

'To do what?'

'To drill the test hole . . . down to kimberlite?'

Kimberlite! This nation of mine will gamble a billion rand to find the next kimberlite in hopes that diamonds will be uncovered. But it won't spend ten rand to find the kimberlite of the human soul. We'll turn the clock back a billion years to find gems worth absolutely nothing in a reasonable world, but we ignore the flint-hard gems in the human conscience that are worth all the raw money in the world. It's an insane society, and if Saltwood does find the new cache of diamonds, everyone in Pretoria and London and Amsterdam and New York will say, 'South Africa has saved itself once more in its time of crisis.' We buy financial credits, but not intelligence.

'I'll keep the mess off to one side,' Philip said in great excitement. 'Not bring in too many vehicles. And the lake poses no problem. We'll go down two or three thousand feet, then fan out our shafts north and south.'

'And the detritus? There's bound to be a lot.'

'There always is when you find diamonds. Ten tons of rubbish for every carat. We'll pile it over there. Never see it from the house.'

The flamingos rose from their small lake, formed their ballet in the air, and danced about the sky in celebration of discoveries about to be made. At the end of one grand sweep, their red feathers blazing in sunlight, they passed the spot at which Philip would place his drills, then headed north. Next year when they returned, the lake would be quite different.

Glossary
and
Genealogical Charts

In writing of a people with a language as evocative as Afrikaans, the temptation is to lard the narrative with a spate of colorful short words like *kloof* (ravine) or astonishing compounds like *onderwyskollegesportsterreine* (education college sports fields). I try to avoid this device, judging it to be exhibitionism which does not aid the reader. However, to write of the Afrikaner without a seasoning of his language would be an injustice. I have, therefore, used those few words without which the narrative would lack verisimilitude, and in this glossary have marked with an asterisk those which can be found in our larger dictionaries as English adoptions.

*ASSEGAI	slender hardwood spear	*Arabic*
BAAS	master; boss	
*BAOBAB	tree with swollen trunk	*Bantu*
BAYETE	royal salute	*Zulu*
*BILTONG	strips of sun-dried, salted meat (jerky)	
*BOBOTIE	ground meat, curry, custard	*Malay*
*BOER	farmer (capitalized: South African of Dutch or Huguenot descent)	
*COMMANDO	Boer military unit (member of such unit)	
*DAGGA	marijuana	*Hottentot*
DANKIE	thanks	
*DISSELBOOM	main shaft of ox wagon	
*DOMINEE	minister of Afrikaner churches	
FONTEIN	natural spring (fountain)	
HARTEBEEST HUT	wattle-and-daub hut with low walls, no windows	
*IMPI	regiment of Zulu warriors	*Bantu*
*INSPAN	harness draft animals	
JA	yes	
*KNOBKERRIE	club with knobbed head	*Hottentot*
*KOPJE	small hill, often flat-topped	
*KRAAL	African village; enclosure for livestock	*Portuguese*
*LAAGER	defensive camp encircled by wagons	

*LOBOLA	cattle paid for bride *Bantu*
*MEALIES	British maize; American corn (hominy grits)
*MEERKAT	small mammal (resembles prairie dog)
MEJUFFROUW	Miss; young unmarried lady
MEVROUW	Mrs.; becomes Mevrou
*MFECANE	the crushing (forced migration following Zulu consolidation) *Bantu*
MIJNHEER	Mr.; becomes Mynheer and Meneer
*MORGEN	land measure (about two acres)
NACHTMAAL	night meal (Holy Communion) (becomes Nagmaal in Afrikaans)
OUBAAS	old boss (old fellow; grandfather)
OUMA	grandmother
*OUTSPAN	unharness draft animals
*PREDIKANT	clergyman (especially of Dutch Reformed churches)
*RAND	unit of currency worth about one dollar (abbreviation of Witwatersrand)
*RONDAVEL	hut with circular floor plan
*SJAMBOK	short whip of rhinoceros or hippopotamus hide *Malay* from *Persian*
SKOLLIE	hooligan (especially Cape Coloured)
*SLIM	clever; crafty; cunning; shrewd (the original English meaning of this word)
*SMOUS	itinerant merchant (peddler) *German*
*SPOOR	track or trail of man or beast
*STOEP	stoop (porch)
*TREK	arduous migration (especially by ox wagon)
TREKBOER	nomadic grazier
TSOTSI	member of street gang *Bantu*
*UITLANDER	outlander (capitalized: foreigner, especially on the gold fields)
*VELD	open grassland with scattered shrubs and trees (veldt is archaic)
*VELDKORNET	minor district official (in military: lieutenant)
*VELDSKOEN	rawhide homemade shoe (also veldtskoen)
VERDOMDE	damned; cursed
V.O.C.	Vereenigde Oostindische Compagnie (United East India Company)
*VOLK	nation; people
VOORTREKKER	forward trekker (member of the 1834–1837 Great Trek)
VRYMEER	Freedom Lake (in Dutch: Vrijmeer)

Pronunciation: In general, words are pronounced as they look, except that J = Y; V = F; W = V; OE = U. The name Van Wyk = Fan Vake; and for no reason that can be explained, Uys = Ace. Vrymeer, of course, is Fraymeer.

The Van Doorns

Nicodemus van Doorn   Joost van Valkenborch

Petrus van Doorn.   Willem van Valkenborch

Titus van Doorn   m. 1613   Hendrickje van Valkenborch
1590–1636   1595–1662

Kornelia   m. 1652   **Karel**   Katje   m. 1658   **Willem**   [1655]   Deborah
Danckaerts   1615–1691   Danckaerts   1625–1693   of Malacca
1626–1680   1633–1691   1638–

(1) Marie   m.1678   **Paul de Pré**   m.1702   (2) Annatjie   m.1678   Marthinus   The
Plon   1660–1713   1651–1714   1659–   Wandering
1661–1688   1702   Coloureds

Henri   Louis   Petronella   m.1694   Bezel   **Hendrik**   m.1709   Johanna   Sarel   m.1710   **Geertruyd**
1679–   1680–   1679–1713   1670–   1681–   1691–   1684–   Steen
                                  1733   1750   1750   1754   1688–1763

Cape Town   Submerged   6 Other   **Adriaan**   m. 1732   Seena van Valck   Trianon
Du Preez   Coloureds   Children   1712–1778   1717–1778   Van Doorn
Family   Family

Son   2 Daughters   (1) Rebecca   m. 1759   **Lodevicus**   m. 1788   (2) Wilhelmina
                      Specx   1739–1815   Heimstra
                      1737–1788   1769–1834

Son   Daughter   **Tjaart**
                              1789–1859

The Nxumalos

Hlenga   m. 1458   **Nxumalo**
1444–1509   of
                     Zimbabwe
                     1437–1514

(1) Thetiwe m. 1824 . Wives (2, 3)   **Nxumalo**   (4) Nonsizi m. 1827   (5) Thandi m. 1828
1805–1827   of   1807–1828   1808–1857
                      iziCwe
                      1788–1849

2 Children   3 Children   Mbengu
                               1829–1880

Mpela   m. 1890   Bildad Magubane   **Micah Nxumalo**
1876–1938   1869–1922   1868–1937

Jefferson   Moses
1901–1959   1908–1969

Matthew   Jonathan   Daniel
1942–   1941–   1949–

The Saltwoods

Captain Nicholas m. 1618 Henrietta
1593–1660   1600–1664

Josiah m. 1781 Emily
1760–1816   1765–1826

Peter m. 1806 Janice   Hilary m. 1821 Emma   Richard m. 1821 Julie   David
1782–   1788–   1785–   1800–   1789–   1799–   1790–
1864   1863   1828   1828   1869   1867   1861

3 Children

Ralph m. 1849 Harriet
1824–1877   1830–1899

Victor   Frank m. 1899 Maud Turner   Anthony
1858–1929   1860–1916   1871–1946   1870–1918

Hilary Roger   Noel m. 1932 Laura   Michael Max·   Timothy m.1919 Clara
1887–   1896–   1906–   Ogilvy· 1910–   1892–   1896–   van Doorn
1916   1975   1954   1912–   1969   1916   1967   1897–1974

Craig m. 1960 Susan Kingsley   Philip Saltwood
1933–   1940–   1948–

Timothy Lenore
1962–   1965–

Travels and Treks

0   200 miles

0   200 kilometers

Vaal Ri

DEATH OF
GUMSTO ×

Orange River

Orange River

Rooi van Valck's ×

Gra*a*

ATLANTIC

OCEAN

1751
×

Golan

1742
×

Cape Town
1648 ●   × 1662   × 1692   1724 ×

Jean Paul Tremblay